Some notes about

MAMA, SING OLD SHEP:

"I laughed, I cried, and I loved *MAMA, SING OLD SHEP.* Charlene Jones knows how it is in Nashville Country Music and she has written it."
___ BRENDA ROBERTS, Songwriter ___

"Ms Jones' first effort is lyrical and rich with Southern characters and subjects. She is an exciting new voice for readers of Bobbie Ann Mason and the "real" South.
___ DOROTHY BALLENGER, Librarian ___

"If you believe in dreams, love a love story, downhome folks and country music, this book is your meat and potatoes. I couldn't put it down."
___ JOAN WHITAKER, Country Music Fan ___

"This picture of *Music City Nashville* is a great read for anyone who loves a good tale and wants to know more about the elusive business of country music."
___ BRAD LEE, Singer/Songwriter ___

"It's been awhile since a book made me do it, but I stayed up nights to finish *MAMA, SING OLD SHEP.*"
___ ANDREA CLINTON, SINGER ___

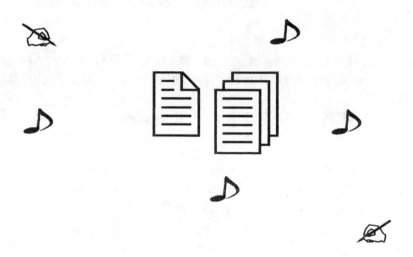

Real songwriting's like plowing, only you're plowing in your soul instead of dirt, trying to make a seed grow.

COPPER JIM QUARRELLS

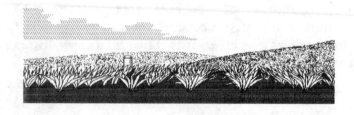

MAMA, SING OLD SHEP

CHARLENE JONES

Edited by
Jonathan Lampley

RED SPRINGS
PUBLISHING

Publisher's Note: This is a work of fiction. Names, characters, places, and incidents are the product of the author's imagination or are used fictitiously. Any resemblance to actual persons, living or dead, events or locales is coincidental or is used fictitiously.

MAMA, SING OLD SHEP
Copyright © 1996 by Charlene Jones

Red Springs Publishing
P O Box 175
Old Hickory, Tennessee, 37138

Grateful acknowledgment to the following for permission to reprint their material: Ryman, Attraction Collage, Music Collage, **Nashville Chamber of Commerce**

Nashville Skyline based on the work of Tennessee Photographic Services. Compliments of **Tennessee Bureau of Tourism**

OLD SHEP Words and Music by Clyde "Red" Foley **Copyright** © 1940 **Duchess Music Corporation. Duchess Music Corporation is an MCA company** All rights reserved. Used by permission. International Copyright secured. Copyright renewed.

First Printing 1996

ISBN # 1-888101-07-5

Library of Congress Catalog Card Number: 95-71411

Cover Design
Big Dot Digital Design, Nashville

Printed in the United States of America

CONTENTS

PART ONE - M IS FOR MAMA

PART TWO - C IS FOR CLAY

PART THREE - A IS FOR ANNA

DEDICATION

Music is our universal language. The heart, the soul, the mission and the appeal of Country Music is people.

MAMA, SING OLD SHEP is about and is dedicated to all people everywhere.

PROLOGUE

Old Mrs. Griffin whispered, "Paw, if there ever is one, this is a fine day for a funeral. I'd sure take sunny April, like today, over old, cold January. I feel so bad for Anna Hill, born here in Greenriver and all."

Old Mr. Griffin whispered, "Yeah, but her son's better off. Clay Hill sure didn't host no kind disease."

"Ain't no kind diseases, Paw. But he's got the biggest funeral Greenriver's seen. Bet Copper Jim's gonna sing, he's getting up with his guitar."

"Don't look right with his hat off, Maw. Ain't many he'd take it off for, even their funeral." James Quarrells, known since boyhood as Copper Jim, stepped under the graveside awning. Clay loved stage clothes, so Jim wore his green, cactus-sequined suit. Standing at the head of the closed coffin, his Scotch-Irish eyes cast a long, blue look at the pall of yellow roses.

Then his guitar began to harmonize with the beauty of the morning, and as only a whiskey and time-worn baritone can, he started singing *Old Shep*.

He'd sung *Old Shep* forever, knew the words by heart. He thought he knew the words to pain. Today was a whole new verse. Like Uncle Ned said, damn devil hit the good like the bad with his bastard son, Pain.

In another part of his mind, he silently prayed: Lord, don't let me bawl in front of Annie. Help me hold it till I'm by myself and I promise, to get by this without getting back on the bottle. Losing Clay is tearing Annie. It'll age her. Living hell sets everybody's wrinkles but don't let it break her. I'd sure be mighty obliged, Lord. Amen.

Annie worshiped Clayboy. All this time by his bed watching him die would done killed most mamas. But Annie had real backbone.

First time Jim ever saw Clayboy, he was a tall kid, happy and rearing to learn music. Second time, Clay was beat and way down blue over his daddy passing his own self away. Took miles of talk to make him see it wasn't his fault. Then Clay jumped into music and let it wash him like a baptizing.

Now, after making the whole world listen, Clayboy was hushed forever. God, what a pity. What a heart-busting, dog-killing pity!

When Jim finished singing, all was quiet. Getting that far helped, now to the rest of it. With his hands on his Gibson, he scanned the crowd. His eyes locked on Anna looking like a young'un blinking in a blinding rain, too lost to cry.

Jim's Adam's apple bobbed spasmodically before he could say, "Clay Manassas Hill was like a son to me, can't nothing fill the hole in my heart his leaving's left. Bad sick and no hope, he was ready. Told me so, told his mama, too. If you love God, you know Clay's in better hands. Know he ain't hurting. Know he's picking and singing if he wants to.

"Clay was the best songwriter and picker I know. After me picking thirty years, he learned all I had in a year. Then swapped licks with the best. Besides Elvis, he was the only perfect performer I've seen.

"The woods was his best place to write. Said the woods sung the best music of all. Said he stole most he wrote copying down sounds in the woods. Folks, I never heard what Clay heard; in the woods or nowhere else. Never imagined it in my mind, less it'd be in God's own Heaven.

"Miss Annie, last night a song hit me on Clay loving you and you loving him. If it suits you, I'd like to sing it now." He waited till Anna nodded yes.

Softly finger picking, he went on, "Clay left this life like he lived it, close to his mama; her singing *Old Shep* to him, after he'd sung it to the world. My song's called, *Mama, Sing Old Shep.*"

MAMA, SING OLD SHEP

Copper Jim Quarrells

His time on a hard bed was fast ticking down.
He lay limp and white as the sheets.
His eyes fluttered open, he knew she knew.
He smiled then asked her so weak:
CHORUS:
Mama, sing Old Shep to me.
Sing, Mama, like you used to sing
When I was a child and bad dreams took my sleep.
Mama, sing Old Shep to me.

There looms a dark tunnel I must walk alone
To light at the far end I see.
Your sweet lullabies walk me through blackest gloom.
Mama, sing Old Shep to me.
(Repeat chorus...
Her high mountain treble was not washed away
By rivers that flooded her eyes.
And into the third verse as her voice refused,
Her boy walked into the light.
(Repeat chorus...

PART ONE

M

IS FOR

MAMA

IN THE EYES OF A CHILD

ANNA HILL

In the eyes of a child I see tomorrow
Not bound by lies, hate, blame or sorrow.
In the eyes of a child, in each boy, in each girl
Lies the faith and the hope and the love of the world.

CHORUS

To this child of mine, I give my best
Trembling that I might fail my quest.
To use all I am for all he needs.
He follows today, tomorrow he leads.

In the eyes of a child lives every nation,
Dawns every dream, crowns all creation.
In the eyes of a child lives the best that we've got.
Part of you, part of me and a whole lot of God.
(Repeat chorus...

~~~~~ **CHAPTER 1** ~~~~~
LAST LULLABY

"Mama, can you hear me?"

"Yes, son," she said, rising from her chair. Standing by his bed, she felt his forehead. His fever wasn't up. "I'm right here, Clay."

"Mama, this ain't the bad dream? We... we really are here?"

His weak voice already had her near tears. Every word seemed to take all he could muster. "Darling, what's wrong?"

"Bad old dreams, Mama. Like when I was little and you'd sing *Old Shep*... I'd go on back to sleep... Mama, sing *Old Shep* now."

"What were you dreaming, Clay?"

"Well it's like this... this real dark tunnel... with a light at the end."

"Might be the medicine. Listen, Copper Jim's bringing his guitar. If you're not up to picking, he'll pick for you. Junior's coming later and Gunnar too."

"Mama, I have to get to the light. Please sing it."

"Clay, darling, I--"

"Mama, sing *Old Shep*. It helps me feel better." Anna swallowed her tears and reached deep in her soul for strength. He only had to plead one more, "Please, Mama," and maternal love let Anna the mother do, what Anna the woman could never have done.

Her voice came lovely as a new kind of bird: *"When he was a boy and Old Shep was a pup."* As she trebled bell-clear and showed where Clay came by his singing, Anna remembered his introduction of the song on stage:

"Folks, a mama's lullaby is the world's sweetest sound. I want to sing a song my Mama sang to me when I was little. Still ask her to sing it, now and then. When you write songs, it's one you take as a standard and try to equal. When I write, I'm trying to share feelings, or paint a story. When I finish a song, I compare it to songs like *Old Shep*. Keeps me from getting too big for my songwriting britches. Red Foley wrote *Old Shep* and painted a Rembrandt of a song. Mama always sung it when I had a skinned knee, or a bad dream. One day she'll be singing it on stage with me. Yes, Mama, don't shake your head.

"Folks, Mama writes, sings like an angel, and bakes the best biscuits in Tennessee. She's the blond lady in row two. Put the light on her, boys. Give her a hand! My mama, Anna Hill! Stand up, Mama. I'm proud of you!" After the hall rocked with applause, Clay went on, "Hope I can sing *Old Shep* half as well for y'all as Mama sang it for me." He always brought down the house.

Singing by rote, an older verse echoed in Anna's mind: "Yea, though I walk through the valley of the shadow of death, I will fear no evil." Suddenly, she knew Clay was dying. His tunnel was that valley, he knew it too. He was too into what he called "the divine energy of the universe" not to know. He said divine energy inspired his music. She felt it some. Never as strong as Clay. It was the strength her childhood church called "the power of Jesus." Drawing on that power had been part of her long as she could remember.

Sometimes, when she and Clay walked the woods, he would stop, cock his head and listen. The first time it happened, he whispered, "Listen. It's the sound of the universe, Mama. Hear it?"

"Son, if you mean that bobwhite whistling, he's probably calling his mate."

"No. If you listen good, it's like a chorus." After he got Shep, she had seen boy and dog exchange eye contact that surpassed words. Now Clay was in some tunnel, resigned to die. When she finished singing he'd be gone like the others she loved. With the bad picture the doctors painted, maybe it was his best blessing, short of a miracle. But maybe they'd get one!

The thought ran through Anna's mind like the oxygen pumped by her fighting heart, that beat on Bible Belt religion, the American dream, and Mama. Still singing, she prayed. Taught prayer at such an early age, her prayers came like breathing: Lord, send a miracle to save Clay. If you need a soul, take mine. He's my only son. You know what that's like. Let him live to be an old man, with lots of kids and grandkids. The world doesn't need the good to die young. Clay brings such joy to me and the world. Lord, please spare him! Amen.

The white room was warm. Still she started the shaking she hated and the weakness it showed. But her voice held strong and Clay was resting. She began to sing softer, dragging out the melody. Her tears overflowed in distinct crystal drops. She started a soft hum as she had when singing Clay the child to sleep, then hushed. He did not protest, his breathing was steady.

With a sigh, she took her sweater from the back of the recliner chair and put it on. She wished for a cigarette, and wished she hadn't promised Clay she'd quit smoking. She couldn't go back on her promise till he got well. What if he don't? He will. What if he don't? He has to! Hush! She tiptoed to the windows.

Like Clay, she loved nature. The month was March but it was a May day. Too nice a day to go insane. She learned to survive the present by thinking of the past. Like a rabbit running from a wolf, her thoughts ran to hide in the past.

Spring brought good fishing to Greenriver Lake. Her folks fished every spring till a freak storm capsized their boat. Daddy made everyone wear life jackets. It made no sense all three bodies were found without life jackets, even her little sister, Marie. She'd have drowned too, if she hadn't been at Aunt Effie's. After the funeral, she rode back to the farm with her aunt.

Sad as that day was, she'd have fared better if she could've stayed. Aunt Effie Fitzgerald's big house was a place she had loved and spent holidays and a month in summer since she could remember. Always full of games, stories and songs, Aunt Effie taught her to play checkers, and to sing *Old Shep* and lots of songs. But in six months Aunt Effie lay dead in her coffin.

For three days and nights the house overflowed with food and folks Anna hardly knew or not at all. She finally got the courage to leave her corner behind the kitchen stove and crept in the parlor to see Aunt Effie. The old lady lying in the pink dress didn't look like anybody Anna knew. Aunt Effie would never wear a lacy dress. Maybe the whole thing was a mistake.

After looking long and hard, Anna saw the angry old lady frowning from the gray coffin was Aunt Effie. Dead, she was old. Her grin and joking black eyes had kept her face young and full of light. Her love for music from Chopin to Bill Monroe, her garden, the mare Sassy Girl, the peach orchard and tending folks and black dirt colored her aura of youth. Her mad look came from some dunce putting her in a dumb dress. She never wore any dress but her good gray suit she wore to town and church. At home she wore jeans like two mornings ago, when she rode off on Sassy saying she had things to do.

That meant she needed time alone, or to see Mr. Charlie on the next farm. His wife was dead, like Aunt Effie's Dumas. Since Aunt Effie went to pains to be sure she didn't know about Mr. Charlie, and her own children too, Anna never let on. Aunt Effie said he was a neighbor and sometimes hired man. Being the one soul she never cussed in front of gave away Mr. Charlie being more. Plus his phone calls; Aunt Effie talked softer when it was him.

The clincher came the day he came to fix the well pump. After Mr. Charlie fixed the pump and water was running in the kitchen sink again, Aunt Effie served him coffee and fried peach pies made fresh that morning. Anna sat at the table and had milk and a pie before going out to the tree swing.

At the back steps, she remembered her ham biscuit, still on the table, she made to take the sweet taste from her mouth. Going back for her biscuit, she stopped at the screen door. They were still at the table, but now he was holding her hand. Aunt Effie smiling at a man holding her hand froze Anna.

Aunt Effie hated all men like she hated her dead husband Dumas the drunkard, as she called him. She was forever saying, "If you want to be punished, marry a drunkard. You'll have a life of worry and weeping. You'll get to raise the crops and the young'uns by yourself. You'll stay busy cleaning up his puke and out of his way when he gets mean, so you don't kill or be killed. Won't know a peaceful hour. You'll amaze yourself to the bitter end, when he drinks his self to death, by not shedding a tear at the burying."

Paralyzed at the door, Anna had a flash: Maybe Mr. Charlie didn't drink.

Maybe too, it was easier to forget her biscuit. She tiptoed backward across the porch, then jumped all four steps and ran just like a spooked fawn for the tree swing.

It was crazy Aunt Effie could get killed riding Sassy Girl. She'd loved and ridden that mare since before Anna was born. No one knew what happened. Sassy just came trotting back in the barn with an empty saddle. Anna went looking for Aunt Effie and found her laying dead in the peach orchard.

Her eldest son, Evan said, "Some snake scared Sassy and she threw Mama. I told her she was too old to ride that mare. Never could tell Mama nothing. I'm thankful she didn't suffer, Doc said a broken neck brings death on instant."

Again, Anna sat in church hearing a preacher preach on the Lord having need of folks. It struck her the Lord was having a run on having need of folks she needed. Taking her aunt took her last relative willing to take her in.

Just past her thirteenth birthday, Anna landed in the God awful "Christian" climate of Give Us This Day Orphanage. Evan and Margaret drove her to her newest new home, justifying every mile to Nashville with how they didn't have room in their Christian home for her and their four boys. It'd be different if she was a boy, they hoped she understood. Anna understood she lost out again by being a girl. But, maybe this time being a girl was a plus.

Living with Evan and Margaret was no more appealing than living in an orphanage where she didn't know a soul. She never liked Evan, Aunt Effie didn't either. She used way more "sons a bitches" and "damnations" when Evan came around. She once said, "Evan's a Baptist elder, so he must be a good man but if souls like Margaret and Evan fill heaven, I'd be a fish out of water! It's the nasty nice folks that take the fun out of religion and living. Can't believe God put us here to be long faced."

In seven months, a happy twelve year old turned into a glum teenager. In a sad world, fighting to survive, she woke one morning and saw she was bleeding to death on top of everything else. With her period, which she hadn't been told a thing about, she was left to the dubious mercies of Mrs. Stokes, the kind, rule-worshiping head of Give Us This Day. With the best a closed mind would allow, Mrs. Stokes comforted her tomboy heart.

But her parents were fun folks like Aunt Effie. She hadn't been raised to cross all her t's and dot all her i's. The boys' games she loved, like softball were forbidden. She couldn't even sit in the fork of a friendly oak to do her thinking. Being a young lady, Mrs. Stokes said, it was time to act like one. Mrs. Stokes had to call her by both names, so Anna Lucy was to play with the young ladies, not the young men. But girls didn't play games worth playing. That's why she played with boys in the first place, for Pete's sake. Girls just talked about boys and when they could wear lipstick and bras. Who gave a rat's rear about that?

She not only felt alone and lonely, but bored as hell. Those first horrible months, she prayed nightly for the Lord to need her, like He needed all her folks. During a less heroic moment, she wondered if she got to needing Mrs. Stokes, if God would need her too. With her luck, if Mrs. Stokes departed, Frankenstein might take her place. After weeks of waking, alive and still at Give Us This Day, she stopped praying for the Lord to need her. She had His answer; a big fat no! She had to find other ways to relieve her pain. Like Aunt Effie said, ain't no glory in a heart mossing over with pain.

She found the orphanage library, read every book she could halfway stand and the good ones several times. Books gave her things to think about besides how lonesome she was and things to dream about besides how she hated the orphanage. Books were her survival till Jeff Hill of the long-legged walk, wheat-colored hair and tender blue eyes came along.

Back then, he was master of the quick smile and really talked to her. She loved Edgar Rice Burroughs, Jeff climbing up and down utility poles in his leg spikes looked like Tarzan. He made her heart race as she sat on the steps with two more girls watching him and the line crew hanging new lights.

Over the next few days, Jeff became interested in her and eventually stole her out of the orphanage. They giggled like two kids stealing watermelons the night she left. After dark, meeting him under that old magnolia was easy. He had his '56 Chevy parked down the road, and she hadn't been in a car in four years. Once they were running fifty miles an hour from Give Us This Day, she was delighted. Those first precious years seemed like another life now. She guessed they were; when Jeff was such joy to be with and their love was warm. Whatever he got in his head during the last years, she had loved him dearly.

After the magic was gone, and he started weirding out, Jeff was still good to her and she was good to him. She cooked his meals, kept his house and son clean and his bed warm. What more could a woman do to show her man she loved him? Till Jeff, she was doomed to stay in the orphanage till she was eighteen, and she'd never regret the man who helped her make Clay. A child had to be the most beautiful thing a man and woman could create together.

From the first, Clay was the light of her life. So was Jeff, as her man for God's sake, not her baby! She never understood why Jeff never understood loving your own flesh and blood wasn't adultery or betrayal! He was so self-assured in the early days and holding down a good job with the electric company. Who would have dreamed he'd turn so insecure after Clay was born or that Jeff could be a man to take his own life in his son's sixteenth year.

She'd been Jeff's wedded wife six months when the authorities found her. By then, she had a noticeable swelling under her skirt. After Jeff had shown their marriage certificate, the authorities, consisting of two policeman and Mrs. Stokes, decided to let well enough alone.

That night she held their eight pound son for the first time, Jeff stood by her bed proud as could be, so still self-assured and macho. Making Clay was pretty macho of them both, if you asked her.

After Clay turned four, Jeff decided it was time for another baby. It struck her as a fine idea and was perfectly willing. After a year or so she hadn't conceived, and they decided to see if somebody was firing blanks.

Dr. Jonas saw no reason they couldn't have another baby. He said relax and let Mother Nature take her course, but they were relaxed, that way. Their bed always bounced warm and did to the last. Clay came easy, actually a fringe benefit. They weren't thinking about a baby the first time Mother Nature took her course. Relaxed and trying at opportune times, no second child came.

After several years and no luck getting pregnant, they really went downhill. Jeff got a nutty notion it was her fault she wasn't pregnant. He said straight out, "You don't want another child. You want to devote all your time to Clay. A blind man could see that." Where Clay was concerned, Jeff was a blind man with twenty-twenty vision. She told him he didn't know shit from sugar.

Clay was the one subject they never saw eye to eye on. She learned to accept her inability to fix Jeff's problem with her love for Clay. She tried her damnedest to reassure him before concluding his feelings were not her fault, or Clay's. As hard as she tried, as sincerely as she talked, she'd have found the way long ago, if she knew how. Only Jeff could change his feelings.

Her folks drowning taught her early to let go of the irrevocable or it would drag her under with it. She accepted her marriage with a grain of salt. Nobody was perfect, that included her and Clay, as well as Jeff. Too much good filled their lives to let the bad destroy them as a family. Most couples lost the "magic" after a while. Jeff was the last man she thought would turn into a jealous fool over his own son, but everybody was a fool about something.

Still Jeff got worse, nothing helped. He grew more moody and his moods turned blacker. She suggested they get counseling. He growled they could handle their problems and wouldn't discuss it. Again she had to accept hard reality. As long as he denied the truth and refused help, there was none.

Clay's pain over Jeff holding him at arms' length was hard enough to cope with, never mind her pain or Jeff's. Clay was so beautiful and the blessing of her life. He was a good boy, and so intelligent. She couldn't unlove him! If there was a villain, it was Jeff. Piss on him when it came to hurting Clay.

It made her heart ache to see how he did things to please his daddy. Clay even watched TV football, which he had no interest in, to share time with Jeff. He loved to ride in the car with Jeff, but errands like a trip to the gas station, that never bothered most dads, were trips Clay was seldom allowed to share.

In spite of her resolutions to the contrary, she tried to discuss with Jeff his coldness to Clay. But he never knew what she was talking about and blew smoke about making a good living and that was being a good father. The last time she asked Jeff to take Clay on an errand, he snarled, "Stop trying to hang that kid around my neck! Give me a break!"

"Okay, ass! I won't bring it up again." And she hadn't, nor had he. But time after time, she watched Clay trot beside the car begging, "Let me go, Daddy. Please let me go! I'll be good!" Nearly always Jeff backed out of the driveway on a routine errand, without answering or slowing down.

She vowed to let their relationship seek its own level. But one day, hurting for Clay and hating Jeff's stupidity, she had to change it one way if she couldn't another. She ran to her sobbing seven year old watching the car go down the hill, turned him to face her and hissed, "Don't ever ask that bastard to take you anywhere again! I mean it! You hear me?"

"Ye... yes'm, but--"

"Come take a bath, we're going to a movie. He's too dumb to know he's hurting himself worse than us. I can't change him. You got to stop crying over your daddy being a fool. Get over it! That's all either of us can do."

After the movie, Clay asked, "Why won't Daddy let me go, Mama?"

"I don't know, but sometimes the answer is no. It doesn't mean it's right, it just means no. A brick wall no is a hard lesson, so learn it now. Don't go through life beating your head against brick walls."

She never suspected then, but Jeff had to be seeing other women. Lord, back then, she didn't know married folks even fantasized about being unfaithful! Now, it was easy to see if Jeff hadn't wound up dead, they would have divorced. Not coming out of the woods that last hunting trip was proof.

Clay was only eleven, but he still didn't get Jeff's praise for earning money to buy the dog of his dreams. Clay had to have a shepherd, but not the kind used since dirt in Tennessee to herd stock, guard the home and for a pet. Till he started reading library books, she thought a German Shepherd was only a Police Dog, and mean and vicious. Besides biting folks, Clay said, the breed was used for herding and tracking lost people. The shepherd he wanted cost fifty dollars and no other dog would do.

All that summer Clay mowed lawns to buy the pup he had picked out. The breeder said "Shep" would be a hundred dollars, but he had a sprained paw when the rest of the litter was sold. Soon it was hard to tell if Clay worshiped Shep more or Shep worshiped him more. For sure she didn't worry as much about Clay when Shep was with him. Course then she had to sing *Old Shep* for the boy and the dog. One night she joked, "If they make a film of this song, I'm going to get y'all auditioned. You're both naturals."

She had ambitions to be a singer and loved to sing before losing her folks. After, she didn't sing till Clay came. Sang and rocked Clay to sleep every night in spite of Jeff complaining, "He's going to get so spoiled we can't stand him."

"Jeff, I love to rock him."

"What about the nights when I want to talk?"

"Honey, we are talking."

"You know what I mean," he said, his eyes pleading.

"He'll be asleep and down for the night in ten minutes, like always. Then we can do what ever you want to, like always. Are you jealous of your own son?"

"Forget it, Anna. Got to change the oil in the car." That was the last of his complaining about her rocking Clay, but it didn't take Einstein to see he didn't like it. She guessed he saw, she was going to rock Clay if he liked it or not! She knew how bad it felt to be raised without affection.

When Jeff came in from the garage, she told him that travesty wasn't happening to her own flesh and blood. He just stomped off to bed but from then on he was depressed. It happened so gradually, it seemed like his nature.

Maybe she never knew Jeff at all. After living single awhile, she suspected she didn't understand men in general. For sure, she didn't understand the ones who seemed to like who she was, then tried to change her, or shame her or something. They made her feel like a toy that needed fixing. She wasn't looking to be fixed. The less painful thing was to forget men.

When Jake stumbled into her life, she told him, up front, she was nuts where men were concerned. He wouldn't take a warning for an answer. Hell, Jake wouldn't take no for an answer. For a time, she was crazy about him. They were so good together, till it all came falling down. He seemed unique, a rare free spirit. Looking back, she could see the war of wills they got into.

Why some men had to be right over women when they were wrong was a fact she couldn't fathom; anybody was wrong some. Insecurity was a trait to change, not aid and abet. If she intimidated anyone, they'd have to get over it or be intimidated. No malice was on her part. She'd never been dumb enough to apologize for having blue eyes. It was just as dumb to apologize for being herself. Playing it straight cost, no getting around that.

After Jake, thinking she had risen above or sunk below her vulnerability, she quit men forever-- again. Then came Gunnar McGuire, an endangered species, ballsy enough to accept her as is. Now he was the beat of her heart, the love of her life and hopefully the last. With Gun, it was no problem she could spell cat, was not the kinkiest body in the bedroom, and didn't pretend to be the village virgin or idiot to keep her man from being intimidated.

Miracle of miracles, he wasn't intimidated. Successful in music and otherwise, he didn't need a hundred and ten pound woman, who had spent her life keeping house and raising a son, playing little, helpless me games to convince him he was competent, needed and loved. Gun founded one of Nashville's most respected publishing and production houses and, evidently, did his bimbo chasing before her time. His character and mature good looks were uncommonly appealing, and she worshiped Gun. He did as much for her in the bedroom as any man could and miles more in the parlor. His libido surged strong enough he didn't need kinky shit to be happily satisfied. Or, he was kind enough to get kinky service elsewhere, without harassing her for bedroom romps she wasn't into. He even understood she had to stay with Clay.

Without Gun, she could never have come this far. Feeling herself falling asleep, she checked her son and softly prayed, "Lord, help Clay. Please. I won't ever beg for another thing. Send the vaccine. Please, please don't let them put dirt in Clay's face! Christ's name, amen."

Clay was so thin, couldn't stand pneumonia again.

Too late to undress or get the folding bed. She adjusted her recliner chair as horizontal as possible. Looking once more at Clay, so handsome, so haggard, her eyes fluttered into merciful sleep. Two new tears slipped from her lids, lingered a moment, then tracked down the sides of her face to hide in her hair.

 CHAPTER 2
SOME DAYS A CHANGE

Clay was having a good day, he ate well at breakfast and lunch. He even joked a little. Now he was napping, she was reading *Gone With the Wind* again. It had been years since she had read the tribulations of Scarlett. A long ago story made a safe place to hide.

Anna's reading was interrupted when Copper Jim sauntered in with his guitar. Seeing Clay was asleep, he set his case by the wall, put a shushing finger to his lips, and eased to the bed to check Clay out.

When Jim took the chair beside her, Anna wondered if he could see how small Clay was getting. Till Jim handed her his red and white bandanna, she didn't know she was crying. She dried her eyes and handed back the bandanna.

Copper Jim whispered, "Hope he feels like picking when he wakes up."

"He's eating today, but he woke up talking wild last night. I... I'm afraid he's tired of fighting." The fear in her voice hit Jim's ears like a scream.

"Need you a break, Annie. Go on to the lunchroom and eat something. Can't be no good for Clay getting down sick yourself."

She tried to smile. "I won't get down sick and I'm not hungry."

"Well, go have you some coffee and a piece of pie. Caffeine and sugar beats nothing. I can't stand seeing you so beat."

"All right, if it'll make you feel better. I won't be long, Jim."

"Take your time, I got all day and all night." After she was gone, he got his guitar and sat beside the bed picking softly and thinking. This damn AIDS was past understanding. Clay was straight as a man was made. It was hell, he was down and victim unto death from such a freak thing. Knocked out most of the time just to stand the pain. Doctors said it coulda laid in him for years.

Staying blind running drunk from dope or alcohol or both made a man hell ragged as he could suffer. Got his own self down to skin and bones when he was boozing and eating pills like a retard. Looked like death eating a cracker. Had the hiccups next to Clay's case. Jim got his bandanna again and wiped his eyes. It was a devil done shame to put a man on top, then strike him down with this pestilence. And it wasn't just the boy-girls or she-hims or whatever was the nice way to put it. He didn't see why a soul hung with back door craving wanted to be called gay. Couldn't be nothing gay about waking up with another damn man, if folks shunned you or not!

Maybe gays couldn't help how they got their jollies, but them back and forth cesspools could. They was the real varmints that loosed the AIDS. You could read on Sodom and Gomorrah if you didn't know that. It was all right there in the Book. Them forked-dick sons a bitches back and forth between the sexes made this abomination. Oughta be horse whipped and public hung. A body could pick men or women one to lay with.

None of this shit belonged to men lusting for women, or women lusting for men. Clap, syphilis, and bastard young'uns rained enough punishment on men and women. Shouldn't be infecting normal folks like Clayboy there, just a shadow of hisself without strength left to sleep. Just months ago, he was busting the charts and knocking folks out at concerts, with the girls fighting to get to him. He didn't know how a man Clay's age could keep from using girls begging to be used, but he didn't. If he had said it since Clay was sixteen, Jim hadn't expected the marvel that came from Clay's first concert till his last.

Once in Louisville, he had the fans hog wild. Taking bows after four encores, Clay said, "They make me feel good, but I need a chocolate shake." He took another bow, and walked off with them screaming for more. Rolling down the highway to Nashville, Clay told Bry to stop at the first exit for chocolate shakes. Chocolate shakes were one of the few eats he still loved.

For a man who was mighty picky about the few females he did pick, who wasn't long past being a boy, who never hurt nobody in his whole life, who just wanted to pick and sing his songs, it didn't make no sense. Didn't make no justice, or show no mercy. Jim wiped his eyes again, and wiped off his guitar. Fretting a chord, he adjusted a string as he studied Clay and decided it looked like another day when Clay had to sleep most of it away.

Copper Jim started picking and prayed, "You know what You're doing if I don't, Lord. But I'd be much obliged if You took this bad cup from Clayboy."

From that first night at the Center, he loved Clay like his own. But raising kids, like raising anything, took a world of cultivating. He never was much on raising kids or crops. Maybe he was a low-life like Leona said. Him and Leona had a daughter named Linda Jean up in her thirties now. It'd been years since he had heard from either. Linda Jean didn't like her daddy much, he couldn't blame her. He was too drunk and too broke to a daddy when she needed one.

Leona bitched she never knew where he was. It was funny what a woman called romantic till a man was her husband. Anyway, Leona sent her letter to his agent. He was on the road so much about that time, he didn't have a home or post office box. Leona's letter said Linda Jean had a baby boy with copper-red hair like his grandpa. Linda Jean had married a rancher and they was all living together in Wyoming. Leona sent the phone number and address but he thought it might be risky to call. He sent a New Mama card and a five hundred dollar check. Never got no answer but the canceled check. Linda Jean was enough like her daddy to know money spends wherever it comes from.

Since the baby, he'd sent money twice a year. Leona finally sent a picture of Linda Jean and the boy and wrote his whole name on the back, Lucas Quarrells Thompson. She wrote his nickname, Lucky, down too. Jim was thinking Linda Jean had done well when Gunnar and Junior walked in.

Gunnar asked, "Clay doing okay?"

"Sleeping since I got here. Glad to see your guitar, Junior."

"Where is Anna?" Gunnar asked.

"Coffee shop," Copper Jim said. "Hospitals and funeral homes make the well sick. Wish you'd get her out for a car ride, or something."

Anna felt a lift from the coffee, the warm pecan pie wasn't such a hot idea. Bad as things were, it did help to have good friends. Jim had made Clay a kind of replacement daddy. Besides God, he had more to do with Clay being a star than anyone. Jim was proud of the three of them being native Tennesseans in music. According to him, they were distant cousins, too. She didn't keep tabs that far removed. In junior high she researched a three generation genealogy chart. As a summer project she planned to go to the state archives and research deeper, but that was the summer she lost her family.

Suddenly, her mind was tracing a memory she had fought to forget. To know what was happening now, she had to remember what it was in the past she couldn't stand to think about.

Course it was her nightmare about Florida and the warning it carried. They were at Daytona, in the beach cottage where Jeff, Clay and herself vacationed the summer Clay was eight and his baby tooth flared up. At four he fell off a swing and killed the nerve in a front tooth. Their dentist wanted to keep it as a spacer. If a problem developed, he said, it would have to come out.

On a holiday it would act up but they finally found a dentist. The extraction ended Clay's pain and there was little bleeding. Other than a gap in his grin, he was fine; they thought. Then no one had heard of AIDS. Driving back to the cottage, Clay wanted to go to the beach and they continued their vacation. It was time to shed the tooth, so he wasn't without it much longer than normal.

The first time she had the nightmare, Clay was in his teens. In the nightmare, Jeff had gone to the dog races, she and Clay were in the beach house. He was in his upstairs bedroom reading. Downstairs in an easy chair with her bare feet on an ottoman, she was into a novel. Then the room darkened. She switched on the lamp and read on till an uneasy feeling possessed her. She hadn't looked out, but she felt a bad storm brewing. Monster waves flashed in her mind, her uneasy feeling rose to impending doom.

She walked out on the porch and searched the Atlantic's horizon. The storm was so far out it was still a pinhead, but it was a killer blowing in to take all in its wake. Its main mission was to kill Clay, they had to get inland fast!

Back inside, she called Clay. Somehow she could see him on the bed, ignoring her. She called again, "A storm's coming. We have to leave!" He was unconcerned as a rock. Near panic, she ran upstairs, screaming "Clay!" When she crested the stairs and could actually see him, he was still reading. "Can't you hear?" she asked as calmly as she could. No response. "Clay, something like a tidal wave is blowing in. We have to get out of here fast!"

Without looking up, "It's okay, Mama, don't worry."

"We have to go!" Clay turned the page of his comic. She ran to the bed and shook him by the shoulder; he was a wet dishrag. She got an arm around him, managed to raise him to a sitting position and screamed, "Help me!" He smiled, serene as a drunk. She had no idea how, but she had to get him downstairs. He was a head taller and outweighed her thirty pounds.

Then the nightmare skipped to her walking Clay through the kitchen to the open back door and the wind howling like something gone mad. As she was about to walk him out the door and down the steps, he braced his arms on either side of the door and said, "Mama, go on, I have to stay here."

"A killer storm's rolling in. Come on!" He stood looking at her, stubborn as a mule. She moved out to the steps for a look around the house at the storm. A wall of water three stories high was at the beach. A rush of terror hit so hard she nearly fainted. Shaking her head for clarity and consciousness, she turned back to Clay and was greeted with a sneering grin. "Clay, let go of the door!"

"You go without me. You don't understand, but it's meant to be this way."

Anna felt a surge of adrenaline and shrieked, "No, you don't understand! I ain't spent my life raising you to let you stay here and drown! I said go and by God you're going!" For leverage she backed down a step, and came around in a haymaker slap that struck Clay in the face. She hated the shape of her hand imprinted in red on his cheek, but desperation called for desperate action. Shocked, Clay dropped his arms. She grabbed his shirt front and with strength they knew she did not possess on her own, Anna jerked the hundred-and-fifty-pound teen through the door and down the steps.

"Run!" she commanded. He stood at the bottom of the steps with an amazed expression on his face. "Clay, I said run, or do I have to pick your tall ass up and carry you?" Suddenly he laughed and was himself.

He started jogging in place and yelled, "Hey, Mama, last one to Atlantic Avenue's a rotten egg." As the black wave crested over the cottage roaring like a dragon from hell, they ran, fleet and free as two deer.

Then she woke from the dream, warning or whatever, but in the middle of the night, in middle Tennessee, the smell of the ocean permeated her nostrils. The taste of salt water washed bitterly in her throat, the face of the Florida dentist leered in her mind, and not a dry thread was on her body. She had to shower and change from the skin out. As long as there was hot water, she stood sobbing like it was Judgment Day and Clay was sentenced to hell.

For days, dread sat like an invisible vulture on the shoulder of her mind. At times, it always tried to flutter its filthy wings back into her conscious mind. Then, she made herself busy doing all the jobs she hated. She washed windows, waxed floors and the most hated job of all-- the dreaded cleaning of the oven. But the vulture always roosted deep in her mind.

Though she could never think the nightmare through, she knew it was a foretelling of horror. Even at the time, the dentist's gay voice bothered her. His prettiness had kept coming back to mind, when she had never been prejudiced about gays. Now she knew he had given Clay this damnation. If she had been into her gift of second sight then, she would have known. Her upbringing was opposed to visions. Till Clay talked about "knowing and seeing things" she gave psychic power little credence. But, God, why this? In desperation she gave the uneaten pecan pie a whack with her fork.

"The idea is to eat pie, not whip it to death," McGuire said as he sat down and smiled. He lifted her hand from the table and kissed it. With his lips on her hand, he said, "I love you." Her eyes were distant. "Where are you, darling?"

Her gaze came into focus. "Bad as Clay's getting, I guess hell."

"Hey, let's ride out to my house so you can rest."

"I don't want to rest," she snapped. "I need to fight somebody."

"Don't make it me. Let's go to Norman's. You love Norman's steak."

"I'm not dressed for Norman's." He sensed hysteria might take her, and once it started, she might not come back. She'd lost way too many folks she loved.

"Anna, I wish there was something useful to do."

"Me too. I keep making conversation, fluffing Clay's pillows, telling stories, singing old songs. I do small things for a man dying for want of a miracle."

"I'm praying for one. Bry's waiting. You need to take a break, before you break. Let's go to my place so you can bathe and rest on a real bed. You're losing weight as fast as Clay."

"But I'm afraid Clay might--"

"Junior and Jim would fight hell for Clay and they're going to pick. Don't fight common sense, or folks that love you. It won't help to get sick and have Clay worried about you." He squeezed her hand before kissing it again. "It's a gorgeous day, and I'm taking you out of here."

"Could we go to Song Farm and walk in the woods?"

"Anywhere you want. You're not the Rock of Gibraltar, and it's no sin to need me." He smiled, but she saw the desire in his eyes. She had ignored her man in an intimate way for weeks.

"I do need you, Gun. I'm just so scared for Clay."

"To think you don't need me scares hell out of me." He hadn't meant to say, "And I want you so." The way she wet her lips and looked down at her hands, gonged like a fire bell. The basic difference had tripped him up. A devastated man craved loving. A devastated woman thought it was the last thing she wanted. When you had someone worth loving, making love helped any time.

Still looking at her hands, she said, "I think it's broke." Her remark was so honest, so Anna, he didn't know whether to laugh or cry. Easy, he told himself, she's like a scared mare. Clay's still her baby. If you don't hold her today, you may tomorrow, but she never has wanted you till she wants you. When Clay was well, she wasn't into sacrificial pieces and you don't want her to be.

He kissed her cheek, saying, "Come on let's join the world awhile." The desperation in her eyes was pitiful. It was the first time he had seen her past tears. She needed him to hold her as much as he needed to. If it happened, he had be careful. This upset, she might beat him to the floor, fly like a dove, or throw a fit. Any songwriter could, that's what made a songwriter. If they made love, it was in his hands. Might be wiser to wait, but waiting when action was needed was bad in love or business.

"Gun, I just want to walk the woods."

"Fine, some days a change beats a rest anyway."

❀ ❀

Riding in the limo with Gun was always great. Bry driving on I-40 to Little Gatlinburg had her on familiar ground. Even after they moved to Woodhill, Clay came to the softly wild acres. He had set the house aside as a haven for aspiring songwriters and called it Song Farm. As Bry drove in the parking area, Gunnar said, "Tell them it's us so they won't worry about trespassers."

"Sure, Boss." It was a marvel what a man will do for a woman. Roughing it wasn't on Boss's list. During their occasional wee hours talks, sharing a fifth of Jack, he said he'd enjoyed all the hot, cold and wet he wanted. Said he got nature burnout in his farming days. Didn't even hang out at Center Hill, fishing like his music buddies. He said, "I catch my fish in the lake at Shelbyhouse or on a plate at Norman's. Ain't missed mosquitoes or chiggers."

Bry watched him follow Anna down the path to the trees. Boss paid good, treated him fine and was a smart dude when he was normal. A man could be a pure fool during a case of the pussy-whippeds, he'd been there. He woulda bet a week's pay there was no way for this shit from Gunnar McGuire, star maker, hit maker, woman maker, mover and shaker of Music Row. Boss walking to raw woods in his five hundred dollar suit and two hundred dollar shoes, after a piece that couldn't make a wart on the young stuff he'd left squalling was unreal. Like when Boss dumped Ginny and here she come. Not that he was too proud to take Boss's leavings. Took some man's leavings most always.

Virginity went with the sixties. Wasn't all that great, anyway. He'd had virginity in Lower Alabama. Left it crying on its front porch one night.

With AIDS around, taking anybody's leavings was a decision. Fooling with Anna Hill was real, deep shit. Being Clay's mama she had to come in contact with his blood. If she didn't take AIDS, she'd go crazy as Christmas when Clay died. Boss hadn't touched another woman since taking the hots for her. A first in six years, and for a damn loser! It wasn't he didn't like Anna, he did. She was somebody. No spring chicken but still good-looking. He'd seen the fire flare and turn her eyes purple when her Irish got up. If a man got her mind off Clay and in a bedroom mood, she'd be a lively piece. But hell, he'd be scared to touch her for a million dollars.

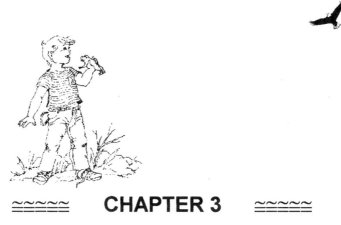

≋≋≋≋≋ **CHAPTER 3** ≋≋≋≋≋

LITTLE GATLINBURG

Her sure footsteps told him she walked familiar ground. Under the trees, strolling a humus carpet woven from an infinity of autumns, he could feel the peace she felt. He sighed, "These old trees are precious giants." Her answer was silently slipping her hand into his.

As they walked deeper into the silver-green world of leaves, he felt her drift more into herself, hearing the echoes of a thousand yesterdays. It was a virginal place, too heavy with shade for undergrowth. There were oak trees with more circumference than the arms of two men could encircle. Towering pine and poplar created a cathedral. The high tree singing of a pair of mockingbirds reminded Gunnar of the balcony choir they heard in Paris. He felt a mood of enduring grace, immune to time, untouched by the woodsman's axe. It was no wonder that Clay loved this place.

The phrase "This is the forest primeval" came to mind. He swallowed his urge to share it. It was enough she asked him to bring her here and imperative to give her the silence she needed. Unlike many women, she didn't have to have him or any man. She made no secret of how much she liked and wanted him. At this point in life, he needed his woman's liking and wanting more than he needed to be needed or even to be loved. For that, he followed her frame of mind as well as her footsteps and not just through a lovely forest. Awhile back, he had accepted, he would follow Anna Hill to hell and here he was. She continued to silently walk the trails, till they came to a huge jagged circle of limestone. She sat down on the rock and lay her hand on it reverently.

Anna's eyes took on the unfocused look they always did when she was seized by a vision or a song. She began to study the fern and surrounding multitude of tiny red and blue and yellow wildflowers. She touched the petals of a white violet growing at the base of the rock. Stroking the heavy moss on top, she said, "Sit down with me, Gun." He sat close and she placed her hand on his thigh, to let him know she appreciated his presence. She fell silent for several minutes before saying, "Clay loves it so here in the woods."

"The limestone looks like it had ancient help to be so round. Like Druids might've worshiped here, but they roamed Europe." Looking up through the trees, he added, "It is magnificent here."

"I hoped you would feel it." Then in a removed voice, she began to tell him things. Long pauses came between her sentences. There were leaps in time between incidents but he did not interrupt. From her tone and her eyes, he knew she was quite apart from him. The flood of the past washing her mind of worry for the present was a break he knew she needed.

All afternoon a man who loved to talk, whose love for conversation was one of his traits endearing to her, said little. Some of what she shared was known to him, but at twilight he knew more than he had ever hoped to about the paradoxes and puzzles within Anna and her rare bond with her son.

Rearing Clay started the healing of her soul, the recovery of her aborted young dreams, and with Clay's triumph she was at last mended from early tragedies. As a man thinks, so is he, echoed in Gunnar's mind. He paraphrased, as a woman thinks, so is she.

Clay's voice matured out baritone, but his style was learned in Anna's lap. Like Copper Jim said, "Blood tells, Clay's just a male version of his mama." Gunnar agreed, but it would take time to harvest Anna's talent, and he had no choice but to wait. Listening to her flood of memories, he was sadly aware she was preparing for another bad goodbye.

Clay was a hyper child and matured into a hyper man. As a boy he was loving and giving, as he was now. One was supposed to be molded by maturity, but she couldn't give credence to that with Clay. Spiritually and emotionally he had changed little to none.

After getting over Jeff's death and feeling guilty, they were happier with him gone, their quality of life, even without Jeff's income, improved. Jeff's mood swings had grown so bad, so gradually, they had not fully realized the pall of depression they lived under. Perhaps from bad house vibes, Clay was drawn early to the woods, the waters, to all things of Nature. Like the white-tailed deer, he lived to travel the green lanes of Little Gatlinburg.

Even as a child, he sang on perfect pitch. From her kitchen window she often heard his singing echoing through the trees, bouncing from hollow to hollow and bluff to bluff. Those echoes were his first stage monitors, the woods made his first amphitheater. That was why he loved performing professionally outside. A soundman's nightmare was Clay's mecca. Outside sound seldom equaled studio quality, but he always outdid himself. Those albums were his most lauded by critics and fans alike.

When he was six or so, he talked about his room in the woods. Initially, she took it for fantasy. He told her it was green and blue and silver with a wishing rock. He could lie on it and look up and see all the animals in the trees. There was a skylight in the roof of the trees to watch for hawks. One day he ran in, piping, "An eagle! A real live eagle! You gotta come see him, Mama!"

"Son, I'm mixing a cake, and he'll be gone by now."

"No," he said, his eyes big. "I feel him. If you come to my rock and we sit still, he'll fly back. Hurry!" Deciding it was time to check out Clay's secret room, she dropped her spoon in the batter and followed.

It all turned out to be real, just as he had described. For the first time, she sat on the rock and waited for an eagle. She didn't have much faith, but in a few minutes the eagle came flying back over.

Time in the woods was prime time for Clay. One fall day, he woke from a nap with the chipmunk on his chest. The tiny animal, with giant courage and trusting brown eyes, was nuzzling for the peanuts in his shirt pocket. He learned by being quiet, with peanuts, or carrots, he could be friends with the creatures from the grass and trees. Birds and rabbits and squirrels came. Even a red fox came to share a cookie. He said, "I had the cookies for me. I didn't know foxes like cookies." She'd never forget his wide-eyed wonder.

Even the shyest of creatures came, the soft-eyed doe and her fawn. Clay saw her watching, moving from tree to tree, twitching her tail, turning her ears to catch any sound before she came to his rock for his apple. They came a few weeks and stopped. He searched and called but they never came back. The day he gave up, he came home crying a hunter had killed his friends and fretted all evening. At bedtime, he was still upset. She tried to comfort him with, "Maybe the mama deer found a new mate and they all went to another part of the woods to live."

"Uh, uh, you want me to feel better, I know you."

"Since we don't know what happened, we can only guess. So why not guess a good thing?" He looked at her an eon, for an eight year old, then the pain and anger in his eyes cooled.

"Yeah! He smiled. "They moved to another part of the woods. Now, Mama, sing *Old Shep* so I can go to sleep." One Saturday after a day in the woods, as she was tucking him in, he said, "I sing for the animals. They like *Old Shep* and *Danny Boy*. I sing all the songs we know and some I made up. They like *Old Shep* best, like me. I know all the words now, but I can't sing it special like you. Mama, sing *Old Shep*."

All his life, he had been her joy and her salvation. From the first moment she held him in her arms, pink and serious and wiggly, she felt something beyond any feeling she had ever known. With Clay's birth she recovered her sense of blood. She loved her mother-in-law like her mother, but it wasn't the same as blood kin. The first time Jeff took her home, up past Sevierville, she fell in love with the farm, the mountains and Mama Hill. The Smoky Mountains reminded her of articles and pictures on the Swiss Alps. Jeff said, "Nobody but an Anna would read up on such places." The paper and detective stories were the only reading he liked. Jeff said she took his mama as a substitute for her own, his mama took her as a substitute for his twin, Janice, who died with polio when they were eight.

She loved blackberry picking with Mama Hill in the summer and hickory nut hunting in the fall. They all loved Mama Hill's blackberry jam and hickory nut pie. Jeff said neither one was worth fighting chiggers and snakes for. When he was a boy he had to help, but picking out nuts drove him crazy. He said he'd settle for a moon pie anytime before doing all that.

Jeff said he wasn't hanging on the plowing and planting cross either. After high school, he answered an ad in the Knoxville paper for work in Nashville and hired on as an apprentice electrician. Later, he wanted his daddy to work in the maintenance section. His daddy could fix anything with a motor, and was still young enough to work out a pension. Nathan Hill died before she and Jeff married, and never would work for the electric company. Jeff said it was like his folks made work a religion, like they thought working like mules would earn them heaven when they died. Even after buying a tractor, his daddy was still at the mercy of every wrong wind.

By the time he turned three, if Jeff did deny it, Clay knew things beyond them and explanation. She thought the Lord's hand lay closer on Clay than on most. Jeff thought she was a too proud mama and her overblown sense of motherhood would settle down as the boy got older. He said she praised anything Clay did all out of proportion. Jeff could be plain shitty.

Clay knew the alphabet at three from her drawing letters on his back and putting each letter with a familiar word; like C is for Clay, M is for Mama, A is for Anna. At four he was reading his encyclopedias, knew all the dinosaurs and how to pronounce their names. Till then she didn't know how to pronounce *brontosaurus* or what one looked like.

In her sixth month with Clay, she bought the set of books from a door-to-door salesman. When Jeff came home from work, he wasn't thrilled. Signing up on the easy payment plan for books his unborn child wouldn't be using for years wasn't his idea of the wisest way to spend. They needed other things more, like a baby crib. But he said they'd make it and he married her to give, not take away. She had it lean as a kid and he hadn't put her in any castle.

Jeff was good to her, it was a shame he wasn't as loving with Clay. The books did give Clay a head start. Like the salesman said, some kids picked up knowledge having encyclopedias. She told Jeff, "Hope you're not too mad at me." Gunnar picked up the fact that Jeff worshiped Anna. A man never got too mad at a woman he worshiped. Besides, Anna was so honest, there was no way to tell her she had bought the snow job of the year.

But as it turned out, the books did all the salesman promised. When Clay started first grade, the whole set was dog-eared, smudged with tiny finger-prints, peanut butter and jelly stains, vanilla wafers, and sweet milk, all his favorite snack foods. After he found the section on music, the most-used book was the "M" volume. At five, he was humming scales as he ran his small finger along the notations. Watching him made her wonder if a child could absorb music by osmosis. She guessed it came from the same source that made a Chopin climb on a piano stool as a child.

The fated day Clay saw a TV commercial selling mail-order guitars left no peace in the house till they ordered one and it was delivered. "Waste of money," Jeff snorted. "His fingers are too short to start picking." But Jeff's love for her, like her love for Clay, made him make her happy. Anna loved Jeff too much to abuse a good thing. He said she always wanted what he wanted unless it wasn't what Clay wanted.

After the guitar came, Clay proved his daddy wrong again. All too often, proving Jeff wrong was a deed done with no malice on Clay's part. Innocent as it was, now she could see how her pride in Clay's triumphs was always a put down to Jeff. At face value, he couldn't give Clay credit, never mind a few high-flying dreams thrown in. Jeff tried to put a lid on what Clay could do. She never could make him see how putting a lid on anyone was cruel, and putting a lid on Clay was impossible. Clay always was gifted.

She never put him on a divine level like Jeff said. More and more he made remarks like, "You think Clay is Jesus Christ." She was too reverent toward God for that, but it crossed her mind Mary must have felt similar feelings about Jesus. A mama knows when her son is special. She remembered saying, "Jeff, don't doubt your own flesh and blood. All he does is half you."

So much she said to Jeff, meant to help, made him mad or intimidated and always depressed. Things were so clear in hindsight. He was probably up there somewhere now, seeing better too. She hoped it didn't chap his ass Clay conquered the music world as bad as it did when he could spell brontosaurus at four. Once when she praised Clay's A report card, Jeff growled, "You think he can change water to wine."

"Naw, he'd get you on his side if he could do that.

After the guitar came, there was no peace in the house till Clay's uninhibited banging progressed to picking and singing. As the days passed and Clay "caught on to it" as Jeff said, his picking and singing brought untold pleasure. If nothing else, Jeff enjoyed Clay's music when it was warm evenings on the front porch with friends joining in.

In senior high, Clay did throw fifty-cent words around, but he got along with the other boys. He enjoyed things they enjoyed, just not as much. He was the best catcher on the team, batted four hundred, and he could be counted on to play a great game. He just couldn't always be counted on. Their house was near the field; if Clay hadn't shown up half an hour before game time, the coach sent some boys to fetch him. Once the boys found Chopin, as they called Clay, and hustled him to the field, he played fine. After his freshman year, if it was game day and he was into a song he couldn't leave, the room in the woods was his haven. No one else knew where it was and she wouldn't give his secret away. Privacy was imperative when he was creating music.

Then he got the idea for a tape recorder. He said he could better practice singing, and when he had a new song going, a recorder would keep him from losing it. For his birthday, Anna saw to it that he got a portable recorder, but he still loved to pick and write in the woods more than anywhere. So many times, she watched him walk off with Shep, guitar case, backpack stocked with paper, pencils and goodies.

Once when Jeff accused her of spoiling him, she said, "Any mother wants her son to have what he wants that's affordable and harmless. The least spoiled soul in this house is Clay and you know it."

Clay was never ashamed to admit his songwriting came hard. He said on stage, "Writing's deep concentration most of the time. When I get into a new song then lose it, it's like I can't concentrate hard enough. Singing's a gift I got listening to Mama sing before and after I was born. Her voice is the sweetest sound and her heartbeat is the purest."

Anna recalled how he loved stories and would listen as long as she would tell. Now and then he said, "Tell the blackberry biscuit story, Mama, when you wasn't supposed to eat anything."

☺

Like most summers, I was spending two weeks with Aunt Effie who was off the wall as a fell picture. You never knew what she'd say or do, but she most always did or said things that kept you giggling or amazed or both. One day, we were going on a mission of mercy to a neighbor. Aunt Effie said, "Mattie's eat up with consumption, there's no cure and it's catching. Don't use the toilet or the dipper. Don't drink or eat a thing. There's ham and biscuits in the warming oven, jam's on the table. Ate my breakfast before you got up. Eat to do till we get back."

"Yes, ma'am, I will."

"It's hot today, but it'll be hotter tomorrow. Told Mattie I'd be back a week ago. Guess I lied. First cold will take her like the morning glories. Ain't much I can do, but make her laugh or clean her house if her twin daughters haven't. Don't get excited about housework, but we do things anyway if we're decent. Tomorrow we'll clean this shanty, bad as it gripes me. Can't live in filth."

"I'll help you clean both houses, Aunt Effie."

"You can help here, but not at Mattie's. Mattie and me have been friends since we were too young to go to the toilet by our self after dark. I should be horse-whipped for staying away."

"You stay real busy around here."

"Damned if I know what at, never am caught up. I do have to go, or wouldn't take you about consumption."

"She's really gonna die?"

"No need to dwell on it, ain't a thing we can do. It's in the Lord's hands and I'm proud of it. Mind about eating and drinking and won't be no problem. Listen to common sense now, so when you're grown it's a habit. You hear?"

"Yes'm, I hear and I won't."

"Pull a chair to the warming oven and get all you want. Sweet milk's poured in the refrigerator, eat while I brush and saddle Sassy. Got us a jug of water and ham biscuit for the saddle bags. Too hot to take more than we'll eat on the way. Fill up full and don't eat or drink at Mattie's." She made the best biscuits, and I ate a big breakfast.

When we boarded Sassy, it was late morning and hot on the gravel road. Our ham biscuit and water was gone before we got there, I was thirsty when we walked in. Mrs. Miller's twin grandsons, about my age, were eating blackberry biscuits, I turned wolf hungry. Seeing my mouth watering, Aunt Effie gave me a don't you dare look, introducing me.

Mrs. Miller said Bart and Art were keeping her company and were playing at the spring branch and I could play too. With her ratty hair stringing from the bun on her head and bad cough, she wasn't anyone I wanted to linger with. As we started out, Aunt Effie said, "Mind you behave," to warn me about the biscuits Bart and Art were finishing.

I followed the twins across the front porch and down the steps of the sizeable house that was peeling for a paint job. They led the way around back and down to the spring branch barely over my ankles. They invited me to ride a spotted goat but I wasn't broke to goat riding. They steered by twisting the goat's tail, and he bleated about it some. The goat had horns and Bart kept insisting I take a ride. I said I was afraid the goat might get mad about his tail getting twisted and start biting or bucking. They laughed, and Art said my city side was showing.

When they tired of the goat, they taught me to play rocks and tin cans, a game that was fun and practical. Scores of cans lay in a discard pile and a blanket of rocks lay along the spring branch. You got ten shots throwing rocks at tin cans stood side by side on a rusty oil drum. The one who knocked down the most cans in a best two out of three set won. I was no goat rider, but I held my own at rocks and tin cans. My undoing was Bart saying he was hungry for another blackberry biscuit. Art said he was too, they both said, "Let's go."

Trailing the twins was my only choice, since they had killed a chicken snake and I didn't want to see another one by myself. They led me in the back way to the cool kitchen smelling of wood smoke and good things to eat. Back then most country folks had little money, but they raised huge gardens and beef and pork. Their food would have graced God's table.

Aunt Effie and their granny talked in the parlor about a quilt pattern, while Bart did the honors in the kitchen.

Being a country boy, Bart took feeding company for granted. He took three biscuits from the warming oven, jam from the pie safe, and a knife from the blue jar on the table. Then he sat on one of the straightback chairs and built three blackberry biscuits. I couldn't keep my eyes off his work and decided he had to be the smartest boy in the world. He left the finished biscuits on the red and white gingham oilcloth to put the fixings away.

Art said, "We can eat if we put things up. Mama said to keep Granny company, not make a mess. Granny won't be here long and ain't able to clean up after herself, much less kids."

I said, "I'm sorry."

"Ain't your fault," Bart said, with serious black eyes. "Ain't nobody's fault."

A copy of his brother, but for serious green eyes, Art said, "Mama said so."

I was thinking if Bart made a biscuit for me, I hoped he wouldn't be mad because I couldn't eat it. When he had everything put away and took a test bite of biscuit, it got jam running down his chin, my mouth to watering and turned my will to mush. After rubbing his belly and shaking his head yes, the black-eyed twin handed a biscuit to Art and one to me.

Eating our scrumptious blackberry biscuits, we moseyed back to the spring branch and I won my first game of rocks and tin cans.

When we left it was cooler and we had fun riding Sassy Girl home. I waited in the barn while Aunt Effie unsaddled Sassy and turned her out to graze.

We walked on to the house and I thought we'd get right to fixing supper. Aunt Effie didn't go to the sink to wash her hands, but to the cupboard where she kept medicine. While she moved bottles around, I felt bad she was sick. But when she took out a castor oil bottle, I was so glad it wasn't for me.

Back then, when a kid got puny, there were three steps to recovery. The first was a good worming with nothing good about swallowing a worm pill the size of a half dollar. The second was a good enema. If you survived the first two steps and wasn't well, the third step was a good dose of castor oil. With all three steps, you spent more time running to the facilities than running to play. After the worming and enema, you acted better, better or not, to avoid castor oil. I was about to extend my sympathy as she measured four tablespoons in a cup, but she said, "Come take your medicine."

I backed off like a dog facing turpentine, moaning, " I don't feel sick".

"What if consumption was on that jam biscuit?"

"Didn't taste like it. Anyway, how did you know?"

"A potato eye could see the jam on your mouth. Need to wipe your mouth when you eat, but I'm damn glad you didn't today. You're a mite hard-headed. We know where you get that. Thank God, I ain't a liar."

"Aunt Effie, caster oil makes me vomit."

"Get consumption, you won't vomit or nothing else."

"If caster oil cures it, let's run take Mrs. Miller a dose."

"It don't. Got to get you cleaned out, so it has no time to set up. You take consumption, it'll kill me if your mama don't. Come on, Anna Lucy," she said coming at me with the cup, "take your medicine!" Aunt Effie was cemetery serious when she said "Anna Lucy."

CHAPTER 4

WHAT'S DONE IS DONE

It was late when Gunnar brought her back, but Clay was sleeping peacefully. Jim said he was awake all evening singing and picking. She hadn't heard Clay sing since he came in the hospital. Junior said he was writing a new song.

Gunnar had been right about her getting out, but going to his place was something else. Shacking up with her lover while her son lay sick wasn't the perfect behavior for a concerned mother. Sitting on Clay's wishing rock started her memories pouring out, Gun's arm around her waist felt too supportive to push away. She picked the worst times to have to lean. Then, of all things, she had to play kissy-face with Gun right there in the woods. One tender fool falling for another tender fool's come on was no way for either to stay sane. That rendered her weak enough to go home with him, that mansion was what got her in his bed in the first place. She knew better than to start trading affection with Gun. Once she got in high gear loving, she never had any brains. Like that first time slipped up on her.

They had so many fights about Clay's contract, she didn't know she even liked the man. Dinner to discuss the details of Clay's first concert was all the evening was supposed to cover. Getting herself covered wasn't on the agenda. After dinner they settled out by the pool for a glass of wine. By the time they moved into his den for their discussion, she knew she wanted him to kiss her. Knowing he knew made her feel all the more vulnerable. He was such a handsome, powerful man, he could have any woman he wanted. Besides, she couldn't be romantically involved with Clay's producer.

Gunnar's lips touching hers were too much then and now. After that first time with Gun, she was again, in a word, addicted. Maybe they both were, there didn't seem to be any stopping place. When Clay got better, she intended to marry Gunnar, like she promised again last night. Something about his house always acted on her like an aphrodisiac.

Maybe it was his studio. It was a magical place and he was like a wizard making music magic in it. Producing hit after hit not only made him rich, it earned him numerous awards and gold records. Besides Clay's singing, those cypress walls echoed with the vocals of most of the stars that had risen from Nashville over the past twenty odd years.

If it wasn't his studio, maybe it was something he had pumped in through the heating and cooling ducts. In any case, she never twisted into that pink marble entry foyer without winding up grinding like some minx and twisting back out with a smile on her face and genteelly satisfied.

When she let him talk her into a hot bath and nap, she should have known she couldn't keep him out of any of it. By the time they got around to the nap, he would have stayed out of that, he knew she needed rest. That last round was her own hot ass coming on. Sometimes she acted like some twenty-year-old bimbo. But after, napping with Gun had been wonderful.

Sometimes her overblown sense of guilt was her worst enemy. It couldn't make Clay worse for her to love Gun. Clay wouldn't object, any more than she would object if he could be lucky enough to have someone's arms around him he cared for in that way. And Gun had been so faithful, such an angel. Every friend Clay had except Gunnar, Jim and Junior ran for their lives.

He wouldn't let her call Rachel. He wanted to see that Luara bitch, but she had no time for Clay after his illness was diagnosed. AIDS had shocked everyone, but he didn't invent the damned disease. Luara sure as shit should have stayed out of bed with a man nearly young enough to be her son.

But yesterday had been a rare good day from first to last. After Copper Jim and Junior said good night, Gunnar stayed awhile with her and the sleeping Clay. Again, Gun said how dearly he loved her, his soulful, brown eyes backing up every word. After he kissed her good night and left, she settled down and slept longer at a time than she had in weeks.

Anna was standing at the window when Maria bid her a cheery good morning and began checking Clay's vital signs.

He woke when she started pumping the blood pressure gauge. As always on waking, the first thing he did was smile. That was one thing about his face that hadn't changed. In a sleepy voice, he said, "You a dream or what?"

"You're feeling chipper," Maria said, smiling.

"What's your name, angel?"

"I told you my name. You're a fickle man, no?"

"No, but lately I do have a fickle memory."

"My name is Maria."

"Always did like pretty girls named Maria, Maria."

Shaking a thermometer, she smiled. "Open; good. I'll tell you something, but one moment first." She went in the bathroom, returned with a washcloth and wiped his face. "Feel good?"

"Uh, huh," he mumbled over the thermometer.

Maria checked the wand and said, "Temperature is normal today."

"What were you going to tell me?"

"Well, I like handsome hombres named Clay Hill. Also I am looking for a husband who sings great, owns his own jet and makes mucho American dollars. And I want a strong son or two, with blond curls."

"I like a shy woman," Clay grinned.

"My friend, selling tortillas on the streets of Madrid takes the shyness. I come to America to be a liberated woman. Also, I am jealous. I won't have other girls putting their hands on what is mine."

"I'm a one-woman, at the time, man. Ask Mama."

"No mama thinks her son can do wrong. Mine thinks my brothers are gods."

"I think you're a goddess."

"You're a silver-tongued devil. I know your love songs about women."

"There's already a love song about you. It's called 'Spanish Eyes.' I'd love to have a daughter someday with eyes like yours."

"When you are well, it's a deal."

His smile faded. "Maria, all we need is a miracle."

"I will pray to Saint Cecilia, patron saint of music, and light a candle. Maybe she can get us a miracle."

Still a master at fantasy, he said, "Thanks, darling. When I get well, I'm buying you the best dinner in town."

"Wonderful! Mrs. Hill, can I get something for you?"

"You're an angel, but I'm fine. I can't thank you enough."

"I see it in your eyes and in Clay's." Turning to Clay, she said, "Breakfast is soon, eat well. Eating is important." As Maria left, the phone rang.

"How are you, darling?" It was Gunnar.

"Much, much better."

"Thanks for loving me," he said, his voice husky.

"My pleasure, Mr. McGuire."

"Wish you were here now for an encore."

"Myself."

"How is Clay?

"Feeling good, he's been flirting with his nurse. Want to talk to him?"

"Yes, and I want you to go have some breakfast."

Anna handed the phone to Clay. "It's Gun. I'm going for coffee."

Clay said, "Hey, man, how you doing?"

"Great. Copper Jim said you wanted me to call."

"Don't mean to be morbid, just got to talk business without Mama. My no win mess is about over, Gun, and I got to make a will. Can you help me?"

"Anything, Clay."

"First, please look after Mama. I know you care for her."

"More than life. You know I've been trying to marry her for some time."

"Just be patient. She isn't as independent as she thinks. That's why I want to make a will without Mama knowing. You got a pen and paper?"

"Yeah, I keep them by my bed," Gunnar managed to croak.

"This is a brutal way to hit a man before he gets out of bed, but here goes. I'm leaving Luara Frazier a hundred thousand. It won't save her if she gets AIDS, but I want her to have the money. I've written a letter to be given to her at my death along with the money. I'll give you the letter when you bring the will. Fake Mama out of here when you do."

"Okay," McGuire said and swallowed.

"Fifty thousand to Copper Jim, twenty to Rachel, a hundred thousand to Vandy AIDS research. The rest to Mama, you be executor. Did I go too fast?"

"Uh, no," Gunnar said, thinking, This thing is going like a cyclone. Hell, maybe I'm just feeling my age.

"Good. That's it for the will. Gunnar, I need one more favor."

"Hold on, my pen's gone bad." He laid aside the perfect pen, muffled the phone with a pillow and wiped his crying eyes. After composing himself, he retrieved the phone. "Clay, let me read this back, want to be sure it's right."

After Gunnar read his notes, Clay said, "That's fine. Now there's a song I'm trying to write that ain't happening. Maybe I'll get lucky and have one last visit from the song fairy. In that case, get a crew in here to record it. We can lay down the vocal and guitar parts. Want two tracks of Jim's rhythm, there's one lead part I have to pick. Later, you and Jim add whatever you hear. Okay?"

Relieved to get off wills, Gunnar said, "I'll have a crew there in two hours."

"It's called *Luara*. If we get it recorded, burn the letter and release the song as soon as possible, even if it's after my death."

"No problem. Does Rachel know you're sick?"

"Doubt it, she never keeps up with current events."

"Could your problem have originated with her?"

"No. We were first for each other. I can't prove it, but I was infected by the gay dentist that treated me as a kid. I exposed Rachel. If she's ignorant of the fact, in my opinion, the merciful thing is to let her be. She didn't want to share my life. Ain't no reason to make her share my damnation till she has to. If she has to. When you bring the will for my signature, do it when Mama ain't looking. Do it soon. This show's about over."

"Clay, I don't know what to say."

"Say you'll do it."

"Consider it done." he couldn't believe Clay's courage.

"When this is over, Mama will need you then more than ever. Marry her. Take her away awhile. When you bring her back, how ever you have to do it, Gunnar, start her career. You and singing will be Mama's salvation."

When Gunnar managed to quit crying, his eyes were drawn to the side of the bed where Anna had lain last night. This separate living wasn't getting it, but she was right. They couldn't marry with Clay sick. The media would make it a circus. That was Clay's reason for saying "after."

Anna had to know Clay's death was imminent. She was too psychic to imagine his recovery was possible.

They were both subject to come down with the same damn thing. He wasn't one to dwell on the negative but he didn't hide from it. Anna was the best thing that had ever happened to him, he wouldn't take back one second with her even if he could. All he regretted was not marrying her before this thing with Clay raised its ugly head. He couldn't be as supportive or as protective toward all that was coming without the two of them being married.

Clay with AIDS would hit the media like a West Tennessee tornado. You needed to be in the storm cellar before it started blowing. For years, Anna hadn't anyone to lean on but Clay. Soon she wouldn't have him.

With its bad side, marriage was still the best way for a couple who wanted to let their love grow and live together. If he came down with AIDS, or any slow terminal illness, he'd never get in the shape Clay was; or down to a skeleton like his brother got with cancer. He would never forget how his Clyde cried and begged him to shoot him before finally dying. There were things a man didn't do, even for his dying brother.

As for checking out of this world ounce by ounce, McGuire knew his balls weren't big enough for that performance-- no sir! Slow death wasn't for him as long as he had his thirty-eight. You could get second opinions, pray for the miracle, try the healer preacher. Your chances were better with inside straights. He quit betting inside straights his first year in Nashville.

He could relate to Jeff Hill's suicide. If a beat bastard was that miserable in this world, he sure as hell had the choice of checking out. That jealous of Clay then, Jeff most likely would have become the world's most publicized nut if he'd hung around to witness Clay's stardom. Gunnar didn't believe he lost all his black hair to silver without learning something. He'd love to live forever, but he had seen worse things than dying.

He hadn't known much about Anna's late husband, but he admired the man for knowing when it was time to run to his own kind of storm cellar. He admired him too for having the guts to pull it off without upsetting his mother more than he had to-- Anna and Clay, too for that matter. Lying here by his side, Anna had finally told him about it.

"Mama, could I go to the Community Center tonight? A flyer was on the school bulletin board. Copper Jim Quarrells is teaching guitar and songwriting. He's a real Grand Ole Opry star. His class is seven to nine."

"Your daddy left early for East Tennessee. He's meeting your Uncle Mike at Mama Hill's to go hunting. He'll be late, I'll take you."

"Hey, it's for all ages. Why not see what you think? Should be fun and you love to sing and write."

"Have to register for my class. I'll drop you by, I won't be over an hour."

"Daddy agreed to you taking the real estate class?"

"Yes. Getting a job later is what he objects to."

"I'm not thrilled about that either. Some of my buddies have working moms. I like you here when I come home. You should get into music more."

"I need something, I'm feeling so useless. I love music with you, I don't want to go past that. You're good to show me a little guitar."

"You don't need me to show you writing songs."

"Thanks, but I'd like to make some extra money."

"There's lots of money to be made with good music."

"I want extra money before that. Clay, even if I had the option, I'd hate to spend my life in a tour bus."

"I'm going to buy my own jet, but I'll have most of my concerts here. Country music fans want to come to Nashville, anyway. I'll build us a mansion with lots of rooms and some acres for concert facilities."

"If you spend that kind of money, I need a job."

"Don't you worry, Mama, I'll be making the money."

"If being positive helps, you will. I think I'd like selling real estate, but I may be too dumb to pass the real estate test.

"There's not a dumb bone in your body, but I can't believe you want to work when you don't need to."

"You don't need me much now and I need something besides housework. Jeff would die if he heard me, but we could use more income. College isn't far away, and you need a nice car, if not a new one, for graduation."

"You know I want to go into music full time."

"Clay, I think you should go to college first."

"I don't have time for college, Mama."

"We don't have to decide tonight. You might change your mind, and I don't want money to be a problem. I have to get dressed. When you finish eating, don't forget to put your dishes in the dishwasher."

That evening, stopping the car to drop Clay, she couldn't stop herself from saying, "Want me to go in with you?"

"Mama, I'm a big boy now."

"Whoops. Have to pardon a hen with one chick, but check before I leave to be sure they're having it."

He soon came loping back, grinning "It's great! They got a stage and all kinds of neat equipment."

"See you in an hour or so. Be careful, Clay."

Adult education was a big thing, the school was packed. It was two hours before she got back to the Center. Clay was sharing an outside bench with a teenage girl. As he walked to the car, Anna was amazed again at how tall he was. It seemed only last week, he was crawling around on the floor making motor sounds and pushing Matchbox cars.

He opened the door and said, "Mama, this is Mary Ellen Morris. She's taking the class too. Can we take her home? She lives near us."

"Sure," Anna said, but she didn't feel sure. The girl had the biggest boobs for a skinny girl she had ever seen, straining under what may have been the tightest T-shirt. It made her seem too old and too fast.

Clay loaded their guitars on the back seat, then opened the front door. Anna said, "Hi." Mary Ellen answered with a slight smile.

Anna was shocked by her son's manly job of helping the girl adjust the seat belt. His Matchbox car days were certainly over.

On the road, Anna began to feel a strange distrust of Mary Ellen. She made herself be nice and said, "Are you a picker too?"

"Not like Clay. I'm a beginner."

"You'll learn," Clay said. "Copper Jim's great. He promised to look at some of my songs. He's something else picking."

The girl said, "He liked your picking, Clay."

"I have a lot to learn. Some of his licks are unbelievable. There's a niche for country rhythm, and he's right on it. Mama, go right at the corner, then left. Mary Ellen lives in Swiss Meadow Apartments."

"Okay. Do you two have classes together at school?"

"Algebra," Clay said. "She moved from Michigan."

"How do you like Tennessee, Mary Ellen?"

"Love it. I've met more nice people, like Clay. Dad's a pilot, we move around a lot. I live in that next building with the night light on."

Anna watched Clay walk his first young lady to her door, his mass of curls gleaming in the moonlight. They stood talking a moment before Mary Ellen kissed him on the cheek and went inside. Anna felt a flash of resentment, and thought, Whoa! Can't stop your baby from growing up or liking big boobs.

But driving on home, she couldn't shake her negative feelings as she made small talk with Clay. Usually she wasn't this torn by her feelings from second sight. She knew it was reliable, but no better than she was able to decipher. She had never felt such revulsion toward a kid.

It was after ten when she turned in the driveway and Clay said, "When is Daddy coming home?"

"Expected him by now," Anna said, frowning at the empty space in the carport. Jeff was never this late.

Shep greeted them at the door, Clay set his guitar down saying, "I better exercise him, Mama."

"I need some coffee. Want a Coke and sandwich?"

"Just a Coke please, ma'am."

When Clay came back, he gave Shep a biscuit then joined Anna at the table. "Mama, I sure wish I coulda seen Mama Hill, but Daddy gets so uptight because I won't shoot the animals."

"You had school and you hate hearing the shotguns."

The phone rang and he answered. With his hand over the receiver, he said, "It's Uncle Mike, Mama. He's upset."

She took the phone. "Hello. I am sitting down. Oh, God! No, I can't wait. We'll watch the fog, don't worry about us, look after Jeff." Handing the phone back to Clay she said, "Your daddy had an accident."

Clay hung up the phone. "It's real bad, Mama."

Rinsing their dishes, she said, "Yes, we have to hurry and go." Her sick smile in her pale face made him want to cry.

"Mama, please, just sit down a minute."

More sympathy shaded his eyes than she needed, but she sat at the table and hid her shaking hands in her lap.

"Listen, Mama, it's really bad, and it was no accident. So don't go racing two hundred miles in fog to help. You can't, and it's what he wanted. I saw it, I even saw a squirrel in a tree looking down at Daddy making it look like he stumbled. I, I'm trying to prepare you, Mama."

"Darling, I should be preparing you," she said from far away.

Seeing she was in shock, he used the softest tone his changing voice could. "Mama, what's done is done. I don't want you hurt too. You hear?"

"Yes, son, I hear. I'll be careful on the road. Now, pack some clothes, your toothbrush and hurry, darling!"

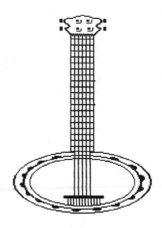

 CHAPTER 5

IF YOU BEEN TO ONE FUNERAL

Fate was merciful and gave them a clear night to Knoxville. In spite of bad fog on up the mountain, they walked into the emergency room of Sevierville Hospital at three a.m. Clay felt their luck stop at the door, and in five minutes Anna felt like killing somebody.

After total confusion from the receptionist, the computer operator and whoever they talked with on the phone, the receptionist said, "I'm sorry, Mrs. Hill, but Mr. Hill came in so recently, the computer isn't updated."

Anna said stiffly, "Where is he?"

"Critical Care on seven south."

"How do we get there?" Anna snapped.

Standing at her side, Clay said, "Easy, Mama."

"Take the elevator in the rear of the lobby. Arrows are on each floor."

On seven south they found Mike Hill in the Critical Care waiting room, in hunting clothes and devastated. As they walked up, he looked at them but gave no sign of recognizing either.

Anna took the chair next to Mike, and Clay took the chair next to his mother. As calmly as she could, Anna said, "Mike?" There was no response, and again she said, "Mike?"

"Yeah?" Mike said, in a vague voice.

She put her hand on his arm and said, "Mike, it's Clay and Anna".

"Hey. Wasn't expecting y'all this soon."

"We got lucky, there wasn't much fog. Are you okay?"

"Yeah, Anna, I'm fine. It ain't me."

"And Jeff?" Mike shook his head no, and his eyes filled. He looked at her a hopeless moment then leaned forward in his chair. Reaching across Anna, he squeezed Clay's knee. Looking in his teenage eyes, Mike shook his head again then looked at the floor between his legs.

"Mike, what about Jeff?" Anna repeated.

With his head still down, Mike said, "Not good."

"Will they let us see him?"

"Yeah, one person in at a time, but you shouldn't go in. You don't know what a twelve-gauge does at close range. Jeff won't know the difference, so it don't make no difference." Mike broke into sobs.

Tears burned Anna's eyes but she was determined not to cry as she said, "Clay, stay with your uncle. I have to go see about your father."

Clay moved over and touched his handkerchief to Mike's hands covering his face and said, "Here, Mike." Mike silently took Clay's handkerchief.

Mike was twenty-eight. He and Clay talked more like brothers than uncle and nephew. Since Clay had reached his teens, he communicated with his uncle like he never could with his dad. But now, not knowing what to do or to say, he sat silently by while Mike cried.

When Mike stood and wiped his eyes, Clay stood with him and they shared a bear hug. Clay saw it was his first time to be taller than Mike as he said, "Mike, can I get you a Coke?"

"No, thanks, man, I'm okay."

"What about Daddy?"

"I love you and him too much to lie. I don't know why they started him back breathing. He couldn't if they didn't have all kinds of contraptions on him and in him. In God's name I don't know why they do all that."

"Well, maybe sometimes it helps, Mike."

"Jeff's brain is gone. They admitted it, in a bunch of fancy words. I knew it when I brought him here in the back of his truck. Doctors can do fine things, nobody but God can make a new brain."

"Uh, did you burn the note and bury the wire?"

"What?" Mike said, startled.

"You know, like his note said."

"Boy, how did you know about that?"

"I saw it in my head as you talked to Mama on the phone."

Mike growled, "I don't believe this, or this whole damn day."

"Did you do the things Daddy wrote in the note he left hanging on the tree?"

He gazed at Clay a burning moment and said, "Yes, damn it, I did. My brother never asked me to do much. What he did ask, I tried to do. I wrapped up what was left of his head in my undershirt. Then in my shirt too because there was so much-- stuff! Then I carried him out of the woods to the truck."

"How? He weights twenty pounds more than you do."

"I don't know, I just did."

"Thanks for doing like he asked."

"He took care of me plenty of times, like he did you." Mike sat back down and stared at the floor. After a while he said, "Hey, I'm sorry, Clay. Don't pay any attention to me. I'm too upset to make sense."

"That's okay, I know."

"Don't keep saying, you know, when you wasn't even there."

"It's like I told you, I saw it. I saw Daddy write the note and tack it up. Then rig the wire and, I saw him after he pulled it."

"Then why ain't you upset? You weird or what?"

"Mama has all she can handle. People have always thought I'm weird. Whatever, I'm like I've always been able to sometimes see things."

"Maybe I'm weird sitting here hoping my one brother won't live. But I wouldn't want to live broke so bad I couldn't be mended. Jeff has brain damage, and other problems too. The way his throat's torn up, he won't ever eat another bite. He wasn't breathing when we got here and I don't know how long he went without breathing. I don't want to be a zombie. Do you?"

"I don't know."

"You don't want your daddy living a vegetable. That ain't no life."

"I really don't know, Mike. I never have thought much about dying. But I know what's here, I don't know what's on the other side."

"How you been talking, I figured you know it all."

"I only know what comes in my mind. I can't make things come, can't keep them from coming and I can't make them go."

"Hell, I'm sorry. I know that's been happening all your life. This has to be bad to see. But hadn't you rather die than live a vegetable?"

"I guess but I'd hate to die. In the first place, I love life and I'd like to live forever. In the second, I'd hate to wake up in hell."

"Why should you be in hell? You're a good person. I think all the Hills are pretty good folks. Don't you?"

"Yeah, but is pretty good, good enough for Jesus?"

"He saved a thief on the cross, so he should have mercy on honest working folks like us. I'd rather take my chances, missing hell in the hereafter, than living it here, with my head broke open like a busted coconut and hooked to a bunch of God damned mechanical mothers. Hell, we shoot rabbits in that shape. Hunters have more mercy than doctors." Mike hid his face in his hands again as his voice broke and his body shook.

"You need a tranquilizer or something, Mike."

Mike said through his hands. "I hate pills." Then he stood and said, "I gotta call Mama and get me a slug of whiskey. When I come back I hope Jeff ain't here. Or if this is a stupid nightmare, I hope I wake up. If Anna gets back first, tell her I had to do some things. But don't say a word about what you saw in your head. If Jeff went to all that trouble to make it look accidental, let it be. I don't want Mama even suspecting he died from anything but an accident. It's going to be hard on her anyway. Might finish her off if she thinks Jeff took his own life. Don't mind telling you, I can't stand the same twelve gauge shell that killed my brother taking Mama, too. Okay?"

"Wouldn't that be cheating? Most insurance don't pay on suicide."

"Mama's old, Clay. Anyway, Jeff worked over twenty years. They got their damn premiums. I don't want Mama to know and I mean it. We can't kill Mama over splitting hairs with some big ass insurance company. Your own mama don't need to know either."

"Mama already knows."

"Anna wasn't there. How could she know?"

"I told her about what I saw. She might not go along with covering up a suicide. Mama hates lies. I'm sorry, I'm more upset than I show. Never thought about how hard it will go with Mama Hill."

"I was the only one there. If I say it was an accident it was, and I sure as hell am going to say it was. You can lay your last dollar down on that. The Hills ain't had no suicides yet. With my brother going to all that trouble to cover his up, it ain't in me to give him away. My poor old Mama's had all the hell she needs. She never got over Daddy dying."

"Okay, I'll get Mama to go along, someway."

"Clay, at first I wasn't going to do that shit in his note. Didn't have time to start burning notes and burying wires. I needed to get to the hospital. But him or something wouldn't let me leave till I did what the note said. It was the worst thing I ever felt. Wouldn't turn me loose till I had things like Jeff wanted. So, that's the way it has to be."

"Okay, Mike."

"Don't start nothing about what you saw on the shit house wall. I'll make a fool out of you in court. If you want to talk extra-sensory, check some of the old mountaineers around. Some say they talk to Daniel Boone and Davy Crockett. Jeff wanted his death to be an accident. He hovered there in the woods till I followed his note. After I got him in his pickup bed, it hit me I forgot to burn the note. I thought it was crazy, with him laying like he was, but I couldn't leave till I went back and burned the damn note. So that's the way it's gonna be! You hear me, Clay?"

"Yes, I said okay."

"I'm sorry for hollering and I hate to leave you alone, but I got to do a few things. I know Mama ain't slept a wink since I called before. She won't till I call back. Course after I do, she sure won't be getting any sleep."

"Why not take a chance she's dozed off?"

"I might. I ain't got the guts to talk to her till I get a drink of whiskey. Need a bottle." He looked at Clay as if wanting a comment.

"Mike, you feel bad enough already."

"Yeah, but after I talk to Mama, I'll need another drink. I got to take a walk. Right now, I ain't fit for the hounds to howl at."

When Anna came back from Critical Care, Mike was gone and Clay was asleep in a chair. Her first instinct was to push his curls back from his forehead. On second thought, she sat several seats away, taking care not to wake him. He needed his rest, and she needed quiet time to give her muddy water a chance to clear.

This morning she was a housewife trying not to become stagnant. Less than twenty-four hours later, she was a widow trying to stand the pain. Life had suddenly jumped in fast forward; if she couldn't push rewind, maybe she could at least push pause for awhile. She had no words to tell Clay his daddy was dead, and he was half an orphan and she was a whole widow.

When Clay woke, her eyes broke the news. He said, "Mama, I'm sorry for what I told you before we left home. Daddy's death has to be an accident."

"But it wasn't, Clay."

"Mike is the only witness, and that's how he wants it. He says it would kill Mama Hill to know Daddy shot himself, and me telling about seeing things will make me look like a nut."

The look that passed between them was their first exchange as peers. Seeing Mike stumble in, she said, "Guess we have no choice."

Two weeks and another life later, Anna walked down the stairs of Mama Hill's house. She had slept better, maybe she was better. For the first time, she could appreciate the smell of good food.

As she walked in the warm kitchen, Mama Hill turned from taking biscuits out of the oven and said, "Morning, Anna. You look some better rested."

"Morning, and I am rested."

"Got biscuits baked, eggs and gravy's on the table and a jar of the jam you love. It's from berries we picked last fall. Let me get my biscuits and we'll eat."

"Can I help you do something?"

"Pour your coffee and set down. Table's all set."

Anna poured a cup then gingerly took a sip and said, "You make the best coffee, and the hottest. You must boil it twice."

"I do hate cold coffee. Try these scrambled eggs. Took them from under the hens this morning. That's back strip sausage there. It ain't floating in sage and pepper either. Sausage made with good lean meat don't need the taste smothered up with seasoning. Try you some." Anna took generous portions knowing the most comforting, loving act she could do for Mama Hill was to eat hearty and compliment her excellent cooking.

Anna asked, "How long have you been up?"

"Five, like always. Got my chickens fed, turned the cow in with the calf. Might leave them together a few days. Don't need the milk and don't feel like milking. Old Arthur Rightus is back in my hands. Comes in cold weather or when I get upset."

"You don't have to get up early or milk either."

"Like to milk when I feel good. Been milking fifty some years. Habit I guess, like getting up early. I been getting up early all my life, ain't no use laying there in the bed awake, and take the backache."

"I didn't know you have back trouble."

"Don't, if I get myself up and don't wallow in the bed. It's a pretty day, sunny and not too cold. Could gather us some hickorys, if you're a mind to. A pie would be good for dinner with you and Clay to help eat it up. Maybe he'd pick them out for us. That boy has always been good to help with picking out nuts or anything else. He's mighty fine, Anna. You can be real proud."

"Thanks, and thanks for the invitation but I'm going home. I won't need dinner with this great breakfast. After Clay gets up and eats, we're leaving. I want him to have some of this wonderful smoked sausage."

"You always was good to brag on my cooking. Have some more eggs and sausage. It's the first appetite you've had."

"No, thanks. I do want more coffee and one more blackberry biscuit. You and my Aunt Effie always did make me pig out on blackberry biscuits."

"Recon you should be going home already?"

"It's time. I can't stay here forever, much as I'd like to. Clay has to get back in school, we all have to try and get on with living."

"Anna, what are you gonna do?"

"Lord, I don't know. Somehow, just do I reckon."

"Yeah, you got to, for your sake and Clay's. Honey, I got me a nest egg. Not a heap but you're welcome to it. I'll be getting another rocking chair check come first of the month."

"Thanks, that's very kind, Mama Hill, but Jeff kept good life insurance with the electric company. We have some savings. I may need to get a job but I was already thinking about that anyway."

"Don't go to work right off. You ain't used to working out and Clay ain't used to you being gone."

"But I miss Jeff already."

"You'll do that, working or not. I know from losing his daddy. Some mornings I still reach for Nathan. Still want to tell him things."

"How do you stand it, Mama Hill?"

"Oh, you start thinking of ways to keep busy. Keeping busy's the best way."

"I stay busy, but Jeff handled everything. I don't even know what we owe. How did you learn to get by all alone?"

"Mike was little and needed tending to. Took it a day at a time. With death you got no choice but to handle it or it will handle you. I did lots and lots of quilting. Always loved quilting. Specially Dutch Doll and Wedding Ring quilts, till my fingers got so bad. Kept my quilting frames in the living room by the stove every winter till old Arthur stopped that."

"You gave us a beautiful Dutch Doll quilt."

"A lady at Knoxville sold some for me. Anna, while you was watching TV last night, Clay said he's making his future from picking music."

"Yes, that's all he will talk about doing."

"You don't sound much like that suits you."

"He's so smart the hard subjects come easy. It seems a shame for him to miss college. The music business is uncertain, but it's all he sees."

"If he is my grandson, Clay is pretty enough to be a music star. Looks more like his granddaddy every day. Nathan had a mane of curly hair like him when he was young. I love to hear Clay pick and sing. Folks around here have been picking since I can remember. Me and my sisters did a trio, way back. We was the Smoky Mountain Maids, sung on the radio some at Knoxville."

"I didn't know y'all performed on the radio."

"Yeah. That's where I met Nathan. He had a fine baritone voice and was mighty pretty back then."

"That's where Clay got his talent."

"Guess it is sort of in the family. We all sung at cake walks, church socials and the like. After that Nathan picked and sung at church for years. We've had several in the family with the hankering after music. Never knew any of us lucky enough to make any decent money at it."

"Clay thinks he's going to make us rich in music. Says he's going to build a mansion and name it Woodhill. I want you to come live with us, if we get to living in that kind of style."

"Well, if Clay does all that, bad as I'd hate to leave my mountains, I'd be mighty tempted. Y'all come on back to see me along. Be berry-picking time before you can say scat."

"Thanks, we will. You know we love you and your mountains."

"Appreciate you being good to my Jeffrey. He's born hard to satisfy, started off with the nine months colic. Never felt anybody cared about him till you. Always bragged how fine you are and how lucky he was to have you.

"Got you just one piece of advice, Anna. Live your life. The older you get, the shorter it seems from sunup till sundown; the sooner from breakfast to bedtime. The days get gone before you turn around. Shotguns get some, cars and jets get some, sickness gets others. If you're lucky enough, or smart enough, or strong enough, or even blessed enough to get by all that, you still ain't home free.

"Old age gets all the leftovers, like it's getting me. It may be the worst fate of all, setting like a grinning crocodile just waiting. You swear you ain't giving in to old age, but it sneaks up when you're sleeping. That's why old folks sleep so light. Trying to hang on, knowing even a bulldog can't. So raise your boy, live your life. Marry a good man when you come across one."

"My Aunt Effie told me the same thing."

"Told you right. The good years and sweet times run off fast as warm molasses out of a syrup bucket. You keep seeing your face every morning looking back at you from the mirror, older every day. Can't do nothing to stop it or even slow it up. So many things can't be saved. They can only be put to good use. Love's one, living's one, and time's another."

"Tell me about time. I can't believe Clay's as old as he is, or me either."

"At my age, you're a baby yourself. Got too many good years left to spend alone. Course, you need time to get used to Jeff being gone, like myself. But we ain't strangers to funeral pain."

Anna sighed, "But that doesn't make it get any easier."

"No, sure don't. But don't let losing Jeff beat you. You're smart and in your prime. Forget funerals once they're over, don't care who it is. You can drag funerals around forever, ain't but one you can't turn loose. We all got one coming and no way out. Give funerals to God."

"You didn't do that, Mama Hill."

"Nope, but I wish I had. I coulda made me a new life. Years ago some real, nice men came around here calling."

"Nothing ever came of it?"

"I never would let nothing come of it. And old loneliness don't leave by itself. It's just like head lice. Anna, if you don't do nothing to stop it, loneliness multiplies and multiplies. Honey, you listen to an old woman who has seen a bunch of funerals. If you been to one funeral, then you have been to them all. Same thing gets done at a rich or a poor funeral. Won't see one even a little bit different. Except maybe your own. Don't know about that, yet."

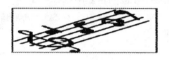

≈≈≈≈≈ **CHAPTER 6** ≈≈≈≈≈

BORN SONGWRITER

Eight weeks passed before Clay would leave his mama alone to go to class. When he walked in, Copper Jim grinned. "Back to pick with us again?"

"Yes, sir," he said, delighted to be remembered

"Sorry about your daddy. Mary Ellen told us. Son, I was impressed with your picking and singing that night you was here."

"I was impressed with your picking, singing and songwriting. Hope I didn't get too far behind the class."

"Ain't missed nothing on guitar, most of the folks are beginners. One feller's a fair picker. He's been helping me teach basic chords. You done your guitar homework and it sure does show."

"Thank you, sir. I love guitar."

"That shows too. We studied on the Nashville number system some. You know the numbers yet?"

"No, sir, but I've heard about it."

"It's so folks who don't note read can communicate. All the session pickers and professional folks use the numbers. Say you're a songwriter?"

"Well, yes, sir, I do try."

"Numbers are good for songwriting too. Shows you how many measures to write and how to arrange a song for a three minute record. The numbers are like another right hand to a songwriter. I'll repeat most of what we covered. What's worth saying once about songwriting's worth saying over. Passed out a list of books. You can have a copy before you leave, if you want one."

"Yes, sir, I sure do."

"Mary Ellen says you sing at school. Perform any time you can. We got more pickers than writers in class. The few writers think they got a done song or two. They ain't, mighta hurt their amateur feelings. Son, if you don't want a critique, don't ask. If you ask, don't argue, listen. Don't have to agree or change a word. Some critiques ain't worth the wind they're mouthed on. Some critics can't outgrow giving bad critiques. Good critics see good and bad. If you aim to be a professional, listen. Then do as you like. After tonight, if you feel behind, we'll meet extra to catch you up. Next week I got a session but come an hour early the next and we'll go over the numbers. If you want, bring some of your songs and I'll look them over."

"I will, and thank you, sir."

"Let's get this bunch started, gonna work on stage tonight. I can go without food a spell but picking's like air to me."

Parking his truck at the Center two weeks later, Jim saw Clay waiting on the bench by the door. With his cowboy hat low over his eyes and carrying his guitar case, he walked his tall frame up and said, "Hey, son, how you doing?"

"Hoping you still have some time to spend with me."

"You look like a hot hound hunting a lap of water. Guess we better give you a cool drink."

"Mr. Jim, you're the first professional music person I've met. I mean that's made lots of money in music." Jim saw the boy had the music bug bad.

"Depends on what you mean by lots, made good money. Ain't done much lately making new money. Lost my rabbit's foot with publishers or don't give a damn, one. Publishers get me raw quick. Still got royalties coming in off old cuts. Ain't made me rich but it's been awhile since I had to work for wages. Course I ain't one to turn my back on big money made fair and square."

"Earning enough money in music you don't have to work at something else, sounds great," Clay said.

"It is. My Uncle Ned said, If you want a dream bad enough you'll find a way if it's fly over or crawl under. Ain't forgot when I had to work a day job I hated and write at night after I was wore out. Get you fine-tuned, you might make it. Ready to learn the numbers I been telling you about?"

"Yes sir, but not right this minute, I guess."

"Whatever it is you wanna say, we're home folks here. Come on out with it."

"Well, would you look at my songs first?"

"Sure will. Let's move to our room and good light."

Clay loved following a real songwriter through the lobby, down the hall to class and setting his guitar case on the floor with Copper Jim's. Jim sat at the desk, Clay took the side chair. "Now," Jim said, "let's see your songs."

Clay took his lyric sheets from his case and handed them to Jim. Flipping through the pages, Jim saw each song was neatly hand-printed on notebook paper. The kid was serious. He went back to the top page, read the lyric and asked, "Can I write on your lyric sheets?"

"I'd be mighty obliged."

Jim read and made notes the longest quarter hour of Clay's life before saying, "Partner, where are you in your schooling?"

"I'm a junior."

"Going to college?"

"Don't tell my mama," Clay grinned, "but no. Mama wants me to go bad. She didn't, and she's always been sorry. There's other folks too. Coach thinks I can get a baseball scholarship, my English teacher thinks I might get a journalism scholarship."

"What do you want?" Copper Jim asked, pushing his cowboy hat back, exposing his mane of copper hair salted with gray.

"I hate disappointing folks who have been good to me, especially Mama. Since Daddy died, I hate it more. But when I graduate, I'm getting into music full time. I've been waiting to grow up forever, I want two years. Then if I don't make it in music, I'll go to college with a good heart."

"Sounds good to me. Course I'm hooked on music too."

"Mr. Jim, you know the score. Do you think I have a chance in music."

"Boy, the last place I want to be is twist you and your mama."

"You won't be. I love Mama more than anything. We get along great, but I have to go easy since Daddy died. You can understand that, can't you?"

Jim said, "Yes, sir, I can. How is she so far?"

"She's lonesome and missing Daddy. Tries to hide it, but I know when her eyes are red from crying and not allergies like she says. I know what she's thinking most of the time, just by her eyes. And she's my hero. Mama's the best person you'll ever known and a real survivor. In time, she'll be fine."

"If there's a thing I can do, let me know."

"I'd like to know what you think of my songs. Mama writes some with me. We're sharing all I learn from you. She sings great and she's been writing poetry for years. She has poems that make you catch your breath."

"Oughta bring her to class."

"I tried, she said maybe later."

"Good. Now, like I was fixing to say, music can be a bad bronc to ride."

"Can't anything?"

"Got a point there." Jim lifted his feet on top of the desk. Clay saw he was careful to hang his boots across a corner so they didn't mar the wood.

"I won't be happy till I do music full time. Is that too off the wall?"

"When you're hot to pick, a year is forever. Just take it a day at a time."

"I will, I just wanted to level. Right now, I need more than anything to know what you think about my songs."

"Ain't no denying a songwriter, but like I told you, music can be tough."

"I know," Clay said evenly, "but it doesn't matter."

"Don't guess doctoring or lawyering is a snap either. Just don't go believing I know it all, don't by a long shot. Son, your mama might hate me if she's set on you going another direction, but I'll be honest. Ain't nothing I wouldn't give to be in high school and where you are picking, songwriting, singing and living in Nashville. Back then, I had no more idea what I wanted to be than a jaybird. Taking too long to know sets lots of young folks back too far to catch up. With any luck, you can make a songwriter. You got a songwriter's head and heart and that's what it takes." Clay thought his heart might jump out of his chest.

"Want to write for love or money?"

"I guess both, Mr. Jim. Is that wrong?"

"Ain't a bit wrong. The best songs get wrote by writers who write that way, but it's hard, most of the time-- awful hard. It's real easy to get knocked off the right songwriting trail by rejection or sometimes to make a little money at it and get greedy. Then you whore yourself into writing like what's playing on the radio instead of writing what you feel, in a knowing, crafted way. From what I can see, you ain't doing but one thing wrong."

"What's that, Mr. Jim?"

"We been friends long enough for you to know I'm Copper Jim, or Jim. Forget mister. I ain't Methuselah, if I do seem like it to a young'un like you. One of the best things about songs, ain't no age, rank, or color."

"Yes, sir."

"Think of writing like a hog farmer who likes hogs. Has a talent for tending hogs. Loves hearing hogs grunt and watching them eat, an grow off. Loves it enough to pay the bill from his own pocket, to start. He knows he has to sell the hogs he's raising today, so he can pay for raising hogs he wants to raise tomorrow. His salvation and his challenge is to start making money before he goes broke, so he can stay in a business he loves. You with me?"

"Yes, sir."

"He can raise any hogs he wants, to any weight he wants, if he's in hogs for meat. If he wants in the hog business, he better raise a top hog the market wants and take it to market in top weight and health. Ain't nobody wanting to buy sick hogs. He ain't apt to run into nobody wanting to buy no rare, no exotic, or no five legged hogs. No horned hogs neither. I hear you laughing, it sounds funny, but songwriting ain't no different. Still, I've known songwriters who never got nowhere and some who went plum nuts trying to get songs cut, with about as much chance as selling five legged hogs.

"Clay, you been putting music and words down how they come-- and you're good. That's fun and fine and when you got a call to write, easy as breathing. Come easy or come hard, all songs are a gift. Any song you write is a part of all the songs you've written. Some are the practice, some are the game-- some are the bush, some are the berry. They come out like a litter of pups getting born, conceived and lined up in a certain order. The ugly pup in the front of the line may be the worst pup his mama ever whelped, but the ugly pup has to come before the great pup behind him has a prayer. Now and then a song comes perfect, like you want it from the get go. Ever felt that happen?"

"Yes, sir, it's the best feeling in the world."

"From a commercial point, may be your best song or your worst. Don't have much control either way. It's a message from On High, you're His instrument to get it said. It's coming so fast and so right, you can't keep your pencil writing fast enough. After you write it and go back and read the words, there's thoughts and things on the paper you can't remember thinking or writing."

"I know that feeling."

"That's not the rule, rewriting's the rule. Songs can be hard to satisfy as a horny hog with no sow. Won't let you sleep at night, won't hush in daylight, and what you write ain't it. It's so far from it, you want to puke. Sometimes you do puke, your bowels get in an uproar, you fall back on the bottle, or your preferred way to punish yourself. You know it's there, cause it won't leave you alone. You're like a gold prospector hot to trot with a fever that don't cool and don't kill-- just suffers hell out of you."

"I know that feeling too, Copper Jim."

"Songwriting can be the most flustering way to make a living a man can choose. But you don't feel you choose, it's like songwriting chooses you. Pitiful part is, ain't no guarantee you'll make a penny at it. I've knowed lots that ain't. Knowed too many that took to the bottle or pills and a few who took their life cause they couldn't. You understand me?"

"Yes, sir, but it doesn't matter."

"There's something else to accept right off. Most folks ain't smart as you, bookwise. If you want to be understood, get the big words out of your lyrics and get down to plain American. Know you like 'Old Shep' and 'Cheating Heart.' We talked about them songs. Remember songs like that when you write and forget the fifty-cent words and use your hook more."

"My what?"

"Music folks call a title a hook. All I got's my opinion, you got a right to your own. Ain't no always or no hard rules in songwriting; just general rules. Sooner or later a great songwriter will break every one, a hack songwriter don't never break none and a no-talent songwriter breaks about every rule in about every line he writes. Best thing for a soul like that's to break all his pencils."

Clay chuckled. "I like your sense of humor about it."

"Keep a sense of humor about all the music business and the business we call living. Won't last till the water gets hot if you don't. Getting too serious to joke is what got most folks locked up in the asylum out on Murfreesboro Road. Lots of folks, who ought to know better, say writing songs is easy. It sounds easy, but it's kept me juggling words most of my life. I still don't know it all and won't never. Don't know how to use all I know, all of the time. Still get to feeling like the more I know, the less I know."

"Can you explain more about that, Copper Jim?"

"Well, write a hit. Then and try to figure out how you done it. That's one to confound Confucius. Great songs are so simple, they're complicated. Great songwriting's complicated but it sounds simple. Anyway, the last line of the verse going into the chorus, the first line of the chorus or last line of the chorus are places to look to use your hook, if it works."

"How do you know if it works, Jim?"

"A gut feeling, like driving a truck and hunting a place. If you turn left and get lost, you turn around and drive back till you know where you are and start over. True test with a song comes when it's cut. If it sells records it's right, if it don't it's wrong. Before that, whether the whole song's any good or not is opinions. First your own, then some artist, producer or publisher."

"What if you want to record your own songs?"

"That's another deal, and I'm getting too long winded. Always do talking songwriting. It's time for class and folks are waiting in the hall. You got enough to study on awhile. What I say is my opinion, anybody starts laying you down hard rules, back off. Less he's hot to cut one of your songs."

"What difference does that make?"

"Don't make a penny till you get recorded. Say an artist wants to record your song and wants some changes. If you want the cut, make the changes if the artist ain't just ripping off your writing royalties."

Clay asked, "Ain't that selling out?"

"Depends. The artist might be right about the changes. No writer always writes the truth and the light. It's somebody dictating what does or don't make good songwriting, over all, you watch out for. And somebody talking a turn on words, or some formula song that sold a million records.

"They'll say fans are too dumb to understand deep lyrics. You'll think of a *MacArthur Park* that sold millions and you'd give your left ball to write. Every time some label guru refuses to record any song over three minutes, here comes a gem like *American Pie* running eight minutes the fans can't get enough of. After the basics, go with your gut. Some nut's always preaching different won't work. I bet the man that made the wheel got told a million times it'd never work before he got it turning right." Jim checked his watch and said, "Gotta hush up, Clayboy. It's done past class time."

"Thanks, Copper Jim. I really appreciate your time."

"Glad to. Check my notes on your lyrics. They're one man's opinion. That's all anybody can give you, don't care who it is. I give you the skeleton of a chick named songwriting. Got to put your own meat and feathers on it. If you want to forget all I said and write for yourself, you don't need me butting in. If you're serious about getting recorded, study what I said."

"I'm dead serious".

"When you're about to graduate, we'll see how you feel, okay?"

"Okay," Clay said, "but I'll feel the same way."

"When the time comes, there's writer's nights and offices down on Music Row I'll take you to. Got folks I might want you to meet, if music's still it."

"It will be. You can count on that."

"Fine, now I got a class to teach. Come on, let's do the teaching so we can pick. Can't meet you early next week, got a session. Might be late for class, tell the folks I'll be on shortly if I am. If you can stay after class in two weeks, I'll show you the numbers."

"I can, Copper Jim, and thanks."

"You're welcome. We need to turn the others in. Especially one young lady." Jim lowered his voice. "Your back's to the door so you ain't seen, but Mary Ellen's stood it about as long as she can. She's been looking in at you, dancing on one foot, then the other. Reckon you got her incensed. Hey, don't be embarrassed, women are the one pleasure better than songwriting." He winked and turned to the students in the hall, "Y'all come set and we'll begin."

Mary Ellen rushed up to Clay and gave him a hug. Copper Jim's grin made Clay blush as she said, "I'm so sorry about your dad."

After they were seated, Jim said, "Want to start on stage presence. We'll do the lesson, then move out to the auditorium and stage. Some of the Center members want to hear us pick and sing. If your ambitions run to performing or not, this part of the class is great for confidence. Even if you don't perform, I want everybody to walk on stage to the mike and introduce yourself. No big deal, just say your name, and why you joined the class.

"When we start doing shows here, I'd like to not just give singers and pickers stage experience. I want you folks who ain't performers to be our masters of ceremonies. Need several MC people. They ain't charging for using the building, but the neighborhood's full of older folks. They want us to give a free monthly show for anybody caring to come.

"Tonight, it's three-quarter time, turn to page ten. Then we'll do the good part. I'm happy as a boy at recess when I'm picking and grinning."

Two weeks later after class, Clay waited in the lobby. Copper Jim always took a few minutes for questions. It was ironic how much more fun it was to listen to him than most teachers and how much more enlightening. The man was a born teacher as well as a born songwriter.

Copper Jim saw Clay waiting eager as a rooster after shelled corn and remembered when he'd been that rearing to go. Hell, maybe the boy could help him get it back. He sat down. "Hey, where's little Mary Ellen?"

"She had to be with kin. Her daddy picked her up."

"Well, Clayboy, can't always have it our own way. Give me one of them sheets of notebook paper in your guitar case."

Clay found a sheet of paper. "You need a pencil?"

"Naw. Run out of paper and forgot to buy more. The last verse come to a song I been writing on a year. It's a waiting game at times, new writer or old."

Laying his guitar case on his lap to write on, Jim said, "Got seven chords in a key. We'll use G. Write G, then A, B, C, D, E, F. Under each chord letter, write one to seven. G's our key, so G is one, A is two, B is three, C is four, D is five, E is six, and F is seven. Before I forget, you done a fine job on stage."

"Thanks," Clay said, flushing with pleasure.

"Welcome. When you use off chords, minors some say, write a minus sign to the right of the number. Got a seventh, write a little seven at the top of the number to the right. For flats, write a little b to the left of the number. Sharps, write a pound sign to the number's upper left- that's it."

"That's all there is to making professionals know how to play my songs?"

"Well, you got augmented and such, but charts with this much give the creative licks to the musicians. It's the same in any key, so it covers transposing. We'll do charts again in class, you done got the gist of it. We better get. They want to close and bet your mama's waiting."

Outside, Clay took a breath of the starry night and saw his mother with Shep parked beside Jim's pickup as he said, "Clay, another thing, and listen hard."

Clay was looking hard, but Jim could see the boy only saw the dreams in his head. "Out of all our jawing, the point is, hold to your singing and picking. It'll bring you pleasure if it don't go past porch picking in the cool of evening or the kitchen on a cold night. As for songwriting, if you don't have to-- don't."

"I do have to. Songwriting's the main thing."

"Yeah. Seen that the first night you hit class. There's an air about a soul serious about songwriting." Feeling sad, Jim started for his pickup.

"Copper Jim, I was wondering if you would teach me how to get the feeling in that rhythm lick you did on stage tonight?"

"I can teach you the lick, teach you the song crafting, teach you all I know about pick and pencil; you gotta pick your own feeling, pick your own rhythm, and write your own words and tune. To be a star, you gotta do it all in a way the record label gurus can use it. They can have a time knowing it when they hear it, but label gurus crave originality, done right. They done got plenty parrots and pitifuls."

"I imagine so."

"You know, real songwriting's like plowing, only you're plowing in your soul instead of dirt, trying to make a seed grow. Plowing songs is ten times hard as plowing dirt, most of the time, when you're serious about it. I done both. Don't mean to dishearten you, just want you to know you ain't took up no candy ass job. When you write a hit that's high on the charts, don't let it throw you. Don't strut around, like some turkeys I could name, thinking they're Jesus. It's the fastest way I know to run off the songwriting fairy."

"The who?"

"Songwriting fairy. The way you write, I know you heard her soft voice whispering to your soul."

Clay smiled. "Yes, sir, she whispers my best songs."

"You got that right! I try to keep her wanting to fly back and whisper again. Getting too big for your songwriting britches runs her off pronto. A writer writing a great song ain't no dearer to God than a soul at the burger joint frying a great burger. Or the worker at the tire plant turning out great tires. It's all a decent way to make a living. You'll be a better songwriter and a better man, to see it that way. When you do get lucky with a number one song, thank God and the fans. Now it does pay better than a burger joint or plant."

"Bet you appreciate that."

"Son, every royalty check I get. One of these days you will too, born songwriter ain't got no choice."

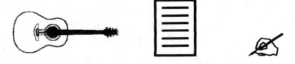

CHAPTER 7

SICK OF LONELYVILLE

Moment to lonely moment, that first winter brought home how far short she had fallen, at convincing Jeff she loved him. Clearly the years she gave him as his faithful wife had counted for nothing. Sometimes she cried, sometimes she cussed, all the time she missed him and felt like running through a wall. Her love for Clay never replaced her love for Jeff. Learning to live without him was a daily battle. She felt as if she was losing the battle and the war.

Jeff's absence changed the simplest things, like grocery shopping, what to cook, when and what bills to pay. From day one, he took charge and it worked great. Jeff loved taking charge and she hated details. Now, she hardly knew what there was to take charge of. Remembering not to listen for his returning footsteps in the evening was a lesson she continued to flunk.

On those days after Clay went off to school, when she could only sit and rock by the bay window and bawl, she suspected she was addicted to bawling. But Jeff had been so warm to sleep next to, their bedroom had been her haven. Now she hated it, his scent was everywhere. Several times she attacked the closet to make disposition of his things. They were good clothes and should be given to someone who needed them.

No matter how she tried, she got claustrophobic the moment she started. His scent was suffocating, the bedroom was suffocating, she couldn't stand it. She started sleeping on the den sofa until one morning she saw there was more than one way to skin a cat. She gathered her courage, commanded herself not to cry and walked into the dreaded closet. Rushing like a thief, she took her things to the spare bedroom closet and slept there that night.

Still, endless blue evenings jerked her back to her orphanage days and feelings of abandonment until Jeff came. No wonder she believed in princes on white horses. If there was life before Jeff, there was life after. Her experience with living after the death of loved ones had taught her salvation was in going through the motions till the motions got going.

The next day she drove to the library for her first card in years. The librarian acquainted her with the new titles and a book on getting past lost loved ones. The book sounded repulsive but she didn't want to hurt the librarian's feelings.

Ironically it was the one book she read. The novels glazed over, the words ran together, the story lines seemed silly. Maybe because her arms were empty, she couldn't give a shit who loved who or didn't, who screwed who or didn't, who was or wasn't successful careerwise, or if same work paid women same as men. Her attitude was purely rotten and killed all the love stories for her.

At least she reckoned they were love stories or an attempt to be. She read enough to learn couples didn't have love anymore. They had relationships, whatever the hell that meant. God, relationship sounded so clinical, like something a counselor or a gynecologist might say, in reference to a man and a woman sharing their most intimate selves. How could anyone call naked, sweaty, get-down love-making a relationship? Course, the English language didn't have even a kitchen word for screwing much less a front parlor word.

Little on TV held her interest. She hated cop shows, game shows, news, sports, weather and raw sex. Seeing men and women in G-strings, renamed swim suits, or naked lovers in her face wasn't her bag; nor was blood, guts, horror, facial expressions during orgasm, or the screams or facial expressions of a rape victim. It was all gross and a waste to someone craving entertainment. Why had all the good dramas, stand-up comics, and concerts gone? Where were the sensitive souls who used to crank the cameras with a sixth sense that told them when to fade? Who had debauched the magical state of film before skin inherited the wide and the small screen?

Continuing the class gave her two nights a week in a neutral if not a positive environment. Real estate didn't excite her but doing something besides fighting the lost and the lonelies kept her going. It beat a TV set that offered little she liked and books she couldn't appreciate.

As she drove to class, sometimes her pain came splashing out. She had to park till it passed. Bawling on the way home was better for her appearance. It just wasn't always possible and later was prime time for rapists. Course, her weeping and wailing and gnashing of teeth should turn the sickest soul off. When she had cried till she couldn't tell if she was wailing over Jeff or the possibility of being attacked, she knew it was time to stuff it and go.

For sure, it was time she quit feeling sorry for herself and went on with living like Mama Hill said. Her blues worried Clay and he had his own problems. They never had much of a father-son relationship, still Clay was having it hard getting used to Jeff's absence. He felt responsible for her and sensed her tears whether he saw her crying or not. She had to get a grip!

About once a day, she told herself it would help when she got her real estate license. That kept her plodding to class. When she finished the course, passed the test and got her license, it made no difference. She didn't get a job as a real estate agent or anything else. Whether her reasons were excuses or reasons, she just couldn't make herself go job hunting.

Clay didn't need an empty house to come home to, she didn't need to be told what to do right now. She couldn't give an employer her best when her heart kept telling her not to go to work. If she was thrifty and lucky and didn't have a financial setback, money wasn't a problem. Jeff had good insurance. Entitled to it or not, she had it. The proverbial wolf was not at the door. Jeff's insurance paid off the mortgage, the bills, and left thirty thousand dollars in savings. There were also the Social Security benefits. Financially they could have been worse off-- and had been.

The teen years could be the most besetting of all. Jeff always wanted her to ·be there when Clay came home from school and it worked. She decided not to change that unless it became unavoidable. Maybe she was chickenshit about working, but it was in Clay's best interest for her to stay at home. When they were better adjusted, she would make another evaluation.

Getting through Christmas was never easy but that year was especially hard where Clay was concerned. They both tried to stop creeping around the house like it was a funeral home or hospital, but neither of them knew how to celebrate. She was glad for Clay's holiday programs at school that kept him busy the first week of his vacation. At breakfast the day before Christmas Eve, he said, "There's a Bette Davis double feature I'd like us to see."

"Son, thanks, but you don't like Bette Davis."

"I like some of her stuff, and it is part of my Christmas gift to you."

Clay always knew how to pet her. At the movie he bought popcorn, Cokes, chocolate bars and they had a fine time. She wore sneakers and jeans like Clay, already a head taller than she. The films were fantastic, and sharing time with her son doing her thing was one of her best Christmas presents.

Between Christmas and New Year's, they spent two nights with Mama Hill, but Christmas morning boiled down to just the two of them and Shep. New Year's Eve boiled down to Anna all by herself with Shep and that boiled down to lonely. She told herself she had such times to chew up and spit out.

She had to look on the bright side. Clay had a New Year's party so she didn't have to go through the evening holding back her feelings for his sake. By midnight, she had cut off her cry, consumed three glasses of Chablis and was reasonably decent for Clay to come back home to.

Music was her best place for hiding and healing. Now that she had time to listen, Reba, Elvis, Chopin and Emmylou and Willie and Rachmaninoff and Julio were her most understanding friends.

One miraculous morning she woke to the fact she had survived the holidays. Since it wasn't her time to die, it was past time to start living. She returned to old literary friends at the library and a few new ones. Browsing one afternoon, she saw a book on the music business and knew it was time to start reading.

One more miraculous morning she gazed out her kitchen window and saw budding proof that spring was rescuing the widow and the fatherless from the long blue of winter. Not that being fatherless wasn't new for Clay.

In many ways, he had to accept long ago not having a father. Minus Jeff watching every word passed with his mother, Clay felt relief. Other than her sadness and the tragedy felt when anyone dies, his world turned happier without Jeff. Guilt feelings from that truth was his hardest part to deal with. Other than the same middle and last name, all he had ever had in common with his father was his mother.

That April, Anna was drawn into life in the fast lane of raising a teen. Till then Clay had expressed no interest in a driver's license and was safely wrapped in the cocoon of music and baseball. Clay becoming a driver brought the curtain down on all that wonderful peace of mind. His "Mama, I know you can teach me," sounded valid. She tried twice.

His first lesson, she took him on the back roads around home and terrified herself. As badly as she hated her fear, it made her so nervous she had to take four aspirins before her head stopped pounding. A novice driver and a novice teacher, even on back roads, wasn't working. In fact, the narrow ridge roads around home were a quick way for her to get them killed. So for the second lesson, she chose the church parking lot, a huge square area with one maple tree in the middle. Nothing could go wrong.

After Clay almost hit the one tree twice, she saw plan B wasn't working, she was no driving teacher, and there must be a better way for him and her nerves.

At such times she hated Jeff for dying, mechanical things were his strong suit and her nemesis. Clay wasn't much better than she was. It hadn't entered her head till nearly too late, he didn't know the gas from the brake. Ultimately Clay solved the problem by enrolling in driver education at school.

One night picking Clay up from music, she saw his getting the hots for Mary Ellen was why he got the hots for a license. That would have been fine if he had been attracted to a stable girl. This soon after losing his daddy, he didn't need the heartbreak. Such things had to happen. Sons did grow up, they did love girls and not always the right one. Still, it wouldn't have been failing any guts test if the two of them had time to adjust before more hell started.

At a bad time and for his first time, if not wisely, Clay did fall hard. Paris fell no harder for Helen, Romeo for Juliet, nor, about two months ago, than did Shep fall for that dumb toy poodle down the road.

Poor Shep was doomed to unrequited love from the start. Size alone destroyed any possibility for a meaningful or a physical relationship. Pebbles barely came to his hocks, and Mrs. Simmons ranting on the phone, "I don't mean to be uncaring. You had true tragedy but my Pebbles is a rare, chocolate, toy poodle, and my dearest companion. My girl's too small and high bred to mate with a German shepherd and too innocent to know it."

"I guess Shep's too innocent to know it, too."

"Pebbles is enchanted with Shep. She runs off in the woods with him and doesn't pay a bit of attention to me calling her. Shep's a wonderful dog too, but y'all have to keep him home till Pebbles goes out of season. He would destroy my little girl if he got to her."

Anna knew the wisest minds were confounded by the eyes of the heart; more accurately the eyes of the libido. She didn't understand but she knew going ape shit over someone was sometimes just ape shit. Clay was ape shit over Mary Ellen. She was pretty, but there was something sly and conniving about Mary Ellen. If she did sound like Mrs. Simmons, Anna would bet Mary Ellen was pulling Clay's strings with sex. For sure Mary Ellen had become Clay's reason for getting up in the morning and he was riding for a fall.

Damn! It was like when he was five. He kept taking his shoes off running barefoot in clover catching bees in jars. She kept warning, "You'll get stung going barefoot. Wear your shoes." Course he didn't and one did. Then it was tears and a small swollen foot on a pillow. When the swelling subsided, Clay still caught honey bees, but he wore shoes.

Mary Ellen looked like her pedigree might be part Holstein. Otherwise pencil slim, she had the biggest boobs on any fifteen year old in creation. They had Clay hypnotized and he was open as a puppy with his feelings. He couldn't keep his eyes off Mary Ellen or her boobs and she couldn't keep her hands off him. The girl instigated holding his hand when Anna drove them places or laying her hand on his thigh. Around the house, she was always touching him on the shoulder or slipping her arm around his waist. Anna had never seen a girl into such open touching of a young man; of course Clay was loving it.

He was fifty thousand feet and still rising when Mary Ellen caused his first crash landing. Anna smelled the girl playing both ends against the middle several times, but Clay refused to be warned. Finally the little cretin lied so blatantly, even Clay couldn't find an excuse for her.

Mary Ellen broke a movie date saying she had to attend a family affair. It was a movie Clay had been excited about and waiting to see since it had first started being filmed. He didn't want to wait any longer and asked Anna to go with him. As they shopped at the concession counter for their goodies, up walked Miss Mary Ellen with another young man. Nobody spoke, Mary Ellen looked like she had swallowed a frog and Anna knew Clay sure felt like one.

Anna doubted anyone enjoyed the movie except maybe the other boy, who probably had no idea what was going on. She hoped Clay had all of Mary Ellen he wanted but all she could get out of him was, "If you don't mind, I don't want to discuss it." A curtain dropped behind his eyes, like his daddy's used to, though his eyes were a darker blue like her own.

After a few days, she tried talking to him again, but he made excuses for Mary Ellen. Too much mother blood ran in his veins, he had to learn the hard way. When he wasn't in school, Clay moped in the house or the woods and never answered the phone. When Mary Ellen called, he refused to speak with her, but Anna knew he was nursing wounded pride. He was not over the girl.

Into the third week, Mary Ellen called, Clay did talk with her and they made up. It wasn't two days till again she was asking for rides to places that had nothing to do with him. Clay was still so blind to the way he was being used, Anna had to say, "Darling, don't be her fool, she doesn't care about you."

"You don't know that. You never have liked her."

"Clay, Mary Ellen is a user and a liar."

"No. She dated the boy in her old school and wasn't sure if she was over him, but she is now. She swore she is and she does have problems. She deserves the benefit of the doubt."

"Problems don't give people a right to mistreat other people."

"Can you understand I'm in love with Mary Ellen?"

"In love nothing, Clay Hill. You're in lust, and so fascinated by a pair of cantaloupe boobs, you can't see straight."

"Is it a crime if I am?" His blindness to the truth was baffling.

"There are lots of normal girls at school. Why can't you like one of those?"

"Where can I find a girl built like Mary Ellen."

"Son, one good thing about learning the hard way, you never forget!"

"Mama, why are you so negative about Mary Ellen?"

"I got bad vibes the first time I saw her, and they're right. Till she came along, you never needed an affidavit when I said something."

After the movie deal, the girl wouldn't look her in the eye. Anna knew she knew she was onto her. Mary Ellen never finished a sentence. It was always "Really," or "You don't say." Anna had rather be told to go to hell, than hear patronizing crap. She wished the little heifer would vanish from Clay's life, but her feelings had to be checked. She tried to throw some verbal speed bumps before his headlong pursuit. His violet eyes always flashed hot with resentment like two beacons to his heart. The truth would make him see when he would accept it. Mary Ellen was like a virus, all a mother could do was be there when the truth cut him in two.

Clay swung between agony and ecstasy while Mary Ellen lied, cheated, took his time and every penny she could get him to spend, while he made excuses for her behavior. In such cases, parental objections often served to accelerate teen feelings into teen marriage. In the case of a single mother with a son near manhood, it was not always clear who was looking after who anyway. Clay was so defensive about the few men she dated, she had to wonder if she was being defensive for the same defensive reasons.

Anyway, she was having hell navigating in single waters. The idea that a man buying her dinner bought him a roll in the hay was repugnant. Apparently there were women who jumped at the chance. The men she fought off in a car or told good night at the door hadn't called back.

Hell, there hadn't been any she wanted to call back. And passion could be more mind-boggling than any drug. Clay was out of his head, it wasn't the time for her to be out of hers. His senior year should be fun. He didn't need to spend it on an emotional seesaw over a psychotic teen vamp.

Mary Ellen had little or no home life. She was always underfoot and lolled on Clay's bed until Anna spoke with Clay about it. When Clay got nowhere, she spoke with the girl like she would have a daughter, "Mary Ellen, a young lady doesn't go to a young man's room, much less lay on his bed."

"Mrs. Hill, we weren't doing anything wrong."

"It still isn't how to behave, if you don't aim to do anything wrong."

"Would that be so horrible?"

"Honey, at y'all's age, it would be totally horrible."

"I don't know that I agree with you, Mrs. Hill."

"Fine! But visit outside my son's bedroom."

When Clay got his license, they agreed he would start solo driving in the neighborhood. That included school, the Center, the mall and Mary Ellen's apartment. His license lightened Anna's chauffeuring job and the situation. He continued to see Mary Ellen, but Anna wasn't forced to witness every date.

In early winter a real ray of sunshine beamed. Mary Ellen's dad was transferring to Atlanta, the whole family was to move at Christmas. Anna held her tongue, her temper and her imagination. Maybe this too would pass.

Anna knew she had to be cool. Mary Ellen didn't want to move, but Clay didn't deserve to be duped into early marriage by her manipulation. After all, Anna wasn't much older when she married Jeff. They had married out of real love, but the orphanage was a factor. Mary Ellen was way down the road from Anna at putting two and two together and coming up with the best answer for herself. Besides, where his girl was concerned, Clay was thinking with a part of his body lower than his head. It crossed Anna's mind that under the influence of passion, men could get as dumbed out as women.

As much living and loving as she thought she had done, she was just before seeing how dumbed out from passion she could get. Nerd dates had rendered her to her new, greatest truth that she was a one man woman. Losing Jeff ended her capacity to feel anything for a man. Then she had to dump her new, greatest truth for her latest, greatest truth.

An evening came when Clay had music, and she had a movie to see. On the way to the Center Mary Ellen was obviously irked about being back to Clay's mama being the appointed drive. Anna couldn't have cared less what Mary, Mary quite contrary Ellen was irked about. The girl sat stretching a pink T-shirt that would have made Marilyn Monroe look like a boy. Her perfect lips stuck out in a pout about as far as her boobs, that were making Clay nervous or horny, one. Anna wasn't sure which, but if he chose to be ding-donged, that was his choice. She wasn't having her cage rattled by a teen tease.

When she dropped them off, Clay said, "Thanks. Enjoy your movie." The girl said nothing, Anna drove on with her mind raging, Son, you end up tied to that, you'll have hell on wheels. If my grandkids have that cat's ways, I won't be baby sitting, or Sunday dinnering. You can bet your Dixie ass on that!

After the movie Anna walked in the Center early. Instead of going to the auditorium to hear Clay, she decided to check on the fitness program. Seeing no one in the office, she started looking on her own and wandered into a huge exercise area. One lone man was across the room exercising on a contraption of weights and wires that had to be effective. His tank top and shorts showed a sweating but gorgeous body. He called, "May I help you?"

"Yes. I'm looking for Brenda Parks."

As he walked over, wiping his face with a towel, his swagger and smile swept through her. "Brenda left early, one of her kids got sick."

"Please, don't let me interrupt your workout."

"No problem. I need a break." He was incredibly handsome, still she was shocked by the ripple of response dancing through her body.

"I'm picking my son up from music and wanted to check on a fitness class for me." He was beautiful, maybe she only needed the right man!

"I run the classes. Jake Dennis," he said, extending his hand.

"I'm Anna Hill." His handshake skipped her heart six beats. Fool, she thought, just ooze into heat right before the poor man's eyes. "Uh, I need something for someone falling apart at the seams."

"You have beautiful body lines, your weight's fine," he said, looking her over as clinically as a doctor.

"Uh, I need to tone up and develop my wind. I sing, also I've heard exercise is good for depression."

"Yes. I would love to design a program just for your goals."

"Yeah. Well, I doubt I could work all the machines."

"They're user friendly. I could explain them now."

"My son is probably wondering if I've run away from home."

"We do group and individual sessions. I feel we can satisfy your needs, Anna." She loved how he said "Anna." Flirting from a man trying to sell her something was no surprise. Her response was the new wrinkle.

She couldn't believe her syrupy, "I'm sure you can."

"Come tomorrow and sign up," he said, flashing that wonderful smile.

Feeling mesmerized, she loved her nonchalant, "I'll see." His eyes were gray velvet. Returning his smile in what she hoped was a cosmopolitan way, she thought, Bet he runs through women like hot sauce on sponge cake. Lord, there may be a woman somewhere smart enough to refuse a man with that smile, those eyes and that build, but tonight; down and blue and sick of Lonelyville, her name sure as hell ain't Anna Hill!

CHAPTER 8

A TENDER MAN

After three weeks she was as fascinated with fitness as she was with Jake. The mood lift alone was worth all the sweat of working out. Exercise was another interest her good girl syndrome robbed her of. How much of herself a woman would let the role of good girl destroy would be funny, if it wasn't so sad. Jeff said he got enough exercise at work and he hated her in anything without him. Always, God help her, she went along with what Jeff wanted. Except where Clay was concerned. Hell, no wonder he was so jealous of Clay!

Anyway, Jake's guidance was paying off. Her body was toning up, she could feel her thighs and breasts firming. Her stomach was flatter and her down moods were always better after workouts. At twilight, if she wasn't careful, if she let her mind dwell on it, she missed Jeff terribly. Physical exertion bathing her brain with new oxygen was her best medicine.

She was too honest to deny her interest in Jake. From the first he piqued her feelings. Still as long as she had been without, a bit of the hornys for an attractive man was normal. She wasn't a stone, he was gorgeous, and he was nice. Besides, a little lust from afar, beat sitting at home too blue to move. It was a big improvement over crying for a husband who offed himself to get away from her ass. And depression sucked.

Day by day, her interest in Jake was growing. She felt it all the way across the room while he conducted class, she felt it when he helped her with an exercise. She felt it when he came to mind no matter where she was or what she was doing. The swagger of his walk, the curve from his wide shoulders down to the nothing of his hips, the ripple of his muscles in the tank tops were all becoming the eighth wonder of her world. Just in a fantasy kind of way, she kept thinking. It just meant she hadn't died on the hoof.

She couldn't take seriously the attention of a man who made his living giving mostly women attention, since few men were in the class. He was any woman's fantasy. Probably any attractive woman's, who wanted him. He might be a sexual athlete like he was a fitness athlete. Letting a womanizer break her heart, blow away her self-esteem and Clay's respect wasn't happening.

Eventually she saw her feelings for Jake went beyond mere lust, innocent or otherwise. He influenced her attitude about life and herself more than anyone since Aunt Effie. Jake believed each day was to be enjoyed, and that time and good health were life's best assets. He taught her perspective and focus. His input would forever color the way she received the gift of life.

His office, the body building machines and the large open space for group exercises was Jake's domain. That first morning, when he smiled and invited her into his office to plan her personal workout, he began to have a profound effect on her. Jake was the first man to make her feel he cared about who she was, and what she was as a woman, rather than as a reflection of himself. It was all heady stuff for an Anna. He made her believe he got a kick out of watching her grow and that toys were not just for kids. Adults needed fun possessions and playtime and deserved both as much as kids. His knowing gray eyes backed his words as he said, "Playtime keeps grownups from getting mean and from caving in when times get rough."

That first day, he checked her weight, measured her bust, waist and hips; totally professional, totally serious and totally a gentleman. After he had written all that down, he went over each answer she had written on her enrollment form, including her comments in the space on the second page for what she wanted to achieve from the class.

Clearly he took fitness seriously, his own physique gave testimony in living color. His attitude was evident in the time he gave her with suggestions and instructions. As he demonstrated the exercise machines, Anna felt his interest was genuine, and knowing it was his job, she still felt flattered.

There had been nothing in her life to prepare her for a Jake Dennis. Probably there had been nothing in his life to prepare him for an Anna. He happened to her so easily; like a good book or good music. But first of all, maybe best of all, he happened to her like a good friend.

After two months in Jake's class, Anna left the Center with him for lunch. She assumed she would drive her car and meet him somewhere. But as they walked out of the building she said, "Where can we met?"

"Let's take my pickup so we can talk on the way. I think you're serious about the program and advanced to the point I should give you a few private tips to work on at home," Jake said smiling reasonably.

Like an everyday thing, she was chauffeured to the outskirts of town, ten miles over the speed limit, in an immaculate pickup with a man she suddenly felt she hardly knew. Hell, she'd never ridden in a pickup, except Aunt Effie's old chugger. Charging up the interstate ramp like a fox chasing hound, he said, "Fitness is all we've talked about. Now tell me about your pretty self."

"Well, I love music, love to read. Lately I've found out I like exercising."

"That keeps the students who hang in hanging in. If you like it, exercise grows on you like a passion."

"As a girl, I loved to play baseball with the best of the boys."

"I'll bet," Jake said and smiled. "What else?"

"As you know I have a son. Clay is in his senior year at West Side."

"Does he play sports?"

"Yes, baseball."

"Woman, you don't seem married."

"My husband was killed in a hunting accident."

"I'm sorry. Was it a good marriage?"

"Yes, in more ways than no. In some ways it was a great marriage."

"Did you love your husband?"

"Yes. He was good to me and a good provider."

"Don't sound like love."

"What do you mean?" Anna said.

"I'm sure that's how a dead husband wants to be remembered."

"What?"

Jake mocked, "He was good to me and a good provider. Woman, give me a break, not to mention him. Was you in love with the man or what?"

"You jump right on it don't you?"

"In a New York minute if you'll let me." His eyes burned into hers. Before she could think of a reply, he grinned, "Don't look so worried, I was kidding."

"With you, sometimes it's hard to tell."

"Hey, I'm sorry. I like you and I only want to ask you for one thing."

"Should I ask what?"

"You won't be sorry." He looked away from the highway to meet her eyes.

"Okay." She couldn't imagine why she trusted him; maybe his smile.

"Just be straight with me. Basically, I think you are damn straight. That's why I asked you to lunch."

"How do you mean basically straight, Jake?

"I think you're an upfront gal. I hate women who play games. I ain't no tea and crumpets guy. You know that if you've been paying attention at all. Let me know where I am. If you don't want to talk about your marriage or anything I bring up, say so."

"So!" Anna said.

"I hear that." He grinned and whipped around the car he was tailgating not a foot away. Once he was back in the right lane of traffic, and she thought they might live, he said, "You seeing anyone special?"

"No."

"Good."

"Good for who?"

"For me." They laughed and he said, "What toys do you play with?"

"Toys?"

"What do you do for fun? What are your hobbies?"

"My son, I guess, and your class."

"That's a start, but kids don't count. I'm not talking work or responsibilities. We love our kids but kids are work and responsibility. How do you play?"

"Since you put it that way, don't guess I do."

"Didn't you say you do some singing?"

"I help Clay write some of his songs. That's where my singing comes in. I do harmonies on his work tapes. Clay wants to be a singer and songwriter."

"Every other soul in town's trying to get in country music. What we enjoy with our kids doesn't count either. What do you do for Anna?" She was silent so long he took his eyes off the road to search her eyes and said, "What?"

"With your conditions, I can't think of anything."

"Why not?" Again she was silent until he said, "That's not a hard question."

She shrugged. "I haven't thought about myself in those terms since I was twelve. You have blown my mind."

"Good, so think about it."

"Now?"

"Why not? I got big ears."

"Fate made choices for me. Do you have kids? You are single, aren't you?"

"Yes to both questions. I have two girls. At least they were caught in my oven, at the time."

"Jake, you don't think the children are yours?"

"Let's say there's doubt. I'm very single. I have faced two divorce judges and two will do. Wham, bam, thank you, ma'am."

"Sounds like you don't believe in marriage."

"I believe in a good marriage and miracles, but I ain't had either one. I could use a good marriage, but I'd rather be in hell with my back broke as in another bad one. Talk about torture, when it goes sour."

"Are both daughters from the same marriage?"

"Yeah, both daughters and both divorces."

"You must have tried hard to make it work."

"That or I hold the record on how long it takes to see a bitch is a bitch. You like steak?"

"Yes, I love steak."

"Good, I'm going to feed you the best steak in captivity." He pushed his right turn signal. His exit put them in an area new to her. She knew it was one of the few rural areas in the county where any farming was still done. They were driving the western edge of Greenriver Lake. Jake was just the man to know an off-beat lakeside eatery.

For conversation more than inquiry, she said, "I don't know this area. Where is this great steak house?"

"At the end of the next driveway," he said, braking to turn in. Then he charged up the driveway to an A-frame house at the crest of a gentle hill.

"Who lives up there?"

"Me," he said, following the curve of the driveway to the back of the house into an attached carport. Riding with him was a course on the wisdom of wearing a seat belt. With a final stomp on the brakes, he was out and around the pickup while it was still rocking. He stood holding the door for her with the unabashed gallantry of a dark haired Prince Charming. Insecure about his bringing her to a residence instead of a restaurant, she hesitated a moment.

Jake gazing directly into her eyes reminded her of an electric toaster she had one time. The damn thing went bad and was subject to give her a small but uncomfortable shock if she pushed the toast button down with her hands the least bit damp. It had gotten her attention with a few good jolts before she realized what was going on. She wasn't sure what was going on now, or how she let herself get in this isolated situation with a man she barely knew. It would have been so simple if she had told him to meet her at McDonald's and let him like it or lump it. Now there he stood with that let's-do-it grin on his lips. Sometimes she was such a fatal female fool.

"You getting out?" Jake drawled.

Lord, she was seeing a let's-do-it look that would fit in a textbook on the subject. She reckoned the ass was at least original. Not even one glass of wine or the steak, and he was coming on like a fast freight. The instant this animal got her to the mouth of his lair, he was primed to rut. Damn! she could be such a dunce about men. Jake seemed so human, so nice all these weeks. Might as well be shot for a goat as a lamb, she thought, and said blandly, "Hey, man?"

"Yeah?" Jake said, using his coolest tone.

"If you're thinking what I think you're thinking, think again. You might as well know right now, I ain't been single that long before or since marriage. If I live a thousand years and every one of them single, I hope to God I never will be. So if you'd be so kind, take my unswinging ass back to town and don't waste more of your precious time."

The last answer she expected was his laugh as he said, "Just checking. A man alone has to be careful what kind of woman he lets in his house."

She didn't feel as secure as she sounded: "Well, Wild Bill, do I pass the entrance test, or do we mosey on back to Dodge?"

"Miss Gutsy, don't get your feathers ruffled, I was playing. You looked so scared the minute we turned up the driveway, I couldn't resist. Come on, darling, I'll behave," he said, trying to look sincere. She saw the devil grin playing at the corners of his mouth. Extending his hand to help her out, he said grandly, "Welcome, my lady, to my humble abode. Consider my house your house and be assured you couldn't be in safer hands with Allstate."

Instead of screaming her lungs out for help like any half-rational half-wit, she took the man's hand and crawled out of his truck. This is how fool women get sliced to bits, she thought as she said, of all things, "You said we were having the best steak in town. This sure doesn't look much like a restaurant."

"Didn't say it was. Said we were going to have the best steak in town. In case you don't know it, woman, it takes me to cook the best steak in town," he said with a cocky grin, "course I thought you'd know that."

"Jake Dennis, I don't know anything and don't go thinking I know anything. I've been out in the boondocks, a long time, raising my son."

"I can see that. Baby, you don't have to have the steak or anything else around here you don't want, now or ever," he said, releasing her hand he still held from helping her out of the truck. His eyes were soft and his voice was tender, "Doll, I'll take you back to town, if that's what you want. I was bugging, didn't mean to scare you. I was wrong, I'm sorry. Believe it or not, I've had one or two women try to force themselves on me. An exercise instructor meets all kinds, but I never forced myself on a woman in my life. My batting average ain't that bad. If you want me to take you out of here, say so."

Seconds passed with him eye to eye before she said, "I want us to be friends. Guess I over react sometimes."

"Good. Come on in, I want to show you some of my toys. They didn't let me play enough as a kid. I'm doing my best to make it up to myself. As uptight as you are, looks like you got some making up to do."

As he unlocked the door, she began to feel okay and grinned, "I'll bet it really isn't all that bad."

"What isn't all that bad?"

"Your batting average."

"Well, guess we all got our little pride to beset us." Leading her by the hand he walked her through his kitchen and on into his living room. "Have a seat," he said, indicating a curve of sectional sofas. He walked to a wall of cedar bookcases stacked floor to ceiling, flipped a switch, and the voice of Julio Iglesias filled the room. Then he took a book from the shelf, brought it to her and said, "This is on fitness. You might browse through it while I fix lunch."

"Let me help."

"I'm a pretty good cook, for a man. Just make yourself at home, darling. Anything here belongs to you."

Anna's eyes drifted to her surroundings. The house wasn't enormous but this was the largest room in a home she had ever been in. Running the length of the house, the room was at least forty feet long. Adjacent to the bookshelves, a huge fireplace of native rock stood a good twelve feet across and rose up through the cathedral ceiling.

He returned with a frosty glass. "Want some iced tea?"

"Thanks," she said, taking the glass as he sat on the sofa beside her. Seeing he waited expectantly, she took a sip from the tea. It had mint of some kind. "Good tea, and this is a wonderful room."

"Had limited funds and love space, so I built four big rooms instead of seven small ones."

"You built this by yourself?"

"It was the only way I could afford what I wanted."

"Do you always get what you want?"

"Yes, unless there's a good reason I can't." She returned his smile, then as always, dropped conversation for music. She didn't know Spanish but she understood Julio's song. The voice of love needed no translator.

After a few moments he said, "Anna, where have you gone?"

"Sorry, music does that to me. I love your stereo."

"It's one of my toys, books are another. That's why I built the shelves."

"It must be nice to be able to build what you want."

"That's the only way I've had of getting what I want. You like Julio?"

"Love him when I'm in a mellow mood."

"Me too. You like Dylan?"

"He's one of my favorites. I like some of most all music. A little hard opera, hard rock or hard bluegrass goes a long way."

"There's more good stuff on that tape. Enjoy yourself while I fix lunch."

"I'm not used to being waited on, I'd be more comfortable helping."

"No, this is my invitation. Kick off your shoes, put your feet up. With the wonders of my microwave and my magic hands, we eat in half an hour. And, if you'll keep your female chauvinism under control, I'll keep my male chauvinism under control. Okay?" It was hard to resist the steel velvet of his eyes. Hell, it was hard to believe he was real.

She could feel his sincerity and said, "Okay."

"That's my girl." Again, he started to the kitchen.

She called, "Jake?"

"Yeah?" He turned back to face her.

"Thanks for being so kind."

"Ma'am, I'm always kind." He smiled wickedly. "Kind is how dear old mammy raised me."

"Then thanks to your mammy and you." She laughed.

"Thanks to you too, woman."

"For letting you wait on me?"

"For being here, and being so beautiful."

"No one ever told me all that before."

"Someone has now." He looked at her a long moment and added, "Someone's going to make you believe it."

"Guess it shows I don't," Anna said.

"Like it'll show when you do." She felt he was going to kiss her, but he walked back to the kitchen. She heard a cabinet drawer open then close on the hard side. Jake started whistling, and she knew if two people could kiss across a room, they had.

When he served what was by then an early dinner, at the cedar table in his kitchen, she had never been more graciously hosted or deliciously fed. The steak, the baked potato and the spinach salad were all scrumptious. He even cut her steak and fed her the first bite. "Like you like it?" he asked, watching her chew as closely as he would have a child.

"It's wonderful."

"Good," he said, sitting down. "Need anything else?"

"Everything's here and you're blowing my mind. I'm not used to such service, especially from a man."

"You'll get where you ain't so spooked by it," he said as casually as saying Pass the butter. She didn't believe the tenderness of the meat or the man.

"Jake, everything's so good."

"Thanks, glad you like it."

The attention he gave her, was a lesson in attention. It was Jake who first taught her a tender man beats the tenderness of a woman, hands down. He insisted she eat every bite with incentives like, "Your salad okay?"

"Great, but I can't stay in weight eating with you."

"You can eat more when you eat smart without gaining. It's all in the balance between calorie intake and calorie burning."

"Sounds like you know what you're talking about."

"Woman, it's my job to know. Body weight's the result of how much eaten, in relationship to how much exercise."

"I never thought about it that way, Jake."

"I've made a life style of doing what I want with no guilt, no punishment and without hurting anyone." Even though he smiled, sadness was in his eyes. "I don't do anything to be punished for. I've been punished enough to pay for any wrong I might have done unaware. Some people deal in punishment, I deal in having fun, without injury or insult to anyone."

"If your philosophy works, I'd like to try it."

"Hanging out with me, you won't be on a guilt trip, out of shape, or hungry. We take a walk after we eat, or a bike ride."

"Lord, I haven't ridden a bicycle in years."

"Then, honey, it's time you did."

The moon painted his sundeck in platinum. Stretched under the stars on a chaise lounge with Jake stretched on another was marvelous. She said, "I'm satisfied as a sultan's cat, I might even start purring."

"Woman, feeling real satisfied myself. I like talking to you."

"Thanks." She had used his phone to tell Clay she was with a friend and would be home presently.

"Ready for another bike ride."

"Oooh, no, I'm much too comfortable now."

"How come that rabbit running across the road scared you?"

"He didn't scare me, he startled me."

"Whatever," he chuckled, "you sure jumped."

"I don't know when I've felt this relaxed." She took a sip from the glass of his juice mix. "You do cook the best steak in town."

"Shoot, Miss Anna, would I lie to you?"

"I don't know. Would you?"

"No, ma'am, I wouldn't." He laid his hand over hers on the arm of her chaise lounge. Her hand tensed slightly but she didn't move it. She knew she probably should, but she didn't want to. He was a master at making a woman feel all woman. She had never felt so female. He said, "I may not volunteer information, but what I do tell, I tell like it is. As far as I know how it is."

"What do you mean by, as far as you know how it is?"

"We're all limited by our visions. My faults don't include consciously lying."

"What do they include?"

"Can't think of a one," he chuckled with a slight pressure on her hand. "Course I don't tell my faults to a first date I want to see again."

"Do you want to see me again?"

"You don't hear me telling my faults, do you?" Their laugh hung on the night, a cozy silence followed. A dog barked on the ridge. The frogs at the pond set up a chorus, a deeper bass frog singing lead now and then. Far away, the lights of a car searched the road up the climb of the wooded hill to the west. When he said "Do you?" she knew what he was asking.

Still she said, "What?"

"Want to see me again?"

"Well, I don't," she said, then realized a man showing her a wonderful time was asking a simple question. She looked in his eyes and said, "Yes."

He grinned and moved nearer. God, it had been a lovely time. He was so untypical, surely he wouldn't spoil it by making the typical pass. Sexy feelings building and sexual action were rivers apart. She wasn't ready for the real thing yet. She did hope he was sensitive to that.

"Turn your face this way," he said gently, so gently that she did. His lips were not three inches from her lips. In the moonlight his eyes were silver velvet, as soft as his voice. There was a pause, only seconds, but long enough to turn her lips away if she didn't want to be kissed. Suddenly she needed to be kissed by Jake. It had been forever since someone she wanted to kiss had wanted to kiss her.

The man of the perfect smile, perfect build and perfect steak kissed the perfect kiss. There was no demand, no question, no probing; only a tender message of affection.

"Woman, you ready to go?" It was the most understanding question any man had ever asked.

"Yes," she said and with a sigh.

"Don't be sighing that relieved sigh. I don't do that on the first date. Not even with a woman as foxy as you. At times not even on the second date. You ain't messing with a man of easy virtue."

"You're rotten," she laughed, as he gave her a hand up from the chaise.

Still holding her hand, looking deep in her eyes, he said, "One night when our feelings are right, when you really trust me, we'll make love out here under the stars." He brushed her lips with his and said, "Ready to go, angel?"

After he walked her to her car at the Center, she rolled down the glass and said, "I had a fine evening."

"My pleasure." He kissed her good night as proper as a high school senior delivering his date back to the proper place after the proper prom. Then, his voice husky with passion, came the last question she expected: "You like dancing?" His question hit her so off the wall, she took a moment to realize he was serious. "Well, do you?"

"I don't know. It was too long ago and too little of it to remember."

"You do like country music, don't you?"

"Love it," Anna said, smiling.

"Tomorrow night, let's refresh your dancing. It's great exercise. If you don't have a ball, I promise not to ask you again. I want to show you a good time, take you around town and show off how gorgeous you are. Especially when you laugh and when you kiss me." Feather soft he touched her lips with his again and brought her feelings fully alive. The light brush of his lips charged an electric reaction that ran through her more intensely than a drawn out kiss.

She kept both hands gripping the steering wheel so he wouldn't see them tremble. His affection was putting her at ease and arousing her at the same time. If she had been scheduled for major surgery or an audience with the Pope, she would have canceled to be with Jake. He was so beautiful inside and out, his feelings were so tender, so touching.

He loved her chuckle as she said, "Man, that's an offer I can't refuse."

"Great, call you in the morning. Night, pretty lady."

Watching him swagger to his truck, her feelings were almost maternal. Still, she felt so feminine and soothed by the male nurturing she had missed. Parts of what some labeled male chauvinism were things she loved. Like the way he waited to see her car started and she left with no problem. For all that swagger, all those muscles, he was a tender man, soft hearted as an orchid, infinitely more exciting and-- he genteelly watered her flowers.

Rolling by his truck, she waved in return to his smile and salute. She had a good time as who she was before she became a wife, a mother and last and for damn sure least, a widow. It had been the nicest day in years for the woman Jake resurrected, and delightfully surprising to find beneath all her roles, there breathed a woman still alive and still passionately kicking. He made her feel desirable and beautifully replenished. The female needed the male presence so badly... to flourish... to flower. And hell, she just really, really liked the man!

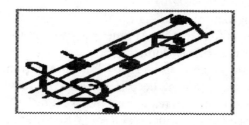

CHAPTER 9

THE WARMEST PLACE

From the first bad days till moments ago on the phone, Mama Hill said, "Live in the past, and you stop the future. Clay don't need a quitter."

It really was time to brace up and try again. Like Jake said, "I waited enough in the corner at school. They preached using time wisely one minute, stood you in the corner the next. Pissed one teacher off asking how to use time wisely standing in the corner. Thanks to my smart mouth, she said to stand in the corner another hour. All she taught me was to hate her and standing in the corner." He chuckled. She smiled back, admiring his living in the now.

He reaped more from being alive than any adult she knew. He was off the wall, and a bit coarse, but he was together. He used each day for what he liked and moved on to new things when his interest cooled. His way would turn her to more than hovering over her son. Clay needed space to grow. His dreams mustn't be broken before he started, like hers. Jake would be a friend for him as well as herself. He'd love Clay's music. Clay could teach Jake guitar.

Much too late, she saw those suppositions were more mistakes in her evaluation of Jake. He did champion personal growth, and good times. Jeff saved for a rainy day, Jake was into living before a rainy day washed away the chance. He had a serious side, but he wore it lightly. It didn't drain his dreams or enthusiasm. Jake's laugh came easily, his interest in others readily. A man not so buckle-down would be good for her. Marriage wasn't the only way to love a man. Now felt like the time to giggle and grin, go with the flow and see where Jake might lead her. He had much to teach with his free living. The anchor on her existence had always hung too heavy.

When he called the next day, she was pleased as a sophomore. As he asked, "How's my woman?" She heard the possession and presumption in his voice.

In a heartbeat she ignored both and cooed, "Fine."

She loved his soft "What are you doing, kitten?"

"Working on a song Clay and I are writing."

"Hey, you're supposed to be thinking of me."

Again she side-stepped. "I'm still up fifty thousand feet from last night."

"Me too. Had to call before I go rob my bees."

"Bees?" Being with her last night hadn't stopped his other interests.

"Yeah. You like honey?"

"No, but my son loves honey."

"I'm not trying to impress your son. We still going out tonight?"

"I'm sorry, I forgot Clay's in a school play tonight. I've seen some rehearsals. The kids are good and Clay's doing some original songs. You could join us."

"I have enough school stuff with my own kids. And getting kids involved too soon can kill a relationship. How about just you and me tomorrow night?"

Feeling put off, she agreed. Jake had a right to his preferences. She was blessed he could say so.

"Want to have dinner or what? It's your night. We all have to do things like the play you have to go see your son in tonight."

"You do understand," Anna said wondrously. Jeff had her trained to expect a fuss about Clay's activities.

"Don't like it, but I understand. Tomorrow night, we do what you want. No one's given much time to doing what you want. Anna, that's changing."

"Don't pet me. I'll be clinging or crying or both." That's it, she thought, be easy. God! She was already shaking from his just being nice.

"Clinging's fine, but crying ain't what I want you doing. Don't believe in making folks cry. We're going out to play, just tell Jake how you want to go."

"I may have to take a class to cope with that. Let's meet after supper at the Center. Say, eight-thirty?"

"Honky tonking in Nashville, honey, means boots and jeans."

His pickup in the lights of the Center gleamed like a new-age Cinderella coach. He was there when she parked, opening her door, smiling his white smile, handsome as a prince dressed western. She loved the gray velvet of his eyes as he smiled and said, "Thought you'd never get here."

"Am I late?" she said, thinking, Lord, he's so beautiful.

"No, foxy lady, I'm just anxious to see you."

"I don't know how to take compliments and service."

"You'll get used to it." Handing her out of the car, frankly looking her over, he added, "You look real great."

Charging for the highway, he took her hand, kissed her palm, then each fingertip and gently laid it back on the red leather seat. "Wanted to do that all day long, sweet darling, and I do love the way you fill those jeans?"

"Thanks, and you're the best looking cowboy I've ridden in a pickup with."

She didn't say, he drove like the truck was a wild mustang that might rear and whinny. It was an imperfect world filled with fragile male egos. Bitching about his driving hurt his feelings. She guessed if they died, they died.

"Woman, I'm a pure fool for flattery. How did your boy's play go?"

"Fine, he's come a ways with stage presence in Copper Jim's class."

"Where do you want to go dancing?"

"I haven't danced in years, never did much."

"Woman loves music, writes music, has a son aspiring to be a country music star. Woman like that should be a natural dancer."

"Woman had a husband who never wanted to go dancing."

"Baby, it's been so damn dry for you."

"Don't," she said, tears flooding her eyes.

"Hey, don't cry, I was just petting you." She dabbed her eyes with a tissue, but his concern made her eyes fill again. Not trusting herself to speak, she shrugged and wiped her tears. He pulled her close and said, "Can't pet you way over there." She snuggled like a kitten saved from the hounds.

His arm around her shoulders felt as warm as a big brother's hug. "Jake, you have to stop being so good to me."

"Being good to each other's what dating's about. It's marriage that chains two in a locked-in deal where they can safely pull each other's wings off." She was silent but he felt her tension leaving. Soon she laid her head on his shoulder and hid her face in the warm hollow of his neck.

When the truck bumped on a gravel road, he said, "This is my house." As they bounced up a driveway that needed grading, he said, "You all right?"

She moved away, saying, "Fine as I ever am. You should know, I'm an emotional wreck and nuts where men are concerned. You'd be smart to take me back to the Center and not bother with me again. My little fit's just me. You wanted to go dancing and hear live music, so let's go."

He charged on in the carport. "Let's dance here tonight. We're starting to care, at least I am. Need to be where we can talk, can't with a band grooving. I'll take you dancing tomorrow night. Okay, angel?"

"Okay, if that's what you want."

He killed the motor and said, "There's a great saloon I want to take you to, but tomorrow night will do. Save your appetite, we're having the biggest lobsters they got." Their eyes locked a moment before he said, "Hope you don't mind, I can't wait any longer to kiss you." She didn't mind at all. Her lips, then her sigh, told him kissing her was a good idea. After, he said, "Woman, I can't take much of that." She had no idea what the proper comment was when someone has kissed you silly. He opened his door, put his arm around her waist and slid her out of the truck with him, and thoroughly kissed her again.

Then he was leading her in his house. If he led her in a lion's den she would have followed. He was the second man she had gone this far with. With Jeff, it was after what she had taken vows to do. Now, she was walking into what she'd have amazed herself at considering a month ago.

None of Jake's tenderness was why she had been turned off by those nerds trying to put a hand down her blouse or up her dress as clinically as a gynecologist. She wasn't frigid like one accused. He had turned her cold as shit with his idea of seduction. Approval rather than taking liberties, affection and the choice of saying no mixed a strong aphrodisiac.

Jake pulled her to him, kissed her long and easy, then moved with her to the sofa. "Need some music," he said, then went to the cedar shelves and turned on the stereo. He didn't want to mess this up rushing. Most women moved about ten heartbeats behind his tempo. When he could, few women would. When he was ready, he wanted a woman to be damned ready. "I'll be right back."

With Jake in the kitchen, the mood was broken. Reality jumped out like a spook to put her on guard and her need for comfort evaporated. Listening to the sounds of the refrigerator and cabinet doors and Jake clinking glassware, she started feeling ill at ease and out of place.

Dylan was singing about lost love when Jake returned with two glasses of purple wine. Seeing she was digging the Dylan lyrics, he silently handed her a glass, set the other on the coffee table and moved to light the readied fireplace. He stood by seeing that the flame was burning well before he walked back to the sofa and sat beside her. "Love a fireplace," she said, admiring the flames.

"Me too." He sipped his wine. The song was ending when he said, "You dig Dylan much as I do." Then he tugged off his beautiful black and gold boots.

"Yes, he's a wonderful songwriter."

"He writes songs I love or hate," Jake said, standing his boots at the end of the sofa. She noticed he had small feet for a man at least six feet tall.

"This wine is great. Who makes wine this delicious?"

"Me," he said, grinning.

"It's nectar. Is there anything you can't do?"

"Sip it slow, darling. It has a big kick."

"Never tasted anything alcoholic this good." She drained her glass.

"Want another?."

"I'm surprised, but I think I do."

"Eat some cheese and sip it slow. Homemade hits slower than store wine, you'll feel it in a minute. Clay wouldn't like me getting you drunk."

"The last thing I need is Clay even suspecting me of being drunk." As he walked back to his kitchen in his sock feet, she saw again how exercise paid off. He had the broadest shoulders and narrowest narrow hips.

When he returned with her glass filled again, a plate of cheese and dark crackers, something sweet and saxophone was weaving through the sound system. Anna's eyes caught on his gray glance-- the music was suggesting all kinds of blood-warming things. "You have wonderful eyes, Jake."

"Appreciate it," he said. Her eyes told him the grapes were hitting her pretty hard. Hell, he didn't want her drunk. He didn't have to get a woman drunk to make out. But she was beginning to relax-- God, she was spooky. Maybe in her case, a little buzz was good. He set the cheese on the coffee table and held the wine to her lips. "Just a sip," he commanded.

"That sax should be against the law," she giggled, then obedient as a beagle, took a sip of wine as he held the glass to her lips and held her with his eyes. He could see she wanted to be kissed but he let her want.

"Honey, that hot sax wants us to dance." He saw her eyes were saying, We might be getting lucky but don't rush... don't ruin it. It's been a long time.

As he took her hand and pulled her to her feet, she giggled, "Wait, big shoulders, gotta get my boots off before I step on your piggies."

"Let me help."

As he knelt removing her boots, she said, "Man, stop looking at me like you know how nuts I am, and all about me."

"I know all I need to know," he said, massaging her feet.

"No, you don't. You don't really know anything about me."

"Know I like being with you, and you got real warm feet."

"Not till you started rubbing them."

"Come on, let's dance." She loved how he led her. When she didn't know what to do, it was nice to be in the arms of a man who did. With each step he led into the feel and the rhythm of the music, he was also leading into the rhythm of their feelings. It was time to speak or hold her peace. It was time to fake off into small talk if she wasn't ready for a love affair. She said not a word. She looked into his eyes and knew it was going to be fine as he moved her in and out of the firelight.

He felt her relax, let him take her, glide her to the music, hold her close with the mood of the sax. He held her closer still and felt her body say yes. She loved the passion in his voice as he said, "Been trying to figure how to get my arms around you since we met."

She felt wonderful, velvet colored her. "Think you got it figured it, Jake."

"You lied to me," he said, kissing her hair. "You dance good."

"I do fine following a strong lead. I get found out trying to dance with a man who thinks I can guess where he wants to go. I hate that."

"I hate it when a woman won't say what she wants and gets mad when my guesses ain't right." Julio's tape started playing again.

He led her into a samba, rumba, some Latin thing. She pulled back. "I can't."

"Yes, you can. Relax." He swayed her to the rhythm, led her into the steps.

"I don't believing this." She was doing what he was doing and loving it.

"Believe it, doll." He turned her several times, holding her closer than ever.

As the music ended, he dipped her till her hair brushed the floor, then led her to the sofa and put a piece of cheese to her lips. After she took a bite, he put the rest in his mouth. She asked, "Where did you learn to dance so well?"

"You don't want to know," he said, working the logs with the fire poker. When he walked back to her, her eyes were locked by his. He took her wine from the coffee table and handed it to her, picked up his own and drank it. As he set his glass back down, she knew the moment was now. Whatever else Jake was he had been her fantasy for years. Countless nights she had dreamed him, his face hidden in the shadows of the moon at his back as he loved her. From the time she was fifteen, she had dreamed this very man.

When she married Jeff, she took him for her dream man. After their marriage went bad the dream returned, he was not the man. She felt as guilty as if she had been physically unfaithful. It wasn't only the dream that filled her with guilt. It was also the knowing, as she had always known things. The man in her dream, with his warm hands and his face lost in shadows except for his sensuous eyes, would hold her someday or some night or some life.

Now he was here beside her on the sofa, smiling so tenderly, coming on ready or not. She wasn't at all sure that she was ready. She wasn't at all sure she was up to contending with the results or the emotional tide warming and rising inside her. Maybe it was easier to hold back, maybe it was smarter to run, if not as thrilling. For sure it was safer, for her and for him. Once she let her defenses fall, she could be such an insecure bitch. Once she let him set her passion free and gave him emotional control, she might be the witch of the world to cope with. She had loved and lost too many. In the years before Jeff turned so cold toward Clay, at times she didn't want him out of her sight.

Soft as a moth wing, he brushed her lips with his. "Got warm lips," he said, kissing them again. Then he was kissing her seriously, but his lips were light, his lips touched without demanding. Then he started to whisper, not demands, or even needs, but praise, laurels, compliments. His words were beautiful and badly needed. If she was too chickenshit to risk her heart, why was she here?

And, Lord, she was being comforted. He was saying everything she was soul dry to hear. All the soft things Jeff could never say, that Mrs. Stokes could never say, or even Aunt Effie. If her mother had said then-- it had been too long. Time and trauma had erased her mother, she couldn't remember Jake's words being said by anyone, anytime, anywhere.

He knew how badly she was in need because he was in need. It was a miracle that he could lavish on her the approving, loving, beautiful, beguiling things-- lyrical things. Things she had stopped herself from even dreaming she needed to hear. But, oh, God, she did. She had been heart-starved for his pretty phrases, his touch, his tender machismo for years and years. He said words for that lonely child inside her, still crying for affection. She said things she had never been able to say, things she had needed to acknowledge ever since the lake took everybody. Then Aunt Effie died too and all she had was that dream-killing, mind-caging, abomination of Give Us This Day! God, how awful!

Jeff left her too. She couldn't blame that on God. Jeff left of his own free will. He didn't have to kill his silly self. How stupid! Sure she loved Clay. Clay was her baby. Hell, it wasn't even like he was a bastard or something! Clay was Jeff's baby too! There wasn't one thing wrong in a mother loving her son; her only begotten son, for God's sake. But Jeff thought so! He put her back amongst the lonely and lost. She thought he was strong, dependable and good. Why did he have to turn into such a chickenshit? Jealous of his own flesh and blood? Who would have guessed the courageous young prince who rescued her from the stupid orphanage was as insecure as a damn guinea hen?

Maybe it was better not to bother loving. She didn't know how many more leavings she could survive. Hell, she didn't know how many more survivals she could survive. She didn't know how many more risings above it, recyclings, or resurrections her mind would bear. Damn the tears! The valleys of depression! Days like dungeons and soul-killing, lonely, lonely, nights! There wasn't enough lonely in the word lonely. Repeated a million times it didn't tell how lonely it gets when you got mind-break blues. When you only have that cold old traveler, Mister Howling Wind.

"Jake, have you met Mister Howling Wind? He knows the lonelies, that's why he moans so long and low. He was all that knew I was alive. Mrs. Stokes always looked through me. Hell, Mrs. Stokes looked through herself."

"Don't cry, woman, I won't let you be lonely. I love you."

"Don't say you love me, don't even whisper you love me. Don't dare love me! He'll take you. Don't kiss me anymore. I commit the unpardonable sin."

"Unpardonable sin?"

"I love my son. I'll make you jealous and crazy. You might go hunting. Ha! Ain't that a rip! What's in your damned wine, darling?"

"Like I warned you, honey, it's a little strong."

"A little strong? I'm shit-faced!"

"Maybe you need to be. Hush and kiss me."

"Listen, maybe loving's too hard a horse for me to ride and He's trying to tell me. Maybe that's why my ass keeps winding up bucked off; crying in the dirt for dead people. Tears don't have to show to be crying. You know that."

"Loving makes up, it's the greatest thing of all."

"But maybe it ain't meant for some. Like some can't eat chocolate. Nothing wrong with chocolate, some just can't tolerate things like chocolate and love."

"Doll, don't blame love for folks and fate. The most beautiful thing is to love, to be loved and make love."

"I can't, Jake, it's too dangerous."

"No danger. It's great. Trust me. No, don't push me off, don't hold back. I can't take that. I won't leave you. Here, touch me. See how bad I want you? Yeah. It's yours. You want to, baby, just like me. I can feel you want Jake to love you; course you do. Wouldn't hurt you for nothing. Relax, pretty Anna."

"I can't relax, I--"

"Shush, darling, sure you can. Kiss me."

"Jake, I--" She was silenced by his mouth on her mouth, kissing her long and deep, exploring with his tongue, then brought her tongue into his mouth.

He did not stop till he felt her relax, heard her breath catch in her throat, felt her rise against him. Some women talked too much. Sometimes women got insecure-- talked it all away, if you didn't take control, and stop them from being their own worst enemy. He eased up as if to move his lips away. He felt her mouth reach for his and knew it was all right now, she was his. He lifted his lips from hers and whispered, "Here, play, just play, angel. That's good, yeah, pretty baby, play. They never let you play enough, like me. They never let us have much fun, made us adults at twelve. Never got to be a little girl much, like I never got to be a little boy."

"It was so cold there, Jake."

"Yes, darling, I know."

"Jake, the North Pole isn't as cold as an orphanage."

"Darling, I know it has to be the coldest place ever. Listen, love me, let me love you. The orphanage is over. Nobody ever hung around to love you much, pretty baby, cry if you need to. Yeah, honey, it's all right to cry Just remember I'm hanging around now. Jake is here, Anna. Jake isn't going to leave you. Here now. Please... listen. Nobody ever hung around to love Jake either. But now I got my Anna. My pretty, pretty Anna to love me... yeah. Make it up to me... let me make it up to you.

"Let me, honey, let me now. I can't wait any longer... relax, let me. Help me... lift up to me-- please. Oh, yeah... so good, baby, feels so good just touching, knowing each other this way. Makes me feel so cared about, baby. Makes me feel so special. Let me love you, now. Okay? Show me... guide me. Help me, this is for both of us... make it sweet... Oh, God, so good. Knew it would be, angel. This is the best there is-- the sweetest. Best, most beautiful a man and woman can do for each other. You know? Oh, honey, you know... know so good. Come on, that's it. Yeah, give it to me. Yeah, now, come! Come on. Come. Oh, baby. Darling!"

He picked her up, stood holding her in his arms a moment to kiss her, then carried her to his bedroom. He laid her on the bed as gently as he would fine china. Then he was beside her, gathering her in his arms and kissing her. Even with the fog of the wine, she knew it was real. This was not her dream or one of those sweet scenarios she sometimes ran through her mind to oil the tears in her heart. It wasn't a new dram of make-believe to comfort her broken soul she learned to concoct as an orphan. It was all being said and done, he was here, he was real. The loving may have been birthed by need, unwound by wine, but it was real and the strongest, most inviting invading ever to touch her.

She wasn't having to do a thing or to solve a thing. She didn't have to be brave, be still, pick the right word out of three, answer true/false questions or take the pop quiz. She hadn't heard "Act responsible" or "Wait for tomorrow" or for someone to come and be her guardian or till she turned twenty-one, even one time. It hadn't been a decision. All she had to do was let it happen, he took care of the rest. He didn't need instructions, suggestions, help or to ask permission. He knew when he had permission, truly he was the perfect lover. He didn't push, he didn't rush. He knew how to arouse her. He was sure, gentle, competent-- Lord, he had her number all the way.

Now again with no help, he had them together; his smooth, hard, muscled self warmly against herself, kissing, touching, tasting, knowing, teaching, demonstrating again how well he knew how to minister to her needs, her pleasure. As he slowly loved her, obviously more sure of her now, she was delighted, amazed and aroused as hell.

When he boldly pushed into her deeper than ever, she loved it, she reached to meet him. Thinking she should break away, run from this power he had over her, she strained up to him more, kissing him like no tomorrow. He was the sweetest, dearest, most loving, warmest place she had ever been. As they seriously began moving to another finale, Jake realized he had never made love to more. All the chases, all the challenges, all the conquests, all the runs and wins and scores, all the days and all the nights, all the women all together had never given more, never taken more-- she was unbelievable!

She was amazed how she was letting her feelings fly, taking opportunity, infinite gratitude and boundless pleasure from all his finesse, his fire, his beautiful control. For the first time, she was aware of control on a man's part. As long as he held off, she found pleasure. As long as she found pleasure, he held off. She felt freedom she had never found before or even knew how to reach for. This was life's most powerful drug, most beautiful high. Then again came the moment she needed to feel his pleasure, just when he could bridle himself no longer as she had in the living room and there was no reason to bridle. As he began riding with total abandonment, he felt her contracting again in perfect sync. As her tears of joy watered his face, he knew he was her perfect ten; as friend, as lover and as man.

He lay on her, too pleased to move. In the dark his smile was in his, "Woman, you're a loving miracle." This one would keep him fascinated for awhile, if she kept up this kind of loving. He murmured, "I love you."

"When love means this much, we can't lose it. Can we, Jake?"

"Course not. Kiss me, woman."

When he at last lay back on his pillow, he could barely tell he was a boy. He was consumed, done, drained. He might not ever want any more. But falling asleep, his lips quivered in a grin, he was mistaken. He felt himself reaching for his warm Anna, pulling her to him to hold her, guard her, keep poachers away from his stuff. He never held a woman like this-- after. Years ago, an old shaman foretold, at the end of a long search and after Jake was mature enough to know her, he would find the one woman who would be all women to him. Jake kissed the sleeping Anna's bare shoulder. Till tonight, he had believed the white-haired psychic was a fake or dealing tarot cards without a full deck. He smiled, his lips still against the woman's shoulder, delighted to be wrong.

Later, he woke and searched the king-sized bed. He heard movement. She was up. "Angel, what're you doing?"

"Well, uh, I have to get home."

"No, you don't," he said, getting up. He found her in the dark and put his arms around her. "What are you doing putting your clothes on? I want you to stay." He fumbled at her bra.

"Please, I have to go." She pulled away and found her jeans in the dark.

"Call and tell Clay you're staying over. That ain't a problem, unless you're ashamed of me." She hated the pain in his voice

But she said, "I can't deal with telling Clay yet."

"I thought tonight was going to be for us."

"It has been, it's three in the morning. You said we'd do what I wanted. It's been great! Now I want to go home."

"You know how many women in class would love to be here? How many I wouldn't even have to go after? How many would come flying out, bring the damn steaks and the wine and beg to say over?"

Dressed after a fashion, she flipped on the light in the joining bath. "No, stud buddy, I don't. But it's so gross to say such a thing. I drug my dumb ass out with you, thinking you're a free spirit and a man of character. Thought your fairness and the chemistry between us was a basis for real love. Goes to show how wrong I thought!" She stormed in the bathroom and slammed the door.

He placed his forehead against the door and said, "Baby, I don't think there's anything wrong with your thinking."

"Ha! We'd be halfway to town if you didn't. Call one of the girls so anxious to fly out here the next time. Hell, call one tonight if you ain't satisfied, one without a son she's trying to raise decent."

"Shit!" he growled, and flipped on the bedside lamp as she came from the bathroom. His anger reminded her of a two year old. As the gray coals of his eyes scorched her, she fought an urge to giggle. He just might hit her. She didn't give a damn, but she didn't want to goad him into that.

He barked, "I know not to fool with married women. Or women with kids! Looks like I'd honor my own damn rules, don't it?"

"I'm not into rules. I've had rules enough for the rest of my life."

"Is that right, Miss Priss?" Hell, she was stealing his lines.

"Check into an orphanage if you want rules. I'm into treating folks like you want to be treated, trading feeling for feeling, love for love if I get lucky." She had to hush, she didn't want this ape making her cry.

Stepping into buckskin moccasins, he said, "I got one better than that, hot stuff, while your hard head is having second thoughts."

"Just take me on home, I don't want to hear it."

"Hear it anyway! From the first, I knew we were right for the love of a lifetime. Knew too you're too talky, too bossy and too libber for me. Did I listen? No! Am I hurt? I'm devastated, and pissed at how I don't listen to me. You got me feeling like a joy boy; like a piece of meat. Hope you're happy."

"I'm ecstatic, Jake."

"Wench, you ready to go?"

"Is a dove ready to fly?"

"Always, darling, when her little ass gets through fucking."

CHAPTER 10

WORSHIP TO WAR TO WORSHIP

She didn't know if her undoing was the man or her glands, but halfway back to town, she was feeling used and too mad to be afraid. Used was the last feeling that should be twisting a woman's gut after such sweet sex, love or whatever they shared all evening. It was her first illegal sex. Jeff wouldn't touch her till after the Justice of the Peace. Maybe this was how it was when you weren't married. Legal or illegal, if you wanted a good time with a damn man, better have it before you crawled in bed with him. Anything your heart desired was fine before; while he was all proud and hotted up. After, the sweetest bastard was subject to bull up.

Hell, if Jeff wasn't too dumb to live, this wouldn't be happening. She was content to spend her whole life with him. He had no right to leave her like this!

Shit, she'd be joining him real soon if she didn't stop riding with Jake. He was close enough to the eighteen wheeler in front of them for the two vehicles to kiss. At the last second, he swerved to the left lane. Luckily no car was in the lane and her seat belt was fastened. Maybe giving her a whiplash would make his night, if he didn't kill them both! At ninety miles an hour, this silly ass she was silly enough to be with was subject to wreck any minute. No wonder he was divorced! When he was pissed he was brain dead!

He shot her a steel glare. She looked away and raised her chin. If he wanted to scare her, he damn well had, but she'd be smeared all over the road before she'd beg! Lord! Talk about the moon shining on the wolfman, or Jekyll and Hyde in living color! The Neanderthal side of men was so hateful.

She could just see Jake sitting by a cave fire wearing some dead animal's hair, mad as murder because he found nothing to kill all day. When temper turned him into an animal, the sweetest male might punch out a female and blame her. Her young, tomboy days taught her that.

Up until puberty, she held her own. Then Mama Nature grew the boys taller and stronger, while pound for pound she grew smaller and weaker. Unless you liked getting beat up, you used an equalizer to play in the streets of Greenriver. A good rock evened things up when the climate got hostile. Once a boy had a testicle attack from a "split tail" win, the best might knock hell out of you, girl or not, honor or not. So you let them know they might whip you, but they'd get a run for their money. Without a rock or stick, it was a loser all the way against someone with the reach, weight and height. All she had was the damned crooked pelvis that make girls weaker.

Another tactic, was to wait to mouth off till she was close enough to home to run inside before she got caught. She was the fastest short distance runner on the block; faster when she was scared. Speaking of scared, this bastard's eyes went from worship to war to worship in a blink. Her mood swings were nuts, but his went sky to dungeon. Naturally, she'd flip over manic depressive, serial killer material. If she got home in one piece, she'd keep her hot ass home!

When he came in for a landing, he hadn't said a word; neither had she. While she was waiting for the truck to stop rocking, he snarled, "Ain't this where you been bitching to be?"

"You got it, Frankenstein!" She slid out of the pickup and slammed the door without a backward glance.

Thinking the door might cave in, Jake barked, "Little, high tempered, bitch," and watched her twist off to her car, then roared off to the scream of tires.

Searching her purse reminded her, she should have car keys in hand. But she had to be too upset to think about living till it was too late. She hated the male chauvinists who designed purses. They loved making a woman prey for the local rapist. Here she was, digging in a bottomless pit for car keys at three in the morning in a deserted parking lot. She willed her hands to stop shaking. All the public service messages warned against showing fear. God, it was dark!

Finally she found the keys and got the car in motion before she gave herself the luxury of feeling relieved. She'd never again be alone on the road this time of night short of an emergency. Out for a good screwing, like a bitch in heat, didn't qualify. This was why women wanted the staying-over bit. Hell, it wasn't the man they hated leaving but the danger being out in the night alone

This was a crock, out in the wee hours without so much as a rolling pin for defense. A flat tire would put her at the mercy of whoever, Jeff always changed tires, Clay changed them now. Truth was, she would be vulnerable broke down on the road, getting stuff out of the trunk even if she knew what to do with it. If the car did betray her, like everything else tonight, she'd lock it and hope for the best. Unless a police car came, she'd sit on the shoulder of the road till daylight, then walk for help. Single life had a bad tails side.

When she pulled in the drive, she was never happier to get home. If she hadn't been so spooked she would have got down and kissed the ground. This time before she unlocked the car, the house key was in her hand.

Shep met her at the door. "Hi, boy," she said, petting his head, then tiptoed down the hall to Clay's room. He was asleep, so she didn't have to come up with an alibi. God did know when a silly woman had put her silly self through all she could stand. Shep brushed past and plopped in his place by Clay's bed.

He gave her a last look before laying his noble head between his paws, after a good night thump of his tail closed his eyes.

In the friendly dark of her bedroom, she sat on the side of her bed to undress. Still wearing her western shirt, she crawled under the covers too tired to bother with a gown. She said "Oh" aloud, feeling the soreness in her buttocks from exercise they were no longer used to. Yeah, hot ass, dash out tomorrow night and find you some more. Get another stallion to shack up with, then scare yourself to death coming home at three in the morning. Lord, I feel like I been chewed up and spit out, she thought, falling asleep.

The next day she got no call. Why want a call from such a nut? She was a big girl, she'd get over it! She'd been forewarned. Jake admitted straight up, women were a hobby. He laid that gem on her in the same sentence he named music, dancing, jogging and beekeeping as hobbies. He had no more interest in one woman than he did in one bee. The crux of the matter was the honey. She didn't know how good a beekeeper he was, but she'd swear on the Bible he knew his woman hobby well. He had read the lesson, could answer the questions at the end of the chapter. He deserved "A" marks and a gold star too.

As Jake expected, she didn't show up the next day or the next. After ten days he was concerned. It wasn't over till he said it was over. He called the shots with his women. No bitch was irreplaceable, but this one was too hot and too good to let go-- yet. Since his divorce, he did the letting go! Anna wasn't going to jack him around if she was great. He was no rookie and he could do without any woman. All damn women if he had to. Hell, he had!

Putting up with Darleen's shit taught him how softly lethal women could be, back when he was dreaming of being a doctor. He'd been too sexed up to see he killed any chance for that when he married her. Darleen couldn't make a pimple on a doctor's wife's ass. That's from kids marrying when they ought to be playing ball or something they were old enough to handle.

This Anna woman was a great new trip. High tempered as hell but wired hot as a microwave oven. Entering Anna was entering a whole new world of making love. Loving Anna was another dimension of loving. She got so excited, that got him so excited-- he loved it. Anna was no tease, no sacrificial lamb, no clinging vine, no raging nymphomaniac. She was the original article, a woman doing what she was born to do as good as it gets. Any better, his heart couldn't stand it. Still, a man had to take it with a grain of salt, once he made up his mind he wasn't going to be run over by any woman ever again.

As he left, Brenda said, "Where is Anna Hill?"

"How the hell do I know?"

Wise to his ways, she said, "Ooh, la, la, someone got to our lady killer." His eyes cut into her's, then he stomped out. "And our token chauvinist is in love," Brenda said to his back already on the far side of the glass door. Shoot, she was only bugging. Jake was honest and did a fine job. She was lucky to have him. As much as he loved women, he never messed with jailbait girls. Brenda had no designs on him nor he on her. Jake knew she was a happily married woman, like she knew he was a happily practicing womanizer. Even if she was looking, she wouldn't be in the market for a Jake. If he could keep it up as long as he could do push-ups, she'd be addicted in one session. He'd move on to the next female in line, she'd be nursing a broken heart.

She wouldn't mean to hurt his feelings for anything. He was already badly burned where women were concerned. Under that macho veneer, there beat a dear heart that just needed the right woman. She hadn't had a clue he had fallen for Anna Hill. Anna was nice and beautiful, but smart and independent as hell. Jake was too insecure to handle a relationship with such a woman. A woman like Anna would drive him crazy, bring out the worst in him and never know why, just going about her own business.

When he finally called, he hated Anna's sleepy, "Hello."

"Guess you're so blue over us, you can't sleep."

"Jake?"

"Who else would be talking about us?" Jake was too much of a health nut to be drunk but there was no mistaking his alcohol slur. Before she could answer, he hissed, "Shit!" and hung up.

She was padding from the bathroom when he rang back. "Woman, don't quit class from hating me."

"I don't hate you, Jake, I just haven't felt like coming."

"Thanks a lot for getting my boss on my ass."

"I'm sorry about your boss but--"

"Forget my boss. Come in the morning." A thousand mean things hit her mind. While she was choosing the meanest one, he said, "You hear me?"

"Say please!" He hung up. "Asshole," she snarled. As she was dropping off again there was another ring and another before she said, "What the hell is it?"

"Please, God damn it! Please! Satisfied?"

"Yes, asshole!" For some dumb reason, she grinned.

There was no grin in his "Don't be late."

She had thrown her pillows on the floor and lay spread-eagled on her stomach, settled for serious sleep when he rang again. "By God! Hello!"

"By God, I'm sorry!"

"Sorry about what, Jake?"

"If you don't kno... know, maybe I don't need to be sorry."

"Big man, with all you've earned to be sorry about, I'd like to know what. You sorry you were such a bully the other night? Sorry you're being such a bully now? Maybe you're sorry you had too much to drink. Or, hell, could you be sorry you care more about me than just a piece of ass?"

"I'm sor... sorry to be a bore, sorry you quit class to prove you were right and I was wrong, sorry you got me in love with your ass. I'm damn sor... sorry I'm not there with your love wrapped all around me. Woman, I'm sorry for any damn thing you need me to be sorry for. So what else for you?" He hung up again, but it was a soft hang up. Like he just pushed down the button.

Lord, she thought, I don't know what I've fallen in, Jake, but I'm sorry too you're not here in bed with me. I want you so.

He made her feel more cared for and more caring, more giving and more receiving than she had even imagined possible. The sex was pure heaven and she felt so alive. The whole wonderful love making-night was a dream come true. At least it was till Armageddon set in.

Actually, the surface of her sexuality had hardly been scratched till Jake. He taught her what heights were possible with a man who wanted to give her those heights. Till Jake, she hadn't touched the beautiful balance of love and lust.

Wherever sexual arousal originated, he had all her responses running on all pistons, cruising at four hundred miles an hour. For sure he knew how to flick her willing little bic. She couldn't remember feeling like such a fool or such a goddess! And probably, he was the typical womanizer so many women got strung out over sooner or later. Mostly later, when they think they know better. When they think they know the score in general; in particular, where a sexual athlete is concerned. But she was too damn far gone to help it.

It was years before she matured and mellowed toward herself enough for a simple truth. Right time, right opportunity renders a love hungry woman or man as vulnerable for love as crossing a desert renders a wanderer for water. When acute thirst reaches acute deprivation, it is far too acute for anyone to stop to test the water. A womanizer senses that and picks up on a hot female like a buck picking up on a doe's heat scent. Shit, it's basic as biscuits!

Still, it was wonderful. She couldn't discount Jake like some dime store diamond she had taken for the real thing. He was the real thing! He started a time she had never felt more sexual release or response, more intimacy or more closeness. All that was worth fighting for.

The next day, knowing he had been as contrite as he could, she went to class. Whether it was to show him she didn't follow orders to the letter, she didn't know, but she walked in forty minutes late.

Jake was holding group exercise, she eased into a place and joined in without looking at him. She felt his eyes on her. They made her remember how warm he was, the feel of his kiss, his hands, his... his....

She thought, Lord, brains hush! But it was impossible to keep her eyes from touching Jake's eyes. Her fixed stare at the fat lady in front of her, struggling valiantly to perform side-straddle hops, as well as two hundred pounds of lard would allow, came undone. Her eyes locked on his and got her into difficulty trying to perform her own side-straddle hops.

Damn! Instantly, his eyes were arousing her. They were like some kind of drug she had evaluated herself too intelligent to touch. After how hateful he could be, she should have some sense. Wrong again, Anna El Stupido Hill!

He began rounds, offering pointers here and there. As he approached her, she was filled with wanting. It was all she could do to continue the exercise. He walked close behind her, breathing on her neck, and she did stop. With the music blaring, smiling his sweetest, there was no way for anyone to see he stood arousing her with his eyes, before he hissed, "Miss Cuntzie had to be late but she did come. Glad to see you can listen once in a while, dummy." His words hit her like he had literally slapped her. She hated the tears that sprang to her eyes, but she looked at him a long, unbelieving moment before she turned and ran. His sharp, "Anna!" did not bring her back.

She was rolling in her driveway before she hardly knew what happened. She ran inside the house and started dropping sweaty clothes, piece by piece, down the hall and across her bedroom carpet all the way to her shower. She showered everything she had from her head to her toes and most of it twice.

When she climbed out of the shower, the phone was ringing. Wrapped in a towel, she padded to the phone as it rang again. "Hello?"

"Hi, Spitfire?" he said, with a low laugh.

"Bastard, I want you to know one thing."

"What's that, sweet ass?"

"I'm not your punching bag, mental or otherwise, and kiss my country ass!"

"You ain't country. You come from working folks, like me."

"My mama and Aunt Effie were. They both had too much backbone and redneck pride to put up with a low down, chauvinistic, womanizing son of a bitch putting them down, no matter how good the loving. I won't either, stud-buddy. And don't you forget it!"

"I love a lady!" Jake sneered. His voice warmed noticeably as he said, "By the way, I'd love to kiss your ass. Can I come over and do it now?"

"Damn!" She hung up, but not before his laugh.

☺☹

She had on her makeup, was dressed in rubbed denim jeans, and her eyes had taken on the purple of her sweater. With a last look in the mirror, she gave her blond hair a shake of her head, patted it into place and was satisfied. Then she went to the kitchen for coffee and took it down the hall.

She and Clay had made the spare bedroom into a songwriting studio. She was anxious to get back to the song they were writing. As she hung her guitar over her shoulders, Shep barked from the kennel. After a few moments, he barked again as someone rang the door bell.

Checking in the peep hole, she saw Jake standing on the stoop. Her knees turn to jelly. Impatient as always, he rang again as she took her guitar off her shoulders and leaned it against the sofa.

When she opened the door, he took a length of tree limb from behind his back with a white handkerchief tied to the end and waved it. She was braced for anger but his grin was so appealing, he looked so sweet and innocent waving his peace offering, he was so handsome, he looked so glad to see her, she was so glad to see him, her anger turned to laughter.

He laughed too. "Woman, am I forgiven?"

"Yes, nut, you're forgiven," she said still laughing, truly delighted now to see him. "Come in and have coffee with me. Just made a fresh pot."

He walked in. "That guitar's a real beauty."

"Oh, thanks, I was writing."

"You play this?" He picked up her guitar and strummed it a time or two.

"Barely. Clay's the picker here. Do you play?"

"Haven't got to it yet." He leaned her guitar back against the sofa.

"I play just enough to write a three chord song that isn't too uptempo."

"Listen, if you're busy--"

"I'm not that busy, come on. Have coffee with me." She turned to lead the way, but he took her by the shoulder and turned her around.

Then the eye thing between them started. His arms went around her waist as he said, "Didn't drive clear out here just for coffee. Kiss me." His mouth covered hers before she could object. He held her tight but his kiss was gentle, she didn't try to turn away. He kissed her long and easy till she was kissing him back and they were both very moved. Taking one of her hands on his chest, he kissed each fingertip. His eyes were velvet, his voice was full with passion as he said, "I want you to know, I'm really sorry."

"I'm sorry too, Jake." Then he was kissing her again and she was kissing him, again and again, and soon there was no control, no stopping, only feeling and love and mounting passion. Their mouths opened and their tongues touched and it was wonderful and he was wonderful and she was wonderful and the world was wonderful and the living room was spinning. Suddenly, his mouth was under her sweater and all that sweet, hot, beautiful magic was happening, brewing, building, warming so sweet again and she felt weak, helpless as some kind of flower before the bee-- willing initially-- then wanting-- aiding-- abetting-- her hands in his hair-- under his tank top-- touching his chest -- caressing his strong, hard back.

And he was so tender, so knowing of the right touch at the right moment. When he took her to the carpet she was needing, wanting, ready to be filled. She helped him as he started, both were undoing confining, delaying clothing. He read her so well. Knowing she had been programmed as a girl to say no, he asked no questions. He knew how to test where and when and if. He knew what pleased her, what moved her, what aroused her. Even more, he knew what was passe and when to move on. He knew to make her wait a bit, till she was gently desperate, writhing with wanting, rising to invite him, crazy for him, moaning for his filling of that void created to be filled with him. Then he did and it was grand, inspiring her to work under him, with him, wild and free and giving; going for it with all the delayed longing driving her as the starving-for- him-woman he had brought her to be.

Even so, this time she knew, this loving, this high heady trip, he was letting her set the pace. He held off to give her time; he held back to give her freedom of movement to keep her mood and her momentum going. He knew the more he gave her, the more he enabled her to give him. Again and again she came, completely amazed, delighted with Jake's ability and her new, multiple self he had led her to discover. She could barely believe it, she had the feeling of being someone else observing herself. In the privacy of her own living room, he was taking her somewhere else, making her someone else. Initially on the carpet, then on to the overstuffed chair, the sofa, standing against the wall, she was discovering new heights, and the marvelous, female animal she could be in the arms of this marvelous animal of a man.

With each orgasm, she felt higher, freer and more loved. As release blessed her again and again, hearing her own moan of ecstasy was like hearing the sounds of a new, unknown, undreamed-of female side of herself. A female side that had been locked away for years like Rapunzel in the tower. Now a prince named Jake had come to release, relieve and rescue-- to love her away from the routine, the adequate, the mundane. His unique sense of duty as a lover was the aphrodisiac of the ages. There would never be another war or another rhino killed for his horn-- if all men only knew!

Finally spent, but for one last finale of ecstasy, she only said "Now" but he knew where she was, and gave to her as she to him. They wrought the ultimate; that sweetest together, in a final blissful joining.

She lay several minutes in euphoria. Then reality returned and rendered her feeling ridiculous, on the living room carpet harsh and scratchy to freshly cooled skin. "Jake, what if Clay came home early?"

"Who cares?" he said lazily but her restlessness made him lift his body enough for her to move out from under. She rolled away and was up like a female on fire, gathering her abandoned clothes and then she was down the hall and under the shower. Damn! she knew, he had crossed the man's eyes with her behavior. His? Hell! she had crossed her own! She couldn't imagine what was getting into her. She didn't know she could be such a slut. If she didn't stop acting so starved for it, she was going to lose him sure. No man wanted to be in love with a pure bitch.

As she turned under the tepid shower for a final rinse, Jake slid the shower door back and stepped in with her. Instantly she was captured by his eyes. She couldn't have taken her eyes from his velvet gaze if the world had ended.

In a heartbeat, she was in his arms, into his kiss and under his tutelage. He moved on from her mouth to kiss wet kisses on her cheek, her neck, her shoulder, her breasts. A thrill shivered through her as he took her breast in his mouth. His unique warmth touched her most vulnerable place, then eased between her legs. When he felt her tense acceptance relax to a swaying welcome, he stiffly but gently began his slow pushing search, easing his way until he was mystically, wonderfully, deeply inside her. She felt him gear down to a holding pattern, to linger a loving moment, while he ran his tongue over her eyelids, her cheeks, her lips, on down the column of her neck to her shoulders, her breasts.

It seemed he took a long time with her breasts. He didn't know how impossibly quick, how beautifully he could love her alive, blissfully afire; and wildly wanting him all over again. But she stood in sync, on board, in rhythm and pumping in perfect harmony with the man as if this might be the last loving of her life. And he stayed for her; how wonderful of him to stay for her to have her time-- time and time again.

Then he moved into a new mode and mood that was his trip, his pace, his control. She was wild to please as he coached, "Not yet, don't rush, darling. No hurry, kitten, easy cruising... hold back for me, pretty Anna, let it last, let it build. You learn fast, that's it. Let it be... gets better and better. Good, that's my woman... so good, darling." She felt totally with him, high on his passion, assenting at his speed, in loving sync; feeling and moving and following his strong climb, building the heat of their flame higher and higher in the rain of the shower, the rain of their feelings, up the long, hot, wet, outer-space flight of passion. "You're wonderful," she moaned as they crested the peak.

At the top of mutual arousal, and the impending eruption of feeling, he commanded, "Now! Let it all go!"

As one voice, they breathed, "I love you."

Then, clinging to him, dizzy from loving, weak with satisfaction, she murmured, "I can't believe me. What if Clay came? What would I do?"

"You'd say, Clay, knock the next time. We love each other, we have to share our love. Woman, the truth don't hurt kids, it's the lies."

After one last kiss, she climbed out of the shower, grabbed her robe and handed him a towel. He kissed her hand, then said, "I'll take that coffee now."

☺☺

At the kitchen table, Jake said, "Didn't picture you living in the sticks."

"Jeff wanted Clay to know the woods." She smiled, but she felt self-conscious. Here she sat having coffee, prim as the village virgin, after an all morning, all over the house orgy. God!

"Woman, when I'm upset I can be an ass. But I do love you, and I'm sorry."

"Darling, you have a lovely way of saying things with no protective phrases." He smiled and sipped his coffee. She had dreamed of him in her kitchen, she had not dreamed of his tenderness. "Jake, you are all I ever wanted in a man, but I may be the last woman you need."

"Well, I'll say one thing for you, honey. You can take your pretty ass out of a room faster than a speeding bullet." His laugh made her laugh.

Still she said, "That's what I mean, I can't take put downs. And however hot I've acted, I don't make love just because it feels good. For me, sex is a special place. And if I'm there-- I care."

"Long as you do it like you do, I'll care and I'll damn sure be there."

"I'm totally serious, Jake. My values are dated, but I can't ruin Clay's respect for me. Maybe you should date the girls at the Center. That was no idle brag you made. They're always talking about what a hunk you are. And you are."

"Hon, when I was blowing off about women, I was mad and being dumb. And then I had a choice. When you were working out yesterday, you were all I could see. It was like the sun fell when you left. You're all I've wanted since that night you walked in hunting an exercise class."

"What are you saying?"

"I guess, maybe marriage. We'll take our time, but I don't need other women. Don't want you with other men. Want you with me. Talking to me, sleeping with me, eating with me. You like fresh catfish?"

"Yes, but it's hard to find."

"I know where we can get it with no bones, plus great slaw, white beans, and Vidalia onion. It ain't fancy but it sets by the Harpeth River. We'll get a river view table." He finished his coffee.

"Sounds great," Anna said, filling his cup.

"Woman, I love how you pouring for me makes me feel, but I had enough coffee. Ready to go eat catfish?"

"You mean right now?"

"You don't have to milk or gather eggs, do you?"

She giggled and said, "No, but I do have plans with Clay tonight."

"Hell, guess I see who's important around here."

"That's not fair," she said softly.

"Got caught in that." He grinned but his gray eyes went dark as slate.

When she turned from placing the coffeepot on the warmer, he was standing. "Jake, I want you to meet Clay. He'll be here shortly."

"Need to get on home and see about my bees."

"There's that appealing spontaneity coming out."

"Thanks, if that means what I think it does. Honey, what does Clay coming home have to do with us going out now?

"Well, we'd be pushed for time and I hate to leave the minute he walks in."

"Anna, he's seventeen. Give him a break, and me."

"You ought to know, I'll give you about anything."

"Then what's the problem?'

"No problem, plans are made for tonight. Okay?"

"Okay. What about tomorrow afternoon?"

"Tomorrow is Thanksgiving Eve. We're going up to Mama Hill's."

"Forgot Thanksgiving. When are you coming back?"

"Sunday night, Clay has school on Monday."

"Must still be pretty tight with your in-laws."

"Mama Hill is like a mother to me. She's getting on and we haven't seen her in ages. You'd think East Tennessee was another hemisphere."

"Well, can you see me Monday?" '

"Darling, I'd love to." Seeing him to the door, she felt his sadness and couldn't stand him leaving blue. "Jake, kiss me bye?"

He stopped without turning, his hand on the doorknob. Clearly, he was in a quandary. She was afraid he would go without a word. Then he did turn, he even grinned. Still something sad was in his "Didn't mean to fall in love-- but I did. Course you know that. Come here, wench."

~~~~~ **CHAPTER 11** ~~~~~

JAKE'S STORY

Hearing Clay at the front door, she called, "We are in the kitchen." She had told Clay about her date with Jake, still as he walked in the room his eyes widened. An eligible man at their table was a seldom sight.

She felt ill at ease making the introduction but she was proud of how Clay held out his hand to Jake. As they shook hands, she was surprised to see Clay was the taller of the two. He wasn't muscled out like Jake, but he was half a head taller. Less than thrilled about seeing Jake, he managed to smile. "Nice to meet you, Mr. Dennis."

"Nice to meet you, Clay. Call me Jake."

"You teach the exercise program at the Center."

"Yes. I've seen you on stage. I hear you want to be in country music."

"I'm going to try. Mama's helping me write, Copper Jim's coaching me. He has been in music for years."

"Still picks on the Opry, doesn't he?"

"Yes, sir. He's the best rhythm picker in Nashville."

"Son, have a seat with us."

"Just came for my guitar, Mama. Josh is waiting in his car. We're going to pick at his house, then go to class, if that's okay."

"Okay. Just be careful and don't stay out late."

"Josh will bring me home after class. Will you be home then?"

Seeing his worry, Jake said, "Yes. We're going for a drive and dinner. I'll take good care of her and I think she'll enjoy herself. She'll be home when you get back from your night out."

Clay smiled again and said, "Okay." But Anna read his negative eyes.

"How about another fillet?"

"Thanks, Jake, the food was all you said, but I've already eaten too much."

"Miss Sally bakes the best peach cobbler you ever tasted."

"Maybe another time. Now I can't eat another bite. Look out there, Jake, the river is just beautiful in the evening sun."

"Yeah. Before the sun is gone, let's take a walk along the river. You might have room for pie after that."

"I'll gain fifty pounds with all this eating."

"I'll keep it worked off, don't worry," he said with a leer and was delighted with her blush. "Hey, no reason to be getting all red. I only meant with the workout class." As he pulled her chair back, he bent his head close to her ear, "Doll, I been looking for a woman warm as you all my life."

They followed a walk around the cafe to the river and started to stroll.

Jake said, "The Harpeth ain't as big as the Cumberland River, but it's got it all when it comes to beauty. The way the sun ripples on the water reminds me of loving you." He caught her eyes with his before he said, "Sweet darling, I crave you so much, I can't think about much of anything else. You eating made me want to love you too." Then he kissed her, the kiss left them breathless. "Anna, we can't fight anymore. I can't stand another two weeks apart."

"Me either," she said and kissed his cheek.

"The way you make me feel makes me doubt I ever was in love. Scares me too. If I do anything wrong, you say so and I'll make it right."

As they walked, she loved the way he took her hand and said, "This wind blowing off the river's getting sharp. Is it too cold on you?"

"I'm cold natured as a canary but I'm fine and I need to walk. Jake, do you miss married life?"

"Not to the bitch I married." His grin softened his words, but anger flashed in his eyes. "Do you?"

"Well, I'm pretty pro marriage."

"You had a good marriage. A bad marriage is like you hate losing a bad tooth but you don't miss the pain."

"Jeff made me feel loved till--"

"How would you feel about getting married again?"

"You proposing?" He was so handsome when he smiled.

"Since my divorce, you're the first female that hasn't made me think marriage is a dirty word. I don't want to be away from you, but I may be bad husband material. My ex-wife and me fought like hell. I may be hard to live with at times but I don't lie and I don't cheat. I am high tempered. I'm getting better but sometimes I still lose it."

Anna chucked, "If you need a witness, I can testify.

"Hey, you have some temper yourself."

"I don't fly off unprovoked."

"But you can fly off in a New York minute. I think righteous anger is a healthy and normal thing. Darleen never learned to get out of a man's face when he's stood all he can and is hanging by a hair to sanity."

They strolled to a picnic table and sat down. He caressed her with his eyes. She said, "I love the easy way we share time."

"I love you." Anna heard her cue to return his words.

"What happened with your wife?" came out of her mouth.

"Two more too young, too broke high school sweethearts who should have left it at that." He gazed at the Harpeth, she knew he didn't see the river. With his anger cooled, maybe he was seeing the true colors of bad memories.

"After high school I started college in Memphis. We were miserable apart and I didn't have money to come home much. We decided if we both got jobs, we could make it. We married and rented two rooms in Memphis. I went to class during the day and worked for a vet at night. She never held up her end but one way. Came up pregnant right off and puking her head off so she couldn't work. We nearly starved, I still hate peanut butter. Finished the one year, then I quit to get a decent job.

"Quitting college was bad. Darlene delivering a red haired daughter was worse. With my black hair and her black hair, the chance of it being my baby was slim to none. Minimum wage was all there was in Memphis so we went back to Jackson and moved in with her folks. Minimum wage was all I found in Jackson too. Finally I got a good paying job in Nashville. We hated moving that far away from Jackson, but we wanted our own place.

"After a year or so, Nashville got to feeling like home and finances improved. We assumed a VA loan on a house from a couple wanting to go back to farming. They let us take up their note for a hundred dollars moving money. We got a good brick house in a nice neighborhood. It was small but it had an acre lot so we could add on and there was already plenty of room for just Darleen, Carol and me. Carol was almost three and beautiful, in spite of her red hair and everybody asking where it came from.

"We started back to church. I talked with the pastor about Carol's red hair. He said that didn't prove she wasn't mine and I'd made a vow to God to stay married for life. I put away my doubts like he advised.

"Then Darleen got where she couldn't stay home like a decent wife. She didn't trust me to make the living. We were doing fine. I was getting raises along. There was talk about me making foreman when the next job came open. We started a five dollar a week Christmas Club savings. Did she take satisfaction in that? No! What we had, never was good enough or soon enough and Darleen never did accept a man needs his pride.

"She slipped out and bought furniture we couldn't afford. A shitty motive was always in Darleen's moves. Now she could justify going to work to help pay for furniture, she knew damn well we couldn't afford.

"Darleen gets a job at a burger joint, leaves me to baby sit, knowing I couldn't work all day and keep Carol at night. It wasn't bad when Carol went off to sleep at eight like she was supposed to, but babies wake up crying when they get sick. Usually nothing serious, unless you're sweating in a factory fourteen hours a day, six and seven days a week. Then a baby's slightest upset is serious. Darleen was just like my mama. Daddy never did a damn thing fast enough to suit Mama."

"Jake, you didn't care much for your mother?"

"I hated her guts after I came home from school one day and saw her all over some plumber on the back porch. Like I was told, I came around to the back door so I wouldn't track up the living room linoleum. There she stood, kissing a bastard I'd never seen, or his Triple A Plumbing truck either."

"They didn't see me, so I slipped around front, wiped my feet good and walked on in. I turned on the TV good and loud. Pronto, here she come, innocent as a nun on Sunday, to jump on me about the TV too loud and coming in the front door. Never said a word about her plumber, but that was when I started seeing most folks are two-faced as hell.

"Daddy always laid out drinking. Maybe Mama had to do what she was doing to stand it, but Darleen was something else. I had treated her like a queen; giving up college, my dream of being a doctor, working like a dog in a factory and taking a redheaded daughter. I deserved better. Told her and told her I didn't want my wife car hopping in a short-tailed skirt. All I got for my trouble was being told I was jealous and old fashioned and cut off till she went to wanting some. When a woman wants sex, she never has a headache or is too tired and her man can't do no wrong.

"Anyway, one night Carol was having a time cutting teeth. All feverish and cranky and couldn't sleep. I rocked and gave her all the baby aspirin I dared. Nothing helped. Then I remembered, she loved vanilla milk shakes and riding in my Maverick. I thought a ride and a shake might soothe her.

"If it did, I might kill two birds with one rock. Seeing what was going on at the Burger Heaven had been in my mind awhile. Carol still had fever when I put her in her car seat, but she hushed right up.

"I got a shake and coffee at a drive-through and headed uptown. She loved the city lights from the time she could sit alone. We had a big time playing the radio and riding. She forgot about hurting, went to pointing and giggling. Sucking on her shake straw without losing a drop. We rode around till she went to sleep, then I headed for the Burger Heaven.

"My Maverick blended with the other clunkers in the used car lot next door, while I found out the score. Carol needed her mama and I needed to work and make a living in peace. Somehow, I'd pay for the furniture Darleen bought, but first I wanted to see what was going on.

"I sat watching her wait on cars, wiggling up to the windows, getting the whistles and grins. Even with the window down, I couldn't hear the remarks but I could hear her laugh. I wasn't fool enough to think the talk was about old Aunt Dinah's quilting party. I saw from her ass twisting up and down the walkway in front of the cars. She was loving it.

"When she came home, Carol was asleep, I was waiting in the living room. I clued her in about her baby daughter being sick and about me watching her ass at play, at work. The bitch started screaming about me spying and she couldn't help it if men thought she was good-looking. Said her job was being nice to customers and she hadn't done one thing wrong.

"I said I didn't give a damn if she was Mother Mary, if she was going to be my wife she was through sashaying around in a short skirt to a bunch of cheap flirting, even if that was all it amounted to.

"She screamed, 'You can't stop it, if I don't want to stop and I don't! There's more in this world than sitting with a baby twenty-four hours a day.'

"I said, 'Carol can't help being here. Since she is, looks like you'd be woman enough to take care of her and if you ain't, I'm leaving.'

"She said, I knew where the door was and not to let it hit me in the ass on my way out! That was one time she had a piece of advice worth taking. I spent the night sleeping like a baby, parked on the hill behind Confederate Park. At sunup, I drove to the plant, washed up in the men's room, hit the cafeteria and ate breakfast. Made me see all I had to do for breakfast was pay for it. Didn't have to fight or eat crap."

Seeing Anna was shivering, he said, "Why didn't you tell me you're cold?"

"I'm okay, go ahead and finish."

"Nope. Got to get you out of this wind first. The cold's coming in fast with the sun about gone." Putting his jacket on her shoulders, he said, "Come on, sweet darling. My fireplace is just waiting for a light."

After the truck warmed up she was fine. Still she was glad to be in his house. Even in a good mood, Jake was the world's worst driver. He struck a big country match from the box on the mantel to light the fire and she held her hands out to warm. He lit any kind of fire faster than lightning.

When he had the coffee made, the fire was burning well and they stood talking, drinking coffee and warming their backsides. It was one of her best memories of Jake. She wanted him so badly, right there on the carpet in front of the fire. Too backward to tell him, she just said, "After spending the night in the park, did you get your divorce?"

"Still hadn't been punished enough." He grinned, laying a huge cushion in front of the fire for them. "Stayed away six months, but I mailed a check every payday. Took Carol out every week or so. Loved taking her to the mall and watching her skip around getting a kick out of stuff.

"Once she went running up to a blue dress hanging at the door of the Kid Toggery. I bought her the dress and a new outfit to go with it. The saleslady helped pick out lacy socks and black patent leather shoes. We found a white straw hat and a little white purse to match and dressed Carol up in all her new finery. She stood turning, admiring herself in the full-view mirror. Then she walked all around for the store ladies to admire her. She's always been real beautiful. Little wench knew it even then.

"When we got ready to go, she didn't want to take off her finery. I thought it'd be my one time to see her dressed in it anyway. The saleslady helped me take off the tags. Carol wore her new duds out of the store, prissing around, showing folks in the mall how great she looked."

"Jake, she must have been precious."

"Could have sold tickets to how cute she looked and the way she hammed it up. The dress was beautiful. Carol hung her purse on her shoulder like a grown lady. Won't ever forget her straw bonnet with the flowers on the brim and her hair curling down her back. She still has beautiful hair, if it is red as a peckerwood. Bet she skipped two miles showing off."

"She sounds adorable."

"She was, still is. When we'd be out having a good time, if she got tired of walking, I'd sit her on my shoulders. I never had to worry about her letting go and falling. Always had a head full of sense. Till you, Anna, she's the only heart in my life that's made me feel I got as much love back as I gave. If I'm her biological daddy or not, Carol's my daughter!"

"What about your other daughter?"

"Jackie ain't mine. Me and Darleen were divorced over six months when I got hooked back in. It was that same day I dressed Carol up at the mall. Carol came running out to meet me when I picked her up, rearing to go. We waved to Darleen at the door, but I didn't look at her.

"When I took Carol home, Darleen came out to meet me and started begging me to come back. I told her to hold on, Carol didn't need to see her mother upset. We went in the house and I turned on the TV in the den and got Carol settled watching cartoons coming on.

"Darleen and me sat down to talk in the living room. I could tell she was in heat to bawl and throw a fit. That whore never cared what kind of shine she cut or what lie she told that upset Carol.

"Anyway, Darleen says she wants me back, says she loves me and Carol loves me. She swears on the Bible she'll do anything to make it work.

"Carol hears talk about me coming home and runs in and crawls up in my lap crying and begging me to come home. So... anyway, I did. Darleen still says I been Carol's fool since she was born. Carol's like me, and I think like you. Some of us can be as wrong as the rest but we show some mercy at some point. Jackie is Darleen made over. Suck you dry, and damn you when there's no more to suck. Anna, you got to be tired of all this."

"No, Jake, I love a man who will talk to me."

"Well you sure got that." He kissed her cheek. "Hey, hang on, baby, we need another cup of coffee."

He brought two more mugs of coffee and put another log on the fire. She smiled at the neat way he kept house. It was her first exposure to the house habits of a single male. After the fire was to his liking, he took the mantel broom and swept bits of wood under the screen toward the fire.

"Looks like you'd make someone a wonderful wife."

"Hey, I got this house cleaning bit down pat."

"I can see that."

He sat beside her. "Okay, so, I'm back at home a month, and my illustrious wife comes up pregnant again. Low and behold, she had a premature, ten-pound, baby girl with fire-red hair."

"Oh, God, no!" Anna moaned.

"Yeah! But Carol ain't crying, so I let it go. Darleen named the new baby Jackie. When Jackie is three months old, I come in from work, and Darleen's sister Linda is with the kids. She says I'm to baby sit till Darleen gets home and heads for the door.

"I say hold on, and ask where Darleen is. Linda walks clear out on the porch before she tells me Darleen's back working at Burger Heaven."

"Oh, Jake, no," Anna said, "how could she?"

"It's like we said, some folks got no mercy. For the moment, I had no choice. The Lord knows when a man's stood all he can-- the new baby was good. Carol was close to four and by then she was good, they were both sound asleep by eight. I was packed and waiting when Darleen came assing in around midnight. She wants to know what I'm doing, I tell her the monkey on her string's out of there.

"She starts hollering, I ain't leaving her trapped with two babies and grabs my suitcase, throws it on the floor and sits on it. When I came to myself, I had her lifted up the wall by her shirt front fixing to throw her out a window that wasn't open. She was screaming, I was calling her all I'd been holding back, the new baby was squalling. Carol was crying, pulling at my pants leg and begging, 'Daddy, don't. I'll be good. Please, Daddy, don't hurt Mama!'

"Carol brought me out of it, or I'd have killed Darleen's ass for sure. Guess I won't ever forget that night."

"I won't ever forget you telling me about it," Anna said and got up for a tissue from her purse.

"A bitch is the lowest form of life to me but this bitch was Carol's mama. Carol loved her and she was a good mama to Carol-- the new baby too. The new baby was Carol's half-sister, whoever the daddy was. None of it was her fault or the new baby's."

"It takes a big man to see that, Jake."

"I took long enough," he said, shrugging. "Never even hit a woman and here I was, ready to kill one. I put Darleen down and patted Carol on the head, I was shaking all over. I picked Carol up and took her back to bed. I told her, I won't hurt your mama, honey, long as she's good to you, and that's a promise. When she was asleep, I left. My suitcase was still on the floor. I walked around it and left without taking one thing."

He sat staring into the fire. He looked exhausted. Ever so gently, Anna touched his cheek. He pressed her hand to his face before he kissed it. Then he checked the schoolhouse clock hanging over the fireplace.

"Bad as I hate to, we better head back to your place. Clay will be home soon and he looked concerned I could be stealing his mama forever. He's already lost his daddy so I don't guess he needs to be worried about losing you too. Even if he is fixing to graduate high school; losing your folks is never easy."

"Are your parents living?"

"Mama died just last year. I was twenty-six when Daddy died with a heart attack. It nearly killed me too and we didn't even like each other. That was almost six years ago."

Till that moment, she had not even suspected that Jake was younger than she was. She couldn't believe it! Course she couldn't believe she was pushing forty!

He got up and held his hand out. When she was standing, he put his arms around her and kissed her till she was on fire and feeling eighteen. "It's a shame we don't have time for some loving."

"I know," she said, her eyes dark with passion.

"Wish I hadn't promised Clay. We'll make it up tomorrow night."

As they rode back to Little Gatlinburg, Jake was quieter than usual and did his best driving ever. She thought he might be feeling overexposed, as she sometimes felt after confiding deep things.

He reached across the seat and took her hand. After a while he smiled and said, "Slip over this way." As they rode close, his arm around her shoulders, she wondered what she was going to do about him being so much younger.

When they pulled in her driveway, Shep trotted into the headlights, barking at the strange truck. Jake said, "Better introduce me to that beautiful monster so he'll know I'm on the home team. I plan on him seeing a lot of me."

Rolling down the glass, Anna called, "Here, boy."

Shep wagged his tail and whined in recognition, then trotted to Anna's side of the truck. He reared up and put his paws on her window and stuck his head inside. Jake breathed, "Damn, what a dog."

"Yeah, good boy. Shep, this is Jake. Yeah, Shep and Jake is our friend. Okay? Now jump down so I can get out. That's right."

In the driveway Anna petted Shep again, saying, "Now, Shep, want you to meet Jake. Yeah, Shep." Then she called, "Jake, it's okay. Come pet him. He's gentle as a lamb when he knows you."

Jake cut his lights, the night was black till the moon took over. He called, "Are you sure, woman?"

"Would I lie to you?"

"Damn sure hope not," he said, leaving the truck.

"Jake, hold the back of your hand out."

"Why, so he can eat it?"

She giggled. "So he can smell it, dogs go on scent. Stop joking and let him smell your hand so he knows you."

After everybody knew everybody, they walked in the house together. Jake and Shep checked the house out.

Anna felt nothing could bother her with Shep around, but it was a good feeling to have a man looking out for her again. He returned to where she stood in the kitchen and kissed her till they were reeling. "Love the way you kiss, baby. Want you at my place all night tomorrow night."

"Uh, well, I--"

"I mean it," he said, watching the fire in her eyes cool to doubt. Her eyes talked almost as well as her mouth, now he knew where she was coming from. He was glad she hadn't been any bastard's bitch that wanted to hunt.

"I don't know how I'd explain being away all night to Clay. I want to, I don't know what to tell him."

"How about the truth?"

"One truth I didn't know before, you're younger than me."

"Hey, haven't you heard age discrimination's against the law? And don't gag on a gnat trying to swallow an elephant. Let me tell you my truth. I like women, but you're the only one who has it all. We are probably going to get married, about the time your boy graduates. I don't guess there's any rush, other than the problem we're trying to work out now."

"Tell me. I love to listen to you talk."

"Well, kitten, you're all a woman should be-- lady, siren; angel, vamp; vixen, virgin. You're a straight ahead, get down, all right, all night, female loving machine. Honey, you're wonderful and I want you to know it. You give your all, I never knew such passion or total fusion loving a woman before. You want to get as much as you give, that's why you make it so good. Anna, there's no reason to be blushing over the way the loving is between us. I need a warm woman, I want and love you because you are."

"I love you too, Jake."

"That's reason to stay and not waste the sweet gift we have." The way he said things sometimes made her want to cry. "I can't treat a woman who tears me up the way you do like a girl I'm taking to the prom. I'm a grown man with a grown man's needs. You sleep on it. Do what you have to do."

Jake put his hand under her chin and lifted it till he could see her eyes. She felt he searched her soul before kissing her. Then as he stroked her nipple, she knew she was being shown how very much he could make her want him.

His voice was hoarse with wanting as he said, "Gotta go before I rape you in your own kitchen, with Shep trying to decide whether to eat me, and Clay due home any minute." She knew he wanted her to say something normal, like "Stay over." She wanted to take him to her bed right now.

Pain shadowed his eyes. He said, "Don't bother seeing me to the door," and left the kitchen. It felt like a bad luck omen every time she let him leave like this. Should she offer him the sofa? Bed down with him in front of Clay?

She stood in torment before calling, "Jake!"

"Yeah?"

She ran to him. "I do love you, Jake."

"Love you too, but don't kiss me. Have to go, if I'm going." His eyes questioned, her answer was silence, then he was out the front door and gone.

After changing to her flannel nightgown, she watched TV and waited for Clay. With Jake's kiss still on her lips and his story playing back in her mind, she missed the ten o'clock news.

Jake had weathered some mean old times. They were both walking around wounded. And not having him stay over was hurting a man who didn't deserve to be hurt. And she was hurting too, probably felt the loss of not making love tonight more than he did.

She was so happy to see Clay when he came home and hugged her. He was so handsome and growing up too fast. She wasn't ready to lose her boy.

They ate a snack in the kitchen together and talked. More than once, she looked in his clear young eyes and tried her hardest to say, Clay, I'm spending the night with Jake tomorrow night. I do love him so. Son, I hope you can understand and be happy for me. Or maybe she should say the loving part first and then get to the spending the night part.

No matter. The words just would not come.

CHAPTER 12

≈≈≈≈≈   ≋≋≋≋≋

EVEN OLD SANTA CLAUS

Copper Jim parked and saw Clay waiting on a bench in front of the Center. Walking up closer, he saw the boy was bad blue around the gills. "Son, you're looking mighty down in the mouth," he said, taking a seat.

"Guess I'm just antsy over graduating and getting the right break." Jim knew Clay was hedging. Sometimes a fellow had to warm up on what he could say, to say what he needed to talk over.

"Won't be long now, Clayboy."

"I read about this group getting ripped off their royalty money by their publisher and manager."

"Well, sons a bitches infest everywhere. They'll try to use you, or knock you down, not cause you're good or bad. Cause they're sons a bitches. Ain't even no use taking it personal."

"How can you keep from taking your music personal?"

"It's personal when you write it, business when you sell it. Can't please all the folks all the time. Pleasing yourself is the best you can hope for, all you need to worry about. Play and sing and write what you like, what you're proud of. If other folks like it, fine. If they don't, you can't help it but you can live with whatever happens, when you like yourself."

"But I want the fans to like my music."

"That's natural. Ain't no doubt in my mind they're gonna go crazy over your music. Wouldn't be egging you on if it was. On music, I know most of the time what I'm talking about. Folks bought a few tickets to hear me in my time. It makes you feel good when you pull a big crowd and they like what you do. Feels even better when you got decent money from doing it."

"If I can make a decent living with my music, I'll be happy."

"Bad hours and work conditions make music one of the hardest jobs."

"I still have to do it," Clay said evenly.

"Well, some folks get lucky and make a decent living in music. A few get rich and famous. Course for every one that does, there's thousands that don't. Too many wind up beat in their back pocket and broke underneath their left front pocket. Seen too many, including me, drunked out or drugged out or give out. Sometimes all three. Music can be a mean bitch, I can tell you that."

"You make it sound awful grim."

"Can be when it goes against you. I've seen it rob folks of anything worth having. Things lots more costly than a decent job. Like wives and husbands and young'uns and even a prayer of having the backbone to face another day sober. That's what pulled me off the road. I was losing my woman, at the time, and it had done cost me my first wife and family."

"You mean just over picking music?"

"Over being broke, being gone, being drunk, and being unfaithful. A drunk fighting music is as drunk as the drunk fighting a plow, a factory, a bulldozer, or any of the ways folks make a living. He's just as costly, and brings just as much pain to his own self and the ones he's supposed to love. Substance abuse ain't nothing but a way of crying like a baby when life ain't going right."

"I don't drink at all, Copper Jim. You know that."

"And you'll be a sight better off to never start drinking or smoking, not to mention doping. Nice part about not starting, don't never have to stop. Lots of pickers don't take in nothing stronger than coffee starting out."

"I know."

"Doubt you do, partner, I'm talking hard addiction. The kind when you can't live without something or somebody dragging you down. Clayboy, you got good brains to see the truth. Always try to have the guts to look at it."

"I will, Copper Jim, don't worry."

"Don't aim to hurt your feelings, but your girlfriend ain't straight. You tried to help. She don't want help. It's like I told you, a rabbit's a rabbit, a squirrel's a squirrel. Try to get rabbits to act like squirrels, or squirrels to act like rabbits, you get troubles. Don't mean to make you mad, but little Mary Ellen's on some kind of shit. Don't believe you are-- hope you ain't. It'll wreck your career and I'm done if you are."

"No, course not, Copper Jim."

"Like I said, I could be wrong. But when you've seen drugging, you can smell it. Hard as it might be, you gotta let go of the wrong kind of folks if you don't want to be the wrong kind of folks yourself. It's like plain two and two ain't nothing but four. Ain't no pitching horseshoes close. You got to use your noggin and know, some categories you can't go along with nobody on."

"Don't ever worry about me with drugs."

"Good. Now what is worrying you?"

"What do you think about Jake Dennis?"

"Don't know much about him past speaking to. Why?"

"He's Mama's boyfriend, but he ain't good enough for her."

Jim pushed his hat back and said, "Reckon who would be?"

Clay grinned. "Nobody, I don't guess."

"She ain't no different than us. I got Miss Roxie, you got Mary Ellen, who she ain't been happy about."

"I know but that man's a chaser."

"Ain't no way in this world to figure why a woman wants a certain man, or a man wants a certain woman. When it comes to knowing why folks pick folks, ain't no knowing. That'd confound old Confucius, let alone us."

"I guess." Copper Jim broke down creation's greatest minds to street talk.

"You want the best for your mama. You worry cause you love her and she's tender. She's tough too, couldn't live what she has otherwise. Takes tender to be tough. Turn bitter and brittle, you break like a dry twig."

"But Mama can do better than Jake Dennis."

"Could be but you want her to stay out of some of your business. Maybe she'd appreciate the same from you."

"But he plays around with the girls in his classes. You know what the grapevine says as well as I do."

"You get the proof, I'll bust that bastard's jaw if I have to use a two by four." Clay saw by Jim's ice eyes he wasn't joking.

"You don't like him either, Copper Jim."

"No, but your mama does. Long as he don't mistreat her, fine. We was picking 'Wild Wood Flower' last week and it's been in my head all day. We got time before class to run through it. This might be a night to have us a performing, even if it ain't the regular night."

"Sounds cool to me."

"Good. Let's forget trouble. Picking and singing's the best medicine for gloom and doom. We got a good crowd of locals coming around hoping we'll pick some. Let's get to it," Jim said, stomping out his cigarette.

"I'll be along in a minute." Knowing the boy needed time to settle with the truth, Jim pulled his hat low on his forehead and walked in the Center.

Clay sat thinking awhile, then remembered Jake would be leaving the building soon to pick up his mama. She said he was taking her dancing and not to expect her till late. Copper Jim was right. For problems, music was the best medicine. Sitting here when that grinning barbell jock came out and having to make conversation would be the pits. He grunted, picked up his guitar case and walked in to join Copper Jim.

It was past midnight when they walked down the hall with their arms around each other's waist. He had gone all out to show her a good time, she hated she couldn't tell Clay she'd be staying over. She hated worse, she hadn't leveled with Jake about not telling Clay. Knowing she should have told him, she heard herself still waltzing, "Had a great time."

"Me too, baby. You're getting to be a fine dancer."

"I have an excellent teacher, Jake."

"Your teacher has a foxy student." Jake stopped for a kiss before leading her by the hand into his bedroom. While he lit the candle and the incense, she thought, Can't tell him now. All they had said and done this evening had built to this, the most precious part for both of them.

Then in the light of the candle, the intriguing aroma of the incense bathing the room in magic, foretelling heaven, and Jake kissing her, any negative thought was unthinkable. His lips were soft, wonderful. This was not the moment to jeopardize her awareness of how her old, not very free and not very easy self was changing. She couldn't hinder her progress to how beautifully free and easy she would be under his influence.

"I love you," he said, kissing her, pulling her body against his; his lips moving on her lips, opening her mouth. Then his tongue was touching, tasting, loving, persuading her tongue to follow in his warm mouth.

He was arousing her so, bringing her to his control with only his lips, touching so knowingly, so sweetly. So softly he was lighting her fire, melting her defenses, making her want him-- respond to him so proudly passionate, so frankly female. She felt desire burning in her eyes. Knowing as never before that feeling to be one of nature's greatest gifts, prompted her not to close her eyes but to let the fire shine. He deserved to know what he was doing for her.

She kissed him with even more appreciation. Loving had never been like this. It had been good-- or so she believed when Jeff was all she knew. But by now, the loving would have all been over with Jeff. The end was paramount and not the means with her late husband. She loved the time Jake took, the obvious way he loved making her ache for him.

Gently, expertly he was exposing, exploring, educating her to an erotic side of herself she had not guessed could be a real, beating, breathing part of her. All of this he did with only his words, his lips, his kisses. She was too under his influence, loving the effect of his influence for any thought of objecting when his lingering fingertips came to caress her hair, her forehead, her ear, her nose, her neck, her shoulders before moving, so slowly, so gracefully, so naturally on down to each individual part of her, waiting impatiently to be caressed. Jake's timing was extraordinary.

He knew exactly the moment to start with the whole of his hand, cupping, kneading, leading, patiently working at teaching her as he had taught her the aerobic exercises in class. One lesson learned led to another lesson but nothing haphazard, nothing rushed, the slightest detail deserved lingering attention.

When he had her in a wild rush of feeling, he moved on at the perfect instant, to frankly making her aware of his passion and his need, gently grinding himself against her, letting his movement tell her where he was, how he was and what he wanted from her, until he had her following with his every movement, as earlier he had led her into dancing with the band. But that was the warm-up, this was the real thing and some kind of new, beautiful, blood-rushing dance. Again, she was finding his tutoring delightfully mesmerizing.

Without a word he was impatiently at her clothes, pulling some up and some down, some open and some off. Then there was the rip of unyielding, tearing fabric and she said, "Let me, angel."

She was wise to the stubborn button that was too big for the buttonhole. After she worked it through the hole, the zipper ran down easily. Then she was stepping out of her skirt, and maybe, she thought, out of her cotton-picking mind, but she was at the point of no return..

When she stood nude before him, his worshiping eyes told her everything she needed to hear. After a few moments, he took her back in his arms and she felt herself become completely nuts with him again-- with the smell of him, the mouth of him-- the strong, tender, callous, gentle, hard, soft, ugly, beautiful, breath-catching, heart-rushing male presence of him.

And his hands were everywhere, the heated excitement they could feel they were building for her were their permission, admission and justification. Then his mouth was everywhere, softly consuming her hungry mouth. Hell, she couldn't open it wide enough to him. She couldn't hold her hands back. She was amazed at how they reached for him, needing him, touching him, discovering him, learning him, loving him; her fingertips oh so tenderly tracing, treasuring, praising, worshiping his hard, smooth, welcoming, quivering, rippling muscles. The wonder of him, the heat of him, his wide shoulders, hard back, smooth buttocks and thighs would never all leave from the memory of her fingertips.

Then it dawned on her; however long they stood kiss for kiss, caress for caress, skin against skin, was her choice. That was his sweetest, most arousing move of all. Feeling him wanting to linger with her and for her was infinitely tantalizing and his greatest strength to accomplish her eager surrender for there was no surrender. With Jake love making was truly a mutual, joyful sharing. Suddenly, she could not wait another second, not another instant. "Jake, please now if you're ready, darling."

"Thought you'd never ask." He smiled in gold candlelight, his velvet eyes looking at her with primal joy. His unmasked delight made her feel so totally female and infinitely proud of it. Then she felt that certain male approval for her uniqueness as his woman that is the strongest aphrodisiac known for the female of the species. He made her literally feel worshiped with his lingering attention; his boundless giving while simultaneously announcing, with simple body language, his need, his expectation, his reward of receiving her all.

Jake anointed her with the strongest sense of approval she had ever felt.

He kissed her a baby-soft kiss that touched her as pure affection before swooping her up in his arms like a pagan and taking her to his loving place. Damn! He knew it all, had it all, used it all!

Her hands had to touch him, to know him, to love him. Their mouths fused like they were only one mouth, one need, one wanting. As the heat of passion took her higher and higher, she was lost and she was found-- she was free and she was bound in that lovely, loving lunacy he knew how to ignite-- so beautifully, so wonderfully, so well. She lay impatient beneath him, lifting up to him, inviting him in. She was touching, guiding, crazy for the closeness of the filling as he began to push in-- held for a moment till he felt her movement beneath him asking for more, before he plunged on to touch, to caress the deepest depths of her-- to let her touch and know the deepest heart of him.

He loved hearing her "Yes, yes, yes!" He loved the sense she gave him of savoring him, of loving him and her joy at his entry, the rise and fall of her pelvis, her strong encircling legs.

Her first orgasm approaching drove her to a frenzy of movement. As it happened, for whatever insane reason, she heard herself hiss, "Damn you, you bastard... angel... devil.... You're the best that ever, ever, ever happened to me! And, darling, you have made me love you so."

As an instant second spasm gripped her, she felt a rush of jubilant tears. Happy, terrible, wonderful, crazy, sane, erotic, loving tears were washing her cheeks and his cheeks. Their salty taste mingled in their kiss, in her mouth and in his mouth as somewhere between a moan and a scream, a sob and a song, erupted her happy hosanna, "Jake, oh, Jake, Jaaake!"

Later he woke holding her, feeling more loved, more loving, more satisfied than he ever had. She stirred as he kissed her shoulder. The last thing he expected was her moving away and off the far side of the bed. The sound of her movements told him she was making a pit stop. When she finished, she didn't come back to bed. Damn it to hell, she was getting dressed!

"Anna, what are you doing?"

"It's late. Clay'll be worried."

"You didn't tell him you're staying?"

"I'm sorry, I tried. I,... couldn't."

"Why?" he asked.

"I just couldn't, I don't know."

"Sure you know!"

She hated the anger in his voice. "Jake, don't spoil tonight by getting mad."

"I'm trying as hard as I know how to understand."

"Maybe lovers who stay over ought to be married."

"When I mention marriage, you don't even answer me. Straight up, do you want to marry me?"

"Yes, if you can stop bullying me."

"Baby, I never been more loving with a woman in my life."

"You're wonderful, as long as I do exactly what you say. Whether you understand it or not, I don't know how to tell my seventeen year old son, nuts for his sixteen year old girlfriend, that I'm making out but he can't."

"Woman, there's a difference in adults and teenagers."

"I agree in a practical sense, but I doubt it in a moral sense. Anyway, I need you to help me work through it, instead of you making demands like some gorilla beating on his chest."

"You didn't think I was a gorilla while ago."

"I was enjoying loving you too much to think. Maybe somewhere in my crazy psyche, I think you'll die and leave me. Don't bug me for answers I don't have. Can't you see your attitude is just male ego?"

"I thought it was just love," he said sadly.

"We're loved out! Why sweat where we sleep?"

"I thought women needed the closeness afterwards."

"That's another thing, stop thinking of me as women. I ain't women. I'm just me! Sometimes I think straight and sometimes I think shitty. Sometimes I think I want you to take me and hold me and never take me home. Sometimes I think I want you to leave me, forget me and let me forget you. But all of the time, I'm sick of feeling like I'll get my behavior test grade from you every time we're together, and I mean it."

"Woman, let's just go ahead and get married now."

"If we can't stop fighting, we don't need to get married. And, grass or grave, I've enjoyed all the widow shit I can stand."

"When can we get married if we can stop fighting?"

"After Clay graduates and I can concentrate on you."

"Fine, call him. Say we're getting married when school's out and you're staying here tonight." He smiled and waited, but her reply was too slow in coming. His velvet eyes turned to steel. "Hell, forget it. You don't want to and I don't want any supreme sacrifice. I'll take your ass home. But like I told you before, I can't treat my woman like some teenage girl I'm taking to the hop. I know what I need to be faithful."

"Jake, listen to me a minute!"

"No! I'm taking you home, but I don't like it. Nothing you can say will make me like it. So hush, if it wouldn't bridle you too much. I don't want to hear any more, and I mean it!"

Driving back home, after walking Anna to her door, Jake began to settle down. He knew what was happening; didn't need to be hit over the head. It was third-grade simple. She didn't stay because the boy was number one. If it wasn't the boy, it'd be something else. While it suited her purpose, she'd love him; but she wasn't going to stand by him and she wasn't going to ever belong to him. When her precious boy got his career going and the money rolling in, Jake Dennis's ass would be grass. It didn't take a brain to figure that out, and his lying mama didn't raise no fool.

All women were two-faced as a mirror, just like Mama till the day the bitch died. When they didn't want to do anything it wasn't right, they had the rag on, or God was watching and you'd go to hell when you died. When they wanted to do something, they made new rules. Like Mama on the back porch kissing the plumber, when she always acted like fornicating was the blackest sin in the Book. Hell, he didn't have to hear a confession to know what she and that bastard were doing before he got home from school.

When Anna got ready to stay over, it'd be fine. She'd come up with a new rule to make it fine. She might twist in any night and decide to stay two weeks. Like all women, she knew who had the pussy. What they had going wouldn't work because she wouldn't let it work and he couldn't do a damn thing about it. No need to be upset, he'd been in this shit before. In the meantime, the sex was great. While it suited her, he might as well get all he could and forget marriage! He'd as soon have his balls hung in a barbed-wire fence anyway. He couldn't spend till death did them part, kissing her kid's ass. Hell!

After that she sometimes drove, other times he brought her out. He stopped objecting to taking her home, or her going home and night after night they loved to perfection. When he drove her home, he walked her to the door, kissed her good night and drove back to his place confident his Prince Charming side had been charming. He left the princess purring and he was purring too. Given a choice, he'd prefer patting her on the ass during the night. Maybe roll her over and knock off another sweet piece. But he was purring his best ever. Any man would purr getting his brains screwed out by a loving miracle. Still, he wasn't dragging around pussy whipped with herds of women up for grabs. Nix to that!

Anna considered Jake a miracle in many ways. She had never felt more cared for, more passion, more freedom and at times never more chained. In an erotic sense, they made heaven. He could look at her with a velvet gaze and make her want him. To put it in street talk: he got all she had to give and he was most welcome. Long as the good felt better than the bad felt bad.

Jake was an addiction she couldn't blow off cold turkey. Not yet. Lord, no! Please not yet! Maybe it would work out. In and out of bed, he took her to places she had never dreamed of. He couldn't help it if he had highs and lows that at times made him the hardest man in creation to get along with. But he was so tender, so protective and a beautiful lover. As pioneers in the old West, they'd have made an ideal couple. She'd have been a flop at fighting Indians and Jake could have totally run the show.

Even after she was aware of how far behind the development of his body his emotions were, she kept hoping. The poets wrote how love finds a way, they did love each other. In many ways they were wonderful together. They loved so many of the same things it was unreal.

Sometimes they hauled in sacks of food and had a carpet picnic in front of the TV, CD, VCR or a new stack of books and magazines. Some times they sat on the deck and talked and never ran out of things to talk about. Jake was as big a talker as she was. One of her major erotic zones had to be her ears. After one of their conversations, sharing all shades of thoughts and feelings, she was subject to find herself flat out coming on to him.

Once or twice a week it was bike riding, then they would cook out on Jake's deck. He might decide to have dinner on the ground by making a pallet from several of the patchwork quilts he collected. After dark, in the privacy of his second level deck, they would make love. As Jake promised before that first time, making love under the stars was a great turn-on.

However, Anna's ability to adapt to an affair different from any she had known made less of Jake emotionally, not more. It threw his whole concept of

women and how they were supposed to be out of balance. Jake needed a
woman to need him. Anna wanted him but she didn't need him. The more
Anna gave, the more she rose above, the more insecure Jake became.

It sounded like a fault when he said, "You don't need anybody."

"Darling, I need you like a river needs water."

"No, woman, you want me. You don't need me."

"Is there a difference?"

"Need better accepts human frailties. Human frailties turn want off." Seeing
the sadness in his eyes made her sense the melting of their forever.

Till late that spring she was crazy for him. She knew now that kind of love
believes anything is possible. In his arms, she lived the promise of all the
soaps, all the movies, all the novels. They made merry, made forever plans and
made ten high loving, but in the valleys of her soul, down where the song fairy
dwelled, she knew it was not to be. This torn and tender man was only a rose
in her life, not her life. When she looked down the road five years or one year,
he wasn't there. It was terrifying. She had to try harder, love harder! She
couldn't bear losing Jake, too!

The glow of love on her face, her easy laughter, her up mood was most
becoming and apparent even to Clay. She was more beautiful, she walked with
a new joy. She was down six pounds and wonderfully toned from exercising.

Clay thought maybe she knew what she was up against. For sure Jake wasn't
straight, but she seemed to be handling it. Butting out was best. Mama not
liking Mary Ellen didn't stop him. No one knew better she wasn't perfect but it
didn't stop his caring. Mama was too perceptive not to know the score. Clay
guessed it didn't stop her from caring for Jake either.

Clay's graduation, the time for Anna and Jake's final binding, fertilized by
Jake refusing to take her, sprouted the seed of their final break. Jake failed to
recognize that whom he manipulated under the name "woman" and whom he
manipulated under the name "mother" were hemispheres apart.

In Jake's mind, Anna had earned it. He drawled, "Hope y'all have a good
time, but I ain't going."

"What do you mean you're not going?"

"Just playing your game, following your rules."

"I don't play games, Jake. What rules?"

"Doing what the hell I want to, like you. When I wanted you to stay over, it
didn't suit you, so you didn't. I want to go to the graduation, but I can't. School
was boring when I was in school, and I told you I'm burned out on kid shit."

"But--"

"But hell! I'm treating you just like you treat me."

"That's the most stubborn bullshit I've ever heard!"

"Thought it would be. Ain't going anyway," he said, watching rage purple
her eyes. The fury of a woman scorned wasn't a hot matchhead next to the fury
of a mama thinking her kid was scorned.

He felt what was coming before the words flamed from her mouth. "That kind of thinking goes to show your mind's about as long as your dick!"

"You should be liking it, you seem to love my dick."

"Asshole!"

"That's telling it like a real lady."

"I'll tell you something else, shit head."

"What's that, darling?" His smile was maddening.

"If they had screwing exercises at commencement, wild horses couldn't hold you off the front row." Lord, she was sounding just like Aunt Effie.

"That's right. And if they had screwing exercises, I'd bet the farm, the mule and the forty acres, your little hot ass would pay attention."

"You ought to know, you love giving me lessons."

"Never had to beg you once to come to class."

"Damn, Jake, you're an angel one minute and Satan the next." She rolled out of bed and started dressing.

"Yeah, doll, it gets rough all over sometimes."

"I'm not here to take your insults. Just get dressed and take me home."

Jake grinned. Revenge was so sweet and so easy sometimes, because what goes around does come around. Knowing it would make her madder, he had to drawl, "Hon, I'd be real glad to. All I want is to take care of you. But, hot stuff, you got your own wheels waiting out back. Miss Libber don't need Jake. She can take her sweet ass home all by herself!"

"Jake Dennis, sometimes I just double hate you!"

"Little darling, I do sympathize, but some nights you liberated ladies would make even old Santa Claus act like a rare son of a bitch."

CHAPTER 13

GRADUATION

At his room in the woods, Clay lay on his wishing rock gazing out the skylight in the roof of leaves. Standing like a circle of centuries, the surrounding oaks were as massive and as mystical as ever, but the rock seemed smaller. "Get on up here, Shep," he said, moving around. "Not as much room as it used to be, but I can lay catty-cornered."

Scratching Shep between the ears, he watched a gray squirrel gone white-faced. The squirrel would run up to his nest in the biggest oak in the circle, look down as if wanting Clay to follow, then run down the huge trunk to stop and stare. "Talk to me, Ben," Clay said. "We all been playing here a long time. You know it's almost over for us both. You're no fool, or you wouldn't have lived to be white-faced." Ben ran to the back of the tree, peeped around and chattered, Shep cocked his head and whined.

Clay chuckled. "Shep, you and Ben know this is a first and a last day. I'm done with school and Mary Ellen. Couldn't figure why she was so moody till I saw the needle marks. It's the first day I'm not due in school on a weekday. Sometimes the things you want most, and take the longest time coming, kind of sneak up on you at the last minute. It's time to start music and stop worrying over a girl doing dope. Never been so happy and unhappy at the same time."

Pacing the kitchen as she talked on the phone, Anna said, "But, Copper Jim, do you truly think Clay has star potential?"

"Yes'm, I truly do. Don't you?"

"Well yes, but a mother can be biased. I don't want to tell Clay he can do things he can't. He has improved so since you took him under your wing."

"Thanks, but I didn't make the apple, just helped put the shine on. Clay's voice alone could make him a star. It's just how soon you want him started."

"Right away, if you think he's ready. That's all he wants, so I want him to take his chance before he gets too old for college if music doesn't work out for him. I've been reading all I can about the music business. For his graduation present, I want to give him his first studio session. Copper Jim, I was just wondering if you would help us record a session?"

"I'd be tickled to, but it can get expensive. Need to cut four sides at least. Could run seven hundred dollars with mixing and buying master tape."

"Then we can do it, but I'd like you to handle it. I was afraid it'd be more."

"Would if you don't know how to book musicians and a studio and stay shed of the Row sharks. You hold your cost down by being ready when you start paying for studio time. We'll have chord charts done, Clay will be rehearsed and we'll book a crack engineer and session musicians. Pickers who know how to shut up, set down and go to picking cost more, but they save money overall. They do a session and get gone. We'll buy master, mix and cassette tape at the wholesale house. No need paying for leg work when we all got legs."

"I have a nest egg saved just for Clay's graduation present. Nothing in the world would mean more to him or me."

"Annie, It'd mean the world to me, too. I been meaning to ask you about Clay performing with my band. One of my pickers is leaving. I'd like Clay to take his place, picking on Saturday nights, if it's okay with you and him."

"Jim, I been knowing one of these days he'd start being gone performing."

"If it wouldn't trouble you, I'd like you to come too. At least the first time with Clay not being twenty-one and still a legal minor. Since it's partly my graduation present, is it okay to invite him tonight?"

"It's fine. Listen, I held off making plans in case he got back with Mary Ellen. I thought she would be moved by now. The last time she called, Clay wouldn't talk to her, but she'll make a final play. She doesn't want to move, but I don't think Clay would do anything foolish, at this point."

"Hope he's done. All the girl knows is conniving-- if dope made it or not."

"If he's alone, I'd like all of us to go somewhere nice for supper."

"Sounds fine to me. I like the Palace mighty well."

"The Palace it is, and my treat."

"Annie, it's my treat and no arguing. I been figuring how to ask y'all without making trouble for Clay or you with your friend." This was the first time Jim had mentioned any inkling that Jake was a member of the planet. "Not nosing in your affairs, but I need to know how many reservations to make."

"Jake isn't interested in tonight. "

"Well, we'll eat, see the floorshow and have us a good time. Clay's done a fine job and deserves to celebrate."

He had sung the alma mater, the tassel swung from the graduate side of his cap and his diploma was in hand. Principle Norris dismissed the class on stage in the gym, and Clay came smiling down the steps to Anna's hug. Looking into her eyes misty with pride, he realized how his six two towered over her five four as she said, "Son, I'm so proud of you."

Then Copper Jim was pumping his hand and saying, "Clayboy, I'm damn proud of you too and you be proud of yourself."

"I'm proud it's over. I want out of this monkey suit, and trying to graduate school for twelve years has made me hungry as a dog."

As they left the gym three abreast with Anna in the middle, she couldn't help wishing Jake had come. All during the program, she almost cried because no Jake sat by her side to celebrate this milestone in her life as well as Clay's. No Jake rushed with her afterward to congratulate her beaming son. Jake could be so shitty. Now, when they could marry, there was no reason to. Jake didn't know beans about being a husband, he didn't care a rat's ass about her son! She knew that when the horny bastard was throwing fits for her to sleep with him right before Clay's eyes. Lord, lightning was striking twice! Torn between love for her son and love for her man, she was losing her man again.

Clay was feeling great that he would never walk back in the gym as a student. Then out of nowhere, Mary Ellen fell in step beside him and said, "I need to talk to you." To allow them privacy, Anna and Jim slowed their pace.

Looking straight ahead, Clay started walking faster. Mary Ellen said, "Could you please slow down a minute? We need to talk."

"I don't talk to people who are mean and lie and do something else I don't want to go into." He quickened his pace more. As he lost her in the crowd, Mary Ellen saw the toughest argument was no argument.

Out in the beauty of the June night, Clay walked off into the shadows here he could watch the door and wait for his mama and Copper Jim. A loser was finally over. His girl was the part of his dream that turned into a nightmare, he just hoped the rest wouldn't. Again he vowed to give people the benefit of the doubt, but bad people had no place in his dream or his life. That was a promise to himself-- forever! He was born one of the unhip tribe like Mama and Jim.

He simply liked doing the "right thing." If he happened to hurt someone, he felt bad, and had nothing in common with the cunning folks in the world. Unfortunately, he had trouble identifying them sometimes. Listening better, to folks who were on his side, was something he had to work on too.

Clay ate his last bite of prime rib, pushed his plate back and said, "I do thank you, Copper Jim. That dinner was super."

"You're welcome. Watching you eat, I see why you keep getting taller. How about desert? The Palace has the best coconut pie this side of heaven."

"In a minute. Guess y'all know I'm glad to be out of school."

"Yes," Anna said, "and that brings us to another thing. For graduation, you get your first studio session and Jim's going to produce it."

"Wow, Mama! That's fantastic! If it won't cost too much."

"Don't worry, I've been saving for this."

"I'm too happy to worry much, Mama. When do we start?"

"It's up to the man who knows a studio."

Busy with his steak, Jim said, "Next few weeks, soon as we can put it together. Had to ask your mama before I could offer you my gift, got her okay this morning. Want you to pick in my band, if you would."

"If I would? Man, that's what I been waiting for all my life!"

"Waiting's over. Come Saturday night, we got a dance to pick for. It's time to head toward picking with the big boys, if that's what you aim to go for."

"I'm happier when I'm picking than any time." A thought took the smile off Clay's face. "You're positive you wouldn't invite me just to be nice?"

"Most positively wouldn't. My music's like my promise; don't allow lies with neither. But music can be rough, even if you luck out and make it big."

Clay said, "I just hope I'm good enough."

"Wouldn't be egging you on if you wasn't. Hell, pardon my French, Miss Annie, you're the best talent I've ever seen. Going over with the industry and the fans can be a rocky road, but you got the reason and the right to take your shot. Just need more stage time and we got plans for that. This summer I want you picking with me. Come fall we'll do the writers nights around the Row."

"Hear that, Mama?"

"I sure do, darling." Anna beamed

"Partner, when you hit the writer's nights, don't want it to be the first time you walk on a strange stage. You know the Center stage like the back of your hand. Gotta walk up to a mike on any stage like that."

"Does a different stage make a big difference?"

"Anything makes a difference to a singer, like different dirt does a race horse-- different stage, different mike. Managing a singer's like managing a boxer. Overmatch him, you'll get him flattened when the last thing he needs is a setback. Heard the saying, paying your dues?"

"Yes, sir."

"Paying your dues means getting you and your songs to a professional level. You don't set foot on stage near the Row sounding like a nervous crow and singing songs not writ. If you want to be a pro, you gotta hit stage performing like a pro, singing songs written tight as a fist. You gotta sing your own songs better than anyone else could and cover songs better than anyone else did."

"How do you do that?" Anna asked.

"Just don't set yourself up to lose. Don't need to sing *Crazy* if you can't do it better than Patsy done. Don't need to sing *Cheating Heart* if you can't beat what Hank done. Folks won't buy you if they got the song, sung better, on a record done bought. I know all about how and why, that's my born gift. My undoing was not whipping the whiskey soon enough."

"But you did beat the bottle."

"Yes'm, but a music factory, like any factory, won't keep a hand drinking or drugging or sluffing off. Ain't no mill gonna keep a hand that can't be counted on to be there and on time, most of the time. No record label ain't either; less you're selling too many records to fire. I wasn't."

Clay said, "I love music too much to let something dumb ruin me."

"That's what kept me coming to the Center after time I had to passed. Love working with folks, who want to learn, if they're great or not."

"After time you had to passed?"

"Yeah, Miss Annie, got a DUI. Fact is, got several. Teaching at the Center was the public service part of my last DUI mess up."

Clay said, "I didn't know that, Copper Jim."

"Most don't, DUIs ain't nothing I'm jumping up and down proud of. We're down to the nitty-gritty now. Your mama's asked me to produce your first session. Y'all need to know, you'll be trusting a man who woulda made more waves and more money if he had left the bottle alone years before he did."

"Jim, it doesn't matter to us," Anna said softly. "We love you."

"Appreciate that, now something else y'all to know. Clay, you coulda got on an independent label the first time I heard you. Major labels don't fool with kids much. Independents ain't the best way to start, but it works at times. I can't see starting small, at sixteen, when taking time to come of age can let you start big. And you needed schooling. When you make big money, you need to know how to take care of it. Your mama might not always be handy to keep track."

"His mama's not all that smart either," Anna said.

"You're smarter than most. I've seen the time I'd rather catch little fish as no fish, but I never went fishing for nothing little. Went home sometimes with a three inch sun perch on a tree fork stringer, but I never fished I wasn't fishing to catch me a Moby Dick. Clay, it's time to start fishing for your Moby Dick. Hope we got it schemed out where there ain't no limit to what you can catch."

"Right, Jim, me too."

"Your singing and writing has to be hit quality when the business folks first hear you. Any record label's hunting hit singers and hit songs. Room's always at the top. You're a ten, real superstar potential. Want the honchos to know that the first note they hear you sing. A star starts ready and don't stop growing. Elvis was tons better when he stopped than when he started. Pop music ain't my category, but next to what he does now, Sinatra started in the primer. That's how it has to be for a star to last. That's how it can be for you."

"You're blowing my mind, but I hope so."

"Always keep growing. That's why some stars shine a lifetime, when others shoot up like a rocket then fall like a rock. Fans love you when you entertain. That's why I don't see you no flash in the pan, you can do any kind of song. When you ain't singing, you can pick. Anyway, I got a standing booking for my band to play a club at Tullahoma on Saturday nights. I want you playing with us Saturday, if it suits you."

"Copper Jim, I'm rearing to go. What do you think, Mama?"

"I'm rearing to go too, if you want me tagging along."

"Tagging, nothing. I want you for my manager and backup singer, too."

"I might make a personal manager. From what I read, you mainly need someone you can trust," she said, wanting to avoid another discussion of backup vocals. "Y'all work out the details for Saturday night, while I make a pit stop before the show starts." She had seen Jake looking in from the lobby several times, looking more and more like an angry bull.

At first she thought, Let him look! But Clay was enjoying every minute of tonight and luckily his back was to the lobby. A scene was never one of her pet things, but tonight of all nights, she had to avoid one at all costs. Clay shouldn't have to remember his graduation as the night his mother had a brawl with her lover before God and everybody. Jake could be such a dumb bastard when he lost his temper. Almost as dumb as she could be, when she lost hers.

She made a right turn at the red arrow pointing to Dolls written on the wall, in case Clay or Jim might be watching. Once she made the turn behind the privacy wall, she saw another route to the lobby and took it.

Hell, there he was, pacing with his thumbs hooked in the pockets of his jeans. As she had been known to do at some of the worst moments, she felt an urge to giggle. The way Jake was breathing, fire might start shooting out his nostrils like a dragon. A giggle would be like pouring coal oil on a flame. Unless she wanted all-out war, she needed to swallow her giggle. His steel glare helped her manage. If looks could kill, she'd drop dead on the spot. Shit! This was too serious to be stupid and too stupid to be serious.

Jake stomped up and snarled, "What's so damn funny?"

She realized the giggle, she thought she had stifled must be leaking out her eyes or somewhere. Hoping offense was the best defense, she snapped, "What are you doing here, Jake Dennis?"

"Miss Cuntzie, it's a free country. You women ain't totally running it yet."

"I don't run anything. You were invited to share tonight. You should be with us, instead of stomping out here like a raging bull."

"Please, I don't aim to lose my temper but I'm close. Just have a drink with me. I need to talk to you a minute."

"I can't, you know this is Clay's night."

"I said a minute. Where is it written Clay Hill has to have every second of tonight?" His eyes pierced hers like gray bullets. She wasn't hot on his idea, but he was mad enough to kill somebody. It was his own stubborn fault, still there was nothing to be gained by provoking him further. Getting shoved up the side of a wall like his ex-wife wasn't a prospect she was crazy about either, especially here. The one wall without a counter or something in front of it was the one with all the autographed pictures of the country music stars.

Looking around for exits, she considered the powder room. As mad as he was, Jake might come in after her. She might as well see what he would come up with. One thing about Jake, he could be ridiculous but he was never boring. And why lie? She deeply wished they could work things out. She said, "I can only stay a minute."

Walking into the bar they looked like lovers. In a booth facing each other they glared like enemies. "Jake, our fights are ruining us!"

"Then why don't you stop?" She saw the fool was suddenly smiling his wonderful smile. Shit and hell!

She spat, "Now, you tell me what's so damn funny."

"Me. I let you make me crazy, then act like an ass."

"Then why don't you stop?"

"I'll be glad to, if you'll stop going out on me."

"I've never gone out on you!"

"You're in this fancy joint with another man tonight."

"Damn, Jake Dennis, Jim isn't another man."

"Well, you sure as hell fooled me."

"He's a friend and associate. When Clay's career takes off, I'll have lots of male associates. And you just have to get used to that, or else."

"Or else what?"

"Or else we're through," she said with resignation.

"Just like that, huh?"

"No, we'll have more asinine fights first and break my heart. But you're letting your insecurity destroy us. I might as well accept it. "

"Hell, I'm not insecure!"

"Yes, you are, Jake, and you refuse to face it. I'll be faithful as a dog, but I won't be dominated, if I have to stay single and celibate the rest of my life!"

What a waste, he thought, watching her eyes go dark like they always did when she was mad or hot. Half the time she didn't know which. Hell, he didn't know which either till he tried. Either way her eyes all purple like that made him want her. She was the best natural fuck in God's world, but she'd be insulted as a preacher's wife if he told her in those words straight up.

She moved to leave. "Wait," he said, taking her hand. "I'm sorry. It makes me crazy to think of you with anyone else. Woman, I love you more than anything. When you get through here come by my place and let me prove it."

She yanked her hand from his. "Damn, Jake, you know I can't. If you want a scene, fine! Have at it! I'm going to the john. Then I'm seeing the floorshow with Clay and Copper Jim."

Copper Jim waited till Anna walked out of sight before saying, "Saw Mary Ellen come up to you back in the gym. You still upset over her?"

"I don't know how any girl that pretty could lie and turn plain mean."

"It happens. Only thing I know, folks been loving and losing since day one and they will till the last day. Like Uncle Ned used to say, ain't no new sins. Same old sins since Adam, just new folk sinning."

"Guess that old cliche is true. Love is blind."

"Loving a woman ain't only blind. When it's in high gear, it's deaf, dumb and stupid. They'll love you and leave you, hate you and won't leave you, kiss you and try to kill you, then try to kiss you again. And you keep coming back for more. Sometimes, they'll kill you with a gun, sometimes with a lie or a chill. Then if you ain't paralyzed or dead, you may crawl back for more."

"Sounds pretty bad." Clay chuckled.

"Don't let it shake you one way or the other. Store it in your mind like all that book school stuff you been storing. Graduation turned you out to the school of hard knocks that ain't got no graduation. When you think you got it all, you'll fall flat on your rear and see you got new lessons to learn. Two things you can't bank on is good weather and good women. A day can start out the sunniest you ever did see, and rain like forty days and nights fore nightfall. Tear up your best plans. Same way with women."

"Right now, I'd just as soon forget women."

"Why, good weather and good women's two wonders this world wouldn't amount to much without!" Jim chuckled.

Suddenly Clay grinned. "Guess not."

"Its the first time you had your heart busted. A busted heart suffers hell out of you. It can make you wish you was dead, but it ain't fatal. Once you're dead, you're just dead. Don't have to worry about the laughing, the crying, the loving or the losing. With a busted heart you do get another chance."

"I don't want another chance with women. I'm quitting while I'm ahead."

"Might as well say you're quitting breathing or a foundered hog won't swill more slop. Ain't no way he kin stop when he's feeling better. Take folks with a grain of salt. Like them or don't, love then or don't, but folks are just folks. You been raised mostly by your mama. She shoots straight, she's nicer than most. Don't go rushing in when you first meet somebody. Use your noggin. Baby rabbits don't grown up without looking out for hawks.

"Son, loving women's like hunting, ain't no way, without chancing chiggers. If folks ain't got no character, sure can't loan them any. I'm one knows the hard way. Get hooked on the wrong woman and you mess yourself up good. Can't let her go, and ain't no way to hold her. Good news is, there's lots of fish. Decide there ain't but one woman you gotta have to live, then learn you can't, pardon me, but you're genteelly fucked!"

"Didn't learn to love her overnight, I can't unlove her overnight. But I won't hurt this way again. I won't love all the way again, I'll hold a little back."

"Most do, when love gets that high and don't work. That's the bad side. The good side, you ain't forty years old with kids bawling cause they hate choosing to live with their mama or daddy. It's a rip nobody gets over. Ain't a birthday or Christmas, folks that once was a family don't wish they still was."

"I wanted to marry her. When my career gets going."

"I know and I sympathize, partner, but remember what you learned out of losing Mary Ellen and profit by it. Judge a woman before you get serious. Any female you court could wind up your young'uns' mama. If she ain't like what you want your kids to be, turn her loose quick. Blood tells-- yours and hers. Once you have a kid, if you have much to do with it or not, you ain't never all the way divorced from its mama. Ain't never divorced from the kid none."

PART TWO

C

IS FOR

CLAY

HONKY TONK SONG

ANNA & CLAY HILL

WE LOVE BANDS AND DANCING,
COWBOY BOOTS AND JEANS.
HONKY TONK LINE DANCE PARTIES,
HEARING SINGERS SING
SONGS ON WORK AND DIXIE DREAMS,
MAMA, LOVE AND HOME.
BUT OUR LOVE AIN'T NO
HONKY TONK SONG.

CHORUS
OUR LOVE AIN'T NO HONKY TONK TWO STEP
FAST DANCE BOOGIE SOON GONE.
WHAT WE GOT BURNS TOO HOT
NOT TO BURN ON AND ON.
WE DO LOVE A HONKY TONK NIGHT,
LINE DANCE DANCING TILL DAWN.
BUT OUR LOVE AIN'T NO
HONKY TONK SONG.

SEE THAT GRAND OLD COUPLE
UP FRONT BY THE BAND.
MARRIED SINCE FOREVER,
STILL DANCING EVERY DANCE.
THEY LOOK LIKE I PICTURE US,
AS THE YEARS ROLL ON.
CAUSE OUR LOVE AIN'T NO
HONKY TONK SONG.
                    (repeat chorus..

BRIDGE: WE'LL WALK OUT TOGETHER,
        WHEN THEY CLOSE THE CLUB.
    WHEN THE BAND DOES ANOTHER DANCE,
YOU CAN BET WE'LL BE IN, ALWAYS BE IN, FOREVER BE IN LOVE.
                    (Repeat chorus..

CHAPTER 14

THE BLUE COLLAR COUNTRY CLUB

It had taken an infinity of time and grease to get the wheels turning, but finally they were en route in Copper Jim's pickup. Deep inside, where there was room for nothing but truth, Clay felt his future in motion.

Time dragging by like between Thanksgiving and Christmas impatient for Santa, made the patient weary. Same old same old; tomorrow, tomorrow. Going through the motions of going through school had gone slow as a sloth, with Mary Ellen his one relief. Then the good part of that gone.

Mama said he'd miss school when autumn started golding and it wasn't his time to go back anymore. She said autumn was a beautiful season that made some folks sad from missing school and the learning that takes the mind off gray winter, youth slipping away and lonely times.

For the first time, he knew she was wrong. Tonight was all the learning he wanted. School left a music mind hungry even in Nashville, the mother city of country music. The musical heritage of Tennessee school children was ignored like a bastard child at a family reunion.

This was his first look at the book on performing on a professional stage. It was his first professional chance to entertain and go feeling with the music, flying with the music, forgetting everything except the high of performing. Tonight had to be the way of all his tomorrows playing the Grand Ole Opry, Mile High Stadium and all the legendary halls and stages around the world.

He wanted live TV coverage of those concerts and the fans feeling and flying and forgetting troubles with him. He wanted them released and renewed in the baptism of music like he was.

It was what he had to have, how he had to spend his energy.

Everything else was a warm up for now. Music was his push and pull, compulsion and addiction, challenge and reward. He was happier about singing tonight than he had ever been.

Now that he had accepted Mary Ellen being out of his life, he was getting over missing her and deeper into who he was musically. He was writing new songs, polishing old ones. When he was creating, he was happy. Free from worrying what lie or drug she was into was relief he hadn't expected. In all fairness, it wasn't all her fault, her parents were real dirt daubs. Knowing about the slugs Mary Ellen had for parents made him see having a suicide father wasn't the world's worse sin. It didn't compare with incest. Mary Ellen denied it, but he felt it really was the case.

Drugging had been a turn off since junior high when his favorite singer over- dosed. He vowed to create and share music without drugs or alcohol and have at least as much backbone as the robins and doves. He'd offer what he had from the heart with no tricks, or gimmicks, or chemicals.

If there came a time he couldn't do that, he'd quit.

He had too much to think about and was too excited to join the conversation Jim and Anna had kept up since leaving home. It seemed far less than the hour and a half they had been rolling when he saw a green and white highway sign reading TULLAHOMA NEXT RIGHT.

Jim was saying, "Worst thing I know is the wanna-be-a-star fever. Makes the Old West gold fever about like hiccups. Star fever can burn every ounce of brains from a body. Mostly, the harder a body starts trying to sing like a star, write like a star and look like a star, the farther they get from anything that favors a star. To me, a star is a mighty high and precious thing."

"It is to me too," Anna said.

"If you got the talent, loving the doing takes you there. All a real star does is shine. When you pick cause you love it, sing cause you love it or write cause you love it, win, lose or draw you get your reward, to a point. Even a mule won't pull without a little hay."

"No wonder you think Jim's right on, Mama. You've said that all my life."

"Don't you agree?"

"Yes, ma'am, and I'm on my way to doing my thing. Be glad for me."

"I am, but I don't want you spending your life in a string of bars.

"Annie," Jim said, "you don't have to worry about the Blue Collar. Hope you know I wouldn't be taking y'all to no rough place. Don't even take me to pick to rough places anymore. You realize after a while it ain't worth it. Course sometimes I think rationalizing's the worst part of getting older. Don't guess you'd know nothing about that yet, Clayboy."

"Hey, man, you rubbing it in?"

"Rubbing it in? I'm jealous as a jaybird at a worm pulling with a sore bill. Anyway, the Blue Collar belongs to an old buddy of mine, Frank Islander. He got tired of being away from his family and waiting on session work. Opened his own place several years back. Runs it right and runs it decent. Good enough for any preacher. Frank's wife and kids work in the Collar."

"How many kids does he have?" Anna asked.

"Six, last count I had. Three boys, three girls. Got one named Rachel about your age, Clay. Pretty as women get and sings like a mockingbird. Frank had it rough starting. Money was short and his temper's short when he's worried for his family. Church folks give him a hard time at first."

"Why was that?" Anna asked.

"It's funny about playing music, Annie. Some places, folks almost worship you. Other places they suspect you like the devil. Up in Kentucky anybody that picks has it made. Kentucky folks like to dance more than Tennessee folks. Old, young, everybody dances in Kentucky. East Tennessee they love you, West Tennessee too. Nashville folks tend to be leery."

"That's wild with the Opry born in Nashville."

"Yep. Frank showed Christians and heathens alike he wasn't running no den of iniquity. Got a sweet business now, says he don't miss the old days. Picking for the stars and union sessions is just a job after a while. Pays good but it's like long distance truck driving, you got no home life. Y'all are right before seeing what a good substitute Frank and Bess come up with."

Jim pulled into a graveled parking area beside a long steel building. A neon sign on the roof flashed THE BLUE COLLAR COUNTRY CLUB.

Clay said, "Copper Jim, this is awesome!"

"Son, I wouldn't take you to a chicken coop to pick."

Inside the club, Jim led them to a table by the stage and seated Anna. Then he and Clay started bringing in the gear. It was early, but a crowd was already eating in the huge room. A wood burning stove stood on a brick hearth in one corner. The lingering smell of burnt wood told the stove was real. Anna doubted anything about the club or the people who ran it was fake.

A good scrubbing wouldn't have been wasted, but she loved the sawbuck dining tables and sea-grass bottom chairs. The tables were covered with red and white gingham oilcloths like Aunt Effie kept on her kitchen table. Anna didn't know oilcloth was still available. The fragrance of smoked pork and something sweet baking was reminiscent of Aunt Effie's kitchen too.

Anna liked the Collar, it made a great neighborhood gathering place. She wished for a similar place at home. After all the tremendous growth in recent years, Nashville still had few family places out of the high-rent district. The separation of alcohol and family was still the rule in Music City.

Without being too obvious, she loved watching Clay love running in and out of the club helping the band set up. Jim brought Frank Islander over and introduced him. He was a dark-haired big man, fifty something, beginning to run to fat. She could see how eating here every day could make anybody run to fat. The kitchen aromas had her looking forward to the dinner they planned to eat at first break.

Driving down, Jim described the place as a working folk's country club; a restaurant and tavern where folks played pool, video games, dating games, danced and had a good time. Membership cards were forty dollars a year for singles and sixty for families that allowed a twenty percent discount on everything. Babies and kids were welcome as well as grandpa, grandma, old maid aunts and fundamentalist preachers. A family of four could eat dinner for the price of a baby sitter.

Frank's wife and daughters ran the kitchen, Frank and his sons ran the stage.

Bess called her menu country soul food. Fresh turnip greens, country ham, corn, pork roast, sweet potatoes, poor man's pudding, banana pudding, corn sticks, biscuits, blackberry and strawberry jam were some of the delicacies offered. The food was served cafeteria style, two beers was the limit with supper, and no hard liquor.

Farmers, factory workers, postal clerks, store clerks, truck drivers, office clerks and lower management made the majority of the customers. The middle and lower income clientele patronized the club with the same social enjoyment and sense of belonging as their richer neighbors patronized The Tullahoma Golf Club two miles down the road.

Frank had designed it so everybody could do their thing without interfering with anyone else. Jim said that was the reason for the Blue Collar's success. When a band wasn't playing, the jukebox was, but neither played too loud.

The right wing of the Blue Collar housed the weekend live music so the conversation of the dinner crowd wasn't drowned out by the dancing crowd's music. Jim said the drums were behind a plexiglass shield so the volume could be controlled and the band could play lower than most live music. Frank always said, "Volume ain't talent, but most amateurs think so." His kids had cut their musician's teeth on Frank's saying and his front porch approach to acoustic volume. Frank wanted the most noticeable sound in the club to be chatter and laughter, except right where the band played.

At the appointed hour of seven p.m., the bandstand was set up to Copper Jim's and Frank's satisfaction. The band members took their places, Frank stepped to the mike and a hush fell over the room. The patrons took listening to country music to heart as much as they did eating country cooking.

When Frank introduced Copper Jim, he tipped his hat and said, "Thank you, Frank. I do appreciate that real nice introduction. It's good to be back. Neighbors, first off, we gonna do y'all a medley. So let's go picking and grinning and dancing! Boys, jump in and pick any time it feels good."

Jim struck a chord and the band was into a fiddle lead buck dance. Then without waiting for the applause to cease he was into his vocal of *San Antonio Rose* and then led the band into *The Tennessee Waltz* to finish the medley.

The crowd gave a generous applause and Copper Jim stepped back up to the mike. "Thank y'all. Y'all are mighty kind and we do appreciate it. Wanna thank Frank and Bess for having us, and we appreciate you folks coming out. Yes, sir, and yes, ma'am, the Blue Collar has been one of our favorite places ever since the night Frank and Bess opened up.

"Better introduce my boys right quick. That's Jess Hawkins on drums, Phil Ryan on fiddle, Foxy Foster on bass, Bob North on mandolin and lead guitar. Most of y'all know Frank's daughter Rachel and big son Milton. They'll be doing harmony, Milton picks dobro too. We got a guest helping Bob on lead guitar tonight, Clay Hill. Later on, Clay'll sing for y'all. Does his own original tunes and some of the old standards too.

"Hope y'all have a good time. If the spirit moves you, sing along anywhere it hits you. We'll take all the help we can get. Saturday night don't come but once a week, so enjoy yourselves and let us know if you got requests. Now, Foxy's doing an Alabama tune, then a Randy Travis song, then we'll do *Foggy Mountain Breakdown*. Folks, Foxy Foster singing *Old Flame* and *On the Other Hand*, back to back. All you round dancers, hit the floor."

Jim's experience was evident, Anna realized Clay had a true professional for a coach. Right before the band's first break, she felt her nerves tighten as he introduced Clay. "Folks, like I told you, Clay Hill's gonna sing. Come around, Clay, and say howdy to the folks."

Clay walked up beside Jim, leaned into the mike with a smile and said, "Hi, folks, it's real nice to be here."

Jim said, "I don't know where this ole boy got all that blond hair, but his songs come from his heart and his mama helping him write. This is his first night at the Blue Collar. But y'all are gonna be hearing a lot from this young man. He's a mite nervous, this being his debut, so give him a good welcome.

"Clayboy, come on around and let these fine folks hear how good you sing. Folks, in his professional debut, Clay Hill from Nashville! Give him a big Blue Collar round of applause!"

To Anna's surprise and delight, Clay said, just like he was supposed to, "Thanks, Copper Jim, thanks, ladies and gentlemen. Appreciate Frank and Bess letting me perform. It's a real pleasure to be here at the Blue Collar Country Club. Hope you all like my music." Clay gave the band a count off and went into a fast number.

The format was two to four songs back to back and rotating pickers on musical breaks to give musician each a solo shot. When a song was done, they played into the next song with a sixteen-bar intro.

Copper Jim had explained to Clay, "Hate to stop when a band's on a roll. Too much talking and announcing pulls down any high you build up with the audience. Folks come to hear music not jawing. Give them a long intro so they know what's coming up, the singer gets a breather and the dancers pick up the beat and decide if they wanna dance or not."

When Clay had sung to the band's solo, the crowd broke into applause. His grin flashing on his applauding mother let her know how happy he was.

After he finished the song, the crowd clapped and whistled through the drummer gearing down to a slow tempo, and the band's intro before Clay went into *Old Shep*. Then they listened quiet as church.

When he ended the song, he brought the house down.

They clapped until Jim said, "Believe they like how you do, Clay. Let's give them *Rocky Top* before we go milk."

Clay loved singing lead with Rachel's high voice vocals and the harmonies of Copper Jim and Milton. The band played the up tempo tune, till when Jim made another attempt to break the dancers had no objection.

"Folks, we gonna takes us a break and eat some of the Blue Collar's fine home cooking. Ain't tasted no real fried chicken or fried apple pie since we was here last. Miss Bess's apple pies are about my favorite eating in the whole world. Hang around, we'll be back here on the Blue Collar stage in twenty minutes. And we sure do thank y'all."

☆

After they navigated the cafeteria line and settled at their table with laden plates, Bess Islander came by with her open face and broad smile. "We sure appreciate Copper Jim bringing y'all down to pick and grin with us."

Jim said, "Don't think y'all met. Bess Islander, meet Anna Hill."

"Met that handsome son of yours in the parking lot, Anna. Nice to meet you. Thanks for coming down."

"Nice to meet you, thanks for having us," Anna said, returning Bess's smile.

"Y'all are welcome. Boy, you're quite a performer." Bess could see that Clay was more interested in his food at the moment than anything else.

"Thank you, ma'am," he said, starting to stand.

"Keep you seat, and eat, breaks between sets don't last long. Jim's been telling us about you a long time. We wanted him to bring you to pick way before now. Said you had to grow up. Jim has his own ideas about things, especially music. Never wanted anybody messing with it, so Frank and me don't. Clay, you're all he said and more."

"Thanks, a bunch, Mrs. Islander."

"Call me Bess. My Rachel loves your music too. She's getting over bad hepatitis. Your music's made her want to sing the first time in ages."

"Thank you, ma'am. Rachel is a real beautiful girl."

"Thanks, Clay. Copper Jim, is that chicken browned to suit?"

"It's so good I can't hardly stop chewing long enough to talk."

"Eat while you can. I know how much work picking and singing is."

"Bess, these pole beans are larruping as the fried chicken. Clayboy, someday I'm stealing Bess from Frank. Woman that cooks like her would be worth straightening up and staying home with."

"He's said that for years, Clay. Pay no mind to kangaroos and musicians. Jim Quarrells wouldn't stay home with Marilyn Monroe."

Clay chuckled. "He says you sing Patsy Cline songs super."

"Singing's mostly behind me, don't hardly know a whole song anymore. Aimed to be a singer about a hundred years ago."

"What happened?"

"Frank Islander, happened, been happening ever since! Kept me too busy having and tending to kids, to sing. Never was content leaving them with sitters when we was on the road. Didn't like taking them with us either. We toured a while after Frank Jr. was born, then here come Linda Gail. Couldn't take honky tonks, drunks, two young'uns and a tour bus of musicians. Got a fairly strong constitution, but I ain't no walking on water miracle."

"Besides your beautiful daughter, you got a great club. Thanks for letting me perform here." Clay's eyes told Bess how much he liked her.

"Keeps the kids busy and Frank at home. You can get a picker off the road but you can't get a picker off the music. How long you been singing?"

"How long, Mama?"

Anna said, "Since he was two and humming before that. He'd lay in his crib and hum himself to sleep with songs on the radio. He couldn't sing words, but you could tell the melodies when he was a year old."

"He has a great career ahead of him."

"Thanks, Bess. Music's all he's ever wanted to do."

"Nothing wrong with that. Clay, let me give you some unsolicited advice."

"Ma'am, anybody with a daughter as pretty as Rachel and fries chicken this good has to be smart. I'll take any advice you'd care to give me."

"Lord, Copper Jim, you didn't tell me this Clayboy of yours, with all his picking and singing and writing, has a silver tongue to boot."

"Bess, you been around enough pickers to know that."

"Ain't that the truth. Clay, get your career going before you get your family going. A family of folks needs a nest same as a family of blue jays. Get some decent money coming in, then make your nest. Talented as you are, won't take forever. So don't get the cart before the horse."

"That's what I been saying," Jim said, buttering a biscuit.

"Thanks, I'll keep that in mind," Clay said.

"No, boy, you'll be a fool like everybody when that ole love bug bites. See that in them big navy blue eyes you got from your mama."

Jim drawled, "Ole love bug's hard to resist."

"Tell me about it, we could both write a book. Well, I better get back to work before I get my own career in trouble."

"Gonna find time to dance with me?"

"Don't I always? Enjoy your supper, folks. See y'all after while." Anna watched her stop at each table to remember folks and say a few words. It was easy to see why the Blue Collar was a huge success.

Driving home, Jim said, "Would Thursday week suit y'all for the session?"

"Yes," Anna and Clay said together.

"Looks like everything will be ready. Booked a sixteen-track studio. Sixteen tracks will be plenty and the rate's ten dollars less an hour than for twenty-four. Don't like every whistle and bell there is on a record. An old road buddy of mine, still on the road, will be in town Monday. Want him to pick on the session if he can. Mac Smith is listed lead picker on lots of hit albums. Mac understands my rhythm and I understand his lead. Speaking of picking, Clay, I figured it'd be okay to tell Frank and Bess you was gonna pick regular. If it ain't, I can call back and let them know."

"I'd love to. What do you think, Mama?"

"I think it's great, darling."

Jim said, "Now that means being tied up coming down to Tullahoma every Saturday. What y'all thank about that?"

"I'm thrilled to death. How about you, Mama?"

"This is what we have talked about for years."

"Good," Jim said. "We'll play the Blue Collar a couple of months, then move in on the writers nights around the Row. We'll have the session behind us and our demo tapes. We'll want tapes with us, in case we meet anybody to hand one off to. Clayboy, tonight was your audition, so that's free. Starting next Saturday you make thirty dollars a night."

"I can't believe it, Jim."

"It's so and you're worth it. Gigs around Nashville just don't pay much."

Clay laughed. "Thanks. This has been the very best night of my life."

Anna said, "I appreciate all you're doing too."

"My pleasure. Clay, all the nights you worked at the Center are paying off."

"Copper Jim, if you have no objections, I'd love to have Rachel's harmony and Milton's dobro on the session."

"Had the same notion, I think they'd be tickled."

"Sounds like things are starting big," Anna said.

"Depends," Jim said, "time, place, luck. My concern ain't been starting. I want Clay started right."

"How do you mean?" Clay asked.

"Started as who you are musically, and staying that way. When we're performing, can't tell who might be listening. Maybe somebody big, maybe not. We need to take some tapes to pass to the right folks if any show up and show interest. That sound all right?"

"Sounds cool, I'm always ready to pick. Can't believe doing my first gig, rehearsing for a session and planning writer's nights on Music Row."

"Let's rehearse at the Center Tuesday night. Pick out your six best songs."

"You know my catalog. Got any suggestions?"

"Pick four up tempo tunes and two ballads. We'll have time to cut four sides. Always take a couple of songs over what you think you'll get done. Line them up in the order of importance. In the studio a song can change, you might not want to do it. Need a few extras just in case. Sometimes you get lucky and have time to do more. I'll be disappointed if we don't get five songs in three hours. Hope we get all six down."

"Does Clay need to learn studio singing first?"

"No, Miss Annie, he's been singing in a mike over two years. Can't learn no better way than doing. Some producers use studio tricks all out of reason. I been wanting a crack at producing with some ideas I've had a long time now. Clay, if you was recording a robin, how'd you want it to sound?"

"Guess I'd want it to sound like a robin."

"Right, and you want a mockingbird to sound like a mockingbird. One in a tree not in a cage or studio. A Clay Hill record ought to sound like Clay Hill live. Let's let the producer, in this case me, do all the studio worrying. I want you to rear back and sing like you do on stage."

Anna said, "I really appreciate all the interest you've taken in Clay."

"I hope you know how much I appreciate it too," Clay said. "Next to Mama, you're the best friend I've ever had. Guess you answered a million questions. I've been full of questions and still am."

"Ain't no thanks necessary, I'm enjoying this. Always did want to produce a hit singer. The good Lord knows, when a feller gets all blued up thinking he's done lived all the good parts. He knows when it's time to send something uplifting. Reckon we all got us a new dream coming true."

☆

As they rehearsed, Jim was moved by Clay's singing. Things were getting down to the nitty-gritty. Clayboy's monster or messiah of success was around the corner. Jim wiped his tears before Clay could see. Lord, talk about a singer too good to be true. The boy got better every time he walked up to a mike.

"Copper Jim, want to go from the top again?"

"Ain't no need rehearsing all the edge off. You sung start to finish without a bobble twice. Let's pack it in."

"You think I'll do all right, Copper Jim?"

"Singing and writing's natural to you as a crow flying. Just handle the success as well as you have the planting and the plowing for it."

"You can't know how I want folks to like my music."

"They will, way sooner than you know. Two years on down the road, you'll be known world-wide."

"You sound kinda worried."

"Like I said countless times, being a star can be heaven or hell. It's all in if you handle it or let it handle you. Seen it ruin some good folks."

"With you and Mama in my corner, I'll be okay. By the way Mama wants you to come eat fried pies she made this morning."

"Tell her thanks, but Miss Roxie's cooking supper. She'll throw it out and me too if I'm too late. Say, did you get you a woman yet?"

"No. It was only Saturday we talked about that."

"That was three nights ago. What's your hold up?"

Clay laughed. "I've been busy rehearsing."

"Sounds like you're putting it off, all cowboys get throwed. Ain't nothing like a high loving woman, not even music. Miss Roxie's a mite high tempered. If I start taking her for granted, all I get's hot lip and cold shoulder. Still a high tempered woman's a high loving woman. I try not to hurt Miss Roxie or make her mad, cause she's good to me. Putting your arms around a guitar holds you, but it's got no warm arms to hold you back. It's a one way love that can get mighty cold all by yourself. Songwriters need loving to keep picking, like they need picking to keep loving."

"Were you kidding me the other night about Rachel?"

"I was serious as taxes about her being pretty."

"I'm talking about you saying she liked me."

"Heck, boy, I was serious about that too."

"How do you know that, Copper Jim?"

"How does a white dove know how to fly?"

"A white dove's born knowing how to fly."

"Ain't smart enough to always pick up on it, but I was born knowing women's feelings. You was too, you're a musician. The ladies like musicians cause we understand their feelings."

"I think you're full of it," Clay grinned.

"Me too, at times. Right now, partner, I'm talking gospel."

CHAPTER 15

IT'S A HIT

"Copper Jim, it isn't fair, you having to drive every Saturday."

"Thanks, Annie, but I'd rather drive than ride. Say, who is that bodacious feller over by the door wearing the red cowboy hat? Or is it wearing him?"

"Like my new hat, Marshall Dillon?" Clay said, pulling his hat low, striking a pose. "Mama got me this for my birthday. I think she done good."

"Yeah, it's sharp as a skinning knife, and goes with my red truck."

Anna said, "I saw it in a western store window and couldn't hold myself. Clay's name was all over it and his birthday was coming up."

Switching lanes to pass, Jim said. "Son, how does it feel to be nineteen?"

"Great. Besides my hat, Mama gave me my own wheels. We found this seventy-six Coupe De Ville without a dent anywhere. They're putting on new tires and doing some upholstery work. We'll get it Monday."

"You're in high cotton now, Clayboy. And this coming Thursday's all set for our demo session. Got Mac Smith, the lead picker I was telling y'all about."

"Hey, that's great," Clay said.

"Be sure and invite Rachel and Milton."

"I will. Rachel could be a star in her own right."

"Yeah, she could, Clay. If she wanted to."

When they arrived at the club, they settled at the table they occupied the previous Saturday. It was clear the Hills had made new friends and new fans. The Islanders and several customers came by to express their appreciation of Clay's music, and a teenage girl requested his first autograph to sign.

At the end of the first set, Jim said, "Folks, we got the up and coming young star who made his debut here at the Blue Collar last Saturday night. For his second time, beat your hands together for Clay Hill!"

Clay opened with an upbeat country rock tune called "Cherokee Eyes." Right off Anna saw how much more he was in control and into his material. He was almost as relaxed as when he rehearsed at home and enchanted the crowd. The dancers sat down, conversation hushed, the noise of the cafeteria line and cash register ceased. It seemed every soul, even babes in arms, stopped everything but breathing.

At the end of his four song medley, they wildly applauded and demanded an encore, then a second encore and a third. As Clay sang his third encore, he looked at Anna and flashed the grin he did when he came from school with an A report card. Standing to applaud with the rest of his fans, Anna looked at her son with the same proud smile she had after reviewing his A report cards.

She knew Clay was on his way to making his fondest dream come alive. Lord, he was wonderful, so tall and handsome. It was hard to believe her little boy was grown. Why, in God's name, did Jake have to be such an ass when she had loved him so! Why did she have to miss the bastard right in the middle of a great moment like this? Hell! she was crazy as Jake!

Clay took his bows and expressed his appreciation. Instead of complying with their demand for another encore, he said, "I know y'all are enjoying the harmony vocals of Rachel and Milton as much as me. They grew up singing on this stage so y'all know their talent. For the record, I love what they do." Clay waited again for quiet then, "To finish the set, there's an old standard called "Blue Eyes Crying In The Rain." I'd like Rachel Islander to sing a duet with me, if she'd be so kind." Clapping hands told the fans approved.

Rachel and Clay brought down the house. Anna rose with the crowd to give them a standing ovation. Instead of complying with the insistent applause for more, Anna saw Clay taking that long low bow she was beginning to see as his trademark for ending his performance. It was another thing he had developed on stage at the Community Center. Last Saturday after his last song, Clay used the exaggerated bow on the Blue Collar stage.

He came out of his bow and without further ado stepped off stage, gave Rachel a hand down and they walked away together. Anna was glad to know Clay knew when enough was enough and was taking Jim's advice about stopping while your audience still wanted to hear you.

Clay smiled down at Rachel and said, "Let's get out for some fresh air."

"Clay, they're having a fit to hear you sing some more."

Walking toward the door, he said, "Honey, I'll be glad to sing after we take a break and give them one. I need to ask you something and it's best to leave before you wear your welcome out." He returned her soft smile. Everything about Rachel struck him as soft and beautiful as he held the door, then followed her out on the sawbuck wood porch.

"I'll say one thing, when you're done, you're sure done."

"We need to talk and eat supper and I've been told to stop while I'm ahead."

"Copper Jim and Daddy have said that all my life."

"Did they say you smile as pretty as wildflowers?"

"What kind of wildflowers?"

"Mostly red and yellow, course there's violets too."

"You talk a pretty picture, Clay Hill."

"Talk's not nearly as pretty as the real thing. You'll have to come see for yourself." As they strolled down the porch, he pushed back his cowboy hat.

"It's a sin for a man to have those blond curls."

"Hey, I hate my hair."

"I love it, it's beautiful. Where is home, Clay?"

"West Nashville."

"You got wildflowers in West Nashville?"

"I live a little ways out on a few acres."

"Is that where you learned to sing so great?"

"Well, I hope. I love your singing. You planning on a singing career?"

"Oh no. Didn't you graduate this year?"

"Yep. You graduated last year?"

"Two years ago. You seem older, Clay. How old are you?"

"Nineteen, last week. I was late starting school. Mama held me back a year."

"I'm twenty-two. I was sick and late starting too. Then I got sick again and lost too many days to pass sixth grade. My senior year I had hepatitis and barely graduated. For a long time I was too dumb to stay healthy. I'm okay, now. I'm going to Paris to study art when my doctor says I can. If I keep improving, he'll release me in a few months."

"Cool, knew you were creative. You write songs too?"

"Daddy and Milton are the songwriters. Mama says I put my songs on canvas instead of paper."

"If you paint like you look and sing, you're great."

"Thanks, but there's so much to learn. I'll start a picture, sure I'm painting a masterpiece. About the time I'm going good, I start thinking it's a master piece of crap. But some of my best finished work, I thought was my worst when I was fighting to paint what was in my soul on canvas."

"What do your folks think about you going to Paris?"

"They hate it like I hate the thought of getting sick in bed again. I'll wait till I'm strong. Hepatitis can make you helpless. I don't want to get over there and get sick because I jumped the gun. Crazy as it may sound, I have to try. I can't stand it if I don't! Being the songwriter you are, you know how I feel."

"Yes, I understand the call of a dream." They reached the end of the porch and sat on a bench. Clay said, "Guess we're both disappointing our folks. Mama wanted me to go to college, I've had it with school for a while. Forever, if I'm lucky. Like you, I've been put off from following my dream too long."

"You're going to be the biggest star ever launched out of Nashville. Everyone needs that first big break, with your talent you'll get it."

"Thanks, that's why I wanted to talk to you, other than just wanting to talk to you. Uh, we're going to record a demo tape of some of my original songs. I wonder, I mean Copper Jim and I wonder if you and Milton would help us out. It will be a full production, like a record."

"Sounds great, Clay!"

"Your high voice singing and harmonies would sure sweeten the tracks."

"I'd love to and I know Milton would too."

"If y'all would, I'd sure be grateful."

"It'll be a blast. Come on, let's go find Milton."

"Wait, girl, you didn't answer my other question." His eyes caught and held hers as he asked, "Would you go out with me, sometime?" He saw the spark of interest he had hoped for in her beautiful fawn eyes.

Her voice was very soft. "Clay, you know I'll go out with you."

"You made my night. Now, I'm ready for supper and to talk to Milton." He loved the way her small hand felt in his. As they walked up the porch, he asked, "Is this the hand that creates the paintings?"

"Yes, I'm afraid it's guilty." He opened her hand and lightly kissed her palm. "That's for good luck, Rachel. Yours and mine."

Lost in his eyes, she said, "Let's go ask Milton about your session."

In the control room of Sixteenth Avenue Studio, Copper Jim couldn't believe how well the session was going. As Clay finished his second vocal, he said, "Clayboy sings as natural as a mockingbird. I'm plumb flabbergasted."

"I'm plumb flabbergasted too," Anna said softly.

Clancy said, "I've engineered on session for the top stars, but this kid is a singing miracle. And he wrote the songs too?"

"Yep, him and his mama here, Clancy."

Clancy said, "Do you know how good your music is?"

Anna said, "I hope it will do. Music's all Clay has ever talked about doing."

"It will do him into a major label contract."

"Clance, you're right about that. Clayboy's natural as a duck in a pond. Just show him the water and turn him loose. Speaking of turning loose, I best turn everybody loose for a break." Jim turned on the PA system, "Clay, your vocal's a hit if I ever heard one. Let's all take a call to nature break, then I want you to come on in here and take a last listen to what we got cut."

"Sure, Jim," Clay said.

"Listen, y'all," Jim said, "If you get any ideas, after we play the tracks, don't be bashful. May not use them but your ideas are welcome. Everybody's doing a super job and we appreciate it."

Clay said to Rachel and Milt, "Let's meet in the control room."

At the mixing board, Clancy said, "Mrs. Hill, Copper Jim and me have seen talent come, seen it go, and seen it stay. Clay's here to stay."

"Thanks, Clancy, I hope so. Clay wants this so much."

"Barring an act of God, I have no doubt about it. He sings, picks, writes; he's young and he's handsome. The ladies like all that and they buy most of the records. He sounds too good to be true, and is. Everybody will like that."

Anna's beaming smile went beyond her words in expressing her feelings. "You don't know how I appreciate your kind words. Clancy, call me Anna."

Jim said, "Annie, that goes to show how struck he is with Clay. Clancy would call the Queen of England, Lizbeth. Clay just laid down a heart stopping vocal. And his idea about Milt playing dobro like he is trying to mock a Baptist piano player is a master touch on that mountain melody."

"Where you been keeping this boy, Jim?"

"Just letting the apple get ripe, Clancy."

"Apple my ass! Pardon me, Anna, He's a superstar and you know it! And the song's a hit. When it comes to hill country with its roots in gospel, something new that sounds like something old is rare. Anymore, ain't many who can write songs like you and Clay do, Anna."

"Clancey, you're very kind. I love Rachel's harmony on that song."

"Me too," Jim said. "Rachel sounds just like her mama did twenty years ago. It's been a spell since I been around this much great talent. Lord, I love it!"

Clay, Rachel and Milton walked in the room together. Anna hugged Clay and said,"You were fantastic, if you are mine."

"Thanks, Mama. I love doing this."

"I know, son, it shows in every note you sing. And the rest of you were all out of this world too," Anna added and sat down.

Copper Jim pushed his cowboy hat back and said, "Got hit product working here. Your and Rachel's duet made the hair on the back of my neck stand up. When music touches your heart, that's the best you can get. All I hear on top of what we got is twin fiddles, see what you think, Clay. Clancy, let her rip."

After the songs played, Anna was crying and everyone was speechless. Clay broke the hush, "I think you're right, Jim, hit product or not. The songs are done except the twin fiddles. They're happening like I want to hear them. Thanks for a fine job on both songs."

"Don't thank me. Thank Annie and you. I'm just cranking the wheels and keeping the music off your vocals. Boy, you and the Islanders made the songs happen. Everybody's doing a real fantastic job."

Clay said, "Rachel, you and Milton are the best."

The Islanders expressed their thanks, and Jim said, "Clay if you're ready let's get them other two songs done. Clock's a running."

"Hey, Mama, and don't be crying now. Be happy."

"Son, I am," Anna said smiling and wiping another tear. "I am so happy, darling. Don't worry about me, go sing me the other songs. Rachel, you and Milton are doing a beautiful job. Y'all have great sibling harmony."

"Thanks, Mrs. Hill," Rachel said.

Milton said, "We appreciate recording in a studio".

Clay said, "Mama, next to you, they sing harmony with me better than we could hope for. You satisfied, Copper Jim?"

"Tickled pink, and rearing to get the other two songs done."

"Me too. Rachel, Milton if y'all are ready, let's go."

Jim sat watching the young singers as they walked back out to the mikes. Then he said to Mac Smith standing by the door finishing a cigarette, "Remember when we was that rearing to go?"

"Like it was yesterday, but it sure as hell wasn't."

"Naw, I don't reckon, but I'm right glad of it."

"You mean you're glad to be over fifty years old?"

"If I could choose, I'd take the years and off the bottle, before twenty-five again and still on it, in a hummingbird minute. Mac, you're hitting some tasty licks, time ain't hurt your picking. Got any thoughts on the tracks?"

"Hell, you know what you're doing. Always did, with music."

"Need harpsichord on one of the next songs, maybe both. Hear Juanita Pitts on them. Know where she is these days?"

"Running and gunning bad when she had money, last I heard."

"Damn! She was going to rehab the last I heard."

"Did, but after detoxing, she walked off. Counselor took her to Human Services to get her welfare money started. Fool counselor went to the can and left her alone, wild from detoxing and Juanita walks."

"Shit!" Copper Jim said.

"She called the next day wanting back in. They told her, because she left she was out. Hell, why throw a dope addict trying to kick the habit out of rehab for acting like a dope addict trying to kick the habit?"

"It's like the numb nuts that used to throw crazy folks in snake pits."

"Juanita was living on the street, sleeping under Victory Bridge in a box."

"That's what caretakers ought to do. Take a woman in hell and next door to dying and give her out to the pimps and pushers. Hell, I ain't the smartest soul breathing but I ain't the dumbest either."

"Jim, the government will be serious at stopping dope and the crime that goes with it when the National Guard's on the streets stopping it.

"Sometimes this country bullshits itself past being. Makes my ass gnaw shucks. Let's make music. When I have time, I'm gonna see about Juanita."

"I'd like to go along, if you wouldn't mind."

"Fine. I'll hunt you up. Mac, let's pick."

After they cut the tracks on the last two songs, Jim had everyone take a final listen. After the play back, he asked, "Clayboy, you happy?"

"Yes. I think they're there. Mama, what do you think?"

"Clay, the whole production is wonderful."

Jim said over the PA, "Folks, we're calling it a night. Meet Miss Anna in the lobby for your pay. Y'all done a fine job and much obliged."

Anna went to the lobby to pay the musicians, Clay, Rachel and Milton walked out to the performing area to talk.

Copper Jim said, "My ears are too full to mix now, Clancy. You booked tomorrow morning, say ten or so?"

"Don't have a thing booked till three."

"Book me at ten. Like always, you done a fine job."

After Anna had written checks for the other musicians, she tried to pay Copper Jim, Rachel and Milton. They refused saying it was their pleasure.

"Well, at least," Anna said, "let me buy supper. I'm hungry and I know Clay is starved. Rachel, you and Milton need to eat something before driving home. If y'all would stay over, we have plenty of room at our house."

Rachel said, "Milton's wife will be needing him. They have a new baby, and my folks will be expecting me."

"Tell y'all what," Jim said, "the Golden Goose has good home cooking. Should still be serving and having the writers night too. Let's blow in, eat supper, and do the songs we recorded. I'd really enjoy that."

♪

Copper Jim led the way to a table with a stage view. He told the waiter, "Bring two coffees, three Cokes and menus if the cook's cooking."

"He is," the waiter smiled, "and in rare form."

"Good, I like his grub and we're about to starve. They still taking names for the songwriter's show?"

"I believe so. Check with Betty at the sound board."

They had eaten and rested when Clay, Rachel, and Milton followed Copper Jim on stage. After they set up, Clay walked to a mike. Looking over his audience, he made Anna think of a runner getting on his mark to race.

"Ladies and gentlemen, my name's Clay Hill. This tall fellow standing beside me is my music guru and my best friend, Copper Jim Quarrells. Copper Jim's the best country rhythm picker I've ever heard. Once you hear him, you'll agree he's the best country rhythm picker you ever heard too. This lady with the big fawn eyes is Miss Rachel Islander and she sings as beautiful as she looks. The big dude with the beard, is her brother Milton. You can almost tell by looking, he was one of the best linebackers Coffee County High ever had. On top of that he sings harmony like I wish I could and plays dobro, like I can't even dream. By the way, the cook here at the Golden Goose, cooks like I wish I could. Earlier, we finished in the studio, then took a notion to come here for supper and perform two of the songs we recorded. Hope y'all like them."

There was polite applause as Clay finger picked his intro solo, then Jim and Milton joined in. Into the third line of Clay's vocal, a hush fell over the club.

Jim knew country music styles changed and went from hard country, to cross-over pop sounds. What was now traditional, was different from how it sounded five years ago and it was over five years since he' been in a listening club. The crowd had lots of college kids he never used to see.

All the old guard like himself shied from it, but the college crowd's likes made a difference these days. However it was dressed, tux or overalls, evening gown or feed sack dress, country music was for people and about people. What the fans you wanted to sell were thinking and doing made the difference, whether they took your album home or left it gathering dust in the store rack.

Jim wasn't sure what the educated bunch wanted, but after a few lines he knew Clay had them listening. With the chorus, regardless of education, occupation or background, the audience was Clay's. He had the educated, the over thirty-fivers and even the show-me songwriters hooked. Impressing your songwriter peers was no easy feat. Even beginning writers knew a well-written piece and the value of a song that pulled at heartfelt emotions. Whether or not they had developed to the point of writing a song well, they heard a fellow writer's skill. Clayboy having everybody listening like they'd been struck dumb was a flying good sign.

When Clay ended his second song, there was a silence followed by a standing ovation from every soul, except an elderly man in a wheelchair, smiling, clapping arthritic hands and demanding in his croaking voice, "More! More! He's good as Eddie Arnold, Roy Acuff too. You're going to give them hell, boy. You're a star. More! More!"

Betty asked, "Y'all want another song?" Applause was her answer. "Clay, how about singing us one more song?"

"My pleasure. Folks, I'd like to sing a song Mama and me wrote for my Grandmama Hill. She's a quarter Cherokee, our song's called *Cherokee Eyes*."

When Clay finished, he was again greeted with applause and demands for more. He bowed, then smiled toward Anna sitting beyond the shallow area of visibility the stage lights permitted. Turning to Jim, his eyes asking whether to continue. Like most neophyte singers high on praise, Clay would have sung all night. Jim gave him a thumbs-up, to signal it was over. Clay stepped to the mike and said, "Thanks. We appreciate it."

He bowed long and low, then gave Rachel a helping hand. They left the stage to more applause and shouts to "Do one more!" As Clay moved through the compliments of the crowd, Betty waved him over to her sound board.

Holding up a finger to wait a moment, she introduced the next songwriter, before saying "Clay, we have an early, invitational show on Thursday evenings. I'd like to have you back for that next week."

He looked at Copper Jim, Jim nodded yes.

When they returned to the table, Anna said, "Y'all were all wonderful."

"Mama, Betty wants us on her early show next week."

"I hope y'all told her yes."

"Sure did. Rachel, Milt, we want y'all to come back, too."

Milton said, "Thanks, but the folks will need us. We can't ask off two Thursdays in a row. They are nearly as busy as Fridays and Saturdays. Rachel, it's getting late, we best be going."

"We best all be going," Copper Jim said, and the Hills agreed.

Clay followed Rachel outside and led her a few steps away from the others. "Rachel, I was wondering if we might catch a movie or something tomorrow?"

"Sounds like fun."

"Call you in the morning, okay?"

"Okay. And, Clay, your *Cherokee Eyes* song is a hit." Her burning brown eyes made him a believer.

CHAPTER 16

LOST LOVE

Following up his driveway, one side of her brain said turn around, while the other fantasized in anticipation. Usually, she went along with gut feelings, but Clay would be in Tullahoma till late. For once, she had all the time in the world. She wanted to be with Jake in the worst way. He braked to his normal grinding stop and was there when she parked with a smile to open her door.

He closed his back door, then pulled her to him and kissed her hard. Desperation colored his "Been wanting you bad. Baby, it's been too long."

"I can't help it if you refuse my invitations."

"You made me nuts for you the minute you walked in class," he said, and kissed her again. Then, holding her close with one arm, he took a fistful of her hair and gently pulled her head back. He searched her eyes for something unknown to her, maybe unknown to him.

"What?" she said, seeing his pain.

He looked a moment more, then moaned, "Woman, I love you something crazy and you know it."

"Man, I don't know anything."

He kissed her passionately, still holding her by the hair with one hand, molding her to him with his other arm. Anna found realizing she was helpless, knowing he could break her neck like a broom straw was arousing rather than intimidating.

When Jake released her mouth, passion had turned her eyes dark as a hot summer storm and he smiled.

She snapped, "Ass, are you satisfied?"

"Yes, baby. I was so afraid it had all gone away. You don't know what you mean to me. I don't guess you ever will."

"Whatever, I doubt it's enough."

"Enough for what, Anna?"

"The rest of our lives," she snapped, but stood on tiptoe to reach his lips. Joy spread through her like warmth from a fire as she felt his passion soar, his hardness against her. She purred, "I've been dying for you, darling."

The honesty of her response set him to trembling. The way she let desire slide into high gear, start her grinding against him, excited him so. There wasn't a coy bone in her body. She went with her feelings and let passion take her over despair and reasoning. She sighed, "For now, this is all there is." For now, there was nothing else in the world for either of them.

All his earlier thoughts, all the demands he meant to put to her, melted in the heat of desire. One more time, she was his or he was hers or they were each other's. He never quibbled over dotting i's or crossing t's, results moved him. With Anna, results were always fantastic.

She gave her tongue to his insistent mouth, then passion had them crazy and high and flying on an irresistible wind of wanting-- wild and captured and so glad of it. Brainwashed by feeling, a mutual surrender burned their bickering into the urgent love-making of knowing it could be their last chance.

Their inability to undress fast enough brought the sound of tearing fabric, her broken bra hook, clothes raining on the counter, clothes raining on the floor, one of his white sweat socks hanging on the dish drainer, her bra on the table draped across the sugar bowl and two in a tangle on the floor.

Then on the turquoise carpet in the space between the range and refrigerator on opposite sides of the kitchen, at times under the table, heaven was in session with two swearing forever, making mind-burning love. It was Jake on top, then rolling to put her on top, again and again. It was moving and marvelous and mesmerizing and felt never-ending. She loved it, he loved it. If loving it made a lasting relationship, they would have stayed together three lifetimes. "Please," she begged, "don't ever leave me."

"Honey, hell's army couldn't drag me away from you."

"I couldn't stand it, I just couldn't stand it."

"Woman, I won't leave you, don't worry. You like?"

"I love... oh, God, yes. Jakey, you're... so good."

"And who do you belong to?"

"I love you. I belong to me."

"No. Tell me the truth."

"I'm telling you the truth. Kiss me."

"Say who you belong to first, then I'll kiss you."

"I belong to me!"

"No kisses for Anna."

"Jake!"

"Who do you belong to, woman?"

"Damn it! Me!"

"Who?"

"Hell, you! Kiss me."

"Say it!"

"I said it."

"No, say, I belong to Jake!"

"Shit! I belong to Jake."

"Say, Anna belongs to Jake like you mean it."

"Anna belongs to Jake. Kiss me! You know I can't without you kissing me."

"Angel, I belong to you, too. I love you, I'll never leave you." Kissing her deep and easy, like he knew she liked, he felt a new tremor take her. "See?" he said, rocking her with all he had, feeling the infinite joy of knowing he had all she wanted, all she needed. There was no way any woman could fake her pleasure, her moans, her spasms. "Woman, you always make me feel ten feet tall. Are you again?"

"Oh, darling, oh... yes!"

"Will you again?"

"Is the sky blue? Don't stop, don't... eeemmmm!"

"Good? Is it? Tell me!"

"It's wonderful! You're wonderful, I love you. Kiss me one more time." It was wonderful and she did love loving him and she could love him as long as he could maintain. It was always more times than she could keep count. Why wouldn't she love him? Hell, any woman would love him. She had to be sure he knew. "Jake, you are a miracle, a loving, male angel."

"You too, tell me again you belong to me."

"You're wonderful, I love you, Jake."

"Tell me. Please!.."

"Okay, I do."

"No, say it, Anna."

"Shit, I belong to you, Jake!"

"I love to hear it. Why is it a bother to say it?"

"I don't know."

"Say how long. How long do you belong to me?"

"Long as you want me... so good... so good."

"Again, Anna? Are you again?"

"Yes! Jake! Oh, Jake!"

When she came down, he said, "I love you," rolling on top again, feeling her ebb, happy he could move her, satisfy her.

"Jake, now you. It's your turn now, angel."

"You sure?"

"Yes, darling. I need... need to feel you thrill."

Feeling she would again, he held back. He had to give her one more time on her own, had to hear her moan, feel the muscle spasm inside possess her and him. He loved feeling that each time it happened. That part of it, when he could feel her grip him, took him beyond the shadow of a doubt that he thrilled her. It gave his pride the surge that was almost better, at least as good, as his own climax. The woman satisfied was the woman true, the woman pleased was the woman who stayed. He never felt such spasms in Darleen.

Then, he had to, he couldn't wait any longer! It slipped up on him. "Anna, honey, I..." but then he felt her rising to him. "Oh, darling, perfect! I love you. You can't know how much I love you."

"I love you," she said. He felt her relax and knew they were both spent, done, wonderfully released and relieved and lifted one more marvelous time.

She came to herself on top, the two of them still in a tangle sharing a foggy afterglow. As her fog lifted, she became acutely aware of the sweat she was bathed in-- actually a second coating to the one she had worked up in exercise class. Neither of them had wanted to take time for showers at the Center. The plan was to shower here first, showering had not been first. Her deodorant failure was bearing witness to that.

Without a word, she left him and went to shower.

The fault, if there was one, lay in too long between lovings. Too much fussing and too little loving would have wrecked Romeo and Juliet. She adjusted the water to a strong tepid spray, stepped in and stood turning and rinsing to cool down. Then she lathered up in Jake's good smelling soap and shampoo, scrubbing until she was squeaky clean and wonderfully refreshed.

Then one more time, she learned showering alone under the same roof with Jake didn't happen. He pulled back the curtain and grinned. Then he stepped in and moved under the water and kissed her shoulder. He silently bathed from head to toe before he took her in his arms and kissed her like he hadn't kissed her in a year. She appreciated the rubber mat on the shower floor as he picked her up and her legs automatically went around his waist. She fit around Jake as if she had been custom made for him. He smiled a happy six year old smile and whispered, "I love you... and this."

"I love you too and your gray eyes."

"You're so good, woman, ease back some, yeah. Okay?"

"Easy, it's big."

"Go with it, you'll like it, that's it. Okay now?"

"Ye .. yes."

"No pain?"

"Not now. Oh, it's good this way too. You're such a beautiful lover. You know so much. How,... how do you know so much?"

"It's my job to please my woman. Doesn't hurt now?"

"It's fantastic, I love it. Am I too heavy?"

"You're a baby feather, darling. Just give it to me. Love me. Relax and let me love you. Yeah... uumm. That's it... you're so damn beautiful. Woman, you please me so. Hey, you want me to wash your back?"

"Like this?" she said, laughing, and heard the joy in her laughter. She was nuts and didn't care! This was the best, the sexiest, the most woman she had ever been or wanted to be.

"Of course, like this. I could."

"Man, I don't doubt it. I do have to give you credit, you know how and what to do with a woman."

"A woman needs the hell loved out of her every day or so."

"I believe it. When we love, you make me the happiest woman in the world," she said, then gasped as he took her nipple into his mouth.

Afterward, he said, "That's right, I want to hear you gasp. I want to make you sigh, moan, cry, giggle. I want to give it all to you. I want to be the only one who can. I'm going to make you so addicted to loving me, you'll be mine-- all mine. I won't have to push getting you to say you belong to me and I won't have to worry about you leaving me ever. I'll tie you to me with loving."

It seemed to Anna that perhaps he already had, as Jake started making love to her seriously, kissing her everywhere endlessly, saying over and over, "You are so beautiful, baby. All I ever wanted in a woman." Endlessly plunging deep inside, then almost all the way back out: "You're so hot, angel,... so good. I love you... love you... yeah... oh, yeah!" If response meant addiction, she already was. He made her moan and cry and all the rest of it like always. "Give it to me again," he demanded-- she couldn't wait.

Cooking supper together, with the kitchen graced by candlelight, they talked, shared secrets, and traded feather kisses. This was as happy as Anna had ever been or needed to be.

Jake had sliced turkey, cantaloupe, fresh peaches and all their favorite garden salad fixings. Making a tub bowl of salad with sinful amounts of onion and garlic, he grinned, "We'll both be eating. What the hell?"

Frying up the batter, she said, "Doubt there's a man south of the Mason-Dixon line who doesn't love hot hoe cakes."

"Yeah, fried in good high-cholesterol bacon grease."

They ate after dark on the deck, shared a bottle of white wine, and the moon-silvered view of the field rolling down to the black top. Occasional car lights flashed on the wooded hills across the road climbing the ridge, then disappeared around the curve.

Feeling royally loved and royally fed, she ate and looked at him through the misty eyes of love. Jake was so considerate in so many ways, like shopping for the food so they didn't have to bother getting it in, when they found the time to be here together. She moved to his lounge and said, "Thank you, darling, for a lovely evening."

"I was thinking the same thing. It has been lovely but, honey, it ain't over yet." He kissed her, then got up and pulled her to her feet. He wrapped her in his arms, kissed her again with fresh wanting, then murmured, "Forgot to tell you what hoe cakes do to me, darling. I need to love you one more time." His news seemed a bit much at the moment.

"Jake, I don't--" He picked her up, put his mouth on hers, walked, still kissing her, all the way to his bed.

Undressing her, his caresses won her over till he brought up again the other thing. Evidently she hadn't made her point before. Frozen, she jerked away, rolled out of bed, collected her scattered clothes and started dressing. In a dead voice, he said, "Anna, what are you doing?"

"Going home. I... I can't please you."

"Nobody said you can't please me."

"I'm saying it." Her near tears were in her voice.

"Hey, don't take it so serious? It's no big deal."

"I told you awhile back, I'm not into that."

"I said it's no big deal."

"Then why do you keep on instigating it?"

"Maybe I think it's something to share. Maybe I think we can if you'll loosen up. I want us to have it all. Maybe sometime you'll grow up."

"No! I won't grow up, as you put it. I have a place for that part of you but it damn sure ain't my mouth."

"How do you know, when you won't give it a chance?"

"Because just the thought's sickening to me."

"It isn't sickening. Lots of couples do."

"Lots of couples swing and do groupies, I'm not into that either. Are you?"

"Hell, no."

"I don't want you to feel deprived, anymore than I want to feel pushed into things. You need a new half of this couple."

"This ain't sixteen ninety. We got new values."

"And new venereal diseases, the most deadly ever. Got a brand new one, or one that's been lost for eons. I imagine AIDS has been around before. Like when the Romans got so perverted."

"You're the worst maze of contradictions I know."

"I don't know if I should say go to hell or thanks."

"And don't give a damn which one you say, woman."

"Wrong! You started out so uncontrolling. That's what made me love you."

"Hey, I don't try to control you or anybody else."

"Control has many names, ways and means. You can always identify it by how put down it makes you feel. You have trouble calling a spade a spade."

"Can't you let labels and spades slide?"

"It's always me taking up the slack when I do."

"Anna, I have no idea what you're talking about."

"Once a friend told me he felt sorry for women. He said a woman's wrong anyway she goes. If she won't allow anything, she's a prude. If she allows affection but won't go all the way, she's a tease. If she goes all the way she's a slut. It's the same, although he didn't get into oral sex. Frankly, my dear, I'm not into every bedroom trick anybody can conjure up, and don't intend to get into it. I thought the fact I have a few values made you want me. According to you, you already divorced one slut."

"And what was this smart friend to you?"

"Not a damn thing. And he was before your time. That makes it none of your business if he was."

"Was what?"

"Everything you're insinuating." His answer was a snort. "And I hear what that snort's saying. Now we're back from let's get kinky to who Anna ain't been a virgin with. The real problem is, you corralled the wrong Eve."

"Anna, would you translate that?"

"This Eve don't eat apples and I'm outta here. With all your hot contacts, you'll fix that in a flash with a phone call."

"I got no idea in hell what you're talking about."

"I'm talking about oral sex, you're into it and I ain't."

"You mean unless you're getting it!"

"Anytime I went along with anyone, it always backfired. It's damned if you do and damned if you don't. I don't care about getting it, that was to make you happy. But I damn sure can't give it. The thought makes me want to puke, so I don't see how we have a future as lovers or anything else."

"Guess you think I'm weird."

"I'm not talking weird or unweird. I'm talking choice, I'm talking preference, I'm talking need. You need someone who needs what you need. I need someone who needs what I need. So we don't need each other."

"Anna, everybody's into oral sex."

"I'm not. I mean it! You hear me?"

"Why can't you be free with yourself?"

"I am! That's why I'm in your bedroom without being married to you. That's why we're having this difference of opinion. That's why I'm getting dressed so I can get the hell out of here. Being free means choices, Jake. The last I heard, a choice still covers no as well as yes."

"You women are so sweet, like little girls and kittens till you start justifying your own shit. Then you'd claw the balls off a brass monkey."

"You don't have to worry about me clawing anymore. I'm not and never have been required company."

"Bitch, that's just how dumb you are!"

"I'm no bitch or dumb, you bastard son of a bitch!"

"I'm sorry, I know you're no bitch, but you can be dumb. You're required company to me and don't even know it. I meant to waltz around, have a great time and great sex with a hot wired woman. I knew not to fall in love with anybody, much less a libber like you. But no! Ole Jake couldn't be that smart or that frigging simple. I had to fall in love with your hot little ass! Ain't that a rip! Ain't that just a wild cat's ass, darling?"

"Guess that's my fault too!"

"Who else? The weatherman?"

All the velvet in his eyes all evening was gone. Now, there was only steel, now there was only Jake looking at her in that way, when she didn't know if it was rape or neck-wringing time. Either way, it was time to go, even if she had to leave without her left tennis shoe. But then she finally saw the damn thing under the edge of the floor-length drape. She jammed her foot in the shoe, grabbed her purse and bolted for the door.

As she turned the doorknob, he thundered, "Don't leave!"

His voice was a command she couldn't ignore, clearly he would get physical if she took another step. Any man could get physical if a woman pushed hard enough. Hell, it's how the bastards are built. She knew from the start he had a short fuse. Wanting to pet the tiger was part of why he attracted her.

She didn't want to push him too far. She didn't want violence between them after all the love and all the good. Shit, she didn't need the pain, he didn't need the guilt. He was already heart-heavy with guilt. Guilt was why he was an emotional wreck. Someone had put a mind-boggling guilt trip on him. That's what made him so insecure. No fear was in her eyes as she looked at him and moaned, "What else is there for us?"

Before she could move, he was out of the bed and she was in his arms. "Anna, in spite of everything, I love you and you love me. That's what there is for us," he said and kissed her like he would never let her go. When he felt her resistance die, he said, "Please, woman, please forgive me. I won't ever bring the other thing up again, darling."

It was late when she woke in his arms. The candle had burned low, but it gave off enough sputtering light for her to see his eyes were open. Vibes told her he had been watching her sleep. She kissed the hard biceps of one of his arms that held her, he pecked her on the forehead. "Jake, I have never been happier or felt more satisfied than when I'm with you."

"Is that why you spend so much time with Quarrells, because you're so damn happy when you're with me?"

Her negative vibes from the afternoon came rushing back and fell in place. Evidently she was going to have to be hit over the head before she really got it. He was never in a good mood when she had been out the night before with Clay and his music.

The little light in her slow mind burned brighter as he said, "Woman, in the first place, you don't have to go every place Clay and that old buzzard go. Clay ain't a baby. Hell, you just want to be with them more than with me."

"You know it's not like that."

"Then what? You tell me!"

"I'm like you, I want it all! You of all people, the original free spirit, the self-professed eternal child should understand that. The axis of your every day sits on doing precisely what you want to do."

"Anna, you still haven't told me why."

"Clay wants me to and I want to. We have dreamed about this forever, and don't slur Copper Jim. He's a fine man and my best friend."

"That old coot's a better friend than me?"

"Surely you know you're more than a friend. If you want to know my feelings toward you as a friend, anymore, you don't feel like a friend."

"Well, I do appreciate that, Anna."

"Well, you asked! Jim never says hateful shit. Jake, I don't know anymore if you're a friend, an enemy, or an addiction."

"What about when he asks for some? Gonna be his friend then?"

"God, man, you're sick!"

"You'll find out how sick when he lays a big paw on you out running the streets with him every night. He ain't doing all this for nothing."

"If you're so worried, why don't you come with us?"

"I don't want to, Anna. Can't you understand that?"

"No problem! If I can understand you don't want to, you can understand I do want to. I've had all your bullying about it I can take. I was right earlier, we need to stop seeing each other awhile."

"No, we don't need to stop seeing each other. You're right about the nuts part. I am. You make me nuts, you always have! You know that, Anna."

"I don't even know what you're talking about."

"I'm nuts about you, that gives you too much power over me."

"If I had power over you, you'd have been at graduation, going to shows with us and at Clay's demo session."

"I have other things I have to do."

"I just want the understanding from you, you want from me."

"The Bible says men are to be over women and run the house."

"Bullshit!"

"That ain't bullshit, that's the truth."

"Here's the truth: Clay's career is something we have talked about, dreamed about, planned on and worked on for years and years. There's no way I can believe God would bitch about me helping my boy make his dream come true. You're sounding too much like a fool husband to suit me."

"Well, I'm the last fool you can plan on blowing my head off over your ass."

"Good! Once was more than enough! Let's quit talking shit, Jake. You can't believe how Clay sang in the studio and the Golden Goose."

"I didn't ask you here to talk about kids."

"It isn't possible for me not to talk about Clay. I love you, but we've gone as far together as we can."

"Anna, you don't mean that, you don't want that."

"No, but that may be the way it has to be. I don't want to be miserable and I won't make you miserable. If we can't be good to each other and good for each other, why prolong the agony?"

"Then don't. Kiss me, and let me love you again."

"We can't keep hiding our incompatibility in sex."

"Incompatible? Lord, you're wired hot and real and beautiful. It don't get more compatible. The other don't matter, it's whatever you want. Come on, doll. Please, baby," he said, moving her to the bed.

"Join me instead of judging me and prove it."

"Prove it how?"

"Go with us tomorrow night to Clay's writers night."

"All right, come on back to bed." She was not convinced but she had to try.
"Jake, I have your word? You promise?"
"Yeah, darling. Come on back to bed now and love me."

The next evening, it was no surprise when he called to cancel. Somewhere in her sub-conscious she had known. It was like a re-run as he told her there was no way he could make it. She had suspected him of lying before. It was her first time to be sure as he said, "Darleen called, I have to take Carol somewhere. Darleen said something came up and she's tied up."
"Bet I know what came up."
"Forgot you're psychic," he growled. "What?"
"A damned lie."
"Well, woman, tempt a man to lie for sex-- he will every time."
"Man, here's you a news flash," she said calmly. He claimed no psychic powers, but he did pick up on how pissed she was though her voice was cool. "Don't lie often to an honest woman." She should have known. Hell, maybe she did! What was one piece, more or less, in an effort to save love that had dripped sweet as ripe watermelon. "One lie too many, lies an honest woman past caring, or wanting to make love to your lying ass. And, stud buddy, I am."
"Little darling, you're as hung up on me as I am on you."
"Yeah, right! But from now on, don't call me, I'll call you."
"You don't mean that. The woman in my arms moaning and loving last night don't mean it either." His conceit was sickening, like the night he bragged about all the girls so hot to come to his house from class.
She snapped, "Asshole, try me!"
"You'll call when you want some of old Jake."
"Don't hold your breath," she fired and hung up.

As Clay thought, when he picked the two ballads, tonight he was more at home on the Golden Goose stage.
His mother listened carefully, as he sang the songs with only a guitar break between. In her mind, in a word, he was great. The crowd gave him a standing ovation, then insisted on two encores. Clay did their new song called "Lost Love" and brought tears to Anna's eyes. Her anger had cooled and she felt sick with missing Jake.
Clay finished with another standing ovation and shouts for more. He would have done another song but Jim motioned it was time to stop and they stepped off the stage. As they took their guitars off and put them in the cases, Clay said, "Thanks for getting us off."
"That's my job. Can't get fascinated by your own voice and hypnotized by applause till folks who hollered more go to thinking, I can't stand no more!

When you hit a crest, it falls. Don't care who you are, human ears tire of the same sound, quit while they want to hear more."

When Clay returned to their table, Anna said, "You get better every time you walk on stage, darling."

"I love to share our songs, Mama."

"That's why you come off so well on stage."

"I don't mean to pry, but at supper something was bothering you. While I was singing 'Lost Love' you were crying. Did you and Jake split?"

"Clay, I... yes. Yes, we did."

"Maybe y'all can patch it up."

"Not this time."

"I'm sorry you're hurt, Mama, but he isn't right for you."

"No, Clay, but I love him so."

"I know," he said, understanding her pain. "Hey, looks like we lost Jim."

"Some man over there stopped him. They're talking like it's someone Jim knows. Maybe you do too."

Clay looked around at Jim talking to an older man wearing a cowboy hat. "Not anyone I know, Copper Jim knows everybody."

The next songwriter, setting up a keyboard, gave Copper Jim and the stranger time to talk. When the songwriter on stage started singing, they walked across the room and out the door.

Clay and Anna had heard two more songwriters when Jim and the stranger came to their table. Jim said, "Want y'all to meet a buddy of mine, Junior Finney. Junior, meet Anna and Clay Hill."

"Ni... nice to meet you, folks. Clay, I had to shake the hand of a ne... new star rising. Yes, sir, a new star rising for a fact."

"Mr. Finney, I thank you. Can you join us?"

"Gotta go, Clay. Call me Junior. Just wanted to say you write, pick and sing great. Knew when I sa... saw you with Copper Jim you was good. He never did fool with no-talent, talent. Miss Anna, it's goo... good to meet you."

"Thank you. Same here, Junior. Won't you sit down?"

"No, ma'am. Got to wa... watch an act in Printer's Alley. Just wanted you all to know how much I enjoyed the music. It's a plea... plea... nice to hear a hit artist. Be seeing y'all." Junior tipped his hat and left.

Jim said, "I need some grapefruit juice, how about y'all?" The Hills agreed. After placing their order, Jim said, "Junior scouts for a big producer."

Anna asked, "Should we have given him a tape?"

"If his boss comes to our next writers night, give him one then. I ain't one to look at eggs and count chickens. Junior's boss don't cotton to me. Wrote songs for him till we agreed to disagree. Might still feel hard, ain't no use wasting tapes. He's a feller by the name of Gunnar McGuire."

"The Gunnar McGuire?" Clay asked.

"Yep, partner. If he meets our terms, ain't nobody better."

Anna said, "But can you work with him, Copper Jim?"

"Well, creative control killed our deal, way back when. My records made some quarters drop in the juke box, but I wasn't ever no superstar potential.. Since Clayboy is, we got big clout in contract negotiating. And, Annie, you got a head on your shoulders. We'll talk it all out and hire us a good music lawyer. If we contract with McGuire or the Pope, we gotta hold creative control."

Anna said, "What if McGuire won't go for it?"

"Oh, he'll growl and holler outrage, use any trick in the book. But, if we just stand our ground, we got old Gunnar."

"How can you be so sure?" Clay asked.

"Because he ain't no fool. Well, except maybe about music. He's a damn sharp fool then. Made a king's fortune in it. He sure knows a twenty-four karat superstar when he gets lucky enough to hear one."

CHAPTER 17

THE NEW LONG BRANCH

Junior sat in front of McGuire's boxcar of a desk. Junior's job meant hanging out in the clubs till two or three in the morning, so his workday seldom started before afternoon. Nobody who was anybody started work before ten but Boss. Boss was always in his office early. He was different about lots of things. That was why Junior worked for him in the first place.

He didn't really have to work for anybody anymore. He still made a thousand or two a quarter in royalties. His old records weren't dead yet. Then Boss got the government check to coming every month; paid him for scouting besides. Junior Finney didn't have to dance to nobody's jig if he didn't want. Like Boss here on the phone all day. Junior didn't know how the man stood it, but Boss wasn't no fool. He could butt heads with the toughest, come out on top most of the time and still be honest.

Junior couldn't sleep most nights till daylight anyway. When a man spent years performing all night, he was likely to get his days and nights crossways. Even before he got his head banged up in a mugging. Coward bastards had to sneak up behind him from a dark alley. Otherwise he woulda put them to sleep permanent. Junior never lost a fair fight, ever.

He was uncomfortable in McGuire's Sixteenth Avenue office, like always in plush places. White carpet two inches tall, he reckoned, made Mr. Gunnar feel rich. It made him feel like maybe he didn't wipe all the cow shit off his boots. Couldn't really figure that one, he hadn't been around cow shit in years. Probably been better off if he'd never left it, like his brother said. But he hadn't missed cows or cow shit either.

Boss would be mad at what he had to say, so he had to say it soft as he could and still do his job. Junior waited, whetting his pocket knife on his boot heel. Some folks could sharpen knives that way. Some folks could shit you, too. He never could tell much difference in his knife, but it occupied his hands. His hands felt left out when they wasn't picking.

Boss hung up again and told Annette to hold his calls. Junior's yellow eyes returned the man's brown glare without fear. McGuire said, "Hang on one more minute," and made another note with a gold pen.

"It's your ni... nickel," Junior cackled. He'd been facing music honchos for years. Boss was honest, some music honchos were crooked as a snake. If they was still alive, Frank and Jesse could throw away their guns and rob legal. Robbing folks who made the music brought way more than bank robbing. If you was a singer, they'd rob you of your singing royalties. If you was a writer, they'd rob you of your writing royalties. If you was a picker, they'd rob you with damn under the table kickbacks.

Lower Broad thugs were saints next to Music Row sharks. Had to be watchful as an old maid in a cat house about who to do business with. Music sharks swam the Row eight days a week and a whiff of money made them attack. They'd who-do their mama if they smelled money in her purse. Anymore, his head was too fuzzy to lay it all out, it wasn't too fuzzy to know it was so. He'd be ashamed if he was some folks, pulling rank to get their names on songs they never wrote a word or note on. Good side to getting past writing, it put the pencil pimps past dogging you.

McGuire laid his gold pen down. "Now, what were you saying?" Junior was off in a memory. "Junior? Hey, Junior!"

"Huh? Wha... what's that you're saying, Boss?"

"I can't believe this about Ginny Ann. I've been in the business too long to start doing everything wrong."

"I... I was saying my opinion you asked for, and doing my job you pay for."

"Damn, I did ask and you told me. When I ask for an opinion, I try to listen to someone who'll be honest. Junior, I am sorry."

"Big business like you got puts a lot on you. Junior don't take exception."

"Ginny Ann is a good young singer. Thought a few months on stage might polish her to recordable. These days there ain't no Patsy Clines. I need a new act that just smells like a star. Since I lost the Duncan Duo, it's been slim pickings. Damn crashing jets to hell, anyway."

"What you ho... hoped ain't come true, she's just another singer. Might sell a few records, but she ain't got the heart to be a star. She's struck on herself and it shows. Like her hassling the band. She was thrilled for a chance when you got her show clothes and pay to sing. Now she's so uppity it's sickening. She's gor... gorgeous, got a decent voice, but getting struck on herself won't get it. We got stars that can't sing no better, but they're nice. Least in public."

"You're telling me, Ginny Ann is a bitch?"

"Hate to say... say it that way."

"Hate, hell! This is business, not a fan club. Give me the bottom line."

"I... I give you the bottom line when you asked me about her last year. You was thinking more on her stu... stuff than her voice then."

"I knew she was no canary. She sings okay and she is a knockout. Girl singers have built careers on less. Hell, how often do you hear a voice?"

"She don't wri... write worth a shit, she's got the heart of a whore. She may be a good lay, so screw her and forget her si... singing. She'll cost more than she'll make. Now, wha... what else for you?"

"Think you covered it, Junior. Got anything else?"

"Found this boy that's a gre... great singer and picker. Him and his mama write great songs. They ju... just started doing the writers nights."

"I don't need a boy, or a mother riding shotgun."

"Ain't no boy boy. He's grown. Co-writes with his mama. On his own, too."

"Family can be a pain. Especially an old mare and her colt."

"Se... seems to me, the Judds done fi... fine."

"The Judds are a rare exception all the way around."

"This kid is too. Som... somebody's gonna sign him. I'd like to see it be you," Junior said, nodding in agreement with his own statement. "They're nice folks. The mama's a lo... long way from being an old mare."

"Wouldn't be struck on the mama, would you?"

"Not enough to warp my judgment of... of her boy's singing. Nice to meet a lady, for a change." He grinned his two front teeth, missing grin.

"Uh, oh! Look out here, Junior."

"Cou... country ain't like pop. Got to do some living to write country right. The mama has, and the boy's a magi... magician with chords and picking. Him being young, keeps their lyrics right for the young fans."

"Who does he sing like?"

"There's something Hank, something Elvis, something black and blue and something I ain't never heard. You li... listen cause he feels and sees things you do and can't put in words. He stands up there singing it all, and pi... picking a Martin like I can't even dream."

"You're describing what I'm looking for."

Junior cackled. "Why you think I'm telling you?"

"Okay, you win. Where can I see them?"

"Gotta have a pro... promise before I tell you."

"What are you talking about?"

"Hell, a promise! I ain't talking Greek. Shi... shit!" McGuire knew when Junior was tired of talking. Junior had spent most of his career bumming around in joints on Lower Broad when he should have been on hit albums. His number one hit hadn't hit, but Junior had an album out making money, and a good paying gig in Printer's Alley. He was staying sober and had investors talking putting big money behind him till one night, he was walking to a joint on Lower Broad to a "git down" picking.

Between Printer's Alley and Lower Broad, two thugs stepped out of the dark and hit Junior in the head one time too many. He still had great ears for talent worth developing before big money got it signed. When Junior had the look of a mischievous child that might not share a secret, you better give your milk down if you wanted in on what he knew. Gunnar said, "What promise?"

"You ta... take them like they are or leave them alone."

"Finney, every singer or writer needs polishing."

"Not Cla... Clay Hill. Somebody's gonna make a bank full of money on these folks. Somebody who knows a gold mine whe... when they see it. All they need's an album out, promotion and bookings."

"Hell, any singer needs polish."

"Who po... polished the singing brakeman, or Roy or Eddie? Who polished Emmylou's treble or Chet's fingers? If you gotta redo their bra... brains, they'll go home. And like I said, I promised a friend."

"I smell something. Do I know this friend?"

"Well, yeah. Guess yo... you do."

"Now, we're getting to the nitty-gritty. What friend?"

"Don't get ma... mad, it's Copper Jim Quarrells."

"You know damn well I know Quarrells. At least I thought I did. You know he wrote for me for a while. Wrote some hits we're still making royalty money from. Jim would've been a Hall of Fame writer if he'd dumped that bitch he was shacked up with, left the bottle alone and listened to reason."

"Wou... woulda if he coulda," Junior said softly.

"Melba was a slut after she got hooked on dope."

"You ever been ho... hooked on a woman?"

"I've loved women, if that's what you mean."

"Ho... hooked on a woman's like whiskey, pills, and coke all put together. You know she's rotten, but you can't stay off her and ca... can't stay on her."

"Nope, I don't guess I have, not like that."

"If you ain't walked in the shoes, you can't understand. That was the case with Jim and Melba Mullenberg when y'all fell out."

"He never told me anything about it."

"Cou.. could you tell something like that?"

"Maybe not. How did he get over her?"

"He di... didn't. She overdosed."

"I remember now. She was a hard country singer. Died a few years back. Never knew she was Copper Jim's woman. Wonder why he didn't tell me?"

"You and him had music differences before he went ape shit over Melba. Then he got so hard to work with, you wouldn't dem... demo none of his songs. For two years, before his contract ran out, you wouldn't look at his so... songs or release him so somebody else could."

"He wasn't writing anything worth demoing."

"Boss, drunk or sober, good times or bad, Copper Jim's a hell of a songwriter. Got his own style and his own way. He ain't into co-writing like you wanted him to, but Jim's a fine songwriter. You was both going through a bad time at the sa... same time. I love you both," Junior said. His yellow eyes were saying, If you don't like that you can kiss my ass.

"That was when I was going through a divorce."

"Anyway, he didn't come to me, I we... went in the Golden Goose. It's one of my now and then stops. Happened to catch Copper Jim and Clay on stage. I couldn't believe my ears so I hung back in the crowd. They was asked to come back again. Waited till the next night before I talked to Jim. Hadn't seen him in a long ti... time. He was Melba's band director and rhythm picker but he was a lot more than that. Melba wouldn't stand before a mike on sta... stage or in a studio without him. After she died, Jim left music and devoted himself fu... full time to the bottle for a spell.

"I'd see him at Lacy's some. He'd always be shit-faced but he ain't a loud dru... drunk. The drunker Jim gets, the quieter he gets. You know how he loves to talk; drinking, he's quiet as a rock. Don't say nothing but "gimme another beer." Lacy stayed open no matter how la... late till he got ready to go, then Lacy'd drive him home. We thought he was a goner. Never expected to see him sober this si... side of Jordan."

"How did he get off the bottle-- or is he?"

"Got a DUI. You know co... cops, once they get your number. A red truck with co... cow horns on the hood ain't hard to spot. Jim wound up with more DUIs and sentenced to community service. Started a music class and Clay Hill was a student. Knowing Clay and his mama got Jim off the bottle. I asked where they were performing next, said you might take a listen. Jim don't want the boy's style cha... changed. Says he coulda got the boy a label at sixteen."

"Why didn't he?"

"Didn't want Clay robbed of ti... time to develop. And his daddy killed himself. Thought the mama thought more of Clay than him."

"Hell, all mamas think more of their babies than they do husbands or themselves. Have to, to keep from pinching their squalling heads off."

Junior chortled, "You ki... kill me, Boss."

"After all this sneaking, I got to hear this boy."

"Jim says just don't let on in front of Clay ti... till you make up your mind. If you ain't interested, he won't be no wiser and won't feel bad. Says they been through hell and don't want them getting fa.. false hopes."

"I can understand that."

"Got your pro... promise on not trying to change them?"

"You got it. Where can I hear this boy wonder?"

"The Ne... New Long Branch writers night."

"Good God, Jim Quarrells can't think much of this kid playing him there. That dump's for writers just off the bus."

"Wasn't on no bus, he's fro... from Nashville."

"Hell, Nashville natives have enough sense to stay out of music. Nobody born in Nashville wants to be a star."

"He does. Ju... just needs a showcase at Connie's."

"I thought you said they just hit the Row."

"Whe.. when he told me they need a showcase at Connie's, it hit me li... like it is you, but he's right. He don't know the new bunch running things on the Row. He ain't got the clout to get a showcase, but that's what the kid needs. Cause a peach ripens early, ain't no call to leave it hanging on the tree. Making a star ain't like seniority at the mill."

"Is their material unpublished?"

"Unpublished as dew. Doubt they know what publishing means."

"Hell, I never figured on another writers night, but if it pukes me I'll be there. You paint too good a picture to miss."

Sign up was at seven, Copper Jim wanted Clay signed to perform by ten. That was the ideal slot to catch anybody who was anybody in the business. Even the Row honchos might drop in for a drink to listen and relax awhile before calling it a day. By ten the business folks had thinned out. The New Long Branch had a bigger listening room than most songwriters nights.

In a hard town for bands, Duke Lee kept his band booked in one of the motel chains at least two nights a week year round. Duke's format was more entertaining for the motel's guests than the typical songwriter fare that was usually a songwriter who wasn't any great shakes as a singer and backed with only his not so great guitar or keyboard accompaniment.

Duke's show consisted of his performance and his five piece band accompanying the writers singing their songs. The writers only had to furnish chord charts to perform original songs. They could also furnish their own accompaniment or sing to music tracks Duke would play through the PA system. Clay and Copper Jim had worked up charts on his original songs and they were excited about a chance to play with a new band.

Remembering Anna liked a table far enough back in the crowd to pick up on audience response, Jim led the way to a table halfway to the stage and said, "This okay with you folks?" Anna and Clay agreed that it was. Jim pulled a chair out for Anna facing the stage. "Set yourself down and relax, Annie, while Clay and me get signed up and put our guitars up."

Clay followed Jim to stash their guitars with the others to the left of the stage. Then they walked over to the bar and Jim signed the yellow legal pad with the spaces already numbered one through twenty-five for the songwriters to sign up. Any performer was free to sign any open space. Jim signed Clay's name on the open number eight line.

"Hey there, Woodrow," Jim said, then introduced Clay to Woodrow Sullivan, a session keyboard player.

When Jim and Clay sat down at the table with Anna, the first songwriter of the night was already on stage. He was picking enough of his song for the drummer to get the feel and tempo. When the songwriter and the drummer understood each other, the drummer signaled Duke to make the introduction.

The songwriter and the band got off to an even start and were performing the songwriter's second tune as Gunnar and Junior walked in. Out of respect for the efforts of an obviously neophyte tunesmith, who would never be a singer, one of the most powerful names in country music stood waiting till the not so young and very unpromising songwriter sang his song.

While applause covered their footsteps, walking on tiptoe so his boots were quiet, McGuire advanced into the room followed by Junior. He spied two vacant stools at the end of the bar.

The bartender was there before they warmed the stools with, "Evening, Mr. McGuire. Can I get you something?"

"Evening. I'll have Black Jack and branch. What's yours, Junior?"

"Take a long ne... neck Falls City."

When their drinks came, knowing it all started with a songwriter, Gunnar settled down, determined to take the program in good grace.

An hour later, after the band had braved the third songwriter and six God awful songs, Gunnar knew all over again why he hated a writers night. Most songwriters were pitiful, till they had written forty or fifty terrible attempts at writing a song. Usually, it took the best prospects five years to learn the craft. Most of those he heard tonight hadn't been weaned off their mama five years. Songwriters had to start somewhere, but he wished they had more sense than to howl their premature babies in public. A Mongolian idiot would know better.

He signaled the bartender and ordered another Jack and branch and Junior another beer. He envied Junior looking around, grinning at the room in general and sucking contentedly on his beer. Junior had a good time anywhere he went, if he didn't drink too much Falls City. He was a crying drunk and obnoxious as hell, but he seldom drank too much. It might be worth getting hit on the head one too many times if it left you that contented. Junior knew good songs as well as himself, but he was sitting there enjoying every note of this shit! The band had to be wanting to pick in the worst way to stand this gig.

He hated pulling rank, but he couldn't stand any more. "Junior, can you get Duke Lee over here?"

"How soon you want him, Boss?"

"Now! And tell him to bring his roster."

Junior slid off his stool, walked to the end of the stage and signaled to Duke waiting for the next writer teaching his song to the drummer. Gunnar saw Duke walk over to Junior and exchange a few words, then go to his lead picker for a brief exchange before walking off stage and following Junior.

The picker was introducing the writer as Junior introduced the two men.

Duke said, "Mr. McGuire, I appreciate you coming to catch my show."

"Duke, call me Gunnar. When is a writer named Clay Hill coming up?"

"I'll check." Duke ran his finger down his clipboard. "Clay Hill has five writers in front of him."

"If you want a week's gig in my Cockfight Club, put him on next and call me tomorrow."

"Gunnar, you got it! And thanks."

"You're welcome. I can't take anymore of this torture."

"What if you had it three nights a week?"

"I'd get a day job! Every songwriter up has been outhouse awful."

"Gotta get back on stage. Gunnar, your boy's up next."

"Junior, this kid better be platinum or your ass is grass."

Junior cackled, "Go... gonna knock your socks off, Boss."

On stage, Duke Lee picked up his guitar and helped finish the song in progress. Then he stepped up to the mike to say, "Ladies and gentlemen, get ready for a real treat. Our next songwriter is Clay Hill."

At their table, Clay said, "I was number eight."

"Yeah, you sure was," Copper Jim confirmed.

Again Duke Lee said, "Clay Hill, you still here?"

Clay threw up his hand and yelled, "Yo!"

"Get on up here, man. Give him a hand, folks. This is Clay's debut on the New Long Branch stage."

Clay said, "Copper Jim, what's going on?"

"Son, looks like we are. Let's go." He had seen Junior and Gunnar, he could smell a McGuire string pulling a mile off. Wasn't no use to make Clay nervous telling him Gunnar was here.

At the bar Junior cackled. "Boss, you do ge... get things done." Gunnar watched Clay Hill and Copper Jim on stage. Jim distributed charts to the musicians while Clay taught the drummer the beat of his songs.

Duke Lee took those moments to say, "This is a workshop for songwriters and performers. The singer songwriter is the most happening form of talent the labels are looking to sign. It makes us proud to give new songwriters and performers a forum to develop their talent. We don't allow any judging or tomato throwing. Folks, our next writer has done his half minute rehearsal. I'm proud of my musicians. They play by the number system written on chord charts. The band has never heard these songs. Now, ladies and gentlemen, for his first time with the Nashville Songwriters Band, Clay Hill!"

Stationed at the mike, Clay gave the band the count off, then started an upbeat song called *Mountain Fiddle Hoedown Rap*. Right off the crowd was clapping and toe tapping. When he ended the song, an avalanche of applause followed. Then the band hit the sixteen bar turnaround leading into his and Anna's new ballad. Clay arranged the song for the band to end the intro on a diamond chord, then he sang the first two lines of the song a cappella. The hush of the band, then Clay's baritone far beyond one so young, brought a reverent silence from the crowd. For four and a half minutes, it seemed no word was spoken and no glass was clinked. When he had sung the tag, strummed an ending diamond chord, Clay bowed his head.

The crowd was on its feet clapping and screaming. Gunnar was on his feet like any fan. He couldn't hear Junior's cackle but he knew the, I told you so look on his face. Junior shouted, "What'd I tell you?" Drowned out by the claps and shouts, McGuire could only nod and smile. When the crowd quieted, Junior said, "What do you think of Clay Hill now, Boss?"

"Junior, you found me a superstar."

As Clay introduced his next song, the crowd fell silent. After he had sung the song and followed with two encores, and while they still demanded more, Clay and Copper Jim left the stage.

McGuire came off his bar stool with tears in his eyes, a man creatively on fire, applauding like the newest country music proselyte. He'd kill to produce this boy! Hill's performance satisfied a craving in his producer heart like a fix does an addict. This all-American looking kid had lifted him higher than any raw performer ever had. Hallelujah!

Clay Hill had it all! His performance reassured McGuire he was still soul deep in love with country music. His lack of passion the last few years was because there hadn't been much to get passionate about. There was so little that lit that special fire in a music lover's heart. Clay was the first singer to bring tears to his eyes since his last Elvis concert.

Even with the mike, Duke Lee was having trouble being heard over the crowd's applause and demands for more. "Clay! Hey! Talk to me, Clay Hill!"

Clay was halfway back to the table when he heard Duke. "Yeah, Mr. Lee?"

"Isn't this your first time to perform with us at the New Long Branch?"

"Yes, sir," Clay answered.

"Then you have dues to pay. Anybody who sings and writes like you do, can't walk away scot-free. Do you promise to pay?"

Suspecting Duke was putting him on, Clay said, "Well, sir, what do I owe?"

"You have to promise to pay, or we feed you to the green monster backstage. Right, folks?"

His question prompted shouts of "Yeah" and "Gotta promise to pay up."

Grinning, Clay agreed, "Okay, guess I better promise."

Duke said, "The price is you come back and be our special guest at the New Long Branch and do forty five minutes of your songs. Okay, Clay?"

"I'd be honored to pay dues like that. Thank you, sir!"

"Give him another hand, folks. Up and coming, multitalented singer songwriter, Claaaaay Hill!"

After Junior introduced him, after he was seated at the table, after he and Jim spoke a few words, Gunnar was still moved by Clay's performance. From the bar, he hadn't seen the mother looked as good as the boy sounded. One look in her purple eyes had him as zonked as her son's music. At that moment he didn't know which he wanted most, the singer or the mother. Maybe he could have both. He decided not to waste time skirting the crux of the matter.

When McGuire gave his milk down right off saying, "Clay, I don't know when I've been so entertained or so impressed," it was hard to know who was more shocked, Junior or Jim. Gunnar went on, "I hear you want to be a star."

"Well, I'm sure hoping."

"I'd like to help that happen." Gunnar's dark eyes boring into Clay's violet look saw his eyes were older than the rest of him. "You won't ever be sorry."

"Sir, I can see that. I'm grateful for your interest and kindness."

"You're welcome. Here's my card. Can you come to my office tomorrow?"

Clay said to Anna and Copper Jim, "Is that convenient?"

Anna said, "I can't. Could I call you tomorrow for an appointment?"

"Of course." He saw she had the same midnight blue eyes as her son.

"I'd like to give you Clay's tape that Copper Jim produced. There are four of Clay's original songs."

"Great, thank you. Anna, would Monday work, say around one?"

"Well, yes, for me. Copper Jim, Clay, what about you all?"

Clay said, "Great. How about you, Copper Jim?"

Clay saw Copper Jim was wearing the poker face he got when something didn't suit, but he said, "Yeah, sounds fine."

"See you all then," Gunnar said. "Again, Clay, thanks for your music."

Watching Gunnar leave, Clay said, "It's so cool getting to meet a legend."

"Could be cool, him getting to meet a legend," Copper Jim drawled.

"What legend?"

"Why, you, Clayboy. Come next year."

CHAPTER 18
CONTRACT

Annette stopped typing and smiled. "Good afternoon."

"Hi, I'm Anna Hill."

"I'm Annett Mosier. Mr. McGuire's expecting you. Please follow me." Anna saw Annette had the figure of a Playboy Bunny as she knocked at the double walnut doors to McGuire's inner sanctum.

Standing at wall of glass, he smiled. "Nice to see you again."

"Thank you." Anna returned his smile.

"You'll find the blue chair comfortable. Would you like coffee or a drink?"

"No, thank you," she said taking the chair.

Annette left them behind closed doors as McGuire said, "How is Clay?"

"He's fine," Anna said. "Thanks for your interest."

"With proper management, he has a brilliant future."

"We already agree on that much."

He returned her smile thinking, She has the most disturbing eyes. "I expected Clay and Jim to be here."

"Clay hates the business of music. He's always said I was his manager. I didn't think he was serious-- it seems he was, and Copper Jim too."

"I've heard his tape and I'm delighted."

"I was hoping you would be. He and Jim put their heart and soul in that session. I think it shows. Honestly, I think it's good enough to press."

"Yes, with some work. The vocals are great, the songs are great. For an album, I'd steer the production more crossover."

"I think Jim wanted it traditional country."

"Country music has to cross over if you like big sales, and I do. It doesn't have to sound less country than jazz has to sound country. You just produce for a broader market. I try not to limit what I do, especially music. Clay has a classic American sound and songs that need to be heard."

"I'm not sure I understand what you mean."

"Songs like *Born To Lose* and *God Bless America* sound right in the country or in town. They sound right for denim or lace and touch the emotions. Clay's sound is so marketable. He has a fantastic future. I'd like to be part of it. I've never heard a raw, young artist on a par with him."

"Thank you, Mr. McGuire. Hopefully, we can work out an agreement."

"I see an enjoyable and profitable relationship," he said, thinking, In more ways than one. "Please call me Gunnar, may I call you Anna?"

"Yes," she said. He really was an attractive man.

"I understand you and Clay are Nashville natives."

"I'm from the Greenriver area. Clay was born on the west side, graduated in June from West Side High."

"Any college plans?"

"Music's all he wants. When a son gets to be over six feet, a mama has to listen more and talk less. I want Clay to be happy."

"I feel the same way about my son. Anna, if being a star will make Clay happy, he has a great chance."

"He thinks it will. But the music business is uncertain, and you hear such bad things. Like folks signing away homes and life savings trying to be a star. The dope, sleeping around and somebody always suing somebody scares me."

"Bad things happen in the music business, as they do in any business. I'm an honest businessman. Ask around and take the contract I plan to offer to your music attorney. I know some good ones, if you haven't retained one."

"We have a lawyer, but thank you."

Feeling she was not reassured, he went on, "There are many reasons for the bad side of the business. Music can make big money in a short time; with a mega artist, literally mountains of money. Many people have a streak of larceny at one price or another. Any contract depends on the integrity of the people involved. I believe we all have integrity, we'll make a fortune, and Clay will be happy."

"Clay being happy is the main thing."

"People work better when they're happy-- even hit artists. You want him to have his dream and so do I. I'm ninety percent sure I can get him a major label. As an independent producer, I work with all the majors. Red Springs is my choice. If we negotiate a contract, that will be my first door to knock on."

"I'd like to ask you one other thing."

"Ask me anything." He smiled to reassure her.

"Is creative control part of a standard contract?"

"No. As producer, I hold creative control."

"Clay wants creative control, and Copper Jim as co-producer with you."

"I'd welcome y'all's ideas. I'd never want Clay doing material he wasn't happy with, but creative control is what I get paid for."

"Clay says he can't function controlled creatively."

"He doesn't have a track record as a producer. Neither does Quarrells."

"He doesn't think of himself as a producer. He thinks in terms of controlling his creations; sounding like he wants to sound. He wants Copper Jim in his career. We both love Jim, he's been like a father to Clay. You should know, before I take any more of your time, these things aren't negotiable."

She heard the edge in his voice and saw the fire light his eyes as he said, "Anna, I don't think y'all realize what you are asking for."

"Yes, we do. Clay must have creative control, Copper Jim for his co-producer and me as his manager. We retain all writer's rights on our songs and half the publishing. The rest is yours."

She hated his condescending smile as he said, "Creative control isn't possible. Don't let Quarrells lead y'all down the yellow brick road, from our old problems."

"He says you're the best producer Clay could have. The stipulations I mentioned are Clay's, and the only way he will sign with anyone."

"Clay is only nineteen. If I agreed to such a contract, I doubt a major label would go along with giving a nineteen year old creative control, much less co-production to a man limited to a track record of penning some good songs and picking great rhythm guitar. Be reasonable. Please?"

"I'm trying to be. Clay isn't your ordinary singer, writer, picker or nineteen year old. So don't be fooled by his youth. He's as easy going as anybody you could meet except with his music. Musically, he won't give an inch."

"I stand in awe of Clay's music. But selling music I do know and I have the track record to prove it."

"He must follow his instincts to create. He can be guided, Copper Jim has been guiding him a long time. Clay has to control his soul. You can't tell the goose how to lay golden eggs, if you're lucky enough to find one that can."

"Anna, I'm a country boy, but we never had geese. I don't know normal or golden goose eggs, I know music. I learned the hard way to survive in a business I love. I mean to go on surviving. I'm more partial to limousines than the worn-out Ford that grunted me to town thirty odd years ago. I keep a picture of it and me. When I think I might be courting stupidity, I take the picture out and look at it to remind me of what being poor is like. I don't have the stomach for suicide, business or otherwise."

Wondering why the meeting was turning so abrasive, she said, "I don't have the stomach for suicide and neither does Clay." She liked McGuire, she knew at the Long Branch she liked him. He had rights, but she was on the other team. Nobody had to be the villain. Trying to sound like a good sport, she said, "Forgive me for taking up your time. Clay won't give up the right to approve of his own creations. You certainly have the right to approach your goals as you see fit. I'm sorry but this meeting's a mistake for all of us. Good day." With a sad smile, she swiftly walked out.

McGuire could not rise or protest. For the first time in his life, he had seen a woman who probably didn't have a hundred dollars ahead of her bills, quietly priss her pretty ass out on a multimillion dollar deal. She didn't even slam the door! He ran his hand through his silver hair and sat immobile for a good five minutes. Good day? Hell! Who did she think she was, Paul Harvey? He barked on the intercom, "Annette, get me Jim Quarrells on the phone."

She buzzed shortly with, "Information has no listing for Mr. Quarrells."

"Try the musicians local, Lacy's Bar and stop Mr. McGuireing and siring. Call me Gunnar, like I've told you several times!"

"I'm sorry, sir. I mean, Gunnar. I was taught in secretarial school not to use my supervisor's given name."

"This ain't school! Call Junior to help you find Quarrells. Find him if you have to hire a posse!"

"A what, sir, uh, Gunnar?"

"Posse. Don't you watch TV? Hold my calls unless it's Quarrells or Finney. Call Bry and tell him to be out front in ten minutes. Set up a meeting with Finney and Quarrells for two tomorrow. I'm going to the gym before I kill somebody. Clock me out, Annette."

"Sir?"

"Clock me out, I'm leaving for the day," Gunnar said as sedately as he could then shut off the intercom. This new girl's work skills were perfect but, God, she had no sense of humor. After a moment, he realized his own sense of humor was in short supply and got back on the intercom. "Annette, please overlook my briskness. When I seem abrupt, mark it down as the crazy nature of the crazy music business."

She giggled. "I've learned that much, Mr. McGuire."

"Gunnar, damn it, Annette! Gunnar!" he thundered.

He walked in Sadie's for lunch starved as usual. He seldom ate breakfast. Sometimes, after a recording session that ran till dawn, he loved breakfast. At five a.m., his normal time to get up, he never had the stomach to look an egg in the eye. For years he wanted to sleep late in the morning. Now that he was rich enough he could-- he couldn't. His workday started at seven before Annette came in at nine. He set aside noon till two for his sustenance meal and preferred to lunch alone.

With half a day's work done, he liked reviewing the morning and previewing the afternoon. This had been his routine since leaving his first office on Division Street. Back then he thought he hadn't time or money for two hour lunches at Sadie's. He could have eaten at a cheaper place, but he should have taken time to think. Like any job, thinking didn't get done without time.

Often someone joined him, but it didn't involve the host commitment of an invited guest. Business or social, he preferred eating with someone at the dinner hour with his day behind him. With the exception of recording, he never planned anything after dinner. He liked to give a dinner engagement whatever time it required, without risking the bad vibes that cutting someone short, of greater or lesser degree, could create. Tonight's peon in music might be tomorrow's winner, and vice versa.

He was enjoying a last cup of coffee when Millie, the mouth of Music Row, bounced up. He didn't mind buying her lunch, or listening to her mouth. In her way, she was a good old gal, and damn good to him. Rumor had it, Millie was into younger men in recent years. It was a hell of a note, but with the so called liberated ladies in powerful music chairs, not just aspiring young girl singers had the couch problem any longer.

Millie ran a major A & R department like a queen. He took care of her at Christmas and birthdays, she took care of him by getting his songs in the right hands. He pitched Millie first rate songs but he had pitched too long to imagine hit material was enough to get cuts. Old and new publishing houses went down the tube with hit material when they didn't know how to navigate the muddy political waters of Music Row.

"Got time for an old buddy, McGuire?"

"Always have time for you. Sit down." He stood and helped her get seated.

"McGuire, you're a monument to my motto."

"What is your motto this week?"

"It doesn't cost a dime to be kind."

"I'll buy that. You're looking good, like the new hair color." He did the flirting bit with Millie, bedding the bitch was out. She was sharp as a computer, but ugly as a frog. She was too old now and always had been too ugly. Surely she knew. Mirrors hung all over.

"You are so sweet," she said, ogling the young waiters. Sadie always hired handsome college boys.

"Try to be. So, what's the latest dirt?"

"Actually, Gunnar, it's about you."

"Me? Hell, I'm celibate as a monk."

"For once it isn't women. It's about your new boy?"

"What new boy?"

"The one with his mama and Copper Jim Quarrells in tow."

"How do you know that?" His surprise gave her a chuckle of satisfaction. She loved being in the know and usually was. Again, it hit his head Millie was a good example of why it wasn't smart business to put females in management. Like that pushy heifer he tried to talk business to yesterday. He'd get that straight when he met with Jim after lunch.

"I have my sources. Come on, what's going on with you and this kid? I hear he's something rare. Is he rare, McGuire?"

The waiter came to ask, "More coffee, sir?"

"Yes, and take Mrs. Hawthorn's order."

"Just coffee," Millie said, admiring the young hunk filling the waiting cup on the table. Then she lit a brown cigarette that looked as long as a pencil.

After the waiter left, Gunnar said, "It's not like you to skip lunch."

"I didn't come to eat. Eat is all I've done all morning. I came to get away from the office. Who is the young Adonis posing as our waiter?"

"His name is Stan. I'll find out about him if you like."

"Not unless he wants to be a star, he looks more like the law student type. With Sadie's connections downtown, she probably has him roped in."

"You don't think Sadie has the hots for young men?"

"Of course not, and oaks don't have acorns."

"Maybe your young Adonis has scruples."

"He's working in Sadie's joint, ain't he?"

"Touche. Does Sadie really have connections at the capitol?"

"Darling, don't be dense. How do you think she got a liquor license this near Alamo's church?"

"What exactly are her connections?"

"Sadie's had an affair for years, with the most influential judge in metro."

"And sex wins again, Millie, my friend."

"Sex or money or both, but don't go heavy on me. My spastic colon won't tolerate it just now. My office is nuts with a birthday bash for our token femme fatale. I can't get my work done. Hell, I can't get my loafing done. Plus, I've been submitting material for an up coming album for weeks. The producers have passed on every song I've picked and time is running out."

"Sounds like a weak act."

"The weaker the act, the harder they pick. We're down to the wire on Eddie Foster's session. They have only two songs and aren't crazy about those. Got a song for Eddie Foster to take folks' breath away?"

"Honey, Eddie's breath taking days are over."

"I know, the bastard sings like a crow. Too much coke, too many beds and too little rest. Eddie's worked way too much overtime as a sniffing and loving machine." McGuire knew Millie knew all about Eddie's loving machine.

"Need traditional stuff, not too rangy?"

"He has the range of a tea kettle. I know you hate to waste material on a has been, but he still makes money with good songs. He has the Opry and Branson. The older gals love Eddie. Actually they may be loving him to death. He never could say no." It amused Gunnar to watch Millie drift a moment with a memory before she said, "If you get a good song out, one of the hat acts may pick it up. They all do what Eddie started years ago."

"I got Copper Jim Quarrells songs that could be talked."

"Dear God, send some over. Speaking of Quarrells, tell me about your new boy. Say he's pretty good?"

"Pretty good, my garter belt. Try megastar."

"McGuire, please, today of all days, I don't need hype."

"No hype. Millie, your wildest recording dream's called Clay Hill."

"Got him signed? You and Quarrells had problems."

"Signed, sealed and delivered," Gunnar lied.

"Clay Hill," she mused. "Is he from Georgia?"

"No, born and raised in Nashville."

"Hush!"

"I'll send you his tape along with Eddie's songs. Junior scouted him. I didn't believe an act could be as good as he said, but the kid blew me away."

"I've never seen those black eyes of yours this excited about an artist. When can I hear him live?"

"When I showcase him at Connie's. For now, his tape is for your ears only."

Millie couldn't resist taunting, "What if I don't like him?"

"You will. You love ten talent as much as I do."

Annette smiled and asked, "How was lunch?"

"Beautiful. Are Junior and Quarrells here?"

"Junior is, Mr. Quarrells is on his way. Joan called, and Pete with Warners."

"Thanks. Send Quarrells in when he arrives." Joan knew when he had lunch, but she just had to call between twelve and two, then and now. Then she bitched when he wasn't in. Not now, thanks to his lawyer.

Gunnar walked in and growled, "Junior, where the hell is Quarrells?"

Junior pushed his hat back, then said, "He'll be here any mi... min... soon."

"Good." Gunnar sat at his desk and turned to look out on Sixteenth Avenue. It was an ordinary looking street but it had kept him fascinated all his adult life. "Junior, it's my time for a mega hit act."

"Yep, and Clay Hi... Hill's it."

Copper Jim irreverently strolled in saying, "This the meeting?"

Gunnar turned. "Yes, finally. You want a drink?"

"Naw. Old John Barleycorn got bigger than me."

"Junior, how about you?"

"Boss, I... I'm fine."

Gunnar said, "Quarrells, what's Anna Hill's problem? She hate money?"

"Hell, I don't know as Annie's got a problem."

"I see you haven't changed any."

"Not a speck, you the one changed. Seeing folks as having problems when they don't agree with you. Reckon you ain't changed back none."

"Back to what?"

"To who you was when you jumped the cotton patch."

"Quarrells, I don't know what you're talking about."

"I'm saying let the music be." Searing Gunnar with his eyes, Jim barked, "Junior, you said he promised not to try to change Clay. Was you lying?"

"Ji... Jim, you know Junior Fi... Finney don't lie!"

"Don't get your shit hot, Junior. Gunnar, you told Junior you'd sign Clay as is, or not at all. So, are you're a man of your word, or are you ain't?"

"You know good and damn well my word is my bond."

"So whatcha giving Annie a hard time for?"

Returning Jim's ice blue stare with dark fire, Gunnar snapped, "I was simply trying to make the woman rich."

"Well, if you don't aim to give Annie a hard time, if you're a man of your word, if you don't aim to change Clay, why fight for creative control?"

"God, they don't know pig wings about business."

"Naw, and business boys don't know pig wings about songwriters, who don't give a shit about the business of the music business. To keep the business side from eating the creative side was why she met with you. Annie ain't asked you for one bit of control on the business side."

"It amounts to the same thing."

"Pitiful part is it don't! Never did! Never will! You still can't see the difference between creating and business. You want to sign a feller to do something you can't do, then tell him how to do it. Some folks'd sign a cow, then tell her how to give milk. We couldn't work together years ago, guess we can't now. Thought you'd be the best producer Clay could get," Copper Jim said, starting to rise.

"You know damn well I am."

"Yeah, if you can accept he ain't broke and don't need fixing. Figured by now you'd signed enough plastic singers and cut enough plastic songs you'd appreciate a real singer singing the real stuff. Reckon not. Reckon you ain't even honest anymore, saying one thing, now dealing for another."

"What in hell makes you say I'm signing plastic?"

"What the hell makes you think you ain't? How long since you had a number one chart song that wasn't bought?"

"I don't buy chart space and you know it."

"Shit, that's why you ain't had nothing big lately. Why do you think name artists are cutting thirty year old copyrights, this day and time?"

"Maybe they like the songs."

"Wrong. They can't find new songs, wrote from the heart. The quack song doctors got the songs so concocted, fans that used to buy new records are buying reissues. Tried to tell you what it was coming to back when, a rock could see it now. The Nashville Sound's seldom as fish feathers, and country music's a endangered species. Use your noggin, man!"

"I don't need to be told how to run my business."

"I'm talking creating, don't know that much on business. But a man too smart to be told anything's in a dumb row of dumplings."

"I know my music," Gunnar growled.

"Thought I knew mine. Last few years, I've learned more from a kid, without all the eggshell pecked off his nose, than anybody. At creating music, Clay Hill was born knowing more than you and me, and a hundred more like us."

"Your point's well taken. Bottom line, do you want these folks with me?"

"Yeah, with creative control. Without it, naw."

"Why want creative control for a kid? As an artist, Hill is soaking wet."

"Take the cotton out of your ears! He's young, not dumb. Ain't been on stage enough to let loose all his energy, but you ain't stood in no line to sign nobody to compare. A Patsy or Elvis don't come along but once or twice a generation."

"And you think Clay Hill is in that league?"

"Know he is. Patsy come along so great, they didn't know what to do with her, either. If it hadn't been for Arthur Godfrey, don't guess they ever woulda. They told Elvis to go home. In house ears can be damn deaf, dumb and blind."

"I think maybe bitterness has made you nuts."

"Maybe, but it ain't made me stupid. And ain't nobody gonna screw with Clay or Annie's brains. You ain't neither."

"Quarrells, you don't even know what you're talking about."

"I know if you got backing money, they'll record your pet pig and hype him as the best act since sound. Let a miracle show up, they wanna mess with it. If they record a owl, they'd wanna tell it how to hoot. It was a sour note that swapped heart for market reports and sure things. Sure things stymie miracles for money farts. It's a blessing they don't run the baby factory. They'd decide the heads oughta look back instead of ahead so everybody could run around falling. That's why me and Clay put it off on Miss Annie to meet with you."

"When you finish blowing off, we'll get to negotiations."

"McGuire, years ago, I had all the negotiations I could eat. Let's just get real. Clay's gonna be the biggest act to hit music since microphones. Do you want him, and him keeping creative control, or do you don't?"

"When can you have Anna Hill back in my office?"

"Now, you listen real good. You come off the backroads of West Tennessee knowing the slop bucket from the water dipper. Somewhere between Sixteenth Avenue, Belle Meade mansions, Tennessee walking horses and Colorado ski slopes, you forgot your young, country raising."

"I haven't forgotten a damn thing. My raising didn't cover negotiating business with a mama's heart. Why wasn't I talking to you and the boy? It's no way to do business and you know it!"

"A contract is just putting on paper what folks agree to. What Bible says a mama can't negotiate for her own young'un?"

"Your kind of logic is why you don't write for me anymore."

Jim drawled, "Yours is why you don't write for you and never did."

"What in hell is that supposed to mean?"

"Tell him, Junior."

"Hey, I'm setting on my own roo... roosting pole, like a good Rhode Island Red. Don't get me in y'all's fight."

"Tell me what, Junior?" McGuire said.

"No use no... now, you ain't still trying to wr... write songs. But too mu... much business runs the song fairy off."

"What?" Gunnar boomed.

Copper Jim boomed, "Can't you hear? Too much business, too much logic, too much control and damn greed runs the song fairy off."

"Y'all know I tried my best to make it as a songwriter. Not everybody can! It has nothing to do with a song fairy."

"Hell, McGuire, that's why I couldn't keep writing for you."

"Let's get off old news and song fairies. I like money, but I'm not greedy. I'm one of the few publishers who gives fifty percent of the publishing on any top ten song to the writer. I give bigger draws and run them longer in a dry spell than anyone."

"And when a song hits, you get it back before the writer sees a penny."

"I do, and I'm not ashamed of it."

"That's why trying to tell you anything is so hard. You got no shame."

"Quarrells, could you accept, I don't want to be told anything? Would it be shameful to get on with business?"

"Nope. You don't have to cut a note Clay sings or Annie, if she ever does agree to sing. But if I'm what you're fighting, I'm after more track record as a producer. I need the clout to get Annie a label when it's time. Know you can't see no sense to that. In your book, a female over twenty's too old for a label."

"We don't have an agreement on the son, and you're talking mama. Can you do one thing at a time?"

"Yeah, but it's boring as hell. Anyhow, outside God Almighty, ain't nobody messing with their material or their minds. Clay don't need nothing but a deal. He's done a diamond, you need to shit or jump off the chamber."

"I asked six pages ago when you can have her here."

"I done had her here, next time you come to her. Draw up a standard record deal, giving you and me co-producing and Clay creative control. They get the writing, y'all split the publishing. She's gonna be Clay's manager. That leaves plenty of pie for everybody, as big a pie as Clay will be."

Knowing Jim could trigger his worst, Gunnar swallowed before saying, "Where is her office?"

"When the contract's done, send it by Junior. He'll find me if I'm amongst the living. If my lawyer says it's according to Hoyle, I'll call you and set up a meeting at her office."

Gunnar said, "You don't trust me?"

"Hell, Mohammed's done been to the mountain and got shit on. Like you told me once, trust is trust, business is business. This ain't my business, else I'd be dumb like always, and sign what you stuck under my nose."

Junior cackled, "Wri... writers don't ever le... learn."

Jim said, "That's the Jesus truth, hope to do better by the Hills. They won't get screwed over and hear it called business if I can help it."

McGuire said, "You make me sound real hard-nosed."

The blue daggers of Jim's eyes dug into the brown inferno of Gunnar's as he growled, "If the shoe fits." Unfolding from his chair, Jim drawled, "Like Uncle Ned used to say, set cramped up in the house too long. Need some fresh air, and a good country shit. You always did get my bowels in a uproar."

"I'm real sorry about that, Copper Jim."

"Yeah, I can see how all tore up you are."

~~~~~ **CHAPTER 19** ~~~~~

LACY'S

Junior knew a songwriter hard at it when he saw one. Copper Jim sat at his favorite table in the back corner, scribbling in a spiral notebook, his cowboy hat on the floor under his chair. Seeing Jim was in songwriting labor, Junior eased to the bar and claimed a stool. Lacy said, "How goes it?"

"Good. Ta... take a long neck Falls City." When Lacy brought the beer, Junior said, "Ho... how long's he been at it?"

"Since I opened at ten this morning."

Taking a swallow of beer, Junior checked the clock behind the bar, before he said, ."Lordy, it's fi... five thirty. Ji... Jim must be writing a good one."

"Yep," Lacy said, checking the clock too. "If he's lucky."

"What's he drinking?"

"Grapefruit juice, just pure grapefruit juice."

"He mu... must be really quit."

"Don't drink alcohol here anymore. If it was me downing all that grapefruit juice, I'd get the runs worse than a goose," Lacy said and walked down the bar to serve a patron. Junior and Copper Jim were his oldest friends, both had been coming in since right after he opened. Lacy's was an in-crowd bar in the alley between Sixteenth and Seventeenth avenues. First it was an army Quonset hut converted into a studio, then a short lived publishing house. Sherman Lacy ran it as a watering hole for folks in music.

Back in his drinking days, Copper Jim strolled in looking for a place to write. The big room with an empty back table felt like a good place. Jim sat down, started drinking and writing. The trick was to drink without getting too drunk to fight the writing. When he rolled down his sleeves and rolled up his spiral notebook, drunk but not too drunk, he told Lacy, "You got a good place. Ain't too pretty, but it's damned agreeable."

"I like that," Lacy said. When the songwriter who made eating money by making plaques came in, Lacy hired him to carve the plaque hanging behind the bar reading LACY'S on top and DAMNED AGREEABLE underneath.

Songwriters liked Lacy's since he didn't play taped music. As a failed songwriter, Lacy knew how hard it was to find a place to fight a pencil and paper war with no music. Another song was the last thing you needed, struggling to hear the song in your head already lower than a whisper.

As a recovered alcoholic, Lacy appreciated recovering chemical abusers. Like the sign behind the bar listed, he served fifty virgin drinks. Juice, coffee, tea, and soft drinks marked up two hundred percent made the same profit as alcohol marked up two hundred percent. When a man accepted he was never going to starve or get rich in his business, wringing every penny possible out of his customers was no temptation.

When all a man really craved was his time, the object wasn't how much-- but enough. Enough wasn't a king's ransom when a man wasn't into rich habits or rich people. Now his dream was to do as he liked, like who he liked, mostly songwriters, mostly broke songwriters and stay healthy.

Even name songwriters were broke or bent most of the time. Only a handful made any on going money. On the average, a songwriter made a one hit windfall that was gone in two or three years. That left the songwriter living on credit, writing for another windfall, and trying to remember how in hell he did it the first time. The music business kept songwriters underpaid and over critiqued. For Lacy, it made more sense to help an endangered songwriter, now and then, than some endangered bird.

He picked bass for the stars till his soul got road weary. He served his time fighting a songwriting pencil. Artists were always hungry for twenty-four carat songs. When you wrote ten carat tunes and that was the best you could do, it was time to break your songwriting pencils. Barkeep was the one secondary trade he knew that didn't feel like hard down work. A reasonable man could earn a reasonable living without working at unreasonable labor. Hard labor was beneath anybody with the brains to find the toilet by himself. Messed up a man's hands for picking even when it was only for fun anymore.

Reading appealed to Lacy, he kept paperback books stashed under the bar for when business was slow. When he finished one, he passed it on to some songwriter who happened in and loved to read, too. Paperbacks only cost a quarter at the Goodwill on Roy Acuff Place.

He had read all Hemingway's stuff. That's where he got the idea to pattern his bar after the writer and artist hangouts in Paris. Running a room where a writer was welcome to write long as he needed, whether he bought over one drink, was a good way to make a living.

He had lost out on his dream of being a name songwriter. But he had tried. It all came out pretty well. Lacy doubted he'd have been happier a millionaire with mansions and women. He had plenty of tables in his place, and a light bill or two ahead laid back in the bank. Long as his customers behaved, they were welcome. If a songwriter, man or woman, came in hungry, a bowl of beans and corn bread could be had free from the sideboard. He cooked up dried beans and corn bread every morning and sold it a dollar a throw.

Copper Jim and Junior were glad for Lacy's place. At their lucky table in the back corner facing the door, they had written well and made good money-- especially Jim. Now enough hit songs had been birthed at Lacy's, it was getting to be an attraction to the new crop of songwriters that blew in every spring green as the leaves budded out. Come October, about as many blew back out like the leaves leaving before winter.

Junior saw Jim hang his pencil in his shirt pocket and close his spiral notebook. He joined Jim at the back table, but his glazed eyes told he was still in his song. Junior worked on his beer till Jim said, "How you doing?"

"Good. Got you a hi... hit song going?"

"Chorus wrap-up line may not be strong enough yet."

"Sometimes it's ha... hard to tell," Junior said.

"It's strong as it's gonna be for now."

"I had some songs take a ye... year. Still be throw-aways."

"Hey, Tony," Jim said to a young man who walked up.

"Finished with your song so I can join you now?"

"Yep, if I'm lucky. Have a seat."s

"Thanks, Copper Jim." Tony sat down.

"Tony, meet one of my best buddies, Junior Finney. Junior, Tony came around awhile ago. I explained I had a songwriting hard on an asked him to come back when he saw me hanging my pencil in my pocket. Me and Tony met yesterday. He's come to Nashville to be a songwriter." Jim's indulgent tone indicated this might be the first time a Tony had crossed his path.

Junior knew the Tonys came to town every day. This Tony looked like the ink on his high school diploma might not be real dry. "Ple... pleased to meet you, Tony." Junior knew you never could tell what dreamer might write tomorrow's hit, stepping on a dream was bad luck like stepping on a grave.

"Pleased to meet you, Junior. I wannabe a songwriter more than anything. I been dying to meet writers like you guys for ages. My heroes are songwriters. Copper Jim has been giving me great feedback. I happened in here and met him yesterday. Came down to Nashville to be a hit songwriter. I know I have to write on napkins and toilet paper, drink booze and not eat right."

"Whe .. when did you get off the bu .. bus, Tony?"

"Monday. Got a room in a flea-bag hotel. Have to soak up all the atmosphere and inspiration I can before my money runs out."

"Don't know how much inspiration you'll so... soak up in a flea-bag hotel. Yo... you'll get a tow sack full of cockroaches."

"You're kidding me, Junior."

"Serious as a stud duck in ma... mating season."

"You don't think much of the legendary places?"

"All I... I think of them places is staying away."

"Well, tell me this, are my new cowboy boots all right?" Tony pulled his feet from under the table for inspection.

"Your bo... boots look fine to me," Junior said.

"To tell the truth they, kind of like, hurt my feet. The man at the store said I have to break them in."

"I like that black cowboy hat you're wearing, too," Jim said, doubting breaking the boots in would stop them hurting. He wouldn't walk out of a store in boots that hurt. Wasn't no use disheartening the boy. He'd done bit on the boots. A heart would bite on crazy things bit by the songwriting bug.

"Thanks. Copper Jim, you promised to tell me the quickest way to get ahead in the songwriting game."

"I did?"

"Yes, sir. Like I analyzed it before I left New Jersey, a hit country song, so much of the time, isn't but twelve lines. You know verse, chorus then verse again, that type song. I mean, how hard can that be? It's only a matter of getting serious and coming to Nashville and talking to the horse's mouth, if you catch the drift of my allegory. Right, fellows?"

A straight-faced Junior said, "Te... tell me too, how to get ahead in songwriting. But... but ho... hold off a day, and I'll sell tickets to it."

"Lots a folks already are selling tickets, one way or another. Yeah, Tony, I was gonna tell you, not that I think there's a chance you'll listen."

"But I will, Copper Jim. Really, I'm all ears."

"All right. Go home."

"Excuse me?"

"Go home, Tony."

"Hey, I only hit Nashville day before yesterday!"

"Boy, could I ask you something?"

"Sure, Copper Jim. Ask me anything you want."

"How many songs you got written?"

"Three and started a new one this morning. It's called 'Coming To Nashville.' You like that title?"

"Don't make no difference. It ain't commercial."

"But how do you know, you haven't heard it?"

"Every songwriter that comes writes a coming to Nashville song. Ain't but one been recorded and none that done any good."

"Well, I got ten more songs I'm working on."

"How many you got demoed?"

"What?"

"How many songs you got on tape, to compete with all Hank or Willie or Kris got recorded?"

"Actually, I don't have any of my tunes demoed yet. That's why I came to Nashville, to learn about the business."

"What instrument you play?" Copper Jim drawled.

"Well, I'm getting started with guitar lessons as soon as I find a teacher."

Jim guessed he'd done this routine two hundred times. "You strike me like somebody, with no learning, wanting to doctor and walking in a hospital hot to take somebody's tonsils out. Can't learn doctoring breathing hospital air or songwriting breathing Nashville air. Learn at home with folks who love you."

"There's nothing there about songwriting and no one there could care less."

Jim saw this kid was as determined as a hard-shelled Baptist at a Catholic convention. "Got yourself a job?"

"Not yet. My dad lent me a thousand dollars till I get started. I want a menial job, one that won't take my mind from songwriting, right away."

"You lose more than weight trying to eat dreams and demos cost. Reckon something menial will feed you and keep you off the streets?"

"Wha... what kind of work you in, Tony?" Junior knew Jim was out of patience and Tony wasn't going home.

"I worked in Dad's pizza place. He was teaching me the business and making me his partner. He isn't keen on me being a songwriter. Dads never do understand songwriters. Right, guys?"

Jim's look at Junior said, You come up with a come back to that. Digging in his jeans for money to pay Lacy, he said, "I gotta git." Like always, Junior was saying things that didn't say much on top, but said tons if a body listened deeper. In writing heat like he was, this kid wasn't listening to nobody.

"It's a bi... big turnover in songwriting. If you need a guitar, try the pawn shops on Lower Broad. At ti... times they got good deals."

As Junior started giving Tony a crash course on guitars, Jim gulped the last of his grapefruit juice and swallowed more than he took from the glass. At times the chute between the ignorance of the ignorant and the ignorance of the college educated was the tightest squeeze a bastard with horse sense oughta be trying to stand in. Hell, he didn't have any right to knock the boy. After all these years and as Row savvy as his ass was, he was fixing to climb on a fresh bronc by the name of Clay Hill.

At times he wished he never had picked up a guitar or a pencil, but he couldn't remember ever being as ignorant as this Yankee kid. At best, songwriting was a lean, long shot. Wasn't no need nobody hitting town till they could pick something besides their nose.

Jim settled up with Lacy then walked back to the table. Junior was still trying to enlighten a kid who didn't want to be enlightened. "An... and go by the Songwriters Association. They got all kinds of info... info... stuff."

"Do you agree with Junior, Copper Jim?"

"Yep, and didn't mean to fly off at you, son. Take you a week or two. Get all the facts you can, take in some writers nights. Get an idea what's going on, and a guitar. But go home to get your lessons. When you can play the one, four and five chords, buy a boombox to lay your songs down on work tapes."

"One and four and five chords, Copper Jim?"

"Yep, and buy a book on the Number System."

Tony jerked a pencil and pad from his shirt pocket. "Number System?"

"Yep. May have them at NSAI. If not, they'll know where to get one."

"Gee, I do appreciate you guys. I mean like these are the things I need to know. Okay, now what's next?"

"Now, be sure you write this down. Go home!"

"Ah, come on, Copper Jim, be serious."

"Never been more serious in my life. Go back in with your dad, write songs in your off time. Takes five years to make a songwriter, on a full belly or empty belly. Tony, you'll enjoy it more on a full belly."

"Five years! Come on, man, give me a break!"

Jim's blue eyes bored into Tony's black Italian plea. "Tony, you seem like a fine young feller, so I'm trying to help. I don't know pizza making. Never heard of pizza till I was past thirty, don't guess you learn to make one overnight."

"No, sir, but--"

"Got much call for half-baked pizza in New Jersey?"

"No, sir," Tony chuckled.

"Ain't no call for half-baked songwriters in Nashville. They're a pestilence to publishers and get run off like flies."

"He... he's telling you like it is," Junior chimed in.

"When you get home and get thirty songs wrote, get them all out and listen again. Pick your three best and get them demoed. Nothing fancy, just a good voice with a guitar or keyboard. Buy a *Billboard* and start writing to publishers on the chart cuts. Ask for permission to send your songs in. When a publisher getting top forty cuts asks you to come to Nashville, come on back."

"But, we talked about it yesterday. That's not how you did it."

"Naw, I was ignorant, like you. I didn't know nobody who knew enough to tell me different. What I just told you took me forty years to learn. Like most advice it's free, and you can take it or leave it. Junior, you got that contract?" Copper Jim stood up, this time Junior knew he was gone.

"Ye... yeah, it's right here," Junior handed Jim an envelope from an inside pocket of his red stage jacket. "Boss wants the contract back by tomorrow."

"Tell Boss he'll get the contract when he gets it. This woulda all been done if he hadn't tried to hog tie Miss Annie. I'll call him and set up the meeting at her place when we're ready."

"He won't like it, but te... telling's my job."

Jim said, "Luck to you, Tony. Think on what I said."

"Thanks, Copper Jim, it's been a privilege to bend your ear." When Jim left, Tony said, "What's he so mad about, Junior?"

"Why, I di... didn't notice a thing."

"He doesn't have the best disposition in the world."

"The music school of ha... hard knocks is ki... kinda hard on folks. That's why he... he wanted you to listen."

"Anybody ever listen to Copper Jim?"

"One young feller does, he's fixing to be a su... superstar."

"You kidding me, Junior!"

"That's the contract I ga... gave Copper Jim."

"Can I ask the name of this about to be superstar?"
"It's a young man by the na... name of Clay Hill."

After their attorney confirmed the contract was according to discussion, fair and equitable, Copper Jim had the meeting at Little Gatlinburg.

Covering her disdain, Anna remained true to her southern heritage of extending hospitality to an invited guest. She seated them at the kitchen table, served coffee and Mississippi mud cake, that happened to be Gunnar's favorite. He hadn't eaten homemade mud cake since his mother passed away. Anna's coffee was as good as the cake, she kept everyone's cup filled.

When she offered more cake, Clay was the taker. "Thanks, Mama, I'd like another slice. But not as big as the first one."

Anna kept pouring coffee until Gunnar had to put a protesting hand over his cup. Though she served him graciously, he saw the carefully subdued fire crackling in the depths of her eyes. There was little deception in this woman-- her honesty was her mystery. He appreciated why Copper Jim was so protective of this pair. He had not felt such vibes of innocence and honesty in a house since his farmboy days.

The woman serving the table was comfortably in charge. Gunnar wondered how long it would take her to adjust to household help. He couldn't help but wonder how a higher level of living might affect her, once Clay's career got going. There would be more money to hire help than time for the doing. Clay would have his music as a buffer to replace the invisible cord that still tied mother and son. She would have nothing. No one at the table realized how fast he expected young Hill's career to take off.

He had looked too long and endured too many near facsimiles not to know the real thing when he found it. An artist of Clay's caliber had been a twenty year search. This kid was going to shoot the moon, so he was in heat to sign a contract he wouldn't consider otherwise. Signing such a contract was not the smartest move in the world, but he was damn sure going to gamble. It wasn't failing to sell product, but not having great product that had been his greatest disappointment. It was lucky he and Anna had their run-in at the office. The German Shepherd lying in the corner watched like a bodyguard. Obviously, he worshiped the mother as well as the son.

Feeling Gunnar's concern, Clay reassured, "Don't worry about Shep, we made you welcome. He's cool unless you jump Mama or me."

"I will behave myself, Shep. Don't you worry." Hearing his name the dog thumped the floor with his tail. Gunnar added, "Clay, he's a gorgeous animal."

"Thanks. I love Shep like a brother."

Knowing it was time to softly acknowledge their prior difference, Gunnar looked at Anna and smiled. "Clay, I wouldn't make an aggressive move toward you with your mama here, never mind the dog."

She held up two fingers in a peace sign. "You better not. I have a standing house rule-- don't mess with my young'un."

"I've already learned that the hard way."

On the edge of his dream coming true, not daring to risk his mother and producer having another fight, Clay broke in, "You should've seen Shep in his prime-- he was awesome."

"I'll bet. Going gray on his muzzle. How old is he?"

"He'll be nine this summer."

"That's getting on up there for a dog. He looks like good stock. I'm a walking horse breeder myself. Really enjoy watching the young of two well bred partners grow off. Have you bred him?"

"No, sir, haven't got around to it. Folks have stopped by, wanting to breed their bitches to Shep. It was always backyard stuff. I'd love to have a pup of his from a good line. His pedigree has some of the best American bred lines. I want to keep something of Shep, he is getting old."

"I have a neighbor at my horse farm who breeds and shows shepherds. Don't know his blood lines, but he has beautiful dogs and a case filled with trophies. He might want to breed one of his bitches to Shep."

"I'd like to check that out."

"I doubt you will have the time this next year for tending a litter yourself, but you can always hire help. I'll be glad to ask him about it or maybe you'd like to come down, visit his kennel and talk with him yourself."

"That would be super."

"Hey," Copper Jim growled, "we got a contract here to sign."

"Good," Gunnar said. "Clay has a showcase at Connie's in eight weeks."

"You got him a showcase before you got a contract?"

"Quarrells, this deal has to be. You knew that from the start, like me."

"How did you get in Connie's on such short notice?"

"That's just one of the reasons y'all need a contract with me. The showcase is booked eight weeks from today. Clay, can you be ready?"

"How about it, Copper Jim, can we?" Clay asked.

"Shucks, we're done ready now."

"I do like confidence," Anna said.

Gunnar returned her smile, their eyes held a moment. "Me too, must be something in the air here."

Anna shot, "We ordinary mortals have to have something to keep the stubborn from inheriting the earth."

"Moving right along," Gunnar grinned, "after y'all have a chance to decide, let me know how many reservations you need."

"Just save one place for me," Jim said.

"Copper Jim, it'd mean a lot to me if Miss Roxie came."

"Clayboy, she keeps the Eighteen Wheeler open twenty-four hours. Says a truckstop ain't worth nothing that don't keep a trucker a hot cup of coffee all the time. But, I'll tell her you want her to come."

"Thanks. How about you, Mama?"

"Just me."

"Mama, it's fine with me, whoever you ask."

"Just me," she repeated, knowing he meant Jake.

"If it's okay with you, Copper Jim, I would like to ask Rachel and Milton to perform with us that night."

"Be mighty fine with me, Clayboy."

"I'd also like to invite the whole Islander clan. They all have been so good to us and I really like them. You think they'd like to come?"

"Don't know about Frank and Bess. Like Miss Roxie, they don't leave their business much. We can ask."

"When we put a band together, I'd like Rachel and Milton to be with us."

"Yeah, that's a good idea, Clay," Jim said.

"Okay. Another think I thought of. What do you think about The Copperhill Band as a name for our band?"

"Hey, son, I like that. Sounds lucky to me. What do you think, Gunnar?"

"I like it too. Who are Rachel and Milton?"

"Rachel and Milton Islander. They're sister and brother, help their folks run the Blue Collar where I pick with Copper Jim. You should come down. We have a great time and love Bess Islander's home cooking. She's the mama."

"Thanks, I might try that, Clay," Gunnar said.

"Rachel and Milton were on my tape. You commented on how good you thought they was."

"Yes, they did a fine job, which reminds me, we should release a side or two of that session."

"On what label, Gunnar?" Copper Jim asked.

"Hope to have a major after the showcase. Millie Hawthorn with Red Springs is sold on Clay. She played his tape for the top brass and they are impressed. They want to see Clay live before they commit. Contracting with them means international distribution. If we should come up without a major, I want to release a side on my Cotton Gin label and negotiate the distribution. That would take longer, Clay needs air play as soon as possible."

"What song would you release first?" Jim asked.

"I'd like to take what you all have in the studio for sweetening and remixing. I like *Cherokee Eyes*. It's first rate country rock and commercial as air. You can't turn on the TV or radio without hearing about Native Americans. After I make my additions, let's listen to all the songs and see which one we all like best. Also, I want our first cassette single to pass out at the showcase."

Jim drawled, "What sweetening you got in mind?"

"Boosting the rhythm tracks; adding some licks. Play with different sounds, maybe a sax."

"Sax on a country song? Have you lost it, McGuire?"

"Knew you wouldn't be hot on the sax idea. Hell, I might try a trumpet. I never know for sure, till I hear what I hear from studio speakers. If y'all don't like what I produce, we dump it and I pay the bill. I still want to pass out a cassette of *Cherokee Eyes* at the showcase. I think it should be our first release. The Red Springs honcho is a quarter Cherokee and loves that song."

"Clayboy, what do you reckon?" Copper Jim asked.

"Sounds far out but, like Mr. McGuire, I don't know till I hear it through speakers. Can't see we have a thing to lose, if it's okay by you."

Copper Jim conceded, "Guess you're right."

Gunnar checked his watch. "Anna, thanks for your hospitality, the cake was fantastic. When you know how many will be in y'all's party, let me know. Connie's is small. We need reservations for those we want to seat. Now, if you folks are ready, let's sign the contract. I have to fire a singer in an hour."

"Sounds like a fine way to spend an afternoon."

"Well, Anna, it's not anything I'm looking forward to, but it has to be done."

Clay said, "Is there time to book a studio, sweeten the tracks and get the cassette copies made by the showcase?"

"That's the beauty of owning a studio. We'll have four sides down within two weeks and time to listen and decide. I want everybody to be satisfied. We'll have the single at Connie's and ready to mail to radio right after."

"You're sending radio a tape after my showcase?"

Gunnar explained, "If we sign with the label, they will do the mailing. We will record eight more songs for a full album."

"Fantastic!" Clay said.

Anna asked, "Why be in such a hurry?"

"Clay is ready and music's like harvesting peaches. You start picking the minute the crop's ready. Chances can go bad like peaches left hanging too long. I'm not one to let that happen."

"I didn't imagine you would be."

"Anna, you have a problem with that?"

"Not at all, Gunnar, I like your logic." Seeing her smile, Clay breathed a silent wheeew-- it was going to work! Finally his music was going to be heard!

CHAPTER 20
CONNIE'S

She couldn't believe this small cafe was the mecca for country music hopefuls from all over. It made the Blue Collar look like a football field. But most anyone that started off the streets of Nashville, started at Connie's. Here you might see the last kid off the bus or a megastar. The walls were papered with gold records and photographs of stars who started to shine here and earned Connie her own celebrity. Connie had the reputation of being culler and cultivator of talent. Having pioneered the forum concept where new talent could develop, Connie had been featured on national TV, and was queried and quoted constantly.

Performing a new song on Connie's stage brought priceless feedback. A latest attempt at being rich and famous and songwriting immortality might need a rewrite. Maybe the idea wasn't strong enough, or a similar song was too recently on the charts. Sometimes a song had hit potential and only needed to be demoed and shopped. After the demo, for too many, the good part died. Songwriters were famous for procrastinating about selling their wares, but to get a song on the radio, the demo had to be shopped.

Connie was quoted as saying the monetary return in the listening club business was minimal, but the right contact for songwriters and artists happened enough to keep her heart inspired and her doors open. Performance money was mostly gratis, for the known or unknown. Money couldn't be the question when performing at Connie's could be the answer. Nashville housed the heart of country, Connie's was a main artery to that heart. The stream of dreamers who thumbed, flew or wheeled to town all came to Connie's.

It was hitting Anna how close her baby boy stood to stardom. If Clay made it here, he could make it in Nashville. That loaded him a shot at making it world-wide. If the world heard him, she knew it would love him. The thought made her giddy! If she meant to get through the evening, she had to think about something else.

McGuire was certainly earning his keep. Clay had said, "I'm so lucky to have this showcase. Mr. McGuire is awesome."

"His interest in your career is supposed to be the best you can get," she said. His interest in her made her nervous, she doubted his sincerity. Still she had no doubt about his interest in Clay. The man was too smart and successful to use his resources flippantly.

When Clay, Roxie, Jim and Anna walked in and Jim asked about their reservation, Connie herself took them to their table. She was in her middle years, still attractive, and her aura of confidence made Anna like her instantly. The star booster's respect for Gunnar was clear. Seating them at a line of tables butted end to end, Connie said, "This is Gunnar's place of choice."

Anna thought, Bet he gets his choice of anything here. She wished for a seat in the shadows with a view of the stage. If word got around about her being Clay's mama, it took any spontaneous audience response to his performance she might pick up. Tonight being so vital, she wanted to watch audience reaction with a sharp eye. That was out, at these tables.

Two men wearing business suits, taking a table on the far side of the room, caught her attention. She wished she knew the faces of the music executives better. Apparel meant nothing. The making it or the faking it might wear business suits or jeans with the knees out. The making it were known to wear the worst clothes and drive the longest Cadillacs.

Twenty chairs were in McGuire's reservation, she had no idea who they were all for. Hell, he knew everybody. God appearing to sit with them wouldn't be a total shock. Clay's audience would be judgmental as some old western hanging judge and competitive as kids for candy. The "show me" vibes in the place would be harder to entertain than the regular fans.

With this night being his trial by fire, Clay's attitude was astounding. She'd be shaking in her boots, but he was so up this morning and still was. He chatted with her and called his friends happy as Christmas morning.

When they picked up Copper Jim and Roxie, Clay was like a boy going fishing. On the way, Jim said, "Record honchos and investors hit Connie's. Backing acts is big business. If it's a winner, an act pays better than the Kentucky Derby. If it's a loser, it's a good tax write-off."

Clay said, "It blows my mind, that every night in Nashville, á club is giving somebody's dream a chance to come true."

Being a native, Anna had absorbed an awareness of Music Row all her life. Now she read everything she could about the music industry. Among other things, it was packed with superstitious people. If an artist was picked up by a label, if a writer landed a staff writing job playing a certain club, if a recording studio cut a hit record, any of this could assure a fringe business of on going success. The songwriting fairy worked in many ways to bless even back row worshipers at the music altar.

Her thoughts were interrupted by the arrival of Rachel, her parents, Milton and his wife, Sue. As Clay seated Rachel, Anna saw again the special way he looked at the girl. Thank God! It was time he looked special at somebody besides Mary Ellen. Rachel came from a solid family and she could look you in the eye. With her big brown eyes and auburn hair curling down her back, Anna saw why Clay was attracted. Rachel was a dreamer like Clay and loved music; he could do worse.

Jim said, "Let's get back to the dressing room. Need to have a powwow before we go on stage." With everyone's good wishes, they left the table.

Anna knew this had to be the most nervous night of her life. Her insides were jumping like a cornered frog. Get your mind on something else, she told herself, taking a sip of wine. The clock ate the bar told twenty minutes till showtime, there was standing room only now. McGuire should be here!

Earlier on the phone, he had said, "Tonight will be a milestone for Clay. He needs to make it with the younger fans, but it's the over thirty-five record buyers that keep country acts recording. The industry people coming tonight are thirty-something and older. Our backs are against the wall."

With their backs against the wall in business, she needed to feel her back against the wall literally. It wasn't often, but she had her scared spells. Right now she was feeling as insecure as molasses. It might be from Gunnar's show of interest in her, the spark of interest she felt for him, or just this showcase meaning what it did to Clay.

McGuire stopped her thoughts with, "Never expected y'all to beat me here, but I expected to be here before now." Anna looked up in his brown eyes, felt them doing something with hers and began to feel better and to feel worse. The responding wiggle somewhere down in her gut wasn't welcome. It felt on the verge of some kind of betrayal. She thought, Be still, my glands! It couldn't be in her best interest to care for a high-roller like McGuire. His picture in the newspapers and on TV told how partial he was to young girls. He was way too fast for an Anna. God, please let me be smarter than this!

With a charmed I'm sure smile, she purred, "I was worried." Hell, think of the devil, he appears every time, smiles like an angel with Finney in tow and two new men who look rich. Naturally he'd bring his lovely secretary with a Clark Kent look alike, even down to black horn rimmed glasses, for cover.

"Anna, you know Annette, this is her husband, Larry. You know Junior, these guys are Ramsey Witt and Seth Ryan. Folks, Anna Hill."

"Nice to meet y'all. Please, sit down."

Gunnar sat at the head of the table next to Anna. In a for her ears only tone, he said, "Don't think we'll be using Ramsey and Seth since Red Springs wants to handle the promotion and booking. I'd just as soon let them. They're tops at Red Springs. As the saying goes, if it ain't broke, don't fix it. Ramsey and Seth understand, but they wanted them to see the showcase. They're the best, and seeing Clay will put them in the know."

"Do they work for you?" Anna asked.

"Sometimes, they're independents and sometimes work for Red Springs. Max Majors wants *Cherokee Eyes* promoted to the hilt."

"By the way," she said, loving his beautiful brown eyes, "I listened again to all the songs. You enhanced the tracks more than I realized."

"Thanks. If Max likes what he hears tonight, we'll have to jump back in the studio and record enough songs for an album."

"Clay will love that."

"Me, too. Didn't mean to run this late, I'm not as good at being in two places at one time as I used to be. So, how is Clay and where is Clay?"

"Thrilled to death. He and Jim are in the dressing room with Rachel and Milton. You going back to say hello?"

"No, it's too close to showtime, and I don't want Jim to think I'm trying to take over. Beside, Clay only needs to think about performing now."

"Gunnar, why do music heads bother with unknowns in clubs like Connie's."

"Money. Talent's cheaper fresh off the bus than from someone else's contract. Top people look for top talent at rock bottom prices. That means getting it before the competition gets it. Scouting new talent is an ongoing quest in the business. Excuse me a moment."

He stood to motion over a leprechaun of a woman, no longer young. Anna doubted she'd ever been beautiful, but the woman had the brightest amber eyes. She was escorted by a handsome younger man. Gunnar introduced her as Millie Hawthorn, head of A & R at Red Springs.

Anna knew Red Springs was a label of recent years that originated as a custom label founded by three widowed triplets in their sixties. The sisters started with their savings and small inheritances back in the seventies. Their father sent them to business school, and got them banking jobs. They never made big money working in banks, but they were privy to great advice about investments and smart enough to profit by it.

After retirement, the triplets wanted to stay busy. They had put a lifetime into doing what they had to do to meet responsibilities. By then, they wanted to do something they loved. As girls, they sang as a trio, and "just loved" music. They had some money and the time and, since Nashville was Music City, they decided to start a custom record label.

The girls were born in Red Boiling Springs, Tennessee and named their label Red Springs Records. Thrifty and honest as three nuns, they developed Red Springs into the most innovative custom company in Nashville. It was knowledge the triplets gave an act more for less. Some of their customers sent their records to DJs. Some started getting air play, and the triplets had a money making company on their hands.

When foreign money made inquiries, the girls were considering doing something else. They had "done" the record thing and were wondering what Las Vegas might do for those who loved and understood the idiosyncrasies of numbers. When a deal was made, the triplets stipulated in the sale conditions that Red Springs would keep its name, red records and logo. The logo was a drawing of three Appalachian women in old-fashioned dresses and sunbonnets sitting on a settle bench. The woman in the middle held a dulcimer. According to the girls, the logo "carried the luck of Red Springs." The woman holding the dulcimer was the triplets' grandmother and her triplet sisters.

During negotiations, the foreign buyers kept smiling at the little old ladies. Little old ladies were revered in their country. To anything the sisters said, the buyers said, "Aah, so" having been reared to listen to wisdom one might profit by. These ladies knew what they were talking about. Red Springs continued to release hit after hit with the women on the settle bench spinning in the center of each red disk they pressed.

Millie said, "Your son is great on tape. Can't wait to hear him live."

"Thank you," Anna said, instantly liking Millie.

"This gorgeous hunk is my protegee, Greg Green. He's lead singer in our next band act at Red Springs. Greg, darling, get acquainted with everyone."

While Greg made rounds, Millie took the chair Gunnar held for her. When they were seated, he said, "Thanks for coming, Millie."

"Wild horses couldn't hold me. I played the tape again. Clay Hill will make record history and platinum money."

"Thanks, I value your opinion. Is Max coming?"

"Yes, Gunnar, and he loves Clay's Indian song."

"Millie, I owe you one. Anna, Max is a vice president at Red Springs."

Millie said, "Max isn't only a VP, he owns a chunk of stock. He also convinced some Texas oil friends to buy stock in Red Springs. What Max says, goes. And don't thank me, Gunnar, I owe you. Your boy's the first talent I've heard with potential to fill the gap Elvis left. Oh, there's Max now."

After the introductions, Max sat at Gunnar's left. Gunnar signaled the waitress. "Champagne for everyone, Debby. See if anyone wants anything else. Put everything on my tab." Anna admired how he took control as he got Junior's attention sitting down the table talking with Frank.

Junior came and said, "What you ne... need, Boss?"

"Get Bry and pass out the singles."

"Su... sure, Boss. Anna, don't you be nervous now, they'll love your boy."

Connie walked on stage, held up a cassette and said, "Does Gunnar McGuire know how to launch an act or what?" Applause broke in, she waited a moment and continued, "Thanks for coming out. For those who don't know, I'm Connie. The last name is so subject to change, I don't bother with it anymore."

The audience laughed, but Anna thought it was a weird joke. Seeing her confusion, Millie said, "Takes time to appreciate Row humor. Connie's had the same husband for two kids and twenty years."

Connie went on, "I haven't heard our guest, but he comes from Gunnar McGuire, a veteran hit maker, publisher and producer. We also have with us from Red Springs Records, Millie Hawthorn and Max Majors. We're proud to have such illustrious guests. Thank you all for coming. Without further ado, Clay Hill and the Copperhill Band. Give them a warm welcome!"

At the sound of the applause, Copper Jim gave the band the down beat for the intro to *Cherokee Eyes*.

Clay bounded on stage, blond, handsome and full of energy as always. Anna knew her son was a pretty boy, but tonight he took her breath away. She wasn't blinded enough by mother love to imagine his good looks and talent. She was too honest, too smart and loved Clay too much to lie.

His blond hair, cut short on the sides and top, cascaded like a waterfall of curls down past his shoulders. The applause after the first two lines he sang kept erupting through his medley and told Anna that her evaluation of his talent was on the mark.

When Clay finished his opening, the packed house rose as one with a standing ovation. He took his bows, then waved in diffidence to the band for their share of the praise.

Then he held up his hands for silence. Then looking over the crowd to make contact, Clay said, "Y'all are looking real good and I do thank you so very much for coming."

"I can't tell you how much it means to be here. I want to thank Mama for putting up with me all these years. Stand up, Mama. Don't be shy." Anna rose slightly in her chair. After the respectful applause, he moved on; "I thank Miss Connie and Mr. McGuire for giving me this chance. I want to extent to a special thanks to Ms. Hawthorn and Mr. Majors for coming.

Now, I want to introduce my best friend, my music guru and my personal hero. Picks the best rhythm lick in country music, Mr. Copper Jim Quarrells!"

After the applause, Clay shouted, "Y'all love country rock?"

"Yeah!" they screamed.

"Like country roll?"

"Yeah!" they screamed again.

Clay screamed, "All right! Gimme that rock and roll country thunder, Copper Jim." He was off and running like a musical train. Anna's heart filled with so much pride and love, she thought it might burst.

Applause thundered and approval roared halfway through the first verse of *Mountain Fiddle Hoedown Rap* like a performer dreams of. Copper Jim had done a great job tutoring Clay. His most repeated instruction was "Always just be your own self. Country music fans feel it when you fake it."

Clay was performing like he had grown up dancing, picking and singing on top of his wishing rock at Little Gatlinburg.

Anna saw the adrenaline accelerate Clay into overdrive-- into the cosmic energy he had always been tuned to-- that would make or break his rising star because once he started he could not draw back until the flow was over. The audience went wild as Clay picked up his volume and sang into the second verse. They were on their feet with standing ovations off and on during the whole set. Thank God they loved him.

After Clay finished the showcase format of six songs, the crowd demanded an encore and then a second. It was breaking a house rule of never more than two encores but Connie had no choice other than to step up to the mike and say, "Clay Hill, you are magnificent and these folks are demanding an encore and frankly, I am, too. Please, give us another song."

Clay stepped back to the mike and looked his audience over. He seemed to be trying to make contact with every eye, every ear and every heart before saying, "I've loved and I've been loved. I been hurt and who-doed like most of you. I doubt any of us are ever more hurt than the first time we get fifty thousand feet over somebody-- then wind up crushed and crashed. There's a woods in back of my house that I grew up in and I still love to roam in. It's where I do my best thinking and it's one of my best places to write. I was sitting on a rock in those woods when this next song came pouring out.

"A lot of you are singer songwriters too, so you know what I mean when I say this next song was a gift. All I did was push the pencil. It was written by cosmic energy, God, or whatever you're the most comfortable calling your higher power. It could be called *Requiem For A Love Affair*. Folks, when this song came down, I don't mind y'all knowing-- I was crying."

Clay sung the first line a cappella. As from the first time she heard him sing this ballad, Anna felt goose flesh rise on her arms. Noticing Gunnar noticed, they shared a smile and he briefly stroked her arm. "Clay wrote this by himself. I think it's his best song so far." Gunnar smiled with understanding.

The song was Clay's tribute to Mary Ellen. Warm as light spring rain, he fingerpicked a guitar solo, Jim brought in the band with a harmonic crescendo, then Clay cried the first word of the next line "Morna!"

He sounded like a heart breaking. Till that moment, Anna had not fully appreciated his sense of the dramatic and of timing. But this was his first performance in a true concert setting. She thought, I never saw a Greek god, but in all honesty, if I needed a model for one, I'd use my son. If a Greek god sings, he wants to sing like Clay Hill. The tears that slipped from the corners of her eyes were not tears of sadness or pride. They were tears of homage, a perfect song, painting, sunrise, or buttercup could bring.

As he caroled into the lovely, sad chorus of *Morna*, the hush that took his audience was more significant than a roar. The club was caught in the spell of Clay Hill's music, even the bartenders and waitresses were still.

As he sung into the final repeat of the chorus, that told of all the pain, heartache and disillusionment of trust destroyed; of love betrayed; of a final farewell to much more than losing a lover-- Clay hit a variation on the melody he had not sung before. The poignancy, the pathos of the moment was almost too much to bear and this was the night he graduated into a style of singing uniquely, and totally Clay Hill.

From that night, he never sang a song the same way twice. He simply signaled the band, as he had just now, to follow his picking. From then on, he performed different approaches that kept his material fresh and new, and praise coming from the critics, the media and the fans.

Clay said, "The fans are the most important critics of all to a singing storyteller. They take it like you sing it. They don't have the Emperor's New Clothes syndrome like some critics and record brass."

Clay ended "Morna" with his arms toward heaven and his head bowed. The crowd was on its feet again with a standing ovation. Followed by applause, screams for "more" and "bravo," he walked off stage and disappeared into the back room. The crowd continued with their demands for "more" and so did Anna until it was clear Clay had finished his concert.

Tonight's performance was done, but what a moment of glory for Clay! As she stood applauding, thrilled to tears, she knew he would conquer the music world. Tonight was one of those corner-turning times. Nothing would be the same. Maybe that was good, but it was scary.

Suddenly, in the midst of all the handshakes, hugs and emotion of the moment, something drew her eyes to the bar. She fell into the gray velvet gaze of Jake Dennis and could not disengage her eyes. She stared mesmerized till he turned and became lost in the departing crowd. Their relationship had ceased-- it was not over.

Anna's flush and eye contact with the man who returned her stricken look with a sardonic grin, before turning his back to leave, was not missed by McGuire. The exchange was mere seconds but one second of that color eye contact would have revealed the man was her unfinished business. It was as revealing as two dogs hung up in the street and just as eye catching. McGuire knew the signs of high passion between a man and a woman. He had built a business on it.

There would be at least one more last goodbye. Last goodbyes were a heartbeat from a new hello. Till this passed, there was no use in his wasting time trying to make time with her. Once lovers generated that degree of passion, giving up on it was hell, no matter how wide the breach or how small the chance to try again. It was what everyone dreamed of, breathed for, lusted for. It inspired all the love songs, all the Samsons and all the Delilahs.

Ten high loving was the oldest, strongest and most natural human addiction. There was no cure unless it cured itself. For the lucky-- it never did!

Taking Anna's arm, he said to everyone standing at their table, "Let's go congratulate our star." As they made their way through the crowded room, Gunnar said to the passing waitress, "Honey, bring two bottles of champagne to the dressing room."

Anna was first to reach the open door. Rachel in Clay's arms, the two of them lost in a kiss, blew her away. She stood with her eyes wide and her mouth open, till Jim saw her and shouted, "We got us a winner," and hugged her.

In her warm bed, away from the crowd and McGuire, Anna stretched down in the covers. Clay was a success, such good things were happening. Red Springs wanted him and reps from two other labels wanted to talk if there was a problem. Gunnar liked Red Springs and predicted clear sailing. After running up and down the emotional ladder all night, her feelings needed to gel. She rolled on her stomach to sleep.

Sleep wouldn't come, she was too wound up. Jake showing up was the last thing she expected. His eyes did still shake the shit out of her, but their lost love needed to stay lost. Letting her recovering heart beat all soft and willing for him to break again would be double dumb! No love was miles above a broken heart. When a woman got past wanting children, having a man might be just a habit anyway. Men were a natural convenience when the loving was good-- damned inconvenient when it turned contrary.

Again, lack of time and opportunity had broken her loving habit. With no male chauvinist to swagger around and tempt her, she hardly thought about sex. When the craving did hit, she got by remembering the hell of withdrawal from cigarettes and a man. She never wanted that much pain again.

She nearly died over losing Jake; Jeff too, but not like Jake. The care and catering to a man took too much effort to wind up emotionally killed. She barely remembered, it had been so long since she'd had any, but it might not be worth it. She did miss a broad back to warm against. A man's back was so warm; especially after a nightmare or when you got scared of growing old, or needed to talk to someone who gave a shit. Like it'd be nice to roll over and talk with Jake or Gunnar. Gunnar would be more hip on music, but Jake had a good grass roots way of seeing things.

God, she was gross, considering two men in her bed on the same night. Hell, Jake was never interested in Clay's music. Strange he came to the showcase. He was handsome; made beautiful love when he stuck to the normal stuff. And he would behave if he wasn't so insecure. If she could reassure him, they would be fine. Loving Jake was pure heaven when it was good. Course it was soured shit when it turned bad.

Hey, it's late, you're tired and thinking stupid. If you could get along with Jake, you would have. You worshiped him, you gave him all you are. Well, I can be wrong too. Like thinking Annette's on the make, Larry's all she wants.

Anna remembered when Jeff was her total horizon. It wasn't a bad way to be, but nights passing too lonely too long caused a metamorphosis. She wasn't who she was then, like she wasn't who she was in kindergarten. She just wished-- she didn't know what. Love was so simple the first time.

The phone didn't startle her, subconsciously she must have expected his call. She didn't know she had been asleep till her hoarse "Hello?"

"Hope I didn't wake you."

"Huh?"

"Woman, I said, I hope I didn't wake you."

"Well, shit you did!"

"Well, shit I'm sorry!"

"So am I!" His chuckle tantalized her fully awake.

"Like always, bitchy as hell when you wake up."

"Then don't wake me up. Call back after while."

"I'm awake. You're no better than me to lose sleep."

"What time-- oh, think I drank too much champagne."

"You were drinking your share and having a ball."

"Would it have made your day if I'd been miserable?"

"Hey, I don't blame you. I believe in a good time."

"Why didn't you come over and join us?"

"Hell, I didn't want to."

"Like always, I guess you told me."

"Baby, I didn't call to fight. I want to say what a fine entertainer Clay is and congratulate y'all. Together, you and Clay could turn Texas over."

"How did you know about his showcase?"

"You can't turn on the tube or read the newspaper without knowing about Clay. Ain't that gray headed dude you were sitting with Gunnar McGuire?"

"Yes. He and Copper Jim are producing Clay."

"I read McGuire's interview. He said Clay's the biggest thing since Elvis. Didn't you read it?"

"Yes, but I didn't dream you did. I'm not used to Clay being news."

"Better get used to it. McGuire said you were one of Clay's studio backup singers, his co-writer and you'd be on stage with him soon."

"That ain't happening. It's Clay's show."

"Nobody messes with Clay, not even his mama. Right?"

"Right!" she snapped.

"Relax, firecracker. I'm on your side, always have been, always will be."

"It's damn hard to tell sometimes."

"Don't know why we men can get so uptight when women make points. If y'all were as dumb as we can try to make you, the world would stop turning."

"Lord! you've learned a lot."

"Went back to the Dennis School of Reason. Falling for you blew my mind. You don't get between a cow and her calf, unless you like to get gored."

"Are you still working out?"

"At home, quit Brenda for the honey business. I'm selling to a chain of health food stores. If you don't, lots of folks like honey. It's good for you."

"So is milk. Don't like milk either."

"I miss you." He waited for her answer. She liked herself better before he taught her how to push his buttons; before he taught her you can't win playing straight in a crooked game. She learned on her own he couldn't stay out of control long. His voice was husky when he said, "You in bed?"

"Uh huh."

"Wish I was laying there with you."

After a moment she said, "What time is it?"

"Ten after five. I said, I miss you. I'm crazy about you."

"So, what do we do now?"

"Anna, I was too hard on you and I'm sorry. Does it still mean enough to talk about over coffee?"

"Not if everything has to be your way."

"Baby, is that what you think?"

"You know all about music, love and kids. Those who disagree with you are dumb and need to repent and accept the gospel according to Jake Dennis."

"Anna, I'm so sorry. I don't mean to be that way. I love you, and you're a hard act to follow, little darling."

"Well, you can't replace loving and making love, with sex."

"Who are you loving? That old bastard pouring you champagne last night?"

"It wouldn't be any of your business if I was doing the Green Bay Packers, but he's just business."

"I saw the way the son of a bitch was looking at you. He might as well have written 'I want in Anna Hill's pants' on the wall."

"Hell, it's too late and I'm too tired to listen to you being gross."

"Baby, don't hang up. I didn't mean to make you mad. But, truly, as brilliant as you are, woman, you are so dumb at times."

"I'm not too dumb for you to call at all hours, or to get a megabucks contract with McGuire. Plus, we're signing with the hottest record label in town and I'm sitting in as Clay's manager. I ain't dumb! You hear me?"

"Yes'm, and I'm sorry." The grin in his voice was maddening.

"I won't put up with your put downs. Bastard, you got that?" She didn't know if his low laugh was a turn on or turn off. He always could make her want to kill him and rape him at the same time.

"Anna, for the tenth time, I am truly sorry."

"Damn you! You were so sweet, so wonderful." Tears she had dammed for months broke free. "Till I was crazy about you, the... then you turned bully on me. I really don't know if I care if you're sor... sorry or not!"

Solemn as heartache, he said, "Woman, please, for what we had and might still have, meet me. I do love you. I really do."

"I-- I don't know," she sniffed.

"Don't guess I meant to you what you do to me. If I did you'd want to try one more time." The pain in his voice made her think, Why not? He was insecure as molasses but he had loved and thrilled her like no one ever had-- probably ever would.

"Oh, Jake, I do wish we could mend it."

"Just meet me for coffee. That's all I'm asking."

She sniffed sedately, "Okay."

"Where and what time?"

"You mean today?"

"Naw, Christmas!" he growled. Shit! He'd never change his spots.

She should hang up on his ass. But that was the problem. Passion! Temper! Hangup! Breakup! Makeup! Breakup again! Then going crazy for a man who could excite her more than anybody.

Deciding Jake was being as humble as he knew how to be, she said, "You listen to me, Jake Dennis. You listen good because I mean what I'm saying. McGuire is supposed to call and let me know, but if there is to be a meeting with Red Springs Records today, I'll damn sure be there with bells on."

"Yeah, I can see you now, all reared back in a limo wrapped in mink, gorgeous as a movie star. Clay's your ultimate thrill, I just have to get used to it. Okay, when is this McGuire supposed to call?"

"By ten. Oh, Jake, all this is so intimidating!"

"Hey, it's what you worked for. Relax and let it happen. I'll call back at eleven, woman." He hung up without saying goodbye.

The way he said "woman" still raced her motor. He always did make her think everything was going to be fine. God!

CHAPTER 21

SHELBYHOUSE

She was having coffee when he called. "Hope I didn't wake you, Anna."

"No. I'm too carried away to sleep late. Clay's still sleeping, he's always exhausted after a show."

"That boy gives it all he's got, and he's as great to watch as he is to hear. That means hit videos and sold out concerts. Max Majors thinks so too. He wants to meet with us Monday at two, if that's convenient."

"It's fine. I can't thank you enough."

"My pleasure, I was wrong to doubt your judgment. Clay does possess God given talent, and I most humbly apologize."

"Apology accepted."

"Good. I've waited all my career for a Clay Hill. No wonder you're proud. Max says Clay needs air play right away. When he wakes up, tell him about Max and also I'm setting up a session."

"He will be so happy."

"I'm waiting for call backs. There's an engineer I want and a bass player. You should find recording at my place comfortable. It's time the fans get to hear Clay and he's so lucky to have a lovely mother, as rare as his talent. You can't imagine how I admire you, you never give up. Tell Clay I'll call back."

When the phone rang again, she thought it was Jake, but McGuire said, "The engineer and bass player are available and so is Copper Jim. Would you have Clay call me when he gets up?"

"He is up, hang on. He's coming from exercising Shep."

Momentarily, Clay answered on the extension.

"Morning, Clay. How does it feel to be a superstar rising?"

"Thank you. It's the best feeling in the world."

"I think we should cut the six songs you did for the showcase and the two you did for encores. I produce twelve song albums. Do you have four more on a par with the eight you sang?"

"Yes, sir."

"By the way, how many songs are in your catalog?"

"What would you say, Mama, four or five hundred?"

"Something like that, son."

"Four or five hundred? How long y'all been writing?"

"How long, Mama?"

Gunnar heard her motherly pride as she said, "Clay's been making up songs and stories since he taught himself to write at three. I write with him some, but he does most of it."

Clay said, "Mama co-wrote half the songs."

"You two pick another dozen you like. We'll all pick sixteen or so to cut and make final choices for the album from those."

"Sir, does Copper Jim know about the session?."

"Yes, I know Jim is a great producer, so don't worry. When you pick material, remember we want each song strong enough to be a hit single."

"Mr. McGuire, we want one gospel or inspirational song on each album."

"Clay, call me Gunnar. In a creative way, I'm not your elder or your junior. Creativity is older than all of us and younger than spring calves. Music folks, nine to ninety, use first names. The kid in music folks dies hard, the music's dead when it does. As for gospel, I'd rather not unless it's big for you."

In his inoffensive way, Clay said, "Sir, it is."

"Well, that's settled. I want to have an album done in five weeks. If you have the songs, it will be. So you have four more good songs, Clay?"

"We trashed the ones that weren't any good."

"Weren't any good? Everything I've heard is a gem."

"Well, Mama and me hate dumb songs, don't you?"

Gunnar stifled a groan, "Uh, yeah, I do." Anna stifled a laugh and leaned back in her chair. Gunnar went on, "Sometimes spur of the moment things work. I need to ride down to Shelbyville and thought y'all might go with me. We can have lunch and discuss things on the way. Clay, we might run over and see my neighbor's shepherd kennel."

"I'd love to but I have plans. Mama could go."

"Clay," Anna said, "he wants you, not me."

"I'll be glad to day after tomorrow. Rachel and I are singing at the Blue Collar tonight. Y'all can talk business. What works for you, Mama, works for me. Gunnar, what Mama says is always fine with me."

"Great. We can discuss business and get to know each other better."

"And I won't worry about you here alone," Clay said.

It seemed to Anna that McGuire had to say, "Would one o'clock be too early to pick you up? It's a lovely day, we should get out and enjoy it."

Clay said. "She's already dressed. Getting out will do her good. Shep won't let anything bother Mama, but if she spends the day with you, she won't be here lonesome." Anna felt her face flame, he was shoving her up McGuire's ass. To be so smart, Clay could act brain dead at times. Hell, he acted like he still thought the stork brought him, when it came to her and men.

"Anna, I promise you'll have fun. See you at one?"

She was blowing it with Jake, but she said, "Fine." Jake would take it like she didn't care about him, but Clay's career came first right now.

"We'll do lunch on the way. Dress casual, I want to show you my horses."

As it turned out, she shouldn't have worried for Jake's feelings. He hadn't phoned when her doorbell rang at one. Someone doing what he said he would, when he said he would, was nice. Jake hated a time clock and so did she, but there was a thing called consideration.

As the chauffeur eased the white stretch limo out of her driveway, she conceded again how nice it was for someone to be on time, and act like he considered it a privilege. She was one to hang loose about the exact minute, but Jake was three hours late. Maybe what she saw in him was a figment from the dumb side of her brain all along. Or maybe, some side of her brain taunted, a figment of your libido.

McGuire said, "Where do you like to have lunch?"

"Uh, well, my palate's easy to please."

"Do you like Emil's?"

"Uh, I love Emil's." She had never set foot in Emil's, but she knew she loved it. Emil's was the richest watering hole in town. Piss on Jake!

"Emil's it is, Anna." Lord, he had the deepest, brown eyes. He was probably the womanizer of the year, but he knew where to eat lunch!

♪

McGuire had been called to the phone again, she walked the long porch of his Shelbyhouse. There had to be a fancier name than porch for a porch running the length of a mansion and furnished with ungodly expensive white wicker, but she didn't know what it was. He had to be manufacturing money. Even a blue light special Kmart shopper like herself could see that.

On the way down, he had explained the phone was a problem anywhere but in the limo. The limo phone only had an out-going line. At the time, she thought only an out-going line was on the rude side. They had been about to start a tour of his stables when he was called to the phone a second time. Now she wished there was only an out going line in his mansion.

He said he valued his limo more than any business tool he owned. Early on, after he realized a limo would be a great office away from the office, he still delayed his order. The thought of a chauffeur driven limo made him feel ostentatious, till he saw his "country boy syndrome" was hurting business. Then ostentatious or not, he bought the car. It ended his guilt about having money. Working while riding made more revenue than any other single effort. When he ordered his next limo, he spared no expense.

"I'd say you got over money guilt. You were buying at Connie's like you own a money machine." She looked serious, then broke into her throaty laugh.

"You got a sexy laugh, Anna Hill."

"Thank you-- I think," she said, thinking she was doing better with single life. She wasn't falling apart from a handsome man's attention.

"It was a compliment, and you're right about my learning to like money. Haywood County cotton pickers get lucky sometimes and it ain't no sin. I love making and spending money. Connie's was a business expense, every cent's deductible. It took years to get in the bracket that dictates spending money to make money. Clay will make mountains of money for all of us." Something like doubt in her eyes made him add, "You see that, don't you?"

"McGuire, I can't even imagine mountains of money."

"Several limos ago, living with money was another lesson I had to learn."

She raised an eyebrow. "I'd say you made all A's."

"Yes, I managed," He smiled. "I like your sense of humor and you're right. I doubt the Man upstairs wants us to live deprived of anything."

"Then wonder why, religiously, money has such a stigma?"

"To keep the rich, rich, and the poor, poor. Maybe to comfort those doomed to poverty. Money has no stigma with those who have it, but you must control money or it controls you. Could I offer a piece of advice?"

"Of course."

"When the money starts, put a percentage away. Don't wake up one day with the IRS throwing y'all out in the street. Don't cop an easy come, easy go attitude. It hasn't come easy, you two have worked for years. If it should go-- it won't go easy. Once you get used to the flushing kind, it's hell to go back to the privy. It can break the heart and the mind. I've seen it happen. Get help with managing income. When it's time, I'll recommend someone if you like."

"Thank you. I'd like very much."

"Making millions at something you love is fantastic, but music can be a fickle bitch."

"Why fickle bitch?"

"Okay, fickle bastard, but once you're on top, you don't know how long you'll stay. Financial security is great, so take care of the money."

"I just hope Clay will make a living and be happy."

"When I was looking ahead at more years than I was looking back, it seemed impossible to make a comfortable living at something I loved."

"Glad you did. This car rides like cloud nine."

"Yes, I finally got my music pump primed. Initially, I thought my start was my end, when I got smart enough to see I couldn't write great songs."

"Ouch! That had to be a low blow."

"Killed me till I realized I know great songs and how rare anybody writes one. My personal pen and paper wars taught me that. Ultimately, I stopped resenting the songs my starving writer friends were writing. Then I got excited for the world to hear songs I considered great."

"How did you know a great song?"

"Like you know your heart beats and tomorrow is coming. But when I decided to do publishing and producing, my first independent records got air play but they didn't make a penny."

"But why not?"

"I didn't know records and songs had to be with a performing rights agency to collect royalties. Finally, I stumbled onto that critical detail and signed with BMI. Then the song plugging I had worn out my shoes doing reaped a cut or two and a little money started trickling in. Every penny I could steal from myself went back in demos and pitch copies."

"Who did you pitch to?"

"Anybody! I'd put a tape in the postman's sack, if I got a chance."

"Must have worked. You're a success."

"There again, it was no overnight success-- a little cut here and a little cut there. With the money just dripping in, to keep going was like balancing a seesaw. Instead of moaning the blues I tried to work smarter. You need luck, but when you pitch and don't sell, something is wrong.

"I did a review of each song in my catalog and culled to the few I felt were across the board hits. I unloaded my files and my mind by giving the other songs back to the writers. I listened again to the fifteen I kept and rated them one through fifteen. Next I pulled out the demos I believed were hooked and filed the others to redemo when I had the money. I took the six songs from that and rated those one through six."

"That didn't leave you much inventory."

"One smash is all you need to start. I made a casting file on each song, made twenty tape copies of each and started knocking on doors again. I worked the Row during the day, the clubs at night, backstage at the Opry Friday and Saturday nights. When I had an extra five bucks, I was trying to bribe some bus driver or musician to give a tape to a name act."

"That must have been hard on your shoe leather."

"Yes, and even harder on my domestic life."

"Wife give you a hard time?"

"Wife gave me a divorce."

"Ooops, excuse me."

"Myself. About that time, I got my first name cut. Then a bucket of money poured in, I had enough to hire my first secretary. That hooked me on the green stuff. The thought of doing my own clerical work again still keeps me ahead of the music game." He chuckled. With his silver hair and years in music, he had to be fifty-something, but he chuckled like a boy.

"So, the American dream does come true."

"With all its faults, we live in a fine country, a fairy tale town, a magical business and I love it. I get high sniffing the air in a studio. My first ex and our son say music is all I love."

She held his eyes and asked, "What do you say?"

"I say no. But if it is, it doesn't keep them from sharing the money. Music is the only thing that gives me back all I put into it, and more."

"What's the best thing music has given you?"

"This car! It's the one place in the world I can listen to music as long and as loud as I want, without being bothered or bothering. Bry, my chauffeur, doesn't have to listen. He has speakers to tune to his liking or turn off."

"Do you listen much?"

"Yes. I listen the thirty minute drive from Belle Meade to Sixteenth Avenue, morning and evening. When I have time, I listen during the day."

"From Belle Meade to Sixteenth to Shelbyville horse country, you do inhabit the best of several worlds."

"In many ways I'm one of the luckiest men alive."

"You've worked hard for what you have."

"Many people work like dogs and never make past groceries. Music folks work hard, but the money's better. You and Clay are just beginning to find out how hard music folks do work. His album will mean hours and hours of hard work. Once the record's released, he'll be on the road and that's hard. When his celebrity starts, living with the world watching ain't no easy job. My job makes me only an inside celebrity, but my office is a target for any nerd who imagines he can sing or write."

"Guess that's why you need the limo."

"That and when I'm trolling for new songs. I hang out in here and listen to tapes while Bry drives.'

"Where does he drive to?"

"I have routes I like, he knows those. When the traffic goes home, I love downtown. On a summer night, when I can lower the windows in comfort, I like the sounds and smells and beat of the streets. I like Church Street, Sixteenth Avenue-- all the Row area. Love to drive by the Ryman where the Opry used to be. Years ago, I picked with the Opry band Friday and Saturday nights. I was broke as a beggar and happy as a clown to play on that stage. I like Union Station and Lower Broad. River Front Park with a docked paddle wheel steamer can put me in a listening frame of mind.

"Cruising after hours, when the street cleaning trucks come and the pedestrians are gone, makes me feel like Nashville's all mine. We roll through Centennial Park, circle the Parthenon, the lake and gardens. I like to ride by the Capitol, like to watch the fountains at the courthouse. One night I'd like you to cruise the city loop with me. It's like a merry-go-round when the lights go flashing by. After a while the same lights come flashing by again. No mistaking the L and C Tower, or the restaurant spinning on top of the hotel."

"You're a real Nashville fan, Gunnar."

"From the first day I drove up Broad moving from West Tennessee, more years ago than it seems possible. I'll never forget the red and gold of that autumn or how bright the sun was shining.

"I thought Nashville was a magical place-- she is. She's a grand gal but she ain't no Miss Muffet sitting on a tuffet. She's a working woman, not too long out of the country. She's down home, up and coming, and she's found out she likes her animal comforts. She likes pulling the chain, flipping the switch, and pouring her milk out of a bottle instead of pulling it out of a cow. She hasn't forgotten what it's like to have to run to the outhouse and light the lamp, and shiver till she gets the fire in the buck stove blazing up again. She hasn't forgotten fighting for that egg under a mean pecking hen or eating sow belly when the smoked hams had to be sold for seed money.

"She knows what it is to lift and tote and reap and sow. She knows what it is to lend a helping hand, and to ask for one in rough weather. She'll give you an even break if you'll give her one. She'll set you down to dinner and feed you if you're hungry. If you'll go to the field with her and help her work for the next meal, she'll share that one with you. But if you're lazy and trifling, she don't want you; not for a friend or for a neighbor. She may tolerate you, but she don't want you. She'll help the helpless but she's worked too hard to be where she is, and she's got too much pride to love the leech or con or parasite."

"You say it like poetry, Gunnar."

"Nashville is music, music's our poetry, songwriters are our poets."

"Do you only listen to country?"

"I listen to all kinds of music, love old forties and fifties pop, some classical and a little jazz-- like Peggy Lee and Ella. Now and then I listen to Madonna, Whitney, Billy Joel. Country's my first love and I'm listening most of the time for music to buy and sell. I'd still listen if I was only listening for music to love. I doubt the world would turn without music. Our lives are lived to a sound track. Music is everywhere."

"Get many tapes from unknown writers?"

"About a bushel basket a week. I play every tape that comes with my name on it and some that don't. It might not be past the intro." She loved his smile as he said, "It won't be past the first screech, but I listen. I'm afraid not to. It's like seeing a penny on the street, have to pick it up. Bad luck if I don't."

"Find any good songs from unknowns?"

"Rarely, but the biggest hit I've had came in the mail from an unknown. It was in the worst looking package and worst demo I've ever heard but the first line of lyric told me I had a diamond in the rough."

"Is the writer known now?"

"One hit seldom makes a known songwriter. Thought I'd found a country Irving Berlin. That one song was all he wrote worth a damn. I was late finishing an album, so I flew him in from Alabama to contract the song. Later, I listened to dozens more. All crap. Junior picked him up at the airport and brought him in my office looking like he didn't know whether to be ticked off or tickled. A songwriter in off the wall clothes isn't unusual, but this guy is sporting new overalls, looking squeaky clean and, as far as he was concerned, dressed in Sunday best. He couldn't have found Sixteenth with a posse, if Junior hadn't picked him up. Our one song songwriter had never been out of lower Alabama. But he made money off his hit. Bought a new truck, a big farm, recorded some better demos, and started spiffying up, as he called it. His taste ran to plaid, his waist ran to forty-six."

"Oh, Lord," Anna chuckled.

"He never wrote anything else I could use, I got scared he had stolen his hit. But the song was out there, getting air play. All I could do was wait and see. No one ever sued. After he saw he couldn't write another hit, I felt sorry for him. Fell into letting him waste my time, till one day when he was moaning and I got hot. Told him I'd never written one hit. He went home in a few days."

"You write too, Gunnar?"

"Tried; like everybody. Wouldn't be any publishers or producers, if it wasn't for failed songwriters. Adequate ain't enough. Like Copper Jim says, you got to be touched by the song fairy to write great songs." He grinned, then spat, "Damn!" Anna turned to see Gracie signaling him again to the phone.

After his phone call, Gunnar found her at the end of the porch. "You look ten miles deep."

"Thinking's hard on me, but I didn't know it shows that bad."

"Lady, nothing could show bad on you. Forgive me, Gracie has her orders. Now, Elvis has left the building."

"Really, I understand."

"I don't. I want to relax with a lovely lady. Let's go see my horses." As they fell into step, he took her hand. Smiling down in her violet eyes, he said, "You're beautiful, and good company in spite of our bad start. I haven't talked this much with a woman in years."

"I may be getting to where talk is what I do best."

"Hey, I'm looking at a passionate lady." She was aware of the jag of sparks that flared as their eyes met. It started that first day she was in his office, and had made her abrasive. Trying to handle Clay's business while attracted to the man she was handling business with made her feel compromised. With the contract signed, she was enjoying him. She loved easy talk with the right man. He broke in, "I didn't mean to embarrass you."

"I wouldn't touch that remark with a ten foot pole."

"Darling, try it, like it or no obligation." When he smiled, McGuire didn't look nearly so dominating.

"Is that a standing invitation?" she flirted back.

"You better believe it." His eyes burned with innuendo as they strolled into the long barn and the welcoming whinny of horses.

Anna said, "They sound happy to see you."

"I'm happy to see them." He walked her through the immaculate barn smelling of sweet feed and alfalfa hay.

The long-necked heads that whinnied at the stall doors testified his involvement went beyond pride of ownership. He stopped to pet each one, to whisper praise in each ear, along with a cut of carrot from his jacket pockets as he talked with her. It was clear he was into a cherished subject as he explained walking horse conformation and strong points of the breed.

For Anna, the most appealing of men was the man's man, sensitive, competent, sincere, interested in the arts, and a healthy belief in God.

Something had to be hiding its ugly head, he was too good to be true. She loved listening to his horse dialog laced with references to nobility, high withers, short backs, running walk, Roan Allen and Midnight Sun.

"Anna, you must come to the Celebration. I have a stallion that's a contender for the championship." His voice had the exuberance of a boy, her response buttons were being punched in a most appealing way.

While she had the choice of a sane decision, it was time to decide if she wanted Jake. He was special, he always would be, but could she reassure his insecurities? Could she watch her every move for the sake of his damaged ego and accept the attitude his losses fostered? She hated to admit it, but much of what she felt for Jake was sex. It was better to face it now, than to live it in the hell of a bad marriage. Bottom line, she doubted Jake could accept Clay.

And McGuire had her feelings on the rise. She might not need a McGuire type. The last thing he needed might be an Anna type who couldn't sit down, shut up and play games. Probably the last thing he wanted was a meaningful relationship. With all the material things he gave himself, it was logical to imagine women were part of that. Besides, two strong willed people seldom sustained a relationship. It wasn't acting that gave Hollywood couples hell, but the iron will it took just to get in films. Most men's egos suffered coupled with iron willed women. She didn't consider herself iron willed, still she would never start again with a man she intimidated.

She already knew Gunnar could be domineering as garlic, but his dark good looks against his silver hair, his broad shoulders and narrow hips made him a hunk. He was the male blend of take charge and sensitivity she was innately attracted to; and maybe innately incompatible with.

She'd be spending long hours with Clay's career. They had dreamed too long for her to let anyone interfere. She hated Jeff's resentment of the attention she gave Clay, Jake had the same problem. She couldn't change that-- then or now. Whatever she had to give to making Clay's career a success-- she had to. Mothers thought with their ovaries as much as their brains. If a man wanted her, he had to accept that she also had a job to do.

In the bright sun of Bedford County on a spread to grace kings, she faced reality. To let change happen without some direction was dumb as letting a car steer itself. Avoidance was not maturity. Coping not only in times of crisis was where she had to grow. With Clay's career riding on her relationship with McGuire, she needed to keep it platonic. And, she had her fill of bad romance. Chemistry was no reason to start a new disaster.

The welfare of too many was involved to risk a time when she and Gunnar would be old flames and new enemies. Forceful as he was, volatile as she was, they had a better chance of not working as lovers than working. Her attraction to him could be her pride on the rebound and her starving libido. Seeing Jake would put that to the test.

That night, when Bry steered into her driveway, she said, "Thanks for a wonderful day. It's late, Gunnar, don't bother seeing me to the door."

With a piercing look, he said, "I see a lady to her door. And I know when a woman hasn't decided whether or not to snuff an old flame."

"How do you know that?" Too late she saw her question was an admission and could have bitten her tongue.

"I've been there. It's hell to lose love that was everything."

"I didn't realize I'm that transparent."

"Anna, I make my living relating to people, and I'm a horse breeder. You're skittish as a mare that wants the stud and doesn't want him. She's making him nuts, he's making her nuts. It's a toss up whether they'll mate or kill each other."

"When it's like that, does the stud truly want the mare?"

"He's crazy for her, he thinks she's great! That's what makes him crazy."

"Then why doesn't he treat her like she wants him to?"

"He doesn't know how. He will jump over the barn to please her. Most females have trouble realizing their male interest has his limitations. A poor bastard's best is all he can do, his best may not solve the problem."

"What do you do?" she said. "With horses, I mean."

"Of course, horses. Some say, horses don't have our reasoning power. Some say none. But a mare won't belabor the point long before she takes the stud or rejects him. I saw who you have to make a decision about in Connie's."

"I thought I was through."

"When love has meant the world, it's tough to let go. A look can change a last goodbye to a new hello. Whatever, you're great company and a beautiful woman. After Clay's album, I'd like you to go horseback riding with me, when you have your situation settled. Remember, we can't change who we are. Forever couples seem to always be together. In a crowded room, their eyes keep finding each other, that seems to be all they need. I need time with other interests-- music, horses. If the woman in my life starts bitching about it, I feel trapped. For me, it isn't worth it, I doubt it is for you."

"Gunnar, thanks again for today. Some days feel as good as music."

"Yes, that's what keeps me going back to the studio. Anna, soon the weather will be fine to swim and fish in the spring lake. I do want you to come back."

"And it has nothing to do with being Clay's producer."

"It simply has to do with the fact that I enjoy your company."

Loving his tan and silver hair, she said, "Ask me again in a few days, and I'll give you a straight answer."

"Good. I see where Clay Hill gets his honesty." He smiled and kissed her cheek, then got out to open her door.

CHAPTER 22

ENDINGS AND BEGINNINGS

Glancing from the road, he said "Slip over here, beautiful." She moved close, touching him along his right side as he drove. He put his arm around her shoulders and said, "Want to see a movie or what?"

"Anything you want," she said, kissing his cheek.

"I just want to be with you. Maybe go somewhere nice to eat. There's one decent movie playing."

"Tullahoma isn't Nashville. A new release probably isn't playing here yet."

"Really, the day's too pretty to hole up in a movie."

"Have you seen the road from here to Lewisburg?"

"I'd never seen Tullahoma till Copper Jim brought me down."

"You'd like driving the old road. A park preserve is on the way, it's rugged and woodsy. Just before the park, there's a store still slicing baloney and cheese off the roll. We could shop there and spend the afternoon in the park, if you like baloney and cheese."

"I love it. Is it warm enough for you?"

"Sure, we can talk and hike and have some privacy."

"Sounds cool."

When he drove inside the park, she said, "Take the next right to the shelters with fireplaces and a view of the lake."

"The timber looks like it's never been cut. You should paint some of this, it's beautiful and my kind of hang out."

"I thought you'd like it."

Parking on the bluff above the lake, he said, "Let's take a hike before lunch. Deer trails are everywhere."

"Okay. Do you hunt deer?"

"Only with my eyes. Had a pet deer once."

After their hike, they spread Shep's blanket on the grass above the lake and ate. Clay said, "The baloney is great."

"Mama and Daddy bought us baloney, cheese, and Moon Pies."

"It's getting a little nippy. You cold?"

"I'm fine, darling, don't fuss over me."

"We should head on back. It's not long till we have to be at the Blue Collar."
She moved closer. "Clay, kiss me."

After several kisses, he pecked her lips lightly and said, "We have to go. I
don't want to be late at the club."

"What's wrong?"

"Everything's fine. I just need a break."

"Why?"

"Rachel, I think you know."

"Don't be like my parents. I'm no invalid so don't treat me like one."

"Honey, how do you want me to treat you?"

"Love me, treat me like a woman. You care for me, don't you?"

"I love you, I want you to be my wife."

"Then quit treating me like a little girl, all you do is kiss me. For your
information, I'm a woman. At least rumor has it I'm a woman."

"No one knows better than me you're a woman."

"Actually, I'd like to find out."

He kissed her again, and said, "If you want to be my woman, you are."

"So make love to me!"

"We got to get back, Rach, help me stash our trash."

♪

She was lovely as the Tullahoma midnight. Holding her hand and sitting
together in the porch swing made a moment when it was enough just to be
alive. Rachel beside him in the car, their time in the park, the Blue Collar for
supper, the show and dancing made a fantastic day. The Islander kids,
grandkids, in-laws, customers and friends was his first exposure to the inner
circle of a big, happy family. They had it all; he was as bewitched with
Rachel's family as he was with her. "Rach, I can't tell you what today has
meant to me."

"Just an ordinary day for the Islanders. I love to hear you sing. You had the
Blue Collar spellbound."

"Thanks. When we get married, we'll have lots of kids, like your folks."

"Are you kidding?"

"Honey, I'm totally serious."

"You don't know the work in raising six kids."

"It isn't when you have money to hire help. By the time we have kids, we
can hire help like the Kennedys and you'll be out with me singing."

"Talk about a dreamer." Rachel smiled. "Would you do me a favor?"

"Sure, Rach, if I can, darling."

"Don't go home in the morning. Stay one more night."

"Okay, if Red Springs doesn't need me. Doubt they've had time to set up a
session yet. I'll call Mama in the morning and see."

♪

Anna was jarred awake by the phone. "Hello?"

"Hate waking you."

"Yeah, Jake, I see you do."

"Thought I'd start early before you had a chance to disappear." His resentment was louder than his words.

"I hate it when you mess up and I'm the villain."

"What're you talking about?" he demanded.

"You know I'm not in a good mood when I first wake and I'm never up this early. You didn't call back yesterday, now you want to blame me."

"Anna, right after I talked with you, I got busy."

"It's okay you got busy and a sin I got busy!"

"Well, you didn't get busy at home. Don't guess you consider where you were any of my business?"

"No, I don't," she snapped.

"Woman, maybe you're right."

"You know I'm right! No damn maybe about it."

"So I screwed up. Do we meet or do I come out?"

"Doubt there's a point in either. I can't put up with your put downs."

"Am I that bad?"

"I can't take feeling bullied anymore."

"Well, Clay's going over the top and you're going to be a rich bitch, so you're too good for me now."

"Hell, I always was, only now I got sense enough to know it," she hissed and hung up. The phone rang back instantly. He wouldn't let this be easy for either of them. The phone rang-- then again. It was never easy when Jake didn't get his way. She answered, "What?"

"Fireball, could we meet and talk about it?"

"Why? Hear you haven't let any grass grow under your feet."

"I told you, I'm a grown man with a grown man's needs."

"Evidently a grown animal's."

"What was I supposed to do? Blow my head off in the woods?"

"Hell," she said wearily and hung up again.

Again he rang back. "That was a cheap shot and I'm ashamed, but I love you. Not seeing you is driving me out of my brains. Anna, I'm sorry."

"You got that right, asshole!"

"You know the City Cafe where we used to get fresh turnip greens and corn bread." She was a fool to keep talking. Talk to Jake was a come on. "Would you meet me there, in an hour?"

"Jake, really-- "

"Please, just a few minutes?"

"Okay," she said, knowing she had to stop letting him talk her into things. Still, this had to be settled. He might come charging up to the house if she didn't meet him.

"Woman, you won't stand me up will you?"

"No, I'll be there at eleven."

She had dozed off when the phone rang again. Jake had to keep on till he got a new fuss started. "Shit," she said, then answered the phone "Hello!"

"Mama? Mama, you okay?"

"Oh, yes, I'm fine. What's wrong, Clay?"

"I'm having a ball. You never sleep late. You're not sick are you?"

"No. I walked more than I'm used to. Gunnar showed me his horses."

"I'm having a blast with Rachel and her family. We picked last night at the Blue Collar. She wants me to stay another night. I'd like to if things are okay with you. Frank and Bess asked me to stay, too."

"I'm fine, have fun while you can. Gunnar says you will get busy with the music real soon."

"I'll be home tomorrow evening. Okay?"

"Have a good time. You deserve it."

After hanging up, Clay joined the Islanders, still sitting around the breakfast table. Talking to Rachel but for all their expectant looks, he said, "Mama's fine and it's okay for me to stay over tonight."

"Good," Bess said. "Now have a fresh cup of coffee."

"Ma'am, I've had plenty, thanks. Rach, I need to walk off some breakfast. I'd get fat if I stayed around your mom's cooking."

"Rachel," Bess said, "don't stay out too long. The sun's bright but it's chilly. Clay, don't keep her out over an hour. The last few weeks are the first time she's been on top of the hepatitis in a year. She'll overdo if we don't help her watch out for herself."

"Thanks a lot, Mama," Rachel said wearily.

"Ma'am, I'll look after her. See y'all after while."

Standing at the window watching Rachel and Clay walk up the hill, Bess said, "Frank, pretty as they both are, they'd have beautiful babies."

"Be a while before Rachel wants a husband or babies."

Bess poured coffee, then sat at the table. "Could do lots worse than marrying Clay Hill."

"You made sure he knows about her trip overseas."

"Frank, you see the way he looks at her. It's plain as pudding he's crazy about her. He deserves to know."

"Maybe Rachel told him," Frank said, and slurped at his too hot coffee.

"You saw his mouth fall open!"

"She's still my baby daughter, Bess."

"Mine too and we been so close to losing her."

"The Lord ain't been ready. She ain't herself yet."

"Much as I hate to say it, we spoiled her, Frank."

"Rachel needed spoiling. She ain't never been strong like our others. Damn chicken pox, not all that bad for most, nearly killed Rachel and her just a toddler. Worse case even the doctor ever saw. Then had mumps twice, which is seldom and her appendix rupturing at nine, then hepatitis when she was trying to get her high school. Rachel won't ever be strong."

"Can't help your heart going out to her, but the hepatitis might be a blessing. Healthy, she would have hit Europe soon as she graduated. She's headstrong from getting her way so much."

"We never done more for Rachel than for the others."

"Might have done less, letting her have her way. But she never was a bit of trouble playing with her Barbie dolls, looking like a redheaded angel. Didn't know she was on the place. We started spoiling her way back. First she was the baby and our last. After Rachel, you got fixed. She's always been our prettiest, then she was sick, then she could sing, then she could paint, then she was sick some more. We overlooked her squalling till she got her way. If the other kids did that, we'd a tanned their bottoms."

"She wasn't like the others, always throwing fits."

"Naw, but she's hell on wheels when she does."

"You siding with Hill against Rachel because a that?"

"No. He's a good man with a future, head over heels in love with her and she thinks the world of him. He'd make her a fine husband, if she'd forget Paris."

"She ain't. She's set her head."

"I don't want her across the waters at the mercy of foreigners. Tennessee's fine to paint in. If anybody can keep her on our side of the world, it's Clay."

"He can't, and he ain't but nineteen. He needs a chance to see some women before he settles down to being married and faithful to just one."

"If it was one of our boys, I'd agree. Clay's different and when a man looks at a woman the way he looks at Rachel, it doesn't have a thing to do with the calendar or wild oats."

"I know," Frank said, getting up from the table. "I know too, she ain't looking that way at him. You might as well realize that-- Clay too. Rachel's a grown woman and I don't think she's been with a man. Clay's got something she wants, but it ain't no wedding ring."

"You should be ashamed slurring your own daughter."

"Hell, she's your daughter too. You think she ain't got humping feelings coming from you and me? Don't kid yourself. Honey, I got to run to Tullahoma to the feed store. Want to go?"

"I need to work on supper for the club."

"Bess, Rachel's grown and Clay won't take any privilege she didn't want him to. I think as much of Clay as you and I trust him with Rachel."

"I just hate to make it look like we don't care."

"They gonna do what they wanna do if they both wanna do it. There ain't a thing we can do to stop it."

"I still feel I ought not leave them here alone."

"Suit yourself. They won't be around long till they'll be gone somewhere. Bess, a sparking couple don't need a bed to get together. They may be up in the

barn loft now. Ain't no better place to knock off a little loving than a loft full
of sweet smelling hay. Your memory ain't that bad yet, is it?"

"Now, that was always your idea, Frank Islander."

"Yeah, and you grinding like a sewing machine."

"Go on, Daddy, and let me do my work."

"Need anything from town?"

"I'm fine, you go on now."

"Okay, fire breaker," he said, walking to the sink where she was scraping
carrots. "Kiss your man bye."

♪

Clay and Rachel walked silently up the hill on past the barn. Strolling
through the orchard, he noticed the apple trees were coming into bloom. The
Herefords grazing kept the grass a good walking height. Seeing she wasn't
going to mention it, Clay was too much his mother's son to let it hang.
"Thought you were going with me and be part of my show."

"I am. I hope."

"Is Paris why you said you would for only a year?"

"Yes, of course," she said.

"But you said you had to finish your education."

"Paris is my education."

"I don't understand why you didn't tell me."

He saw her frown as she said, "I thought you knew. Maybe it was because
when we talked about going on the road, we were in a room full of people."

"We weren't with people in the park or driving to the Blue Collar or sitting
in the porch swing after we got back. You never mentioned Paris."

"We were talking about your deal, not Paris. I told you that first night on the
porch at the Blue Collar."

"That was before we fell in love. Girl, you haven't said a word since."

"Clay, you would have had that hurt look and the edge in your voice like
now. I hate spoiling a good thing."

"Rach, it's okay if you don't care, but don't mess with me."

"I hate to argue, so all my life I've been called easy-going, till I set my head.
When I don't want to be changed and sometimes when sad or bad things
happen, I can't talk about it. But I'm crazy about you."

"Yeah. That's why you're going off to Paris."

"Not for a while. I don't have enough money yet."

"Is that why you're going to work with me?"

"Yes, but I want to be with you, and working with your show will be fun
and a great experience."

"As soon as my career takes off and the money starts coming in, Rachel, I
want you to marry me. I was going to ask you tonight after the show."

"Clay, you aren't old enough to get married."

"I'm nineteen by the calendar and a thousand by another kind of clock. Lots of men get married at nineteen and make fine husbands. I love you, and soon I can take care of you."

"You're headed for life in the fast lane. You have no idea who you are or what you want."

"I know how I feel. Rachel, will you marry me?"

She looked in his eyes and said, "I can't that soon."

"Then going to Paris means more to you than me?"

"Does performing mean more to you than me?"

"That's different."

"Why?" she said. "Because you are a man?"

"Because it's my dream. A man can marry and still have his dream."

"And a woman can't?"

"I don't want you to stop dreaming or painting. Paint here."

"I simply can't get what I need in this country."

"I can't get what I need with you out of it. I feel like I'm standing on a mountain, taking time to catch my wind before I start climbing another mountain. I need you to help me make this last climb."

"All you need is to get out there and sing."

"I want you with me, Rachel."

"I'm going to be with you, for a while."

"I can't do my thing in France."

"And I can't do mine in Nashville."

"Rach, if I blow this shot, nobody will touch me."

"God willing, within a year, I'll have money and health to do my thing. By then you'll be a star with girls running out your ears. You won't throw rocks at some old country girl like me."

"I'm asking you to be my wife."

"I'm honored, but I'm going. Anyway, I doubt I'm emotionally secure enough to set myself up to be another Mrs. Presley."

"Hey, I don't do dope!"

"I'm not talking dope. You have no idea how many women will want to do you. You don't have a kid's notion of how gorgeous you are, how compelling you are, or what an aphrodisiac you are to females when you swagger out on stage and get in your music."

"Ain't it who I want to do that counts?"

"You're a man, honey. I'm only your first woman. As a star you'll have to fight the women off like bees after clover. They'll be hiding under the floormats of your Cadillac."

"That old seventy-nine?"

"You'll have a dozen new Cadillacs, plenty of money and anything else you want. I've been waiting since I was in the fourth grade to go to Paris to paint and study art. Everything has worked against me, from being sick to falling in love too soon, but I'm going if it harelips hell. You're doing your thing. You, of all people, should understand."

"I understand you just want to fool around with me."

"I love you! I'll marry you right now, but I'm going to Paris."

"No wife of mine's going off to Paris."

"Of course not! Superstar or not, you were raised too much a Bubba for that. That's why I haven't suggested it."

"Okay, you tell me, Rachel."

"I can't. I love you, I'll make love to you, I'll marry you, but I won't give up Paris. Here, I won't ever be treated like anything but an invalid with a stupid urge to go paint in Paris, when I should settle down and make some good man a wife. And you, who I thought was so original, are as bad as my family."

"Girl, what are you talking about?"

"You want to do what you want to do, but you're not taking my painting seriously, like Mama and Daddy. You think it can be done on the kitchen table in whatever fifteen minutes you don't need me. Folks say all kinds of things, maybe they believe them. It's what they do that talks. Someday, I'll paint the difference between what we say and what we do."

"How can you paint that?"

"I can't. That's why I need to go where they take art as seriously as music and don't know about my health and won't treat me like I'll break."

"Honey, I don't treat you like you will break."

"Then make love to me. Clay, I need you so. That's all I think about every time you kiss me."

"I need you too, Rach, you know that."

"If you did, we'd be in the loft loving right now."

"Heck, I didn't know that was what you wanted now."

"Nobody cares what I want. Like the hour Mama gave me is up, and I don't want to go inside. She'll be standing on her ear if I don't, and I've worried her enough." Looking drained, Rachel started to the house. Clay knew he had hurt her feelings and she looked so small walking off in a huff all by herself. Without turning she called, "You coming?"

"Nope."

She turned and said, "You wanted to know how I feel. I didn't tell you to make you mad."

"You didn't. Do me a favor."

"What, Clay?"

"Come show me the barn loft." He was amazed to see her grin and come running. You just never knew with women.

♪

Jake occupied a booth by the row of windows. Lord, he was beautiful and he had picked her kind of spot. He smiled and stood as she approached, but he had to bark, "Felt like I was getting stood up. You're late, as usual."

"Dock my paycheck!"

"Hey, Anna, I was just bugging."

"That doesn't mean I want to be bugged. I bought a new used car and I'm not used to it yet."

"What happened to your station wagon?"

"Clay's using it," she said without thinking. She did think before saying Clay was out of town.

"You let him have the best car?"

"The wagon hauls more and he might do some camping."

"You look great. Not seeing me hasn't hurt you."

"Thanks," she said. He was handsome as a dream and still turning her mind to mush with his velvet eyes.

They sat down and he said, "One of the iced teas is yours, if the ice hasn't all melted. Want lunch?"

"No, the tea is fine. You go ahead and order."

"I'm not hungry. Woman, I miss you." He waited a moment to give her a chance to answer. When she had no comment, he said, "I want you back."

"It's time to take it like it is or not at all."

"There you go, speaking in a parable again. I hate it when you evade me with things I don't understand."

"See if this is plain enough. I was in love with you, but you have a male chauvinist side I never loved or liked. When you're in love it enlarges the pluses and diminishes the minuses. Then I could overlook your chauvinism. I can't now. It turns me off. Like it or not, I'm over you, Jake. I've felt claustrophobic since the minute I sat down here with you."

"Well, thanks a lot. I needed that."

"I'm sorry. I'm trying to be upfront with you."

"What are my pluses, if you got time."

"Give me a break, Jake."

"I'm trying to see what you see." Her eyes hung on his, remembering when that look made her beat him to the floor.

"Jake, in a word, you're gorgeous."

"Woman, I'm not asking you to blow smoke up my ass."

"Man, if you want to know how I see you, shut up and listen. But I've told you all this before."

"That was bedtalk. Say it in daylight."

"All right, you're handsome, you have a Mr. America build and wonderful gray eyes. You are a wonderful lover. You stay involved in a variety of things, that makes you an interesting and fun person."

"If I have such good points, why can't we make it?"

"I haven't gone into all your minuses. I'd rather just say that I don't want your pluses enough to put up with your minuses. I'm sorry."

"But you take your boy's minuses with no problem."

"Clay was born to me, I don't have any choice. And no, I don't think he has any major minuses."

"Yeah, how well I know."

"Jake, you never tried to cultivate a relationship with Clay. He would have followed you like a puppy. You never gave him a chance."

"You won't let him be treated like an ordinary kid."

"Don't you know yet Clay isn't an ordinary kid? Clay has more talent in his little finger than most of us. Ordinary kids don't have major record labels at nineteen. His high I.Q. is why you never gave him a chance. If he was just a good old boy type, begging you to sneak him a beer, you'd have liked him fine. God, I was crazy to get mixed up with you."

"You were crazy about what I got. Be honest, like you were bragging your honest kid is. Ain't that it?"

"Yes, till you got so conceited about how I was panting for you, you thought I wanted to eat it! But you broke my rose-colored glasses."

"You don't mean that, Anna. Why lie to yourself?"

"I'm over letting my libido run me. Great sex is not enough! Besides, you never meant to marry me."

"Wrong! I planned big on marrying you."

"No. That's why, after you found out it wasn't my thing, you pushed me about oral sex, and my unpardonable sin of being a mother. That was how you blamed me for your wanting out. Love accepts the innocent quirks of people."

"Anna, I don't know what you're talking about."

"When I was talking about something you didn't agree with, you never did know what I was talking about. I'm talking about letting your ex take all the faith out of you. I'm talking about you've lost your spontaneity by always having to control. Jake, you're too bright and too nice, when your paranoia doesn't have you by the brains, not to realize what I'm saying is true. I frankly think you know it already."

"Well, Anna, you can't lose what you don't have."

"There you go in defensive mode. Ever since you fell in love with me, you had to start tearing me down."

"Why would I do that if I was in love with you?"

"You never meant to fall in love with me or anyone else. You're scared shitless of marriage. You meant to use me as long as it suited and leave me when it didn't. But like most of us, Jake, you got a heart you can't control."

"You make me sound bad," he said. She saw she had and she had chosen between as is-- or not at all.

"In spite of your good points, and you have many, I can't fight the rest of my life to be who I am. I don't mean to make you sound bad. You just punched one of my major fault buttons on the screen."

"There's the parable stuff again." She saw a man who hated to lose, trying to lose gracefully.

"Guess my bad side's showing. Ask my opinion and I'm dumb enough to think you want it."

"Yeah, honey, I did ask."

"When we were good, Jake, we were unbelievable."

"That's the only reason I'm here."

"Well, maybe it is me. Maybe I do think too much of Clay."

"Maybe you needed sex, you like to screw more than any woman I know. Maybe you needed somebody till Clay went over. Maybe since you'll be a rich bitch, you think you're too good for me."

"Oh, hell," she started, then changed her mind. "Yeah, I do think I'm too good for you now. I thought I was too good for you then. That's why I could cry and moan and touch heaven in your arms. But now, old stud buddy," she hissed, her eyes blazing, "I got enough sense to know it."

"Guess you told me." He was the one person who grinned when he cried. She was going to cry or forgive him if she didn't get the hell gone.

In the car she had to hold her shaking right hand with her shaking left hand to get the key in the ignition. She drove away thinking, Lord, I'm glad to get that over. If you're so glad why cry? I'm not! Hey, those are tears on your cheeks, if it ain't raining inside this new, used car.

A mile later, Clay flashed in her mind. She thought it was because Jake was jealous of him and she ended their relationship.

She couldn't know that, in the hay-tinted shadows of a barn loft, Clay had started a love affair he wanted to last forever.

She couldn't hear Rachel saying, "Oh, Clay, it was like I dreamed."

"Yeah, me, too. I knew you were beautiful. I didn't know the half of how marvelous you are, till now." They kissed passionately.

Then she said, "What are you thinking? Your eyes look dark as midnight."

"What a nice ring the name Rachel Hill has to it."

"Everybody says the first time hurts bad, you hardly hurt me at all."

"Mama said go easy, a woman would let me know when."

"This is your first time, too?"

"Honey, what do you think I been so nervous about?"

"I was afraid you didn't want me."

"That's why we're here, I wanted to wait till we married. Now, so you know for sure how much I want you, could we go for our second loving?"

She laughed. "Darling, I thought you'd never ask."

CHEROKEE EYES

Clay Hill

Cherokee Eyes was half redneck,
Half pure Cherokee red.
She rode a red pinto pony,
Black haired hussy, some said.
She could gun down a fast cowboy
Shooting his silver tongue lies
Firing just a dark eyed lady's
Outraged Cherokee eyes.

CHORUS:
Cherokee Eyes, Cherokee Eyes,
Soft as a fawn, deep as the night.
Innocent child of guilty times
Only love will let guilt die,
Cherokee Eyes.

One night a broad shouldered stranger
Tall as Tennessee pride
On a look into dark fire
Fell for Cherokee Eyes.
Honest sweet talk was the one way
Love could touch the wild and afraid
Soft as a baritone angel,
Cherokee heard him say:
(Repeat chorus...

CHAPTER 23
PARIS

Three years later, Rachel's predictions had all come true but one. Clay was the superstar, had the money, had the Cadillacs, had the women after him, but still he was only after Rachel. She was right predicting *Cherokee Eyes* would be a hit. It went number one on the country charts and adult contemporary. A North Carolina Cherokee tribe adopted *Cherokee Eyes* as their anthem and invited Clay to perform at their annual festival. His concert broke records in the southeast and launched him into international stardom.

His first album, *A Tennessee Hill*, went platinum, won the Horizon Award, his first Grammy, and *Cherokee Eyes* won Song of the Year. Clay's career skyrocketed. His name was a household word in most of the known world. He sang for presidents, royalty, and best of all, the fans couldn't get enough of one Tennessee Hill and his music.

All that first year, Rachel traveled with Clay, sang backup with Clay, made love with Clay, was true to Clay, and steadily refused to become his wife. Clay steadily refused to understand she needed to pursue her dream as badly as he did his. Every time she tried to talk it out with him, it led to the same dead end and she learned to quietly plan and paint.

One sunny morning, she stepped out of a taxi and boarded a jet to France. Till then, Clay had been one of those lucky people denied little by life. He was stunned when he was handed the note Rachel asked a band member to deliver. Only one line registered: "I have to do this. I love you, I always will. I'll be waiting when you want to come be with me."

Now and then he flew to Paris, but he was weary with Rachel's way of conducting a love affair. He had done the European tour and history was repeating itself. In the major cities of the continent, Rachel traveled with him, sang with him, slept with him, and still refused to marry him. It had been a great tour, the Europeans had been good to him. He loved being dubbed the Tennessee Caruso by the press. Careerwise, he had never been happier, but his time with Rachel was running out and he felt helpless to stop it.

They had two weeks together after the tour. Clay thought with some time together, he could convince her to come home with him and be his wife. He was wrong. Their time was ending. Today was their last together before he flew home. The last two weeks, the two of them taking in Paris and making unbelievable love were a sample of what a good life they could build together.

He loved so many things about Rachel. When she was free, she was great company. She was a compulsive painter but he loved to watch her work.

During his stay, she was assaulted by a creative onslaught. She would wake early, make coffee and be at her easel when Clay got up. He would get coffee and sink in an easy chair at the far end of the studio. The first morning, she said, "Darling, let me finish with this blue paint and I'll be right with you."

Knowing that far away voice, that feeling, that danger of never being able to come back to where she was, Clay said, "Let it flow. You could lose it if you quit too soon. I love to read and watch you, if I don't distract you."

"Clay, I love having you here. When I want to make love I only have to curl up in your lap." She smiled at him, then started painting again.

He enjoyed watching her sail to that high of total involvement that shut out everything for the joy of expressing something indescribable till the visible or audible expression was born. It made him feel close to her. Ironically, their twin spirits that brought them together were now tearing them apart. He explained more than once, "I'm tired of marking time. No matter what you say or how much I understand, I feel if you love me, your place is with me. I've waited as long as I can, I want you in my life or out of it."

"I am in your life, Clay."

"Another spring has passed with an ocean between us. I don't know when, if ever, you're coming home." Rachel's painting was no passive dream. The studio was filled with her work-- tremendously moving work, all started and finished in Paris. She was learning and growing to the point even his untrained eye could see the improvement from her Tullahoma paintings. After lunch she said, "I have one last painting to show you."

Clay had no idea why he said, "Is it finished?"

"Yes. I'm a little shy about this one." She led him to the far corner of her studio. "Did you ever write a song you wanted so badly to be good, and gave you such hell to get right, it was hard to judge it yourself and excruciating to chance a critique?"

"Yes, I know the feeling."

"Be brutally honest. I didn't want to risk hurt feelings between us, so I waited. I don't mean to put you on the spot, but if you don't think this painting is any good-- it isn't."

"I like your stuff, but I'm no authority on art."

"You're an excellent critic. This is the biggest thing I've attempted in more ways than one." She undraped a huge canvas.

Recognizing the scene, Clay looked at her and grinned. Then he stood looking at the canvas a few moments. He walked back and forth from end to end of the canvas before stepping back for an overall view. The four by eight foot oil of the showcase at Connie's painted in great detail touched him deeper and happier and sadder than any of Rachel's work ever had.

In the foreground he stood singing, Copper Jim was a step behind to his left as they were that night. Jim's demeanor conveyed his interest and influence on Clay's career. Rachel's eyes were on Clay as she stood singing harmony beside Milton, two steps back and to Clay's right. The Copperhill Band played across the background. In the lower right corner, she had written *Showcase* and signed it with the single word, Rachel.

He had not understood how well she understood. He was amazed at how she had caught the emotion of that first critical performance. She painted in the passionate vein he tried to express in music. He was heart touched she was inspired to paint his showcase and thrilled by the display of her talent. Her love for him was in living color for all the world to see.

As he explored each detail, a vision lit his mind of a silver-haired Rachel, still slim, still beautiful, still painting, still single and still in Paris. Her face was blessed with the glow of a love affair. Her passion was for no lover, it was lavished on painting. She stood at the head of a class, teaching a group of art students. In the art world she was revered far beyond Paris. But Paris was truly home to a Tennessean held by the velvet chains of creativity.

Something beyond art kept her in Paris, but his vision failed to see what. It was clear she would never leave the city that helped her give birth to her creative self. It broke his heart not to be in her life, but he couldn't blame her. It took an artist to know an artist, he was not unloved by this girl who was such a departure from her family and her heritage. Her love for him was in every brush stroke of *Showcase*, as it was in her every kiss. It burned a gentle fire in her dark eyes as he looked at her now. He had not lost her, he had not been bested. There must be a competition to win or to lose, his love taking Rachel from her Parisian passion was no contest.

"Clay, I can't stand it. What do you think?"

"It takes longer to be brutally honest."

"Come on, stop kidding. Do you like it or what?"

"Rach, how long have you been working on this?"

"Mentally, the morning after we made love in the loft. I woke with it in my head but I hadn't developed enough as a painter to paint what I saw. I started with a brush last Christmas."

"Why haven't you shown me this before now?"

"Scared you wouldn't like it. This means more to me than anything I've done. This alone was worth coming to Paris for. So, what do you think?"

"Rach, I don't know if I want to laugh or cry. If your picture was a song, I'd call it a hit. With a painting, I think it's called a masterpiece."

"Oh, I so wanted you to like it."

"I love it. Could I use a copy on my next album cover?"

"I'd be honored, Clay, and probably made as an artist."

"That's what makes me want to cry. You are and I've lost you."

"Darling, you haven't lost me."

"In the way I want you, I never had you."

She hugged him. "Clay, I'm right here."

"That's the trouble, you'll always be right here. Right here in Paris. My home is Nashville. I really have lost you."

"No! Clay, you haven't lost me, you're dumping me."

"Like I been telling you, I need your love. Love, to me, is marriage. Listen, I have to place a call. We've worn out this subject anyway."

"I'll get my bath while you make your call."

Waiting for the ring back on his call, he remembered invading Luara's office. He had no idea it was half closed on a Saturday afternoon. After a moment, he heard someone in the back and called, "Anybody home?"

A female voice said, "Be with you in a minute."

"Thanks." He sat down and leafed through a magazine till a beautiful brunette emerged. She greeted him with her white smile, her sapphire eyes, her extended hand and, "Hello, I'm Luara Frazier."

He stood and took her hand. "I'm Clay Hill."

"I know, I'm one of your biggest fans. You cost me a mint in albums." Luara smiled and took a chair. "Please sit down. Seriously, Clay, I love your music."

"Thank you, ma'am."

"Sorry you walked in an empty office. My staff works till noon on Saturdays, and all my sales people are out with clients."

"I wanted to talk with you. I want to buy a home. I hear you're the best real estate broker in town."

"Thanks. May I ask who recommended me, Mr. Hill?"

"Call me Clay, ma'am, if you would."

"On one condition."

"Ma'am, with your sapphire eyes, you got it."

"Don't call me ma'am. My name's Luara."

"Luara, Gunnar McGuire, my producer, recommended you. You sold him a great house. The better places for sale seem to have Luara Frazier signs."

"Thank you, it was good of Gunnar to recommend me."

"Judging by your office, you don't need me bad as I need you."

"I doubt anybody in business ever has too much business. I'm sure you know that from record sales."

"I hear that. I want to buy my mama a home."

"I have several estates I'd like to show you."

"I'm leaving for a European tour, I'll be gone several weeks. Thought I'd give you an idea of what I want and you might be on the lookout while I'm gone. Then maybe you'd show me some places when I get home."

"I'd love to. What do you want in your home?"

"A home for Mama, with lots of room inside and out. Mama wouldn't be near as picky as me and wouldn't think about spending near as much money. That's why she isn't here. I want this to be her refuge, her home, and her nest egg. Something she could turn over to good advantage if anything happened to me and she needed money."

"Clay, are you ill?"

"I'm healthy as a horse. I won't live to be an old man, but that's no news.

"No?"

"No. Mama's spent so much time and money taking care of me and I want to treat her like she's treated me. Besides finding the right home, I'll need help decorating and hiring household help and whatever needs to be done to put a place in top shape to move in and start living." Clay grinned self-consciously as he admitted, "Haven't had much experience with mansions but I been in lots of motel rooms the last few years. I want the place ready like a motel room. When you walk in, all you do's unpack. Can you help with all that?"

"We do decorating and remodeling for our clients."

"Cool. I don't want Mama worried about what it costs or anything that goes with it. She ain't used to the fact we don't have to worry about money anymore. I don't want her to have to lift a finger. Also, I have a German Shepherd I love like a brother. After the tour, I'm planning on him having a family. We need kennel space, an acre or two for exercise and a perimeter fence. When we don't have company, the dogs will have the run of the whole place."

"You're planning on your own security force?"

"Shep's getting old, I don't want to lose all of him. I'm going to buy him a mate and hope they have a big litter."

"Clay, your mom and your dog are lucky to have you."

"Thanks. All my life, Mama's life has been about me. Now I want to do something special for her. After the tour, I'll be in Paris two weeks. After that, I hope you'll have something right for all of us."

"That sounds divine."

"I hope," he said wistfully. She was moved by his voice. Only the fear of losing a lover caused that tone. "If the girl I want to marry comes home with me, it might affect the size of the house. But in a mansion, guess there's always room for one more."

"Yes, but your bride might have decorating ideas."

"Oh. Well, I'll call you when I know for sure."

"Good. As a rule, homes like you're considering take awhile to move. I have some properties I'd like to show you, if they're still on the market when you return. In the meantime, I'll look further and make your needs my first priority. Tell me more about your tastes, if you have time."

"That's what brought me barging in here. Found a few hours I'm not supposed to be in two places at once."

Then his thoughts were stopped by the phone. He answered, then heard Luara's husky, "How are you, Clay Hill?"

"Homesick, but I'm leaving in the morning. Luara, I only need a home for Mama and me."

Hearing his sadness, she said, "I'm so sorry."

"Yeah, tell me about it."

"I have three properties that meet your needs. They're all lovely. When can I show them to you?"

"Wednesday. I'll call you Wednesday morning."

"I'll give you my home number. Got a pen handy?"

"Lord, girl, a songaholic always has a pen handy."

When Rachel came from her bath wrapped in a silk robe, he was sitting on a lounge chair having coffee. He smiled and said, "Want a fresh cup, baby?"

She sat on his lap. "I want you." She kissed him long and tender, then moaned, "There must be a way for us."

"It's called marriage, kiss me again like that in the bedroom."

As they made love for what he accepted as the final time, she said, "I love you too much to lose you, there's never been anyone else. There never will be anyone else for me. Not like this."

"Nor me," he said, but his vision made him see they had no future together. Seeing did not stay his tears or hers as they lost themselves in loving.

After was another thing. After, he said, "You are the only woman I've ever made love to. Wish there never had to be another."

"There doesn't have to be another, Clay."

"You here and me there won't work."

"It would if you'd let it."

"I told you, Rach, I can't live this way any longer."

"Darling, the only argument I have is my love for you."

Again, she began to make love to him. Desperation carried them higher than ever. When neither could hold back any longer, they gave each other heaven, to hover in a heart holding eternity, then floated softly down, the most satisfied the human condition ever feels. It was their most moving time of all, perhaps because neither could relent and both knew they were over without loving any the less. It was simply that all hearts do not beat the same. Some hearts beat from the creative power of the universe and would no more cut the cord maintaining that heartbeat than a fetus. The connection was as vital to a creative soul as life itself.

Knowing her answer, he still said, "Please, come home with me. Let's get married and start our family."

"I am home, let's marry now. Let your base be Nashville and mine Paris."

"No, Rachel." She saw his blue eyes turn dark.

Still she said, "What makes France so wrong for us?"

"Honey, France ain't home. France ain't Tennessee. I ain't no Frenchman and you ain't no Frenchwoman and I don't want my young'uns to be raised French young'uns. I'm sick of France."

"But why? We've had a great time."

"France made you a better painter and robbed me of a wife. So, what else for you?" He spoke bitterly, smiling the smile of one trying to be a good sport about being broken in two.

The woman knew there was not a more final smile and trembled. The artist computed his smile as the male version of a Mona Lisa smile and filed it for future use in a painting. Unable to accept their last goodbye, she moaned, "Don't burn bridges we don't have to. I still love you and you love me."

"For the last time I'm begging you, come home. I'm buying a house for you and me and Mama and our kids. I'll build a studio to make this place look like a chicken coop. I'll even buy it, tear it down, ship it home and rebuild it."

"No. It wouldn't be the same. You don't have to do anything, darling, I'll come home to you when I can."

"We take our chance now, or it won't happen, Rach."

"What makes you say that?"

"Darling, you know I know things."

"If I leave Paris now, I won't be able to paint. As much as I love you, that would make me hate you. True love doesn't ask for blood sacrifices. Whatever it makes me, your dream isn't more important than mine."

"Don't make you or me anything, just makes us over."

"I am so sorry, Clay."

"Me too, darling, but I can't wait any longer. Haven't written a word since I left Nashville."

"Then you understand how I feel."

"Yes. That's why I've hung in this long. As over used as the phrase is, Rachel, I'll always love you."

"And I'll always love you."

He kissed her lips, then took his finger and traced her forehead, down the side of her face, across her chin, up the other side back to her forehead. He smoothed back the auburn curls still damp on her forehead from loving. He could not deny his tears as he traced the bridge of her nose, across her top lip then across her bottom lip. "Thought my little girl would have lips like this and your big fawn eyes. I don't expect to always get what I want, but sometimes it hurts so bad when I don't." Then she was crying and holding him and fresh tears blurred his eyes. He couldn't believe they could love so much and let each other go, but he kissed her cheek and got out of bed.

Gathering his clothes off the floor, he wished he had gone with Mama and Gunnar. Wild horses couldn't drag Rachel out of Paris. Stepping in the shower, he was so glad Jim had decided to keep the hotel suite and see more of Europe. At least he didn't have to fly home alone.

When he was dressed, the painter saw and saved for future use what the woman could not bear: a lover with the look of a last goodbye. As he moved about packing his things in the suitcase he had unpacked two weeks earlier, the woman wanted to say, I'll go with you before I'll lose you. The painter fighting for life possessed the woman and held her silent. When he snapped his suitcase shut, the painter couldn't stop the weeping woman from pleading, "Why not leave things open?"

"I'm a simple man, Rach. I need my woman where I can see her and love her and touch her most every day and night. She can paint, sew, go to the mall or whatever, if she's faithful, home most nights, and gives me a kid or two. It breaks my heart, but I can't let you rob me of love any longer and I don't have time to cheat on the side."

"Clay, don't--"

"I wanted you the first night I played in your daddy's club. I can't go on wanting and waiting."

"A little longer won't make that much difference."

"All the fame, all the glory, all the money don't buy a day of time."

"Clay, just give me a little more time till--"

"Where's Van Gogh's time? Where's Elvis's time? I've waited too long now. You're my first woman, I'm your first man. I wanted it to stay that way, that's why I wrote "First And Last." Course what you want and what you get is often two different deals. Guess this is one of those deals."

"Clay, you're so wrong and--"

"I'm done putting off till tomorrow any dream I can make come true today. I'm going home, buy Mama a house, and Shep a mate . Then I'm going to find me a woman who wants what I want as much as what she wants at the least enough to compromise. If you change your mind in the near future, call. I'll come running in a hummingbird minute."

He put on his cowboy hat and picked up his suitcase. Standing tall and slim in his boots and jeans and hat, Rachel thought he had never looked more handsome. Smiling sadly, he made a thumbs up sign.

She moaned, "I always thought we'd work it out."

"Me too." He blew her a kiss and closed the door. She knew he was hers if she only called his name and agreed to his terms. But she just couldn't.

Paris was turning sickly Rachel Islander from Tullahoma, Tennessee into an artist! She couldn't be on a time clock and she was doomed to be an old maid. She could never love or give herself to another man. She had given all she had to Clay. If that was the price, so be it. She refused to give up her soul.

All she could do was cry and question, like her soul sisters through the ages, why does a woman have to look like some hard line bitch to follow her dream? If he was the artist and she was the performer, she'd still be expected to leave her thing for his! It had been that way for so long, few questioned the injustice of it. No one even understood, except other artists, that for now, for however long it took, she couldn't breath without painting, and she couldn't paint without Paris. Oh, please, God, make him see Paris is to painting what Nashville is to country music.

He walked the streets aimlessly, remembering Rachel. He would always remember all the things they saw and shared, the fire in her eyes when she was loving him. But of all the dreams he dreamed for them, he never dreamed they would be over. As many times as he had imagined a showdown, because he had been fair, because he had been patient, because he loved her and believed she loved him, because he was right-- he never considered life without her or when he ran out of patience, she would refuse to be fair.

He came to a rock wall running along a river. The river was brown, the sun was setting, and he was limp with heartache. He had no idea where he was, but getting lost and his broken heart hadn't disabled his gnawing stomach. He saw a street vendor and bought something to eat that looked close to a orange icee.

Back at the rock wall, he set his suitcase at the base of the wall and himself on top. First things first, he thought and started eating the concoction that was made from fresh oranges and tasted delicious.

The wall he sat on looked as old and used as he felt. It had probably seen old Napoleon running low. He could relate to that. Meeting one's Waterloo couldn't be anybody's favorite way to kill time. There was little traffic on the river, he guessed rivers looked alike the world over. This one made him want to see the Cumberland, and glad he was going home. Sitting by a river, close enough to hear the water flow, was a good place to rest and to cool out. When he finished his orange treat, he sat idly thinking he might buy another.

Then he felt the voice of the song fairy in the river at his feet start a song in his head. He took his pad and pen from his pocket and began to write:

Rachel, I can't stay in Paris France.
Your music man's home base is Tennessee.
I know painting means the world to you.
If I do too, come home and marry me.

Above the first four lines, he wrote: First Verse. He skipped down six lines, wrote the word Chorus and underneath wrote the chorus playing in his head:

Come back home, Rachel. I can't stay, Rachel.
You know how it is with me, far away from Tennessee
I can't write and sing her country shades of Green.
I beg you, Rachel. Oh please, Rachel,
Let's pack all your painting things, live our love in Tennessee
And I'll be there for you eternally.

Skipping six spaces again, he wrote: Second Verse. Suddenly the voice of the song fairy hushed, the music died and again he was alone. He sat and listened. He tried to just hum the melody. But the song fairy was gone and the melody went with her. If he was lucky she'd return, she could write this one better than he could. If he finished it without her, he couldn't make it the song he wanted, anymore than he could make his heart beat.

Lingering with the river, he pondered. This would be a song rooted in truth, like all his best work. When it started again it would be time for his guitar. He would go with the wings of creative freedom, let it fly where it wanted to.

Some of the emotion he was feeling needed to ebb. At the moment the song was a downer. If he waited for the song fairy, she might whisper how the lovers could get back together.

A riverboat horn blared and he was beset by the sounds around him. Nothing else would be coming down for now. He signed his name, dated it, put the pad and pen in his pocket and stood up on the rock wall. Paris was a magical city, he could feel her strong creative vibes. He had nothing against Paris, he was just in love with another town and his heart was broken.

He had lost his girl, his dream of them together, he was hurt and he needed home. He wanted to walk the woods with his dog and talk to his mama. Also, he wanted another icee and to see Copper Jim. Yanking his cowboy hat low on his forehead, he jumped from the wall and picked up his suitcase. The street vendor would know which way to the hotel.

When Clay found the hotel, Copper Jim couldn't get a word in edgeways. Pacing with a truckload of words and feelings pouring out, Clay said, "Bad as I hate it, we released all claims on each other."

"Clayboy, I'm damn sorry."

"Thanks. And I apologize, Copper Jim. I know Rachel's the daughter of two of your best friends." Clay flopped on a chair by the windows.

"Son, you been drinking?"

Clay frowned. "You know I don't drink."

"I'm glad to still know it, cause from where I am it's clear as clouds, you got no reason to apologize to me. Anyway, she's doing the breaking up."

"Just don't want you thinking I dumped your best friend's daughter. I know what Frank means to you."

"Well, ain't she who decided to come to Europe and study painting?"

"Yes, sir," Clay confirmed, still gazing out the windows.

"Ain't she the one been gone something like two years and still don't give no time to come home? Ain't she the one told you plain out she didn't care about running all over everywhere on no country music show?"

"Yeah, she did."

"Didn't you say you asked her again to come home, so you could give her your name, put her in a fine home you're fixing to buy, plus offering to build any kind of a studio her little picture painting hands'd want?"

"Yes, so what are you saying?"

"What do you mean, what am I saying? I ain't been over here so long I'm a wee, weeing and parley vooing like these Frenchies, have I?"

"Doubt it's possible to parley voo with a Tennessee twang like you got."

"You might be right there, but this is plain as the nose on your face. You can tie excuses up in all kinds of higher aspirations and yeller ribbons and ole Aunt Sadie's sunbonnet, but sooner or later you get down to facts. Don't mean to hurt your feelings, son, but Rachel don't want you. You offered her the world, and there's just so much any man can do. Can't hogtie her and make her. Writing and painting and plowing and building buildings are fine, long as they don't trouble two loving each other. Anything's fine long as two want to be together enough to love around what else they want besides each other. Don't care what the songs say, each other ain't all no two lovers want all the time."

"Guess not."

"Ain't no guess to it, no couple can stay in bed twenty-four hours a day. Least, not after the first two or three days. Most of loving happens out of the bed, I'm sorry to say," Jim chuckled.

"We do love each other but maybe how people need to spend their time doesn't have much to do with love."

"Don't. I like women good as most. Ain't one to run with every woman I could, or to want a bunch on the string. Can't remember when I didn't need a good woman and a good guitar. Nobody needs a raft of neither. Can't play on but one at a time decent. Seen a dude on TV playing two guitars at once, not playing neither worth a shit. Like the tomcats trying to keep a string of women. Don't advise that, but see you some women. See enough till you find one you like that likes you and thinks like you think, feels like you feel and wants what you want. Big star like you, blue over a woman wanting to smear paint in Paris more than being with you in a home in Nashville's pure pitiful to me."

"Jim, don't be hard on Rachel. She's a dreamer like us."

"Wouldn't be hard on her for the world. She's being hard on herself and you! Frank's daughter or the president's, I got no patience with it. Ain't said a word cause it ain't my business. Since you opened it up, I don't like it or understand it. Ain't even patriotic. We got artist schools in our country."

"Painting's her dream. I can't feel hard at her for not wanting to give up her dream. You don't understand."

"Hell, I just said I don't! And I don't know why you can't feel hard at her when it's plain as mustard on a frog's back she's broke your heart."

"I wish I hated her but I don't."

"Course not, but some things are a woman's place and some a man's. Don't matter how liberated anybody is. I've seen male and female liberate their self plum out of having anybody. When it comes to the man making a living, it's the woman's place to go along."

"Lots of women would argue the point."

"Lots of women wind up alone, like lots of men. Ain't hard to set up a loser. Rules against nature can turn a winner to a loser on a pencil lead. Rachel's made a bad mistake. You can't stop living so she can follow her dream. If she cares, she oughta come home with you."

"She painted our Connie's showcase. Painted you, me, herself and the whole band. It's great. She's going to let me use it on my next album cover. Maybe it wasn't fair giving her an ultimatum."

"Rachel may be good as Al Capp or Walt Disney. Hell, you ain't asked her to quit. You asked her to paint where y'all can have a life and you can make her a living. When it comes to women, you still come off simple sometimes. Don't mean to hurt your feelings, but I been trying to tell you since your Mary Ellen days. Loving's something you do, so you don't do without. You're loving and still doing without."

"That's it," Clay said, searching for the pad in his jacket.

"That's what?" Copper Jim asked.

"The hook of my new song." Clay wrote and repeated, "Loving's something you do, so you don't do without."

"Hell's bells, if you still got balls to write, you got balls to live without Rachel. When you're done, let's hunt supper. I'm hungry as a hog. Course we can't get no pinto beans or cornbread. I need Miss Roxie's home cooking bad. Staying here extra wasn't a hot idea for neither one of us. Gunnar's jumped around the world so much he don't care, but I could gnaw a nail. This Tennessee withdrawal's killing me."

"He's at home anywhere Mama is."

"Yep. You feel all right about that?"

"Long as he's good to her, it's fine with me."

"I sure don't want no more pancakes the Frenchies call Crepe Suzies. Pancakes is pancakes and lay on my stomach like lead. Ready?"

"Wait. Let me write this down. And gripe some more, maybe you'll give us a line. *Tennessee Withdrawal* sure sounds like a song title to me."

"Hell, that ain't a title, that's a fact."

"Rachel said Nashville ain't the only town where I can base my career."

"Wrong, " Jim barked."

"Yeah, and I'm homesick as a hound in a high rise apartment."

Walking to the elevator, Jim said, "Europe's seen all it's gonna see of me."

"You ain't performing for these nice folks anymore?"

"Not less they come to the good ole U.S. of A."

"Copper Jim, I do believe you're missing Miss Roxie."

"I'm about starved for her good homecooking."

"Bet it's Miss Roxie's loving you're missing."

"I'd be hard pressed to choose, wish we was leaving now. California is foreign as I'm gonna get again. You can write that down in your daybook. Ain't even gonna mind flying over nothing but water tomorrow. I'd try to walk on it to get back to Nashville."

CHAPTER 24

WOODHILL

After the bomb search and four-hour wait in New York, he still hated getting back on the plane. As impatient as he was to get home, the delay increased his fear of flying. He took comfort in at having a window seat, although he and Jim had been separated. Jim was toward the front and he sat two rows from the rear. Once in the air, he could fake his mind off flying by looking down at the toy world. It was wild how height brought nature down in size. As a kid, he'd learned that in the woods. Up high in the branches of that tallest oak had been one of his best places to think and write. The death of his daddy sent him up there to think things through. Maybe he was watching, maybe he was finally proud of his son.

Everyone was seated when the woman walked down the aisle and took the outside seat on Clay's row. She wore a flight attendant uniform and filled the neat uniform like the designer meant it to be. From her hair curling up to the envelope hat, to her shoulders narrowing down to her waist, the curve of her hips, and her shapely legs sloping into blue pumps, she wore the company colors perfectly. Her one flaw was an old face. Her body was so perfect, it was like the wrong face was on the right body.

Clay had hoped for someone to talk with to take his mind off the flight, but now the cat had his tongue. She settled in her seat, crossing her lovely legs, and took a magazine from the holder on the seat in front of them. He realized he was staring, forced his eyes to the window and fought an urge to cry. Get over it, he chided himself. Instead of feeling sorry for her, hope you look as good if you live to be her age, if you do know you won't.

The sun was weaving pink and gold through the heavens. Dwarfed at this altitude, the city below reminded him of a Grandma Moses painting. As always, he was awed by how neat the houses and buildings looked from a plane. It looked impossible dirt, dope, poverty and murder could be a part of the scene. There was the river; every city skyview needed a river running like a green silk ribbon. The lights from a baseball field flashed on, flashing back memories of his own games. Then lights started flashing on all over town like eyes winking back at the stars.

In moments the town was left behind, leaving him thinking, Somewhere in time, we were returned to Eden and don't even know it. Now instead of apples, we're losing paradise to garbage. If I could write that and not sound preachy, it would make a great song.

Clay got his bag stashed under his seat and took out the clipboard holding Blue Horse loose-leaf paper like he had used for writing since grade school. He found his pencil sharpener shaped like a miniature dog house, twisted a new point on a number-one lead pencil and started writing. He didn't know what part of a song he was writing first. It was so easy for the four chord to be the one chord in another key.

Then he started hearing the chorus. In parentheses, he wrote "Chorus," skipped down two lines and wrote the words. The chorus was a gift, it came whole. But then the voice went away. Clay frowned. He sat listening to the depths of himself so intently he could almost hear his heart beat and the creak of the creative wheels turning in his head. Nothing was happening. The song was gone, like a radio out of power. Knowing he would have to wait till the song came back, he put his writing tools away and settled back.

When the attendants served dinner, Clay noticed his attendant failed to take an order from the lady on the aisle seat. He took it for an oversight. The second time around, the attendant ignored her again. Since the woman was in uniform, he thought it might be company policy to serve employees last. But where he came from, older folks ate at the first table.

The attendants were trained not to make a to-do over celebrities-- if that was what he was. They weren't making any public announcements, but both attendants were falling all over themselves to make sure he was served and still ignoring the lady. Then an attendant came back and said, "Mr. Hill, would you care for anything else?"

Clay smiled. "Yes, darling, y'all missed this lady here by me. If y'all are running short on food, I'll be glad to share mine."

"Excuse me?" the attendant said.

"Darling, I may be selling some records now, but I'm still a down home boy. I don't eat before folks doing without."

The blonde was cool except for the faint flush of her cheeks. "Sorry, Mr. Hill, we will take care of her right away."

After the meal, as if they had talked all along, the woman said, "Is it very hard to write songs?"

"Well, sometimes, ma'am."

"Clay, I've seen your TV shows and concerts. I've been a fan ever since I saw your benefit for the Cherokees."

"Appreciate that. Folks like you keep me going."

"As a retiree, I fly free and love it. Don't you?"

"To be honest, ma'am, flying scares me to death."

"I had to scrounge too long for any way I could travel not to love flying. I have all your albums. You have a talent for writing indelicate subjects in a delicate way. I bet everybody you meet has a song idea for you."

"Yes'm, but I mostly can't write other folks' ideas much."

"That's why your music is personal. Have you written about child abuse?"

"No, ma'am, can't say that I have."

"A victim of child abuse never gets over it. It should be aired and stopped."

"You were abused as a child," Clay said gently.

"Yes. You and my mother are two of three people I've admitted that to. She never believed me, but the abuser is often a family member. One reason it goes on and on is denial by the child and anyone the child might confide in. I wish you would put it in a song. Music carries a message people hear, they never would otherwise. Your abortion song is a masterpiece."

"Ma'am, you know my name but I don't know yours."

"It's Peggy. My dad named me Princess when I was born. I left at sixteen and changed my name to Peggy."

"I don't know if I can write it but I'd like to hear your story."

"He first came on to me when I was fourteen. I told my mom. She accused him, he denied it and she pretended to believe him. Maybe she did. Anyway, he beat me and they lectured me about lying. After that, I tried to avoid him and stayed away from home all I could.

"I thought it was over. When I turned sixteen, my mom started working midnights. One night he tied my hands to my bedposts and raped me. He said if I told anyone, he would beat me worse than before. So I left."

"Couldn't you tell police or a teacher?"

"His best friend was the police chief, I knew he'd be like Mom. I told my gym teacher when she asked about the bruises on my legs after the first time. She said she was sorry but she couldn't get involved."

"Who did you turn to?"

"I tried again to tell my mother. She cried, told me to stop lying and to go on to school, if I knew what was good for me. It was a Friday, she grocery shopped on Friday mornings. I circled back and hid in the garage till she left in the car. Then I went in and packed a suitcase, took money I had saved and robbed a cookie jar where she kept household cash. I went to their bedroom and got the quarters he saved. I figured they owed me the money, since it was all they would ever give me.

"I walked to the bus station a back way so no one would see me. At the station, I sat down and counted the money. I had a hundred and twenty dollars in bills and change. I put fifty dollars back for food. Since I hated Michigan winters, I bought the most miles south my traveling money would buy. I looked older than sixteen, so the ticket agent didn't question my buying a ticket. He wasn't crazy about my forty dollars in quarters. I thought it was great Dad's mad money bought my ticket.

"I wound up in Atlanta with a job in a food chain in the bus station. Till I got a paycheck, I slipped around living in the station and on the streets. Then I met a man on the street just waiting for runaways. He asked if I'd like a job making big money. I said no. After a while, I saw my job only paid enough to keep me fed and my rent paid. I was too young to get much else and was terrified my parents would find me if I was visible. The man on the streets kept offering me big money. Eventually, I worked for him and hated it, but it did pay better. I saved up to go to Europe and start a new life. That never happened, but prostitution gave me a better life than I'd ever known.

"After two years, one of my tricks turned out to be a partner in the company that owns this plane. He gave me a job and an apartment. I was his mistress till he died last year. That's why they snub me. Over the years, word leaked out about us to everyone but his wife, thank goodness."

"Ma'am, that's quite a story."

With pleading eyes, she asked, "Can you write my story and the story of countless others?"

"Let me sleep on it. Do you like *Honky Tonk Princess* for a title?"

"Yes, very much. It's an apt title."

Clay put his hat over his eyes. In two minutes, he was in a crazy dream that would half wake him, but before his mind cleared, he would fall back in the dream. He had not dreamed of Shep in a long time.

In the dream, Shep had a mate, a beautiful black and tan bitch. There was a whelping box of pups about three weeks old. There were too many for one litter, nineteen or so and couldn't be Shep's. They were all red like Irish Setters, and Shep's eyes were full of tears. Clay woke himself saying, "Shep, it's not your fault, she bred to another dog."

Peggy said, "Clay, are you all right?"

"I... I was having a bad dream. Excuse me, I need to go wash my face."

When he returned, she was reading and his dream of the off-breed litter started nagging him again. His talent for interpreting dreams came up nil.

When they landed, he didn't feel his normal relief. Leaving the plane, Peggy said, "I enjoyed our visit, Clay."

"Me too. Got something I can write on?"

"Yes," she said, and took a pad from her purse.

Writing his number down, he said, "Call me for tickets anytime. When *Honky Tonk Princess* is released, call and let me know if you like it."

Clay woke at dawn in the bed he had slept in since junior high. He expected to wake glad to be home. But he was engulfed again in the pain of losing Rachel. Home wasn't going to fix things as he had hoped.

Mama, Gunnar and Miss Roxie had been waiting at the airport for Copper Jim and himself. Funny, he never noticed how good love looked on Mama, or Gunnar's satisfied glow. Had to give Gunnar credit-- he knew how to get along with Mama after he figured out she was a pushover for a man who would accept her as is. After they left Jim and Miss Roxie, Bry drove Mama, Gunnar and himself home. They were up late, it was still only five thirty.

He closed his eyes and tried to sleep, but the dream of Shep's litter filled his mind. A message was in the dream, his subconscious was fighting to tell him. As he saw himself standing, looking down at the mongrel pups, part of the message came. It was time to breed Shep if he was going to.

The other thing he was through putting off was buying Woodhill. Calling Luara from Rachel's had that started. The dream was a reminder not to renege. It was too early yet to call Luara. It wasn't too early to call Gunnar when he was at Shelbyhouse. After two rings Gunnar answered. "Morning, man."

"Good morning, Clay, how are you?"

"A little weary but fine."

"What are you doing up this early?"

"Jet lag I guess. What's your excuse?"

"Before the sun gets hot and the grass is still wet, this is paradise. If you're not too tired, you ought to come on down and enjoy it with me."

"That shepherd breeder who breeds and shows still live next door?"

"Yeah. You couldn't blow Raymond Moses out of Bedford County."

"Reckon he'll be around today?"

"We'll see. I was at his place last week, looking at a new litter. He asked when you were bringing Shep."

"Think he might have a nice bitch for Shep?"

"I imagine. He wants a Shep pup. Says he let his old stock get away from him and Shep's pedigree is closer to blood he doesn't want to lose."

"Sounds like we're on the same beam. I'm moving on some things I've put off. I'm buying a bigger house."

"You and Rachel must be getting married."

"No such luck. I'm afraid Rachel and I are over."

"Y'all were great during the tour."

"I'm buying a house around your place up here. I love the neighborhood."

"That's great, but damn, I'm sorry about you and Rachel."

"I begged her to come home and marry me. If you don't mind my asking, as we speak, when are you and Mama getting married?"

"Her latest excuse is you. Says you're losing too much weight."

"That's Mama. Ran out of vitamins and I'm tired from the tour. I'll rest now."

"Is that the bottom line, Clay?"

"That's it. Listen, buying a bigger home doesn't mean I'm trying to keep Mama from marrying you or anything."

"I know. I'm hoping she'll marry me within the year. Either way, you need a bigger house to fill with Anna's and my grandchildren someday."

"I intend to as soon as I can."

"I was kidding. You got plenty of time, Clay."

"For some reason I don't feel like I have."

"Load Shep up and come on down here and relax."

"If it won't inconvenience you, I will. There's another thing or two I want to talk with you about in private. How about after lunch sometime?"

"Sounds good. Bring Anna and plan on staying over."

"I'll call back after I talk with Mama."

"No need to call, come on when you get ready. I'll be here at the house or at the barn with the horses."

"How is old Laughing Man doing?"

"Got a mare in for him, he knows it so he's happy."

"Give him a brush stroke for me. He's a fine hunk of horse flesh."

After hanging up, Clay said, "Okay, Shep, I know you want to go outside. Hang on till I get my britches on."

Loving the woodsy smell of the Tennessee morning, he walked the dog. With or without Rachel, he had missed home, he felt funky and he had been out of the country far too long to spend the day indoors. When he returned to the kitchen, he filled Shep's bowls.

Feeling better after a shower, he dialed Luara and smiled at her warm hello. "Morning, Luara, this is Clay Hill."

"Hey, good morning, nice to have you back."

"It's nice to be back. Hope I didn't wake you."

"I've been up awhile, drinking coffee and relaxing. How are you?"

"Glad to be home. I did love performing over there. Europeans understand country music. How are you?"

"Fine, real estate has been good to me lately. Saw your Berlin concert on cable. You were fantastic."

"I appreciate that. You're one kind lady."

"Not at all, I love music and especially yours."

"Thanks. I'll be in town several weeks. I have an interview, an album and I don't know what all. I'm ready to get Mama's house squared away."

"Great, I'm excited about another place. It's a gorgeous house with dog kennels and six acres of fenced grounds. The former owner had Dobermans."

"It sounds right on, Luara."

"I think it is what you have in mind. The house is southern colonial, with a huge pool and all the amenities we discussed. The owner's about to remarry and move to his fiancee's home in Florida. Actually, he's already in Florida. I thought about you when I got the listing. Tried to reach you last week, but you were still out of the country."

"Sounds like Woodhill."

"Excuse me?"

"Woodhill will be the name of the place I buy."

"Woodhill," she repeated. "I like that, it describes the place. It's loaded with trees and the house stands on a rise. There's maple, oak, two huge magnolia trees and a small orchard in the back."

"No apple trees, I hope."

"Clay, I think I did see a few. You don't like apple trees?"

"Sometime when you have at least a week, I'll explain."

"Sounds like another sad love story."

"You got it. Starts out, once upon a time I proposed in an apple orchard, got turned down and was too dense to know it. Anyway, I'm driving down to Shelbyville today and I'll be gone overnight."

"So tomorrow or the next day, Clay?"

"Darling, I'm feeling restless, need to get out awhile. I'm free till noon or so. Could you, like, show me this place with the kennels in an hour or so?"

"You mean from now?"

"If it wouldn't be too much of an imposition."

"I should have known. When you music people decide to make a move, you're ready to move."

"Guess music folks are off the wall. We can set another time, but it'd be cool if you could. The place sounds fine and I want a house for Mama soon."

She was too perceptive to miss the anxiety or maybe urgency in his voice. "Clay, I can handle it. I'll do some shuffling with my schedule but it won't be the first time. The owner's out of town, so it's no imposition on him."

"Thanks, Luara. Where do I pick you up?"

"Normally, I pick clients up, or we meet at the property."

"Normally, they don't ask you to show property on an hour's notice. Tell me where to pick you up, girl."

The "girl" word did it. It was awhile since anyone had called her girl. Few in the business world called a female "girl" who wasn't anymore. Her tailored business image and wearing her hair up was a factor. Another factor was owning Luara Frazier Properties. But, she thought, giving him directions to her home, some days the magic word is please, some days the magic word is thank you. Always, with a woman who has just turned thirty-six and not feeling secure or ravishingly wonderful about it, the magic word always-- is girl.

When Luara opened her door to a hunk with a wind-blown mane of blond curls, wearing jeans, a red football jersey and sneakers, he didn't come off as mysterious as the entertainer she had seen on TV. The real thing smiling down on her had an accessible look that made him all the more breath-taking as he said, "Good morning, Luara." Clay Hill was all American, she had thought she was addicted to Italians.

"Good morning," she said, wishing he was ten years older or she was ten years younger. Another thought whispered: While you're wishing, go for fifteen. I'll take either. Walking out on the stoop, she said, "It's a lovely day to go house shopping." Clay smiled, shaking her offered hand.

"Is it proper to tell a real estate lady she's gorgeous?"

"It's most proper, and coming from a young man as gorgeous as you, it's wonderful. This real estate lady has just had her thirty-sixth birthday and isn't feeling too swift about it." She closed her door and started to lead the way to the silver Mercedes in the driveway.

"Luara, if you don't mind, let's take my convertible. It hasn't been out to play since I went to Europe. It needs the exercise and I need to drive."

She eyed the car. "If you can oblige an old lady and put the top up."

"Lady, they don't put old ladies on magazine covers, that's where you belong. I'll be happy to put the top up. I'll be happy to go get another car if you don't like the color of this one." Luara's laugh blessed his morning.

"No, but you are so sweet. I love red convertibles when I'm not working. It's atrocious what one does to my hair, and I have clients all day."

"Won't take but a hummingbird minute to fix that little detail."

As Clay opened the door for her, she smiled and said, "We're only going three miles but that's long enough to turn me to a hag for the day."

"No problem." He already had the top of the car coming up. "We'll ride with the top down one day when you're not working." After they were on their way, the coziness with the top up suited him better.

"Drive to Belle Meade Boulevard and take a right at the intersection," she said, thinking, At least he isn't pissed about having to put the top up.

"Being gone has made me see all over again how much I love Nashville."

"You sound like a man glad to be home."

"You better believe it. The fans anywhere keep my creative juices pumping. I need that, but it will be awhile before I'm gone that long and far again."

"You see so many great places. You don't like that?"

"I'm not much of a traveler, but I've had to do my share in the last three years. Do you like to travel?"

"Love it now and then. Love Nashville too, and my work. Unlike your career, mine keeps me at home. By the way, this is a sharp car."

"My car collection is one more nice thing the fans have done for me."

"Watch for the corner. The magnolias cover the turn till you get close. The street's past that last tree."

"Okay." He flipped on the turn blinker.

"It's the third mailbox on the high side. You won't see the house at first, it's back off the street. The privacy is a great plus for a celebrity."

Rolling up the winding drive, he said, "I love the trees."

"I thought you would."

As he crested the long driveway that rounded a curve to the front of a white mansion with six columns, his, "Wow!" made her smile. He sounded more like a delighted boy than a hunk who had flocks of women chasing him.

"You like?"

"It's awesome, I love it. You mean it's got all this," Clay said, waving his arm to indicate the house, "dog kennels, six acres, and a pool?"

"Yes, and servant quarters."

"I'll take it!"

Luara chuckled. "You haven't seen the inside."

He got out and opened her door. "So, let's do that now."

"It is a lovely home. We can write a contract with the stipulation the seller guarantees the structural soundness, if you do decide you want to make an offer. First, let me show you the entire property."

From the moment he saw the two-story foyer with the hand-carved railing and winding staircase, Clay knew it was his. As they walked from room to room, he felt he had been here before. The high ceilings, the feeling of space and freedom that permeated the house convinced him further. Out back there were four eight-by-thirty-foot kennels, with an exercise area, a huge pool and three giant magnolias. "Luara, this is everything I want for me and Mama."

"I was hoping you'd be pleased." She saw the shadows of sadness that shaded his long gaze at the blooming apple trees. She was touched by the way his eyes changed from blue to darkly brooding, like the sun smothered by clouds. "Clay, if the trees bother you, they can come down."

"No. Trees are precious to me, I haven't cut one down yet. I'll get used to the apple trees being here and the girl they remind me of, being absent."

Later, Luara would remember this was the first time she broke a business rule with Clay as she said, "I'm sorry she broke your heart."

"It was the last thing I expected."

"It always is, Clay. No one expects a broken heart." She saw pain mix with acquiescence and the effort it took for him to smile.

"I want this big old house, I love it already."

"Good, I thought you would. I love it, too."

Then he smiled and said, "Hey, covering the back forty has made me dry as a desert in summer. Let's talk over a Coke at some drive through."

"Sounds great, if you won't be mobbed by your fans."

"Not as long as I keep changing cars and patronize drive throughs."

He was moved by her throaty laugh. "Okay, Clay, let me lock up."

"You got a great laugh. Are you always this happy?"

"No. It must be you, or your youth." As he followed, she made herself busy securing doors and windows. She was scared he would make a pass and twice as scared she would.

"Luara, can I help?"

"No. Just hang on." She didn't mind seeing a man a few years younger but he was much too young. She didn't know why she had to chime, "I love how you make me laugh."

"My pleasure, call anytime and ask for the man who makes Luara laugh. With you, darling, I laugh, too."

When they were parked at a fast-food having Cokes, he said, "You're the real estate doctor, what do I offer?"

"Not the asking price, of course."

"What about ten percent off the asking price?"

"That might buy it. You may want to think it over."

"No, I been dreaming this since I was sixteen."

"Clay, at ten percent off, the property is an excellent buy."

"Cool. Listen, I need help getting the house ready for Mama, don't want her to lift a finger. I want to keep it a secret and throw a surprise party when it's ready. Would you help me?"

"Of course. Right now, it would give your secret away, but I do want to meet this mama of yours. She must be a super person to rear a superstar and a son who cares for her so."

"Mama's super all the way. So are you, Luara."

"Thank you, kind sir. You've made my day."

"Luara," he murmured looking out his window.

When he looked back at her, his eyes were like he was drugged as he sang, "Luaaara, Luuaaara, the sapphire shines so lovely in your eyes. Luuaaara, Luuaaara, I hear the sound of love sing in your name. Ooh, ooh, Luuaaara, Luuaaara, my lovely Luuaaara."

Luara had never before been aroused by violet eyes gazing at some distant planet. By the time he took a small tape recorder from the console and sang what he had into it, his throes of inspiration had her totally mesmerized.

Still, when he turned off the recorder and asked, "What do you think?" his voice was innocent as a boy's.

"Uh, well, I think I've seen a miracle. How do you do that?"

"I don't. Just happens sometimes when something moves me. Darling, you really think *Luara* might make a good song?"

"It's marvelous. I couldn't write a song if my life depended on it."

"You don't have to. I'll write it, just for you, if you like it."

"Actually, Clay, I think it's wonderful."

CHAPTER 25

LUARA

The kennels worked well and Shep was so taken with Star Lady, the bitch Raymond recommended, Clay bought her. Like Shep, she had the blood and was also past her prime. With two female puppies coming back to his kennel, Raymond agreed to let her go. Now, Shep had Lady and three ten week old puppies left at Woodhill. Gunnar wanted one and Frank wanted one but Clay wasn't in any hurry to see them leave. He was keeping the male marked like Shep and named him Shep Junior.

Shep was a good and proud papa but at times the years and the puppies were too much. When he got cranky and growled at the pups, he needed a break.

Little Gatlinburg was where they both could heal. In dog years, Shep was past ninety and the years were showing. Twenty-three was young for a man, but Clay couldn't remember feeling as beat as he had lately.

He sat on the wishing rock, Shep napped on a bed of fern, comfortable as some canine potentate. Woodhill was beautiful but Little Gatlinburg was where he and Shep needed to be now and then. All of it had caught up with him. Depression alone could cause exhaustion quicker than ditch digging, and he needed to fix that. The Rachel thing was over, he might as well try someone new, it was futile to go on all alone.

There had been one great thing; Mama loved Woodhill. Course she had to cry a little when he had taken her in to the surprise house party, but he had loved announcing to her, in front of all their guests, that Woodhill belonged to her. And it did; every nail and every piece of furniture was paid for and in Mama's name. Whatever happened or didn't happen, she would be financially secure with a beautiful home.

The day they moved out of Little Gatlinburg, she had to cry again. Actually, he cried too, and realized they could never sell Little Gatlinburg. These hills and trees had been a part of his life too long. The green solitude meant too much to lose. Wherever he went, when he thought of green he always thought of Tennessee and Little Gatlinburg.

Luara had been super helping him get Woodhill decorated. He offered to pay for all the work she did, but she wouldn't take an extra dime. Besides being a beautiful lady, Luara was a great gal and a fine friend. It would be easy to get serious about a woman like that. She was so sexy in her special, sophisticated way and definitely perceptive.

Like the way she anticipated Mama might want some of the old furniture, and having him sneak her into the Little Gatlinburg house while Mama was out with Gunnar. Getting an idea of the pieces Mama had, helped to decorate at Woodhill with an idea of what Mama might want to keep. Luara left one bedroom at Woodhill empty, and when Mama added her touch of decorating, the open bedroom had been used to good advantage.

Slipping around with Luara at Little Gatlinburg, driving her around, shopping for furnishings they needed, hiring the right people to take care of Woodhill and then getting everything ready for Mama's surprise party had been great fun. Without Luara, it all never would have happened.

He wasn't that experienced with having the money to buy a Woodhill. Without the competent servants Luara helped hire, a home that size would be a total drag. The last thing he wanted for Mama was any kind of drag; she deserved to be happy. By now, he thought she'd have married Gunnar, but when he asked her about it she always said, "One of these days, Clay." The psychic vibes weren't right for her yet.

Now with Woodhill squared away, he was ready to handle another matter. If he wanted a new woman, it was time to get serious and get one. No matter how bad he hated it, it was over with Rachel. In the four months since they said goodbye in Paris, she hadn't called once. He'd about got it through his head she wasn't going to call and he'd done all the begging he was going to before he left her in Paris. She just didn't want what he wanted and hadn't blown any smoke about it. She told him straight up how she felt. Accepting last goodbyes was always a problem for him.

Being on top was great, he was hot to record the new album. Gunnar and Jim had everything ready to start in two weeks. Three weeks after that, he'd be starting the new tour with the opening concert at Mile High again. He was looking forward to going back, he loved the clear Colorado air.

Anywhere he was playing music felt good, but good as it felt, man did not live by number-one records alone. The right woman was vital. In spite of the gold records, fame and money, he was lonely for someone to love. During the last U.S. tour, he saw a girl or two-- nothing worth pursuing. For the hundredth time, Copper Jim said he was too picky about women, and he might be. After knowing Luara, other women were boring.

Copper Jim was right. Music with no warm arms to hold you back made a cold bed partner. Rachel was bound to come to a night when she realized a paintbrush didn't have arms, but it would be too late for them.

Shep had his mate and young family, Mama and Gunnar were tight, Jim had Miss Roxie. Clay Hill, close to being the best selling artist of all time, was lonesome as a street person for the right woman. Like Mama always said, when you get to wanting something bad enough, you'll make a move.

He gathered his gear. He had a good melody and some lyrics but the song he came hoping to finish wasn't happening. When it started, that day by the river in Paris, he wouldn't have believed it would be so elusive. Not being able to accept it was over with Rachel was the reason. He wanted *Goodbye, Rachel* on the album and needed the song fairy to get it right. Today she was working somebody else's wishing rock evidently.

His *Luara* song wasn't written either. What he had was good, but it had to ripen and it made him miss Luara. Maybe she was missing him, he knew she liked him. She had to be one fantastic lover, she laughed too sexy to be cold.

Anyway, at least they could be friends. Maybe it was time to see what a quarter and a phone call would do. The woman couldn't say anything worse than no. As off the wall as it might be, and if she laughed in his face, there wasn't but one woman he really wanted to see.

Might as well quit the woods, nothing was happening with the music. "Shep, it's time to call a certain lady."

♥

Swapping cars gave him the anonymity to cruise Nashville like any citizen as long as he watched where he stopped. At a drive-up pay phone, he kissed his quarter for luck, and dropped it in the box. Luckily, Luara was in, her secretary put him right through.

He loved the sound of Luara's low, "Hello, Clay Hill. How are you?"

"Missing getting to see you, since we finished Woodhill. And thanks again, it wouldn't have happened without you."

"You have thanked me enough. I'm wearing the gold bracelet you gave me, it is so beautiful. I love it."

"Good. Luara, I'm feeling kind of bummed out, and I need a friend. Guess you're already booked for lunch."

"Actually, I was about to send out for a salad."

"How about me picking you up for a visit and a bite to eat? I love the brunch at the Opryland Hotel but I seldom get the chance to enjoy it. The management is great about privacy. If the fans give us any trouble, they'll move us in a private room while we eat."

"That sounds great but I have an appointment at two and it's almost noon now. It doesn't sound like the kind of luncheon you want to rush."

"We'll do that another day. Let's do a take-out Percy Warner Park picnic."

He loved the laugh in her voice as she said, "You come up with such original ideas. I could use the fresh air and I'd love to see you, but I must be back by one forty-five. I can't chance blowing this deal."

"I'll be there in a few minutes. I'll have you back in your office on time, or whenever you say. And that's a promise."

He dropped Shep in the exercise fence at Woodhill, away from the pups. They were getting rowdy, he didn't want Shep taking one of their heads off.

Making the left hand turn off Harding Road into the paved area at Luara's office, he saw her standing under the awning at her building. As she walked toward him, he saw again how stunning she was. He was out of the car to meet her at the end of the sidewalk. "Hi, beautiful lady, do I get a hug?"

"You better believe you do."

He ended their hug with a kiss on her cheek and said, "A man could get lost in your sapphire eyes. Girl, you are so beautiful. Tell me something."

"Anything, after such compliments, my tall friend."

"What are those eyes of yours always smiling about?" Her laugh made his heart jump. "Luara, you can't know how I missed you."

"I missed you," she said, and cut his chains of depression with three words.

Feeling happier than he had in a long time, he caught her eyes and felt his spirits rise on her smile. As he drove the refurbished sixty-eight Cadillac through the noon traffic, an exchange of smiles was the sum of their conversation. The aura of mutual joy from just being together made the best communication possible.

On out Harding Road beyond the traffic, before turning into the park entrance, he asked, "Would it make you mad if I ask you a question that isn't any of my business?"

"Not if it won't make you mad if I don't answer."

He glanced at her and said, "You seeing anyone special?" His question surprised her. He had never made a pass.

She searched his eyes, then asked, "Why?"

"I want to see you, if I have to buy another house." It was great to hear her laugh again. "And I'd buy a ticket to hear you laugh like that. Is someone standing between us spending some time together? Don't tell me his name if there is. I'm subject to put a contract out on him."

"Save your money, honey. There's no one special."

"Fantastic." It felt so good to laugh with Luara.

As he drove around a wooded hill, she said, "Looks as if we're going to have a glorious fall."

"There's a great picnic place on top of one of these hills if I can remember where. Mama and me used to come here to see the colors."

"How is your mama?"

"Fine. She spends a lot of time with Gunnar, at the house you sold him and his farm in Shelbyville."

"Does that bother you?"

"No, Gunnar's real good to Mama, good for her, and may be the first man to understand her besides me. Sensitive as a rose petal, opinionated and a strong personality, I think she missed her calling not being a performer. I'm still hoping to get her to do some concerts."

"Is she interested?"

"I wish. She sings and writes like an angel. The place I want to show you is around this curve."

When they cleared the curve, they were high above the tree tops. The land descended like a natural carpet of fields and woods and roads and homes to the valley of Nashville in the distance. Luara said, "I'm supposed to know Nashville real estate but I've never seen this. The view is breathtaking."

"I thought you'd like it," he said, getting out of the car.

He walked her to a picnic table by a stand of maples. "Hold on a second." He dusted off a place on the bench. "Now, you won't get your skirt dusty. Have a seat and I'll be right back." He loped to the car and came back loaded with food bags.

"Clay, can I help?"

"Yes. Let me look at you and rest yourself. You're the one who has to go back to work. Mama didn't raise no fool. I can handle lunch even when I don't have it ready in take-out sacks. Oops, be right back, forgot the napkins." She smiled watching him again lope to the car and back. There was about Clay Hill something very young and very old.

He smiled at her as he arranged the food. Then with a sweep of his arm toward the view, he said, "I love that look at Nashville. It's like a concert of nature. Mama brought me here the first time years ago. She always packed a lunch. This was our first place to visit after Daddy's funeral. We always brought Shep and the guitars. We'd pick and write-- eat and hike. If it turned cool, we'd build a fire. There's always plenty of dead wood around. I cool out with grass and trees and hills."

"It is nice here."

"I finally thought of who you remind me of. It's been bugging me for a long time. Your black hair threw me off but it's finally hit me. You are a dark-haired, olive-skinned Marilyn Monroe look alike."

"You're laying it on thick for broad daylight," she chided, but her smile said she was pleased.

"While I'm at it, I love your wonderful sapphire eyes. They hold laughter and whisper beautiful things."

"Like what?" Their eyes met and held.

"Like anything's possible. They remind me of a picture of a lake hanging over my grandmama's sofa. It has a hundred shades of blue, like your eyes."

"Thank you."

He was lost in her eyes a moment before saying, "If I remembered right, you like white meat chicken, ranch dressing and your tea straight."

"I'm flattered you remembered." He was too much and too handsome and she had to stay away from him.

"Hope it's okay I picked the food up to save time."

"Young man, it's fine with me."

"Don't you think it's time to stop hiding behind young man preambles?"

There was an exchange of electric eyes before she said, "I don't know. You have me fluttering like a sixteen year old." He was afraid he'd gone too fast but an imp danced in her eyes and she said, "I never do well on an empty stomach. Let a working girl eat."

"Okay, but tomorrow we lunch at the Opryland Hotel."

She looked at him so long, he doubted his chances, but she said, "I have clients all afternoon."

"How about the next day?"

"Can't you find a way back to the love you're trying to get over?"

"No," he moaned, with his heart in his eyes. Sales training had taught her the finality of a no without justification.

"I am truly sorry," she said sadly.

"Thanks. Now, as friends if nothing else, what about the next day?"

She warned herself: What this beautiful young man needs is much more than a friend and you haven't been this attracted to anyone in ages. Don't be an imbecile. A broken heart is no picnic! You'll fall in love and it's hopeless. You watched his Berlin concert in a fog. You could barely keep your feelings hidden doing the house for his mother. Unless you crave to be crushed, just say no. She said, "Okay, Clay."

At the hotel, there were four bus loads of Iowa 4-H Club members and their parents who thought Clay Hill was the best thing since corn. To his delight, they had to be served in a private room. Clay felt like a bit of an imposter since it was obviously a room reserved for the rich and famous. He was in the shoes, but he still wasn't comfortable when the waiter said, "Mr. Hill, my name is Robert. Is there anything else?"

"Looks like we got it all but a little time, thank you."

"Sir, if there's anything before I check back, push the buzzer by the door."

"We will and thank you again." As he walked with Robert to the door, he slipped a twenty-dollar bill in his hand and said in a low voice, "Be a buddy, Robert, and don't come back unless I do buzz."

"Of course. Thank you." Robert smiled and left.

Luara said, "We have enough food for a Red Cross crisis."

"Let's check out how it tastes." He held a chair for her. "When I picked you up, you stunned me so, I forgot to say you look stunning."

"Thanks," she said, sitting down. "This is the first time I've seen you in a business suit. I like how it makes you look older."

"Thanks. Mrs. Frazier, I want you to know I'm old enough."

"For what, Mr. Hill?"

"For you, darling."

"Clay, I don't know."

"Would I lie? I do everything a forty year old does and some things better," he leered, and loved her laugh.

"I don't doubt that."

"As the English say, shall we dig in?"

"You bet. Lunch is my main meal."

"You a dieting lady?"

"I try to watch my figure."

"Been watching it myself," he said innocently, but that look was in his eyes.

"Clay, give me a break."

"Okay. Let's have some country ham, it looks great."

"I don't need the salt."

"Me either, but once or twice a year won't hurt."

"Clay, I was serious about watching my figure."

"Darling, I was too."

Luara knew she was blushing like she hadn't in years. Irritation colored her tone, she used the word purposefully, "Boy, how old are you anyway?"

Undaunted, he grinned. "Old enough, like I said."

"No. I mean it, Clay."

"Well, by this life's calendar, twenty-three."

"You think you've lived other lives?"

"Know so." He took another bite of the biscuit and red-eye gravy he was clearly enjoying. Then he went on, "Like sometimes you know you got a sale before you get a contract. Like you knew I'd buy a house from you."

"Well, I certainly hoped."

"Naw, you knew. You're too successful to miss such vibes. Be honest."

"Okay, I knew." She couldn't help smiling.

"You knew we'd be friends, and maybe more."

"Oh, no. You can't pull me into that."

"I still know the answer. Like I know I've had other lives. Like I know I won't live to be an old man in this one."

"Knowing all that doesn't bother you?"

"Course not. I think it's a plus everyone had in earlier times. Over the eons, civilization and the invention of weapons taught most souls out of it."

"How is it you weren't taught out of it?"

"Mama has the gift, lucky for me. Also, she let me be alone some, like she needs to be alone some. You know Little Gatlinburg is forty acres of the softest old woods, too rough to farm or develop. So I got to grow up there. My folks couldn't have afforded it otherwise. I spent every minute I could in those woods. Mama went too, but when I was only six she would let me go alone."

"Were you ever afraid?"

"No. That's one thing about me Daddy liked, he grew up with the woods. If you sit quiet, the animals start coming out. Animals in the wild depend on natural abilities for survival. The little guys have to know when the big guys are coming or they never grow up."

"I like your way of seeing things. Did you learn that from your dad?"

"He wasn't much interested in me. Guess Mama raised me in her own image. You know Mama."

"Not well. I know you two have a great relationship and talk at times without saying a word. But I saw her so little, we had Woodhill ready before I met her, then you went on tour. I'm still not sure she was too happy about not having more say about the house."

"But she was. She's still talking about what a fine decorator you are. Mama likes things nice, but she could care less about decorating."

"That's unusual for a woman."

"Mama grew up in an orphanage. That put her in touch with divine energy and gut feelings. It's like our religion, in a way."

"Does she go along with you on living other lives?"

"Mama feels she's been places before and she's open minded."

"I doubt she would be open minded about you seeing someone thirty-six."

"She knows I'm grown and who I see is my business." He started filling his plate again. Luara watched, amused at how he still ate with the relish of a teen. He was handsome, talented and truly decent. No wonder his music broke all records. "What?" he asked, cocking his head to one side.

She smiled. "You remind me of my son."

"How's he doing?"

"This year, for the first time, he's living with his dad and going to school in California."

"How long have you been divorced?"

"Nine years. I really hate Kyle being so far away."

"Then why did you let him go?"

"He asked," she said lightly, but pain clouded her eyes. "Some boys miss a male image badly. I married again. Lynning was a wonderful husband and father to Kyle. All that ended with his heart attack."

"How long since he died?"

"Five years. I can't remarry just to give my son a male image." Her statement sounded like a question.

"That's like Mama, but we're more like brother and sister. She was barely eighteen when I was born."

"What about your dad?"

"He committed suicide when I was sixteen."

"That must have been hard on you and your mom."

"Hard on Mama. The hard part for me was dealing with my guilt feelings. My life was better with him gone. He didn't like me because Mama loved me."

"That's strange."

"In the wild, most males run off or kill their sons before they're competition. That's another thing Daddy hated. I never would kill things."

"No, I don't imagine you could," she said softly.

"I was home, but I saw it all in the time it takes a phone to ring twice. I don't want to go into it now, I'll tell you about it another time. Mama and me are a little psychic. She was real depressed for a time. Later she had a vision and saw Daddy's suicide."

"I don't think I would want such a gift."

"It's a human version of animal instinct. Originally, we were created with it."

"What makes you think that?"

"Basic logic. Animals know you're coming long before they see you. I doubt He'd create us any less perfect, do you?"

"You're over my head, I can see to you it's simple."

He placed his knife and fork across his empty plate and said, "May be repeating myself but truth is simple. May not make you happy, but it's simple." Luara watched his eyes burn to purple, and felt he was reading her mind.

Searching for something witty to vanilla the moment she hated the inadequacy of, "Guess that's right." Lynning taught her to think on her feet. He never taught her how to hide her feelings from a clairvoyant.

Clay held her eyes a few moments before saying, "The truth here and now is, I want to make love to you and you want to make love to me. I don't think we are immature enough to let a hangnail like a calendar rob us of the privilege." She could not say a word, and he had captured her eyes. Try as she might, she could not drag her gaze away from his.

Timing had always been one of Clay's strong points. He let the moment ascend to its highest before he drawled, "Honey, we going to your place, chance the waiter stumbling in on us here, or see if the hotel has a vacancy?"

Without waiting for her answer, he went to her. As he bent to kiss her, she said, "Please, Clay."

"Girl, we can't fight nature." He kissed her long and soft. Then taking her by the arm, pulling her to her feet, he said, "I just want to kiss you some, precious. Have since I first saw you and you know it. I can be satisfied with just kisses if I have to. When I heard you on the phone this morning, I knew I had to have some of your kisses today."

"I'm too old to-- "

"Hush, I'm old as water, lived ten other lives, loved twenty wives, thirty concubines and sixty children. Kiss me, darling."

"But, Clay-- "

"Trust me. I know what I'm doing." His lips covered her mouth again.

She was never more moved by a man's kiss. Soon she was breathing in a rush, trembling like a bird, behaving like a fool, feeling like sixteen and saying, "Let's go to my place."

"Cool, angel, we got to happen."

♥

When they reached the condo, she said, "I need to call the office."

"Kiss me first?" He kissed her knowingly, taking full possession of her mouth. There was no mistaking the message in his kiss, her answer or that he was opening her blouse as they kissed. His mouth kissed down her neck to her breasts. After a moment, his mouth at her breast, he said, "Make the call, darling, and cancel all your evening appointments."

As he kissed back up to her lips, her arms went around his neck. By the calendar, their ages might not work, but their feelings were working like sun and seed, the fire they were building was timeless.

Locking his arms around her waist, Clay stood straight to his full height. Luara felt her feet clear the floor and knew she had never been in the arms of more man, had never felt stronger desire.

When Clay lifted his lips, he laughed, spun joyfully with her in his arms singing, "Luara's got good sugar, I never been surer." He set her on her feet, with a hug and said, "Foxy lady, if you gotta call, you gotta hurry."

"But we need to wait--"

"Sweet, darling I'm the world's worst at waiting."

Suddenly she smiled. "I'm a bit impatient myself." She unbuttoned his jacket, pushed it off his shoulders, he shrugged it to the floor. "I don't do ties, darling." Happily, he loosened his tie. She opened his shirt and kissed his chest. "You're so handsome," she said, kissing the strong column of his neck. "Clay, everything about you is beautiful."

"Luara, baby, I... uh... honey,... you gonna call your office?"

"After while, precious," she murmured, touching her lips across his chest.

~~~~~ **CHAPTER 26** ~~~~~

SHEP

It had been the longest two weeks of his career, but now he was back with Luara and reassured she was real. They had just showered together and scrubbed each other's backs. That led to more of the love making they thought they had exhausted. After, she rubbed the good smelling lotion over his body. With a towel around his middle, he lay on her bed watching her execute Operation Makeup. He found it fascinating; he found anything and everything about Luara fascinating.

She sat at her dressing table like a goddess, wearing the silky robe he brought her, sapphire like her eyes. Her dressing table was set up as precisely as any creator's workplace. He wished his home studio was set up as well.

Luara was good for him in so many ways. She was smart as she was beautiful, wonderfully organized and he was learning. The mirror she worked before was a great piece of engineering she designed herself and had installed. It reflected a three-way view with one panel magnified.

Clay lay propped up on a pile of satin pillows watching her with the same deep interest he focused on life in the woods from his wishing rock. He realized she was as involved at putting on her makeup as he was working on a song. "Luara, you really enjoy working with makeup."

"Yes, it's something I picked up from my mother. She acted and did makeup with a little theater group-- among other less admirable things."

"Evidently. You should see the anger in your eyes."

"That's another story. Synopsis: Mother falls for other man, leaves with man, leaves daughter with father. Daughter's fourteen and shattered."

"How do some parents do what they do to kids?"

"I don't know, except I think passion may short-circuit the brain. She was great to me before that. We were so close, or I thought so. We did so much together, and she was so beautiful. Sometimes she took me to the theater and taught me makeup. For fun we dressed up in all sorts of wigs and getups, I loved it. When I got older, she let me help her with makeup at the theater. She said I'd be better than she was; said I had a gift for it. Even now, when I'm putting my face on, I feel close to Mother."

"Did you consider makeup or acting as a career?"

"Yes, but I got married. Then I got pregnant, then I got divorced with a son to support. Then I married a marvelous man with money and I got lazy. I learned the real estate business to please Lynning. Then he died and left me plenty of money with no way back to my early dream. Someday, I might try and get a job doing makeup. I'd love to do an eighteenth-century play with all the powder and wigs. But as we speak, I'm still busy and having a wonderful time with a mesmerizing hunk of male."

There was no way to look at her she wasn't beautiful. Made up, unmade up; dressed up, dressed down; dressed for business, a night on the town or-- undressed. Undressed, she was divine, and when she touched him, he could hear angels sing. He smiled at the memory not more than twenty minutes old and said, "There are no perfect people. Something has to be wrong with you, but I don't know what it is."

"Speaking of perfect, you look like a young god with that gold hair curling down your back. All you need is a cluster of grapes, a chalice of wine and two slave girls fanning you."

"Seriously, darling, you are perfect."

"Baby, I can tell you a baker's dozen of things wrong with me. After last night, I've never hated them more."

"What reasons?"

"Thirteen years, precious."

"Luara, that isn't fair to you or to me."

"I couldn't agree with you more, still it's true."

"Years don't matter to people who love each other."

"If you were forty-three and I was fifty-six, they wouldn't matter too much. Now, they count against me almost as badly as being dead."

"Come on, get real."

"Darling, I am and I'm having a time with reality in this fairy tale romance of ours. Only weeks ago I'd have sworn I was smarter than this. It's perfect and it's wonderful but it's love in a box. It can't go anywhere. Don't shake your head. You can't help it and I can't help it, but it's true and we can't change it. All we can change is the subject."

"I'll buy that. Are you coming to Woodhill this afternoon for my interview?"

"What time did you say?"

"Two o'clock. You haven't been in Woodhill since you did the decorating for Mama's party, and you missed that. I want you to get to know her. She knows I'm seeing someone and thinks it's weird I don't bring you around."

"She'll think it's more weird if you do."

"Hey, don't get back on age. Why don't you come on out about one? When the interview's over, we'll take off somewhere nice and have dinner."

"I don't know, Clay."

"If you aren't interested, guess it's no big sin."

"I'm interested in anything you do."

"What then?"

"The interview's at Woodhill."

"So?" he pressed.

"Clay, isn't doing a TV interview stressful?"

"You changed the subject. Don't oil around, I can take it straight."

"All right!" she said, gave her lips a final dab with the lipstick brush and turned on her stool to face him. "I can't handle us yet, in front of your mother, the media or my fifteen year old son."

"Luara, you--"

"You wanted it straight. I need to keep us private awhile longer."

"Copper Jim, in an earthy kind of way, is the smartest person I've ever known. He says love is something you do so you don't do without. I don't know why I keep falling in love with women who want to put me off for one dumb reason or another."

"Clay, angel, I'm not talking about forever."

"When you feel like I feel, a day is forever. I'm crazy about you, I want you with me. I want to touch you and love you when I want to."

"How about till after your Mile High concert?"

"That means you won't be going to Denver with me."

"Wouldn't have much time for me, anyway. You know how hectic concerts are. And I need to stay out of the spotlight for the time being."

"And when I come back?"

"I'll have my head on straight."

"And you promise to go everywhere with me?"

"I... yes, Clay, I promise."

"You got a deal," he said happily. She saw he was coming on again. She didn't want her make up mussed this soon-- or anything else.

"Clay, now it's your turn to answer my question."

"What?" he said settling back on the pillows.

"Isn't appearing on national TV cameras, touring and recording, stressful?"

"Isn't showing houses or working at the factory?"

"Yes, but you just did three weeks on the road with a windup live televised concert. You have the interview, the new album, the videos that go with it, and rehearsals for Mile High. You're beautiful and I love your lanky build, but, darling, you don't need to lose any more weight."

"Please, Luara, not you, too.

"Listen, I know you're young and full of it, but too much is too much. You're taking on too much stress."

"What's even more stressful is trying to sustain a career as an entertainer and not being asked on TV and all the rest of it. It goes with the territory, I didn't get drafted. I've been wanting and dreaming it since I was a kid. Sure, it's been a little busy and I'm a little whacked out. But it'll slack off after Mile High. I'm like Joe down at the loading dock, having to pull overtime. If you want it, you get it while you can. It's part of holding down any job."

"After Mile High, you get a medical checkup."

"Lord, Luara, you sound like Mama."

"That's normal, I'm closer to her age than yours."

"Come on--"

"If you're okay, we'll go anywhere you say."

"And meet my mama?"

"And meet your mama."

"Lady, that's a done deal."

"Good! Listen, I need to go to my office and see if it's still there."

"Honey, I'm gonna miss you."

"Your interview will keep you busy enough without entertaining me. And there is such a thing as loving each other to death, my young friend."

"Hey, what are you saying?"

"The last two days and two nights, practically ever since you came off your tour, darling, we've been at it. I, for one, need a break. Your mom would probably like to spend some time with you. I think it might be a good idea all around if we take tonight and tomorrow off from each other. That way, you can do things you need to and so can I."

"I was gone two weeks, you trained Hannah to run things just like you."

"I know, but--"

"Girl, when did you ever get or give more love?"

"Never."

"When did you ever have better sex?"

"Never, Clay, but--"

"No buts, darling, we feel the same way. Come here."

"It isn't that long till two."

"I know," he said, getting out of bed to kneel in front of her. He picked up a raven tress, rubbed it between his thumb and forefinger and kissed it. "I love your hair, it's so black, so alive."

"Alive? You ought to try fighting it to stay in a business bun during the day. I need to have it cut."

"Nope! No hair cutting. Promise me." His eyes bored into hers.

"Okay," she smiled, "no hair cutting."

He eased open the top of her robe, held only by a tie at her waist. She knew she was had again as he smiled with wonder, then said, "Darling, they're so beautiful," even before he started the kissing, back and forth, taking turns and time with each, until he heard her gasp of pleasure. "That's my girl and that's my cue. You can't know how I love to make you want me, to feel you trembling for me. You make me feel ten feet tall."

"Right now, I think you're going for eleven."

Clay chuckled, "Good!" and kissed her long and lingering on the mouth. Then he gathered her to himself and stood with her in his arms, still kissing her until all she could think of and all she could feel was how much she wanted him. Responding to Clay's caresses was as unavoidable as responding to the licks of a loving puppy.

Without another word or even the hint of a struggle, he had her out of the robe, on the bed and wild for him in spite of her common sense, her business acumen and her acute awareness of how asinine she was going to look when their affair became public. The headlines she could see in the tabloids all burned to ashes in the fire of his touch, his undeniable affection and her uncontrollable response.

Then, as right, as easy, as essential as a breath, he was easing himself inside and up and filling.

Totally inside now, he was giving and he was taking. He was holding her as close, as life sustaining, as dew on a rose. And somehow for him, with him, the mechanics were not mechanical. Love with him was a natural progression, like dinner, then dessert. Kisses brought caresses, caress brought loving. His lovemaking, like his singing, was not a lesson learned, but a natural heartfelt talent. He was mesmerizing with his encouraging white smile, his soul glowing in bottomless violet eyes.

His soft kisses covered her shoulders as he slipped a hand under her buttocks and pulled her closer and fuller to him. She felt their souls were touching when he said, "This is the biggest deal of all."

And when she could hold off no longer, to hear him say "I love you" made perfect sense, perfect paradise.

"I love you," she whispered, knowing her words were not a lie but they were a fantasy. Clay was a child of fire and fantasy. Evidently, she was too, because she heard herself say, "In some other time, with our birthdays right, we would have been married. I would never have been able to keep you out of my pants and we'd have begat twelve kids."

"And me wanting every one to be as loving and beautiful as you. Oh, Luara, I truly do love you."

"No! Clay, you mus--"

"Girl, don't tell me not to love you. I already do, you know it. You love me, too. That's all there is... for all lovers and you know why."

"Yes, but tell me again, darling."

"Love doesn't care about time, love doesn't care about place, or about birthdays. Love just cares about loving. And who loves Clay?"

"Luara loves Clay."

"And who does Clay love?"

"Clay loves Luara."

"Luara, darling, can you now?"

"Oh, yes, darling. Right now!"

Smiling at the camera, Stacy Collins said, "The last ten years, country music has been rolling to the top of the mainstream of American music. Since the forties, with Eddie Arnold, Kitty Wells, Hank Williams, Patsy Cline, and the list goes on, Nashville has been the source. In more recent years, Alabama, Reba, Dolly and many more have made country music the music of America.

"Nashville continues to give us music to work, love and live by. With the superstar we're about to bring you tonight, Mama Nashville has outdone herself. In a short period of time, no star has become more of a household word than our guest.

"Billed as the Country Caruso, this young man has burst on the musical scene like the brightest shooting star to ever stand in front of a mike. His albums top the country and adult contemporary charts. Since his first release, a self-penned song called *Cherokee Eyes*, he continues to break record selling history. The record stores can't keep his records stocked. His concerts are televised live, and are still sold out the day tickets go on sale. He is a man of values and morals. He doesn't do drugs, cigarettes or alcohol and-- he loves his mother, his producers and his record label. On paper, he's too good to be true or interesting, but he is true and very interesting.

"Normally, we show segments devoted to two or more celebrities. Tonight is devoted entirely to the Clay Hill phenomenon. We are bringing you interviews with Clay's mother, Anna Hill, his co-producers Gunnar McGuire and Copper Jim Quarrells, who discovered Clay when he was in high school.

"Our first crew came to Nashville to set up interviewing Clay Hill only. They reported back this is the biggest story concerning a country music star we have produced and to tell it well, we had to cover his mother and his producers. We spent some time deciding how to begin, then we decided the way to tell any story is from the beginning. The beginning of Clay Hill is his mother, who is also his co-writer."

Gunnar was so proud of how beautiful Anna looked as Stacy said, "Anna, you taught Clay to sing as a child."

"Clay passed anything I had to teach years ago."

"But Clay often mentions learning to sing at your knee. Were you preparing him then for superstardom?"

"Oh, Lord, no, Stacy. Singing for me, like so many Southerners, is a way of life. Singing to our babies is part of how we raise kids. Most babies in the South are rocked and sung to sleep at least once a day."

"Was it evident to you early that Clay had talent?"

"From the time he was two, Clay was beyond himself musically and academically. He was very bright but he can tell you better than me. Let's get him in here with us."

"I hope our cameras get the look in your eyes. The eyes of a proud mama are the world's brightest light."

Anna chuckled. "Well, I am real proud of Clay."

"I would be, too. Now we'll talk with the walking, picking, singing epitome of the word Superstar. His TV specials outrate anything on television. In a day of variety shows, talk shows with singing spots and the like, this young man has resurrected the one-hour concert."

As the camera swung on Clay, Stacy said, "Good evening, Clay Hill. How are you?"

"Fine, and obliged to you and Mama for saying nice things about me."

"In a word, how does it feel to be the top performer in the world?"

"In a word, awesome."

"I must tell you, I'm not a fan of what is typically called country music but I'm a most devoted fan of yours. If there is one word that doesn't apply to you, it's typical. Would you agree?"

"The worst person to describe a person is the person. I just do what I have to do, the best I can, and hope folks want to hear it."

"I bought my first album of your music when 'Honky Tonk Princess' came out. Your lyrics are so touching to women in general. It's rare for a man to be so knowing about our feelings. And you're so young. Twenty-three?"

"Yes'm, and a Nashville native."

"I love the way you speak. I know southern etiquette teaches 'yes'm' and 'ma'am.' To a New Yorker it sounds out of *Gone With The Wind* and flows off the tongue so beautifully."

"Thank you, ma'am."

"Tell me, how do you know so much about female feelings?"

"Well, I try to write the truth and how it is when real life situations happen. When you try to write it true, like how it was when it first hit you, it doesn't have much to do with male or female. It's just how it feels and how it is. Course many of the lines are Mama's. Mama can write such tender lines."

"You and your mother are inordinately close. How do you account for that?"

"Well, besides loving Mama, I like her-- she's good company. She's always there for me. And we are so much alike in how we feel things."

"Are the songs usually your ideas or hers?"

"Both. Mama's a born story teller."

"How would you describe your writing, Clay?"

"I'm singing a story like the troubadours back in history. Even kings like to hear stories told or sung. Like I loved to hear the stories Mama read and told and sung when I was a kid. All she had to say was 'Once upon a time' and I couldn't wait to hear what came next."

"You don't consider yourself a man with a rare empathy for women's feelings?"

"Ma'am, the unique thing about once upon a time, it don't matter if it tells about a man, woman, child or bird. The story's told from the narrator's point of view. The narrator's like a god; you make it all happen like you want it to. If the story goes deep into how a woman feels, I talk with Mama. Sometimes she writes it out in prose to draw on. We want it to be honest and probable."

"It's common knowledge your mother is part of and a huge influence on your career. We hear rumors she's going to start performing with you."

"Mama's a little stage shy, but she'll be a performer one of these days."

"We will be looking forward to it. You sometimes write on controversial subjects. Why did you decide to get into controversial subject matter?"

"I didn't decide to be controversial."

Stacy's eyebrows met, "Clay, abortion is about as controversial as you can get. What about your *Rosy* song?"

"That's just a story about one particular abortion. *Rosy* doesn't take sides. Stacy, I'm a troubadour, not a crusader."

"Then why did you write about abortion."

"Abortion's most always in the news. Naturally I gave it some thought, formed some opinions. Then a friend was involved in an abortion, and *Rosy* came to me. Sometimes a song just uses a writer to get written."

"Then it was an inspired song?"

"Well, it may sound pompous, but, yes'm."

"Are you for abortion?"

"Abortion is heavy however it goes down. I've heard even married couples having a natural abortion rarely have a funeral. Hospitals have been taking care of such since day one. Now, some folks are making any stage of conception a big deal."

"You don't consider early abortion a big deal?"

"Not unless it involves me. Only God knows when living starts. If I had a sister who wanted an abortion, I wouldn't want her forced to go to some butcher. If men conceived, abortion would be legal. If men conceived, it never would been illegal."

"You are such a fair minded man."

"If I am, it's because I was raised by Mama."

"Don't most of us feel that way about our mothers?"

Clay grinned. "With mine, it's fact not brag."

Stacy smiled. "Do you write by schedule?"

"Well, I like to sit with my guitar and write on Blue Horse notebook paper when I first wake up."

"What's Blue Horse notebook paper?"

"Like we used in school. I like to write before a given day rattles my head. But a song can happen anytime. I just try to go with it when it does."

"Then you try not to plan too much?"

"Not initially. The planning and the crafting comes in the rewrite. In the beginning, I write however I can write. It may be my story or someone else's. A song idea may come from a movie or TV program that didn't go like I wanted it to. In my song, I make it go my way. With some of my songs, I have no idea where they come from unless it's other lives."

"Then you don't write your own feelings?"

"I try to write the feelings in a story whether it's your story or my story. I try to put myself in the mood the person or persons in the song would be in."

"Who helped with your success?"

"God, Mama, Copper Jim Quarrells and Gunnar McGuire."

Standing out of camera range, Gunnar saw Kevin at the door motioning for him. He eased away and followed Kevin to the study. "Mr. McGuire, we have a real emergency. Shep's down and in a bad way. The vet's on his way."

"We can't alarm Clay now. Kevin, wait for the vet outside and come get me after he examines Shep."

Just before time for Gunnar and Copper Jim to join the interview, Kevin stood at the door and signaled again. Gunnar found him waiting in the hall. "Sir, Shep's gone. The vet says he was dead when I found him, but he didn't suffer. He said that old boy got lucky and died in his sleep."

Very late Anna heard Clay walk by her door and his steps fade away down the stairs. It was so awful about Shep. Maybe she should get up and see if she could comfort him. But they had discussed it for hours before they went to bed. Maybe she should leave him alone. He hadn't knocked at her door. He wasn't shy about coming to her when he wanted to talk.

She was dressed to go downstairs when she heard a car go by the house and down the driveway. Shep was the brother Clay never had and he was shattered. But it wasn't mother comfort he needed now. She didn't know how that Luara woman could see a man so much younger, but if her broken hearted boy could find comfort tonight, so be it.

In ten minutes, Luara was awakened by her door chime. She slipped on a robe and checked through the peep hole before opening the door. Clay was ashen. God, his mama must have died!

"What is it, Clay?"

"Shep," he said, coming into her arms.

She held him. "What's happened?"

"He's dead."

"Oh, no. My poor darling. How?"

"He just died. The vet said mostly old age."

"Baby, I'm so sorry, you want some coke or coffee?"

"No. I just want you."

The next morning, it was late when Luara got up and later still when Clay joined her in the kitchen. He was fresh from the shower, in jeans, shirtless and barefoot. His sadness was like another garment.

His coffee was poured, Luara was dressed for work and about to leave when she said, "Did you sleep any at all?"

"No." The circles under his eyes proved his word.

"I have an appointment at one. I'll be back soon. I wouldn't go but this is an important meeting I've been working on for months."

"Cancel it." His sad eyes a silent plea.

"Clay, I really need--" She stopped as he put his hand in his pocket and came out with a quarter.

Holding the coin out in the palm of his hand, he groaned, "Please?" His voice said he was past desperate. She had a flash of her appointment, a crucial meeting on a million dollar deal, ripe for closing.

Helpless before the violet pain in his eyes, she hesitated only a moment before taking the holding combs from her hair that fell like a dark shawl around her shoulders. "I'll be right back."

Dialing the phone, Luara couldn't believe herself. She didn't risk business for pleasure. It didn't make a dime's worth of sense to risk her commission on a million dollars. Explaining to Hannah how to explain to the client, Luara wished someone would explain to her.

When she hung up, he was right there, saying, "Baby, you can't imagine how I worship you." As his kisses seduced her sanity, she thought, How could I let myself get so nuts over this... boy!

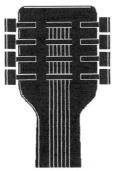

CHAPTER 27

SOME PLACE TO HIDE

The band hit his theme. He stood just off stage letting the music lift him from the physical slump he felt more and more often. Tonight he felt really rotten. When he got home, he'd pack some clothes, buy some groceries and move in for a week or two at Little Gatlinburg. Maybe Luara would take off and stay with him. He had the cabin built in the woods. No one had to know she was there if it made her uncomfortable. She promised to meet Mama after this. Anyway, the woods would heal him; they always had.

Woodhill was beautiful and he wanted Mama to have it, but it might have been a mistake for him. Little Gatlinburg was his source. Shep might still be alive if they'd stayed there. Thank God, Shep Junior was just waiting to worship him, if he'd only give the pup a chance. When he got home, he'd take Shep Junior to the woods for the first time.

Then he felt the music begin doing its magic, the adrenaline was starting to lift him. Still behind the curtain, he started singing his warm up with the band as always. He knew it was going all right; it was all happening for him as he chanted, "Yeah! two, three, four. Yeah! two, three, four. Yeah! Yeah! Yeah!"

He turned on his mike. As always they heard him before they saw him, and the Mile High fans sent him mile high with applause, screams and whistles.

Clay bounded on stage, once again the dynamo of energy music rendered him. Working the stage from end to end, he hit his high screaming chorus on perfect pitch and smiled. He performed as happy as a kid one more time.

Starting out, he looked fine to Anna. Into his third medley, a sense of alarm spread like thick hot oil in her gut. She hadn't wanted to come to Denver, Clay had insisted. Denver wasn't going well. She'd seen the shadows, felt the bad vibes-- Shep's death had been a warning of worse to come.

Sitting in sixth row center beside Gunnar, she slipped her hand in his. The icy coldness of her hand made him look at her with deep concern, a question in his dark eyes. Anna whispered she was okay, he held her hand to warm it but in seconds it started again-- apprehension, concern.

Suddenly she felt raw terror. Clay was in mortal danger! She knew it, she could feel it. A sniper? A bomb? Damn! As big as this place was, anybody could hide a freight engine and six boxcars. But she wasn't saying anymore to Gunnar. She'd worried him with her worry enough, and she had put him off again about marriage. So he was half pissed already. He was a saint to put up with a witch as crazy as she was.

Clay was too pale and too thin, but he was singing beautifully and had never performed better. From his first fantastic night on stage, he'd never failed to thrill her with his music or his way with an audience. She understood the adoration of his fans in the packed stadium. In concert, Clay was like another kind of fire that warmed and lifted and saved the human spirit. That was precisely the point, Clay was human, and he was worn out. He was pushing himself above and beyond and she was sick of it!

When they got home, he would have a checkup and a vacation, if she had to whip his ass and Gunnar's. Enough was enough! She hated to cry on Clay's shoulder. She would if she had to. Manipulation wasn't her bag, but this was her child! No one would see after him if she didn't.

By the time he started his finale, her breath was coming in jerks, her hands were cold as winter mud and no amount of rubbing on Gunnar's part made them warm. Clay had never been so thin in his life! God! He looked like he had been sent out to starve. Hell, it was too much humping with that Luara woman. If he was taken with her, he didn't have to wear it out. That bitch could sure as hell look up longer than he could look down. Men didn't ever know that, but it was true as high noon. Clay didn't even know she knew about Luara. He went to such pains to keep it a secret, she went along.

This was his first concert she couldn't get lost in the music. She felt like a witness at an execution, but he was doing his last song now. His condition hadn't shown, adrenaline kept that from happening. If it wasn't for his passion for performing, Clay Hill wouldn't be able to stand alone. She sat gritting her teeth while he sang encores. The fans didn't want him to leave, but Clay never did more than four encores. Now he was into his second encore. Maybe he'd get through it tonight, but he had to have a checkup!

The Daytona dream came fluttering through her mind. No! By God, she wasn't going through that again! She had enough emotional black clouds and tidal waves without going back to that old nightmare.

He was into the last chorus, hold on, she prayed feeling his weakness. He sang into the tag. She was taking his butt to the doctor if it hare-lipped hell. He bent into his last long bow, he was ending it now. Thank, God! His bow was too long, he was hamming it up too much. Come on, son, end it!

She was the first to see his weave and slight stagger as he attempted to rise. She felt his pain, his floating feeling, his fight not to faint as real as she had felt his kick in her womb. She felt the sweat from his fight to rise from the bow and walk off stage. She watched him weave again and clenched Gunnar's hand. Her other hand went to her mouth to stifle her scream.

As Clay crumpled, her scream pierced the air, but it was lost in the adulation from the packed stadium. They thought it was part of the show. God, they thought Clay was joking!

Then she was on her way to the stage, screaming, "Clay!" shoving through the crowd. Gunnar followed, but he failed to move out of the stands as quickly as she did. When he got to the aisle, he couldn't work his larger frame through the crowd as well. He followed as closely as he could, roaring, "Anna! Wait! Anna!" Then he realized she couldn't hear him. Even if she could, she wouldn't pay any attention. Anna was wild with worry before tonight, now she was berserk. Some coke head would kill her, the way she was shoving. Damn!

Luara's cue was confirmation on which hospital Clay had been flown to. For now, she had to go incognito. Her early years of makeup training would insure that. Anna and the media were more than she could face right now. She pulled two wig boxes down from her closet, then sat at her dressing table. Trying on the red and then the blond wig, she decided to be a redhead for this visit.

A few hours later, she sat in the waiting room of Memorial's intensive care unit, feeling strangely like a spectator at a play. Probably she could have saved her disguise. McGuire and Anna were in and out of the room but they were too concerned about Clay to look her way. She was there when Anna, McGuire and Copper Jim came in together, with a magazine to hide behind. But her own mother wouldn't know her in the redhaired wig and makeup.

Drifting in and out of the waiting room, she kept up with Clay's condition. He had stabilized and was out of immediate danger. Overheard conversations told they were testing. Pneumonia and exhaustion were established facts and perhaps his only problems. They couldn't be sure till all tests were in. She heard Anna say she wanted every test possible since it was impossible to get Clay to see a doctor. Luara hadn't realized how much Clay favored Anna, same classic features, same eyes, hair and gold-toned skin.

All night and all the next day, Luara was there. She read, walked the halls and ate in the cafeteria. After supper she went home to clean up. Clay had left a message on her answering set among the other messages. She called Hannah, asked her to cancel her appointments and take charge for a few days, explaining she couldn't explain right now. Hannah, God bless her, said fine and didn't ask any personal questions.

After a bath, she stretched out for a nap and lay unsure of why she wouldn't see Clay or return his calls. Maybe it was respect for Anna. If it were Kyle, a stupid love interest barging in might be the last thing she could cope with.

Luara stayed incognito at the hospital those first days and nights, till the day all Clay's tests were final. She knew it was dire, but it took a while after the others knew for her to overhear what the diagnosis was. It sounded like cancer! When McGuire tried to comfort Clay's hysterical mother, Luara was there. After Anna was sedated, put to bed in an adjoining room and McGuire stepped back out to go down the hall and cry, Luara was there. When Copper Jim, weather tough as a cattle driving cowboy, bent over in his chair, hid his face in his hands and sobbed between his knees, Luara had to take a break.

She was there when both men put up false hopes to Anna. She didn't know why, she did know when someone was being patronized. Whatever Clay had, it was terrible. Maybe he could never sing again. Luara kept trying to brace herself for the worst, kept meaning to identify herself so she might see Clay. Something kept holding her back.

The last time she was in the waiting room, Gunnar escorted the devastated Anna in from Clay's room. Luara sat by while he tried to comfort the agonizing mother, and overheard enough between Anna's sobs, to hear the dreaded word "AIDS." AIDS had not entered Luara's head.

She sat stunned, unable to rise. A young doctor came in and sat beside Anna. Luara heard him say every test confirmed Clay had AIDS, he had had it for some time, and was in a very advanced stage of the disease. The doctor said it was a mystery how Clay could have been on his feet, much less performing. Sometimes human drive was past explanation.

Luara silently went nuts with terror, silently rose from her chair, silently walked to the elevators, silently rode down to the great cave of the three story lobby and silently walked out of the hospital.

When she had the Mercedes rolling, she couldn't cry. She could and did scream. Her soul outraged, her eyes dry, her mouth wide, she screamed until she couldn't. Still she had not drained her anger. She yanked the red wig off and threw it in the back seat. The masquerade was over. She couldn't face this; with or without her disguise. Luara had left the hospital building forever.

Over the next day and night, she sat silently and watched the Clay Hill news shows on TV. That's all you could call it. It was like the President was mysteriously stricken. Listening numbly to her phone ring, she let the callers put their messages on the set or hang up as they saw fit.

Two days later, Luara sat silently while news about Clay Hill, the all-American male, having AIDS exploded on the world. She sat silently and watched the TV story of his life, and the galloping graveness of his affliction. She sat silently and watched the side news of AIDS, graphically showing the disfiguring effects of the illness as it progressed. She saw patients looking as if they were dying from starvation like Jews in the Nazi holocaust.

She sat through the safe sex messages-- the condom using placebo advice. Half the world's population came strained through a condom; one case in point, her son, Kyle. If sperm got through a condom, she knew an AIDS germ, or gremlin or virus or whatever gave it to you, could too!

Then there were the many like herself, worn out after years of fighting to get and give good sex, in spite of skin-chaffing, rash-causing, unreliable condoms; mood-killing diaphragms; lubricant-destroying douches; friction-taking gels; water-retention birth control pills that made one swell like a frog, hate everything in sight, including sex-- plus the abstaining, jerking, masturbating, and God only knew how many more pleasure-robbing, ecstasy-taking, orgasm-killing, self-image destroying, obnoxious practices to avoid conception, who reluctantly chose surgery. Hating to burn a bridge, but deciding she would never have another child (since her biological clock was running out and no marriage was in sight), she had a tubal ligation. Good idea or bad idea, people were going to have sex and she was people. She couldn't kick the habit but she didn't have to produce a bastard or set herself up for an abortion. She would hate to kill her own flesh and blood and would never get over the guilt.

After, she was so happy with her operation. The surgery didn't amount to as much as an extracted tooth, and sex was wonderful! Finally, she could make love and roll over free as a man. With no more effort than using a few tissues, or sometimes with somebody very special, as she always had with Clay, just lying there or taking a nap with the essence of her partner still present, still somehow bringing her pleasure.

She had reveled in her new freedom; she wasn't reveling now. Lord, she had dosed herself royally with Clay Hill. She had never so much as taken a douche after. Now she was a dead woman. It was time to get ready for her own demise. Damn her luck, and his! They were both too young to die!

She sat listening to the messages on her answer set as they came in and put a new tape in when the one on the machine filled. When she could handle it, she would call everyone and apologize.

Then Clay's voice said, "Luara, I've asked you to call me. I know why you haven't and haven't been here. I understand, I don't blame you. But, darling, I had no idea or I wouldn't have touched you for anything in this world. You know I never had a gay relationship. I don't know anything to say other than I love you and I'm sorry. Sorry for you and, I don't mind saying, sorry for me. I'm here if you ever can stand to come and see me or if you should need me. I'd give anything to see you, for just a moment. If..." The tape ran out. She listened for his call back; there was none.

Well after midnight, she dressed and donned the blond wig. If Clay could stand it, she would too. If his mother was with him, she wouldn't go in his room. There was a chance Anna wouldn't be with him this time of night. Luara had no idea what kind of other security she might run into. There had been nothing in the media about any problem with the fans. Nobody wanted AIDS. A last check in her mirror told she was as ready as she'd ever be.

With the best of intentions, she drove to Memorial. Like always, she parked in the hospital parking lot, walked across the street to the front lobby, walked over to the row of elevators and punched an up arrow. When the stainless steel door yawned open, just like a normal person, just like hundreds of times before, she walked inside. She punched the number of the floor Clay was on.

When the elevator stopped rising, when the door opened at Clay's floor, Luara could not move. She could not make herself take even one step out of the elevator. She stood frozen, desperately trying to move her body out of the elevator box and onto Clay's floor. Her feet were paralyzed.

She watched helplessly as the elevator door slowly closed and continued to ascend. When it had opened and closed and made its way up the next six floors, floor by floor, to the top and then started back down; again it stopped and opened itself on Clay's floor. Luara tried to step out but again her feet were made of stone and would not take one step. As in a dream where she couldn't move, she watched the door close.

As the elevator descended, she felt the early flood and crossed her legs until the elevator opened at ground level. Miraculously her feet worked, she stepped out and hurried to the door marked WOMEN.

There were plenty of paper towels and toilet tissue. With trembling hands, she cleaned up as well as she could then made an emergency sanitary napkin.

At last, feeling too weak to faint, she was back in her car and driving away. She took a deep breath-- it was so strange. All that desire she had felt for Clay, all that love... lust... was no more. All the magic was consumed by horror and-- God, yes, by regret and infinite dread.

And, Clay, I hope you pick up on my thought message. I did try, honey. I did come close but I couldn't go through with seeing you. I don't know what to say, except I feel numb and befuddled and betrayed. I'm sorry too we're in this mess, just like you. I know it isn't your fault but I'm not going to lie to you. I can't take it like losing at tennis... like someone steps on your toe on the dance floor. I feel raped and brutalized and I don't even know who to blame!

I remember saying to you one time, I loved you so much I could die. I thought I was sincere, darling, but I lied. That was bedtalk; one of those things lovers say to each other. Truth is, Clay, I want to live and I want to keep my looks. I want to live forever, and even then if I have to be a corpse, I want to be a beautiful corpse. I abhor the thought of looking like a rotting corpse before I'm dead. I don't want gray skin. I can't stand getting all emaciated and covered with scabs and sores. God, please! You know I'm vain, I was born vain, I'll die vain. I can't stand looking like an AIDS victim.

Clay, I'm sorry you're sick, you know that. You know I care for you. I wish to God I wasn't such a coward. I love you, but all I can feel since they diagnosed you with AIDS is terror!

By the time Luara walked into her foyer, she was totally panicked. Like a zombie, she walked mesmerized through the rooms, unplugging the two TV sets and the two radios. Trembling like she was, she decided not to bother with a shower until she saw she had soaked again through the toilet paper sanitary pad. After her shower, feeling fresh in a soft nightgown, the red tide dammed by a tampon plus a sanitary pad, Luara swallowed two sleeping pills, then climbed in bed and covered up her head.

❧❧

The morning was dark with a cold drizzle, but she forced herself to the grocery anyway. There must be a way out of this thing. When problems had her this rattled, she had to think things through, one thing at a time. That would be impossible with the whole world yammering at her. She had to stay out of the picture till she could make some decisions.

Driving home, she turned on the radio. Clay was singing, wonderful as usual. Then the song was over and the DJ started talking about Clay. When he introduced a Dr. Adams to enlighten the listening audience about AIDS, Luara punched the radio off. So she wouldn't make the same mistake, she stopped by a service station and had the fuse removed from the radio. She couldn't bear hearing about AIDS or Clay Hill-- doomed superstar.

For the next week, Luara existed stoically terrified. She felt as if she had been unplugged like the TV and hardly moved or ate. She didn't bathe. She was too intimidated to get naked that long. Normally, she was an avid reader, but when she could make herself pick up a book, she found herself staring at the wall or out the window or sitting in her back garden paralyzed with fright.

All week, she listened to the hang ups and messages left on her machine. There were the calls from her office, her friends, her brother, her mother, more calls from her office, a call from Kyle, safe in California. How lucky that he had been in California during her involvement with Clay.

She sat feeling mummified, and listened to another call from Clay, then a message from his mother. Anna said Clay wanted to see her and in case Luara thought there might be a problem, there was none. Clay had a special, private room. All she wanted, like any mother, was to see her son happy-- and especially now. Anna ended the message with, "Since you have a son, I know you understand and will be kind."

That was when Luara was first able to cry. Anna's plea broke the lock off her tears and that was when she unplugged the answering machine. During that week, the only call Luara made was to her office manager. She instructed Hannah to pay the bills and the payroll, to give herself a bonus and not to expect her back in the office for another week. That was the first and last lie Luara ever told Hannah.

The rest of her messages fell into two categories. Those she didn't want to answer and those she didn't know how to answer. Kyle was doing fine, happy with his father and right now she didn't know how to talk with Kyle. She most certainly did not want him exposed to what she was exposed to. She'd hardly heard of AIDS before Clay got sick and would have to do some research before she could begin to know how to protect Kyle. Whatever was required, she must protect Kyle! She couldn't stand to face what Anna Hill was facing!

As for Clay, she couldn't blame him. He had more integrity, more character and was more moral than anyone she knew. He was the one soul in her world she believed to be in worse jeopardy than herself, she accepted his apologies. He took responsibility and begged her to come see him or to call. Evidently, he got none of her thought messages. She could not deal with Clay. She learned the other night, she couldn't make herself see him.

He always got her to doing things against her better judgment. Apparently extreme heat melted the female brain and backbone, a woman in love always lost her independence. She had seen brilliant career women fall for some loser and lose it all. She couldn't risk any more with Clay. If she hadn't listened to him, she would not have been intimate with him. His youth alone made her guilty, and her judgment bad.

He knew her well enough to know she didn't think it was his fault. But she was incapable of being big about it. What was she supposed to say, that's okay, honey, no big deal? She had her routine medical checkup six weeks ago and knew she was clear, for now. But now, she couldn't whistle in the dark, even for her own sake. Right now, suppressing her hysteria was all she could handle knowing she had been exposed to a killer disease

That last morning, awakened by a nightmare, she was bathed in perspiration. THEY were coming for her! In the dream, she had been a fly on the wall and she had seen and heard it all. THEY had been putting Clay through the third degree about who all he had slept with. THEY wouldn't give him his medicine till he told them. In the dream, THEY were coming for her and THEY were ringing her front door chime now!

Then she realized someone really was at her door. She found herself on the floor with a pillow and blanket. She made herself answer the door; it was a messenger with a card and a note from Clay. Suddenly, for the first time since the AIDS cloud had devastated her, Luara was fully awake. One more time, she was the living, feeling, moving, thinking, analytical individual of logic and at her best. Somehow, instead of waking to find herself dead as she had expected, she had awakened to resurrection day.

Finally she knew what time it was. It was time to run! They would be coming for her like they came for lepers. She remembered in the Bible, they did horrible things with lepers. There was a movie about it years ago. She could see Ann Baxter or somebody rescuing a relative from this awful island.

AIDS was the new leprosy, it was exactly like it. You looked terrible and there was no cure. She couldn't sit terrified till they came for her. She had to decide what to do and make a plan! Time was short. She could feel it like she could feel a real estate deal. There was a time to ask for the sale, to get it consummated and turned into a black and white reality if you ever expected to.

With a will, she made coffee and was having a second cup when the door chime exploded through the house again. It used to sound so melodic. Now the damn thing sounded like a police siren. Maybe it was the police! Maybe it was the AIDS police and she'd taken too long making up her mind! The chime sounded again, her hand was visibly shaking as she set her cup down.

Tiptoeing, she slipped through the house to a window where she could peep at the front stoop. God, it was her! Anna Hill! Standing at the front door looking like the wrath of God and backed up by Gunnar McGuire! The woman rang the chime again, waited a few seconds and then rang it several times straight. Luara could see the angry way Anna jabbed the button.

Suddenly, afraid they might spot her spying, she slid down the wall and crouched on the floor. Then Anna was shouting, "Luara? Please, Luara, open the door!" Luara started to cry. She couldn't choke back all the sound. Afraid they would hear, she scooted backward from the window to the far corner.

Anna called again, "Luara? Luara, listen, I know you're there!" How did she know? Could she see through brick? Could they hear her outside? Luara didn't think so but she took the bottom of her robe and stuffed it in her mouth.

Anna screamed, "Please, I'm begging you! Open the door!" Then Anna was crying, Luara still couldn't open the door. She couldn't move. "Luara, listen, we need to talk with you." Talk with her? What was there to talk about? Did they think she'd given Clay AIDS? Mothers could think so crazy when their kids were in mortal danger. If Kyle lay dying from AIDS, she'd be ready to kill.

"Luara, please!" Then Anna was sobbing and banging on her door. Luara sobbed harder and stuffed more robe in her mouth. She was sorry but she couldn't make herself endure a meeting with Clay's mother. Luara thought, Please, go away! We can't help each other. Can't you see we're all dead? It's just a matter of time. Her thoughts were interrupted by McGuire's voice.

She couldn't make out what he was saying. She held her breath so she couldn't cry and could hear. Maybe he was telling Anna to step back so he could break down the door. Then she realized Anna's sobs were going away and crawled back to the window. Raising herself to the bottom window pane, Luara stole a look outside.

McGuire was walking Anna from the door. "Merciful God, thank you," Luara muttered from behind the robe she had gagged herself with. "Sweet Jesus, thank you too." Leaning on McGuire, Anna looked totally broken as she blindly walked to the limo where the chauffeur stood holding the door.

With her eyes enormous behind her nose, behind her mouth, behind the bottom of her robe, Luara watched till they disappeared behind the black glass when the chauffeur closed the door. He walked around to the driver's side, then backed the limo out of her driveway and rolled down the street and out of sight. She took the robe out of her mouth, panic had dried her tears.

She had to escape! There was no medical escape. There would be no public escape if the media got wind of her affair with Clay. As scared as Anna was running, the media might to pick up on that at any moment. She had to hide before the world knew her identity! She couldn't deal with this as it was, now she was about to be sucked into it publicly. It wasn't like she and Clay were engaged, the age thing made marriage impossible from the start.

She moved through the house stripping off the robe she had worn for she didn't know how many days. But she was alert enough to realize she smelled purely rank. She ran a hard cold shower and stepped in. Gasping from the shock, she felt her brain kick in. Then she turned the water as hot as she could stand, let it run a few seconds, then adjusted the stream to a nice temperature and washed her hair. With a backbrush, she scrubbed herself all over with lots of lather, then shaved her legs, her armpits and planned.

Lynning always said, when it felt right to cash in your chips, to cash in your chips. Following hunches would make you right more than wrong, and being right more than wrong was the core of good business.

Wrapped in a towel, she took four aspirins and got two more cups of coffee into herself. For the first day in three weeks, her hands were steady. Her plan would work, it was all that would work. As famous as Clay was, they would make someone else guilty. Since he wasn't gay, an older woman who was his lover would be the next best choice. She refused to be fuel for a witch burning.

At noon, she walked in her bank and withdrew ten thousand dollars in cash, twenty thousand in traveler checks, and put the balance of her cash in cashier's checks made payable to Allison Lynning. After closing her accounts, she left the bank and the life of the woman named Luara Frazier.

On the outskirts of town, Allison Lynning stopped in a service station and asked the attendant to check out the Mercedes.

"Ma'am, you must be taking a road trip. Me and my wife want to see California. Can't this year with two kids in college. Never been past Memphis. We hear California has fine weather. Bet that's where you're going."

"How could you tell?" California sounded fine.

"Working out, you learn to read folks. Getting the car checked's a big clue."

"By the way, do you have maps to the West Coast?"

"Inside, by the Coke machine, got all kinds and no charge with a fill up."

Back on the road, having made a hard decision was making her feel better. She had stopped searching for some place where horror could be forgotten and had found a destination. She hadn't had the guts to swallow the pills but they were packed and time was still on her side. They might find a cure. Also, she might luck out and not get AIDS. If she did, California was overrun with gays and more up than anywhere on AIDS. If she got it, and the doctors couldn't do more with it than they could now, she was ready.

Enough Valium was in that bottle to off a bull elephant. She'd never look like an AIDS victim. Vain was her middle name. As shallow as it might be, she loved being beautiful. She had come in this world without much but her looks. She just simply couldn't bear being ugly!

At least, she would be near Kyle. Maybe he shouldn't be near her. She would have to check that out; someway. She didn't know too much about the West Coast. Maybe she would finally see some movie stars.

Pressing her red pump harder to the gas, she picked up speed and meshed into the westbound traffic with a will. Surely there was some place where love didn't keep leading to hell. There had to be some place happy, some place to forget, some place... Some place to hide!

~~~~~ **CHAPTER 28** ~~~~~

MAMA, SING OLD SHEP

Clay pushed the button to raise his bed and got his clipboard. His movements woke Anna from her own after lunch nap. Seeing he was writing, she settled back in her chair and closed her eyes. She couldn't go back to sleep, but Clay didn't need to feel anyone was watching him write. He would get it this time, she could feel it happening without watching. The song fairy vibes were as real as the air.

He felt rotten, but he had to write the Luara song. It had been a long song coming, and time was short. The lyric was coming all in a piece, almost faster than he could write. It was a simple lyric, simple songs were always the hardest. The melody had been right since that first day in the car with Luara. Except for her name and wisps of words here and there, he had fished for the lyric wrong. He had fished for a love song. *Luara* was a goodbye song.

He wrote another ten minutes and said, "Mama, would you try to get Copper Jim or Gunnar? The Luara song is done. I'd like to record it today if possible."

"Clay, are you sure you're up to recording?"

"The tracks will be minimal, the vocal will be the softest I've ever sung. And this song isn't just for Luara, it's for all AIDS victims. Till there's a cure, there will be too many victims and too few who understand."

"Oh, Clay, you don't need to be worrying now."

"I'm not, Mama, but I do need to do this song. My relationship with Luara wasn't the same as with Rachel. In certain ways I love Luara even more. She gave it all to me. She laid her career on the line for me and I would have done anything for her even before I got sick and knew what I exposed her to."

"Son, she was old enough to know what she was doing."

"I chased her. Luara Frazier didn't do one thing to me but love me."

"She left you," Anna said stubbornly.

"I don't blame her, I'd leave myself if I could. Mama, don't give me a hard time." Exhausted, he lay back on his pillows. "Please make the call?"

"It beats me, but whatever you want and I'm sorry."

When Anna got off the phone, she said, "Gun says they'll be here in two hours to record your song."

"Thanks, Mama. Now, I want you to understand something. I've told Jim and Gunnar. No matter what, I want this song released right away."

"But, Clay--"

"No matter what, Mama, I want it released. Promise me!"

"I... I promise." He knew her too well to imagine she was pleased.

"Mama, have you ever been so crushed you thought you'd die, till someone came along and touched you and put you back together?"

"Darling, you have been that for me all your life."

"Then you know what Luara did for me, and you can get by without me. That kind of love gets you by."

The next morning started like a good day. Clay was sleeping, recording his Luara song had relaxed him. As Anna rested and read in her recliner, her eyes strayed occasionally to Clay, to see that he slept safely. It made no difference to her vigilant eyes that now, she guarded a sleeping man rather than a boy. Her actions were still fueled by his need and her love. Sensing another presence, Anna looked toward the door. Rachel Islander stood in the doorway, looking undecided whether to advance or retreat. "Rachel?"

"Yes, Mrs. Hill."

"Well, don't stand out in the hall. Come in."

"I'm afraid I'm not welcome, Mrs. Hill, but I had to come."

"Course you're welcome." Anna walked to the door, hugged Rachel and said, "Clay will be a awake any minute and delighted to see you. You look tired, come have a seat. " She walked Rachel to the chair nearest Clay's bed.

"Mrs. Hill, are you sure it's okay?"

"You can't catch anything just having a seat."

"I didn't mean that, Mrs. Hill."

"I remember a time when you called me Anna."

"You might have a few things you want to call me after you know the truth. You might not even want me in Clay's room."

Rachel realized her words weren't registering as Anna said, "Clay wouldn't let me call you."

"Copper Jim called. I've been sick so much, I got bitter about losing time. Still I had to see Clay, no matter what. So much could have been different if my coping skills had been better. Illness stopped me so much from doing what I wanted, I got where I shut anything out that might stop me again."

"Mama, did I hear Rachel or am I dreaming again?" Clay asked.

"No, son, she's here this time. She came all the way from Paris to see you."

"Hey, Clay," Rachel said, standing by the bed.

"Oh, Rach, I did want to see you. And you're still so beautiful-- so beautiful. I... I didn't want you to see me... like this. But the last few days every time I go to sleep I wake up dreaming you're here. So I knew you were coming. I told Mama. I didn't know when or... if you'd come in time."

"I had no idea you were ill till Jim called. Why didn't you call me?"

"Because there isn't anything you can do but cry. I don't want to make anyone else cry. Like you're crying now, and Mama's crying now. Like I cry too sometimes. It's awful, the way I've made Mama cry. And I'm sorry, Rachel. You can't imagine how I've prayed you won't take this hell. I loved you so, but now I wish to God I'd never touched you."

"Oh, Clay. Oh, my Clay," she moaned as sobs took her. "Hold me, please hold me." Looking more girl than woman, she laid her head on the pillow next to Clay's, her arm across his chest holding him as she cried.

"It's all right, I've accepted it. Rach, please, don't cry. Accept it, honey." Rachel fell across his chest and he held her as she sobbed, saying things Anna couldn't hear for she was sobbing too.

Then for a time there were no sounds but the sounds of sorrow and the courageous sounds a dying man was making to comfort his weeping women.

After a while, Rachel raised her head and said, "I can't live without telling you, Clay. This is all my fault."

"No, Rach."

"Oh, yes-- yes, it really is."

"It's okay if it is. No one knows better than me, you only meant to love me."

Rachel saw how loving he was looking at her. Something of the deep understanding they had once shared was reborn. Her soul was in the sound of her "Clay, I love you so and I was so wrong."

"Rach, if I had understood what bad health does, things would have been different. I had no idea how illness immobilizes you and scares you and all you can do is accept it. Even after you accept it and you're not scared anymore, I didn't know how it bores you because you can't dream anymore. If I'd known, we could have worked it out."

"We should have. That's part of what I came to tell you."

Anna broke in, "Maybe I should leave you two alone."

Rachel said, "No, I want you to know, Clay may be too upset to tell you later. I can't say it but once." Anna sat back down.

Rachel went on, "Clay, a few weeks after you left, I thought I might be pregnant. But, with my health problems, nauseous mornings aren't new. I felt awful over losing you and thought I was anaemic again. But, if there was a baby, I didn't want it to be damaged. I decided if I was pregnant, it was God's way of telling me I was to be your wife. I went to this doctor and--"

"And what did he say?"

"He... he said I was pregnant."

"Pregnant? We... we have a baby?"

"We started a baby. I never had it. The examination included a blood test and... I came up HIV positive."

"But you don't show any signs that I can see."

"I'm a carrier. I have no visible symptoms yet. I might at any time or I may never. There's so much they don't know about AIDS. But I continue to check positive and take the treatment. Clay, you were the first for me and I was the first for you, so somewhere along the line I was given contaminated blood. It's my fault, I want you to know how sorry I am."

"I never blamed you, I was treated by a gay dentist who died with AIDS. Rach, I didn't call you because there's nothing anyone can do."

"I understand, that's why I didn't call you. I saw no help in you knowing any sooner than you had to. And I kept thinking you would call. But, Clay, with so many more chances taking blood than you, I had to be the one."

"No. It could've been either of us, it doesn't make any difference now. It's something we have to accept, but what happened with the baby?"

"Well, I... I had an abortion."

"Abortion?" he said, incredulously.

"Carrying such a horrible disease, I had to."

"You aborted our baby?"

"I knew by your "Rosy" song you don't think abortion is the worst thing in the world. There was nothing else I could do with no cure for AIDS."

"I know, but how could you kill our baby?"

"The baby could have been born with AIDS!"

"But it might not."

"Clay, what if it did?"

"Rachel, at least it had a chance."

"I didn't want to take that chance."

"What if I did? What if our baby had been born clear?"

"Guess bad luck took me to a new low. Blowing our relationship. Seeing how wrong I was-- how wrong we both were. Not knowing what to do, then coming up pregnant, and you never called. Worst of all, coming up with HIV. Knowing there was every chance I'd given it to you. I didn't think there was a prayer our baby wouldn't have it. Now, you're down with it. Anymore, my belief in miracles is nonexistent. Painting is the only thing that's worked out the way I wanted. In the face of all the rest, it's a hollow victory."

Through it all, ready to die and she felt sure praying to die, if her son had shed a tear before this day, Anna hadn't seen it. With the news of his aborted baby, Clay wept without shame. Rachel felt the stiffening of his frail body with his rejection of her decision; felt the withdrawal of his feelings. She knew she had lost him again-- this time forever. Too devastated and shocked by this last to cry out loud, but blinded by the silent tears pouring from her eyes, Rachel found her feet, found her purse and found her way out of Clay's room.

She rushed past Copper Jim in the waiting room to the chair in the corner and sat down crying. Seeing how upset she was, Jim thought, Best let her cry it out. Clay's looks were real upsetting to folks who hadn't seen him in a spell.

Rachel cried a long time. When she settled down, Jim moved to the chair next to her. "Hon, I tried to ready you for seeing Clayboy. It's something you can't believe till you see it. You'll feel better after you rest. Let's go on down to your folks now. They'll be real proud to see you after all this time."

"No, Copper Jim, I'm too upset, I need just one last favor."

"Anything, if I can."

"Say no if you can't, but don't ask me to justify what I need because I can't. It's what I have to do. Promise you won't argue."

"Why sure, Rachel. You got my promise."

"Take me to the airport, I want to go home."

"But you don't need no plane to go to Tullahoma."

"I'm talking about Paris." Then he saw a change had come over Rachel.

On the way from the airport, she talked about how she loved Clay and wanted to stay as long as he needed her. He couldn't imagine what happened while she'd been in to see Clay, but she was sure changed and tore up. He'd seen that shocked look in the eyes of a small boy lying by the road waiting for the ambulance with both legs broken. He had been hit by a car and wasn't making a sound but his eyes had the shocked look Rachel's had now. She was hog killing serious about flying back to Paris. He had a feeling he was right before, wishing he had let her stay in Paris in the first damn place. At times the best you could do didn't work out worth a weasel's shit. Wearily he stood and said, "Wished, since you come this far, you'd go see Frank and Bess if it ain't but thirty minutes." He waited, hoping she might change her mind.

She just kept on wiping tears that just kept on falling. Jim sighed, "Honey, if flying straight back to Paris is what you gotta do, guess we'd best go."

◆

She woke strangely minus her usual sluggishness. The clock said three a.m., she looked at Clay. He was awake, his eyes were lucid-- not squinted from pain or hazy from drugs. His eyes were talking to her, full of love and tenderness. She knew he had willed her awake, knew he was not in pain even as she asked, "Are you hurting? Do you need the nurse?"

"No, but tell Rachel she was right. No one sane would risk putting this illness on a baby. I can't rest; can't get well. I want peace, Mama."

"Clay, darling, we can't give up."

"We're not, it's finished. My mission is over."

"No, we can't quit." Even to her ears, her voice had no conviction.

"Mama, it's time for me to go back. I was there before I was here... so were you and everyone. You taught me that."

"A mother needs to go back before her son."

"Not always, your mission isn't done. In my mind I've seen it. Mama, you know you're supposed to sing. Today's the first day I've been able to talk this much in weeks, I may not be able to again. Don't make me wait in living death any longer. Let me go. Please! Have mercy, Mama."

"Oh, God, please!" Anna put her hands to her head that felt about to explode. The scream of raw agony rolling up from her gut was suddenly shut off from her throat by a new threatening flood of tears.

"Mama, please don't cry! Don't fight me anymore. I'm not as strong as you, I hate this. You're strong enough to let me go, to help me go."

"I'm not nearly as strong as you think, darling. I faked it a lot."

"You have always been stronger than you know. I can't get better. You know me too well to imagine I want to live this way. Release us from this white room." His voice was fading. His eyes, as always, were windows to his weary soul. "Mama, I love you, always have, always will. Like I said, there's a light I have to reach... Please, Mama,... help me to walk to the light."

"I... I don't know what you're talking about, Clay."

"I'll be close... music will draw me closer. I'll be closest... when you sing."

"Darling, you're the singer in the family."

"You're the singer now." His eyes clouded, consciousness was leaving, but his eyes burned like two begging beacons as he whispered, "Please, Mama, sing *Old Shep*." The hardest thing in the world for her was to give in and give up before she gave out. Clay had always understood that about his mama.

"Clay, I know what you want, but I can't."

"You can. Mama, I know you can for me." In memory, the hum that rose in her throat seemed involuntary to Anna. Smiling faintly, in the softest of whispers, Clay said, "I love you more than roses, Mama. All my life... your love has warmed me like another sun. Mama, I'll be close... and the closest when you sing. Now, please... Mama, sing *Old Shep*."

Like it was someone else, Anna heard her hum lift to la's, her la's trill into lyrics and somehow, she was singing the beloved old lines. Clay smiled. His smile had always been her strength, her rhyme, her reason. He lay looking at her with more love than she had ever felt from anyone till his eyes fluttered and closed. As she sang on, she saw the glow of tranquility spreading over his face. As she had watched and sung over the child he had been, frightened by a bad dream, she watched and sang now, while the man found peace. The glow on his face grew deeper, it was as if a light came on from within. A light reflected in a beam of color on his cheeks they had not held in months.

Anna sang slowly, but the high Appalachian lace of her voice had never been more beautiful. She sang bravely and well till the third verse.

Without warning, her voice refused. A heart ripping roar of silence fell like the end of time. Her constricted throat, her paralyzed lips, could not move. She swallowed and struggled to sing... she could not utter a sound. She had reached can't! Her strength was finite! Soon he would open his eyes and look at her disappointed like the other times she could not finish. She would never be able to finish! It was impossible! She would never try again! Never! It was too much to ask! Clay always imagined she was stronger than she was.

Like how he talked just now and always had about her singing on stage. Lord, she didn't have the confidence, so much more was needed than a decent voice. And she was dreadfully sorry she couldn't sing *Old Shep* while he died, damn it! But she could not! Hell, she'd call somebody from the singer's union but he better not start with her again! She closed her eyes and hung her head, miserable at failing, ashamed of the tears that escaped her eyes. No matter how hard she tried to hold back, they came rolling down.

Suddenly, she felt feeling returning from her depths; up from her womb, to the back of her throat and on out to the end of her tongue and then tingling on her numb lips. She cleared her throat and swallowed, maybe she could sing now. She lifted her eyes from her lap and looked apologetically at her son.

He wasn't looking at her with disappointed eyes as he had before when she tried to grant this same request. He was asleep and his face was serene, not pinched with pain. He lay with a faint smile on his lips. That one damp curl lay in a ringlet on his forehead as it had when he was a boy. If Clay was her son, truly he was the most handsome man she had ever seen. As she sat proudly beholding him the old dream at the beach house came roaring in. But it wasn't Florida, it was home. It wasn't years ago, it was now! Then the dream twisted as dreams do, she stood in the place of the beach house. The black wave came crushing, sucking, smothering down on her; all the way down to her very soul.

As she was left emotionally dead in its wake, she saw the black wave was a black wave of truth. She was not looking at a beautiful man, but at a beautiful corpse. The corpse was her Clay! The corpse was her baby! She had not saved him from the wave or herself. She was drowning and somewhere a hysterical woman was screaming: "No! Nooo! Noooo! Not my baby! Anything! Anybody! Not my son! You hear me? You can't have him! Nooooo!"

In Anna's mind Clay was three years old and being wrenched from her arms by the raging kidnaper, Death. Then Death was running with her child and she was screaming and she was cussing and she was running after them. She was running faster than she had ever run-- faster than the minute mile, but it was like she was standing still. She couldn't catch Death. She could only scream, "My baby! Come back. He's mine! You can't have him!"

But she was losing ground, they were leaving her farther and farther behind. She could see herself growing small in the distance. Her feet weighed tons and were plodding along, making her stagger. Then she was down and she couldn't get up and she couldn't stop falling-- down and down and down.

Then came the shriek of utter defeat. Defeat invading down to the taproot of her being; to that secret place where the song fairy visits; on down where, In His Own Image dwells and a mother's love lives. Permeating the hallways, eons from the first time, Anna's cries erupted and joined old kindred echoes in the building. The world heard again the sounds of a mother's soul breaking as she screamed, "Yaaaaaaaaah," then gasped for breath. Then a longer "yaaaaaaaaaaaaaaaaah" and breath; gaining in duration and momentum, "yaaaaaaaaaaaaaaaaaaaaaaaah," breath.

Over and over the sound erupted from her, as it has from mother to mother, from century to century, as old as Eve, as young as the just slapped newborn. The tone varies as does the duration, but the gut-grinding screams never stop until the mother is sedated by unconsciousness, death, dementia, exhaustion or the tender mercies of a doctor. One sound universally uttered, universally understood, universally debilitating are the primal wails of the mother who has lost the fruit of her ovaries, her womb and her breasts. Mother of one or of twenty, with the death of her child, be it adult or infant, saint or sinner, fool or pharaoh, the loss is irrevocable. From the dawn of creation till the end of time and throughout the world, the loss is infinitely female. It has erupted and been understood from the mother in the jogging suit, the flapper dress, the pantaloons, kimono, sarong, sari, tiger skin and mammoth hide. All the long road back to the first mother in fig leaves, a mother's love for her young lives as simple, as profound, as enduring and as vital as Mother Earth herself.

Just the thought of the "Yaaah" sound from his mate reduces the strongest male of any tribe to terror. A long "Yaaaaaaaaaaaah!" was the first sound Gunnar heard as the elevator opened, and he knew. Alarm for his woman seized the man in the business suit and broke him into a run as it had his forerunner in the loincloth. Unabashed, he ran dodging nurses, visitors, a patriarch on a walker, a woman pushing her life on an intravenous pole, till he shoved open the door to Clay's room.

Anna was only whimpering now. He was confused about where her sounds were coming from, till he realized she was in the corner behind the door. He scooped her from the fetal position he found her in, then sat on a chair with her on his lap, rocking her, speaking to her, comforting her as he would a sobbing hysterical child. He was so glad he had decided to come by from a late session.

He saw the dead Clay, still in the bed, and realized death had just happened. God! in here by herself with her dead son, no wonder she was crazy. He got to his feet with Anna in his arms. Blinded by his own tears, he almost collided with Maria running from another emergency to the sound of Anna's screams. Two nurses called in sick, one crisis after the other had happened all night.

Gunnar cried, "I'm taking Anna to the waiting room. Send a doctor with a sedative when you can."

Before a second nurse came on Maria's heels, before Maria ordered, "Get the doctor, stat!" before she took his pulse, before she reverted to Spanish and commanded the second nurse "*Venga, muerta! Mon Dios!* Woman, hurry!" Maria knew what she would find.

In the waiting room, fighting to console the inconsolable, all Gunnar could make out of Anna's avalanche of protest was, "He was bor... born here. They gave my baby life here. I never thought he'd di... die here too. Oh, God! Oh, God! Yaaaaaaaaaaaaaaaah! Yaaaaaaaaaaaaaaaaaaaaaaaaaaah!"

Rocking with her in his arms, nothing he said helped. He doubted she heard, he doubted she would survive. If she did, he didn't see how she could ever draw another sane breath. Through his own sobs, Gunnar vowed, "If you live, however you are... whatever you are... you're mine." Every scream that ripped through her sounded like her mind breaking beyond repair. Suddenly, his luck improved. Mercifully, she fainted.

PART
THREE

A

IS FOR

ANNA

LUARA

Clay Hill

I know you never meant to let me love you.
Your first kiss was for my shattered heart.
But when you laid your beauty down to heal me
I thanked a tender god for pity on your part.

Sometimes it seems no good deed goes unpunished.
My best to you turned out to be my worst.
But if my last most precious prayer is answered
No bad from loving me will ever touch you, girl.

CHORUS:
Luara, Luara
I took the laughing sapphire from your eyes.
Luara, forgive me, Luara.
I never dreamed my love would make you cry.

You left and didn't let me say I'm sorry.
You didn't even let me say goodbye.
I'm left reduced to this recorded message,
Girl, if I could make it right, I'd make it right tonight.
Repeat chorus...

~~~~~ **CHAPTER 29** ~~~~~

FAREWELL WOODHILL

As everywhere, in sunny California, Clay's posthumous hit *Luara* was dominating the airways. Luara had her TV and radios plugged in, but she never tuned in country radio. Clay still sang on country radio every hour.

One day in the car, her rock station played *Luara*. She managed to keep driving while Clay was singing. Blinded by tears, she had to pull over. It was her first time to cry in California. That day at the drive in, when Clay started writing *Luara* she hadn't thought he was serious about her or the song.

Parked on the shoulder of the freeway, she wept and remembered till the traffic and blaring horns brought her back to reality. She dried her eyes. The song was lovely, but songs passed, love passed, life passed. Death was all that was forever, and never needed two consenting adults to do its thing.

As Allison, she vowed not to look or live like the dead while she was alive. She was comfortable with her new name and loved being a blond. All Allison retained of Luara was the sleeping pills, but she had scratched Luara's name off the bottle. If AIDS struck, there was help.

Thank God, that bulldog mother of Clay's kept any last days pictures out of the paper. Clay looked like a Greek god and should be remembered that way. All AIDS victims got to looking the same, like babies and old folks. They were intimate only a short while, maybe she'd stay lucky. You didn't get pregnant, every time you had sex. Lynning wanted a son, but she never conceived with the best doctors saying there was no reason they couldn't have a child.

In California as Allison Lynning, she had put old lives behind her. Now she had to put them out of her mind. Since getting a job doing makeup for a theater group, she hardly thought of Clay. Two TV stations and occasional fashion shows were calling her for makeup jobs and word was getting out she was good. She might market her own line of cosmetics. Vitamins A and E worked magic used with the right things. The original mixes she used on clients were well received. She might start a company-- if she escaped AIDS.

Till *Luara* passed, she would listen to jazz. Clay wrote a beautiful apology, and she accepted. He couldn't help having AIDS, she couldn't go on crying. While she had time, it was time to live. Testing clear didn't make her home free. Luara cranked her new red Mercedes.

At Woodhill, Anna stood at her glass wall staring down at the swimming pool and the grounds. For over two months, dawn had found her awake or never having gone to sleep. Time was supposed to help, but in hell it was always day one. Pain was still stomping in her soft parts with spiked boots.

She doubted ever seeing a day that would feel like the second day without Clay in it. She was getting less and less normal sleep, caring less and less about dealing with the irrevocable. There was no way to deal with this, or to recover. When God took Clay, He took her soul. She had nothing to recover with. She hated the sound of her sobs and the unceasing negative thoughts grinding in her broken brain. Gunnar had horses put to sleep that couldn't get well!

If she lay back down, she might sleep now. She was doing everything hind part before these days. Till Clay got sick, she'd never been a day sleeper. When the long night passed, sometimes now, she could nap.

She dragged her body back to bed and realized Katy had used satin sheets again. Damn! Katy knew she hated satin sheets! A woman couldn't sleep a lifetime on cotton and then get any sleep on satin. Rolling to her side, her cheek touched the wet pillow. She didn't remember crying, so she must have slept at some point. God, she was sick of crying asleep, awake, tranquilized or not. She had tried wine. She cried drunk just like she did sober, washed or unwashed, alone or with someone.

She hated it most when she cried with someone and stopped seeing anyone, not even Gunnar. Most of all not Gunnar. She fell apart when he petted her. Gunnar's pity broke her will quicker than anything.

Rolling to the other pillow, she found it as wet as its mate. "Damn," she muttered, got up and started stripping her bed. If there was one thing she hated worse than satin sheets, it was wet satin pillow cases. She threw all the bed linens on the floor and lay back down on the bare mattress.

The recessed light in the ceiling above her bed started spinning. It was from those last little yellow son of a bitches the quack prescribed. Yellow pills made an idiot out of her like the red and the black and the blue ones had. Whatever the doctor said, she'd be damned if she'd swallow another tranq. She couldn't take them. Something had to give! Rack and ruin was horrible, but life in limbo was class A shit.

Better to be dead than a live chemical corpse. Pills or nothing else could ease or erase the fact that her Clay was dead. Her only begotten son, in whom she had always been so well pleased.

Far from the first time, she thought again: Oh, no! You couldn't take me. He could have gotten over losing me. I'll never get over losing him. I've been dead for years anyway, except where Clay was concerned. He was young. Clay would have always been young, I was old at twelve.

Clay had his music, Clay was my music! You know that? Of course, You know that! You created that! You created a beautiful human being, sent him to me to love as my son, got me hooked on him and then You took him back.

You have taken everybody back I ever loved. You don't do something that mean without malice and forethought.

Oh, hell, stop! Anna Lucy, all it's gonna do is make you start squalling again, tears don't change nothing. You just get red eyes, and look bad as you feel. Don't make a thimbleful of difference.

She struggled out of the naked bed, stumbled to the windows and opened the drapes again. Out there the sun was smiling, the grass was green, the sky was blue, the trees were beautiful. Especially the magnolias, they were her favorite. Next time maybe she'd be a magnolia. Sure wasn't strong enough to be a God damned woman again.

Whatever bad deed she did had to be hellacious to be punished like this. She pled aloud, "Stop torturing me! Take me out of my misery and be done with it. Yes, I'm telling You how to run Your business. Used to think You could run things and I could depend on You. Maybe You need some R and R like me. Maybe You're asleep at the wheel or losing it too. Folks down here wouldn't let a cockroach live hurting this bad."

Fighting for sanity, she shook her head and grabbed one of the velvet drapes for support. She wiped the tears that were streaming again with the sleeve of the big sweat shirt she wore and noticed it was her Gunnar shirt.

Suddenly, still clutching the drape for support, she looked out at the sky and growled, "I ain't no Job!" Then raising her voice: "You hear me? I ain't no Job! No, sir, I ain't. Doubt you ever made but one who could take all you put on him. If you have, it ain't me and You can put that in Your daybook. And if this is the guts test, I'm flunking something fierce." She screamed, "You hear me? I'm whipped! Beat! I'm hollering uncle! You see? I'm eating dirt! If that's what You been hammering for, You got it!"

Damn! she thought, do you want to scare Katy to death with your blaspheming? Get a grip! She walked to her night table for a cigarette, lit one with trembling fingers, then took a deep drag. From the pile of bed linen on the floor, she took a soiled pillow case, blew her nose, wiped her eyes and then walked back to the window. Staring out, she smoked silently, absently thinking it would be nice if she had the energy to go down to the pool for a swim. It would be nice if she could do a lot of things.

Aloud, she said, "Don't know if I'm nuts or blaspheming or what but You know. You know what I'm thinking, before I think it. Don't make it worse to say it. Understand something. If You're trying to see how much I can take, You reached it. You filled my craw several hells and several years ago! I'm belly flat. Can't get back up-- not by myself. If You want me up, You got to help me... I got no reason... You got to help me more than ever. I'm lost, Lord. Like the Jews in Egypt stomping out bricks for old Pharaoh too long. I'm weak-- weary. If You want me to be more than this sniveling mess I am, You gonna have to lead me. Don't mean no disrespect. I just damn well had it-- Sir."

Someone was knocking. From the sound of the knock, someone had been knocking awhile. "Wha-- what?"

"Miss Anna?" It was Katy.

"Yeah?" she said, weaving to the locked door.

"Mr. Gunnar is on the phone again."

"Oh, no! Tell him I'm bad luck. Bad luck to everyone I ever loved. Tell him to run for his life. And leave me alone. You hear?"

"Yes'm, Miss Anna, but I don't like it."

"Me neither." Anna weaved back to the window and moaned, "And leave Gun alone! Ain't gonna love him no more. Don't kill him off too. I'm done loving Gun-- and that's a promise."

The rational side of her mind saw her behavior was the pills. They kept her awake when she should be sleeping, sleeping when she should be awake. They made her move when she ought to be still and still when she ought to be moving. Like now, she needed a shower and some coffee. She needed to get away! Away from Gun, and this moaning mansion. It missed Clay! It cried day and night for Clay! She never wanted it, never felt at home in it. He bought it for her and if that made him happy, she was happy to accept it and to fake it. It was fine with Clay living in it, but it never would be home or acceptable with him dead. With Clay dead, it was too damned big or she was too damned little. Either way, it wouldn't work!

From the first day he brought her here, she knew this son of a bitch of a house was too long for her vacuum cleaner cord. But Clay, so proud and needing to do something for her, was too full of himself to turn down when he grinned, "You always looked out for me. Now I want to look out for you. I think you're a queen, a queen deserves a palace."

And Woodhill was a palace, but it was Clay's palace. Palaces spooked her! They were too big and too lonesome. Like the orphanage. And this palace had lost its prince. That made it unbearable.

She had to get somewhere where no one knew her, where folks didn't keep saying I'm sorry... and, You got to get something else on your mind. If she ever got something else on her mind, she had to get somewhere, that what she had to get off her mind wasn't thrown in her face constantly. She had to get where she could do her grieving and her bleeding without being corrected so she could get it all out and get to her healing-- if there was going to be one. Here healing was impossible, going on was impossible, accepting she couldn't change the unchangeable was impossible. Crawling up on some life raft to tomorrow was impossible in this catastrophic, claustrophobic orgy of pity and petting and sympathy in every eye, in every hushed voice and in this sad, sad palace without its prince.

Anymore, she couldn't function with Gun. At first he was a comfort. She loved him dearly but every time he touched her, she started crying, sometimes her pain made him cry. He was losing weight-- beginning to look old. It was her fault, Gunnar loved Clay too. He couldn't heal around her, she might never heal. Gun was too fine to be burdened with a nut.

And, God, she wished folks would stop sending damn sympathy cards! All they did was remind you. Any fool knew if you were getting stacks of sympathy cards for weeks on end, folks must think you were broken up enough to die. But you don't die cause your son dies, you just wish you could. You keep waking up with stacks of new sympathy cards to suffocate you.

Thank God, if Jeff had to die, he died before so many knew him or her! She had learned to hate sympathy cards and anybody who manufactured the bastards. She hated the discount store in Hackberry Mall, where she used to buy those nice looking, two for a dollar cards back when a dollar was at a premium. Back then she didn't know any better, when folks lost someone, than to buy shit to remind them they lost someone, just on the chance they might have it off their mind for a minute.

It was ludicrous what etiquette's nerd mouth could puke out in the name of caring. When you're broken in two, you have a hard enough time forgetting the pain for a second, with the strongest goof balls they dared give you, without damn sympathy cards to keep you reminded. Every time she managed to fake her mind off with the TV or VCR or book or writing a song, there would stand a new stack of sympathy cards.

Then, here came pictures of the long weeks in the hospital; Clay weighing hardly a hundred pounds, dying an ounce at a time. Then that suffocating blue coffin with smothering satin and velvet; the death scent of flowers; that turbulent ocean of mourners and misfits. She told Katy not to put any more sympathy cards on the foyer table with the normal mail. When Katy asked where to put them, she almost snarled: Put them where the sun don't shine. Instead she said, "Get a trash sack and put them in the pantry."

"Some are hard to tell from regular mail."

"If you can't tell, trash it. But keep those damn cards out of my sight."

She knew Gunnar, Jim, Junior, friends and fans all meant well, but this was like trying to have a baby with witnesses you had to hold up for and pretend it didn't hurt. Hell, labor was no spectator sport, she didn't want anyone in her delivery room. The first good scream she let out with Clay turned Jeff sixty shades of green. His next words were something to the effect, not to let it get to her. It had already got to her, she remembered screaming at him. She couldn't help it getting to her or him. Anybody thought your pelvis widening enough to deliver an eight pound baby didn't get to you was stupid.

She would stand her pain and be as serious about surviving. But, damn it, she had to cry, scream, cuss, bitch, moan, or whatever it took to get her through. She couldn't hush to save someone else the grief. Birth or death, excruciating pain felt the same. Everybody moaned she had to stop crying, get her mind off Clay, and live her life. They kept mouthing Clay wanted her to be okay. She knew Clay wanted her to be okay. Shit, she wanted her to be okay. She wasn't nuts enough yet to enjoy being nuts!

It had only been two months; that wasn't time enough to get over a case of the flux, but she had to get off the poor Annas, the cigarettes, the goof balls and out of this house. She had to get away from these people, away from missing Clay, away from all of it! Everything here was making her crazy. She had to run or let her environment finish her off.

Neutral ground to tap that fountain of "in His own image" deep inside herself was what she needed. She had struggled so hard to key into it, and wasn't even close. With folks and vibes constantly echoing all she had to put behind her, she never would touch that healing inner bit of God.

Here, she was drowning in a Poor Me sea of sympathy. The cowgirl had to ride out of Dodge if she ever wanted to ride again. Didn't look like she was going to die from devastation. The shrink she had consulted was too dumb to know a crazy woman when he saw one. If her suffering was relieved, she had to be her own doctor and she had things to do. She couldn't get the hell out of Dodge looking as crazy as she did.

She found a suitcase, threw in some toilet articles, packed a sweat suit, underwear, tennis shoes, and a few clothes hanging handy. That was all the packing she could stand. She had to smear a little paint on her face. She'd put off that part till last, but her hands were still shaking like she had palsy. No matter how much she rubbed them together, they wouldn't stop; and if she took another pill she couldn't drive.

In the dressing room, she took a deep breath and willed herself to be calm. Then she sat down on the stool and opened the bottle of foundation looking at herself in the mirror. She couldn't go out bare faced and she couldn't stay at Woodhill another day. With her finger over the bottle opening, she tipped makeup on her finger and began.

When she had on a walking out in public face, with no worse casualty than gouging her eye with a mascara brush, she knew it was now or never. She hadn't packed enough clothes, she'd buy what she needed. At least she had money. She'd never get away with hauling much stuff out of the house under Katy's nose on her best day.

Anna found the five thousand cash she kept stashed since she had known what it was to have five thousand dollars to keep stashed and hid it in her purse. Then she sat at her writing table to scribble Gunnar a note.

It was so hard to keep a pencil and paper from causing an attitude. She wanted to write it straight, not prose it up. She wanted to put it down like she would say it if she had the guts to call the man. There was no way she could do that, she barely had the guts for this. He'd never understand; he'd never let her go. She wasn't strong enough to argue and she wasn't strong enough to stay another night. No matter what she wrote or how she wrote it, he'd be hurt. She had to let it flow; let it happen without too much thinking. She did her best writing when she could let it roll straight up from her ovaries, through her arm, down her hand to the pencil and laid it on paper like she felt it.

Gunnar, darling:
 The Indians are attacking, I must retreat or be scalped. We can't talk this over, you would talk me out of it. Please pay the help what you think is generous in the way of severance pay and close the house. I'll never spend another day in Woodhill. I want to sell it but I can't deal with that now.
 Don't be mad and don't be hurt. Please understand and don't worry. This is the first sane move, I have made since—
 I think I told you, when I'm beat belly flat, I have to heal alone. I will be all right— or all wrong, but I have got to get the hell out of limbo. I have to go somewhere where I can get better or worse. I don't know where, but truly I believe I am going to be fine.
 I love you, I have from the first time you took me to see your horses. You have been the man of my life since I watched you stroke and talk to your "babies." I wanted your hands on me right then. I'll call you, when I do again; when I can be a woman to you again. If you can't wait, I can't blame you. All my love, always.
  Your Anna

Driving the yellow Cadillac Clay had delighted in giving her, Anna started her escape. Literally driving for sanity, she wound down the long driveway. Woodhill was beautiful, but it was Clay! It was insane to think she could live here without him. Maybe she couldn't live anywhere with Clay gone, but she had to find out. Bawling and squalling and limping around had to stop!

It was well past lunch when she got it together. Dragging the chains of depression made the simplest task monumental. Taking a shower, dressing in fresh warm-ups, doing her makeup and combing her hair was like crawling up a mountain. Sneaking around like an underage runaway, without making noises that would alert Katy, hadn't helped either.

Katy might call Gunnar or Jim or that dumb doctor who didn't have one trick in his bag that wasn't in a pill bottle. She couldn't make him understand if she was going nuts or to the next world, she'd rather go sober! She couldn't take dope and stay on her feet and she couldn't stay flat on her ass and get stronger! Certain folks would be offended but she couldn't escape and say nice goodbyes to folks who would try to talk her out of leaving.

Her short breath, like she had run too far, made her sit down and rest every few minutes. Plus, she had the cramps so bad she could hardly move. Four aspirins hadn't helped, but that was normal. She'd never made a trip in her life without the rag on. It was time for that shit to cease, instead of flooding like a fountain. She never understood why emotional upsets didn't cut down on a period instead of increasing it. Her gynecologist said birth control pills delayed the change. God, she needed a change and she couldn't put it off any longer!

As she packed, rasping like an old woman was the price of not working out. Sure as fish feathers, she was going nuts if she didn't do something. If she was going to die, she already would have. Being ready to die had little to do with dying-- of natural causes. She wasn't pulling a Jeff. Clay wouldn't want his mama to be a suicide too. If running was the choice of a coward, so be it. Running felt smarter than staying!

Driving up the access ramp to the interstate brought a sigh of relief. She would smoke a cigarette to celebrate, but she smoked her last one putting on her makeup. She glanced in the rear view mirror for a quick inspection-- not too bad, considering her face was put on by a near nut. She dabbed at her mascara with her pinky finger and decided her face was fine to run away from home in. It was plain she'd been voting awhile. If she was lucky, nobody she knew would see her. She looked good enough to stop and buy cigarettes.

Depression had got her to start smoking again, but she never bought over two packs of cigarettes at once. To a point it restricted her cigarette consumption. If she bought a carton, she smoked the carton, one right after the other. If she bought two packs she smoked them, one right after the other. So like now, she couldn't smoke cigarettes she didn't have. Ultra lights weren't nearly as good but she got by with them. Like diet cola, it wasn't as good as the real thing, but it didn't have the sugar and she didn't want the weight. Since she wasn't perfect, maybe some control was better than none.

Now that she was finally in motion, she was going to put some distance between her and Woodhill before she stopped for anything. She had no idea where she was going but, God, she felt good to be on the road. This wasn't another weird dream the pills had her dreaming.

After a while, Anna realized if she had no idea of her destination, the Cadillac was doing fine on its own. It rolled along the twenty odd miles from the south side of Nashville, plus the twenty odd miles to the north side of Nashville without getting lost one time. The spotless coupe rolled in Golden Glen Cemetery with no problem and without gaining a smudge.

At Clay's funeral, she had taken no notice of where she was. Consumed by grief, she hardly knew who she was. There had been three burial lots remaining in the family plot where her folks were buried. One of those seemed as good as anything she could think of at the time for Clay.

Now she felt better about laying him with family rather than off by himself somewhere. Her baby's body would lie as safe from desecration here as any place. Nashvillians were as used to country music stars as stars in the sky and took little more notice. They gave music folks the live and let live southern respect they wanted to receive. Known or unknown, folks deserved to walk the streets and go about their business in peace.

As if fate had been running her affairs, knowing she wasn't able, she realized Clay resting here was appropriate. Her family would have loved Clay. He would have become the son her daddy never had. Her daddy would have taken great pride in his grandson's accomplishments. As she walked to each grave, placing yellow roses she bought from the Chinese man at the gate, she read the four headstones.

She ended a silent prayer: Lord, please forgive the fool shit I said from pain and pills. I'm through with pills. There was a time, I had to have them. But they keep me rattled. Make me strong enough to stand the pain on my own. Amen.

Anna sat down on the concrete bench at the foot of Clay's grave and the one she would fill someday. She realized, when it's your own, the graveyard jokes and fears and phobias lose their punch. In a graveyard, there's nothing to laugh about and nothing to fear, only a sad sameness.

The spirit of Clay Manassas Hill, the part that made him who he was and who she loved, did not lie here conquered and held prisoner in the dark by dirt. Now that she had come, she knew there was no way he could still be here. Graves were honorable places to house empty bodies. If there were ghosts in these quiet green grounds, they were friendly. Clay wouldn't let them harm her. She'd love to talk with even his ghost one more time.

As much as she dreaded coming, she hurt here no worse or no less than anywhere else. She had thought she would spend time here; but still she didn't want to be here. There was nowhere she wanted to be, since sealing herself in Woodhill after the funeral. If she had planned yesterday to come here today, she wouldn't have come.

But coming to Golden Glen helped her see that Clay Hill's spirit was too tuned to the infinite universe to be lying here in dirt that was a cornfield when she was a girl. Nashville City Cemetery was the one graveyard that seemed like it had always been a graveyard. Clay loved to go there and read old tombstones, dating back to the seventeen hundreds.

She dug in her purse for her cigarettes, lit up and waited for the tears. Cemeteries were appropriate places to cry.

But instead of tears, a river of memories flooded her eyes. Wonderful pictures of Clay as a baby, as a boy, as a man; happy times, tender times flashed on the screen of her mind for her to love like a grand old movie. And yes, in spite of the final outcome, vividly chiseled before her eyes in stone, there were times of triumph! Clay Hill had made musical history!

AIDS had not gobbled it all! The word alone was horrendous, but it had not eaten her memories or Clay's glory.

Grief had made her forget there was victory and the rare reality of a man having done what he wanted to do with his talent.

He made those around him happy, he won honors and awards in his field. Not bad, my son, not bad at all, especially for a five year career. Five years, nothing-- not bad for fifty years.

Clay, you were everything I ever dreamed of, I think you were everything you ever dreamed of-- except for more life.

Opinion here has it you're in a better place. I hope so. Maybe you have a woods to run and dream in-- maybe Shep's there. Maybe you have a stage to perform on. Maybe the baby Rachel aborted is there and I'm a grandmother. Maybe you have your health. Oh, darling, I dearly hope so.

You were better at accepting the last goodbye than me. Maybe that's the way I have to think of it to retain any sanity at all. You were the best of the best, and the best part of my life. Anna almost smiled as she said aloud, "I hope it brings you no pain to know I miss you like hell."

Then she felt the shadows and saw the pink twilight was gone. An evening star was winking at her and her stomach was grumbling on empty. It was time to eat something and decide where to spend the night. It wasn't going to be at Woodhill. She'd sleep in the car first!

Leaving Golden Glen released her tears. She found a convenience store where she could park till she could see again. Her tears were softer, the first close to acceptance. She left the cemetery in a better frame of mind than she had going in. She knew her boy wasn't just lying there in the ground, but she had seen his grave her last time till the final time, when she'd be hauled in to stay. Thank God, she had a small grip on accepting another unchangeable.

Knowing when enough was enough, she wiped her eyes and drove back into traffic. Maybe the motel a mile or so out would have a vacancy. She sniffed and looked in the rear view mirror. Her reflection prompted her to fish a lipstick from her purse. No use walking in the motel looking as bad as she felt. Right or wrong, she had taken a baby step toward resignation, she had to take another and another. Any direction was right climbing up from bottom while she found a way to live, in this her newest life.

Clay wouldn't want her broken. She had to keep running and blocking out the pain till someday when she would be strong enough to remember him for all he was without going berserk. The memory of all that good shouldn't be shunned because of the irrevocable and her weakness. Till she could will a stronger self into a reality, somehow she simply had to survive.

The motel had a vacancy, a shower, a dining room and a lounge. The room was clean, well decorated and her steak dinner tasted better than anything she had eaten in weeks. The salesman who hit on her in the bar wasn't too bad, and the band did for two glasses of wine that helped her mood considerably.

At eleven she was in bed, pounding the pillows, threatening to remove the plastic covers under the pillow cases. Finally she got her nest made, knowing she wouldn't be able to sleep alone in a motel, even if it was on the outskirts of Nashville and near Clay's place. Thinking she would be wide-eyed all night, her tired eyes closed and she slept.

CHAPTER 30
RETURN TO GREENRIVER

When morning came, she could hardly believe it was after nine. Lord, that was more running sleep than she had enjoyed in over a year. Her pillows were dry and her stomach wanted to go back to the dining room. After she showered and dressed, she walked to the dining room, hungry and craving a good cup of coffee. When she left, she had devoured three slices of bacon, scrambled eggs, home style biscuits with the most luscious strawberry jam, and three cups of coffee. Then, miracle of miracles, she was able to actually smile at the young desk clerk when she left. He couldn't help it if he was young, blond, handsome and reminded her of Clay! He was a nice desk clerk.

The moment she took the road to Greenriver, she had a feeling of traveling friendly ground. She'd never lived over fifty miles from her birthplace, but fifty miles and thirty years made a hell of a journey. Till now, she had never returned, had never felt any need to and didn't know why she was now. She was running on instruments, letting her subconscious guide her. It always came into play when her conscious mind played out. She was moving with the feeling she was doing what she was supposed to be doing. That made it right.

When she drove up Main Street, it was plain to see the village had grown without changing. The A & P, Village Drug and Maude's Ice Cream Shop, where Maude used to serve the best banana splits and french fries in the world, were all still operating.

Some new shopping facilities had been built, or so she thought. She didn't remember the building housing a Salvation Army store. Knowing she would need more clothes and wanting to avoid the hassle of a boutique, she stopped in. Boutiques never understood: "I'd like three sets of whatever colors you have except yellow. Give me size ten if they run small, size eight if they run large. I can't wear yellow. Most blonds look like a case of jaundice in yellow." A purchase, instead of being sold, and a little joke blew a boutique saleswoman's mind. The girls in school who never chewed gum, passed a note or read a comic book behind their loose leaf binder grew up to be boutique salesladies. She found several things to extend the limited wardrobe she packed. Returning to Woodhill for clothes or anything was unthinkable. Hell, it was impossible!

With little time wasted, she left the thrift store with a sack of clothes, having spent only nineteen dollars and hadn't heard a word of, "That looks dawling on you, dawling" crap. She tossed her sack of purchases on the back seat and continued her tour of Greenriver.

The old fire station looked the same; there was a new bank and community center. It wasn't as large as West Side, where Clay and Copper Jim had met. And where she had met Jake, come to think of it. God, now he was another life. It was a wonder the poor man hadn't killed her. A relationship between two wills as strong as hers and his was doomed from the start. A woman in love had to be the world's worst for thinking she could turn water into wine.

The First Methodist Church looked as it did when she went to vacation Bible school there one summer thirty years ago. Churches had always overrun Greenriver. For its size, it probably had more churches than any town in the state; maybe the whole South. The Baptist and Church of Christ had grown and looked prosperous. The Presbyterian, Church of God and Catholic churches had the faces they had when she was a girl-- too bad she didn't.

Passing her old elementary school slowed her to a crawl. She circled the block and parked. Thornton Grammar School! Lord, she walked those halls the first through the eighth grades. Except for some portable rooms toward the back of the building, the school was as she remembered.

Lighting a cigarette, she remembered the happiness and sense of home and well-being she felt as a kid here. And no wonder, the place is a Norman Rockwell painting of small town U.S.A.

That return to Eden feeling soothing her was a wonder she felt at special times and places. It was always so risky, trying to share that feeling. It disintegrated in the presence of eyes that had to see to believe. Some things were always born of faith and phantoms, some of the best and most precious things. Exposing and trying to share them with the totally literal mind was like trying to share Christ's ascension with an atheist. Aunt Effie was the first to mention and to share those feelings. There had been a few others along the way-- Clay, Copper Jim, Jake to a point, and Gunnar. The cornerstone of his publishing empire stood on faith and phantoms. For music folks, imagination and dreams made stronger building blocks than steel beams. Faith and phantoms kept all the songwriters' hearts from dying as children.

Her reel of grade school memories flipped on. She remembered Mrs. Nancy Burnette, who taught her fourth grade and about books and dreams and writing. Lord, she had loved Mrs. Burnette.

Clay's innate way of relating to things unseen was the reason a lid was never on his creativity or his career. It was one of the things that had made the two of them close and think so much alike. That sharing often dissolved the eighteen years between them, let them escape the mother-son role and be friends and confidants. Oh, Clay, I miss you so, darling. No! she told herself, swallowing the tears rising in her throat. "That shit ain't happening today," she said aloud and cranked the car.

On down Main Street, she saw Thornton High where she planned big on going. But that was the summer her world was blown off its axis-- the first time. Thornton High had a new wing and two portable classrooms.

Further on, she noticed that Thornton Chemical Limited had expanded. The sprawling plant now covered considerably more ground and its towering smokestacks zoomed even higher in the summer sky. World War Two boomed Thornton into a facility never conceived in its original blueprints. The one thing smaller at Thornton was the parking lot. Updated technology had eliminated a great many jobs and people, and therefore automobiles.

Some of those laid off by updated techniques no doubt saw hard times. In the long run, Thornton's remodeling and updating was a blessing. The acid Thornton used in manufacturing, not only emitted fumes that smelled awful and earned Greenriver the nickname Stink Town, it literally ate the workers' clothes, turned the silver coins in their pockets green and kept her mother constantly patching her daddy's work pants.

Though she could no longer remember the girl's name, Thornton cost her a new playmate. After her playmate's daddy worked at the plant awhile, he quit, and since Thornton owned the house, they had to move. A few days after they moved, she heard her daddy telling her mother that Fred said he was getting out while he could because if the acid turned the silver in his pocket green, no telling what it was doing to his insides.

At the end of the Thornton site, Anna took a left and drove on to Greenriver Lake. The perfect day brought the water worshipers out in flocks. The lake was beautifully clear and offered recreation for those who favored it. Over the years, Anna's fair skin had finally convinced her it was never going to tan; it was never going to do anything but burn when exposed to much sun. The drowning of her family hadn't done much to make her care for water sports or the lake, but she parked for a walk along the beach to stretch her legs.

Driving back into Greenriver's business section, she saw the post office and parked to look it over. Not a brick had changed, she didn't reckon, as she read the date on the cornerstone: AD 1932.

Sadly, the movie house next door was gone without a trace. She did regret that fact. Downtown Nashville had nothing to compare with the old Greenriver Theater. Thornton had gone all out. The nerds had won again. Deeds done in the name of progress all too often were just the reverse. The movie house could have been a community playhouse and historical landmark.

Anna drove into the small parking area in front of the site where the theater had stood. In those distant days of her childhood, most movie fans came on foot, so there had been no need for much parking space. Automobiles were rare when the village was young, those who could afford them rarer still. Thornton had built the village close knit and with good sidewalks.

Anna was aware of the volumes written about the stereotyped company store and the bondage that could come from such situations. But it was well known, that in the days when Thornton ran things in Greenriver, a child going cold or hungry or without medical attention was virtually unheard of. Thornton would not tolerate those kind of conditions within a family where the head of the house was an employee. If below par circumstances came to light, Thornton would extend help. If it continued to happen for no good reason, Thornton fired the employee. The employee had to move and Greenriver continued to have virtually no cold or hungry children.

Anna got out of her car and walked up to the old movie site, remembering with something close to reverence with each step the wide circular walk that had led up to the four huge white columns standing on the long front porch from each side of the building. The front had been some Yankee architect's concept of the pre-Civil War South. Anna had loved the front of the building almost as much as the magic of the movies she had seen inside. A good film, then and now, gave her imagination tracks to dream on for weeks.

Walking the clover of the vacant lot, Anna remembered the jobs she had come up with to earn admission money. Her way of turning effort into dreams was returning empty bottles for the deposit. She kept a check on the trash bins, taller than she was then, behind the A & P grocery for discarded wooden fruit boxes. Apple boxes were the best but orange crates would do. Both varieties cut up into excellent kindling Anna sold in the neighborhood for thirty-five cents a bushel basket full. Back then folks needed kindling year round to start fires in their hot water heaters and cook stoves. Thirty-five cents was enough for the twelve-cent movie admission, a nickel for popcorn and a nickel for a Milky Way. A Milky Way or Payday were her favorite candy bars most of the time to go with popcorn. She always saved a few cents to drop in the coin slot she had punched with her mama's butcher knife in the lid of an empty pickle jar. This was her mad money bank she kept back under her bed in a shoe box.

Sometimes she bought blow gum, but the theater manager called you down if you popped bubbles during the movie. She never did figure out how to blow bubbles without popping one once in a while. Sometimes she bought a penny's worth of licorice. There wasn't anything she loved better than licorice. God was in His heaven and all was right with her world when she could see a Saturday double feature, stocked with goodies to eat. She would share begrudgingly with her little sister Marie with remarks like: "You won't help me cut the kindling, why should I share?"

"I'll tell Mama," was Marie's smug, so true answer.

Anna adored the cartoons and The Three Stooges. There were so many she liked but she didn't remember their names. Cowboy movies were her favorite. The Lone Ranger and Roy Rogers had righted wrongs and busied her mind with wonderful visions of the Old West many a Saturday afternoon while she busied her mouth with up to the minute new treats.

But it was all such a long time ago and an even longer frame of mind ago. Here she started out to be what Clay was. For the first time, she could remember singing in every school play or program she could possibly get into and the joy performing had brought her. Timing, she remembered reading somewhere, was the essence of the twist of fate in all things. Be late; be sick; be devastated; be the hunting dog that stopped to run the rabbit and lost the hunter; it was all the same; you missed your bus, or chance, or geranium, or whatever. Suddenly, she felt a new urge to cry. "Don't start that!" she growled aloud, shook her head to clear it, then decided it was time for a change of scene and started walking to the car.

She scrambled through the console between the seats for the Chopin tape and popped it in the cassette player. With trembling fingers, she adjusted the bass and treble, then turned the volume up full blast, letting it fill every crevice and every corner of the car and of her mind. Lord, Detroit did put a wonderful sound system in a Cadillac.

She relaxed and let her head drop to the back of the seat, the music washed over her like a baptism. In moments she felt it ease her mind and soothe her writhing soul. The piano tinkled out of the nocturne and into the sonata, then thundered into the polonaise that was, of all music, her most cherished piece. It was another sanctuary she had forgotten. No wonder her spirit was sagging. Here was another of her true allies she had not asked to come to her rescue. She had not listened to this friend in a year, maybe two.

Anna was not informed as to what Chopin's inspiration had been and had never wanted to know for fear it might take her own inspiration when she listened to his music. For her, when his polonaise was playing, all things were possible. For her, it was the sound of living and loving, of passion and creation, of survival and of victory. It was the sound of infinite wonders. The fact a human being could create that kind of sound was enduring proof God was near. The human spirit could perform miracles; could overcome pain, could be, in the words of Martin Luther King, "Free at last!" Free not only from the injustices of society, but from the slavery of deprivation and pain.

As the polonaise came to its crashing finish, Anna realized the day was almost gone and she was too unless she firmly proceeded with lifting herself out of her valley of despair. It was time to burn some bridges and to build others. She could not continue with life as she was. Hell, they didn't punish criminals like this. "God," she uttered desperately, "start me or stop me, kill me or cure me, but give me some relief!"

Realizing she had spoken aloud made her think to light a cigarette. She was feeling close to feeling comforted by this village of her childhood. The old street was a place she remembered being happy. Here there had been a before the boat accident, a before Aunt Effie's death, a before the orphanage, a before Jeff's death and yes, even a before Clay's death.

In spite of the cigarette, her stomach told her she was hungry, then her watch told her it was almost six o'clock. She cranked the Cadillac.

Greenriver was her first choice for supper, but she wound up at the motel asking for the room back she left that morning.

"How long will you be staying with us this time, Mrs. Hill?"

His question put her in touch with a thought she hadn't thought. "Uh, I have more business than I supposed. Listen, book me for two nights, then I'll let you know, if that's okay."

"That's fine, ma'am."

After getting settled in her room, she went to the snack station, where she filled the ice bucket, and checked the snack machines. She walked back in her room with two diet Cokes, a Mr. Goodbar and a pack of cheese crackers. A few goodies would let her take her time about dressing for supper.

It was amazing-- after a shower, a change of clothes and some TV, she'd proven she could do everyday things again without the dubious help of goof balls or the capable help of Katy at Woodhill. Hell, she'd been taking care of herself a long time before there had been money to hire a Katy.

Once she was on her way in her thrift store finds, Anna enjoyed her second evening in the confines of the motel. Again, dinner was delicious at a table on the terrace overlooking the pool. Several families in the water kept her from feeling lonely. The kids were having a ball, she wasn't sure about the parents.

It was a little past ten when she sat on a stool in the bar and ordered wine. After a while, the band played one of Clay's songs. It brought tears to her eyes but she was glad they played it. Clay would have been delighted.

Two glasses of wine and another talk with the salesman revealed he was a tired husband, promiscuous from boredom, more bored than promiscuous. He said she was going through a divorce and he could spot that situation every time. Unwilling to break his faith in his ability to judge women, or to tell her real story, Anna said she didn't want to talk about problems.

Later, with the TV at low volume for company, she pounded the plastic protected pillows, and started to drift off to sleep.

Then the thought crossed her mind, Maybe there was life after Clay's death after all. It depended on whether she had strength to draw on her in His own image strength and live, or let pain waste her chance.

God, she was sick of pain! Pain was no respecter of persons, places, situations or douche bags. She heard herself giggle. Maybe she'd had more than two glasses of wine. At least she hadn't let the salesman seduce her. She giggled again thinking, At least, I didn't seduce him. Don't like pot bellied men. She giggled once more then fell asleep.

At four in the morning some late arrivals next door woke her. She padded barefoot to the bathroom and went back to bed but her eyes got wider and wider. Since there was no sleeping for the moment, she got up again, lit a cigarette and wished for coffee.

She turned up the TV. An old Bette Davis movie was playing. She tried watching till she finished her cigarette. She couldn't get into the movie, she couldn't get back in bed either. She felt wide awake as a country Shriner at a Chicago convention. Maybe the deck would be nice.

Anna opened the sliding glass door to the night and walked out into the night cool and clear. The embryo of dawn was already dim on the horizon but she left the deck after smoking half a cigarette. A full moon and a patchwork quilt of stars always made a lonely night more lonely. Beautiful wonders needed to be shared.

Inside, the movie was still playing. She became fascinated watching the Bette Davis way of smoking. That was a movie within itself. She climbed in bed, propped against the pillows and tried to watch the movie again. A feeling there was something she was supposed to do kept bugging her till she couldn't stay in the bed or the motel room any longer.

Driving Greenriver Road, she knew it was strange she wasn't afraid to be out roaming at four in the morning.

She stopped in an all night diner for coffee. Coffee was the only thing she dared to order in the dingy little place. The greasy look and smell of it made her hesitant to try the coffee but she was hurting bad for a cup. The questioning eyes of a questionable looking man soon drove her out-- along with the feeling of something she was supposed to do.

Turning the key brought the comforting sound of the car to life. Once moving, she punched in her favorite station and turned the car's direction over to the universe. With the feeling still bugging her about something she was supposed to do, she surrendered as much as possible to divine energy for direction. Never as strong as Clay at picking up divine vibes, she still felt she had or needed little power over the direction her life was taking. The Cadillac rolled again as straight for Greenriver as a rock from a slingshot. The feeling there was something she must do subsided. She was doing it.

The night was turning silver as she entered the village and drove up Main Street. She rolled by the churches, the schools and the shopping center gathering her memories. Taking a right off Main Street, she drove past the old red brick library. She recalled the day her first grade teacher took the class to the library for orientation and their first library card. The building was larger, it might be a good place to visit when the day began.

She began tracking the residential streets for old landmarks. In the days of her childhood, the children of Greenriver were pretty much free to roam the village. Rape and murder and pillage and dope were unheard of in Greenriver then. She wondered if they still were as she started cruising toward the site of the old park and the swimming pool.

Where the park and pool had been was a vacant lot. All that was left were the two street lights that lit the area on those long gone summer nights. She let pictures of it all flood through her mind-- the monkey bars and slide and seesaws and swings and merry-go-round-- the craft shack where she made the squirrel shaped what-not with the one tiny shelf for her mama for Mother's

Day one summer-- how she picked up trash paper for a free pass to the pool, now one more amenity gone, like the movie house Thornton's sell out cost.

Still, it was a miracle and the saving grace of out of the way property that let as much remain of Greenriver as there was. It had improved in private ownership without losing its small town feel. Owner occupied homes were remodeled above what Thornton maintained. Rental units had gone, in most cases, far below Thornton's standards.

Being only twelve miles from Nashville without the traffic, Greenriver was a good place for one in need of anonymity, peace, sky and trees. It was also one of the few places a single Anna Hill could be out after dark and not be afraid. The media would never look for her here, if it even looked. Actually, Greenriver was the one place she felt she could stand to be, at the moment.

When Anna stopped the car again, her search and her mission was over. It was early morning, the beginning of her third day back. Her something-she-was-supposed-to do feeling was satisfied. She or some higher power had parked on Mulberry Street across from the house where she was born. That green shingled cottage had provided her a happy home the first twelve years of her life. It looked like it had been waiting, all the years in between, for her to come back and take care of it and let it take care of her.

The mulberry trees her daddy planted were there. A for sale sign graced the front yard like a welcoming party of one. Its message came as loud and clear as if it had been shouted by a hundred: you have come home again! For now, maybe for always, here is where you belong. All day you remembered a good life before Clay. If you won't be defeated, if you can believe in faith and phantoms, you will find life after Clay.

Aunt Effie always said, "When things get rough get busy. Just because you get knocked down don't mean you lay down." Then she heard Aunt Effie say, "Step on out of that Cadillac. Come on, hon, it's now or never!"

Taking a deep breath, Anna gathered herself with strength born of faith and phantoms. Her shaking hands gave her a problem with unlocking the car door. After a confused moment, she shoved the door open and felt the morning wind softly kiss her face.

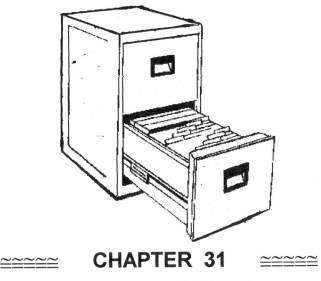

CHAPTER 31

CURBSTONE MEMORIES

Knowing she might look like a nut, Anna sat on the curbstone at the house where she was born. Most grown women didn't sit on curbstones at dawn, but she never had been most grown women. She still didn't claim to be grown.

Besides, in the throes of trying to escape the long arm of nutdom, just looking like a nut was the least of her worries. When you were trying to make your mental getaway through the hole of your imagination, what others thought wasn't the point. Hell, it wasn't even open for a motion. In a fight for survival, what others thought was tabled for the duration, which probably meant forever in her case.

Strange, but now the old house was a cottage to her adult eyes. The For Sale sign looked as if it had been there awhile. The porch still had a swing but the place was looking pretty used. In too many ways she was feeling about as used as the house looked.

A tiger cat slunk up for a pat; she had never liked cats. They wanted affection when they wanted it and to hell with you and what you wanted in between times. She tried to ignore the animal but his meow and sliding against her leg made her stomp her foot and shoo him with a "Git."

Here the sun was blinking awake the bright June day it was beginning to be. Since April, every day at Woodhill, no matter what the weather, felt cold and wet, like Tennessee in the grips of a January drizzle.

At least a hundred years ago, and God only knew how many lives ago, she had sat on this curbstone and made herself a rubber gun. She had an orange crate from the A & P trash bin, she could spare for gun parts instead of cutting up to sell for kindling. She also had one of her daddy's used car tire inner tubes she had saved from the trash can and hidden under the house to make bullets when rubber gun season came around.

Making the gun was a secret, like most of her projects back then. The inner tube had to be saved in secret because Daddy didn't like her playing with "boy things." He never had tried playing with dolls and dishes all the time. In fact, he gave her a hard warning about "sass" the time she tried to explain as polite as she knew how. That was before she got it through her head Daddy didn't want "back-talk," polite or impolite.

A half inch wide circle of rubber cut off the inner tube served as bullets. Stretched the thirty-inch length of the gun, from the clothespin hammer at the butt and hooked over the end of the barrel, a rubber bullet carried enough sting that if you got hit you knew you had been "killed" in the neighborhood games of cops and robbers. You looped extra bullets on your belt, in case you got cornered by gangsters. It was a favorite game of all the kids in the fall before cold weather. At least it was a favorite game of hers and all the boy kids.

She never could play with girls much, she still couldn't. The men, like the boys, played the good games. The preference of the few girls in her neighborhood to play dolls and dishes and Mother and children bored her to death then. Now, women living only to accommodate some nerd Neanderthal, his house and food gave her the sour belches.

Guess you're always going to be an off the wall bitch. I guess. You might be happier if you'd go with the flow. Let's don't get in that shit. You'd be better off to call McGuire and let him help you. He can't help me. Why? He pets me and makes me cry, so get off that. Dunce, he can't help it if you cry. I can't either, but I can stay away from him. Just get off Gunnar! If I call him, I'll wind up a basket case and he sure as hell doesn't need more hell!

I love Gun and I'll call him when I'm feeling better. You mean about getting back in the sack with him? Well, yeah. I don't think you'll ever call him. I don't think you would have pushed him out of your life, if you intended to keep him in it. Most folks reach for people they love when they're hurt. I ain't most people. Nope, you ain't and you work hard at not being. You're too insecure about calling men in the first place and even more so about calling a man you're nuts over. Could be. If Clay had gotten well, you still would have found an excuse to break off with McGuire. You think something bad might happen to him, with you caring so much. Hell, it's happened enough.

What you really need is to find you some nice man to spend quality time with and not to go nuts over. I might when I'm up to it and have time. So hush!

She sipped from her Styrofoam cup of coffee, then lit a cigarette from the pocket of her thrift store shirt. Thinking she should go get breakfast and come back later, she kept smoking, drinking coffee and sitting.

Echoes of the voices of kids and their games still played. Sounds of roller skates, bicycles, the popsicle boy, the market truck, all came rolling back. God, she had loved this neighborhood and that small house! There had been bad times and good times; horribly confining times, but there were also cherished times. Greenriver had given her a sense of home and family she never felt anywhere else. When she ran away from Give Us This Day, life with Jeff was infinitely better than life at the orphanage. Greenriver was a memory mostly blocked out from fighting pain. Now, she could remember a long ago morning sitting on this very curbstone, watching that old sun wake up.

She sat munching on a handful of saltine crackers, the good brand her Daddy got at the grocery. She felt lucky to wake up early and sneak out to watch the sun come up before "they" got up and started the "Do this and do thats" and the "let me plays." Knowing dern well she was too little, Marie always hollered to play.

She had a hard enough way to go sometimes herself. Some boys who didn't live on her block didn't think girls could do anything. If a hot game of softball with them was getting under way, she always had to prove herself. If Marie started horning in, and striking out like always, Anna didn't have a prayer to keep playing herself.

Girl stuff, like dolls and dishes, was all Marie knew how to play. She was good at that! Anna got enough dolls and dishes minding Marie and doing her Mama's dishes. She had to wash and Marie had to dry after every meal. She couldn't guess why anybody would want to play dishes.

Marie didn't like baseball or marbles or rubber guns or cowboys. She just wanted to play when she didn't have anyone else to play with or wanted to cause trouble. She could be so hateful at times. She was always getting behind Mama and Daddy making faces. When she got on one of her sprees, she usually needed a good sock to behave.

Mama and Daddy didn't understand about defending your honor. Gene or Roy wouldn't let some dumb sister make faces at them. When honor or cattle was at risk, you had to risk whippings. She loved Marie, but she could be contrary. Course when Marie and Jan next door played house, they had good snacks for the dishes. To get in on the snacks, she might have to play some.

Anna crunched another saltine, fascinated with the pink sun waking up behind the top of Mr. Cook's peach tree. She was also fascinated with Mr. Cook's tree loaded with coming ripe peaches. She was also afraid of Mr. Cook and Billy Cook who was half a head taller than she was and in her third grade room. She held her own with most of the boys on her block, but she was no match for Billy's height and long arms.

It was hard to win against somebody taller and especially with longer arms. You had to stay out of people's way who were bigger or have you a rock or a stick or be close enough you could run home. If you couldn't reach them, you couldn't hit them. Even if she wasn't chicken, a girl could get her nose bloodied learning that the hard way.

Right after school was out, a bully from Bryant Street jumped on Marie when she wouldn't give him one of her cookies. You couldn't right a wrong with your bare hands against somebody four inches taller and fifteen pounds heavier. The Bryant Street boy already had her nose bleeding when she got her hands on a big stick and laid him one up side of his head. That made up his mind to go on and leave Marie and her be.

If you couldn't beat them, you could show they had a fight on their hands if they messed with you or yours. Daddy taught her that. The boy was Bubba and she was glad he'd moved out of the village. He started the stupid tale about the crazy girl on Mulberry Street that fought with two-by-fours and knives.

She didn't know if John Wayne would handle a fight with a weapon, but he wouldn't let a bully take his little sister's cookies. After she got her nose bloodied saving the cookies, Marie was too stingy to give her one, till she threatened to bloody her nose. Her dumb sister was so stingy.

John Wayne was who she learned righting wrongs from. Her personal code of honor was like John's. She didn't fight till she had to. When she had to, she fought to win, even if she had to pick up a stick against somebody bigger.

It was easy not to fight Billy Cook if you left the peach tree alone. Billy was known to be able to handle himself, he was also known as a quiet kind of boy. If he ever picked a fight or caused trouble, she never heard about it. Billy was a loner and kept to himself, although she never knew why.

Treating her mouth to the salt of another cracker, she started thinking on something else. She needed to plan out her day. If she didn't sort of lay things out and be kind of nimble, her daddy was off from work again today and he'd plan it all for her. She thought he was planning on working on that old thirty-seven Plymouth of his some more. It was still up on blocks with parts all over the back yard. She sure didn't want to get hog-tied into helping with that again. No matter what she did or how she did it, she never suited Daddy. Some folks you never could please, and when you knew you couldn't and you couldn't slip off, once they got you, the best thing to do was just hush, unless you could make yourself invisible.

Yesterday, she'd sat at the steering wheel and held in the brake pedal for him. It seemed liked forever and she started trying to make herself invisible. It never did happen. Daddy just kept hollering from under the car to stop letting the brake pedal slip. She was holding it in with all her might. After holding the pedal for so long, her leg would go to shaking and give out. She would have to stomp her foot against the floorboard to keep it from going to sleep. Then Daddy would start hollering again. When she tried to explain, he'd holler, "Hush talking back and hold the pedal if you know what's good for you."

"Let's go fishing," she hollered back sometimes, hoping to get him into something they both liked. He didn't let her go with him fishing much, but she loved it when he did.

"How the hell can we go fishing with no brakes on the car?" She knew when he used that tone, it was best not to answer.

She knew too how he hated not having a son. She heard him, when he didn't know she was listening, tell Mama, "Looks like Anna or Marie one could have been a boy. Gritty as Anna is, she would have made a fine boy." He didn't hate her being a girl any worse than she did. She'd wished a million times she was a boy. Wishing didn't make it so. She didn't know a thing either one of them could do about that. Anyway, she better get her day planned before he got her back helping work on the Plymouth.

She might go to the park and get a job picking up waste paper to earn a pass to the swimming pool. That would work if she could slip off from Marie. You had to be seven before they'd let you pick up paper. Marie was only six and wouldn't work if she had been seven, she was too sissified. She wouldn't want the scratchy tow sack touching her legs that Zeke the park manager gave you to put trash in. Anna wore jeans instead of shorts or dresses, to keep the sack from scratching her legs. She liked the feel of the sack dragging the ground, hanging on the rope across her shoulder, and using the paper picker-upper too. It looked like a broomstick with the spike part of an ice pick sticking out. She made her own picker-upper once.

Mama wouldn't let her pull the metal part out of their ice pick, and couldn't see the need of having their own picker- upper. "Young lady, pick our paper up with your hands," was Mama's answer. The way grownups said "young lady" always sounded like they really meant "asshole."

She had to beat the head of a big nail to a point. Then she hammered it into an old broomstick she found in a neighbor's trash can after she sawed off the broom part. Too late she realized it would have been better to have driven the nail in the broom handle point first. Then she could have sawed off the nail head and filed it off sharp. After she hammered it into the broomstick with the head sawed off first, she had dulled the point and still had to file it.

Then Mama jumped her case with, "Anna Lucy, that thing looks dangerous. You be careful and you got no business rummaging in trash cans. You stop it and I mean it. Don't you know you can catch anything playing in garbage?"

"I wasn't playing. I couldn't saw the broom off our broomstick."

"If you want to make something, let me show you how to make you a dress. And I have new stencils for dresser scarfs. You could embroider one for your dresser and choose your colors from my embroidery thread."

"Mama, I appreciate it but I don't like sewing." At which point Mama shook her head, like maybe she was raising a Martian or something, and went back in the house. Mama was kind of sissified. Course, some things you thought and some things you said.

Anna spotted the Crawford boys coming across Cedar Street's back alley. She hoped Bud was looking for a game of Big Ring marbles. If he wanted to play Goose, she was going to pass. She never won much at Goose; Big Ring was her best game. Taking empty milk bottles back to the A & P for the deposit till she got a dime to buy more marbles took too long to lose them playing Goose. Bud was the best Goose shooter in Greenriver. She could tear him up at Big Ring.

"Hey, Anna," Bud said.

"Hey, Bud," Anna answered.

Sammy, the younger Crawford, took a seat next to his brother sitting next to Anna. All three sat looking longingly at Mr. Cook's peach tree.

Bud said, "Wish I had me a peach."

"Bud, you get a peach and don't get me one, I'll tell."

"Hush, Sammy. I ain't getting no peach. Anna, wanna play Goose?"

"Do I look crazy, Bud? You always win at Goose."

"Can't help it if I'm good and you're chicken."

"Not getting beat ain't chicken. Like Daddy's tried to teach me, it's using a little horse sense."

"How about a cracker?" Bud knew when to change the subject. If she was a girl, Anna wasn't no fool.

"Me, too," Sammy chimed. Sammy was only five and he was sticking his lower lip out like he might start to snivel if he didn't get a cracker. Besides, Anna knew they were always hungry. Their mama, Agnes, hardly ever cooked and their daddy was hardly ever home. They were better off when he wasn't. Mr. Crawford beat up on Agnes a lot when he was home and drank beer.

Anna knew because she sometimes found empties in their trash can she took and got the deposit back on. Beer bottles were a great find. They brought two cents deposit instead of the penny that milk bottles brought. One time she was taking a long necked empty out of the Crawford trash. It was early one Saturday, like this morning, and she had heard the Crawfords in an awful fuss. There was a sound like chairs knocked over and Mrs. Crawford screamed like she was being killed.

She heard Bud yell, "Leave my mama alone!" Then Bud screamed like he was being killed. Anna grabbed the bottle and got her stick horse galloping faster than any stick horse had ever run between the houses, two streets over to her own yard. When she finally got Silver to whoa, she got off and hitched him by his saw grass bridle to the back steps. "You hold on, Silver, till I get this bottle cleaned up," she told her trusty mount.

Then she turned on the garden hose and washed the beer bottle. When the drug store opened, she planned on trading it in for jaw breakers and blow gum. Maybe she could find a milk bottle in Mama's pantry to go with it and get herself a Tootsie Roll too.

Anna's good fortune made her keep an eye on the Crawford trash. Once she found three empties that reaped a whopping six cents in one sweep. That's when she started saving for the cocker pup. Now, she had four dollars saved in the jar under her bed in a shoe box. The box also kept the calendar where she kept track of the additions to her treasure.

"I said I want a cracker." Sammy's whine got Anna back to the moment.

"Here's y'all a cracker each. I ain't got but two left and I can't go back in the house. Mama might catch me and make me dust, or God knows what before I get out again. Your mama don't make y'all do nothing and she don't care how long you stay out. Boys got it made. Y'all don't have to do none of that dumb stuff." Bud didn't know how to answer that one. Anna could get real windy, he didn't want to give her any more to go on.

Before she changed her mind, Bud popped his cracker in his mouth and said, "Gonna play me some Goose?"

"Play you a game of Big Ring, then a game of Goose. We'll play back and forth. That's a fair deal. Take it or leave it."

"I'm taking it," Bud assured.

"I wanna play," Sammy said.

"Naw, Anna's too good for you. She'll win your marbles and you'll bawl. If you want to give them to her, hand them over but don't bawl." Sammy screwed his face up to bawl anyway.

Anna said, "Sammy, if you're gonna be a crybaby, just go home!"

Bud said, "I gotta watch him. Mama's working today."

"I know what a pain that is, I get so tired of watching Marie. You want another cracker, Sammy?" Sammy nodded his head yes to indicate he truly did. "Will you shut up while me and Bud play marbles?" Anna said, holding the coveted cracker in front of Sammy's eyes. He nodded again. "Cross your heart and hope to die?"

"Yeah," Sammy said, nodding harder. Anna handed him her last cracker.

"Bud, let's get to the Carters' yard and play before I get called for chores."

"Anna, I got to go home for my marbles. You got yours?"

"Got some in a cigar box in the coal shed. My best toy ain't in it, but if I go in the house, I might get stuck. Meet you in a minute."

"Lady? Lady, could I help you?" Anna looked up at the elderly man who had broken her memories. "Miss, you been sitting on the curb here in front of my house a good while. Could I help you?"

"I... uh, I see by the sign that it's for sale."

"Put off selling long as I can. You need a house?"

"Maybe." She got to her feet. "Lived here when I was a kid."

Grinning sadly, he said, "When you was a kid's a long time ago at your age, like yesterday at mine. Lots of young folks move back. Learn Greenriver suits better than they thought. It's a good place, but my Polly died, I got to go to the old folk's home. Call it the retirement home now. Same thing. When a man gets so forgetful he forgets to eat, it's time."

"I'm sorry," Anna said in a small voice.

"My kids don't want me-- can't blame them. Don't want to live with them either, since they got grown. Some were a pill to live with before they got grown. Big man with a mess of kids and a skinny bred-out wife wanted the place. He'd be uncaring about it like he is his wife. Drove him a hard bargain to run him off. You might be the right one. My name's Fambro."

"I'm Anna Woods Hill. I was born in your house."

"Woods? Uh, was your daddy Robert Woods?"

"Yes, sir. Did you know him?"

"Worked with him at Thornton. You're his girl that was in Maury County. That's where Polly and me come from. He was a fine bass fisherman."

"I lived there with my aunt till she died."

"Let's call the real estate lady, I can't remember details. Want to come in and look things over while I call?"

"Yes, thank you, I really would."

"If you decide you want the place, I'll make you a good deal. My mind would rest easy with Robert's girl back in the house. This new breed moving in for the low rent ain't our kind. Hate old washing machines and sofas setting on the porches, flat tire cars making the streets ugly. Hate folks able to work with food stamps at the Piggly Wiggly like hogs for the rest of us to feed. Ain't American, Franklin D. wouldn't have put up with it."

"My aunt loved President Roosevelt." She followed him into the house and into an ocean of memories.

"Nobody but Harry S held a light to Franklin D. He taught Harry everything he knew. There's a Philco radio I found under the house that belonged to your folks. We had it refinished but it's the same cabinet. While I call the real estate lady, look at it in the middle room by the TV. It's yours if you want it. Found two old inner tubes under there too, but they were no good. I was putting out rat poison and found them around the turn under the pantry. Don't know who would drag a used inner tube back that far."

"Sir, where did you say that old Philco is?"

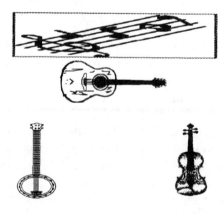

~~~~~ **CHAPTER 32** ~~~~~

RENAISSANCE

Mr. Fambro was in his apartment at the Retirement Center, and Mulberry House was empty and finally hers. She inspected the small rooms that had looked enormous to the child she used to be. She knew there were many lives in a life span, but this was her first old life to re-enter.

Climbing the steps upstairs, she remembered how Marie used to play dolls on those steps. There was carpet on them now that needed to be replaced. In the days of Marie and her dolls, the wooden steps were bare but she had found them a great place to set up her doll collection. It crossed Anna's mind how she loved to sneak back out of bed and listen in the turn at the top of the steps to the grownups talk when her parents were up late with company. She never got caught when Marie slept through and didn't get up with her. Marie could never stay still or quiet for long.

The upstairs of the house remained as it was. The lion-footed bathtub, old-fashioned door locks and electric light bulbs on drop cords hanging down from the ceilings took her back thirty-odd years like a time machine. She went down to the kitchen and stood in the eating area, remembering her mother's white enamel table and chairs. As she walked in the pantry, she pictured the rows of canned goods and staples that used to stand on the shelves. Graham and saltine crackers were always there in a tin for Marie and herself to snack on. Clay had loved graham crackers too.

The porch swing Mr. Fambro left for her was a twin for the one her mother had swung and read and sung to Marie and herself in. Mulberry House was full of things that were as they had been when she was a child. The simple reality of the house enduring through the years brought back feelings of sanity and planted seeds of hope. The Fambros did little but maintain the place, but it was so cared for. The vibes in the house gave silent witness to the love of the Fambros. Like so many who came to work for Thornton, they were good stock. Their one unpardonable sin was getting old.

They were partial to dark colors of paint. That would have to change, she needed light colors. She walked back to the radio Mr. Fambro had left on the kitchen counter. She tuned it in to WSM-AM, like in the old days when they listened to the Opry, and continued her inspection. Evaluating what to remodel, Anna saw there was much to be done.

Some of the work she wanted to do herself. Plumbing, wiring and electrical upgrading would require professional craftsmen. Jeff and she did some remodeling in the tender years. It was one of the few things, after Jeff started with his thing about Clay, they enjoyed together. One of the houses they remodeled had a basement they made into a den, a bedroom and a second bath. Profits from that made the money to build Little Gatlinburg, never dreaming it would be their last home together.

Her Scottish blood was pumping as she walked and made notes. It was in her to be thrifty without stinting. Taking time to get the feel of each room told her something in the house wouldn't work. The kitchen and bath needed a total remodeling. The front door had too much glass for her to feel secure, the back door was plain worn out. New storm doors and windows were needed throughout. The heating system, as well as the wiring and plumbing, needed updating. New woodwork in broken places, wallpaper here and there, and off-white paint would make a wonderful difference. Those were absolutes, might as well throw in a new kitchen and bathroom-- plus more insulation. Couldn't have too much insulation.

She made several more trips inspecting the rooms upstairs and downstairs. Something still wasn't right. She checked all her notes. Right now, she couldn't put her finger on what she was dissatisfied with, but it was past noon. Maybe she needed to run have a salad bar and let this much settle in. Every   detail didn't have to be decided this minute, but it was time to start hiring craftsmen. They would undoubtedly have suggestions, they always did. Usually suggestions about why something she wanted couldn't be done. Load-bearing walls had a way of halting some of her best dreams.

After satisfying herself from the salad bar, Anna sat in her booth and wrote more questions and ideas about remodeling Mulberry House. The wiggle to write songs was twitching again, she planned to use the dining room for her songwriting studio. There was good light, windows to see out and she could also see the front door. Shelves would store her writing tools. They could be constructed to be an overall asset. No former Thornton house had much storage space. If she ever left Greenriver, she wanted her improvements to enhance the property and be an asset to the village.

She wanted to plant some shrubs and a small garden. The front porch was a great place to sit and watch the street traffic, or work over a verse or chorus. She wanted the garden in the back yard for the throes of inspiration. In Paris, she had seen how adept the French were at doing things on limited space. Ground was as scarce over there as in Greenriver.

The library could help her research landscaping small areas. The librarians were wonderful to help her find things. Camping at the motel, waiting out Mr. Fambro's thirty days to vacate, got her back to reading. Poor old thing put off moving till the last day.

Early the next morning, she was walking Mulberry House again. Something was still wrong, it woke her at five. She had bounced out of bed, showered, dressed, put on her face and hurried out of the motel room as happy as a kid going to the playground.

She stopped at the Kwik Sac and bought the thirty-two ounce, fifty-nine cent coffee special on her way in and found a smaller plastic cup in the car. Now she poured coffee from the big cup into the smaller one and kept the lid on the big cup to keep her coffee warm. Taking a thoughtful sip, it hit her-- space in her studio was lacking. She needed space for writing, for picking and pacing while she wrote. Her creativity couldn't flow in a close room.

The old dining room was too close and she wouldn't feel comfortable that far away from the outside doors, especially at night. So that idea was out; but the pantry between the dinning room and kitchen wasn't needed. Actually it was wasting space, since she was putting new kitchen cabinets in with a built-in broom closet. That wall could come down and make more floor space in her studio, plus the window in the pantry would make more natural light and sense of the outside. Then she could breathe and it would be perfect.

Her thoughts were interrupted by a knock at the door. It was Sam Smith, the carpenter she had called. Sam said the wall she wanted to come down wasn't a load-bearing wall. He impressed her as a carpenter who knew his craft and he had honest eyes. His price seemed in line and her gut feelings told her he was a man she could work with. "Sam, when can you start?"

"In the morning." Those magic words got Sam the job.

Anna felt good hiring her first craftsman. As the days passed and the work went along, she discovered she had a sixth sense about hiring and an easy manner working with people. It helped her get the rest of her crew together as easily as she had Sam the carpenter. The renaissance of her old home was as rewarding as any project she had ever taken on.

Barely four weeks later, she was all moved in. Mulberry House stood as a revelation of what ideas, time, craftsmen and money could accomplish. It was amazing how fast walls could come down, old decorating sins could be washed away in fresh paint, and it was great seeing the old house reborn. At least it had been before she dismissed the professionals and started on the work she thought she could do herself.

She didn't want the men banging around making her self-conscious while she was doing her part of the remodeling, and she needed to play music. She wanted to play it loud, with lots of bass like she loved it. You couldn't do that in a motel room and you couldn't do that with any pleasure with folks who didn't dig it standing around breathing.

She bought a new sound system, and after much reading of manuals and even more gnashing of teeth and swearing, she had it rigged up now. Slot A into slot B had always blown her mind but making herself read and follow the instructions, working on her music when her mind locked up and she was ready to throw the whole damn thing in the trash, the system was assembled and playing beautifully. Now, when she wrote, she could grab up her guitar and start picking and singing without a carpenter's eyes popping. Popping eyes, pop quizzes and doubting hearts scared the song fairy off.

"Shit!" she swore, banging her thumb with the hammer, stuck the throbbing thumb in her mouth, backed down the ladder and started looking for a cigarette. It took some walking before she found them in the window over the kitchen sink. After lighting one up to soothe herself, she walked back to the studio to inspect the shelf she was building. "That's just double-damn dandy," she said, "your shelf's crooked as a dog's hind leg." She needed a break. She had been at it since five a.m. with no break and no breakfast.

You know when you work too long without a break, you start screwing up. Maybe you need a professional to build the shelves. You paint and beat down old walls pretty good, but you ain't much of a carpenter and never was.

Jeff always said you couldn't saw straight and he was right. The equal thing, not being same as, was sometimes hard to identify. She always did have trouble seeing where her ability ended and when getting help was the better part of common sense.

The new bath and new roof and new wiring were cut and dried deals. Anna knew she was no roofer, no plumber and no electrician. It was the gray area of remodeling she liked to work with. She was a reasonably good painter and did a good job with simple carpenter work. Most of the time now, she was driving nails straight; it was a matter of concentration. Maybe the bookshelves were too much for her amateur talents.

Anyway it was time to go down to Hardee's and have some breakfast. Slinging a hammer and paintbrush made a body hungry. "Shit!" she said, inspecting her throbbing thumb again. She was eating like a carpenter, whether she was hammering like one or not, and this thumb mashing business was for the birds. God! she didn't reckon it was ever going to stop hurting. She had to wash up and find her purse.

Walking past the Cadillac in the driveway wasn't easy. Damn, she thought, you're spoiled. You used to walk all over this village and be glad for the chance. Two blocks down the street, she began to breath deeper, walk easier and felt herself relax. That was the day she realized that walking in good weather was not punishment but enjoyable.

Anna placed her order at the counter and was seated in a booth before she could have gotten herself psyched up at home to get her spatula out. Come to think of it, she might not have a spatula. She got a box of stainless tableware and kitchen tools at a yard sale for two dollars, but she hadn't gone through it.

The coffee and cinnamon biscuits were scrumptious. The biscuits had to have a million calories to taste so good. Anna knew she couldn't indulge herself with this kind of breakfast often, unless she wanted to walk around with a lot more of her than she was walking around with now. Remodeling Mulberry House was making her eat too much. Sweets were as addictive as sex and smoking, and harder to do without if she got started.

The new restaurant was great for the locals to have an economical source of good food, especially the elderly. Some thought the chemicals Thornton used to use caused some of the health problems of the retirees. Course, like her neighbor Norma said, where else would you find so many in their eighties.

An elderly pair sat across from her, going to town on jam and biscuits. No one wanted to get old, but they seemed to be enjoying themselves. Anna bet the wife had spend countless hot days over a coal-fired kitchen range making jam that wasn't any better than what came free with the biscuits. Her husband didn't have to hear her fuss about slaving over a hot stove, either.

Anna noticed something familiar about an elderly man on a cane, shuffling around the glass front of the store, and thought, God, that was Hunt Hogan. She had overheard a conversation her mama and a neighbor had about Hunt. She would have sworn the conversation, that happened a few days before the accident, was gone from her mind forever. She remembered little about her mother. It was weird having that old memory jump out. The scene came back as plain as the evening she'd overheard it.

Thornton had printed an article and a picture in the plant magazine about Hunt saving a child from a burning house trailer on the outskirts of Greenriver.

Her mother and Jewel went on to discuss how Hunt had migrated from up north for a position as fire chief of the Thornton owned Greenriver Fire Department. Rumor had it that Hunt had also become hopelessly addicted to Southern women. Anna remembered hearing Jewel say he was probably born addicted to anything in a skirt North or South, and evidently the red fire chief's car was irresistible to some.

The women hadn't seen Anna in the upper branches of a mulberry tree. They went on to discuss how during World War Two, Hunt did more to put out home fires than any other single effort in Greenriver. His flat feet got him a 4F classification and he volunteered to be responsible for looking after several of the war widows. Jewel bet everything else was in good working order, since Hunt and some of his responsibilities took years and several divorces to know the war was over. According to Jewel, when a skirt chaser looks like Clark Gable and a woman's man is off at war, a saint could act a fool.

Watching Hunt struggle in, Anna decided that whoever he looked like back then, he looked awful now. Time had not been kind.

It was nice that since moving back to Greenriver, she could take a walk and before walking two blocks some old memory would cross her mind. Surely before dope and giving teenagers a choice about sex, life had been nicer. The old innocence of the kids, the reverence for God and country echoed on Mulberry Street. She could feel it there, real as the sun, the blue sky and her initials she scratched with a nail on a foundation brick of Mulberry House.

She hadn't changed much either, she might be an old child. Hell, maybe she'd never been a child. So much of the time, she saw through the smoke adults blew for kids. Surviving childhood was some challenge whatever the circumstances. Now that she could do as she pleased, and think as she pleased, living in her hometown was fine. As a kid, you did as you were told. Parents, teachers, preachers and the President ran the world.

She was born an owl. As a child, the only nights the owl could hunt was when her daddy worked the graveyard shift. As long as she didn't give her mama trouble, that week was hers to read or write as she pleased. Mama's rule was, if you want to stay up, behave! Anna and Marie did their best to behave so they could stay up, and they truly didn't want to worry Mama. Then at the orphanage, Mrs. Stokes was on the job twenty-four hours, so the owl's hunts were all over.

With all the money Clay earned, she didn't have to worry now about working. The bad side of being able to live for the first time, at her own pace and in her own way, was that it came from Clay's death.

Returning to Greenriver to try and heal and go on living was the best thing she could have done. Clay would love it here. Strange, but she had never wanted to return, even for a look-see, when he was alive. She regretted that. She regretted little where Clay was concerned except that he wasn't alive. She had allowed him his time growing up. With the wonderful son God had given her so freely, she had tried to be custodian, not remodeler. Clay had never needed either. He only needed to be loved and nurtured and allowed to grow. She believed that was all any normal child needed.

Realizing by digging into her immediate past she was playing hostess to pain and inviting tears, Anna was glad to see Amy Lou Harris, now Amy Lou Smith, waddling up to her booth.

"Anna Woods, you look a million miles away."

"Actually, I was in another life. Sit down."

"Looked like you were doing some heavy thinking."

"I was but I don't need to be. Sit down, Amy Lou. To tell the truth, I could use some good company."

Amy Lou sat down heavily, then arranged her two steak biscuits, two cinnamon biscuits and large milk on the table. Anna watched, fascinated by Amy Lou's fascination with food, till she said, "Hadn't seen you since that day at the A & P. You doing all right?"

"Yeah, pretty good, Amy Lou. How's your family?"

"Fine. Guess you're bored with Greenriver."

"No. Given a choice, doubt I'd ever left."

"Be thankful for your time away, Anna."

"You don't like it here?"

"Well, I just never have lived anywhere else."

"Maybe you could move, if it's a big deal."

"Not while Albert's my husband. He loves his job and Greenriver. It would upset him to mention not being happy about something. He says it's sinful not to count our blessings. I haven't seen you at church, you didn't turn infidel, did you?" Amy Lou always had a left-handed tongue, like her left-handed body.

Anna sipped her coffee, then simply said, "No."

Taking a bit of biscuit, Amy Lou said, "Praise God."

"But, maybe I have, according to some that used to rule Greenriver. I haven't been to a church for years. I worship in my own way. I don't think any one church, or all the churches together, have God cornered."

"You always got far out, Anna. I've thought a million times about gym, when your giggling made Mrs. Massey think you were lying."

"Hell, what teenage girl can help giggling?"

Uncomfortable around swearing, Amy Lou said, "What is this new religion you got going for yourself?"

"Oh, I don't know who's going to heaven or hell. And I don't have any hot line to heaven like some, but I know I didn't create myself."

"Hot line to heaven?"

"Some blame everything on God. They're always saying God told me to do this, or not to do that. Maybe I'm jealous, He don't tell me. I sort of have to figure it out for myself, with His help. Got enough hellfire and brimstone preaching as a girl. I need to hear messages like the Sermon on the Mount. I gather enough guilt and low self-esteem on my own."

"Lord knows, I do too," Amy Lou agreed.

Anna lit a cigarette. "I like music, in church or out. I doubt He cares one way or another. Out of context, you could use the Bible to justify murder. I'm not perfect and nobody else is either."

"And we have a right to our feelings despite my family or husband."

"Did you marry a preacher?"

"Not quite, Albert's an elder and works for a church publication. He is a good man, I'm lucky to have him. I know that. Truly, I know that."

"You were lucky too, getting to go to college."

"Christian college? Give me a break."

"You got a diploma that says you learned things. Maybe Christian college was where you needed to go."

"I always did love your honesty, Anna."

"Thanks, but you're honest too."

"I wonder, I can't stand to fuss. You always did say what you think."

"I've learned not to say everything I think."

"I heard what you used to say about me in gym class."

"What?"

"Anna, don't try to deny it at this late date."

"Hell, I can't remember what I said years ago right off. Some days my Alzheimer's in high gear."

Amy Lou chuckled. "Your sense of humor always got you by. You told the girls I was raised on a paper." Anna laughed. "You did say it, Anna."

"Well, you were. You always had to sit around like a lady, and not get dirty. Your mama thought you'd die and go to hell, or maybe she'd die and go to hell, if she let you get off the front porch and play like an ordinary girl. I remember when she taught our Sunday school class. She was real sweet, but I sure felt so sorry for you having her for your mama!"

"My mother was a fine Christian lady."

"Yes, and never wanted you doing a thing but learning John three sixteen."

"That's why you didn't want me on your team in gym?"

"Amy Lou, I wanted to win, you made us lose. I still want to win. I don't cheat, won't play if I know someone else is, but I do love to win."

"It didn't matter to me."

"I know. Most girls weren't tomboys like me, but you were the only one who couldn't bounce a ball twice in succession. I don't know how you learned to screw as poorly coordinated as you were."

Amy Lou giggled and blushed. "How do you know I did?"

"Darling, you got kids."

Amy Lou giggled again. "Yeah, and these biscuits are so fabulous, Anna."

"Yes'm, they are and I've finally heard you giggle like an ordinary girl, Amy Lou." Then the two women finally giggled together like ordinary girls.

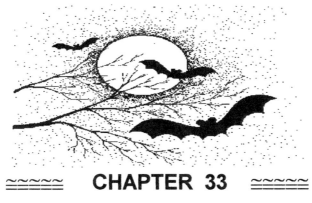

CHAPTER 33

HELL HITS EVERYBODY

Mulberry House was standing proof of what time, work and money could do. Now the house was cheery with the smell of new wood and fresh paint. Anna was especially delighted with the beautiful wall of shelves in her studio. Suddenly, she realized her idea for the shelves came straight from Jake's house. It was a wonder she hadn't bought cedar to build them. She could still smell the cedar in Jake's living room.

The little house was really beginning to feel like home. Shopping yard sales paid off with some country collectibles unavailable anymore in retail stores. The old house was looking good, if she did say so herself. It looked like where some normal person might lie down at night and get the normal sleep; eat the normal breakfast; wash the normal dishes; run the normal vacuum cleaner; read the normal newspaper; live what was left of her normal life and pick up her guitar and write the above normal song.

It was also looking like a place where a person would take her laundry to the washette no matter how bad she hated to. Actually, she had to take her clothes to the laundromat, shop for clothes or a washer and dryer. None of the above felt like anything she was jumping up and down to do.

She made herself start gathering laundry paraphernalia. Rain was supposed to start late in the day with a freeze warning out for after dark. Dragging laundry around would be less depressing while it was only cold, rather than waiting till she had to fight rain too. A true Southerner; winter had never been her time of the year. Before another winter, she would know if she wanted to stay in Greenriver. If she did, she would buy a washer and dryer. Right now, she didn't feel like rushing in to buy too much. All that stuff was still at Woodhill she dumped on poor Gunnar.

That was no way to do a friend, much less the man you loved. That was no way to do your worst enemy. He probably hated her by now; probably had someone else. She couldn't blame him if he did. Shit, she couldn't get into that right now either. It wasn't the day for heavy thinking, she'd see about Woodhill when she was up to it. If the state took it over in the meantime, so be it. At the moment, pitiful as it might be, this was the best she could do.

Taking a place, somewhere warm in January and February, made sense. She hated cold days and freezing nights. Thanksgiving would be a pip alone, not to mention Christmas. Even when she didn't have anything in particular to be depressed about, she was always a near basket case by the new year. Without Clay, Thanksgiving would be hell-- Christmas might just finish her off.

Clay had kept her baking turkeys, making traditional dishes, decorating Christmas trees and hanging stockings. This year there would be no one to cook for, no one to be with and nothing to be thankful for. Maybe she could adopt a personal policy to cancel Thanksgiving and Christmas.

Maybe she'd stay home and hide out like a criminal and not answer the door if anyone knocked-- which they hardly ever did. She might rent some movies, buy some new albums and a new novel or two. She might try to get into some song rewriting and fake herself off through the holidays that way. It would be great if she could pretend some of her favorite things and not come conscious till April, then wake one sunny morning with spring all over the place.

Remodeling Mulberry House was all over but the shouting. A few decorative touches was all she lacked. She didn't know why, but she wanted all the finishing touches done before Christmas Eve.

If the songwriting jag she was into didn't play out, that was her best place to hide. Her pencil was pushing some pretty good stuff right now. It was all too down to be commercial but commercial wasn't the point-- survival was the point. Writing was her salvation, commercial or not.

Suddenly, she wondered where Copper Jim was. It'd be great to lay down the songs she was working on with that country rhythm lick of his. Jim was one more person who had been good to her and she hadn't been considerate of. Someday she would make it up to everybody. Now, she was doing the best she could. If she didn't get the hell out of this house, she was going to be doing the bawling and squalling routine, and that didn't help her or anyone else. For now, she hoped Gunnar and Jim understood.

She read holiday depression was sometimes from childhood Santa Claus disappointment. The article also suggested trying to decipher if bad personal experiences caused holiday blues. Any fool knew good experiences didn't cause depression. Christmas at Give Us This Day was bad enough to kill a mule and every kid there got disappointed every Christmas. When she had parents, some of her requests were larger than their pocketbook. Still, parents could come up with near facsimiles that just didn't get it.

Like the near facsimile doll she got one year instead of the genuine Shirley Temple doll she asked for. A doll with lots of curly hair constituted a Shirley Temple doll to the Santas in her life. Only an ungrateful girl would complain about the doll she got, there were hungry kids who got nothing for Christmas. So her complaints were short lived, but her disappointment lived for years. Clay was the only one who gave her what she wanted for Christmas.

Jeff had a habit of giving practical gifts. Things they needed, but not by herself anymore than any member of the household. She hadn't appreciated the vacuum cleaner one time, another time a washing machine or that dumb electric fry pan you couldn't submerge to wash. Jeff did give her a great gift the year he gave her the Martin guitar. And oh how happy it made her.

They bought Clay his Martin a few years before and he was playing well by then. Clay taught her to play enough to write songs. Her guitar was one of her few personal possessions still in her possession. Taking some lessons would be a way to help get through the holidays.

She still had Substitute Shirley too. Disappointed as she was finding the substitute Shirley Temple doll under the tree, it was ironic the doll was her one remaining childhood possession. The Christmas Santa left her the doll, she was seven. Shattering as life had been, Substitute Shirley came along through it all. She started to love Shirley dearly during the years at Give Us This Day.

When she left Woodhill, she couldn't remember grabbing the doll off her bed or loading the Martin. Strangely, both were in the Cadillac when she got settled enough to unload the trunk. That wasn't the first time she had wondered if they were magic and could transport themselves to where she wound up. Now the guitar stood in a corner of the studio and the doll lay against the throw pillows on the bed.

Several times she planned on Shirley having a new dress but it never happened. Knowing her favorite movie was *Gone With The Wind,* Clay decided what kind of dress. She could still hear his excited, "Mama, Shirley would look great in a green velvet dress like Scarlett wore to Atlanta."

This Christmas she would get someone to make Shirley's dress. Alma might know a seamstress, she knew everybody.

Driving down Main, she was looking forward to seeing Alma, the laundry attendant. Alma was a character and one of her heroes. Parking in front of the building, Anna guessed it looked low-rent to park a Cadillac at a laundromat. Folks would wonder how much she got from the government for food stamps.

Lugging the first of her baskets out of the car, she again read the Greenriver Washette sign. It had a nice flavor about it from that first morning she drove in. Pushing backward through the door with her basket, Anna saw Alma across the room folding clothes out of a dryer.

Alma greeted, "How in the world is Miss Anna this cold day?"

"Hating to stop what I like doing to do laundry."

"Working on your house or your songs?"

"Both. You doing all right?"

"Might as well. It's easier doing your job on your feet than dragging." Alma talked without interrupting herself folding and hanging clothes.

"I hear that," Anna said. Alma chattered like a blue jay and stayed busy all the time. When she wasn't doing her main job washing and drying laundry left by customers, she was wiping machines, sweeping, mopping or emptying trash. She always explained she wasn't hired to empty trash. Her boss, Mr. Burr, would do that, but she kept busy to pass the time.

Alma was seventy-five and still in good working order. She had smiling yellow eyes, and kept a good perm in her rusty graying hair, red hair has a way of turning. As always, she wore a spotless white pantsuit uniform. Being a people person who had not lost her sense of humor with time made Alma a natural laundry attendant. If Anna wanted to talk, Alma would talk her head off. If she brought a lyric to work on, Alma fell silent as a mute.

After Anna got her clothes washing, she stood reading the bulletin board on the back wall. Carrying a broom and a dustpan, Alma walked halfway back to Anna to sweep up the spilled contents of an ashtray.

Anna said, "Bet you hate cleaning up after smokers like me."

"Part of my job; some smoke, some do worse. Hear it's freezing tonight."

"Yeah. I hate cold weather with a passion."

"You sound down in your voice, honey. You okay?"

"Just a little lonesome. Missing my boy." Alma was one of the few people in Greenriver who had mentioned Clay. Using Anna Woods, her maiden name, kept her privacy most of the time. Alma wasn't one to ask a lot of questions, and having someone to talk to was a comfort. Alma understood heartache. She understood that sometimes a person needed to talk, sometimes she needed to hush and sometimes she needed to listen to somebody else talk. Alma was too wise and too sincere to bullshit with that dumb time takes care of things routine. She was one of Anna's favorite people in Greenriver.

Alma said, "Some things hurt and always do. Ain't no statute of limitations on missing somebody. Like me, I was one of five kids and I still take spells missing my folks. Holidays always bring to mind folks we love and don't see much, or not at all. Ain't no way you can keep it from hurting when you care. Like they say, gone but not forgot. Day comes you miss somebody, gone for years, and it hurts like the first day. Like the boy who fell down and bad skinned his knee. Old man come along and said, Big boys don't cry. Boy said, I know, but I got to cry anyway." Alma chuckled at her own story. "It can get like that sometimes. You just gotta cry anyway."

"Yes, I know. Alma, were you born here in Tennessee?"

"Been living in Tennessee forever, born in Arkansas. Raised a few miles from Little Rock out in the country. Course it ain't country now. We had a beautiful place, we all worked to keep it up. Daddy kept us busy growing most of what we ate. I loved working in the garden watching green things grow. Green always has been my favorite color. Farming's hard work and time came I left, but I was happy. Even if I did carry heavy responsibility. Being the oldest, I had to help raise the others. Me and Daddy did the most of it."

"What about your mama?"

"Mama worked in town lawyering and was one smart lady. I didn't take much after her, she was a real beauty. Used to have her auburn hair color, but Mama's was curly and thick as a beaver's pelt. I got the color and the thickness. Mine's straight as a fire poker and hard to curl as straw."

"Bet there wasn't many lady lawyers in Arkansas."

"She came from Virginia, close to Washington, D. C., where her daddy was a lawyer. She was his only child and they just worshiped one another. That's how Mama came to be a lawyer, wanted to be like her daddy. Guess it was a good thing, she never liked minding kids. Didn't like housekeeping, so she worked in town at law work, don't you know."

"Lord, how did she get to Arkansas from Virginia?"

"Mama had kin with a big farm close to where Daddy was raised. He was a doctor. Just had schooling papers to doctor animals. Times like they was back then in the country, Daddy was all the doctor there was. He never refused nobody any accommodation he had. Anyway that's how him and Mama met. The folks with the farm had something sick; mare in foal, best I remember."

"He must've been an understanding husband."

"Daddy worshiped Mama and she did him too. Everybody loved Daddy. He was such a kindly man and real musical. Daddy could play anything musical and taught all us kids. Taught us all a different instrument."

"Sounds like you had your own family band."

"I played piano and sung alto but my older brother and younger sister were the real voices in the family. Would have thought Danny was an Irishman from the Old Country, to hear him sing. Course we got a lot of Irish blood in our family. Colleen sawed the fiddle and sung like an angel. Her voice was clear's the ring of crystal. Homer played bass and Erma Lee played banjo and guitar. Daddy could play all the instruments and sing all the parts."

"What did your mom play?"

"Oh, Mama wasn't musical, except her ears. But, Lord, she was smart. She'd sit and study stacks of legal papers. And Daddy made his own medicine."

"Medicine for what?"

"Anything. He cooked it up on the kitchen stove, always meant to get his recipe. Epsom salts was the root, plus herbs and things he learned from his mama. Daddy's mama, don't you know, was half Cherokee. Knew all their medicine ways. Daddy learned from her. Over the years, treating folks and animals, he developed his own ways."

"He didn't write down how he made his medicine?"

"Nope, it was all in Daddy's head. I got to gathering with him in the woods sometimes, for the herbs and roots he needed to make his mineral water and to doctor with. Daddy raised some of his things for doctoring right there in the garden. It kept everybody around home going. You could rub it on your skin; made it smooth as silk. When it dried, it left a powdery coating fine as dust."

"Then it was good for problems on the outside?"

"Good in or out, directions right on the label. Never no complaints, sold more than he could keep made up."

"Is it still on the market?"

"No, it died with Daddy. He was a seldom soul, I can testify to that."

"He raised a wonderful daughter. I can testify to that," Anna said, hanging the last blouse on a hanger.

"I appreciate that."

"You're welcome." Anna laid her detergent box on top of the basket with the sheets and towels and took the basket to the car.

When she made her last trip, with her clothes on hangers, Anna smiled and said, "Well, Alma, guess I got it all clean one more time."

"Hon, if I don't see you before, have you a real good Thanksgiving."

"You too. Say, Alma, is there a seamstress in the village?"

"Yeah, Mrs. May, if she ain't got too old. Her man died last year, she's been going down ever since. Sewing might do her good, if you ain't in a hurry. Can't hurry old folks, we're all trying to back up."

"I want a new dress made for an old doll by Christmas. If this lady isn't too feeble to sew at all, she'd do fine."

"Mrs. May used to come wash drapes and heavy laundry. Lots of folks do that. Even when they have a washer and dryer. Last few years, her and Mr. May came in together. Older folks come in part of the time just to have somewhere to go. Especially older men like Mr. May who spent their younger days cavorting with wine and women on the side. When that kind get too old to cavort, they run out of anywhere to go. Between you and me, he was a rounder long as he was able to round. Mrs. May never bothered about it, but that's how come so many men die before their time. Wearing their bodies out like racing two hundred thousand miles on a car."

"You remind me of my favorite aunt. She called a spade a spade."

"Well, men drink and fornicate, then wonder why they drop dead at fifty. You can wear a body out like anything else."

"Guess that's right."

"Course, you can live too long. Old Dr. Abner's office girl comes to wash. Says old folks drop in with no appointment in the morning, with a complaint and sit all day. They know it might be after five before Dr. Abner can see them. He tends scheduled folks first, less it's an emergency. Sally, his girl, says he can't get to the drop ins, at times. They got no medical sickness anyway. His waiting room's good as he has to give for old and lonesome. That's what I call pitiful. Ain't seen Mrs. May since Mr. May died. She's like me, too close to eighty. You can be in decent shape one day and down the next; maybe out."

A dryer squawked, one of Alma's pickup customer's clothes were dry. "Hold on, honey, let me get my clothes before they wrinkle like elephant hide." She pushed a cart to the dryer and hung the clothes over the sides. "Now. That'll hold them till I get hangers. Mrs. May lives on Wilson Street, in the ten hundred block. Had a sign out front. Can't miss it, if it still is. Anna, have you a good afternoon and a good Thanksgiving."

"You too." Anna smiled, wishing Alma would hush about Thanksgiving!

It drizzled a cold rain Thanksgiving Day but she got through reasonably well. She ate her holiday meal in a tearoom called Rachel's Table. It was ten miles from Greenriver on the old Knoxville road and named for Andrew Jackson's wife. Village faces were all over the place and she had a table close enough to the fireplace to feel the warmth.

Amy Lou and family were finishing their Thanksgiving meal as Anna was seated. On their way out, she introduced Albert. With his stiff manner and apparent shyness, Albert was a male version of Amy Lou. Whether she could do relay races or not, Amy Lou had always been a gentle soul. Her tall Albert with his polite smile and honest eyes had to be a good man. He faintly reminded Anna of John Lennon; maybe it was his gold rimmed glasses.

After the traditional meal, she had more coffee with her cigarette. For once, not feeling funny about dining alone, she decided to have a slice of carrot cake. The cake was heavenly and afforded her another half hour to enjoy the fire. Then the fire reminded her of Jake. He reminded her of one more good dream gone bad and she left.

Songwriting, six rented movies, countless cigarettes and a bottle of white wine got her through the weekend without a tear-- not many anyway. On Monday, the weather cleared and she took advantage of a sunny morning for a walk. Several bikers were out, two joggers wished her good morning and she spoke to an elderly couple out walking. The elders were so brave it made her sad. All couldn't be pleasant in Greenriver, nor was she naive enough to expect it to be, but the aging of the villagers was a hard reality.

Hardy stock filled the job rush when Thornton opened in the twenties. Now, under their load of years, they tried so hard to remain independent. Daily she saw elderly women mostly, but a few elderly men trudged by too, struggling home with grocery sacks. They looked like they needed to be waited on instead of lugging groceries. Damn getting old, anyway.

And you couldn't get through the village for the churches. Where are the caring Christians now, when the old folks need help? The good brothers and sisters didn't need to be running to foreign lands to minister. Their work was cut out for them here, if they really wanted to do good works. Fixed income old folks had to go begging in more ways than not.

Seeing the older couple reminded her to walk over on Wilson Street and see if Mrs. May's sewing sign was out. On such a nice day someone might be in the yard; if not, she'd jot down the phone number. She always carried a pencil and paper tucked in a pocket, in case a song started coming down. She got caught out once with a pencil and no paper-- writing on her hands and blouse didn't work too well.

On Wilson Street the drone of an auctioneer hit her ears and she realized this was the day they were auctioning off a house and furnishings. The auction company's signs advertising a coming sale were posted all over Greenriver. There were some things she could use in Mulberry House and loved a bargain, so she decided to walk on to the sound of the sale.

A seamstress sign was in the yard. It was Mrs. May's house, and personal effects being auctioned. Furniture, dishes, leftovers from a lifetime were dumped irreverently on the porch and yard. Knives, forks and spoons in a red plastic tray on an ugly green Formica table stood in overgrown winter grass. Looking at the items made her feel as if she was invading someone's privacy. She remembered feeling the same way when she was ten and found a used condom in the dead end of Mulberry Street. Witnessing the passing of the independent part of Mrs. May's life made her think of Give Us This Day.

Several good cherry pieces were up for sale. Three lovely marbletop tables and one cherry gate-leg table waited for the auctioneer. There was a washing machine she needed, a wonderful wardrobe and a blue glass hurricane lamp.

When the bidding started, she found herself unable to bid, knowing Mrs. May was bound for the nursing home. Mrs. May was sitting on the porch swing and seemed to be taking it all fairly well. On closer scrutiny, Anna saw the elderly woman was in the near trance that helpless acceptance can sometimes bring.

They auctioned the late Mr. May's potty chair for five dollars. Some enterprising soul had probably bid the five dollars to get on to the next item.

Anna saw Betty May, who seemed to be the only one out of the five May kids at the sale. Betty had been some years ahead of Anna in school, but she had lived close by. She had been sent to Anna's room once from the junior high classes when the teacher went home sick. As older students occasionally did, Betty kept the class the rest of that day.

During the auction Anna and Betty renewed their acquaintance. Glancing at the liver spots on her hands, Betty said, "Mama fought the nursing home as long as she could. Almost burned the house down twice, then fell and sprained her hip bad. Got third degree burns from spilling hot bacon grease on her arm. I feel sorry for her but not sorry enough to live with her. We never got along. As they get older, folks get harder to get along with. I don't have the nerves to cope with her anymore."

Anna said, "I'm sorry."

"Thanks, but this day's been coming for years. It's coming to us too, if we live that long. Mama's begged to live with me; begged to live with Billie Jean first. That's where she belongs. Billie Jean's her favorite and they get along. Billie Jean could do more for Mama than any of us. She married money and has a big home. She won't even talk about it. I never saw the baby of any family that wasn't loved the most and worth the least. Course I married a fool and put up with him for twenty-odd years till he drank himself to death last fall. He's at Sweet Final Rest now, and I'm getting some rest. If there's a way to get whiskey on the other side, Harold's somewhere drunk as sin."

Anna said, "I stopped by to see if your mother might sew for me but I see that's out of the question."

"I know someone who sews. She's a move-in, but she's nice anyway. Married some crazy musician and got tired of him beating her up. If you'll call, I'll give you her number. It ain't listed, but Beth will do a good job. Like me, she ain't a widow of the retired from Thornton left with a decent living. Mama decided she didn't have to sew, everybody knew that. I don't care what Daddy did, he made a good living. Mama liked sewing. Old folks get to be their own worst enemy-- won't eat, won't walk. Mama was the sweetest soul in the world till she turned seventy. Anna, there's coffee's in the kitchen. Let's leave these hateful loudspeakers a few minutes."

"Don't let me interfere if you have work to do."

"Naw. It's Rob White's baby now. He knows where to find me if he needs to, I'm a coffee hound. Let's talk while Mama's mind's on the sale. It'll be bad when it's over. Tried to get her to go to the retirement home last night and not watch today. No way, short of chaining her to the bedpost."

Following Betty, Anna said, "It's a nice house."

"Daddy and Mama kept the house up good. Have a seat." She indicated a picnic table pushed endways against a wall. "Keeping this old table myself. It's rough but it's yellow poplar and Daddy made it."

"I don't blame you, it's wonderful wood."

"Thanks. Anna, you remember Rob. Went by Bob White in school. Kids used to tease him with the bobwhite whistle. For some reason they just loved to see Rob cry. He ain't crying now, made a killing in real estate."

Anna said, "Didn't he have a rough time back then?"

"Old man White wasn't worth a damn. Rob and his brothers and sisters went hungry a lot. Old man White didn't work at the plant, or Thornton would've put a stop to a bastard letting his kids go hungry. Rob don't want for nothing now. Worth a million if he's worth a dime. And right now he's single. You might can look out for yourself fine, don't know you that well, but watch out. Rob got a late start. He was shy as a possum in school, but he's a heartbreaker now. Anna, some men are just too much to contend with, I don't care how long they can keep it up. You know what I mean?"

"The last thing I need is a man-- specially one that plays bed hopscotch. Betty, when you've been gone, you remember names. It's sometimes hard to put a face with them but I remember that whistle. Kids really can be mean."

"Second childhood kids can too. Hope I go with a quick heart attack, instead of humping around going a grunt at a time. Doctors keep Thornton retirees hanging on when they don't folks without good insurance. Daddy got so pitiful before he died. Mama went nuts seeing him like that, she always thought he was God. After, I thought she might get better, not seeing him that way. But in her mind, he died in his prime. When someone's been bad sick a long time, you think letting go will be easier. You're never ready to lose folks you love."

"I know." Anna smiled sadly.

"I'm sorry. Heard about your boy, I forgot. You can get wooled in this life till it sucks the charity right out of you. I'm like a cow that's been run till she can't give milk. Moaning over my problems, and you had more than your share. I really am sorry."

"It's time I sympathized with somebody besides me."

"After all you've seen, I doubt Greenriver will suit."

From the doorway behind Anna, a male voice said, "Hey, Betty."

"Hi, Rob. You remember Anna? Used to be Anna Woods?"

Anna returned the smile of the hunk she had seen in the yard as he said, "I always notice pretty women. Saw her on the porch." He had to be the local stud of record, handsome as hell and twice as ready to sin.

"Anna Hill, this is Rob White, and watch out for him. He's been rode, ain't never been broke."

"Anna, you're looking good. How you doing?"

"Fine, Rob. Nice to see you."

"You too, Anna. Betty, we got a problem. Auctioned off the porch swing, but your mama won't give it up. We can give the man his ten dollars back, but he lives in Hickman County and wants to get home to milk before dark."

"We got to clear out. The retirement home won't hold Mama's room past Friday. Lord, help me. Come on, Anna."

Out on the porch, Betty said, "Mama, honey, let's go have coffee."

"You know I don't drink coffee after breakfast."

"Okay, but Rob brought a chocolate cake and we'll hunt you a Coke-cola if you can't drink coffee, Mama."

"Ain't hungry, ain't thirsty, and got a right to see my life auctioned off."

"Mama, we been through this a hundred times. We can't keep it all, you picked out what you want most. If you have to stay on the porch, sit in the lawn chair. We can fold it up and take it." Mrs. May shuffled to the chair.

When the farmer climbed a ladder and unhooked the swing from the ceiling, she started sobbing like she might never stop. In a rush of her own tears, Betty said, "Mama, hush. You can live with me and finish driving me crazy if that'll help. But you got to hush or I'm jumping off the Greenriver Bridge and I mean it. I can't stand it, now! You hear me?"

Anna couldn't stand it either. Hell hit everybody, but this hell wasn't hers to stand. Hurrying down the steps and up the block like a thief running from a crime, she had all she could do not to break into a dead run. Damn, she had felt too sorry for herself too long. She wiped her tears with a Greenriver tissue, the back of her hand, murmuring, Lord, help Betty and help Mrs. May. Hell, she can live with me if she'll just hush crying and smile!

 CHAPTER 34
GUNNAR

She crawled out of bed a deeper shade of heartache. Not the ongoing dull devastation that would continue the rest of her life the moment she woke and remembered Clay was really... dead. She would have to fight off that terrible truth day by day, if she survived. No, survival wasn't that important. The nut of that walnut was, she didn't know what the hell else to do with herself.

If she was smart, she would accept the irrevocable and be thankful she was coping with her unsolicited challenge of going through the motions of living with something inside forever broken. Lots of people had broken parts, inside and out. They didn't let poor-me feelings wreck what was left, even if life was like some nightmare car with bad steering that kept rolling toward the cliff.

Still, it wasn't that hell, when she was unable to face getting up till after it was dark and all that was left to think about was using the facilities, swallowing another tranq and staggering back to bed.

She had to kick this latest setback, even if this was Christmas Eve morning and her first Christmas without Clay. She was as over losing him as she ever would be. Thanksgiving had passed badly but she did get through it. Anyway, there was something besides her unhappy holidays grinding her gut, something she couldn't decipher. But, she told herself stepping into the shower, it will come. You couldn't run away from it on a Harley Davidson.

A half hour later, wrapped in the red robe she had given herself for Christmas, Anna poured herself a cup of coffee. She read that red was the courage color, and when she saw the robe in the thrift store window, she went in and bought it knowing she needed tons of courage to make it till spring. She sat down with her coffee to enjoy the small tree she hadn't meant to decorate. Thinking Christmas might go less noticed, she had decided to forget a tree. That was before she picked up Substitute Shirley from Betty's seamstress friend. Shirley looked so beautiful in her green velvet Scarlett dress, she had to have a tree to spend Christmas under.

Anna reached out and adjusted Shirley's long flowing skirt, glad she had redressed her. Preening under the little Christmas tree in all her finery, how the doll would have made Clay smile. Sometimes you had to fake it till you felt it, if you ever wanted to feel again. She touched one of Shirley's black velvet slippers. Buying the tiny shoes looked hopeless till Alma thought of the woman who collected dolls. The woman had hundreds of dolls displayed floor to ceiling all over her house and she had bargained hard to buy Shirley before she consented to sell the slippers.

Anna took a sip of coffee and said, "Shirley, you look beautiful, like a true Old South belle. Clay would have loved your new clothes. You look grand enough to priss on down to Atlanta. Merry Christmas to you, Shirley."

Suddenly near tears, she got up for more coffee. There was a time when she could have a good cry and feel better. That was back before her weeping and wailing and gnashing of teeth mode, that might run all night. Once she let herself get started anymore, she couldn't bawl like a human, so she wasn't about to bawl. Tears were no relief for inconsolable pain. A little walk and some fresh air was her best medicine right now.

Outside wasn't as cold as she felt in the house. Past Thornton, the last mile down the lake road was a gray picture she could relate to. The leaves had fallen to expose a black woods in keeping with her mood.

At the lake, after two fishermen launched their boat and went roaring across the water, she had it to herself. A log furnished a seat and she started crumbling the bag of bread she brought for the ducks.

Their craws were too full to be hungry but they went after the bread. She giggled at the birds competing like pigs for the crumbs and was surprised at how normal her giggle sounded.

When the bread was gone, she started a brisk walk along the lake. The white ducks followed, the green-head mallards swam out in the lake to adventures of their own. She felt charged with nervous energy. Maybe, since she had parked in Greenriver with the old folks, she was falling apart along with them.

Hell, don't start feeling sorry for yourself! I know you're lonely and miss Clay and you're too hard headed to call a friend. I don't have any friends! What about Gunnar? I can't call him. Why? I don't know, leave me alone!

The day was sunny and in the fifties like a Tennessee Christmas was, more often than not. For her, a fifties day made better Jesus birthday weather than a confining blanket of snow and ice. Christmas at Give Us This Day without a family had finally become normal. Life without Jeff had settled into normal. Without Clay nothing would ever be normal again.

Christmas when Clay was two came to mind. That was a good year. Clay got an electric train, Jeff got his dreaded shotgun, she got her cherry bedroom suite and Christmas felt like Christmas. An all is calm all is bright feeling filled their house all Christmas week.

It was a few years before Jeff started reacting to Clay like a rival lover or bastard baby she had run in over him. It was the first good memory of her marriage after Clay was born that had crossed her mind in ages. There had to have been more good memories. When the mind fought for survival by blocking out killing pain, it blocked out the good as well.

She remembered those first days after the one triple funeral she'd ever been part of. Aunt Effie simply let her cry, while comforting her as best she could. Never at a loss for words, sometimes she talked endlessly, other times she cried as hard and as openly as that twelve year old Anna.

She often took Anna on her lap and told her stories, or rocked and sang her to sleep. There was plenty of room in the old rocker, Aunt Effie had given Uncle Dumas one Christmas. He had slept off many a drunk in his rocker, by the fireplace in the living room. Aunt Effie said that old chair had been the most useful piece of furniture in the house. Now it was helping her help her niece rock and cry off more than a young and tender heart needed.

After several weeks, Anna seemed better. They went to town, she picked out a yellow dress and ate a good lunch at the City Cafe. Some of the library books they brought home by the stacks seemed to hold her attention. She was watching TV, riding Sassy and making a dandy little horsewoman.

Then, going into the third month, Anna woke one morning with a crying jag on as bad as the first day. Aunt Effie heard her all the way from the kitchen downstairs. She came with a washcloth and washed Anna's face; tried to talk to her, tried to soothe her. She was inconsolable.

Finally, Aunt Effie gave her a hug, then gathered clothes and dressed her like she was a baby. All Anna could remember Aunt Effie saying during all this was, "I love you and this too shall pass. I love you and this too shall pass," over and over. When she was dressed in a clean shirt and jeans, socks and tennis shoes, Aunt Effie washed the tears from her face one more time.

Then she led the sobbing girl child from the bedroom, down through the kitchen and out to the back yard tree swing. In seconds Anna was swinging so high, she had to concentrate more on holding on to the ropes than crying.

Aunt Effie started talking in a somber tone Anna had not heard her use before. Her words came back into her heart during bleak times all her life.

"Child, we all go through pain we don't get over. Go on and do your weeping and wailing. Let it all drain; may take awhile. Then, if the hurt don't kill you and you ain't crazy enough for the asylum, there'll be time to put it all behind you as far as you can, and go on. Your heart broke by pain will make you as nuts as you crave to be. All you got to do is keep swilling on it. It won't change and won't go away. You got to go away in your mind to new things.

"You got a bad dose of tragedy, awful young. You're a strong, brave girl, you ain't crazy already. If it had to come, you might be better off you are so young. I do believe there's a reason for it. God don't mean for it to kill you or run you crazy, or it already would have. Most everybody that don't die in the cradle gets knocked flat-- and I mean belly flat, sooner or later. You got yours sooner, and they're all gone; your mama, your daddy and little Marie. There ain't one thing we can do about it, but do the best we can. All the crying time it takes for us to get back to living is more good time gone after bad. You might be feeling so blue right now, you're thinking, So what. So, I'll tell you what.

"Anybody that lives to a hundred is a wonder. They say this old world's been turning trillions of years. Honey, compared to that, a hundred years ain't a ripple on the water. Countless, like Christopher Columbus and millions more, been dead lots longer than they lived. I don't know for sure where they've been all this time, or what they have been doing. Hope they ain't been just dead, because we all wind up the same way.

"Ain't got nothing to say about coming in this world, and damn little say about leaving. Can't nobody make time but God, so time's a precious deal. We need to enjoy time while we still have time. Darling, I do! Decided on that a million tears ago. It ain't in your Aunt Effie to lie to you on purpose. You know me well enough to know that. Some tears never completely dry, some heartbreak never completely mends, but a brave soldier would rather live with one leg than not live at all. Good memories get you through blue hell, and a good belly laugh beats medicine.

"He made us to have a good time. When you think of your folks, think back to good times and good days when you were all together. Think on ahead to when you'll all be together again. Could you do that for your old Aunt Effie?"

"Yes'm, I'll try. Could you please stop swinging me so we can talk?"

"Why sure, child." When the swing stopped, Aunt Effie walked around to face her and said, "Now, what is it you want to say?"

"Well, thinking good things is real hard when you're sad."

"But it's your only way out. Don't be feeling bad because you're alive and they ain't. Coulda been you; woulda been if that was the way He wanted it. If it had been, would you want them with a long face forever?"

"No, ma'am, I reckon not."

"They don't want you to either, so don't hold your heart in torment hanging in hurtful yesterdays. Long as we got our health, we can have a good time most of the time. Think on the good in today, dream on the good in tomorrow."

"But I feel so bad I think I'm gonna break. Could you please tell me something good about right now?"

"Well, we ain't sick or hungry. We got a roof over our heads, and there's a cowboy movie in town and Joe's hamburgers. I think it'd be good to treat ourselves to both and buttered popcorn. How about you?"

In spite of her red eyes, Anna grinned. "Okay."

"Come on to the barn and keep me company till I get Sassy Girl seen to. Then we'll get to the kitchen for breakfast, then we'll take us to town. That old pickup of mine needs the trip as much as we do. Evan's been at me again for riding Sassy instead of exercising the truck."

When Aunt Effie had the feed bag on Sassy Girl, she started with the brush and curry comb and said to Anna sitting on a nearby stool, "You've always been a bright girl. I'd love you even if you was dumb, being my sister's daughter and all. But one of the things I like about you, you've always been smart. A body learns to appreciate brains, especially when she's bred out young'uns as dumb as some of mine.

"You look like your mama, got her complexion, same blue-black eyes but you're built lanky and limber like me and think like me. Thank God you don't freckle like me, but your ways are more like me than Reba. We used to talk about that back when you was only three or four. You'd always walk around a doll to pick up a cap pistol. Guess that's why you liked to stay with me, even if I didn't have any girls.

"There was always plenty of toys from my boys for you to play with. Your mama was the lady type. You and me are what I call the female type. Like with mares, there ain't no ladies, just females. You're more like me than your mama or any of my own. Happens that way in folks, like it happens in stock. Genes come out anywhere they take a notion.

"Take my Sassy, tried to get out of her what she is. Been bred to the best walking horse flesh in Tennessee. When you're talking the best walking horse flesh in Tennessee, you're talking the best walking horse flesh in the world. Sassy not only couldn't throw what the studs were, she couldn't throw what she is. Bred her four times to four of the finest, before I gave up and gave out.

"Throwing duds was too hard on her and me. She actually had one white foal. Couldn't believe my eyes when she came out, but that filly was white as snow. White as horse flesh ever gets without being albino; thought she was, at first. But, for a rich, whiteheaded horsewoman, in Rutherford County, she grew into a beautiful mare. Think the woman's hair had some help from Miss Clairol but they made a pretty pair. We all have our likes. White's the last color I want in a walking horse, even Sassy didn't want a white foal. Had to do some hard talking and petting to get her to let it nurse. Sassy only put up with the little thing because of me, so I sold it off soon as it was weaned.

"That ended my horse breeding. Takes work, money and time to care for a pregnant mare, not to mention a high bred foal, when you do it right.

"Course, Sassy did have one beautiful black stud colt. You could tell while he was still wet, he was put together perfect. Lord, the night he was born, I was thrilled to death. Thought I'd bred out the million dollar foal. Took awhile to tell but that was the spookiest bastard I ever saw. Never was more disappointed in my life!

"Dumas always fussed, I expected too much. Well, I don't appreciate an idiot brain in a big beautiful colt, anymore than I do a drunkard's brain in a big beautiful man. Don't guess you remember, but your Uncle Dumas was a good looking man. Set me afire in the beginning. But I can't abide fools; fool folks or fool animals. Sold that colt off to a walking horse fancier that later on did some serious winning with him. Woulda won the Celebration, if he'd had a nickel's worth of brains."

"Who did you sell him to?"

"Man named Jonathan Cunningham-- handsome man. Widower from down around Lookout Mountain. That was a year or two after your Uncle Dumas died. Jonathan tried his best to court me and I liked him. But I couldn't get in no frame of mind for courting right then, or another husband either."

"If you liked him, why not?"

"Don't know. Girl, I appreciate good loving with a man I care about, much as any woman ever does. That's why your five cousins got in the world. Only reason I put up with Dumas, I was trying to stay scriptural and legal with my manning. Course, Dumas the drunkard got where he couldn't do that either. I thought it was bad when he just couldn't stay sober.

"Jonathan called me now and then to let me know how the colt was doing. Named him Sassy Gentleman, after his mama. Came back around a few times. Took me to Columbia for dinner at the Confederate Club; finest eating place in Maury County at that time. Still is, I guess. Anyway, that was far as I'd go with Jonathan, right then.

"After Sassy Gentleman started winning in the show ring, he tried to buy Sassy too. Had all kinds of money. Said flat out he wanted Sassy and money was no object. I had to tell him, some things ain't for sale and money ain't no object either. I love Sassy more than I do most folks. You're an exception. Sassy is all Dumas ever had sense enough to buy me worth a shit.

"Jonathan's frankness was one of the things I loved about him. Takes a frank and honest man, to appreciate a frank and honest woman. He knew I wasn't trying to jack up a price for Sassy. From all indications, he would have given whatever price I'd have been willing to watch her trucked off from here for."

"You should have married him."

Effie smiled sadly. "I know. He stood right here in this barn and told me he was lonely and he loved me. Talking sweet and looking handsome as a prince in a fairy tale, he said he was looking for a wife and wanted her to be me. I wanted him too, but I was still too mad over the bad years romance had already dealt me. When you love a drunkard, you think you can help him. Girl, when you're in love, you're subject to think you can walk on water, but you're walking into hell on earth. When he drinks his winker soft and his heart hard, you find out what misery's all about.

"Bitterness wouldn't let me see, Jonathan was all I thought I was marrying when I married Dumas. That's love for you. When you're shot full of love, it makes you see things that ain't there, ain't ever been and won't never be. Keeps you from seeing things that are. Things you can't do nothing about on your best day and you're pledging yourself into a situation that won't have no mercy on you. Love is the worst fool producing potion in the world. Makes whiskey come off like a cup of whey.

"Course I had to make a joke. Told him it was a hell of a note, when a man would marry a woman to get her mare. Guess I hurt his feelings. He smiled real sad, shook his head and left, and that was it.

"Worst thing about harboring old mistakes, they cause you to make new ones. When I finally got over Dumas, I called Jonathan long distance and invited him to Sunday dinner. In the saddest voice, he told me he was sorry. Truly sorry, Effie, he said the second time. Then he said he had given up on me and remarried. He wasn't half as sorry as I was. Jonathan was a good man."

"Did you cry, Aunt Effie?"

"Not on the phone, I wished him well and meant it. But I was broke in two and later I did cry. I was blue over that deal a spell. Yes'm, a long spell. Just goes to show what a mess of festering old bitterness can cost. Robbed me of the sweetest chance heaven ever sent my way."

Aunt Effie's story was still in her mind when she walked through the village and realized the new shade of blue she had felt all morning wasn't just from her first Christmas without Clay. She was lonely for someone to talk with and to be with. She needed someone to care about and, yes, forever and always yes, someone to care about her.

As Clay's mother, show dates, press conferences, recording sessions, affairs of all kinds had crowded her life. She was busier then than she cared to be. She and Clay had to plan for writing time and alone time. Now, all her time was alone. Of the two, she preferred not enough time alone as this overload that spelled lonely in big, blue letters.

Greenriver, lovely and unaffected as she found it, was a family town. It turned around couples and kids and kin. Many of the crowd from her childhood lived locally. No longer young birds driven to prove they could leave the nest, they identified as somebody's daughter or son, wife or husband, mother, father, sister or brother. She was probably the only native in Greenriver with no family tie at all. Her tie was her feelings of familiarity, love, respect and security.

Greenriver was a small piece of geography that had stood almost still since the fifties with morals and values. That had taken her back to a time before pain and helped her heal. But even here, a single woman over ten and under ninety brought out the worst in wives, like anywhere else.

That evening she went out with Bud Crawford, who matured into a nice and a handsome man, was the one time she ventured into local dating waters. The dinner was nice, but wearing out the night talking about old marble games got to be a drag. Bud was as thankful as she was when it was finally time he could reasonably take her home. She didn't chance prolonging a boring evening by asking him in and he didn't phone again.

That's why none of the songs she was writing now worked. You could only hide in writing so long without touching life. Writing had to do with people and living and loving and being moved by happenings around you.

Poor-me songs had never been strong themes in her writing. Too much pain lay in her past to dwell on. When she wrote, she tried to keep her mind off demons that cut too deep. The world was full of souls struggling to live beyond their wounds received in the action of living. Heartbreak was not good ongoing subject matter, though too many mornings she woke with personal monsters stomping on her chest, as frightening and as shattering as ever. Saving today from burning in yesterday's hell was a forever, world-wide war.

In Hardee's, she thought, While you're in all this inner truth, you should face up to how lonely you are for Gunnar. Shit! Well, is it unthinkable to admit how much you want to talk to him and to feel his arms around you? His arms around you my ass, you'd love to screw the man. Hell! It's a normal thing to want. Is it less painful to go on without anyone, rather than risk losing someone you love again? Yes! A thousand times yes!

Okay, but you're subject to make history repeat itself. What? You could go on running scared till you lose the man you love, like Aunt Effie. When you coach your coward heart to let Gunnar know you're dying to see him, you may find you made him wait too long, like she did her Jonathan. Then you can live the rest of your life knowing you missed the sweetest chance heaven ever sent your way. Aunt Effie always tried to help you. Maybe she still is or why would that old story come to mind after all these years? Why can't you pick up the phone and call the man? I... just don't know.

Might be like that article you read at the library said, it's the right and left side of the brain arguing. Whatever, it's getting too profound for me to follow right now. I'm hungry and I'm going to pig out at the salad bar, if you'll shut up spoiling my appetite. You gonna call him? God, give me a break, I'll call him. When? Hush and let me eat!

She loved the veggies, and fresh strawberries made a great dessert. As long as she stuck to the fresh stuff, she could graze the goodies all she wanted without getting stuffed with calories.

When she got home, maybe she could finish the love song she was writing. It was hard to believe she was into a love song with a happy ending that wasn't a story song. Positive love songs were rare in her song catalog and her life.

She refilled her diet Coke and sat back down to have a cigarette. The mile between Hardee's and home would give her lunch a chance to settle.

When she rounded the corner of Fourteenth and started down Mulberry, she stopped at the sight parked in front of Mulberry House. She stood a second, then whispered, "Oh, God!" There was only one white limo in the world like that. Come to think of it, there probably wasn't another car that long in any color. Lord, this was the moment she had been in a heart to heart talk with herself about all morning. This was the moment she had been dreading and anticipating for weeks. Feeling her insides turn to mush, she didn't know if she wanted to charge or run.

Shaking now, she spat, "Well, fool, stay or go but damn it, do something!" With a dozen thoughts muddying her mind, Anna charged.

When she was within a few paces of the limo long enough for a hinge in the middle, its white exterior in contrast with the black windows, she felt it provoke her old feelings of foreboding.

Suddenly the rear door opened and Gunnar stepped out. He looked taller than his six feet as he stood glaring at her, his eyes blazing like black fire.

Then he took her by the arm, and not too gently set her on the car seat. Slamming down beside her, he barked, "Drive, Bry!"

"Where to, Boss?"

"I don't give a damn. Drive!" The limo squealed from the curb.

Unnerved by his rage, Anna said nothing.

When they were rolling north on I-65, he still had said nothing. Anna looked straight ahead, feeling him eyeball her, and wondered if he was considering carnage, rape or both.

After another ten minutes passed like a week, her temper was on the rise. Digging in her jacket for a cigarette, she remembered he despised cigarette smoke and allowed no one to smoke in his limo. Thinking, Who gives a shit, she fired up. Exhaling a cloud of smoke, she snarled, "Well, hell, McGuire, am I being kidded, kidnapped or what?"

"Lady, don't push your luck. I ain't decided yet."

"While you're thinking it over, if you don't mind, I need to piss! So, unless this train has a can, would you have your partner in crime find me one? Oh, yeah," she added, her eyes flashing, "please?"

He chuckled. "Only you would sit scared out of your wits, ask to take a leak and be insulting about it."

"Whatever happens, happens. I prefer not to meet it with my pants wet."

"Such a lady."

"I ain't never pretended to be a lady. I'm a back alley broad, one generation off the farm, back in the alleys I came from. A cotton-patch kid like you ought to be able to see that."

"This kid beat the cotton patch and ain't about to run back to it."

"Come to think of it, money really don't make a gentleman."

"Angel eyes, where I come from, they make tenant farmers not gentlemen. Hell, if you make enough money, it don't matter if you're a gentleman or not," he said happily. "By the way, it's great just hearing you bitch again. You're still full of piss and vinegar. No wonder I've missed you."

"Don't know about the vinegar, the other is a rising fact."

He chuckled, and said, "Bry, find a restaurant for coffee."

"Yeah, right. I could use a cup of coffee, too."

When Bry parked at a cafe, she was out of the limo before either of the men could open the car door for her. Bry said, "That lady moves, Boss."

"I know. But I don't know whether to whip her butt or get down on my knees and kiss her ass."

"Boss, some women are like some mares. Can't rein too hard if you don't want your butt dumped or their spirit broke. My mama was like that; skirt tail popping all the time. This country never woulda got past Plymouth Rock without womankind like Mama and Anna. Can't let them get too far out of sight, is what Daddy used to say. Anna might slip out the back. I'd follow her."

When Anna came from the women's room, he was waiting in a booth. She smiled and sat down beside him, then laid her hand on his thigh to let him know she was all right. "Feeling better?" he asked in a husky voice.

"If I can have a cup of coffee, I might survive."

"It's coming. I'll take care of you, if you will just let me."

The waitress came with coffee and asked, "Y'all need anything else?"

"Anna, would you like some dinner?"

"Just coffee, thank you."

"I'll check back," the waitress said and left.

"Why did you run away? You said you loved me."

"I told you why in my note, and that I'll always love you. You've seen a dog run off and hide when it's hurt. I can't stand burying anybody else I love. I feel like some bad luck bird. I won't be the cause of your death too."

"Anna, that's crazy."

"I said I'm crazy. Listen, this is no place to spend Christmas or go into all this. Take me home and I'll answer all your questions, if I can."

"Thought you'd never ask. Want coffee to go?"

"I'll make some at home. Got any tapes in the limo?"

"Has Texas got oil?"

"How about Bry driving around Nashville, and you play tapes like you used to. I'd like to ride the city loop and see all the lights. I've missed you so, Gun."

"If that's half as much as I've missed you and women are weaker than men, I don't know how you're alive."

"Gun, wish me a Merry Christmas, then kiss me a Merry Christmas."

"Merry Christmas, angel, and don't ever leave me again. We're meant to be together." After he kissed her, he said, "Ready to go see Nashville?"

"Yes. Let music do the talking while you hold my hand and I get used to how wonderful you are again. After that, I want you to take me to Mulberry House and hold me."

"My pleasure," he said, loving the sparkle in her eyes, hating the underlying shade of sadness. She was trying hard, but she still had much healing to do. This broken, she wouldn't live two years, he needed her around forever.

He punched on a cassette and she settled back in his arms. Till they were married, he couldn't take care of her like he wanted to. Together, there would be new ways to make her happy and he would see to it. If there was a God in heaven, with His help, he would see to it!

~~~~~ **CHAPTER 35** ~~~~~

FOR MY OWN

When Bry parked, Gunnar said, "Mrs. Hill, if you'll please sit still, I'd like to open the door for you."

"Whatever you say, Mr. McGuire."

Following her up the steps, he admired the Mulberry House plaque over the door. Inside each color and piece of furniture was Anna." I like your house."

"Thanks. Let me hang your coat."

"No, let me hang yours." He took her jacket and hung it with his on the clothes tree by the stairs.

"While I make coffee, you should find the sofa comfortable. Won't take but a minute." She disappeared around the dog leg to the dining room.

Waiting on the sofa, he was surprised to see nothing of Clay, no awards, not even a picture.

Soon she was back with two mugs of coffee and curled beside him. He took a sip and smiled. "You still make great coffee, but I can't understand why you didn't let me know where you were."

"You can't let someone know when you don't know, except you're going nuts. I'm beginning to get half a handle on things. I didn't plan to come here. It was like the Caddy had a mind of its own. Good thing too, I didn't."

"I'd have taken you anywhere you wanted to go."

"I didn't know where I wanted to go, Gun. I was just moving on instruments and wound up here. But driving the old streets felt right, and food tasted like food. One day just led to another, and here I am."

"And I've been out of my mind worrying about you."

"You don't look like worrying hurt, handsome as ever. Bet you've been driving the women crazy."

"I thought I could forget any woman. I've forgotten several, but I can't forget you. It's so damn wonderful to see you, and to see you smiling again." He squeezed her hand softly.

"Didn't smile till lately. But I didn't cry constantly, like at Woodhill. You wouldn't think forty miles could make a difference, but Greenriver's like another world. I lock my doors, it's a habit from life amongst the Philistines, but folks who never left don't lock theirs. I don't have to fight traffic to get a loaf of bread. I can even take a walk after dark."

"Without you, I can't do anything after dark."

"Gun, you always say the sweetest things."

"It's the truth; surely you know it." She kissed him and all the longing, the love and the passion once more warmed free. His voice husky with feeling, he said, "I'm spending the night here. No arguments."

"I'll die if you don't, but your limo parked out front all night will make my neighbors think the Martians have landed," she giggled. "Here women don't openly allow men to stay over they're not married to."

"I know small town Tennessee as well as you. We'll fix that as soon as we can get to a preacher." He kissed her again and said, "I'll get Bry situated. We'll be discreet, but neighbors or not, this is our night."

At dawn he woke alone, momentarily alarmed. Then he was reassured by her singing from downstairs. It was a small house, but like she said, there was plenty of room for one person. He guessed there was plenty of room for two people. He'd been raised with a brother, three sisters, and his parents in a house not half as big.

Anna's house was lovely from the warmth of her touch a professional decorator could never match. Her mix of city and country that was crystal and chintz, weathered wood and Queen Anne cherry was charming. He found her white and gold and blue, with fire-engine red here and there, pretty and peaceful. He loved being in Anna's house, he loved even more being in her bed. It had been a warm Christmas night.

At the beginning, talk about two jack rabbits. It must have been as long for her as it had been for him. Now that they had the edge loved off, tonight would be long and slow and unbelievable. After, she started backing down again about marriage. You had to be careful but at times you had to tell Anna how it was. Like he said, "Anytime after the first time, the only reason for a couple to get married is they can't stand it if they don't. Anna, I can't stand it."

"Uh, I don't kno--"

"Really, I can't stand it anymore if you don't marry me. The only word I want to hear out of you is yes. If you can't give it to me, I'm outta here." Lying in his arms, she felt his body stiffen and his arms loosen. She had never been more terrified of a decision.

"Gun, you can't leave in the middle of the night."

"Unless you say what I came to hear, watch me!" Even in the dim light, his black eyes told her it was now or never. She didn't know if she could stand it if he stayed. She damn sure couldn't stand it if he left.

Remembering Aunt Effie losing Jonathan, she said, "I can't survive losing you again. I know I can't survive losing you tonight. So... yes."

Now, happy as a prodigal come home, he lay listening to her song. It was impossible for him to listen without evaluating. He hadn't heard her sing since Clay's death, her sound was still so lovely. She was into something new that probably woke her. Knowing songwriters too well to interrupt, he decided to take his time about getting up.

Creation was like a rival lover that never caused trouble, if you could accept that when creation caressed your songwriter, you stayed out of the damn way. A heart that beat with the gift of creativity reserved a personal chamber or two. If you didn't want hurt feelings or the staff writer salary you paid out wasted, when the writing ruts went to raging, you let it rage and prayed your writer wrote a hit.

When a song was coming down, a songwriter was truly not of this world. They were like women who couldn't be bought, they did what they did for love. Money, if there was any, had to come after the fact. A gifted songwriter writing from the heart composed legendary songs. Clay, Anna and others like them kept publishers like him listening and dedicated.

Others could save the whales and the redwoods. Out of the thousands of songwriters he had heard in thirty years, he didn't need a calculator to add up the rare few who wrote from the heart in a commercial vein.

Those were the only songwriters he looked to sign now. He had plenty of commercial songs in his catalog. Now, he heard too many of them as products of over schooled and overdoctored pencils with too much soul erased by aiming too directly for the almighty dollar. A third grade child could be taught to write a song with an obvious play on words or a hook hanging out like a shirt tail. Soul was the gold. It took precious time for most songwriters to come into their own. With wisdom beyond his young years, Clay Hill was a rare exception. Obviously Clay had lived other lives.

It took five years, but one night, two-thirds drunk, Gunnar did the best thing he could for his own songwriting. He faced the truth. What he felt never came out on paper, he didn't have the gift to make it come out on paper. First, he broke all his pencils, dumped them in the waste can, then staggered out to the dumpster and dumped waste can and all. The next evening he woke up sobered up, with the good sense to never try to write songs again.

But defeat led to ultimate victory and his proper place in music. Seeing he didn't have the talent to write great songs, let him see he did have the talent to hear great songs. The money and power was in publishing and production, and he could hear how to produce a song. He could hear the seed of a great song and song doctor the songwriter into growing that seed to harvest. He could cultivate a songwriter without turning him or her into a parrot.

Songwriting was like singing. If you didn't have the basic talent, it couldn't be taught. You couldn't manufacture a hit standard, anymore than you could Granny's Wedding Ring quilt. What made her quilts worth handing down generation to generation couldn't be rolled off an assembly line. Granny's hands taught by great-granny at great-great-granny's quilting frames made her quilts a treasure worth handing down.

Machines do great things. Thank you, sweet Jesus, it don't all have to be done by hand anymore, and especially picking cotton. But machines don't produce heart and soul. That's why he listened for hours to an unending flow of tapes from an unending flow of unknown writers. Mostly he found mud. Gold mining was always mostly mud.

Bottom line music involved personal preference. Denim and lace, chocolate and vanilla, brass and gold all sold. Like that beauty downstairs, pouring her heart into a new song. He was sold on her that first day she twisted in his office. When she looked him in the eye and told him, without saying a word, that he might be God in the business, but she was going to make damn sure he didn't deform her son's career.

Fluff had fascinated him for years, sex and all its games. Anna touched him like a great country song: beautiful and earthy, warm and real with all the heart-lifting highs and soul-tearing lows. Till Anna, he hadn't wanted to have only one woman since his last marriage. But he was stuck and he wouldn't let her get away this time. The games, the lookers, the genteel hookers didn't get it. Anna was in his gut.

Hearing a lovely melodic line put him listening again to her Appalachian soprano. As he had for years, he thought again what a shame her sound wasn't on vinyl. He had asked to produce her numerous times, she always declined. He kept bringing it up till she said, "Thank you, but one singer in the family's enough." She hadn't said, she may not have known, but he saw then how her own album would give her a sense of competing with Clay. She would never do anything to compete with Clay. Maybe she was right, certainly she had the right to her feelings.

Then he had Clay. Now, with Clay's talent gone, he couldn't let Anna's die on the vine. It would be tedious, he had to be hair trigger careful. It would be the gamble of his life. If he spooked her again, he could lose her forever, but it was an abomination to let her waste herself.

Still, first things first. First, he meant to make her his wife, if she never sang another note. It would be as bad as hiding in Greenriver, to let her waste her talent as just his wife. Anna's kind of woman needed so much more, getting her around music again would make the difference.

The phone by the bed made him realize he'd be wolf hungry in an hour. When Anna worked through the spell of her song, he wanted her to himself, not distracted cooking breakfast. He dialed Bry and got a sleepy "Hello." After normal pleasantries, he asked Bry to deliver two country ham breakfasts. Then he settled back in bed to catnap while she was writing.

A few minutes later, he snarled, "Damn it, Anna, no! You ain't doing that." Her song had been on love lost and love found. Now her lyric was taking a twist into love lost forever. He barked, "You ain't screwing us up or the song!" He got into his pants, snarling, "Hell, I got you, and this time I'm keeping you," and bounded down the steps to the sound of her voice.

She sat facing a window, picking and singing into a boombox. Cassette tapes and cabinets told the room was her studio. A born songwriter may stop pitching, but rarely stops writing. During bad times, writing is a songwriter's haven. Sensing him, she turned. Her glaring eyes looked at him with the ire of the interrupted writer.

He glared back, then growled, "You had something beautiful nearly done! Now you're killing it. That ain't no sad song! Listen to your first two verses and chorus. You're letting fear whore up a great song. It's yours, ruin it if you must, but it's not like you to prostitute a lyric. You know to write a great song, like making great love, you have to do it without guarding your heart."

"Damn it, McGuire, I am!"

"You were till a few minutes ago. That song ain't about what happen last week or last year or to folks down the block. It's about you and me and the fact we love each other and it makes us belong to each other. If I stroke out in the next two seconds, we still do. Last night happened. It was beautiful and we were wonderful. Nothing will take or change last night, Anna. If you can't live it, at least have the guts to write it!"

He left her and followed coffee aroma to the kitchen. After filling the cup she left by the pot, he sat at the table and gingerly took a sip. Damn, it was hot, but it was good. Stove perked coffee was something else he had not enjoyed in so long he had forgotten how good it was.

Anna's beautiful old sawbuck table and straight backed chairs could have been the set he grew up eating on, except this one was sanded and finished. Most folks, like his own, had evicted tables and chairs similar to the barn or woodpile when the chrome and plastic tables came in. He was responsible for that happening in his mama's kitchen.

It was another Christmas and his first year to make good money picking sessions. He was going home driving his first new pickup truck. Session work had kept him so tied up, he hadn't had time to shop. Since he had money, he wanted to give something extra nice to his parents. There were still a few shopping days, Memphis was only fifty miles from home, he would shop there.

Headed west out of Nashville, a radio commercial caught his ear selling Formica kitchen sets. In thirty minutes, he had a set loaded on his pickup and was rolling west again. Formica was easy to keep clean and he was tired of seeing Mama work her guts out. That was years before he made enough money to set his folks up on bottom land. By then they were worn out, but they had ten good years of doing what they wanted to do. One of the best albums he ever produced had his parents sitting in the white rockers on the front porch of their all-modern house.

Rubbing his hand across the walnut table top, he saw it took an Anna to see how warm a rough old table could be. It was probably hauled in by some farmer who left farm for factory. Fifty cents an hour against fifty cents a day was a big raise. Then and now.

His daddy might have lived longer if he had come to work for Thornton. It was always better crops next year with Daddy. Farming had been glorified in country music like the Old West had in movies. The side Gunnar knew was far from glory. Country poor had no more glory than city poor. For every farming family who managed to own their land, there were thousands who never beat sharecropping. In West Tennessee, most folks who picked up a chopping hoe never laid it down till the grave. Without music, that would have been the story of his life.

She was singing again, taking it from the top, evaluating every word. It was important to him that she finish the song in a positive way. He had his say, she had listened, that was all he could do. As any businessman trains himself to do once he makes his play, he put his mind on other things.

The kitchen pleased him as much as the other rooms. The carpet felt good under his bare feet. The country table and chairs set the decorative mode of the room. A blue porcelain dipper hung on the utility board above the stove among other sundry kitchen tools he was unacquainted with. He did know the black iron cornstick pan and black iron skillet.

Gunnar went to the stove for more coffee. When he sat back down at the table, she was standing in the doorway with an attitude in her eyes. He wasn't sure whether he was going to be raped or run off. She was damn hot about something. Her blue eyes had deepened to that black violet they turned to when her passion or her temper was fired. He dearly wished for the former instead of the latter, but he was probably too rough on her about her song.

After several seconds, she conceded, "You're right about us and my song."

Her faint smile reminded him of a scared child as she came to sit on his lap and kiss him. After, she said, "It's just that I love you so, and I'm terrified of losing you." Then she was crying and he was crying and they were kissing again and wonderfully crazy again. There was no time for the faraway bed upstairs, but was only now, on carpet rough to tender skin, neither could stop.

Anna whispered, "Never dreamed it could be this good. Did you, darling?"

"Yes, the first time I saw you. Why do you think I've been running after you all this time? You need to listen to your old man."

"I intend to, and love you like this, always."

Later, when he had her lying spent in his arms, he said, "You can't begin to know how I've missed you."

"I missed you too, and you've solved an old mystery. I loved Jeff but I wasn't in love with him. I didn't know till you what it was to be in love in a sexy as well as a loving way. His suicide was my fault."

"No, you were a virgin, he had a clean slate. You were his to teach loving his way. If he didn't totally fire your passion, that was his fault, not yours."

"It was more than that, Gunnar. Till you, I never realized I loved Jeff in a sisterly kind of way. He was good to me and I was young and hungry. I shared sex with him willingly and lovingly, but I was never head over heels in love. We never had what you and I have, that's why he became so unhappy. He knew it, but as God is my witness, I didn't."

"You can't control love. It doesn't make you guilty of anything. You did love him, and you were faithful, warm and good to him. Many couples have less."

"Why didn't he tell me? We might have changed it."

"Knowing you, he probably never put that fact into words because he was afraid you'd leave him."

"But we had a nice home, a wonderful son. That was more than I'd ever had and that was enough for me."

"How could Jeff be sure of that, Anna?"

"Like you said, knowing me."

"He did know you, you're a warm woman. He knew what you were capable of, but he wasn't capable of bringing out the vixen in you."

"You do, Gun, and I'm so glad." She moved in closer and kissed him. Then she said, "Love me again. Please?"

"I'd love to, but in bed. Even with this nice carpet, the floor is getting hard. And that ain't all that's getting hard around here."

Anna giggled. "Let's go."

"Didn't I see a stereo in your studio?"

"Best I could find."

"First, let's put on some music."

"Oh, Gun, of all times, someone's at the front door."

"I imagine it's Bry with our breakfast. Hussy, I have to keep my strength up to stay around you." Her laughter was his Christmas.

"Baby, you sleeping?"

"Uuuumm, I'm in paradise, it was so good, Gun."

"Me too. I want us to spend the night making carpet love in front of the fireplace at the lodge. Gatlinburg at Christmas is so beautiful."

"Sounds great. Course you got me love hypnotized."

"Got you on my side and I'm gonna keep you this way, but truly I love it up there. The Christmas lights are beautiful from the mountain. I've been planning our Gatlinburg honeymoon for years. By the way, Merry Christmas."

"Merry to you. You're the most romantic man alive."

"I hope so, for you. I've had wives and I've had women, a time or two I thought I had love, but what I feel with you is what I was looking for."

"Gunnar, just promise you won't die and leave me."

"You got it, and I'll make you another promise."

"You don't have to make a bunch of promises."

"I want to make this one. Darling, tonight you get the best loving you ever had. You ain't made love till you make it on top of Old Smoky."

"McGuire, everybody knows Old Smoky is only a song."

"That's my name for the mountain the lodge sits on. I never think of that old song till I'm up there. Gatlinburg makes you believe the star in the East, the wise men, Mary and Joseph and Jesus. You feel like when you were five and there is a Santa Claus, Virginia, and he's coming any minute."

"No wonder he laughs so much, if he loves coming like I do with you."

"Angel, you got a lot of vixen in you."

"Yes, ain't you lucky?" Her velvet laugh was happy as jingle bells.

"You better believe it. Loving you is the luckiest I've ever been." He kissed her neck, then her mouth. "Anna, you want to again?"

"If you'll kiss me like that three more times."

An hour later when he said, "Baby?" Anna didn't move. He shook his arm she was sleeping on; no response. He kissed her forehead. It was great to see her at peace, but they had to get to the mountains before the roads iced. Also, they had a stop on the way that could be real ticklish. He cuddled her closer and said, "Sleeping Beauty, wake up. We got things to do."

"Huumm," she sighed, "let's just make love all day."

"I'm spending the rest of my life loving you. By this time tomorrow, I want us to be married. We need to get up the mountain before it freezes tonight."

Kissing his shoulder, she asked, "Is a marriage contract so important?"

"Contracts are imperative when you want something to work and endure. Besides, my precious, we are marrying kind of people."

"Gun, what if you aren't happy?"

"That's the chance we both take. As for me, Anna, I'd risk hell every day to hold you for my own every night and feel like a king doing it."

≈≈≈≈≈ **CHAPTER 36** ≈≈≈≈≈

RED AND GREEN

Light snow was falling when Bry eased away from Mulberry House. The early twilight was already silvered by the moon. A hard freeze was expected after midnight. Greenriver Road running to I-40 east to Gatlinburg also ran by Golden Glen Cemetery. There was another route; he hoped Anna wouldn't notice the route they were on before the point of no return. If she could see the green and red bags before her emotions took over, he believed she'd draw comfort as he had. He had to keep her distracted two more minutes.

At the moment, he had her listening to a female Christmas album he was impressed with. She was digging the album but she knew him too well. It was clear his ulterior motive was no secret as she said, "The songs are good, and the singer, but why do you play only female artists for me?"

Because this is a fine album, a terrific singer, singing some hit songs. She's Nashville's top female artist, and doesn't approach what you could do."

"But I'm not doing anything."

"Darling, I said, could."

"I hear what you ain't saying."

Responding to the edge in her voice, he said, "It's no secret I think you should be doing your own thing. Aside from that, I think this is the best album a female has done in a while. I wanted to share it with you. And, yes, I'm hoping that hearing what some of the other girl singers are doing might inspire you. So, what else for you?"

"Gun, bad as I hate to admit it, we can't turn back the clock. They want their girl singers under twenty-five and built thirty-six, eighteen and thirty-six. Time ain't on my side and I'm not built like that, then or now. Plus, when I should have been singing, I was pinning on diapers." She looked out the window for a moment before she added, "Can't you just accept it, Gun? I did, several years ago, and I have no regrets."

"You can still have a recording career. Anna, if you can accept you have a choice, I can accept whatever you choose."

"Damn! we're on the cemetery road. Did you tell Bry to go the other way?"

"No, I told him to go this way."

"You know I can't stand-- look. There are red and green bags along the entrance. Can you tell Bry to stop a minute?"

Gunnar's knock on the glass partition pulled Bry to the shoulder of the road. Anna said, "There must be a thousand red and green bags lit with candles. I had no idea it could ever look like Christmas in a cemetery."

"Me either, till I saw this. They're just five pound bags with sand holding up a candle in each one. Coming into Greenriver, I stopped by for a few minutes. Lighting the graveyard for Christmas touched me as a beautiful and comforting gesture. I hoped you might want to go in."

"Yes, I think I do," she murmured, gripping his hand. He couldn't decipher the look in her eyes. "Gun, I don't want to die anymore. Living nuts like I got at Woodhill is what I can't bear. Now I understand why Clay didn't want to live after he got so bad. Christmas red and green bags is the first positive touch I've felt in a cemetery." Admiring the rows of quietly dancing candles in red and green bags, she said with gentle certainty, "I'll be fine."

"Good. Give me a hug," He signaled Bry; the limo rolled through the stone entry and down the candle lit lane. The bags were staggered at intervals on either shoulder along the lane. They rolled around the curve up the rise, turned to the left and on up the lane to the cedar tree near Clay's grave and parked.

Anna sat a moment looking out the window across the landscape at the gentle sea of glowing red and green Merry Christmas bags. The candles seemed to dance out a message of hope. She had the feeling God had not forgotten Clay, or the thousands more buried here or those who came to remember. For once, she felt a touch of solace and a kind of peace in a cemetery. Then the concrete bench told her they were near Clay's grave and the graves of the rest of her family.

Gunnar did not correct her for opening her door and sliding out on her own. He fondly watched her those few moments, knowing she had been on hold in Greenriver. He knew who and what Anna was beneath all her grit and fire. Her writing had told him how sensitive and loving she was long before he loved her. It was so easy to pick out her experienced lines in the songs she had co-written with Clay. For once in his life, he knew the abiding joy of loving the inside of a woman as well as the outside.

This dear heart was facing the aftermath of choosing life, and refusing to surrender to the death of her son. He was not jealous of her love for Clay. He understood the turmoil of her challenge in choosing to live and the strength it took. Anna stood leaning against the side of the car taking a deep breath and a moment to steel herself. He was by her side when she shook her blond mane away from her face and threw her head back. Holding her hand out to him, she looked in his eyes and said for his dark concern, "I'm okay."

"You sure?"

"Yes. I want to see Clay's place again."

"Good," he said, holding her hand, aware of her urge to get back in the car.

But she looked at the rolling acres and said, "Clay got a kick out of Christmas. He'd love the red and green bags and the visitors."

"Yes. We're not alone."

"Coming must help, or all these folks wouldn't."

"There is no right way to accept death. We all have to find our own way."

"The hard part is finding what our own way is, after realizing we can't jump in the grave too. Who are all the people standing around Clay's grave?"

"The fans still love Clay, still buy his records. They're here all the time."

"No one was here the day I came."

"Maybe they weren't supposed to be here that day, darling. The folks in the office say, they never bother anything. A few fans have been here every time I have." He fell into step as she started walking across the grass to Clay's lot.

"The miniature Christmas trees with the multicolored lights on the graves are nice. Who put that one on Clay's?"

"That's my Christmas present to Clay." Gunnar saw her eyes widen as she saw the monument. He had wondered for months if she would be pleased.

Shining in a single floodlight, a white marble replica of Clay's guitar stood in a guitar stand on top of the black monument. Copper Jim's song, "Mama, Sing Old Shep" was engraved on a plaque standing beside the guitar. Anna didn't have to ask who did the guitar. That was a McGuire touch, he loved guitar music as much as Clay. She was even less prepared for the people quietly paying their respects to Clay. She sat on the bench and Gunnar stood by. Clay's fans had been more faithful in coming than his mother.

"Gun, who had the guitar installed?"

"You did, darling. It was in your note, the day you left Woodhill. You asked me to take care of everything that needed to be done."

"I'd never have thought of this. Thank you. It's so right for Clay."

"Copper Jim helped, and that's what he said."

"Clay never liked to go long without a guitar. From the bottom of my heart, thank you. I have to thank Copper Jim too, when I get the chance."

He took his hand out of his overcoat pocket and pressed her shoulder. "We were glad to do it. He will be as pleased as I am you like it."

She took his hand on her shoulder, kissed it and pressed it to her cheek. "I knew you were the sweetest man in creation. I've always loved you, now I love you more than I thought I could love anything or anybody again."

"I feel the same way," he said, then noticed a fan who had apparently come to pay his respects to Clay, but was looking with more interest at Anna.

The man was wearing green warm-ups and running shoes. Somehow Gunnar knew he was no stranger as he walked up and said, "Hello, Anna."

Her glazed eyes looked through him, then changed to recognition. She smiled sadly. "Hi, Jake."

"It's been awhile." His tone said it should have been last night.

"And rivers of water. How are you?"

"I'm okay, how about you?"

"Better, but still not right. I'd like you to meet my fiance, Gunnar McGuire. Gun, this is an old friend, Jake Dennis."

As the two men made polite responses, Gunnar realized this was the man who had been at Clay's showcase at Connie's, and the man on Anna's mind that first day she had ridden down to Shelbyhouse. He was acutely aware of their eye contact now, these two had been to a high loving place. They still didn't understand, as ex-best of lovers never understand, how it can be possible to lose that kind of love, with no road back. Gunnar had reason to know perfect lovers can burn every bridge.

Anna felt as if she was watching a sad old movie. Jake's hair was graying at the temples, but he was still in shape and handsome as Adonis.

Gunnar knew she had fought like an Amazon to keep her relationship with Dennis. He also knew she was well past this part of her past. There was no reason for jealousy on his part nor did he feel any. He only felt sorry for the poor bastard standing there with egg on his face, his heart on his sleeve and that how-the-hell-did-I-ever-lose-her look in his eyes.

The answer to Jake's quandary was first-grade simple, yet profoundly hard for some men to accept. Some women will give a man all they have, if he will hold a loose rein and let her give. In any failed love, the guilty party was always the last to understand. Now it was plain to see Jake understood who the guilty and the deprived party was.

"Woman, I looked all over for you. I didn't know Clay was even sick till I saw it on TV. Honey, I'm so sorry."

"Thank you, Jake."

Trying to smile, he said, "I'm sorry for so much about us. Losing you was the worst move I ever made. Merry Christmas to you, Anna."

This time her smile wasn't quite so sad. "Merry Christmas to you, Jake."

Years had passed since Gunnar had put a pencil to paper. He learned his lesson too well to try it now, but a hit song was happening right before his eyes. It would go something like: Getting over it's all my fault we are over. It was an idea he might pass along to one of his writers.

Anna had mentioned Jake being younger. She had a thing about age, but she had a point in this case. A man five years younger than a woman was no big deal, unless it was a woman like Anna and a man like Jake.

Occasionally, Gunnar was grateful for his years. Learning about love was like learning about anything. If you halfway paid attention, experience made you smarter. When he was younger, he would have blown it too. Anna was a hell of a strong woman, a hell of a gutsy woman, a hell of a passionate woman. You could kill her, you could turn her off, you could run her off. There was no way to control her. She didn't deal in control, she didn't take it or give it. The only way to hold a woman like Anna was to let her go and let her grow. He had paid dearly in time to learn that.

Jon, his fellow walking horse aficionado, taught him you can't break a fiery walker's spirit and expect a winner in the show ring, like you can't break a fiery woman's spirit and expect a winner in the bedroom. Jon also said, "There's lots of giving in keeping a good horse or a good women, but I wouldn't give a dime for a dull horse or a dull woman."

Anna broke in on his thoughts. "Gun, you might take heed. Jake was going to marry me awhile back, till he found out what a witch I can be."

She was shocked to hear Jake say, "You mean before we both found out what a bully I was." Anna could only shrug. Giving her all sometimes made her a hard loser. He went on, "You tried to tell me, wish I had listened, honey. Good luck, McGuire, you're a lucky man."

"Thanks. I know I am, Jake."

"Take good care of her. She's the best thing that ever happened to me. Wish I'd had sense enough to know it when I had the chance. Better go. Parked my truck down the road a mile so I could jog by the Christmas bags. Real nice to see you again, Anna. You're beautiful as ever."

"Thanks, Jake, take care."

"Have a happy marriage," he said, then jogged off.

McGuire watched Jake cutting the light from each bag as he jogged past, growing small and dim down the lane before disappearing around the curve.

"Anna, what kind of man stops his truck on the spur of the moment to jog past Christmas candles in a graveyard?"

"A Jake Dennis kind of man, darling."

"He never had a relationship with Clay, did he?"

"No. Their interest in nature would have been enough to build a friendship."

"Missing out with Clay was another great chance he blew."

When they settled back in the limo, snow was falling again. As they rode away, Anna said, "It's a fine memorial. Y'all did a beautiful job."

"Thanks, hon, I'm glad you're pleased."

Her voice was heavy with sadness. "Maybe we'll have a white Christmas."

"Not in Nashville, the ground's still too warm. Should in Gatlinburg."

"If I hadn't seen it with my own eyes, it would sound so blue, but the bags flickering along the lanes give the cemetery a silent night, holy night feel."

She snuggled up to him still looking out the window. Ever so softly she hummed a bit of "Silent Night." Then she kissed him on the cheek for performing the most tender act anyone could by helping her accept the irrevocable. There was relief in accepting the unchangeable. The loss, the might have beens would always haunt her, but life went on. Life even went on for the bereaved, if they could let it.

Bry had driven almost to the Golden Glen entrance when he saw Copper Jim's truck with the bull horns on the hood. Copper Jim saw McGuire's limo with Bry wearing the black chauffeur cap. Both vehicles stopped and had their window glasses down at the same moment.

Copper Jim said, "That you, Miss Annie?"

"It sure is, Copper Jim."

"How are you, honey?"

"I'm okay." She smiled to show she was and said, "Merry Christmas." As Gunnar slid over to her window, Anna saw Copper Jim's companion and added, "Merry Christmas to you, Roxie."

"Merry Christmas to y'all," Roxie and Copper Jim said together.

Then Jim said, "We been admiring the decorations all over. This looks more like Christmas than any we been to. We was by last night and decided to take another look see before we went home tonight. Clayboy did like a show. We think he woulda liked this, Miss Annie."

"I do too; and the memorial. Thanks ever so much."

"You're mighty welcome. Say, you're doing all right?"

"Yes. We're on our way to Gatlinburg to be married."

"That's mighty fine, been hoping y'all would marry. Clay did too."

Gunnar asked, "When are you two going to get married?"

"We are married," Roxie said with a big smile.

"You're kidding me!"

"Nope, Gunnar," Jim answered with a shy grin. "We're sure nuff married. She's been putting up with me, full time, now on to four months."

"Congratulations to you both."

"Gunnar, when y'all get back, want you to come down to the Eighteen Wheeler and let me cook your wedding supper."

"Thanks, Roxie. I'd love that," Gunnar said.

"I'm getting country hams right off the farm from some of Jim's folks in Jackson County. They cure hams that fry up tender and not too salty."

"We better move on," Jim said. "We're blocking up traffic."

"Call me in a couple of weeks. Got a project coming down you might like to produce with me," Gunnar said.

"I'll do it," Copper Jim said and rolled on.

Whatever doubt Anna had about marrying McGuire passed as they rolled by the last of the bags lighting the entrance to Golden Glen. Clay was in favor of her relationship with Gunnar and he had been right. The Lord giveth and the Lord taketh away, tiptoed through her mind as her quiet tears started to fall. Tonight had taught her it was okay to cry for Clay. It was all right to mourn his passing if she could morn like somebody. It was the weeping and wailing and gnashing of teeth that was damaging and futile.

She took the tissues Gunnar offered, then moved onto his lap to weep. He put his arms around her and let her cry. His only words were, "I love you so."

When he felt her tears subsiding, he asked, "You okay?" She nodded yes. "Mad at me for bringing you to the cemetery?" She shook her head no and settled against his chest. "You know I love you?" She nodded yes, and he thought, All I have to do to hold Anna for my own is to love her.

After she was still long enough for him to hope she might be napping, she said, "I'm mad at me for not coming back to Clay's place sooner. Haven't been since I left from Woodhill. Wouldn't have come then if I hadn't been crazy."

"We all have things we can't face alone, things we might not be able to face with an army." Anna loved the way his eyes were looking at her.

"Man, sometimes you look like a brown-eyed angel; you make the crazy things I do sound okay."

"People are just people. You expect a lot of yourself, you give a lot. But, hon, you're just people too. Feeling some better now?"

"Much better, thanks to you."

"Good. Slip over, got something I want to give you."

She scooted off his lap and he took a gift wrapped box from his jacket pocket and placed it in her hand. "You want me to open it now?"

"Please, ma'am."

After tearing the gold paper off the small package, Anna had an idea of what the velvet box contained. When she saw the ring, she could only look at him incredulously and say, "When you buy a diamond, you buy a diamond. It takes my breath. I didn't know they made diamonds this big."

"The best for the best," Gunnar smiled, pleased with himself. It wasn't often he made her eyes pop.

"I want you to know, I truly loved Jake at one time."

"Love is the most precious natural resource we have. If we saved the love, there wouldn't be any endangered species, or wars."

"Gun, you should know something else."

"Whatever I should know, there's no way, I'm not going to marry you."

"I want you to know up front, if you don't already. If you'll pardon the expression, before it causes hard feelings, I don't do blow jobs."

"What?" he said, to be sure she was serious.

"I'm not into oral sex. I can't, and that's that!"

"All right." Now he knew why Dennis lost her.

"It doesn't matter?" she said, obviously relieved.

"I would never want you to do one thing with me that you don't want to. So kindly put the ring on your finger."

"Please, you do it." She held out the box.

He slipped the diamond on, kissed her hand, then her mouth. Holding her hand out to admire the ring, she said, "I don't believe this."

"I get such a kick out of your reaction to things. Now, my soon to be wife, could your soon to be husband have another kiss?"

"My pleasure." She moved back onto his lap, to kiss him with all her heart.

After, he said, "I love you so, if you didn't screw, not to mention being the loving machine you are, I'd want you anyway. And one more kiss like that, we will have to get a motel before we get to Gatlinburg." Her laughter rippled through the limo, but she scooted off his lap. He made it sound so romantic to marry in Gatlinburg and make love in front of the fireplace, she thought she had better move while she was ahead.

As she sat turning her hand to watch the diamond sparkle, he loaded a tape in the player. She noticed he was playing another girl singer as she moved into his outstretched arms. He said, "Wear the ring forever?"

"Forever, darling." He saw more love shining in her eyes for him than he had ever hoped for as she flirted, "Now, Mr. McGuire, do we have the makings for a legal contract?"

"Better believe we do. If you would be so kind, let's seal it with a kiss. You got one ole boy happy." After their kiss, he kissed the top of her hair and felt her relax. Maybe she would nap. It had been a stressful night, he thought, and let his own eyes close.

When they were driving through Knoxville, she moved from his arms and started digging in her purse. Her "damn" told him she had a problem.

"What?" he asked.

"I need some writing paper." He opened the console, and gave her a pad.

As she began to write, he asked, "Want more light?"

"No. I'm fine," she sighed.

A man outside music might have been offended by how she moved away and turned her back. McGuire tried to avoid breaking mirrors and songwriting spells. He knew, by the frantic way she was writing, a song was coming down almost faster than she could write. For now, his part was to wait. When she started humming, he subtly activated the tape recorder.

Several minutes later, her humming became lyrics and she sang, *"On a dark, blue Christmas Day, at the cemetery gate; she parked her car and prayed for strength to hold on. She had lost her son that year, now more helpless mother's tears, made her want to take her broken heart and go home."*

Then, not hearing all the words yet to the melody playing in her head, Anna went back to humming, singing words intermittently and writing them down..

Gunnar smiled. She was writing truth laced with fantasy, and finally venting her loss of Clay without tears. Straight from her heart, he was hearing a very special Christmas song in the making. It was only a matter of time now. Come next Christmas, if he had any clout with Anna Hill McGuire, they'd have a new album out and his wife would be singing her own Christmas song.

=⇒ ♪ ⇐=

At the Eighteen Wheeler Truck Stop, Roxie said, "Copper Jim, want ice cream on your apple pie?"

"Nope, hon, don't believe I do. This is mighty tasty."

"Think Anna and McGuire can make a go of it?"

"It'd be mighty good if they can."

"Aimed to warm your coffee before I sat down."

"Coffee's fine, enjoy your pie. It's mighty good."

"Thanks. Gunnar's the only man Anna's been serious about, except that Jake she got all lit up over for awhile."

"Jake was too much like Huey Bledsoe," Jim said, taking a bit of pie.

"Who is Huey Bledsoe?"

"A neighbor Uncle Ned said had a hummingbird. Hummingbirds and songwriters both fly backwards half the time, but they gotta do their thing. Huey found out the hard way. Uncle Ned told him to let the bird go."

"Did he?" Roxie asked.

"Naw. Had a popsicle stick cage he made for a baby crow he caught. Made a pet out of the crow, kept it for years till it died. He got lonesome for the crow and tried to catch another, caught a hummingbird instead. It was a fine cage but the hummingbird kept flying against the sides. Two days and nights, Uncle Ned kept telling him to set the bird free, ain't no taming a hummingbird. Huey went on putting food and water in the cage the bird wouldn't touch. Third morning he woke up shocked to tears, the hummingbird beat itself to death struggling to get free."

"How cruel," Roxie said, pouring more coffee.

"Huey never meant to be cruel, just born a few marbles shy of a full sack. Jake never meant to be cruel, he didn't understand about Annie's love for Clay or music. I'm sure glad she's marrying Gunnar."

"The way he was grinning, he is too."

"He's been struck on Annie since he first laid eyes on her. When she told him to stick Clay's contract where the sun don't shine, that done it. That old boy's been wrapped around her finger ever since."

RED AND GREEN SAYS MERRY CHRISTMAS

ANNA HILL MCGUIRE

On a dark, blue Christmas Day, at the cemetery gate,
She parked her car and prayed for strength to hold on.
She had lost her son that year, now more helpless mother's tears
Made her want to take her broken heart and go home.

But along the busy lanes, she saw Christmas candle flames
In red and green lit bags like beacons beaming.
Then a strolling carol choir set her shattered soul on fire,
With this Christmas song they stood by her car singing:

CHORUS
Once upon a manager long ago,
Starts a story every school child knows.
When an everlasting star, led three wise men from afar
To the baby Jesus wrapped in swaddling clothes.
Now red and green says Merry Christmas everywhere,
From the cities, farms and village squares.
Long as people light the lights, celebrate his birthday night
Red and green says Merry Christmas everywhere/

Filled with new faith she began, thinking she could drive on in,
As His holy presence took her spirit higher.
Then the joy of Christmas cheer, stronger with two thousand years,
Gave her strength to sing the carol with the choir.
(Repeat chorus....

352

≈≈≈≈≈ **CHAPTER 37** ≈≈≈≈≈

MR. AND MRS. MCGUIRE

The glow of love covered her face like magical makeup. Marrying McGuire was the best favor she had ever done for herself, and rocking on the porch at Shelbyhouse was where she belonged. After two years, they were still as good as love gets and life after Clay had more meaning than she ever hoped for.

Gun said, "It's time to live first as Anna."

She frowned. "You'll have to break that down."

"I need the Anna who survived the orphanage, widowhood and the pain of Woodhill. Don't play the classic wife role. When it comes to your love, I'm a greedy man and I waited for my time. Now that you're mine, I want your all. I can get more from a woman called Anna than from a woman who thinks of herself as only Mrs. Gunnar McGuire. I want the woman who fought me for her son's creative freedom like a tigress defending her cub."

"Lord, I must have shown my ass that day."

"You showed me my future and what was wrong with my past. I fell in love on the spot and decided to marry you right then."

Remembering, she smiled and continued to rock, appreciating the green of spring coloring the lush pastures of Shelbyhouse. Her eyes lingered on the horse barn, picturing Gunnar there now, happy as a boy gone out to play, in spite of his silver hair, caring for his beloved horses.

With a fantastic husband and their marriage working beautifully, she felt she should be settling down to some kind of settling in. But Gunnar kept rocking her ovaries with talk about her singing career. For hours on end, he listened to tapes of the unrecorded songs she and Clay had co-written, as well as those she had written in the last two years. She knew him too well to imagine all that listening was for pleasure alone.

His faith and ambition for her as an artist was flattering. Being married to such a wonderful man who wanted to give her a second chance at an aborted dream was as pleasing as getting two cherries on your chocolate sundae. But for now, she lived to be loved and petted by her husband and to love and pet him back. It felt like more than enough. In fact it felt wonderful.

She was indeed fortunate to have the chance to make a new choice, but simply because the music was playing didn't mean she had to dance. Choices once made had a life and a way of their own. Maybe she chose only to be Gunnar's wife. That alone would make any woman's life full. There was never a dull moment in McGuire's music menagerie.

Of course, sooner or later she would have to accommodate him about her music, or put her foot down. She wasn't ready to face a showdown. She tried to tell him how lacking she was as a singer and as a performer.

Till Clay, she'd never been to a mass attendance concert, much less thought about performing one. Still, Gunnar wanted to put her on stage, he was supposed to be a guru of the music business. Other than staying close to him, she didn't know what she wanted, if anything.

He was so good to her. Like, he thought it was eccentric of her to want to spend an occasional night at Mulberry House, but they did.

He backed her idea to make Woodhill a school for painters. She had known too much pain to ever live there again. They had money and Clay had been too proud of Woodhill to sell it.

Rachel had refused to come help open or supervise The Woodhill School for Artists. Via long distance and letters she had been most helpful with advice about the right people to hire and getting the school started.

Somehow, she had to waltz through this recording thing with Gunnar. Where music was concerned, he was less than open minded. His first two marriages had failed because of wives who wanted a nine-to-five husband. Anyone who knew music or knew Gunnar at all, knew there was nothing nine-to-five about either.

She couldn't help but wonder, if his wanting her to have a career had to do with his fear she might start hounding him to keep her company more than he could and keep his musical boat floating. She understood music was his life's work and his life's blood. He just needed to understand how well she understood that without music there could be no Gunnar McGuire.

Besides, she did not want a man under foot all the time. On a regular basis, she had fried all the eggs she wanted to and Gracy was a fantastic cook. When it was what she chose to do, Anna loved to cook and to pamper Gunnar. On occasion she would broil his steak, cut it up and feed it to him, wash his back and his feet. But such things were not everyday compulsions. She didn't consider them her duty and was damn thankful he didn't, or equate such services as proof of her love.

As Gunnar said, what one gave was evidence of what one expected to receive. But he had no worry about her wanting his time twenty-four hours a day, day in, day out. She told him, "Don't think you need to occupy me with a singing career. I need time to write and read and keep the muddy bottoms of my emotional waters settled. Darling, I can occupy myself."

"It's not that. Surely, you don't think that."

"Well, hell, how many women my age, or men for that matter, would you consider a record deal with?"

"On your level, all I can find. A ten is a ten, at any age. You and Junior tried to tell me that about Clay. I said no eighteen year old could be a ten, and learned how wrong I was. When it's great music, music fans don't care how old it is. That's dollar fans trying to analyze who will buy. When you get too smart about creative things, you're half a step from outsmarting yourself. Bottom line, you can't put creativity in a bottle, and cream rises to the top."

"If it's that easy, why all the bull and hype?"

"Honey, it's the sevens and below who wrinkle the works and make the politics. Hype is part of selling any product, good or bad. You can't sell gold at a dime on the dollar if no one knows it's for sale."

"And that's the world according to Gunnar McGuire."

He grinned. "Seriously, there is always room at the top, but you still have to let the consumer know. That's true as Sunday morning."

"According to who?" Anna grinned.

"According to anyone who's worked in sales."

"Gun, I don't always agree with you, but you always agree I have a right to my opinion. That's one of the things I love about you most."

"Thanks, but when it comes to doubting you can make it as an artist, your opinion is wrong, in my opinion."

"Name a winner who ever got anywhere at over forty."

"Grandma Moses, Colonel Sanders, K.T. Oslin; Anna McGuire, if she tries. If you're dead set against it, okay, but don't deny yourself a shot by age discriminating against yourself, baby."

"Speaking of baby--"

"What baby?"

"Our baby."

"Anna, you're not pregnant. Are you?"

"No, but what if I was?"

"If you was, we would do the best we could."

"Don't sound like you'd be thrilled."

"The last thing I need is to raise another kid."

"You mean you really wouldn't want our baby?"

"If a baby happens, yes. If I have a choice, no!"

"Well, what's so horrible about having a baby?"

"Horrible's too strong. If you should get pregnant, we'll handle it."

"If we want a baby, we have to start one soon. My clock's running out."

"If you have to have one, I'll have to. But I don't want our time divided with raising a kid. I have three kids and don't want any more. If you do, hear this, I'm bad at fathering. I don't like colic, homework, Little League or any of it. Thank God, mine are grown. That's one consolation for the years. I hate raising kids in a country overrun with dope. Just say no don't get it. Till Congress puts the Guard on the streets to wipe out dope, the police are trying to empty an ocean with a dipper and the American family is under siege."

Anna said, "You're saying adult kids back home on parents, or grandkids left on grandparents, is caused by dope?"

"For the most part, and parents are sick of it. We let the young inherit the Western World, they let it go to hell. Eastern cultures have never worshiped youth like ours, and ours is finally changing. The fifty plus folks have money and are tired of wasting it on addicted adult children. Drugs ain't cheap. Even social users find it hard to pay rent and buy groceries.

"Take a stroll on the Row, see who fill the souvenir shops and tour buses. Check Fan Fare, Opryland, Branson and concert ticket sales. The silver haired daddies and mamas are out like never before. We've had the Black Revolution, the Women's Revolution, the Sex Revolution and God only knows what else, but we ain't seen nothing till the Senior Revolution gets in high gear. It will be damned healthy for the economy, the country and the people as a whole."

"Hate to bust your bubble, Gun, but you're wrong."

"Don't think because I'm nuts about you, I'm nuts about business. Consider the success of TV shows starring older people. Seniors are taking time while they have time, the marketplace is keenly aware of it. If you don't want to be part of it, fine. I hope you won't look back, years from now and be sorry, because you're wrong. You're wrong for me, for music fans, for older people, and for women. You're wrong for yourself and for Clay. You hit notes and phrases so like him, or maybe he was so like you. It's like the chicken and the egg, but it doesn't matter. What matters is not letting your talent go to waste."

"If I was such a hot singer, someone would've signed me way before now."

"Kellogg's wouldn't have sold corn flakes if they had stayed in the kitchen. There's a time for everything, and your time is now. Twenty years ago, seniors weren't a viable factor in the marketplace, that's why you're such a doubting Thomas. Now, the door is wide open for older entertainers."

She was speechless. It wasn't easy to render her speechless, it made him feel bad. "Anna, I'm not on your case. I just need to know you know." He saw the pain in her frown. "If you don't want a record deal, that's your choice. Still I want us to do an album if it never plays any farther than my studio. Okay?"

"I'll think about it," she said quietly.

He knew when to leave. "Listen, I mentioned Jon Cunningham is coming with a mare to be bred. You two will have a chance to meet. Jon is older, but he has a hell of a mind. Send him on down to the barn when he gets here."

The young driver rolled the green pickup pulling a matching horse trailer to a stop and raised his hand in greeting. The handsome older man on the passenger side got out and came striding up the walk to the porch.

Anna felt a twinge of deja vu as she smiled and said, "Good morning, you must be Jon Cunningham."

"Yes. Good morning to you, it is a fine morning."

"I'm Anna McGuire. Gunnar said to be expecting you."

"It's a pleasure to meet you, Mrs. McGuire."

She loved his green eyes and liked him instantly. "Nice to meet you. Gun says you're one of his best friends."

"I hope so. He certainly is one of mine."

"He's down at the barn, left word for you to join him."

"Thank you. I'll do that, Mrs. McGuire."

She watched Jon Cunningham walk back to the truck with the morning sun glinting off his still dark hair, trying to remember where she knew him from. As his driver rolled past the house, she still couldn't place the man. But it was no surprise when Gunnar called from the barn to say Jon would be staying with them for lunch.

Two hours after lunch, still sitting at the dining room table, Gunnar and Jon were talking walkers. As usual with passionate breeders, conversation ran into pedigrees all the way back to Strolling Jim, Midnight Sun and other greats of the breed. Anna had been exposed to horse breeders enough to know talk could run on forever, like when songwriters rapped.

She invited Jon to stay for supper and was about to excuse herself when he mentioned Sassy Gentleman. The hair rose on the back of her neck. She knew there could be only one Sassy Gentleman even as she asked, "Jon, have you heard of a mare named Sassy Girl?"

"I owned her. I didn't know you are a fancier."

"I love to ride, enjoy a show occasionally, especially the open stallion class. The festivity of the Celebration is awesome, but I'm not into it like y'all."

Jon said, "Sassy Girl is a respected name in the breed. Her pedigree's impeccable. My champion, Sassy Gentleman, was out of her. I bought him and later got a chance to buy his dam. Sassy was a gorgeous black mare with conformation as near the standard as it gets. The mare I brought today is line bred on both animals. Gunnar also has progeny from her."

Gunnar said, "My foundation stock came from Sassy Girl. My first brood mare was a Sassy daughter. When I bought her from you, Jon, you said she was what I needed in my barn. Remember?"

"Yes, she produced your first champion. Anna, if I might ask, what do you know about Sassy Girl?"

"She belonged to Effie Fitzgerald."

Jon heard the urgency in Anna's voice and in his own as he said, "How do you know my Sassy?"

"I learned to ride on her. My Aunt Effie taught me."

"You were that devastated child Evan and Margaret had such a time trying to comfort at the funeral?"

It was a moment before Anna could say, "I guess so. I loved Aunt Effie more than anybody right then."

"So did I. Did she ever mention me to you?"

"Yes, but she called you Jonathan. That's why I failed to know your name till you mentioned Sassy."

"Effie was one of the few people to call me Jonathan. She said she loved the sound of it. You may or may not know, I tried my best to marry your aunt. I loved her for years. Actually, I never got over her."

"I've never forgotten her saying, you were the sweetest chance heaven ever sent her way. Remembering that convinced me not to miss the chance to marry Gunnar. Timing was bad for you two."

"Always. The woman I did marry died a few weeks before Effie. I was waiting for a respectable time to pass before I called. I hoped we might try again. Then I saw Effie's obituary in the paper. We weren't supposed to be; or that's the way I had to accept it. Anyway, that's why I was at the funeral and later bought Sassy from Evan."

"Did you marry again?" Anna asked.

"Yes. Most any romantic believes it's the chances we miss that won't mend. It's never chances we take that haunt us on lonely nights, bemoaning the waste after it's too late. Effie was some older than me, that bothered her. Since we had all the family we wanted, I couldn't see that age mattered."

"Of course not," Anna agreed.

"I loved Effie not as a widower in need of a companion. She was a woman of passion and strength, I loved her like eighteen." Anna saw something sad happen in his green eyes before he went on, "None of us are strangers to heartbreak. A man fate has forced to play the courting game to keep a wife as much as myself, has to dance a bit. Even so, I was never a music buff till I watched your son on TV because Gunnar was producing him. After that, I never missed anything Clay did. I have all his albums and never tire of hearing them now and then, especially the lyrics. I hear Effie in some of those lines and he was a master with a guitar."

"Thank you," Anna said softly.

"Thank you, for producing a son who has brought infinite pleasure to millions. When you ran away, Gunnar and I talked about that over sipping bourbon several times when he didn't know where or how you were. Out of eighty years of living, I have learned two things well, my children."

"Children, my foot," Anna said.

"Age is relative, like most everything. A bowl of soup may be ambrosia to the hungry and dishwater to the gods. Folks forty something are babies when you're eighty something. One thing I know, life isn't worth living without love. That's why I'm married to my third wife. Why, I'd toddle to the altar again if something happened to my present wife."

"Jon, I see why Aunt Effie loved you."

"Thank you. Effie refusing to marry me is my one regret. I've never been a womanizer, but I need a loving woman like air. I can't be faithful to a memory, or a love that wouldn't be mine. I still hate sleeping alone."

"I hear that," Gunnar said.

Jon chuckled. "Anna, Gunnar and I may have been around horses too long. But I'm still walking with a good stride, loving with a strong heart and have my sense of humor. I was born an earthy man, life has made me a practical man."

"Those are other things you and Aunt Effie shared. I use her advice about keeping a sense of humor."

"I hope you two are old enough, and don't be grinning, I mean this sincerely, that you won't be offended by what I'm about to say. It takes a great amount of time and maturity to accept that as we live our lives, we lose things and we gain things. Like the poets have said, it's sunshine and rain, roses and thorns."

"It's the rain and thorns I hate," Gunnar said.

Jon smiled. "I don't mean to be negative but I'm talking about things we lose. We'll discuss things we gain another time, when y'all are in a mood to hear me bend your ears all afternoon again. Gaining is another volume. We lose time, we lose our Effies and Clays, our Sassys and Sheps. That's the price of survival. We were created to endure, to rise above, and continue in a meaningful way. With love, we can."

Anna said, "Have you ever been so hurt, all you could feel was pain?"

"I'm afraid so, it's part of devastation. It's the emotional shock factor that initially saves your sanity. We all writhe through that when we're devastated. The best help is forcing yourself to work at something you love. If I may get a bit heavy, love is the healer and the resurrection. Like the Book says, God is love, love is God. I can't live without it." Jon's green eyes saw Anna's blue eyes agree. He smiled as her gaze moved to Gunnar's dark eyes like a shadow darting to its own image. It was such a relief to know that McGuire had found his right other half; a compatible and proper loving mate.

Looking back at Jon, she said, "That's a wonderful way to look at it."

"Thanks, Anna, but enough of philosophy. Gunnar says you two are about to launch your recording career."

Searching Gunnar's eyes, she said, "Gun loves me too much to be objective. Performers are a young breed."

"Music isn't my field of expertise, but I respect Gunnar's judgment. Probably judging if a singer can be a star is much like judging if a walker can champion out. It takes a fantastic animal, a good eye, money, work and luck."

"In the horse business," she said evenly, "or the record business, it would take a double miracle to make a champion out of an old mare."

"If Gunnar thinks you can, and you have the heart for it, I know you can."

"While y'all are into all this discussion," Gunnar drawled, "there's one small detail you might want to consider."

"What's that, old friend?" Cunningham asked.

"If for my ears only, I want an album of my wife singing her songs, and by God, I intend to have it!" His eyes blazed into Anna's as he added, "Mrs. McGuire, my darling, you got that?"

Anna rolled her eyes heavenward. Jon was elated to see her acquiescence, she was not weak or a fool. Gunnar had married a woman who knew when conceding meant victory as his wife. Jon loved the echo of Effie's humor in her voice as she held her husband with her eyes, suddenly a deep violet, and flirted, "Yeah, big stud hoss, I sure do got that."

"Wonderful!" Gunnar growled. A faint smile crossed his lips and his eyes mellowed as he said, "I was beginning to think you'd never understand."

"Believe me, Mr. McGuire, honey, I do understand. When do we start?"

"Mrs. McGuire, my saucy angel, I'll let you know."

~~~~~ **CHAPTER 38** ~~~~~
THE PRODUCER

It had taken two years, but she was standing right before his eyes, in his vocal booth. She was happy, relaxed and singing like one of God's own angels. Sometimes still she had bad dreams, but she was mended, she was wonderful, she was sincerely beautiful and best of all-- she was his. The high point of his life was marrying her, and now the high point of his career was producing her.

Anna had graced his nights and his days beyond his wildest dreams. In the horse game, she was what was called an easy keeper. She stayed in good health and good spirits most of the time. Two of the worst things a man could have was a woman always running to a doctor and a walker that needed a vet every week. Anna didn't cling or bitch. She was quite capable of raising hell at times, mostly because he was quite capable of pushing too hard at times. When he went into what she called his producer mode, she was probably right.

For sure this was the album he had to produce. Hell, it was the album he was born to produce and she was the singer. The songs wouldn't be just hits, they would be standards; even her Christmas song and that hadn't been done by anyone in a while. They had chosen twenty songs they both loved, then Anna turned the selection over to him. For the final twelve, he evaluated every word, note and tempo. He had to. He might never get her in the studio again.

He could feel the worth of the songs and the singer. His challenge was to get it on vinyl right. He was never this bewitched with producing, being in love with the singer gave him a fantastic edge. As she smiled uncertainly from the booth, it hit him again how crazy he was about her.

Anna was feeling weird and thinking she could walk into more fixes than a fool would volunteer for. She was feeling as naked as a jaybird in a cat store, and wasn't this nervous in labor with Clay. There was just no limit to what a woman in love would do to please her man. If she didn't watch her step, McGuire would have her ass tripping out of a boat trying to walk on water! She'd always been a fool for good loving.

Listen, Clay Hill, you said you'd be with me. Darling, your mama needs you. I don't know how I got myself in this mess. It's like that night driving to Sevierville when your daddy died. I need you to help me hold it in the road.

Gunnar felt like the luckiest man alive. Looking like a scared robin, totally dependant on him, Anna was the world's loveliest natural wonder. As a man and as a producer, this was the happiest time of his life. Recording Clay had been a thrill he thought could never be equaled. That was before he felt the thrill of working with the mother. When Anna was singing, the input from all her joy, her devastation, her will to survive, and the divinity of the human spirit came alive to grace the air, to touch the ear and to lift the heart.

The woman was a ten! Tens were as rare as perfect love or perfect diamonds. They made a recorder of such talent shudder from the awesomeness of his luck. He felt touched by the hand of God. Country music was an art form as laudable as any. Art that could be produced for a price affordable to the masses made it all the more worthwhile. He was raised too close to the earth to appreciate art affordable only to the affluent. Creating art rooted in the glory and the heritage of everyday people for the everyday budget was his passion. Whether it be art or apples, he believed in a fair market price.

A big production number or groove tune required more, but Mama, trains, prison, honky tonks, and love gone right or wrong didn't need every whistle and bell in hell. He didn't need or believe in the astronomical budgets the artist wound up paying for. At twelve bucks a pop and rising, the fans were entitled to a top CD. For a few dollars more, he planned to be the first to produce video albums telling a loose story line, like a mini-movie.

Anna didn't know she was going to be the break artist in his new concept. Actually, she didn't know she was going to be breaking. It was hard enough to get her to go along this far. He would bet his life God would help him. He was already betting a marriage, that meant more to him than life, that she would be hooked on singing after her album was a hit.

More than once he braced up to tell her he was going to release what they recorded, but the moment was never right. At some point, she would know she was a star. Hell, she was a star who had given birth to a star. Stars ran in her family. He had to make her believe in herself like she believed in Clay. Life had kept her from her own destiny too long and had left its mark. Making Anna believe in her talent was his job. He knew her infinite passion, they shared the same bed!

He had worked on his studio for years to comply with his personal preferences. The sound system was wired so he could direct the musicians without Anna hearing, direct Anna without the musicians hearing and direct everybody with everybody hearing.

He tuned in everyone and said, "Most of you have worked with me before, but pretend this is day one and feel like this is your product. If you hear something good or bad, less or more, tell me. Your expertise is a matter of record. All of you have played on hit albums so go with the flow. Correct picking don't give nobody goose bumps. We want your creative heart and soul. That isn't always easy; with master musicians, it's always good.

"The lady in the vocal booth is Anna McGuire, my wife and the late Clay Hill's mother. She has a delivery and a style like you never heard before. That's what we want on tape. Think of yourselves as enhancers of what she sings. If she pauses, you pause. If she stops, you stop. Take your licks on the intro, in the holes, on the turnarounds and tags. Don't cover her vocals. Don't cop any notions about what we're going to cut. If it's been a hit, don't repeat what's been done. If it wasn't a hit, there's no winning in repeating losers.

"The heart of this album is feelings. Feel what you do, what Anna does and what I'm trying to do. You have chord charts, but where you feel something, play it. It may not make the mix, but we welcome your contributions. Copper Jim is floor director and co-producer. Okay, Anna, remember to forget everything but the feelings in the songs."

"What about the mike? I don't know how to work a mike."

"Forget the mike. Concentrate on who you are and the different lives you have lived. After the intro, the band will vamp on the one chord. Listen till you want to sing, we want a live effect. When you finish a song, if we don't say it's a take, we rest sixteen counts, then take it from the top again. After three takes, if we don't get what we want, we take ten. We do the same thing over till we get what we want. Anna, this is your music, give it your heart and soul and your vocal. Copper Jim, it's all yours."

"Okay, Gunnar. Hank, like on the chord chart, play sixteen bars of kick bass to open. Like a live rock concert starts."

"Okay," Hank answered.

"Elmer, you'll come in like a screaming guitar would, but you'll be coming in with your banjo. Okay?"

"Yep, got you covered."

"Any questions?" Jim polled the band with his eyes. "Well, just follow your noses. Ready, Miss Annie?"

"Yes, I guess."

"Okay," Jim said, "one two three four."

Hank came down on the bass drum like a sledge hammer and Anna's heart was beating every kick of the drum. The banjo hit the lead intro. Then the total band was into the production and so was she.

As Gunnar hoped, when the band started the vamp, Anna closed her eyes and felt when to start singing at the right moment. After the first verse, she was in a rush and fifty thousand feet high on music.

Gunnar was ecstatic, she was perfect and still rising on the tag. When the last note died, Gunnar and Copper Jim cried, as a duet, "That's a take!"

By the end of the week, the satisfaction on Anna's face testified to Gunnar that she was as enthralled with the project as he was. They had four songs down and they were beyond fantastic. If she sang entire album as well, it would make her a star and his finest production.

His wife was the first female he had recorded who worked as well in the studio as she did in the bedroom. She didn't waste a man's time or her own and gave as good as she got. She was as wonderful at loving or recording as either could get. He had to let her know how proud he was of her.

She was sitting on the chair in the vocal booth crying. Seeing his anxious face, she said, "Oh, darling, you were right. I do love singing, and Clay is so close. Once we get started, I forget who I am, where I am and even how old I am. It makes me that happy."

"Your vocals are the stuff megahits are made of."

"Every note of the way, I feel Clay. You said this is something I've wanted and needed for just about forever. You were right and I love you so. I'll be back in a few minutes, I have to go cry some."

"Honey, I don't--"

"Gun, I'm okay. I'm just... so full. I... I have to cry some. I'll be back soon."

He saw the new flood rising in her eyes. "I'll come with you."

"No! Please, I... I need to be alone." He could see that she did.

"All right, Anna. When you feel up to it, come listen to your vocals. They are beyond even my wildest dreams." Gunnar watched her rush from the studio then returned to the control room. Sitting at the mixing board, he pushed the PA switch. "Copper Jim, could you come in here a minute, please."

"Sure, Gunnar. Boys, take a break, be back shortly." Jim joined Gunnar in the control room and asked, "Miss Annie feeling bad?"

"No. She says, tears of joy. One of those female things, I guess."

"Well, if it is, it is. Ain't no understanding nothing about women, except it ain't no decent life without them. What say we call it a night?"

"Okay. You open to a session same time tomorrow night?"

"Yep, suits me."

"Let's hear the playback again, then go out and eat. Anna needs to eat. She didn't eat supper."

"First let me schedule the pickers."

During the playback, Gunnar made adjustments on the mixing board but both men were silent as concrete. Then there was a full minute of silence before Copper Jim said, "If that ain't a hit album, I'll eat Texas."

Gunnar stood to reach in his back pocket for his handkerchief and dried his eyes. "Sorry, but that woman tears me all to hell and always has. She sings like nothing I've ever heard. Not even Clay got to me like his mama does."

"Well, hellfire, you wasn't in love with Clay. Miss Annie sounds great; don't know about her being better. Clayboy was sure something seldom."

"Listen, Jim, it has to stay between you and me, for now. But I want you to know something. Anna may divorce me, but I have to release this album."

Copper Jim drawled, "Thought it was for in-house ears only."

"Well, I... I changed my mind."

"Changed your mind, or lied in the first place?"

"I didn't mean to lie. She's just too good to be hidden away on a home album. I don't have to tell you, her writing is the best of her career. You helped her lay down work tapes on most of it."

"Miss Annie is for sure one fine singer songwriter."

"The fans deserve to hear her and she deserves a chance."

"What if she don't want no chance?"

"She has some hangups about it but in her heart of hearts, she craves to do it. I wouldn't think of releasing it if I didn't believe that. Don't you?"

"Don't ask me. The last woman I wanted to sing wanted to be a corpse, I reckon. She wound up overdosing."

"If Anna was going to kill herself, she would have long ago. As talented as she is, just being my wife and writing for fun won't sustain her over the long haul. Once it happens, I know a recording career will make her happy and fill a big hole in her heart. I'd hate for her to look back someday and hate missing the chance. I doubt any bird that can fly is happy sitting on the ground."

"Maybe not, but this bird happens to hate being run over. Looks like you drew a damned if you do and damned if you don't deal."

"I know. I need you on the album, but I truly don't want you offended."

"Hell, I don't blame you a bit."

"Then you think what I'm planning is right?"

"Don't know about right, I just don't blame you. I'd be tempted to do the same thing. Gunnar, it ain't me you got to worry about offending."

"Do you think Anna will leave me?"

Looking at the ceiling, Jim drawled, "I'd say there's a damn good chance."

"I'd say you're right, but I have to do it."

"I been expecting you to pull this. You always was a gambler."

"I've gambled on much worse odds and won."

"Yep, but I doubt you had as much to lose."

"I hear that. Want to listen to her vocals again?"

"That's why I'm setting here. Shit, you're gonna do as you please about her album, come hell or high water."

Out back by the pool, Anna had shed her shoes and let down her tears. Shep Junior lay beside her while she sat with her feet in the water and cried. Over and over, she murmured, "Thank you, Clay. This is the closest I've felt to you since... oh, Clay." She put her arms around the dog's neck and cried and talked to Clay as she cried. Sometimes she talked to Shep Junior about Clay, knowing the dog probably didn't remember Clay or that Clay had given him his name.

When Gunnar came, she had stopped crying. She tried to smile as she took her feet out of the pool, saying, "I'll be ready in just a minute."

"Baby, take your time. Everyone's gone but Jim and Bry."

"But I want to do the rest of it."

"Anna, I don't want to make you cry. I want you to be happy. Maybe I'm wrong. Maybe we should just stop the project."

"Damn! It's bad, you're just letting me down easy!"

"Darling, it's magnificent. Swear and cross my heart. I have another session booked for tomorrow night."

"Then I want to do the rest of it, now that I know Clay will help me."

"Want to hear what we cut?"

"Yes," she said, putting her sneakers on. "Gun, you really do know me better than anyone in my whole life."

"I hope so," he said, tying her shoelaces. "Give me a kiss and we'll hear your vocals. Then I'm taking everyone out to eat. You know how making music makes me hungry or horny. Tonight I'm starved for both."

♥

After the playback, she sat mute, staring at something in her mind. Gunnar said, "Jim and I are blown away. Are you satisfied?" She looked at him with that lost-in-a-song look still in her eyes. "Hey, lady, where did you go on me?"

Her eyes came back to the real world, she smiled and said, "Y'all are magicians. Your tracks are fantastic."

"Darling, I told you, you're the best."

"Copper Jim, bottom line, what do you think?"

"Told you that years ago, Annie. Honey, you're a star if you want to be. Now you finally heard yourself sing with the music behind you like Gunnar and me did. Like Clayboy did too. He always did want you to sing. Annie, you know singing, you got good ears. The Lord's been working here tonight-- or Clayboy, one. You got his phrasing and feeling made over."

"I agree," Gunnar said, "except Clay's voice was Anna's made over."

"Well, y'all know both are a mighty wonder to me."

"My Clay was here as real as anybody, singing every note I did."

"Baby, let's call the album, *Another Tennessee Hill*," Gunnar said.

"Whatever, Gun." Anna missed the guilty glance between Gunnar and Jim.

"But do you like that title?"

"Darling, it's fine. Hey, I thought you were going to feed us."

"Lady, we're just waiting on you."

"Then let's go. Where is Bry? This late, I know he's starving too."

"Waiting on you, like us," Jim said. "I'm hungry as a hog and it's too late to wake Miss Roxie to feed me."

"Have you quit cooking, Copper Jim?" Anna asked.

"Since we married, my apron's been hung up. She cooks me anything I want. Says she married me to cook for me, loves doing it and don't love me prowling her kitchen. Lord knows, I don't aim to bother her kitchen, less she gets down sick or something."

CHAPTER 39
TEN

Gunnar had lied like a dog! In house album, be damned! He had no right, no right at all! He had her at the top and knew exactly what he was going to do from the start. She had told him and told him, she didn't know how to live at the top. She wasn't Clay! She couldn't run around swapping cars, changing hats and taking it all in with a grin and a grain of salt. It would make her nuts!

When she found out he released the album behind her back, like a thief in the night, she wasn't too upset. She thought it would die a natural death. Then Gunnar would be left standing in his own shit, needing a wire brush to get it off his feet. When he saw he let loving her screw up his judgment, and nobody cared to hear an old gal sing, he'd be glad to leave her singing to the shower. When the stupid album bombed, at last he would see the world didn't love her like he did. With that behind them, they could go on with a normal life.

But no! this freak thing was happening. She'd always been a master at attracting freak things. *Another Tennessee Hill* was selling like coffee at a hog killing and Gunnar was just getting started. He had hypnotized her into doing a Nashville talk show that went all over the world. Now he was talking tours, TV specials and another album. When it came to country music, he could sell *Coming Round The Mountain* to the New York Opera.

Clearly, Gun was a music marketing magician. He had the fans buying her music when they had all those young girls to choose from. Surely he had called in some heavy favors to pull off selling her shit. But she was worn out with him running over her ass. She couldn't tell her illustrious husband a thing! For the first time, he absolutely refused to consider her opinion or her needs. He listened like he cared when she pitched her bitch about the whole mess, but he didn't consider her for two seconds. He was on a roll; might as well try and stop a dog from pissing on fireplugs.

She could like it or lump it! That wasn't exactly what he said. He was too slick for that, but it was what he meant. She didn't know about lumping it, but she didn't like a whole lot. She didn't like being treated like one of his ex-bimbos, or having their first bad fight. She told him straight out, "Whatever it takes, you're through pushing me around and calling it love."

"Darling, I don't push you around," he protested.

"What in hell would you call it?"

"I'd call it gentle persuasion."

"Gentle? Gentle! When you release a woman's album, all over the world, behind her back? Where I come from, that ain't gentle."

"Why are you afraid to live, or to let Clay live?"

"What in the name of God, are you talking about?"

"You sing too well not to want to. I don't get your hang-up about it, but it's still your turn to do Clay the favor he did you. For years you lived through him, he actually gave you a reason to get up in the morning. Now it's his turn to live through you. Other singers can sing his songs but no one can sing them like you. Your vocals are the only way Clay's songs will ever be sung like he sung them. I'm sorry you're offended; even sorrier you're so afraid of success."

"Then why did you manipulate me into this thing?"

"It had to be done, for your sake," he said with the burning eyes of a man with a mission. "Baby, someday you'll thank me."

"Bullshit!" she snarled.

"Have to go, got things to do at the office."

"Every time I try to discuss this mess, you get busy as a cat hunting the litter box." His laugh over his departing shoulder got him the last word. He always had a way of laughing when she was the maddest; like when they fought over Clay's contract. Even then he was pushing for his way and calling it business.

He knew he had her loving him too much to leave him. Letting him know that had been a mega mistake! Then she threw the gate to her damnation wide open standing in his studio singing like a parrot.

Now, he had the album and her crazy about him to boot. She really hoped he was happy because he had a rude awakening coming.

She absolutely wasn't touring. Touring with Clay taught her about touring. It was murder. Up before thousands, never knowing if they were going to throw stones or laurels. Clay loved it, but concerts made a wreck out of her, bumping around on planes gave her constipation. There was no way she was going to be a jet jumper or bus prisoner. Gunnar better get it through his hard head: she didn't do tours! Just thinking about a tour popped her bra hook. There would be no end to it if she didn't protect herself from her music addict husband.

In the beginning he had been so considerate of her space. In the beginning? God! she was beginning to sound like Genesis. And wasn't that just like her ass, when she was right before pulling an Exodus? Anyway, she loved singing in the studio. Gunnar was a recording wizard, he even made her sound good and was happy as a boy playing with his toys. Lord, he was so handsome when he was happy. Then she got high on hearing her vocals in her headphones.

Singing songs she and Clay had written was pure joy. Then working out the harmony parts with her own leads was like they were singing together again. In her head, she could hear him singing right along. It was so fantastic three new songs had come and she just imagined Clay picking to enhance the melodies.

But that was before her trusted husband released her album and all hell broke loose. That alone was bound to be grounds for divorce. Course, she knew she didn't need grounds. She could leave their marriage anytime she wanted, and so could he. Their pact was, nobody had to stay.

Helping Clay make his dream a reality was one thing, it was born in a mother to help her child. Her status then, was just part of being Clay's mother. Her own celebrity, wasn't anything she had aspired to since she was a girl.

Gunnar was so wrong saying, "You have the worst fear of success I've ever witnessed." She was only interested in the joy of singing. The pride she had taken in doing it well, the lift Gunnar's praise had given her, motivating her to reach even higher, had taken her down the Yellow Brick Road.

She put her guitar in the stand and turned off the recorder. Her concentration was gone. There would be no more writing now; maybe never if she didn't get away from Gunnar. When it came to her music, he didn't hear a word she said. Success beyond her wildest dreams would simply destroy her. She couldn't make Gunnar understand, and she couldn't stand to argue with him anymore.

She believed she knew how to love a man. She had loved Jeff, she had loved Jake even more, and she loved Gunnar most of all. But, over the long haul, she had never known how to get along with any of them. Maybe she never would, maybe she was doomed to live alone. Even so, she would not be bullied!

She could best avoid another scene, by leaving while Gunnar was gone and writing him a note. If she wrote her feelings down in black and white, he would know she was serious, and he would leave her alone. Accepting what she had to do, Anna left the studio and rushed upstairs.

She hoped she wouldn't be throwing clothes in a suitcase and running away from home the rest of her life. She didn't think she was a coward, when being overrun, armies retreated. It beat hell out of surrender!

Mulberry House had been her home again for over four months. Past mansions, luxury hotel suites, private limousines and jets, the curbstone was still her favorite place to think. Her Daddy had planted the mulberry trees one day when she was five. She got mad because he wouldn't let her help dig with his red handled shovel. He told her, "Anna, you're too little to dig with a shovel this big. It's too hard on your female parts. Sit there and watch me and be a good girl. When I cover the roots up, you can help."

Daddy did let her help cover the roots, and for years the mulberries had stood taller than the house. For years Daddy had been gone, like all the others and now Gunnar. And oh, Clay, I miss you so. Stop thinking like that! Do you like doing the weep? You're upset enough! Let it go!

It was awful to always be on guard with her thoughts to keep from getting re-devastated by some past devastation. There had been a time, she could let her mind walk any mental street it fancied. Hell, that was long gone.

She shook her head and got up from the curbstone. Her hair was piled under a Peterbilt cap and she wore her Gunnar sweat shirt, sneakers and jeans. Walking to the middle of the street, she kicked a pebble, thinking further about how rank it was to have to guard her thoughts.

Across the street against the curbstone, she spied an abandoned Greenriver baseball bat. When she was a kid, a cut-off broomstick was used for a bat. She picked up the stick and took a few swings. Then she picked up a pebble, pitched it in the air, swung and missed. "Strike one," she said aloud, then pitched up a bigger pebble. She swung again and heard a satisfying whack as her bat connected. She stood pitching up pebbles without having much luck hitting them away, but it beat sifting memories and squalling. She took more practice swings to revive her coordination. Then she found a rock to pitch up, swung and connected, then jumped as a car horn blared behind her.

As she turned, Gunnar stuck his silver head out the limo window and shouted, "Hey, tomboy, get out of the street before you get run over."

"Better take your ass back to Belle Meade before folks get the wrong idea," she barked. "Cruising the poor side of town in a limo, they might think you're God. Course you already do."

"Heifer, you ain't in a pasture or a ball diamond."

"Hollywood, how would you know?"

He had forgotten he was wearing the reflector sunglasses she hated. He snatched off the glasses as he walked up to her and commanded, "Come here!"

Hearing the edge in his voice she still snarled, "You gray-headed bastard! You almost ran over me, I'm sick of you running over me in more ways than one." How wrong she was to think all her challenges were over. They would never be over as long as she was screwing around with Gunnar McGuire.

"You needed a good shaking up. You get way too sassy without somebody to shiver your timbers now and then and screw your sexy ass down to size."

"Guess you think that's what God made you for?"

"Who does it better?" He yanked her in his arms.

"I didn't say you could hold me," she said, in a futile struggle.

"I didn't ask," he said, pulling her closer.

"Let me go! Who do you think you are?"

"Your husband! And I'm tired of having to stump break you every time I turn around." The black hell in his eyes gave her a clue he was outdone.

Still she hissed, "I didn't ask you to come here. Take your hands off me right now! I don't have to put up--"

"Hush, Miss Piss and Vinegar, before I whip your butt right here in your precious Mulberry Street."

"You wouldn't really do that?" Anna hated the way her statement came out like a dumb blond question.

"Not unless you go too far. Leaving me is damn sure going way too far." The pain in him drained the fight out of her. He really couldn't comprehend her not wanting to be in music in a public way. And she had missed him so.

She was all heart saying, "Gun, you push too hard."

"I know, and I'm sorry. Please, just hush and kiss me." Knowing she was giving in, she was still glad to melt in his arms. That was the way it always was for her when she loved a man.

After their kiss, she said, "Baby, I just don't have the brass to be a star. You proved your point about me making it. Now I want to retire."

"Anna, are you hungry?"

"Hungry for what?"

"Food, what do you think?"

"With you, I never know."

"Well, are you?"

"Well, I could eat."

"Good. I been fishing a lot since you been gone. I'll call Gracy to fry us up a fish supper. Come on. Let's let our differences slide for a while and go pig out on fish, vinegar-water slaw and hoe cakes."

"Gun, that's a deal I can't resist."

When they were rolling west from Greenriver, sure he had his wife in a situation where she couldn't run, he said, "To answer your question back there, if you have to announce your retirement before you halfway get started, it has to be fine with me. More than anything else, I want you to be happy. I don't know if it will be fine with the President."

"What president?"

"The President of the United States invited you to sing at the White House."

"You're going too far. Quit bugging me and stop lying."

"I swear." His dark eyes told her he was not joking.

"My God, you're graveyard serious. Shit!"

"Angel, I've told you all along you're a star. Still, if you gotta quit, guess you gotta quit. I don't have the balls to turn down the President, if he is a Republican. So you call him up and have at it!"

"Gunnar!"

"Truly, honey, I'm not kidding."

"Well, ain't that just new ground great! I don't know how to talk to the President. I wouldn't know how to tell him yes, much less no!"

"Call the man and cancel, or start rehearsals to sing at the White House."

"Gun, you have to help me. You have to tell him."

"I already told him. I told him yes."

"Call back. Say we changed our minds." He looked out the window and said nothing. "Gunnar, now call him and say we changed our minds."

"Like I said, my balls aren't big enough to say no to the President."

"Damn it, Gunnar McGuire, you know I can't."

"Then, heart of my heart, you have a singing date with the President."

"I'll die! I'll just die!"

"Die? I think it's an infinite compliment."

"Yeah, you would!"

McGuire laughed. "Angel, how many folks born on Mulberry Street get asked to sing at the White House?"

"Damn, I don't know."

"I do. None. It's a high honor and you should be proud and gracious enough to go. In all seriousness, Anna, don't you?"

"That in-all-seriousness routine just means you're trying to bend me over."

"Forget the attitude. Don't you feel honored?"

"Well, I guess. Reckon he knows how old I am?" He began to laugh again. "Gunnar, don't laugh. I'm scared to death and serious as I can be!"

"I know you are," he said, still chuckling.

"Well, hell, do you?"

"I'm sure the President, and White House security, knows more about us than we do ourselves. And your age has been well publicized. With your attitude, I wouldn't mention age to the President."

"I never bring up age, but what are you saying?"

"Well, national security could be at stake."

"Satan's in your eyes, but I'll bite. What?"

"If you make excuses based on age, the President might think he can't do his job. After all, he's well over forty-five and most of Congress is, too."

"Gunnar, this is no time to joke!"

"I'm not joking. He is human."

"All right! I'll do it! But after the President, you have to promise to cut this shit off, and I mean it. I can't take the pressure."

"What about the Opry, honey?"

"The evil way you're grinning, I'm afraid to ask."

"Maybe I shouldn't tell you." His grin told he most surely had another rabbit to pull out of his hat.

"Guess you're trying to kill me, but lay it on me."

"They want you to sing on the Opry-- then there's the Queen."

"Oh shit! What queen?"

"The Queen of England; folks in high places are older. Seems they appreciate an older artist's debut album going platinum overnight."

"Platinum?"

"Then there's the final news." Seeing her look of dread, he smiled. "Relax. You'll like this part."

"I'm too weak to ask, but what?"

"Then there's the benefit concert."

"You know I can't do big concerts. It ain't like singing in the studio where you can do it over and over till it's right. Making conversation or singing a song or two on TV is another. Even singing for the President and the Queen is easy compared to mass concerts where you don't know what in the cat hair your audience is subject to do. You know they sometimes get carried away. It was all security could do to keep them off the stage with Clay."

"Clay thrived on performing live."

"Damn, don't you know by now I'm no Clay!"

"Why not? You taught him, his dearest dream was for you to perform."

"I'm too insecure to do stage shows. I hate to put a pin in your balloon but your imagination's on a runaway horse. McGuire, get a grip. You need a Dolly or a Reba to perform in that environment."

"I can't believe you can pass up a half million dollar AIDS benefit."

"Gunnar, what are you talking about now?"

"We discussed a concert at Vanderbilt for months."

"And got turned down flat."

"Baby, that was before your album went platinum."

"Gun, even with all your expertise, they won't let me yodel in their stadium. They already said no."

"You only had a hot album when we approached them before. Your public image and financial picture has changed. They called me. Now they see you filling the stadium and a half million net."

"You beat the drums on this till you got opening Pandora's box looking like opening a box of Cracker Jacks."

"Hey, who got the original idea? Who said she would give a concert, if she could do it for AIDS, in Vanderbilt Stadium where the gate would be big enough to make it pay and bring AIDS to public awareness?"

"I never thought they'd let us do a benefit."

"You got your chance. Vandy might be a drop in the bucket next to what you can raise after you perform for the President. We not only got Vanderbilt's okay, we got a contract like you wanted. We got a date and half a million for AIDS made, if you do the concert. We got nothing if you don't. The date we specified for an answer to our proposal has expired. Darling, if you don't want to, you don't have to sing a note."

"God, Gun, you're incredible."

"No big deal, darling."

"No big deal? It's a miracle."

"For a promotion man, miracles are a dime a dozen."

"Is that right?" Anna said with a leer.

"Actually, this time it isn't. This time they did call me. They still had our contract. They called again this morning to say they put the signed contract in the mail. You didn't ask me the date, darling."

"Gun, you got a I-know-something you-don't-know grin. When is the date?"

"July first."

"Clay's birthday!"

"Yes," he said, as she moved close and kissed him.

"You know I have to do it now."

"Yes, Anna, I know, and you're a ten all the way."

"Darling, why do you have to keep pushing me?"

"Because tens are too rare to waste, and you need me to push you. I've seen heaven in your eyes when you sing, from the first time you sang backup tracks with Clay. The day you woke me singing at Mulberry House, I saw it again. Anna, music transports you like it does me. It can't replace Clay. But, in a special way, it brings him back to you. Music is your healer. It was Clay's salvation, and he was yours. Now, what y'all wrote together and what you will write is your salvation. And you are mine."

"That's the sweetest thing anyone has ever said to me. But why can't just you be my salvation?"

"Because we both need the music."

"Gunnar McGuire, you're slick as satin and weird as hell."

"And I'm in love with my woman and her music. So, kiss me."

Sitting on the patio overlooking the lake, after they had feasted on fish, he said, "I have to check on the mare about to foal. While I'm at the barn, you might call Suzy Allen about your stage clothes. We want lots of changes."

"Whatever you say, Gun." Her smile told he was all of it. He had brought her approval, acceptance, and understanding. In a creative way, he understood her better than she understood herself.

"We'll book the Nashville Symphony along with my studio pickers. Got a progressive country show in mind."

"You're the producer," she said, grateful he wouldn't allow her to place limitations on herself. He filled her cup to overflowing. His love had given her sweet erotica that touched her very soul. She had to do the show for several reasons, but most of all she wanted her man to be happy.

Gunnar took her hand. "I love that look in your eyes".

"Man, don't drag back here too tired to love me."

"Ain't too tired now, if you just have to have me."

She giggled. "No, tonight I want the works; my bath, my Chanel perfume and my new, red negligee you bought me. I want champagne and candlelight and music. Everything will be ready when you come back."

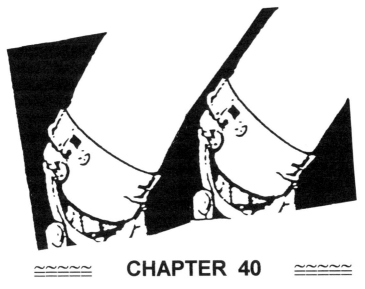

CHAPTER 40

ANNA

The lights went out... the stadium hushed and was in total darkness. Then above the stage, new lights flashed on spelling ANNA in letters twelve feet tall. Extending the width of the stage, the lights repeated her name three times. Their giant flashes came in silent, rotating announcements like mute carolers singing ANNA!... ANNA!... ANNA!...

A roar of approval erupted from the crowd that sounded to Anna like the raging of some carnivorous monster. The ovation that followed thundered like the end of the world. Lord! she needed the nearest exit. She was terrified!

Then the light from the repeating ANNA ANNA ANNA flashed across her face and she was drawn into her job for the night.

Standing in the wing on the opposite side of the stage, Gunnar searched out Anna's eyes, but she made no eye contact. Seeing she was into performing and no longer conscious of him or them, he felt relieved.

Feeling the energy of her lights, the crowd began clapping and chanting, "Anna, Anna, Anna," in time with the flashing. It was as Gunnar had planned.

Anna felt they were on her side before she set foot on stage or sang a note. At his signal, the drummer joined the rhythm of the crowd's hand claps and Anna chant. Then Gunnar signaled to Copper Jim directing the orchestra that the show was all his.

Anna stood as Clay used to stand, hyping herself at the edge of the curtain. Remembering the night she had borne a son... and the night she had lost him, she waited to feel the right moment to walk out on stage.

Feeling Clay near, she smiled. Then, through his eyes, watching the enormous spotlight pan the stadium exposing the bobbing ocean of folks clapping and chanting, she felt them hungering for music as she did. Her foot began to tap the rhythm of the drum, her body began to sway. It was time.

Suddenly, her stage fright turned to the soul-saving happiness of doing something she loved. Clay's presence had come to help and to welcome her!

Now she knew what had been so terrifying about performing. She had no role to hide behind. In concert, she was no daughter, no orphan, no wife, no mother, no widow. Here, there was only Anna.

Instead of hiding her light under a bushel, it was time to let it shine! The stage was one of the rare plateaus above sex, race, rank, Social Security number, and even age.

As Jake would have verbalized it, she had found her best toy. God, it was about time! If she had enough lives, she might actually learn past the primer about living. In his own way and for his own sake, Jake was smart as people get about using time wisely.

The kick drum hit double time, the clapping hands followed, lifting the volume, driving the momentum of the night and her adrenaline. Her heart was pumping in time with the drum and the hand claps of her vast audience. The moment was hers.

She looked at Gunnar smiling at her from the opposite wing and blew him a kiss. He saw her eyes shadow down to purple as Clay's had when the music took hold and took him into that other somewhere.

Still behind the curtain, Anna lifted her mike and started to sing for effect, not out of fear. The chants and claps ceased. Feeling the need of the fifty thousand who had lent her their ears, Clay Hill's mother smiled. For an instant, as she skipped out on stage, Gunnar thought it was Clay.

Hearing her, watching her rise out of stage fright and into her performance, he whispered, "Thank you, sweet Jesus."

As she became something miraculous before his eyes, he saw with mother and son, it was more than fantastic songs and fabulous voices. It was faith and phantoms, it was trust and believing, it was taking the magic carpet ride of once upon a time and open, sesame.

In spite of all the pain, all the fear, all the heartache, it was the human spirit that could still rise to create as freely as the unbroken faith of a three year old child. It was the ageless, infinite magic of Merlin and Scheherazade and Aesop and all the long, forgotten names of all the long, forgotten troubadours and minstrels and jesters and storytellers down through the ages, loved by the mighty and the humble, known throughout time as entertainment.

Anna finished her opening medley, took her bows and caught her breath as they stood and showered her with praise and applause.

Into singing her second three song medley, she felt strong and secure.

When she ended the medley with *Mountain Fiddle Hoedown Rap*, they stood again just for her, applauding wildly and chanting, "A N N A! A N N A! A N N A!" Never had she felt this approved of, this alive, or this certain kind of wonderful. It was habit forming!

Gunnar watched his wife dance to the edge of the stage to greet them, then extend her arms wide as if she embraced them. Obviously, she was riding a rush. But her hands were steady. She was high in that stratosphere that could turn even mediocrity into magnificence. Most remarkable of all, Anna was enjoying herself! Clay was right, she loved singing for them. Finally, she was in her element. She was Anna!

When her audience quieted down, he loved the velvet iron of her voice as she said, "Thank you. Thank you so very much. You make me feel so good. God bless you all. I don't know when I've felt this good. You must have sensed how nervous I walked out here; how badly I need your approval."

After another ovation, she said, "We thank you and appreciate you buying those tickets. We all know how much AIDS research needs financing. Every penny of your admission money will go to AIDS research.

"Folks, you done real good. Thanks to you, tonight means a half million dollars worth of help. Give yourselves a huge round of applause!"

She waited for the applause to subside, and continued, "We're sure going to try and do you a good show for your time and money."

At her signal, the band played the soft intro to her next song, then vamped as she said, "With money for the research and prayers for the miracle, we'll find the cure for this horrendous plague."

Applause came again, then she signaled the band for the downbeat and went into an uptempo country rock tune.

As she danced and swayed, working the stage end to end like some kind of singing enchantress, it was clear to McGuire her fear about age was unfounded. Her white Grecian gown was timeless and so was she.

Suzy Allen did know how to dress a star. Anna's blond hair was pulled back and up and cascaded down the back of her gown. On stage she could pass for sixteen. She could be a new Venus, or a model for a statue signifying all women. She was an original. As her name in the lights he designed for her proclaimed, she was Anna, with her own aura, her own uniqueness, and the special beauty, not of a girl, but of a woman.

When she finished the medley, their standing ovation told her they loved her. She held up her hands for silence.

Soft as a mother's touch, she sang a cappella a high Appalachian melody telling a story of home. Gunnar knew it was what she could remember of her childhood in Mulberry House. He smiled, thinking again how soft and strong and beautifully she sang. Her tone was as pure as the fiddle that started to harmonize with her. For him, her voice was the sound of love. You are the real thing, a living ten, he thought, and, baby, you have come a long, long way.

The night was on fire with the flame of survival in her God blessed voice. Her maturity let it treble all the sweeter, all the stronger, like vintage wine, from the aging and long aching in the kegs of her heart.

As the beauty of her singing poured forth, not one fan enjoyed her concert more than Gunnar. He was moved heart deep by every song she caroled. He'd told her she was great, he had not said the half of it. She was unbelievable!

Anna felt the music healing her as Gunnar promised, she felt Clay there as he said he would be. In her heart she heard him singing with her as when they had written and sung songs together just for the love of it. As Clay had let the music wash him, now she let it wash her. She felt the baptism of music take her, lift her, save her, deliver her born again. Truly now she knew and accepted-- her destiny was to sing!

Done with the program for the first half but not finished, Anna backed up to Copper Jim leading the band and said something. Then she moved back to center stage, waited for silence and said, "Ladies and gentlemen, y'all are such a great audience, I'm dedicating my last song before break to you all.

"Everyone is, or has been a child. Of all the wrong things, I believe child abuse is the lowest, and deserves the hottest fires in hell. Of all the right things, I believe the highest is raising a child, in the way he or she should go. My next song is called *In The Eyes of a Child*. I dedicate it to those who used to be children and to those who still are."

As the orchestra played the introduction, Anna beamed at her husband standing at the edge of the curtain. She had written the song years ago for Clay and for all children. Though she didn't want to, Gunnar had begged her to sing it. So they had rehearsed it, or tried to, several times. She always broke down. Three nights ago they decided to exclude it from the program.

Gunnar was honored by her gesture, but her performance was going too well to mess up. He prayed she could get through it as she began to sing: *"In the eyes of a child I see tomorrow. Not bound by lies, hate, blame or sorrow..."*

When Anna hit the chorus, the crowd and Gunnar were spellbound. He had never felt so loved or heard anything so lovely in his life. Anna was more woman, more singer, more of everything than even he had dreamed.

After the break, as she started the second half of her show, the stage felt as familiar and as mystical as the rainbow woods at Little Gatlinburg. She danced with the hard driving opening song, sure footed and strong voiced, loving the sharing of her talent and her art.

Gunnar knew, there under the stars of a new first of July, a new star rose, not to shadow, not to replace but to replenish the stardom of Clay Hill.

In another form, Anna felt that Clay was born again.

Gunnar picked up on her feelings. She moved like a female Clay as she went about her performing miracle. She was a fountain of performance energy.

On the wings of music, she felt magical! Ageless! Infinite! Clay said he was a troubadour in other lives. Now she felt she had entertained in other times and other courts. She felt herself walking on creative waters, buoyed by passion for music, and sharing her artistry with her audience like lovers share their bodies.

Watching fascinated, Gunnar applauded his wife's performance with all the rest of her fans. Anna was living proof, like so many greats schooled in the unheralded classrooms in session twenty-four hours a day around Music Row, Nashville was the Juilliard of country music songwriting.

When Anna finished her last medley before the finale, to a new avalanche of applause, she had been on stage two hours. She looked and felt tireless, but she did thank God she had gone back to working out.

When they honored her upheld hands for silence, she said, "Thank you. From the bottom of my heart, thank you. Y'all are mighty kind to me and to the victims of AIDS. Most gratefully I thank you and humbly commend you. You're a wonderful and generous audience. Give yourselves another hand. Yeah! That's right. You deserve it!"

She knew now how applause could warm, how much it could mean. She felt like a kid with an all A's report card.

She went on, "Folks, I didn't write this next song. It was written by a dear friend, I consider family. The song he's going to sing is truly a song written from the heart, and with love. Clay Hill's love for Red Foley's song *Old Shep* is no secret. Clay recorded a number one hit on the song.

"Inspired by a request Clay made of me for as long as he lived, Copper Jim Quarrells wrote *Mama, Sing Old Shep.* Now Copper Jim is going to sing it for you, and he has asked me to help out a little with the harmony.

"I'm sure y'all have already seen him over there running the band. Although I'm told with the symphony helping out, it's called an orchestra. Anyway, folks, if you would, welcome a fine artist, writer, producer, orchestra director and best rhythm picker in country music, Copper Jim Quarrells!"

As they applauded, Copper Jim walked up beside Anna. She hugged him, then said, "It's real good to have you here, Copper Jim. You and the whole orchestra are doing a mega fine job."

"Thanks, Miss Annie. It's mighty good to be here."

"All right then, Copper Jim, if you're ready let's do it!"

When the applause quieted, a steel guitar swayed in for a short solo, then an oboe solo, next a crisp Appalachian guitar, followed by a fiddle. They played eight measures together before the entire orchestra fell into an overture.

When the overture ended on a diamond chord, Copper Jim started singing, "*His time on a hard bed was fast ticking down...*"

At the chorus Anna joined in with her high harmony. As the fifty thousand sat enthralled, from the stage wing Gunnar discovered the tender solace of thankful tears. This was the happiest night of his life. It was all coming true, all he had dreamed, all he had prayed... for his Anna.

After *Mama, Sing Old Shep* and a standing ovation, followed by their duet encore, Anna asked Copper Jim to sing a medley of his past chart songs.

As always, from mansions to shanties, in tuxedos or blue jeans, the fans loved Copper Jim's stone country chronicles of home, prison, hard whiskey, soft women, bad times, good times, and love gone wrong.

When Copper Jim had taken his bows, Anna rejoined him on stage. He led her into the finale of the evening with: "Miss Annie, you ready to let me help you do your *The Rise Is Worth the Fall* song? I'd love to hear you sing it."

"Thanks, Copper Jim, I'd love to sing it."

Anna looked out at the audience in the stadium that the lights kept her from seeing. But she could feel them as she said, "Folks, I guess we've all seen times when the pain of losing someone we love just broke us in two. Pain like that can make us think love ain't worth the heartbreak that losing it can bring.

"I don't mind telling you that if it hadn't been for one special person in my life, I'd still be feeling that way. But God saw my need and blessed me and sent me that one special person, my husband, Gunnar McGuire.

"Gun made me see that love is really what makes life worth living. He made me see that when you stop loving, you start dying. That's how come I was inspired to write *The Rise Is Worth the Fall*. So, I want to dedicate this song to my husband and to everyone who has lost someone they love more than life and has lived through how bad it hurts.

"Copper Jim, if you'd help me with the harmony and that fine fingerpicking you do, I'd be mighty obliged."

She stood with her head bowed, listening to the intro, letting the music take her until she had to sing, "*You're my love forever. Darling, as we speak, I want your love for as long as I have breath to breath.*"

Her vocal touched Gunnar as lovely as something in a dream. The reality before his eyes, his Anna performing perfectly, the most magical material a song poet's pen could paint was almost too sweet to bear.

He stood smiling, feeling his soul wash in the healing waters of Anna and her music and the happy roll of his unabashed tears. This was what she was born to be. This was what she was born to give and to take. Lord, she was so real, so beautiful! He was so proud! God, how he loved her!

When they applauded with whistles, screams, shouts of "More!" and "Bravo!" Anna ran to Gunnar and took him by the hand, dragging him back out on stage with her. She was crying and laughing and happier than he had seen her since losing Clay.

She almost sang: "Gun, baby, you were so right, and oh, darling, I love you so. I've got to introduce you. I want the fans to know who you are. "

Before the screaming, applauding fifty thousand, he kissed her passionately, lingeringly. "I worship you, Anna McGuire. You're performing magic, a walking, talking, living miracle. You always have been, angel. Now I hope you finally realize, you truly are a star!"

Feeling divinely blessed, Anna stood in the circle of his arms before the multitude and proudly admitted, "Darling, as a performer, I never would have been anything without you and Clay."

"Baby, I appreciate it. But I had my thanks just watching you perform."

"I had to say it anyway. And, oh, Gun, it's so amazing. Don't some nights still, just come around so awesome?"

"Yes, ma'am. Married to you, my darling, some nights sure do come around awesome and some days. Clay would have been so happy, and so proud of you. I only wish he could have been here."

"Hey, Clay Hill's here as big as anybody!"

"Truly, Anna, I hope so."

"Trust me, Gun, Clay really is here. And it's so great to know, in spite of anything, as long as we live, if we don't let a broken heart break our soul, if we just can hold on, God still sends the night down, like always. So grand, so beautiful and still... just so plain ole country, blackberry biscuit sweet!"

THE RISE IS WORTH THE FALL

Anna Hill

You're my love forever,
Darling, as we speak.
I want your love for as long
As I have breath to breath.
If fate should betray us,
Rob us of it all,
I'll have no regret because
The rise is worth the fall.

CHORUS:
The rise is worth the heartbreak
If our love should crash down.
You're the one I've hungered for
And never found till now.
I will be there for you
Committed past recall.
Love conquers all.
The rise is worth the fall.

I'll share my possessions.
I'll share all of me.
When it comes to love, your love
Is what I'll always need.
If you ever leave me,
God forbid the thought,
My heart will remind me
The rise is worth the fall.
(Repeat Chorus...

ORDER FORM

✍ RED SPRINGS PUBLISHING

P O Box 175B - Old Hickory, Tn 37138
(615)   847-1707

I would like to order: **MAMA, SING OLD SHEP $12.95**

Please add **Shipping**: **$3.00** for first book ($4.00 outside continental U.S.)

Add **$1.00 Shipping** for each additional book ($2.00 outside continental U.S.)

I would like to order: **SOUNDTRACK CASSETTE OF THE TWELVE SONGS**
AND MUSIC FROM MAMA, SING OLD SHEP $8.95

Add **Shipping $1.50** for first cassette **(Add $2.50 outside continental U.S.)**

Add **$.75** for each additional cassette **(Add $1.25 outside continental U.S.)**

SPECIAL VALUE:

Book and CASSETTE $20.00

Please add shipping as above

Continental U.S. send check or money order payable to:

Red Springs Publishing.

No cash or C.O.D.'s.

OUTSIDE CONTINENTAL U. S. : Send check drawn on U.S. bank
payable to: RED SPRINGS PUBLISHING

If I am not fully satisfied, I may return the book and/or cassette for a full refund

Name: (Print)_____

Address:(Print)_____

City (Print)_____

State (Print)_____

Prices and availability subject to change without notice.
Please allow four to six weeks for delivery
THANK YOU

Coming in 96

HOFFA'S WOMEN

Working Women Fighting for Love
as They Fight Against Inequity and Harassment

The next exciting title from

RED SPRINGS

by

CHARLENE JONES

IF YOU LIKED **MAMA, SING OLD SHEP,**
YOU SHOULD ALSO LIKE **HOFFA'S WOMEN**

RED SPRINGS PUBLISHING
P O BOX 175
OLD HICKORY, TN. 37138